THE
JOURNEY

THE
JOURNEY

Kazia Myers

Matador
9 Priory Business Park
Kibworth Beauchamp
Leicestershire LE8 0RX, UK
Tel: (+44) 116 279 2299
Fax: (+44) 116 279 2277
Email: books@troubador.co.uk
Web: www.troubador.co.uk/matador

ISBN 978 1783064 434

British Library Cataloguing in Publication Data.
A catalogue record for this book is available from the British Library.

Typeset in StempelGaramond Roman by Troubador Publishing Ltd
Printed and bound in the UK by TJ International, Padstow, Cornwall

Matador is an imprint of Troubador Publishing Ltd

*For my parents Anastazia and Tadeusz
and their generation
so that their wartime experiences
imposed upon them by their oppressors
should not be forgotten*

Also written by Kazia Myers:

Stolen Years

VOLUME 1

JULIAN

Poland – Siberia,
1940

CHAPTER 1

Saturday, 10th February 1940. I'm yanked out of sleep by a frightening din. Someone is yelling and hammering at the door, and Korek is barking like mad.

I jump out of bed, my mind groggy with sleep.

'Korek! Settle down!' My reaction is automatic as I stagger towards the table in the middle of our room. I can just make out the shape of the lamp in the pale glow from the snow outside our windows. The banging increases. My hands shake, the matches breaking in my fingers, refusing to light. Then at last, the lamp flares up.

I glance up at the wall clock. The time is three in the morning.

'What's happening?' Nastusha sits up in bed her dark hair falling about her shoulders. There's alarm in her face, then she too jumps out of bed and rushes to the cot where our Dorotka is sleeping. I hold Korek back by his collar. My heart pounds as I raise my voice to cut through the noise.

'Who is it?'

'*Atrista!* Open up!' someone shouts back.

Russian soldiers. There's nowhere to hide. I have no choice but to open the door. Even before I turn the key right round, the door is hit with such force, that I grab at the handle to stop myself falling over. Korek jumps up and barks at the three men who push into our home and crowd our little room.

'Control *vasha sobaka*, or I will!' one of them shouts, aiming his rifle at Korek.

'Korek! *Do nogi*! At heel!' I pull him back.

In the sallow light of the paraffin light their faces look sinister with their flat features and slanting eyes. Kazakhs. From the outer reaches of the vast motherland Russia. The third man is not a soldier. He is muffled right up to his eyes against the freezing cold. His eyes are cast down, avoiding mine. I recognise my Ukrainian friend, Demitrey.

'Demitrey? What's all this about?'

He bows his head, shrinking behind the soldiers. One of them waves a sheet of paper at me.

'Kalinski Family. Forester's Lodge. Old Mizun. Dolina!' he barks. I stare back, speechless.

'Answer me!' he yells. 'Julian Kalinski, age twenty- nine!'

'Present!' I mock.

He glances at Nastusha, standing against the cot, holding her wrap tight around her nightgown.

'Anastazia Kalinska. Age twenty-six!'

'That's me!' Her voice is barely audible.

'Dorota Kalinska. Six months old!'

'Our child,' I confirm. I sense Nastusha trembling.

He runs his gaze over us, round our room.

'We've got orders to arrest you!' His shout is like a physical blow. I know enough Russian to understand his mission. The shock strikes me dumb for a split second then instinct takes over,

'It's some misunderstanding!' I protest, 'I haven't done anything wrong. My friend Demitrey will vouch for me!' Even as I speak, Demitrey slips out of the room and disappears into the night. Something drops inside me and my voice takes on a desperate note as I attempt to remonstrate. 'Just look around you. I'm an ordinary man, leading an ordinary life. What's the charge against me?'

He gives me a hard intimidating look before shouting again,

'You're an enemy of the state! Any self-respecting citizen knows that working for a *bourgois kulak*, makes you an enemy of the people!'

'For Christ's sake!' I can't hide my anger. 'You know as well as I do that this estate is in the control of your superiors, so how could my work be in any way subversive?'

He does not reply, just comes towards me and pushing me back with his rifle makes me stand against the wall, close to Nastusha. I hear her stifled whimper. Korek begins to bark.

'Get rid of the bloody dog!' he shouts to his partner.

We watch helpless the other man's rough handling of our dog, Korek's growling resistance, the pushing and the shoving till they are both outside the door.

'Korek! Go to Henryk's house! Go!' One last hopeful order, before the door is banged shut. There follows the sound of a shot and the barking ceases. Nastusha cries out then clamps her hand over her mouth. I feel a jolt in my stomach. A surge of anger runs up my spine, so powerful that I'm ready to take on this bastard, both of them, the whole blasted lot of them. Yet I can do nothing, just stand pinned against the wall and fear for my wife and my child's life.

When his companion re-enters, without a word they begin to search our one-roomed house. We watch them rummaging through our wardrobe, throwing its contents on the floor, pulling out the chest drawers and emptying them in a heap, looking under the table, under our bed, even under Dorotka's cot, pushing Nastusha out of the way.

'What are you searching for?' I can barely contain my outrage.

They come up close to us, their faces almost touching ours, the stink from their clothes overpowering, nauseous. Nastusha cowers over the cot.

'Guns! Rifles! Where have you hidden them?' the senior one demands, his face ugly with rage.

It is an effort to steady my voice.

'From your papers you must know that I'm employed in the forestry,' I tell them, 'my rifle was taken off me the very day your army entered our land.' For a moment I fear that I've overstepped my outspokenness, but to my relief he takes my words as praise and nods. I assure him, 'You won't find any weapons here. Where would I hide them in a tiny place like ours?' Only Henryk, my best mate and I know of the secret places, that will remain hidden until he and I take charge of the forest again.

They step back, signal each other with a nod, then the senior one shouts again,

'You've got half an hour to pack your belongings. We've got orders to take you away!'

'But you can't!' This cry from Nastusha surprises them, as much as it does me. 'You can't take us away right now!' her voice trembles, 'I've got dough ready and rising in the tins. I've got to bake bread in the morning!'

They follow her gaze to the shelf above the warm oven, where the dough-domed tins stand in a neat row.

'*Nye vazhne*! Not important!' one of them growls. 'Start packing right away!'

For a brief moment my fury overpowers my caution.

'And what if I refuse?' I speak through clenched teeth.

He raises his rifle unambiguously.

'Any resistance, and we have orders to shoot!'

I do not doubt him.

The next half hour is a blur of frantic activity dominated by fear. In their watchful, menacing presence, there is no chance of changing out of our night clothes with dignity. We pull on top of them our thick winter woollens, our long overcoats and the fur hats. Then we begin to gather everything that is possible to take with us, in such a short time. Our only suitcase is filled immediately. We use hessian sacks for groceries; our meagre, hard-obtained stores of lentils, barley, flour, macaroni, sugar and tea. Dorotka's semolina is of prime importance now that she has matured to taking solids.

Nastusha's sighs are heavy every time she glances with longing at the baking tins filled with the rising dough. 'It breaks my heart. What a waste!' the words tumble silent under her breath.

I explain to our captors that we have a store of vegetables in a specially constructed compartment underneath the floorboards in the shed. One of them escorts me outside. There is a sleigh on the path with a horse snorting and shivering in the freezing air. Korek's body is stretched out on the snow, his head resting against a mound, that is red with his blood. Something howls inside me and I feel a pain like an iron hand gripping my heart, when I imagine his ever trusting eyes widened in bewilderment as he falls to the ground. I blink hard through the fuzziness in my eyes when I fill the sack with vegetables that we have grown in the summer: potatoes, carrots, parsnips, turnips and beetroot. The other sack I use to cover up Korek's body, to shield Nastusha from this sight. Farewell my faithful friend…I want my thoughts to follow him to his animal heaven.

Indoors, our room looks naked, divested of all Nastusha's embroidered linen covers. She has packed them in a carton box with all our little mementos and family photographs taken off the walls. Dorotka is barely visible inside the soft ball of a down-filled cover on top of our stripped bed. Miraculously she is still sleeping.

'Time to go!' one of the soldiers shouts consulting his watch. The watch is gold and shines with a newness incongruous with his shabby appearance. A prized looting find, no doubt, I note.

'Where are you taking us?' I ask.

He eyes me up and down.

'V *drugoi raion*. Another region. A long way from here. Where your work will be truly honest. Where you'll be working for the benefit of the people. Not for the benefit of your oppressors, the decadent *kulaks!*'

A feeling of utter despondency sweeps over me. But I have to be strong for my wife, for my child. I make a sheltered seat for them on the sleigh amidst our belongings, and send one last glance at the house that has been our home for the past year, that was meant to be the beginning of a new exciting phase for us into our future.

The soldier at the front cracks his whip, the other one at the back shouts '*Yadim*!' I pity the poor skinny horse that struggles to pull us on the slippery path, his vision obscured by his own milky breath that hangs like fog around his head.

Our sleigh picks up speed slowly and the familiar pine trees begin to pass by. The forest crackles with frost and night time sounds, like echoes of sad farewells. Our little house, the forester's lodge, with its shuttered door and windows, looks like a melancholic face, watching us to the end till we become a blur in the distance.

'Who will tell our families?' Nastusha whispers, her head close to mine, her arm protective around Dorotka's form, cradled between us, inside Nastusha's overcoat.

'Henryk and Eva.' I suggest hopefully. 'They'll soon realise.'

'But how will they get the message through?'

I have no idea. Geographically we all live very close, both our families. In peacetime, the river Bug separating us can be easily crossed at various points. Now it has become a dangerous border between the Germans occupying the western bank and the Russians staying put on all the land east of the river.

'I don't know,' I answer truthfully, 'we just have to trust their enterprise.' Nastusha sighs and I feel her anguish, her fear. 'Nastusha, *moja kochana*, my dearest,' I force persuasive fervency into my whisper, 'we're together. I shall protect you. I'll never leave you! Never!'

'I know. I know.' She clutches my hand and in that gesture I feel her utter love for me. But her faith in me does not lift my own anxiety. I would never leave her of my own free will, but what if that freedom is taken from me? What if she and our little baby are thrown at the mercy of our oppressors? My promise then may just as well be an utterance of hollow words!

'Please God,' my prayer is desperate, 'please, don't let that ever happen!'

CHAPTER 2

Our captors stop the sleigh at the village school in Old Mizun, a large, sprawling wooden building, surrounded by a wide belt of gravel, now roughly frozen over and crowded with horses and sleighs. It has ceased to be a place of learning since the Soviet troops requisitioned it for their own purposes last September.

We are baffled. The place is lit up. At four in the morning. There are sounds of voices from within. Hundreds. As if the entire village population is crammed into this one hall. A group of armed soldiers stand around the entrance stamping their feet against the cold, while their colleagues, in twos, patrol the neighbourhood. There's no chance of escape.

'*Yitieez*! Get off!' our guards shout at us.

Fearful, we follow their orders, struggling with our boxes and sacks, till the sleigh is free of our possessions and ready to move off. The cold bites my face. My fingers are numb. I worry for Nastusha and our little Dorotka.

'Go indoors,' I say, 'I'll bring our stuff in.'

I begin to move our pile of belongings, two, three sacks at a time, closer to the entrance, while the soldiers look on. Bastards! I curse them in my mind. Then suddenly a pair of helping hands pick up the rest of my things and Henryk's voice whispers in my ear,

'Kalinski, bloody hell, and you too?'

'And you!' I repeat his words in shock. So many shocks in such a short time. I'm overwhelmed with relief at his presence and follow him like my saviour inside the building.

The hall is crowded with civilians, people of all ages. The elderly huddle together sitting on top of their cases and bundles, the men stand against the walls their faces set with anger and defeat, some smoking furiously. Mothers call to their children, desperate to calm them down, babies are crying, little voices wailing, 'I want to go home...' I see familiar faces, as anxious and bewildered as I am.

Nastusha has found Eva and they're sitting together on top of their joint baggage, sheltering Dorotka and little Stella between them. An elderly man shifts his things against the wall to make space for Henryk and me. His wife is resting on a wooden box. She's bent over, as if in pain, with one leg stretched out and the crutches beside her.

'Sprained ankle,' the man explains, 'they have no mercy for us old folk! I

8

did all the packing, and they just stood over my wife as if she was able to run! Vronovicz is our name.'

We introduce ourselves, Nastusha and I, and our friends Eva and Henryk Bzovski.

'And we both have a little girl each,' Nastusha adds, maternal pride softening her anxious face. She and Eva lift the covers off their overcoats, and show off their babies strapped to them, our Dorotka and little Stella.

Henryk gives me a brotherly hug.

'Bloody hell, Julian! We're such fools! I want to kick myself!' He makes a fist and hits his open palm. 'We had a chance and we blew it! We should have left right at the beginning, when the others did!'

Memories of last September flash through my mind; first the anxious wait to be called up, then within days of the ferocious German attack, absolute chaos as remnants of our defeated army and civilians made their way in droves towards the Romanian border. An escape to France to join Sikorski's forming army appeared to be the only salvation left. We started our frantic preparations, Henryk and I, and the construction of carts for transporting our possessions across the border. But events overtook our efforts faster than we could have imagined. The day before our departure, just seventeen days after the German planes began to destroy our cities without any warning, the Red Army entered our land from the east, and like a vast flood, cut us off from the free world.

'You're telling me, Henryk!' I return his bear hug. 'We can all be wise afterwards. But who would have thought at the time that things were going to move so fast?'

'It was on the cards.' Mr. Vronovicz joins in, his bushy eyebrows overshadowing his eyes. 'History repeats itself. Time and time again. How many times has this happened in the past? When one of our neighbours strikes, the other one immediately does the same. How many times have our borders been chopped and changed and moved about at the hands of …' he lowers his voice to a whisper, though there are no guards nearby to eavesdrop in the general noise, '…the blasted, accursed Soviets and Huns!'

We contemplate his words in silence. I'm in agreement and berate myself for my lack of foresight last summer when we could have saved ourselves.

'And what now?' I ask.

His droopy Pilsudski moustache twitches in consternation.

'At best,' he says, 'they'll send us to some remote *kolhoz* and force us to hard labour. At worst…' he shrugs, 'God knows, they've not shown much care for their own people, the millions they've starved to death.'

'Stop it Vitold!' His wife comes to life with surprising energy. Her face is almost totally hidden in the folds of her thick shawl. 'These are young people! Don't fill their heads with black thoughts!'

Even without his over-honest pessimism I'm filled with dread. Why have we all been rounded up here? What destination have they got planned for us? What if they separate the men from their wives and children? I look at

Nastusha and Eva sitting close together, their sides and shoulders touching for comfort and I cannot bear the thought.

Henryk and I light our cigarettes. My hands can't stop shaking until the first deep inhalation and the warmth in my lungs and the calming in my brain.

Six hours later and we're still here, a subdued crowd cramped in a tight space, in temperatures that freeze your breath. What was the point of that impatient hurry in the first place?

'Those are their tactics. Exactly.' Mr. Vronovicz explains. He's experienced it all before when captured by the Bolsheviks in 1920. 'They make you wait. You never know what you're waiting for. You become weary. Exhausted. Then it makes it easier for them to break your spirit. I was saved in time. When Pilsudski sent them packing with that final blow. Stalin never forgave the Poles,' he says and I feel darkness enter my soul.

There's a strange hush over the crowd, exhausted by the night's extraordinary happenings. The children have quietened down, many sleeping now as they cling to their mothers, or curled up on their fathers' laps. Nastusha and Eva have managed to feed and change our babies once. This required dexterity and speed. The tiny delicate bodies trembled in the vicious cold, the wailing from the little lungs rang out and pulled hard at my heart, filling me with utter grief at the insanity of it all.

It was a relief when they slept again, little Dorotka and Stella, strapped to their mothers and warmed underneath the overcoats. Nastusha and Eva organised a little hot tea in the aluminium mugs and slices of buttered bread for our breakfast. It is a miracle, an incredible miracle, that there is hot water available in one of the back rooms.

But the toilets are a problem. Only four, two each for the girls and the boys normally, and now having to be used by a crowd of, in my estimation, two hundred.

It's easier for the men. Even in this cutting cold it's possible for them to go behind the row of bushes at the fence, though the leafless branches and twigs are no screen from the ever watchful eyes of the armed guards.

'They treat us like animals,' I mutter to Henryk, as we stand in the hot vapours rising from our urine.

'If they want to bloody watch us, let them!' he's philosophical, 'we'll show them something else to be jealous of!' he brags.

Despite my black mood I manage a smile.

'We could teach them a thing or two, couldn't we Henryk?' I know him like a twin; his pride in his physique and his physical achievements, his need to prove his indisputable prowess. I don't begrudge him his delight in being able to outswim me; my long legs can outrun his. He's an excellent horseman, but I'm a pretty good shot with the rifle. 'We're a good partnership, aren't we?' I say.

10

'The best,' he agrees.

We light our cigarettes before crossing the yard among the sleighs and the horses. There's a sudden outburst of noise. Guards around the entrance shout and give orders.

'*Vryema! Yadim*! Time! To go!'

We stub our cigarettes and save the butts for later. We're thrown into nervous activity: men dragging their luggage back to the sleighs, women carrying babies and bundles, tearful children clinging to their parents, getting in the way, being scolded by adults, themselves stretched to breaking point by stress.

We are allotted a sleigh with two horses, large enough to take us four. We squeeze and shove and make room for Mr. and Mrs. Vronovicz. Her face is contorted with pain as Henryk helps me lift her to sit on top of her suitcase. She should be at home by the fire nursing her sprained ankle in comfort and peace.

There's no sun this morning. The sky is dark with impending snow, the air bites painfully every centimetre of exposed skin. We are muffled up to our eyes and the convoy starts out in silence.

We are taken to Dolina station. The sight that meets our eyes is alarming. Armed Russian soldiers and crowds of people like ourselves being pushed and hurried along to climb up onto the waiting train. It is a goods train; hundreds of trucks for transporting cattle.

'Cattle! That's all we are to them!' Eva's voice rasps with bitterness.

Nastusha covers up her fear with anger, I know her well. 'This is inhuman! Diabolical!' Her eyes narrow with disgust.

Henryk is swearing under his breath. Mr. Vronovicz nods sadly.

'Nothing surprises me any more!' he says.

'Listen everyone!' I speak with forced verve. 'Don't panic! We've got to stick together. We'll be all right as long as we stick together!'

'If they bloody let you!' Henryk mutters.

'Come on Bzovzki,' I chide him, 'I can't do this without you!'

And as we climb down and pull and shove and drag our belongings yet again, and help Mrs. Vronovicz to balance on her crutches, and the crowd mills around us amidst shouts and yells and orders from the guards, my whole being cries out for justice from heaven.

It is the next day, 11th February, day two since this nightmare began. Sunday. Our holy day. We would have been ready to go to church.

Our train is stationary and locked on the outside. It has been so since late yesterday afternoon, when convoys of newly arrested civilians had been herded onto the platform and amidst shouting, swearing and shoving with

11

guns, ordered to get onto the train. There were constant cries from terrified children and older women, and I'm ashamed to admit, I felt like one of them.

By then even my subconscious hopes of saving ourselves from this catastrophe had died down. The grim reality of our situation had beaten me into accepting what only two days ago would have been unimaginable. It pained me to see fear in Nastusha's eyes, it pained me even more to be so helpless, so inadequate, and something twisted inside me with a sharp tug when I looked inside the wraps around my daughter's innocent, unknowing little face. *Stay calm, stay practical*, I kept repeating like a spell, *save your sanity for your wife and child*.

We, the younger men in our carriage, Henryk and I and our new friend Roman Zastavny, threw ourselves with zeal into a feverish activity, that would numb our minds for a while. We helped all other families allotted to our carriage to lug the baggage across the platform and to hoist it up to waiting hands. We carried poor Mrs. Vronovicz with her sprained ankle and crutches, and laid her down on her bunk. She cried with pain, silent tears and choked sobs, and I cursed the merciless oppressors, whose families and old relations were surely no different from ours. Mr. Vronovicz's talkative mood had left him. There was fury in his eyes underneath his bushy eyebrows and unspoken rage in the twitching of his droopy moustache.

Henryk's mutterings under his breath were reduced to relief-giving expletives, as we rushed there and back, dragging, carrying, lifting, till I felt the warmth from this frantic exercise seep into my frozen hands and feet.

'Beats the marathon,' I made some feeble attempt to humour him. In return I heard something about bastards and sons of bitches and swine and skunks.

Once we were all aboard our cattle truck, the guards pushed the sliding door across the entrance with a clang, and we heard the metal bolt click into place. We were plunged into darkness until our eyes got adjusted to the murky light filtering through the slits of the tiny barred windows near the ceiling.

'God Almighty!' Henryk's pent-up anger exploded. 'You watch and You do nothing!'

'Hush... my friend' Roman Zastavny placed a hand on Henryk's shoulder. 'You're right. God watches. He does not forget. Trust him, my friend.'

Henryk shrugged off Roman's hand and stepped back.

'What are you, young puppy? A bloody priest, or something?'

Roman's face betrayed no annoyance. He answered with a hint of indulgence in his tone.

'Not a priest yet. Just a seminarian. Studying.'

Henryk's eyes widened with interest and I could have sworn I glimpsed in them a look of begrudged reverence.

'Well, well,' he said, 'a young priest! You've truly got your work cut out here. We need someone to pray day and night for us.'

'I won't let you down,' Roman answered good-naturedly, ignoring Henryk's barb.

Roman is young, perhaps twenty-two, but there's something confident and mature about his calm manner. As he turned towards me, the pencil thin beam of light shone straight into his eyes. They were exceptionally blue, truly cerulean. For no reason at all I had a flashback of bluebells in our forest.

We set about organising our wagon, pushing all the bundles underneath the bunks and stacking the rectangular shaped cases and boxes in columns against the walls, to free central passages of unnecessary clutter. Despite our best efforts, the space is very cramped.

Our wagon is nothing more than a large wooden container. There are four two-tier bunks to house eight families. The older people have requested us, younger ones for access to the lower levels, to avoid the problems for them, associated with climbing. Thus, Henryk and Eva occupy the top bunk, like us, near the ceiling across the narrow passage. Below them, we've helped Mr. and Mrs. Vronovicz to settle as comfortably as it is possible in these inhuman conditions on their hard bed softened with her feather-filled eiderdown.

Below us we've got Roman and his uncle and aunt, Mr. and Mrs. Zastavny. He is an architect. He and his wife are so delicately spoken, it is as if their minds are still inhabiting their world of gentility, that has been snatched from them. Roman is their nephew. He was visiting them when the NKVD tore into their house and despite his attempts to explain that his address was elsewhere, the Russian soldiers arrested all three of them.

Between the two halves of our wagon, there's an iron stove in the middle. The women take it in turns to cook basic meals for their families. Nastusha and I had a bowl of porridge for our supper last night, but our main concern is Dorotka. She still breast feeds, thank God, and there's enough semolina for a week or so, but to cook that we'll need fresh milk and water. We've been given a bucket of hot water, yesterday and today, but for the thirty-three occupants of our carriage it has to be rationed with strict fairness.

We've asked Roman's uncle, the eloquent Mr. Zastavny to be our spokesman and arbitrator, but he declined, saying this office will require much energy and nerve, neither of which he is capable of resurrecting at the moment. We asked the other senior men in our carriage, Mr. Vronovicz and Mr. Bogusz. They are both very subdued, as they struggle to come to terms with this inexplicable catastrophe that has befallen them. There are two younger, family men, Dorodny and Yavorski. They declined too. They are barely coping with their children's demands.

'We'll share this role between us,' Henryk suggested, 'take it in turns, you Julian, Roman and I.' That seemed fair.

The other side of our wagon mirrors ours, a two tier bunk-bed on each side with a passage in the middle. There's the numerous Yavorski family with five children, packed like little fledglings on their bunk, and Bronia Yavorska's advanced pregnancy of their sixth child heralding an imminent confinement.

13

We've adopted their eldest Aniela, twelve, who sleeps on our bunk at night. Her brother Pavel, ten, has taken a liking to Roman, and so the Zastavnys have made room for him on their bunk. We all sleep fully clothed, hats and boots protecting our extremities. The heat from the stove is inadequate to melt the perpetual frost that covers the wagon walls.

Above the Yavorskis, there are two young boys, Aleks and Artur, their mother Mrs. Novitzka and their grandmother. The old lady has a hacking cough and every fit of coughing sounds as if it's her last.

Opposite the Yavorskis and the Novitzkis, there's a family of three old sisters, all widows, and their brother Mr. Bogusz, whose mournful expression is accentuated by his grey droopy eyebrows and droopy moustache. I'm in awe of their calm, stoical acceptance especially when I imagine them in their childhood, four happy siblings together. They're again together, four old people sentenced to undeserved bewildering hardship. Above them the Dorodnys have padded their bunk with sheets and towels for the comfort of their three young daughters, Agata, Natalia and Halinka.

In the corner, behind their bunk, there's a hole in the floor. Initially, there was shock and indignation that anyone should be expected to make use of it for their most personal needs. But as the wagon remains now permanently locked, our best resolutions crumble against the urgent demands of our bodies. Henryk and I have nailed a screen of an old blanket around the hole and have constructed a seat from a wooden box for women and children. Nastusha dreads visiting the corner. It's diabolical for women, she says, having to expose yourself to the freezing cold blowing through the hole, all the while being aware of the fellow travellers on the other side of the screen, dying with embarrassment at the inevitable bodily sounds.

Young children are afraid of falling through the hole; their mothers resort to sitting them on the chamber pots. The air is foul with the reek from the corner, dirty nappies, stale clothes, unwashed bodies, smoke that escapes through the crack in the metal chimney.

Mr. Vronovicz and Mr. Bogusz light their pipes, now and again. To kill time. For me, the tobbacco smoke is preferable to the stench. Henryk and I test our willpower by pacing out our cigarette pleasures. I'm not at all proud of myself when in the end I succumb to the craving which becomes as strong as the hunger. But the mothers complain about the air getting thick and unbreathable. Wretchedly, I find myself wishing for the journey to begin, if only to deliver us from this stagnant impasse.

Henryk and I sit on a box pushed against the wall in the middle section of our carriage. We're both tall men and the constant stooping on our bunks makes our backs ache. He's calmed down now a little, while cradling his little Stella, all wrapped up in a feather-filled cover. Eva is boiling a little semolina and fretting about the shortage of water and no visible chance of buying milk.

Standing next to her at the stove is Bronia Yavorska, with her three youngest ones clutching at the coat that covers her pregnant belly.

'When's your baby due?' I hear Eva ask.

'Any day now.' She gives Eva a fearful look. Her eyes are blotchy and tired.

I've never been much interested in women's stuff, but her fear has a strange effect on me. I push away disturbing thoughts that crowd my mind.

'There's nowhere to hide, when my time comes,' her voice rasps with concern, 'and what if they drag me off the train?'

'You're among friends,' I reassure her, 'we'll all look out for each other.'

'And besides,' Eva adds, 'your little one may just wait until there's a more homely place to receive him.'

Bronia's gaze is intense, and I guess she wants to believe us.

There's a shout from the two boys, Artur and Aleks on their high bunk. They've been glued to their spy hole most of the day, commenting on the additional numbers of people being brought to the station and forced onto the train.

'They're punching and kicking them!' they inform with alarm.

'Who?' There's shock and fear in our wagon.

The boys observe for a moment longer, then one of them cries out.

'It looks like friends and relatives. They've brought food for the people on the train. But the soldiers won't let them near us. They're hitting them with rifles. Pushing them off the platform!'

I climb up onto our bunk where Nastusha is feeding Dorotka, covered up for modesty as well as against the cold. Henryk hands over little Stella to Eva and climbs up beside me. We watch the scene on the platform through a slit near the ceiling. The small crowd is being dispersed in no uncertain manner, prodded and hit with rifles and truncheons. Mainly old women and men. Their distressed faces turn back for one last desperate look as they scurry away with their lovingly prepared parcels undelivered. A dog, not unlike Korek stands on the edge of the platform and howls. A mighty kick from one of the soldiers sends him running away. There's an outburst of wild laughter.

'God forgive me,' Henryk says with that stifled voice which I know so well when he's angry, 'I'd murder him! All of them! If only I could. The bastards! The bloody bastards!' I'm in full empathy with him.

'Who would have thought…' I can't think of anything to say and I feel my hatred hardening with each passing minute and my need for revenge like a burning fire within me, for making our children and our wives suffer, for rendering me so inadequate.

There's a loud banging further down the train with the guards shouting *Keepiatok!* Hot water! We see a group of men being let out with buckets and directed inside the station building. They come out one by one, their buckets steaming in the freezing air. This is repeated till the banging and the clanging of opening doors reaches our wagon. We're prepared with empty buckets, all the men in our carriage. It is incredible how happy this fresh supply of hot water makes us all feel, even after the doors are banged shut and bolted. We store the buckets underneath the bunks, infinitely more precious than liquid gold.

When I climb up to sit beside Nastusha she wears that stoical, resigned look, her dark eyes staring at one spot as she rocks with Dorotka tucked inside her overcoat. I place my arm around her shoulders and draw her close and feel her shudder and see her eyes fill up and tears fall down her cheeks.

'Nastusha, *moja kochana*, my dearest,' I whisper, 'please don't cry.' I can't bear it, seeing her upset. She composes herself and with a deep sigh asks,

'Whatever have we done to deserve this?' There's no answer to this question. I remember with sudden clarity passages from my history books, unimaginable and therefore remote numbers of previous deportees to Siberia throughout the decades of Russian domination of our country; numbers and accounts of those wretched victims that were just a passing impression in my young mind for the duration of a history lesson. With a flash and acute understanding, I feel their pain and suffering, and like Nastusha, I can only ask, why us?

There's a sudden jolt and a spontaneous silence befalls our carriage as we feel the train's slow pull gather speed and hear the metallic thudding of the wheels along the track.

'We're off! We're off!' Artur and Aleks inform from their high bunk, their voices coloured with excitement.

'God save us all!' one of the old ladies cries out. This is like a sign for everyone to let go of their emotions. There's much anger and fear and frustration, there's loud sobbing, there's unrestrained cursing and swearing.

Roman gets up from his bunk and raises his arms.

'Listen all you good people!' he cries, 'please listen for a moment!' The side flaps of his fur hat cover most of his face, but not his eyes that flash blue and defiant in the dimness of our confined space. He waits with his arms raised and strangely his still pose takes effect and the noise dies down.

All move to the edge of their bunks, their expressions expectant, as if awaiting a miracle.

'Good people!' Roman repeats, the arc of his arms encompassing his audience, 'I'm only a young cleric, I know, but spare me a minute of your time.' His compassionate gaze, mature beyond his years, commands their attention. 'Like all of you here, I too, have been taken unawares. With my uncle and aunt. My parents won't know what's happened to us.' He pauses, then resumes with unrestrained passion. 'They've taken us physically, but they can't take away our hearts and minds! I suggest we pray together. We'll gain strength from unity. We'll find strength to stick together, to stick up for each other, even when all this...' he runs his gaze around our prison on wheels, 'when all this is intended to rob us of our humanity, of our dignity!'

There's a reverent silence in contemplation of his words, cut by the rhythmic beat of the carriage wheels. Roman intones the first line of a familiar hymn and everyone joins in:

'Pod Twa obrone...'

'Into your protection
O Father in heaven
Your children place
Their fate...'

I feel a lump in my throat. I swallow hard. Dorotka sneezes and I see Nastusha's face soften with maternal love. She cleans Dorotka's nose, raises her eyes to mine and we sing together with all our strength. I experience relief, brief though it may be. The words of the hymn are like a soothing breath over my agitated heart.

'Bless us O Father
Help us in our need
Save us from a blow
That threatens to destroy us...'

CHAPTER 3

We are in the third day of our imprisonment, the second day of our journey. No one has informed us yet of our destination. The guards have a wagon of their own and only unlock ours when the train stops briefly once a day for us to collect *keepiatok*, hot water, firewood for the stove, and to make use of the toilet at the station. The waiting crowds are worn beyond endurance and many resort to relieving themselves on the other side of the train under the ever watchful eyes and the raucous jeering of the guards. It is degrading and flames up my rage.

Everything irritates me; the constant proximity of others, the itching on my scalp underneath my fur hat, the painful numbness in my hands and feet as I wake in the morning, as the cold air sits razor-sharp on my exposed face. We huddle together, Nastusha and I, underneath our feather-filled cover, with Dorotka between us, with Yavorskis' Aniela clinging to Nastusha's back. The wagon wall is permanently frosted over and we have all rolled sheets and towels to form a barrier between the walls and the people sleeping next to them. Further down the train a small child froze to the wall in his sleep at night. The mother was distraught, and her screams haunted me all day, and the sight of the guards snatching the body of her little boy from her and pushing her back onto the train.

Dread like a tapeworm is eating through my sanity. What's going to happen to us? To our little Dorotka? She's developed a cold. It interferes with her breathing, interrupts her sleep, makes her restless, complaining in the only way that babies can. Her cries are drowned in the more robust protestations of other children, a cacophony that tests the endurance of the most patient among us. Nastusha rocks her inside the covers around her arms, makes soothing sounds, sings a lullaby and I make a conscious effort to regain composure, to choke my frustration.

The eye-stinging stench from the toilet corner makes me want to puke. I long for fresh air, for a good scrub, for a clean shave, for all the ordinary comforts at home. How do women stand it all? How do they cope with their monthly cycle that demands hygiene and frequent changes of underwear?

'I feel itchy all over,' Nastusha complains every night, scratching her head underneath her hat, moving her shoulders inside her stale scratchy garments. 'I dream of heaven,' she says, 'and do you know what that is? A long relaxing soak and a plate full of good food.'

With self imposed restraint we ration our depleting reserves of groceries and vegetables and can only hope they'll last the length of our journey. Our daily meal of a hot soup is the highlight of our existence. We delay this pleasure till the evening so we can settle for the night with a semblance of comfort, when our bodies still tingle with warmth and improved circulation. My stomach feels permanently empty. It must be worse for Nastusha as she still breast-feeds our Dorotka. She does not complain, but I already see a change in her face, the soft contours becoming taut, her dark eyes darting about nervously. We fool our stomachs with frequent sips of water, just moistening sips, so that our ration of water lasts till the next day.

I couldn't have ever imagined what torture boredom and curtailed physical movement could be. Hours are long, days are infinite and our bodies get ever more tired and aching from sitting in bent positions. Nastusha and Eva keep each other company on one bunk, with their legs crossed, their backs arched as they rock their babies and dream up plans of making the new place a real home. Henryk and I sit on the opposite bunk, our legs dangling over Mr. and Mrs. Vronovicz.

The poor old lady hardly moves at all. Her sprained ankle should have medical care, but in these conditions it is unsafe even to unwrap it for inspection. She lies back with her eyes closed, as if already preparing for her final journey. Henryk and I help her up onto her crutches for the unavoidable toilet visits. Her face twists with pain, she camouflages her cries with coughing, but when she reaches her bunk, her lips tremble with the effort and there are droplets of sweat on her brow.

It is hard for Mr. Vronovicz. He tucks all their covers over and around her and offers her water and bread. He wears a perpetual frown exaggerated by his droopy moustache and his bushy eyebrows. 'Damn them! The sons of bitches! Damn them!' can be heard frequently from under his breath. He has no idea about cooking. Nastusha and Eva help him daily to prepare a hot meal for himself and his wife.

In the lull when even the children's energy is exhausted into silence, he sits with the pipe-sucking Mr. Bogusz and they reminisce about the bad old times. They were young men at the turn of the century; eager hot-heads, impatient to take on life with all its adventures. Some adventures, *jasna cholera*! A plague more likely! Army and fighting and then more fighting. And what of the time between the wars? Hardly time to breathe and recover! It was all right for some, those with their money stashed away in Swiss banks, but poor wretches like themselves had to start from zero. And what now? More of the same again!

Mr. Bogusz rocks and nods, his lips clamped around the pipe, his grey eyes watery underneath their white eyebrows. His sisters, three old ladies, clustered on their bunk, communicate in stage whispers, the shock of their incarceration stifling all liveliness they may have previously enjoyed. The eldest, looking about eighty, is lost in the folds of the numerous layers of clothing and her face is like a dried apple peeking from underneath her thick woollen hat. Why are they here at all? What possible jobs will they be capable of carrying out at the end of our journey? What mind has dreamed up such cruelty to those who should be enjoying their last years in comfort?

Roman has gathered the older children on his bunk and entertains them with tales of the Greek heroes or with the escapades of the Three Musketeers. Even the Bible stories in his version become touched with magic and come with a promise that anything is possible if they really believe. I don't question his optimism; how can I when I've nothing better to offer.

Behind him, his uncle Mr. Zastavny, sits crouched and wrapped in a blanket around his shoulders. He attempts to sketch in his notebook. It's not an easy task with cold and gloved hands, nor is his wife's attempt at knitting. I'm constantly amused and touched at the same time by their endearments to each other. He calls her *mój kotek*! 'my little kitten', she reciprocates with '*Rafałek*', 'my dear little Rafał' contained in one diminutive word. Their words are like stardust in this dark world of ours.

The old lady, Aleks and Artur's grandmother is racked with a hacking cough. Her daughter makes concoctions for her with hot water and honey. 'For goodness sake!' the old lady scolds her, 'save the honey for the boys!'

The Dorodny family, with their three girls remain as unobtrusive as it's possible in this confined cramped space. Ryszard Dorodny has been used to a life of comfort in his high position in the railway management. The present discomforts, the dirt, the cold, the air thick with reeking odours are too much for him to bear. His frequent curses are cut short by his wife's sharp reminders, 'Ryszard! Not in front of the girls!' His two younger daughters, Natalia and Halinka spend their time making dolls out of handkerchiefs and string. The older Agata, about nine, has joined Roman's little crowd for free lessons and a little entertainment, as vital as a shot of adrenaline to survive each day.

The train slows down and comes to a halt. Have we arrived or is it another stop for the *keepiatok?* The hot water, surprisingly, the one thing available at all stations.

'It's Szepetovka!' Artur and Aleks shout from their high bunk.

'The Russian border,' Mr. Zastavny informs.

Even before his words are out, there's much banging of rifles against the train doors.

'*Vitieez!* Out! All change!'

The doors are unbolted and pushed back, letting in the light that blinds us for a moment. There's no time to think or ask questions. A guard jumps inside our carriage and shouts,

'Pack everything! Move your stuff to the train on the other side of the platform!'

It is all baffling and surreal. It's like redreaming the nightmare of only a few days ago except that it's all real; the confusion, the rush, the fear, the shouts, the shoving and pushing, the transfer of all our stuff, of the crying children, of the distressed elderly, carrying Mrs. Vronovicz with her sprained ankle, and not forgetting her indispensable crutches.

As we are plunged into the freezing, foggy air, it transpires that the reason for this upheaval is the fact that the Russian rail tracks are set wider apart and therefore prohibitive to enter by any foreign train built for the standard European tracks.

Our carriage is a replica of the one we have just vacated, and after the worst part of transferring all our possessions is over, we all settle again into our corners and bunks. Henryk and I nail the old blanket around the corner with the toilet hole, while Roman and Ryszard get the stove going with the wood that's available at the station. The most welcome blessing in this inhuman situation, is the chance to fill up our buckets with hot water. There's someone from the town's collective milk farm selling milk. For the first time in this worsening nightmare, there's animation in Nastusha's and Eva's faces as they return with their containers filled.

In the late afternoon, the guards' shouting resumes on the platform, the doors are banged shut and bolted and the train moves on. I'm overcome with a feeling of defeat, but when I hug Nastusha close to me, she looks up and smiles,

'As long as I've got milk for Dorotka, and enough food for us to last out this journey, we'll be all right, Yuleczek.' She calls me by my diminutive, *dear little Julian*, and I wish with all my might that I could share her simple faith.

Roman intones a hymn and we all hum along with him, as the train takes us further away from home.

CHAPTER 4

We have passed Kiev today, the fourth day of our journey. Our cattle truck train does not stop in the cities but hurtles across the frozen plains, away from civilisation, stopping only once a day at some remote station, just long enough for us to refill our buckets with hot water, pick up some firewood, and if we're lucky, to trade some of our possessions for bread or milk. The vendors at the stations look like tramps in their rags, their feet wrapped in felt strips. The Soviet prosperity proclaimed from thousands of billboards on the way, along with giant images of the godly, philanthropic, smiling great Stalin, has not filtered through to these miserable wretches. The men's faces, with their sunken eyes are haggard, the women's are old beyond their years.

Mrs. Vronovicz is very ill. She has a high temperature and has not moved from her bunk all day.

'It may be pneumonia, it may be an infection in her sprained ankle,' Mrs. Zastavna guesses. Her brother back in Poland is a doctor and some of his knowledge has rubbed off on her. 'She should be in hospital, not in this forsaken place!' But there's no one to ask for medical help. Even when the train stops, none of the guards are interested in Mrs. Vronovicz's condition; they are too busy removing dead bodies from the briefly open wagons, and stacking them on the waiting carts, while at the same time restraining grieving relatives and forcing them back on the train. It is unbearable to watch and I fear the worst for her.

Mr. Vronovicz lifts his wife's head and brings a cup of hot water to her blue lips. Doggedly, he makes these attempts through the day, but she is unable to exert the slightest effort. He has to be satisfied with just stroking her hand, and at the end of the day, himself exhausted, he lies down beside her, and pulls layers of covering over both of them.

Under our covers on our high bunk, I stroke Dorotka's little form between us, then I seek Nastusha's hand. There's no contact, flesh to flesh, but I need to hold her gloved hand. Yavorski's Aniela, on the other side, is mercifully asleep against Nastusha's back. Nastusha responds by lifting my hand to her lips and kissing it through the layer of fur.

'I love you,' she whispers, 'I couldn't bear it if we became like Mr. and Mrs. Vronovicz.'

In the morning Mrs. Vronovicz is dead when her husband wakes up. He remains by her side all day clasping her inert hand and rocking to and fro, his eyes invisible in the shadow of his bushy eyebrows inside the flaps of his fur hat. Nastusha and Eva offer him hot drinks and what little food we've got. There's no reaction from him. Mrs. Zastavna attempts to pull him out of his trance with a magically produced cup of rice. Henryk and Roman and I take turns to sit beside him and talk. To no avail. Mr. Bogusz, his newly acquired old pal, lights his pipe for him and keeps him company with a continuous, incredibly inexhaustible monologue on the subject of his family's strife between the wars to rebuild their lives. 'And look where it's got us! The devil's taken it all again!'

Even when the train stops in the evening and the soldiers come to take his wife away, Mr. Vronovicz does not move, but remains sitting on the same spot, his shoulders bent, his gaze fixed on the floor. For a brief moment, before the door is pushed shut, Roman stands on the threshold and sends away Mrs. Vronovicz with prayers and the sign of the cross.

My throat suffers a spasm when I think of her body dumped into a hole in the frozen ground, thousands of miles away from her family. No one will ever find her. A lifetime of experiences, emotions, achievements, friendships, her own uniqueness lost without a trace.

When night time comes we throw a blanket over Mr. Vronovicz, wrapping him tight on all sides. The next day we find him curled up and frozen to the wagon floor. The blanket is folded neatly on his bunk bed.

Their deaths have a profound effect on our little community; even the children talk and play in whispers. Nastusha and Eva sit cross-legged on our bunk, their babies tucked inside their overcoats and go through all possible scenarios affecting their families at home. Nastusha's eyes are reddened with handkerchief dabbing.

'I can't help it', she answers my look of concern, 'I can't help thinking about my Mama and my Tato. What if..?' She does not have to say any more. I have the same concerns for my mother and my siblings, left behind on the west side of the river Bug, under the German occupation. My father has already paid the price of being caught in the wrong place at the wrong time, singled out at random in the street by the German soldiers, lined up by the wall with other unfortunate men and shot dead. His death haunts me most nights, his body found and brought down to our house and laid out in the front room, the wound in his chest, the stillness of his limbs, the wax-like pallor of his face. And my mother's grief. Night after night, the stifled moaning in her room.

I lower and screw my eyes to squeeze out the painful memory.

I hear Nastusha sigh,

'Merciful God... how I miss them!'

'Don't fret so!' Eva scolds her, 'what good will it do?'

Henryk nudges me,

'Bloody hell, Kalinski, let's talk about normal stuff or we'll all turn loony. Do you remember that last boar hunt?' His grey eyes squint with nostalgia. I summon to my mind images of our forest, the whiteness of the snow sharpening the shapes of trees, alerting the eye to the slightest movement, making it dead easy to follow identifying trails of hooves or sharp-clawed paws.

'I'd give anything to be back to how it was *before*,' he says, 'we'd be organising the hunts.'

His words rub off on me. I recall the excitement at the meeting place, the shivering anticipation of the hounds straining to run, the gentry in their winter furs astride the well-groomed mounts, the elegant ladies and their tinkling laughter and their pleasure in the carefree gallop through the forest, the bugle sounds echoing on and on.

'The warmed up beer. Just before the start. That was the best,' I reminisce, longing for that bitter-sweet taste, longing for the warmth that it would send to all parts of my body.

'The hunter's stew at the end. Now that was really worth the wait,' Henryk adds, rubbing his stomach.

Nastusha and Eva listen with pity to our musings, but Henryk's crazy mood is infectious. Eva indulges him with a promise:

'We'll make a feast in our new place. It'll be the best hunter's stew ever!'

We have passed Kursk in the sixth day of our journey. It is five in the morning. There's commotion on the Yavorskis' bunk, and as I lean over Nastusha and Aniela on our bunk, Oleg Yavorsk's face peers up at me. Even in the permanent semi-darkness in our wagon, I detect panic in his stricken eyes.

'Bronia's waters have just broken,' his whisper is frantic, 'we must move the children.'

My mind is instantly clear, racing ahead with the dread of the event about to unfold. Nastusha is awake, and so is Aniela, and on the opposite bunk Eva's already climbing down. They remove the sleeping children from around Bronia and carry them to our half of the wagon, leaving us men in charge, while they get on with preparations for Bronia's confinement.

'I want to stay with my Mum,' Aniela touches Nastusha's arm, her voice pleading.

'Dear child,' Nastusha replies gently, 'it's not a sight for a young girl of twelve.'

'Please,' Aniela sounds close to tears, 'I want to help.'

She helps with securing a screening sheet around their family bunk, but Bronia's cries of pain, her panting, Nastusha's and Eva's questions and instructions leave nothing to the imagination. One can only hope that the process will be completed quickly, before the children in the wagon begin to wake up.

Oleg has filled two pots with water to boil, but the fire in the stove is slow going. The cold air pinches all exposed skin. I can barely think of Bronia's soaked garments underneath her, of her baby being born into this paralysing cold. From Nastusha's and Eva's comments behind the screen I gather they're doing their best to keep her warm with additional blankets and a feather filled eiderdown. Oleg walks around the stove, willing the heat to intensify and permeate the wagon. He rubs his hands, he stamps his feet, he hugs himself and sighs,

'God, who would have imagined this a week ago? Why couldn't they have left us to lead a normal life?'

It is the evening, fifteen hours later and Bronia is still in labour. I feel her exhaustion, I'm weary with her suffering, with Oleg's desperation, with my own frustration at being so utterly helpless. Bronia should be in hospital tended by expert hands, but no amount of banging on the door to draw attention to her plight has any effect on the speed of the train that thunders relentlessly across the vastness of Russian lands.

Aniela's eyes are red with crying. She has been patrolling the passage between the bunks, keeping her little siblings out of the way, comforting Pavel, whose reading sessions with Roman have lost all their attraction against his mother's anguished cries.

For everyone else, confined and cramped in this wagon, the day has made routine, unstoppable demands: long hours standing at the stove, feeding the family, keeping the children occupied, assisting the elderly, most of whom have become dazed with events.

Ryszard Dorodny has problems of his own; his wife is bedridden with high fever. He has no remedy for her except additional covering and sips of hot water. His girls, alarmed by the sounds in Yavorski's corner all day, have been silenced with fear over their own mother's condition.

Mrs. Novitzka's old mother looks like a corpse between fits of violent coughing that produces blood. She fears for her boys, Artur and Aleks, in case it's infectious tuberculosis, and keeps them away on the other end of their bunk bed. But the fact is that we're all breathing the same old, stale, contaminated air, which is purified only at stops, when the doors are left open.

Nastusha and Eva have taken short breaks from keeping watch over Bronia to tend to the needs of their babies. Little Stella, at nine months, is no longer so easily rocked to sleep. She has become curious of her surroundings and protests irritably to be allowed to look out and above the covers that keep her strapped to Henryk's chest. I marvel at the tenderness with which his bear-like arms handle her, and at how his gruff voice becomes soft with endearments to her. His eye catches mine and his mouth curls wryly.

'Who would have thought it,' he says, 'from a horseman to a wet nurse!'

'Your secret's safe with me,' I pretend to jest. I feel despair in my heart.

I attempt to spoon a little warmed up milk into Dorotka's tiny mouth. She turns away, whimpers, cries, she wants her mother's milk. Nastusha hears her, detaches herself from the Yavorski's bunk, climbs up on ours and, with relief, I hand her our little daughter.

Mrs. Zastavna, Roman's gently spoken aunt, takes her place behind the screen by Bronia's side.

'She's not pushing,' Oleg's voice is heavy with dread, 'she's hardly breathing. She's lost so much blood. Please, Mrs. Zastavna, please, if you can, do whatever's necessary…'

There's a pause before Mrs. Zastavna replies,

'I'm not a doctor… I'm just thinking what my brother would suggest… this may be a breech birth… this may be why it's taking so long… In the hospital they'd make an incision… they'd use forceps…'

'Please do something, Mrs. Zastavna,' Oleg begs.

Mrs. Zastavna fetches a bag from her bunk and brings out a pair of scissors. She wipes the pointed blades with cotton wool dipped in iodine. I want to shut my eyes tight, I want to block my ears, but Nastusha hands me back our baby.

'Bronia needs me,' she says.

She joins Mrs. Zastavna behind the screen.

'Eva, can you hold the covers up above the knees,' Mrs. Zastavna instructs in her ever gentle manner, 'and you Anastazia, could you shine the torch?'

Images flood my mind, brutally clear of what is about to follow. I catch Henryk's expression; a reflection of my own feeling of sickness. I must remain strong. Manly. I brace myself for Bronia's scream, but all I can hear are the muffled sounds of Mrs. Zastavna's movements between Bronia's thighs. There's one metallic snip but still no cry from Bronia. Wet, slurpy sounds, then, 'Breech birth…as I thought…the umbilical cord … round her neck…' another metallic snip then, 'Quick, wrap her up' from Mrs. Zastavna, 'Ready!' from Nastusha. I feel their panic in the urgent whispers, in the nervous activity behind the screen.

Henryk's eyes are fixed on mine as we wait for the baby's cry. There's none.

'She's not breathing!' we hear Oleg's agonised cry, 'Bronia's not breathing!'

The train stops at the first station in the morning. There's much banging on the doors along its length with shouts: 'Any dead bodies?' My arm tightens around Nastusha who is bent over our little Dorotka, cocooned in layers of covers.

Our wagon's door is pushed back with a deafening clang. The wagon is filled with brightness intensified by the snow's glare. I'm blinded for a moment. A guard jumps up inside.

'A quick stop for *keepiatok*. Hurry!' he orders, his eyes roving round the wagon, stopping on Yavorski's bunk.

Bronia's body is wrapped in a sheet. A small bundle is resting on her chest. Her family are sitting around her, as still as frozen shapes, even the little ones, their faces hidden inside their fur hats.

'The body's got to be moved!' the guard shouts, stepping towards them.

Oleg Yavorski comes to life, slips off the bunk and stretches out his arms to shield his family.

'No! Never!' he cries, 'we'll give her a proper burial in our new place!'

The soldier stares at him then turns round and jumps off the wagon floor. People begin to move, carrying their containers for the hot water. I pick up the Yavorskis' bucket together with mine, and just as we are about to leave the carriage with Henryk, the guard returns with his companion. The two of them stride over to Yavorski's bunk, push the children off the edge and lift Bronia's body by the ends of the sheet. Oleg throws his arms around one guard's waist and digs in his heels to stop him. The guard kicks out backwards with his hard-booted heel and catches Oleg in the groin, sending him doubled up to the floor. There's an eruption of shock and protestation and of children's screaming. Two more guards appear and with their raised guns clear the passage and escort their body-bearing colleagues onto the platform, to a horse and cart, onto which bodies brought out of other carriages are being stacked in a pile.

Oleg picks himself up and runs after them. His cries are gut-wrenching. A dignified burial. That's all he's asking for. This time a vicious blow to his face with a rifle sends him reeling backwards. Henryk and I drop our buckets and rush to help him up and to escort him inside the wagon. Nastusha and Eva are doing their best to console Oleg's children, who cling to each other sobbing and wailing.

Later, when the train moves off with all doors shut and bolted, Oleg presses his swollen cheek against the frost- covered wall of the wagon to catch the last glimpse of his wife's body through a spy hole. I'm looking out through the draughty slit above our bunk. I'm still too numbed to resurrect any emotion, except a wish to bid Bronia a silent farewell. I cannot pick her out of all the corpses thrown together. The cart pulls away shaking the bodies like sacks of potatoes.

CHAPTER 5

We are nine days into our journey. We have passed Yelec and Kotovosk, and hundreds of miles of snow-frozen plains, stopping at remote stations in between, where rag-dressed people and children ran up to our briefly opened doors and begged for food. We had nothing to give them except a yield of dead bodies.

I fear I'm on the brink of madness. I fear this abominable journey was never meant to have a destination. With each passing day I become fearfully more convinced that this nightmare of unrelenting intense cold, of the diminishing food supplies, of the germ-spreading fetid odour that pervades every centimetre of our confined space, has been cunningly created to kill us all off. Since the first day, it seems so remote now, none of us has been able to undress or wash. I feel like an old tramp, my body itching all over, my hair matted and infested with lice, my clothes rancid, my unshaved face like that of a wild man.

Nastusha's initial complaints have given in to stoical acceptance.

'Just think of the pleasure, Julian, when we all have a good soak. It may be sooner than we think. Won't that be pure heaven?' I know she's trying to jolly me along, like when she makes up dreams of running away at the next stop, when we lie close together on the bunk with Dorotka asleep between us and Aniela huddled against Nastusha's back.

She's still in shock, poor child, and though it breaks your heart to watch her, it is a good thing that she has younger siblings to worry about. Her father Oleg seems to have fallen into a permanent daze, and only comes alive when Aniela tugs at his arm to help her fill the buckets with hot water at the stops.

As I hear children cry out with stomach pains every night and listen to their hacking coughs, I feel stricken with terror for our Dorotka. Imagined worst possibilities attack my brain from all sides. Keeping Dorotka warm and dry is a constant worry. Her nappies are dried at the stove on the floor level, but without thorough washing, they've given Dorotka a nappy rash. Thankfully we've still got a little lard left to protect her delicate skin.

Nastusha's milk has dried up the day after Bronia's death. All that day we both felt ill with worry, but Eva suggested giving her watered down semolina. To our immense relief she accepts her new diet. Nevertheless her weight loss is visible. She appears to have shrunk to the size of a new-born, with her sunken cheeks and her matchstick fingers. We keep telling ourselves (against my worst fears) that when we reach our destination, life can be recaptured as normal as possible and that our children will regain their health and weight.

Following Bronia and her stillborn baby, the eldest of the three old sisters died in our carriage, and further down the train two small children died of cold, and a baby suffocated in a fit of coughing. All the older children in our carriage are coughing now. It sounds like the whooping cough. Nastusha and Eva keep our babies well away from the others, but is immunity possible in such a confined space? Dark thoughts plague me mercilessly, but I force myself to hope that our journey is close to an end.

Roman Zastavny is kept busy. In the absence of a real priest and no possibility of a proper church burial, he is constantly asked to pray and to bless the corpses of the loved ones as they are dragged off by the guards at each stop of the train.

'Where's your God now?' I can't help the anger and the bitterness, even as Nastusha pulls me by the sleeve to stop me from blaspheming.

Roman's clear blue eyes, the only true colour in the surrounding gloom, study me with sadness.

'I have no answers,' he replies. 'It is not God who has allowed Stalin to sow his evil. It is the indifference of all the good people, who have stood back and done nothing. His tyranny is nothing new. All through the thirties he has oppressed his own people, destroyed hundreds of villages, and sent thousands of families to their deaths. Through a cunningly created famine. And did the West show any interest? Any compassion? Their indifference was like a tacit approval. They'll wake up one day, too late, when the Red Army appears at their doors.'

His words are like nails in my coffin. Is there no hope for us? I look around our wagon. All ordinary, God-fearing, law-abiding, loved and loving citizens.

'Roman,' I protest, 'we're not some worms or ants. We're human beings.'

Roman's eyes shine moist, like a clear mountain stream.

'Trust Him, Julian. He's got a destiny planned out for each one of us. Whatever ours will be, we have to accept that He knows best.'

I like Roman, I don't want to argue with him and despite my anger, I have to admit that his regular, communal prayers, inject hope into our microcosm of a community.

Dorotka and Stella both have caught the cough. I'm churned with anxiety. Henryk puts up a brave front as he takes turns with Eva to nurse their daughter, but I read fear in the tenseness around his eyes.

It is heart stopping to watch Dorotka's face turn red, then purple when she gasps for breath, her eyes flooded with the effort. When the attack passes and she settles into a feverish sleep, her paper-thin eyelids flickering over her sunken eyes, her rose-bud mouth flaked like a dried up blister, Nastusha cries. I'm left inflamed with anger against those who are inflicting this suffering on our child. I want to break down the walls and the doors of this prison on wheels. I want to rage and roar, but all I can do is to stop myself from crying too. I can do nothing. Nothing for my child. Nothing for my wife. Nothing for those around me.

My stomach feels constantly empty. We are down to just a few bags of rice, lentils and flour. All our vegetables are gone, despite Nastusha's careful rationing. When we lie down for the night, we whisper our dreams to each other. Our dreams of platefuls of *pierogi* and *placki*, or bowls of thick stew. When I sit on the bunk with Henryk, cradling our daughters, while Nastusha and Eva improvise soups on the stove, he and I reminisce about our Sunday afternoons at home, the plump bread covered with slices of ham and cheese, the home-baked apple and plum and blackberry cakes. We reminisce as if we are old men remembering things from our childhood.

Nastusha guards Dorotka's semolina like treasure. Concern and relief play cruel games with our emotions; concern with her lack of appetite, guilty relief that her saved feed will stretch to the next day.

It is fifteen days now, since this torment has been inflicted upon us. We have passed Gorkiy and have been left standing all day in Semenov, on some side track with all doors bolted, no explanations, no hot water. The children got restless, their coughing increased, jarring nerves, testing endurance to the limits. Tempers flared, swearing, like ever faster ping-pong balls, cut through the thick air.

'People! Dear people! Stop!' Roman's voice rose above the din. He stood by the stove amongst the clutter of rancid nappies draped over empty buckets and lifted his arms. He intoned

Serdeczna Matko, Opiekunko ludzi...
Sweet Mother, Protector of people
The children of Eve are calling to You
Have mercy on us.

Miraculously a hush descended upon his captive congregation, then one by one they joined him. After the third hymn had been sung with all the twelve verses, Roman asked the children to join him on the Vronovicz empty bunk. He closed his palms together and opened them like a book, which he pretended to read.

'Nell, *do you know..?' said Stasiu.* A spark of recognition lit up their thin faces. Through the continual interruptions of hacking coughs they listened with avid attention to *The Desert and the Jungle,* that tells the adventures of the two young children, a Polish boy, Stashu, and an English girl, Nell, who escape their abductors and bravely make their way to freedom.

Karolina, Ryszard Dorodny's wife, is not getting better. She has a high temperature and pains in her muscles and bones. Semi-conscious with fever, she is unable to move from the bunk. Mrs. Novitzka's mother is coughing up more blood. There's no doctor or nurse to diagnose their illnesses, no medication to reduce their suffering.

I dread an epidemic, but I keep my fears to myself.

The little Dorodny girls, as thin as marionettes, are comforted by Roman's gently spoken uncle and aunt. The girls' shoulders shake persistently as the coughs rattle in their chests.

Roman, as always, thinks of ways of distracting his little class. He's drawn two circles on a piece of wrapping paper, a piece from the sugar bag, two halves of the globe with the continents outlined on them.

'Will there be wolves and bears where we're going?' Aleks asks, following our route on the improvised map. He's twelve, inquisitive, not easily fobbed off. He needs detailed information.

'They live in the wild,' Roman assures him, 'they won't come close to our town.'

The influenza-like illness has moved to our half of the wagon. Mr. Zastavny looks like a mummy all wrapped up, the rectangle of his forehead showing unnaturally chalky white above the covers. Roman helps his aunt to tend to his uncle's needs, but in his comatose state his uncle is unaware of all their endeavours.

Then something terrible happens, as if the children's unrelenting coughs and the adults' sickness were not plagues enough. When the train stops at a minor station, on the vast open snow-frozen land stretching to the horizon, we all rush out with our buckets for the hot water. There are no toilets. People cross the track between the wagons to the other side to relieve themselves, partly hidden but never free of the guards' prying eyes. Henryk and I stand in the queue for the hot water. There's a crowd surrounding two women selling milk, there's a larger crowd pushing for bread.

'Henryk, if you stay here, I'll queue for the milk. And the bread, if I can get through,' I suggest, giving him my bucket.

There's the usual frantic activity of people running around, anxious to meet all their needs in limited time. Without warning, the train begins to move off.

'Henryk! Julian!' we shout simultaneously to each other above the noise of the panicked crowd. There's a surge of bodies, a rush of running feet, buckets slopping hot water all over the place, raised hands, outstretched arms, shouts and cries. My instinct takes over. I sprint at the side of our open moving carriage and with an all-effort jump propel myself inside. 'Henryk!

Roman!' I shout, and to my relief, they're already beside me and Nastusha is clinging to me, with Dorotka at her chest. The train is gaining speed, the doors slide back with sharp clangs. I look around and count. We're all in. Then my gaze falls on the Yavorski bunk. Three pairs of eyes are looking up at me, Pavel's huge with fear.

'Where's my dad?' he asks, 'where's Aniela? She took Marysia out for a wee.'

God Almighty! This can't be happening. I wonder how many people have been left behind. I walk over and sit beside Pavel. Nastusha sits down on the other side, with the toddlers, Daniel and Tomek between us.

'Pavel,' I stroke his furry head, 'don't worry. They've probably jumped on another wagon. They'll come back to us when the train stops at the next station.'

His brown eyes fill with tears.

'But that's a whole day away! Maybe two! Who'll look after us?'

'We will,' Nasusha comforts him, drawing the little ones close to her.

'But what if they've been left back at the station?' He brushes the tears away with his sleeve.

'There's only one track here, Pavel,' I feign calm, 'the train that follows will catch up with us on the way. We'll soon be together again, you'll see.'

I force a smile as my mind conjures up frozen bodies in the snow.

Henryk gets it first among the four of us; the mind-numbing, the body debilitating illness. He is feverish and shakes violently. His teeth chatter as he curls up underneath all the covers they can find. Eva looks worn out dividing her time between her sick child and her stricken husband. I notice, with a shock, how this once beautiful girl, with her enviable blue-bell eyes and hair the colour of bleached corn, has been reduced to this worn-looking woman with protruding cheek and chin bones and all freshness gone from her eyes.

'I couldn't bear it if anything happened to him,' she whispers through a silent weep.

Nastusha embraces her and holds her close for a moment. What can anyone say?

'Eva, you're not alone, you've got us...'

'And us...' two small voices confirm. They cling to Nastusha's coat. They've not left our side since their father's disappearance.

There's been one stop since then, but no sign of him, only tales from people in the other wagons. People have been left behind. A woman has been crushed to death between the suddenly moving wagons. Mr. Koval from about six wagons down is becoming a familiar figure, the services of his axe more frequently in demand, as toes become frost-bitten, inflamed, purple, black, then gangrenous.

Nastusha checks religiously the feet of our little charges, every night, hurriedly, wrapping them up in bandages torn from an old sheet, before pulling on their fur-lined boots. She's made comforters for the two little boys, which they suck at night time to help them sleep: knots in handkerchiefs filled with a little sugar. Soothing for their flaking lips. Daniel and Tomek sleep wedged between us; their older brother Pavel has been adopted by Roman and his aunt, on the lower bunk. Every day he spends hours at the spy hole, waiting for the train to stop, waiting for his father and his two sisters to rejoin him and his brothers.

The day after Henryk is stricken with the illness, I get the symptoms too. Strong pains attack my whole body; my face is cold yet my head throbs unbearably, threatening to explode. The violent shivering intensifies the stiffness in my joints. I feel totally defeated.

'Nastusha,' my voice rasps, 'I'll be up as soon as I can…'

'Hush, Julian, hush…' she places a warm towel over my face. 'You need to sweat it out to reduce the fever…'

The towel barely warms my face, but I experience a fleetingly pleasant sensation as I drift off into a void. Blackness engulfs me.

When I open my eyes, my eyelids are heavy, my eyeballs feel bruised. The rhythmic swaying of our wagon drives the pain deeper with every thud. Slowly I turn sideways. Nastusha is stretched out beside me covered up to her chin. She's caught the illness too. Her sallow skin and her closed eyes, like dark indentations in her face, give her the appearance of a corpse. Fear grips my heart. I make an effort to raise myself on my elbow.

'Nastusha, Nastusha…' I whisper, willing her to respond.

'Let her sleep, Julian,' Henryk's voice comes from across the passage, 'it's the only treatment we've got…' He's sitting up, cradling little Stella in his arms. He's got a haunted look in his eyes, a ghostly pallor in his face. Eva is comatose beside him, underneath a mound of covers. 'It's inevitable,' he adds, 'in this cramped space, all of us breathing the same rotten air.'

'How long have I been like this?' I ask.

'Three days.'

'Three days!' I have no sense of time. A thought strikes me and with it a jab of panic. 'Who's looking after our Dorotka?'

He looks me straight in the eye and then lowers his gaze. I know him too well.

'Is anything wrong? Has something happened? Henryk! Tell me!'

Before he replies, Roman's head pops up from the lower bunk.

'Are you well enough to look after her?' he asks. My head feels like a container half full of water, making me dizzy and nauseous with the slightest movement. My tongue is dry, like a rattle in my mouth.

'I need some water,' I request, laying my head down with a groan. He climbs up high enough to hold my head up, to press the cup to my lips.

'There now,' he says, 'you're not ready yet. Give yourself a little more time.'

'And Dorotka?'

'All children are being looked after by the Bogusz sisters,' he assures me.

'How come they haven't caught the bug?'

'God only knows, but let's be grateful for that.'

It's too much of an effort to keep my eyes open. I feel Nastusha beside me and Dorotka's in good hands. My heavy eyelids come down like shutters and I feel myself falling into darkness.

It must be morning the next day when I wake up. A sunbeam falls through a slit in the wall above me and forms a pencil thin rectangle on the adjacent wall, an iridescent neon in the permanent gloom of our wagon. I lie still waiting for the pains to resume in my muscles and bones, but to my surprise, all I feel is an emptiness inside me, as if my belly has collapsed against my spine. I feel a scratchiness all over my body clad in my foul smelling clothes, stiff as wood shavings, with dried sweat. I balance shakily on my elbow and look around. Nastusha lies very still beside me, alarmingly still, but then, to my relief, I see her eyelids flicker as a feverish spasm crosses her face, a shrunken face, ravaged by fear and hunger. I have to get up, I tell myself, to take control again, to help her to recover, to look after our baby.

There are all the signs around me of people waking up. I hear children's whispers, subdued by parental reminders of consideration for others; Mrs. Zastavna and one of the old Bogusz sisters are already at the stove, resurrecting the fire with logs, their pots ready, waiting.

'I feel as if I've been chewed and spat out,' I remark to Henryk, who appears to have stayed glued to his spot since yesterday. Eva is curled up beside him, motionless underneath the covers. Henryk nods, but does not say anything. I climb down, my whole body trembling as I hold to the pole. Roman is already waiting for me.

'Sit down for a minute, Julian, beside me,' he invites.

My anxious gaze skims all the bunks. Ryszard Dorodny is lying down on his side with his face to the wall. His wife is missing. His three little girls are being comforted by the elderly Bogusz siblings. Pavel, on his family's empty bunk, is wiping the snot off Tomek's face, while Daniel hangs on to his coat with both hands. Good God! I'm supposed to be looking after them, the poor little orphans! Aleks and Artur sit like vigilant guards over their sick mother. Where's their grandmother? With a sickening feeling, worse than my shaky weakness, I search for our child.

'Where is she?' my voice is hoarse.

'Julian, sit down. Please.' Roman is gentle, his hand coaxing on my arm. I shake it off.

I see hurt in his eyes. I sit down and glimpse behind him his aunt's mournful face as she leans over her dying husband.

34

'Julian,' Roman says, 'things have been happening while you were down with fever. Mrs. Novitzka's mother died. Now she's got the illness. Ryszard's wife died too…' I look up at their bunks and swallow hard. My throat hurts. I begin to understand their silence, heavy with grief.

'Dorotka. Where are you hiding Dorotka?' I struggle with a surge of hysteria.

'Just bear with me…' Roman's blue eyes turn dark. I hurry him. He clears his throat and speaks, halting with each phrase: 'when the guards came… in the morning…to collect the bodies… I pretended that Dorotka was very ill…'

Pretended? Why did he have to pretend? I don't understand.

'She had that dreadful cough,' I remind him.

'Yes, she did,' Roman's nod is nervous, 'I ran out with her inside the station and begged for milk from anyone who listened, I begged for milk for a dying baby…'

I stare at him.

'A dying baby? Why did you say such things?'

'Because…' Roman's voice drops, 'because, I wanted to save your baby from being thrown on the cart with other bodies…'

We hold each other's gazes for a long time. His eyes begin to water. Then, without warning, a terrible pain tears through my body and a roaring noise pierces my eardrums, growing louder and shriller, like the roar of a wild beast. I become one with the howling and the agony.

'Julian, Julian…' Roman sounds distant. My body doubles up, my palms press against my face, the terrifying noise is stifled. I'm suddenly aware of a strange hush around me. I cannot look up. I rock to and fro, in unison with the running train as if somehow this rhythmic action could take away my pain.

It calms me down, enough for me to beg Roman to tell me everything again. I want to know every little detail. I cannot control the sobs that escape my chest, yet I need to listen with acute attention to his every word.

'Julian, Anastazia went down just hours after you did. She collapsed by the stove. Ryszard and I helped her to your bunk and Mr. Bogusz' sisters took charge of Dorotka. She must have already been very ill…' he pauses as if formulating words in his mind, phrases that will deliver a lesser blow. 'The two ladies did their best to nurse her through the night. They took turns to hold her, to keep her warm. She was refusing food. They dampened her mouth, they tried to coax her with drops of milk. She just coughed all the more. In the early hours all the coughing suddenly stopped. There was no doubt…' Roman's voice is shaky, 'she had stopped breathing. We did all the usual checks. The pulse, the heart, the mirror against her mouth. Not a trace of moisture on the glass…'

None of it sounds real, but I need to know more.

'How did she look?'

'Peaceful. Sweet. We crossed her little hands on her chest. Her face was like white porcelain. Like a little cherub from the paintings in the church'. He chooses his words carefully for my benefit, but my mind rejects them. This cannot be true. He must be speaking another language, with another meaning to his words.

Yesterday, only yesterday, or maybe the day before, Dorotka was here, with us... so small yet so big in our lives, her presence filling every minute of every day and night. I long for the baby smell of her, for the softness of her skin, for her gurgling laughter, for the heart-swelling happiness every time I held her to my chest.

'I must find her,' I tell him. Shakily I get up to my feet. Roman does not try to stop me only his eyes watch me worried and sad.

I stagger between the bunks and poke my head inside every space. Some last vestige of common sense pulls me back from this futile search, but my instinct drives me on to check every hidden corner and peer underneath the bunks into the dark recesses stuffed with people's belongings. When there's nowhere else left to look, I drag myself back to Roman and sit down heavily beside him. I hide my face in my palms and press hard, harder and harder, willing this nightmare to be gone when I uncover my eyes. I feel Roman's arm across my bent back and hear his voice, cautiously low.

'Julian... hear me out...'

I nod and sway with the rhythm of the running train.

He takes a deep breath.

'When the train stopped,' he tells me, 'when the guards came in to collect the dead bodies, I hid Dorotka underneath my coat and went out with the others for the hot water. I already had a plan. I had my silver chain and cross ready in my pocket to bribe anyone willing to listen. It was a bigger station. Lots of people. I looked around. There was a Russian couple on the edge of a long queue. I took my chance. It was totally crazy, but I had no choice. I said I needed milk for my dying baby, but if they knew a doctor or a nurse, I needed someone to have a look. I showed them, so that no one else would see, the silver in my hand. This was all the payment I could give them, I said, if only they'd help me. The silver did the trick. They came up close to me. There was no doctor at the station, they said, but they knew someone who worked at the hospital nearby. I opened the coat and showed them Dorotka. For a split second I feared the worst, but they did not call the guards. *I beg you*, I said, *I beg you to give my child a decent burial.* They eyed each other and nodded, then the woman took Dorotka from me and hid her inside her overcoat. *We'll do it*, she said. I believed her. I think they were decent people. And I think the silver more than compensated for their abandoned journey. They left the station straight away and were gone before I joined the water queue.'

We sit in silence for a long while, Roman and I. I uncurl myself and straighten my back. I'm only vaguely aware of the sounds of life around me, subdued, fearful, I think, of my unpredictable reaction. My mind goes over every single word of Roman's account, again and again. Each time my anguish deepens, until it becomes like a raw, agonising wound, spreading, unsparing to every part of me.

'Julian, I did everything I could. Dorotka was saved...' Roman does not have to add 'from a mass grave,' but I know he means to comfort me. I cannot be comforted. I feel like a traitor to my own child. I wasn't there when it mattered most. And now, like a tiny abandoned bundle she lies buried in the frozen ground, a microscopic dot, never to be found, in the depths of the vast land of Russia. Our child.

A violent shudder runs the length of my body.

What will I tell Nastusha?

CHAPTER 6

Nastusha refuses to come down from the bunk. It's two days now since I've told her. Buried under her covers, she ignores my entreaties, my offers of porridge and tea. God knows, she needs all the strength she can get to get back on her feet.

I still feel limp and washed out from the illness. But worse than that is the rawness inside me, which at times is intolerable. I beg God to wipe out all my memory, and with it all my agony, so I can wake up new and strong and capable of taking care of my wife and our little adopted brood. I'm ahead of Nastusha a day or two in our recovery from the illness that had attacked us out of nowhere. Hardly surprising though, with our immune systems undermined, in this filth and stale air and lack of vital nourishment and deprivation of sun and light.

Inexplicably some of us have been spared; the elderly Bogusz siblings, Roman's aunt and Roman.

'How come you're so lucky?' I ask, each word oozing like burning acid.

'God has plans for each one of us,' he answers with a smile. His faith is so simple.

'God can keep his plans,' I retort, 'what good are they to any of us?'

'I pray for you Julian.' He never loses his calm.

'You can keep your prayers!'

'I do. For all of us here.'

Raging anger eats me, and hatred, like black mould, against the perpetrators of crimes against us. When I close my eyes at night I dream of revenge and torture and death for the monster and his henchmen who have hatched out this inhuman plan. I hate him with such force, I can barely bring myself to say his name. Savage. Psychopath. Murderer. I call him all the worst names. Something twists inside me at the very shape of the letters of his name: Stalin.

Undeterred by my uncontrolled outbursts, Roman is standing beside me now, pleading with Nastusha to come down. As have Henryk and Eva in turn, to no avail.

'Leave me alone! I want to die! Please, let me die!' Her cry is like a voice from purgatory. It gives me the shivers. I feel her pain. It intensifies mine. At the same time I feel a surge of resentment against her, a sense of betrayal. As if I and my pain did not matter. 'What about me?' I want to shout, already regretting this self-pitiful, if only mental, rant. I'm supposed to be the strong one. Her rock. I take a deep breath and attempt an assertive tone.

'Anastazia! You can't go on like this! Whether you like it or not, I'm getting you some food, and you'll eat it even if I have to force it down you!'

There's no sound from her, no movement. Roman nudges me then places his finger on his lips as if he had a secret that he wants to be kept from Nastusha. It's all unnecessary, for she does not care about what is going on around her.

While I busy myself at the stove cooking porridge, Roman picks up Daniel first, then Tomek and helps them climb up onto our bunk. They settle themselves on each side of Nastusha's reclining form, and coughing profusely, stroke her covered shoulder and arm, planting slobbery kisses all over her head.

'Aunt Nastusha, are you better yet?' Daniel asks. 'We want you to be well. You've got to look after us. Please get up. Please!'

Daniel repeats his pleas several times. I'm racked with uncertainty. Is this such a good idea? What if she's incapable of making decisions just yet? What if the boys' presence makes Dorotka's absence even more acutely felt? What further damage will her rejection cause these poor little orphans?

I take a deep breath. There's a movement from her. She pushes off her covers and pulls herself up slowly to sit up. Her face is ash-grey and there are dark circles underneath her eyes. She extends her arms around Daniel and Tomek and draws them close to her sides. They look up expectantly, unsure. She does not say anything just rocks with them in her embrace.

'Aunt Nastusha,' Daniel speaks to her, 'are you better now? Will you look after us?'

Her mouth trembles and tears escape her eyes.

'I made a promise to your Mum', she says, 'and promises must be kept, mustn't they?'

We're in the fourth week of our journey. The sameness of our days does not make us any more used to our conditions: the incessant rumbling of the metal wheels, the rocking of our wagon, at times violent with unexpected, sudden stops, the frozen walls, the perpetual stench, the lice, the fear of starvation as the remnants of our food supplies are dwindling daily, the persistent gnawing hunger, the stale clothes, the scratchy underwear, stiff with a month's dried sweat, the feeling of being forgotten and abandoned by the rest of the world; no, one can't ever get used to such things. Yet our stoical acceptance is our only hope of surviving this once unimaginable journey, and now a grim, incessant reality.

The stops for hot water are our chance of exchanging any possessions for food, with the rag-dressed vendors, who can be seduced with items as insignificant as an embroidered handkerchief. The only obtainable bread is black, hard and heavy like a brick. We make it palatable and lasting longer by cutting it very thin, and dampening it with tea or milk. Obtaining an egg or two is a prayed-for luxury. At times soup is available, 'soup' being a misnomer for a cabbage leaf floating in oily water. Dried fish is hard to resist when sporadically it makes an appearance, except that its salt content requires litres upon litres of water to wash it down. We haven't got litres, only the limited amounts contained in the only buckets we've got.

Nastusha has parted with Dorotka's garments in exchange for food. She has kept just one baby bonnet which she carries tucked inside her camisole on her chest, close to her heart. She uses the left-overs of Dorotka's cream to treat the boys' reddened, flaky faces and their swollen toes.

Nastusha suffers severe attacks of grief. Her whole body trembles with the effort of stifling her cries. She stuffs her gloved hand in her mouth and bites hard, her eyes shut tight until the attack passes. I feel utterly helpless. At night, with Tomek and Daniel asleep between us, I stroke her face, until her sighs die down, until her form becomes still. I'm weary of my own pretence of having to be strong at all times. In the middle of the night, when all human sounds are soothed into silence by all-forgetting sleep, and only the metallic rhythm of the train wheels relentlessly pounds on, I cry. It's all so stupid! I get no relief. My eyes still sting the next day, my nose gets clogged up, and the weight on my chest never shifts for a moment, day or night.

Henryk has changed. Gone are the anti-Soviet quips and the bravado, all a defiant act, I know, put on for our sakes, yet inspiring hope in our dreams of returning home one day. I need him to talk, to dream with me, to come alive with plans of an escape, impossible as it is. When I talk to him, he just nods. When I ask him questions he gives me back a reluctant Yes or No. I'd prefer him to rage, to shout and swear. I'd even wrestle with him given the space. His quiet is unnatural. Unsettling.

Eva has that perpetual haunted look about her eyes and avoids mine. When she and Nastusha stand by the stove, like optimistic magicians attempting to create a nourishing concoction out of a handful of remaining grains, they stand side by side, not looking at each other, exchanging small talk, predominantly about food. She has stopped climbing up to our bunk with Stella, as she did before, when she and Nastusha would while away the long hours, chatting and rocking their babies. Stella is very frail, with tiny blue veins marking the pale skin on her hands that are no bigger than a doll's hands. It is a miracle that she's still alive. Her cough appears less intense and she is able to hold down her food and sleep for longer periods of time.

I sometimes catch Nastusha looking at her with longing and something twists in my heart. I can't stop questioning fate; why our child? Why not theirs? It's just a reaction, not a wish. In this tight crammed community anyone's loss is everyone's loss. Their pain would be our pain. Just look at the Yavorski orphans or the Dorodny girls. Why them? I could ask. Why any of us? Why this monstrous evil thrust upon us? I question Roman for answers. He's honest at least.

'Julian, I don't understand any of it, but you must never let go of your trust in God.'

'I wish He'd hurry up and deliver us from this hell.'

'All in good time. He's got His own plans. Slow but sure. Trust Him!'

'Roman, for goodness sake! Are you blind to what's happening around you?!'

Roman's eyes shine, impossibly blue, in the murkiness of the thick, stale air, then he turns round to help his aunt lift his uncle's shoulders and prop them up against a bundle of rolled up sheets, so she can feed him. Mr. Zastavny, the ever gently spoken man, is very ill. The feeding routine is just an attempt at raising hope. Each time Mrs. Zastavna touches her husband's blue lips with a spoon of warm gruel, she prays that he'll have the strength to swallow the food and so make the first step to recovery. Her attempt is futile. Mr. Zastavny is comatose with high fever and there's no medication for him. Roman helps his aunt to lay him back flat, then all she can do is place on his forehead a scarf, which she has cooled against the frosted wall. A wet compress would freeze to his face.

'Julian,' Roman straightens up, 'I have no answers to any of this. We are all battered and bewildered here. It's natural to start doubting God. But you've still got yourself. And for as long as you're alive, you've only got one realistic choice. To go on. No matter what. Or would you rather curl up and wait to die?' He pauses and his clear eyes bore into mine and though my whole being tingles with anger and irritation, I cannot deny a twinge of envy for his dignified calm.

'I'll go on Roman,' I reply bitterly, 'but I swear to God, if I ever get the chance to get hold of one of the bastards who are doing this to us, I'll kill him! Chop him up into bits. With an axe!' It's stupid talk, and I know it, but momentarily my threats of revenge give me a satisfying feeling.

'Count me in!' Henryk's voice comes from his bunk.

'And me! And me!' other voices join in.

Roman looks around.

'Revenge is dangerous,' he says, 'you end up hurting more people than you have bargained for. Often innocent ones. What you need is justice. And properly, legally apportioned punishment.'

'Oh really? And who's going to take our side in this forsaken land. Who's going to listen to us? Stalin?' There, I've said his name and I pretend to spit as I utter the hated word.

'He's not invincible,' Roman says, 'his time will come. And all his crimes will catch up with him in the end. He'll be tried and sentenced.'

That's news to me.

'Really? And how will that be possible?'

'There is an international court,' Roman informs us, with his ever patient,

41

ever pleasant manner, 'a court that deals with dictators like him, and with crimes against humanity.'

I don't wish to dispute Roman's information, but his words sound like a fantasy tale.

'I hope to God, you're right Roman,' I say, 'but I also hope that we'll live to see this happen.'

Roman's reply is simple. 'I pray every day and every night for justice to be done.'

It is early morning. Tomek and Daniel are still asleep, their faces protected from the chill air by scarves which Nastusha has tucked inside their fur-lined hats. She is getting up, ready to boil some water for porridge. Across the passage on their bunk, Henryk and Eva are getting up too.

'Keep her well wrapped up,' Eva instructs Henryk, giving him the bundle of soft blankets, with their little Stella cocooned inside them. She needs to visit the corner behind the screen.

'Let me hold her,' Nastusha says suddenly surprising us all. There's an awkward silence and I see hesitation in Eva's worn face.

'You've got enough on your hands,' she says gently, 'and anyway, Henryk's become quite a baby expert with nothing else to do.' She attempts a smile.

'I know,' Nastusha agrees, 'and what would we have done without our men?' There's no rancour in her words. 'I just want to hold your Stella. Just for a while. Please.'

Eva hands over her precious child and Nastusha cradles her in her arms with so much warmth and reverence, as if Stella was the most wonderful gift on earth. She brings her face down to the tiny features and brushes Stella's cheek with her lips. Then she looks up and smiles, her eyes reddening round the rims of her eyelids.

'This is what I miss,' she says, 'it's like a constant pain.'

Eva's mouth trembles, she hides her face in her hands, and suppresses a sob.

'Don't cry, Eva. Please don't cry.'

Eva looks up and wipes her eyes.

'I'd give anything for things to go back to as they were before...' she says.

'I know that, Eva. Whatever happens to any of us here, affects us all.'

'I was afraid, that you'd hate me...' Eva's haunted look returns to her eyes.

Nastusha shakes her head.

'Eva... what little faith you've got in me...' she reprimands her gently. 'How could I hate anyone here, when we're all victims of the same enemy. No, we must not allow their mistreatment of us destroy anything that's good, that still holds us together.'

Nastusha's clarity of thought surprises me. It surprises Henryk too, I notice. There's an almost imperceptible change in his face, but I recognise it. Haven't I been his inseparable companion in our other life? Haven't I witnessed a hundred times all the changes in his expressions in all his moods?

'Julian,' he says, 'I had a strange dream. I dreamed we were on a barge. On a fast running river. We were escaping to freedom...'

'Henryk,' I lighten my tone, 'that's the best piece of news I've heard for a long time. We must start planning that escape. But first, we must find a river.'

There's a trace of a smile in the crinkles around his eyes, and I know that he knows and is relieved that we can start talking again without reservations.

CHAPTER 7

It has become a noticeable fact, that the further and deeper into the Russian land our cattle-truck train hurtles, the guards' supervision, so severe and intimidating at first, appears to become more lax, at stops on remote stations. It does not require a genius to work out why. They are certain now of our total helplessness. There's not the slightest chance of an escape. On the vast and frozen plains we'd be visible targets for miles around. In the intermittent forests, we'd become easy prey and fodder for the wolves and the bears. The guards' tasks of supervising us at all times are helped by the environment.

Also our numbers have visibly dwindled. When the thinned crowd runs out for the hot water at stops, the normally trigger-happy vigilance of the guards gives in to standing back and feet stamping for warmth, and even to the odd smoke.

Then something strange happens, though nothing by this stage should surprise me in this country ruled by a madman. We can only assume, in our deliberations, Henryk, Roman and I, that there must have been a directive to the officer in charge of our train, to make up the numbers of those lost on the way.

This morning, just after we check everyone's presence following a stop at a station for hot water, and just before the metal door is slid back in place and bolted, three people are pushed inside our carriage. They are Russians. Ordinary citizens, going about their business, waiting for their train. Their own soldiers have kidnapped them.

They stand in the middle, confused, bewildered, looking at us with fear in their eyes, clinging together for support and balance as the carriage begins to rock with acceleration. The two older ones may be a couple. They are wearing padded jackets, *koofayki*, thick trousers and *valonki*, felt boots worn over shoes. They are wrapped additionally in thick shawls. Their faces look ancient, with numerous wrinkles like folds of gathered leather. The younger woman, who may be their daughter is dressed in similar attire. She dabs her eyes and quietly cries. My smattering of Russian enables me to catch the gist of her concern.

'Who'll tell our Ninotchka? And Aloysha? They won't know what's happened to us. And who'll look after them?'

I come forward to tell them that there's room on the Vronovicz vacated bunk, but they shrink back from me as if I were a dangerous beast.

'*Pozhaista*, please, I mean no harm,' I assure them, 'look there's a space for you there if you want to sit down.'

The old couple cling together and don't budge. The woman says,

'*Atyets, Mat*, Father, Mother, sit down and rest while you can.'

We all watch them, the children from the high bunks too, as they move nervously towards the empty bunk. Roman greets them with the old Polish saying,

'*Gość w dom, Bóg w dom*. A visitor at home is like God with you at home.'

They stare back but he does not give up,

'So where are you travelling to?' he asks in Russian.

The old couple look at each other and remain silent. The woman, surprisingly, answers,

'We've volunteered to work at a labour camp. They've got a shortage of workers there.'

'And where's that?' I'm eager to know. Perhaps at last we'll find out our destination.

The woman shakes her head.

'That, we've not been told yet...'

Roman comes forward and asks,

'And you've volunteered? Your elderly parents too? That's very noble of you.' His tone is friendly but I detect a hint of irony in his words. The woman does not appear to notice this and replies in all seriousness.

'The great Soviet Union needs us. It is our privilege to work for the common good. Our benefactor, our great leader Stalin, like a loving father will provide everything that we need.'

I want to vomit on this propaganda, instilled in these poor wretches by repression and fear. There is no need to contradict the woman. Time spent in our cramped conditions, lack of food and water, the guards' indifference will soon open her eyes.

'Perhaps we too can enjoy all the benefits at the end of this journey?' I suggest with challenging sarcasm.

Her eyes flash and she retorts angrily,

'You have to work first, to enjoy the benefits, but what would you know about that, you criminal lot!'

Criminal! My blood boils, but Roman's restraining hand calms me down momentarily.

'Is that what you've been told?' he asks, 'Criminals? Look around you, good lady, and make up your own mind. See these three boys here? They've lost their parents and their three siblings on this journey. What crimes do you think they'd committed to deserve that? See this man behind me? My uncle. Too ill to move. The gentlest person I know. There's a baby up there, and two more boys, and three little girls. Criminals? Really? Just think about that.'

The woman appears decent enough to look uncomfortable with Roman's gentle tone. She looks away and joins the old couple on the empty bunk.

She'll find out soon enough. I can't help an inappropriate smirk of satisfaction.

It is 8th of March, the twenty-seventh day of our journey. Three weeks and six days. A blink of an eye in my normal busy life. An eternity of hell in our prison on wheels.

Our train stops in Kotlas at four in the morning in the barely awakened dawn. Why this unearthly hour? I wonder, as we are let out with our buckets for the *keepiatok*. The size of the station is my answer, one of the major stations on our route and they don't want us to be seen, a train load of foul smelling, bedraggled tramps. Even in the half-light the kindly face of Comrade Stalin looks down on us from the tall walls of the sprawling complex of buildings. There's a sharp wind blowing along the platform. Save for the uniformed station guards and our own armed henchmen there's no one else about.

Panic grips me. Where will I get some food? For three hungry boys. I picture their expectant eyes and something twists inside me. Roman helps out with Pavel, but the boy is naturally drawn to his younger siblings and we often end up with the three of them sleeping with Nastusha, while I climb down and rest for the night next to Roman. His uncle, Mr. Zastavny, looks dead most of the time. Roman and his aunt check the old man's pulse regularly to stop the guards removing him from the train. I don't get it. There he is, a frail old man, lingering on and on...while our little Dorotka... why this miracle for him? And not for her?

My head is filled with grumbles and angry thoughts as I rush with Henryk to join the queue for the hot water. Suddenly, the bundles of rags and torn blankets piled against the wall begin to move and people emerge from them. Even in my tramp-like state I feel like a prince compared to them.

They're wrapped from head to toe in hole-ridden shawls, malting furs and crumbling leathers. The *valonki* on their feet are held together with string. They rush towards us with their wares. They are the station vendors, the fortunate beneficiaries of Stalin's great regime.

My face burns with anger turning the icy air around my head to white vapour, but stronger than my anger for the moment, is my need to obtain food. I leave Henryk with the buckets, and join the bread queue. I get two loaves, the usual black bricks, in exchange for my worn and favourite khaki shorts, and hurry back to free our girls. Nastusha parts with one of her small embroidered tablecloths and comes back with a bag of flour and a jug of milk. The boys crowd round her with anticipation, as she promises.

'I'll make you some delicious noodles!'

Her face lights up like a passing ray. I'd give anything to bring back sunshine to her face, to erase the shadows from underneath her eyes, to hear her laugh, to hear her sing again.

For a moment my mind jumps ahead into the future. Will there ever come a day when all this is left behind us, when we can start again, fresh and optimistic, impatient to follow our dreams? Even as I think these thoughts, I know that our tarnished life can never regain its sparkle, how can it, with Dorotka gone? The pain deep inside me surfaces again.

Our train is locked and bolted, only to stop in the sidings well away from the station buildings. Trains come and go all morning, the steam billowing above the platforms, the sounds of guards' whistles echoing the bustle of a normal life elsewhere, as we are left stationary, abandoned.

'They've left us to die here,' the older Bogusz sister, the herb medic, declares.

'Nonsense!' the younger sister contradicts her, 'why would they do such a horrible crime right in the middle of a large town, when they've got countless forests to hide their dirty deeds in?'

She's got a point and I hang on to it, though nothing is ever certain, as there's no sense in anything that's happened to us.

'What do you think, *Gazpazha* Ivanova?' Henryk climbs down and greets the new tenant below his bunk with a deep bow. She hates being called *gazpazha,* she has told him so. It's bourgeois. Demeaning. She is a comrade, like the rest of her people.

Her parents remain uncommunicative, even after we've put together a collection of covers for them and shared our meagre rations. They spend their days huddled together, making occasional dialogue in subdued whispers. Their daughter, comrade Ivanova, appears to be thawing out towards us, and though never first to speak, gives guarded replies to our questions. Like the rest of us she has developed that weary look around her eyes and mouth, and I've seen her scratching underneath her fur hat. Lice have no respect for anyone.

'Why do you think they've stopped us here?' Henryk pursues.

Her eyes widen and she shrugs.

'It is not for me to question their wisdom.'

'Sweet Jesus!' Henryk's tone and sky-ward glance say it all.

'Go easy on her, Henryk,' I say, 'what do you expect? They've never experienced our kind of life, our freedom.'

Her defiance comes fast.

'That's not true! In our system all people are free and all are treated equally!'

Roman swings his legs over and settles beside me. He nods to her.

'In our system, Comrade Ivanova, innocent people don't get arrested in the middle of the night. In our system people are free to choose what they want to do with their life. They are free to travel anywhere they like, they are free to buy what they like. The shops are full of merchandise, food, clothes, furniture, anything you think of.'

'I don't believe you. You're making up these lies to taunt me. Your system is corrupt with injustices. The *kulaks* have it all at the expense of the oppressed poor people.'

Henryk shakes his head.

'No, you've got it all wrong,' he says, 'we are the ordinary people, we've not been oppressed by any *kulaks* or land owners. In fact, they provide livelihood for villages around their estates. Oppression came only recently with the German invasion, and now with your own people.'

'That was to defend you!' she argues, but her voice trails off.

'Then what are we doing here?' Henryk asks.

'I've told you already, it's not for me to question such things. The state will look after all of us fairly.' It's pointless to go on with this inane conversation. We leave Comrade Ivanova in peace.

There's a sudden jerk and the three of us bump into one another, like falling dominoes. The children shout 'hurrah', the train moves out of the station and gains speed. My watch shows midday, and Roman's scouts compass indicates that our east-bound journey has changed course. We are going south. But not for long. The train slows down after an hour and a half and stops.

'We're in the middle of nowhere!' Artur shouts from his high bunk.

'Just a thick forest around us!' Alex adds as they take turns to spy through the peep hole.

It's the Russian taiga, denser and by far more immense than our forests at home.

The boys' words are drowned in the clanging of sliding doors and the shouting of the guards.

'*Bistra! Spisheet*! Hurry! Everyone out!'

The brightness of the snow blinds me for a moment, then we all begin to jump out of the wagon, one by one, men going first to help women and children. The virgin snow soon becomes trodden into a hard, slippery mass. Nastusha carries little Daniel, I carry Tomek and Pavel clings to us both.

It is a strange sight, hundreds of people spilling out of the cattle trucks. There's no sun, only the steel-cold sky hanging heavy above us. The surrounding landscape of conifers and pine trees is etched hard in black and white. We check and tighten the scarves around the children's faces. The cold is intense, penetrating all layers of clothing to the skin, even the flesh to the bones.

'Keep your faces covered up all the time,' I remind the children.

'Or your noses will drop off,' Artur laughs through his muffler, then stops with his mother's smack.

We all have itchy, chillblained toes and fingers. Mr. Koval's axe has saved a few lives, but I don't even want to think about resorting to such dire measures.

We leave the children sitting on top of a suitcase and cover them up with all the blankets we've got, before emptying the wagon of all remaining luggage. Mrs. Zastavna, distressed and distracted with worry, and Eva cradling her baby underneath her overcoat, sit with the children, while Henryk, Nastusha and I help Roman to lift his uncle off the bunk and carry him onto the eiderdown spread out on the snow. His closed eyes are sunken deep in his ashen face. It is heart wrenching to watch him in this state, to drag him along with us like an inanimate object.

There's hardly a sound from the crowd sprawled on the snow in the middle of a forest. The guards stomp around, no doubt, I suspect, as fed up as we are.

'So what now?' I ask, anger, my constant companion, hotting up inside me.

'We're in bloody Archangielsk region,' Henryk says, 'I've asked the guard.'

'Christ! That's what? Two thousand kilometres from home?' I guess.

'More like three,' Roman says.

I catch Nastusha's glance above her muffler, the pained expression in her eyes, and something squeezes my chest. Only four weeks ago, God, is that all it is? – we inhabited a normal world filled with our child's presence and our happiness. Grown man that I am, I long suddenly for my mother's comforting embrace, I feel a desperate need for my father, as I swallow hard to choke my moment of weakness.

'I'm so hungry...' Pavel's whisper pulls me back to reality.

'And me...' Tomek adds anxiously. Daniel is quiet in Nastusha's arms as he sucks the silken edge of his baby blanket.

Nastusha sits him down to rummage through our food bag and produces a slice of black bread. She breaks a quarter each for the boys and tucks the pieces inside their scarves.

'Suck to soften it first,' she tells them, 'then chew for a long time. Don't swallow it all at once.'

The last quarter of the slice she breaks in two and shares it between us. Even this small morsel, tasting like cardboard and feeling like dry clay is heaven on my tongue. My stomach does a strange twist as I struggle to follow her instructions.

'Will there be a supper waiting for us?' Pavel asks.

This is torment. I cannot bear the disappointment in his eyes when I answer truthfully.

'I don't know.'

'Here, have some of mine.' Roman offers him a portion of his bread. Tomek wants some too. Roman breaks the piece into two equal halves and my stomach yearns for more as I watch his act of kindness.

Our attention is distracted by the sudden movement of the train. We watch the cattle trucks roll by in a line that appears to have no beginning and no end. Then after a while the locomotive comes into view, passes us with much hissing in clouds of steam, diminishes in the distance to a dot and disappears. The prison on wheels that has been our home for a month has vanished, and with it all evidence of our existence has gone. Who will ever find us here, thousands of miles away, hidden in the depths of Russian forests?

Eva sidles up to Nastusha, her arms tight around the tiny form sheltered under her overcoat, and only their eyes, visible above their mufflers, exchange wordless messages of fear and grief.

Just then there is a tinkling sound like the sleigh bells back home in Poland. It's not just my own imagination, because Henryk and Roman jump up, stamp their feet and beat their arms against their bodies for warmth as they strain their eyes through the shadowy gloom of the forest. Dark figures emerge, ten, twenty, then more, pulling empty sledges.

Our guards return to their groups and shout,

'Baggage and children on the sledges! All adults to walk and pull!'

CHAPTER 8

It is five in the afternoon and already dark. We've been walking for over two hours along the swathe that cuts through the forest, pulling sledges with our possessions on top of which the children and the infirm huddle together under covers. The guard walking between Nastusha and me makes it impossible to talk. I cast her frequent sideways glances and note helplessly how laboured her breathing is, and how often she stumbles with exertion. Ahead of us Henryk and Eva are pulling their sledge, and behind us Roman struggles with his, even with the Russian guard helping to pull his aunt and uncle. Mrs. Zastavna is bent over her husband's inert form, keeping the quilt down and tucked in all around him.

Lights appear in the distance, dim but sure. Images of candlelight in the windows at home come to mind. My blurred vision sharpens, my tired legs regain their spring and I fall in step with the guard. He speaks through the scarf wound around his face:

'This is it. *Vash kolhoz.* Your camp. Your home from now on. Here you'll live. Here you'll work. Here you'll die.'

His words are like stabs through my heart but I shout back mentally, Never! It takes all my effort to ask him calmly,

'Where are we?'

'Your nearest town is Yugovo,' he informs me, 'close to the river Yuga. And your camp is called Svoboda.'

I want to thump him, but even as I rage inwardly, I realise that there's no intended malice in his information. He's just carrying out his orders. *Svoboda*, indeed! A forced labour camp called Freedom!

The whiteness of the snow is the main source of light at the camp when we arrive. My first impressions are of a central square, darkened with wood ash to prevent slipping, lined with log cabins on two adjacent sides, and on the facing sides, lined with larger wooden buildings, which I guess to be the administration or community blocks. The odd paraffin lamp hung from the eaves does not dispel my apprehension as I look around and take in the thick wall of the pine forest surrounding us.

Our convoy fills the square and even our youngest travellers, hushed with tiredness and hunger, perk up now and look around. A sudden blaring voice makes us all jump and I notice now there are loudspeakers attached to the gables above the doors. The voice shouts instructions:

'You'll go to your lodgings now! Leave your possessions there and proceed immediately to the *banya*. Your clothes will be fumigated and you'll rid yourselves of dirt and lice! Only then you may visit the canteen where you'll be given a meal!'

Nastusha catches my eye and from the sparkle in hers, I know she is smiling underneath the scarf. My spirit soars madly. Food at long last! And a bath! And clean clothes!

Our guard motions us to follow him to our block. At the door he orders, 'Four families on this side and four in the other half!'

Our families stick together; the Zastavnys, the Bzovskis and us. Ryszard Dorodny runs up to us with his three girls.

'Mrs. Anastazia, Mrs. Eva,' he pleads, 'my girls will need a woman to take them to the baths…' his gaze darts nervously around our group. Who could refuse him, the poor, bereft man?

Nastusha and Eva bend down to his motherless daughters and gather them close. Three pairs of luminous eyes look up from three thin faces and the familiar ache tightens my chest.

'Of course you must stay with us,' Nastusha assures them with a soothing tone, 'soon we'll be warm and clean, with our tummies as full as pumpkins.'

We unload our sledges before our block so the waiting men can take them away. It's at this moment we notice that it's too late for Mr. Zastavny. His wife sits beside him rocking with grief.

'*Bistra!* I need my sledge back!' The Russian shouts, watching his companions walking away with theirs. He slides his hands under her armpits and with a rough jerk pulls her off the sledge. Before he can repeat this with Mr. Zastavny, Roman cries out and we all lunge forward.

'Don't touch him! He's ours! We can manage perfectly on our own!'

We lift up Mr. Zastavny together with his covers and carry him indoors.

It is like walking into a current of warm summer air. I feel weak with the sensation and exert all my strength to hold on tight to Mr. Zastavny's blanket stretcher. It is only when we lay him down on a bed covered with straw that I straighten up and look around.

Our little group has followed us indoors and stands around a stove in the central hall. The stove is burning hot, the first object of comfort in a month. Four open doors reveal four small rooms, about three metres by two, at the most. Each room has two wooden bunks covered with hay, a small roughly hewn table with two chairs, a clay cooking stove in the corner and a paraffin lamp in the window.

Hurriedly we choose our rooms at random, bring in our belongings and gather by the entrance door to await further orders.

Mrs. Zastavna does not want to leave her dead husband. She sits beside him, resting her head on his chest. Her face has a startling pallor, her red-rimmed eyes stare unblinking into space.

'Auntie,' Roman speaks gently, 'let's go. No harm can ever touch him now.'

She closes her eyes shut and a strange keening sound escapes her chest. It gives me the creeps and goose pimples. Roman hugs her. 'Please Auntie, let's not give them any cause to make our situation worse than it is. I promise, tomorrow we'll give uncle the best possible funeral we can.'

The residents of the first two log cabins are called to the *banya* first. That includes us. We are all herded, the men, the women and the children, into the annexe called the *vshoboyka*, the delousing room, and ordered to take off all of our clothes. There's a moment's indecision as the reality of this new surprise sinks in. With uncomfortable self-awareness we naturally separate ourselves from the opposite sex, and form two groups, huddling away from each other in the opposite sides of the room.

This seems to amuse the two attending workers, Mongolian men, in grey, baggy uniforms, their hair oily, their teeth decaying brown, that they expose in raucous laughter. They make me think of hyenas. They make lewd gestures towards our women. My vision flashes red for a split second.

'I want to kill the bastards!' I mutter to Roman, as I step out of my trousers and pants, grimy and stiff with a month's continuous wear.

'Me too,' Roman replies, 'chop them to bits and grind them into the soil with my own boots!'

This uncharacteristic outburst from him makes me smile inwardly. I help Pavel to peel off his clothes, and together, with our bundles covering our groins we proceed to the trestle table on which some garments are already spread out. The two Mongolian men are sprinkling them with some powder from a bucket.

'A good soak and a blast of fresh wind is what our clothes need, not this bloody muck!' Henryk mutters beside me. Men crowd around us, self-conscious in their nakedness, their bubbling anger almost audible.

'I'd prefer to wash my own clothes,' Roman speaks in Russian to one of the Mongolians. He laughs showing his rotting teeth.

'This is far more advanced,' he says, 'what, have you no *vshoboykas* in your country? You must be very backward!'

Roman does not laugh. He raises his eyebrows in a disdainful gesture, lost on the other man, shrugs his thin shoulders and we return to our dark corner and turn to the wall, in a show of honouring our women's modesty.

There's a subdued rumble of voices as we wait for the *banya* doors to be open, for that first plunge into the warm, cleansing water. How many tubs can there be for this number of people? There must be at least fifty people from our two log cabins.

At last, the double door is pushed open and clouds of billowing steam fill the *vshoboyka*. This acts as a screen between our two groups and is most welcome, when we follow the women and the small children into the other room. I don't stare deliberately, yet it's hard to avoid the sight of wasted bodies before us, with protruding bones and hanging loose skin. Nastusha and Eva are somewhere at the front with the little boys and the little Dorodny girls, and I can only imagine Nastusha's distress at this enforced nudity. Pavel clings to my hand, his skinny body like a grasshopper's, his eyes looking too huge in his thin face.

'Don't worry pal,' I give his hand a fatherly squeeze, 'we'll soon be as fresh and clean as the morning dew!'

The *banya* is the size of a small school hall, its low ceiling forcing the milky steam to swirl around us, as we are directed to the benches that form a continuous line around the walls. The men go to the far end, away from the women, and are given limp rags to dry themselves later. I cannot help wondering how many bodies as filthy as mine this rag in my hand has wiped before me. We sit together, Ryszard, Roman, Henryk, Pavel and I and I peer through the steam to catch the first sight of a tub. There are no tubs. There is a row of round metal man-hole covers, heated from beneath the floor, with large stones arranged on top of them. The stones sound alive with hissing as the *banya* workers, men and women in identical grey baggy uniforms, sprinkle them continually with generous amounts of water, amidst the endlessly rising steam.

All my dreams of a good healthy soak evaporate in a blink. Blurred in the steam, the forms of women at the far end move like pale apparitions. Beside me Henryk mutters something about feeling like a bloody steamed fish. Indeed, there is a fish smell in the air, which was particularly noticeable in the *vshoboyka*.

'This is horrible,' Pavel says, his thin body close to my side, 'it's like smothering yourself with lard. I feel dirtier than before. And my hair..!' his fingers rummage through his sticky, matted hair, 'I'll never be able to comb it now.'

'Don't you worry about anything,' I feign cheeriness, 'tomorrow we'll all have a good scrub in real water. A long soak. And I'll trim your hair as well. We'll all need to do that!' I run my hand across my face covered with a month's growth and compare my friends' appearances. We all look like wild creatures escaped from a jungle.

Then something happens. Our heads jerk in the direction of screaming sounds and before I can register the noise, two running figures emerge from the clouds of steam and stop close to us, because there's nowhere else for them to run.

The man worker, a huge man, spreads out his arms and forms a barrier around the woman worker, who's screaming, 'He's mine! He's mine!' as she presses a small naked child to her chest. The child's face is red from wailing.

'That's Daniel!' Pavel shouts jumping up, then holding back with fear.

I sprint towards them, losing my loin cloth, forgetting my nakedness, at the same time as Nastusha appears out of the steam. She is crying aloud, her hands instinctively covering her breasts and her groin. I place my arm around her shoulders, protective yet infinitely frustrated that I can't do anything for her. Things are happening fast.

'Yana!' the man's voice is sharp, 'give the woman back her child!'

'*Niet!*' Yana answers back and turns away from him, pressing screaming Daniel harder to her chest.

'Yana, do I need to remind you of the penalty for insubordination? Do you want to spend a night in the *kartzer*?' Despite his severe tone, I could swear I detect a note of pleading.

For a moment nothing happens. We all stand still like bewitched characters in a Grimm's tale, only Daniel sobs, his face wet with snot and tears. Then Yana turns towards us. It is hard to guess her age in that terribly worn look, in the dull eyes, in the lines that criss-cross her face.

Her lower lip trembles and tears flood her eyes. She hands over Daniel to Nastusha and walks away, her hand clamped over her mouth. Daniel clings like a tick to Nastusha's arm, his matchstick fingers digging into her flesh. He gives out an exhausted, shuddering sigh.

'What's all this been about?' I ask Nastusha.

'I've no idea. She just snatched him from me. I better get back.' She disappears with haste into the steam.

I look at the big man and anger boils inside me, too overwhelming to restrain.

'Have you any idea what we've just been through?' I shout. I know I've overstepped the mark and expect the man to punch me or at least to shout back. But all he says is, 'Go back to your place,' and as I obey and take Pavel with me, the big man plonks himself beside me on the bench.

'I'm Yurey,' he says. He has straight spiky hair, white, as are his eyebrows over his grey eyes. 'We're all Ukrainian, us four workers here. My wife Meela, another man, Sirgey, Yana, whom you've just met, and I. Believe me, I know what you've just been through. Consider yourself lucky. When they dumped us here, there was nothing. Nothing at all. Not even a shack for shelter.'

I stare at him with suspicion. Why is he taking me into his confidence? A total stranger. Is this some sort of a trick?

His grey eyes consider me.

'There was a trainload of us at the beginning. Just like you. Now there's only a handful of us left... Our cabin is right in the farthest corner of the camp, close to the forest. Come over tomorrow... we can talk...'

I must look exceedingly surprised and not a little alarmed, for there's a sudden softening in his features.

'Don't worry, we don't bite. We just want some news of the world outside,' he says.

55

'But what about *them*?' I ask, not having to explain.

He nods.

'There are no rules against workers mingling and talking. We're thousands of miles away from civilisation. They're armed, and we're not. What have they got to fear?'

I digest this slowly.

'What about Yana?' I ask, 'what's the matter with her?'

'Come over tomorrow,' he says, 'and I'll tell you her story. She's a little mad. But it's not surprising after what's happened to her.' He gets up. 'Till tomorrow then,' he says and walks away.

CHAPTER 9

Back in our cabin, we all sort ourselves out in our rooms. The heap of fumigated garments, emanating a mixture of reeking odours, is dumped by the entrance hall, ready for washing tomorrow.

I've moved our table, the size of a small working bench against the foot of one of the bunks. Nastusha has sat Tomek and Daniel at it, in anticipation of our longed for supper. The freezing sledge journey, followed by the contrasting thawing warmth in our cabin have proved too much for them to stay awake. They're fast asleep with their heads resting on their folded arms, their faces steamed pink, their hair dried stiff with a month's unremoved dirt.

'I'll give them a good scrub tomorrow, poor mites,' Nastusha strokes their heads gently, 'now go Julian and see what's on offer at the canteen.'

I put on all of my outdoor clothing and look out for my friends. Pavel stands at the stove in the central hallway and chats to Agata, about ten, like himself, the oldest of the Dorodny girls. Henryk and Ryszard are ready, but Roman lingers at his open door, through which we glimpse Mr. Zastavny laid out on his bunk, his hands crossed on his chest, a rosary wound round his fingers. Whispers of fervent prayers float over from his wife, who is kneeling at his side.

'Roman...' I whisper.

He raises his hand in acknowledgement, gives his oblivious aunt a hug then comes out to join us. Outside he says to us,

'We'll organise a funeral tomorrow.'

'And what about tonight?' Henryk asks. I guess his train of thought. I've got the same misgivings. A dead body amongst us, in warm temperature.

'I don't know what to do,' Roman is truly concerned, 'I can't leave him outside. The body will freeze solid. And the wolves?...'

'They must have some place in this camp,' Henryk says, 'for situations like this one. We'll have to ask.'

We ask the guard just inside the door of the canteen. He listens to Roman's predicament with his gaze fixed on the back wall, then without the slightest expression he says,

'Bring the body to the *kartzer*. I'll be there with the keys at ten!'

I can see that Roman is upset.

'In the *kartzer*? A prison? My uncle has never done anything wrong in his life. It's an affront to treat him like this now.'

The guard remains staring at the far wall.

'Your choice. Take it or leave it,' he says.

After a moment's hesitation Roman asks,

'And where's that?'

'The small shed next to the smithy. You'll smell the horses.' He turns on his heel and walks away dismissively.

The canteen is a large wooden barrack with a kitchen at the far end, a counter for giving out food, and a few roughly hewn tables and chairs for anyone needing to eat in. We join the long queue at the counter. Tonight our meal is free. Tomorrow everything will be explained at a compulsory meeting at ten.

Right from the very first step inside the canteen all my dreams of a decent meal evaporate. There's a cloying odour of stale cabbage and fish that blunts your appetite despite your rumbling stomach. When our group arrives at the counter, two women are ladling soup from two identical metal vats on the stove. Their greasy hair hangs in strings and this sight sours the unappetising aura that hangs over the counter covered in spills and soaked crumbs.

'Two adults and three children,' I inform one of the women, when my turn comes. She takes my pot and pours exactly five ladles of soup. She throws a chunk of black bread before me, just thick enough to cut five slices.

I check the contents of the pot. It holds fatty water with fish tails, fisheyes and a few ribbons of cabbage floating on the surface. I cannot hold back.

'Is this a joke?' I ask her in Russian.

Her wizened face shows no reaction.

'Next!' she shouts.

'Excuse me,' I insist, 'did you hear me?'

She turns round and shrugs.

'Give it back then! If you don't want it, someone else will!'

I'm livid. I feel humiliated, trampled on like trash. I feel totally inadequate in my role as a provider for my family, having to bring this shit back to Nastusha and our little foster boys. Henryk's arm on my shoulder steers me away.

'Come on, Julian,' he says, 'save your energy for the big fish.' His pun does not amuse me, but I realise the revolting woman is only the smallest cog in this inhuman machine.

Pavel's pinched face lights up when we return, bearing our gifts like a parody of the three kings. He tears himself away from Agata and follows me inside our room. I place the pot on the table and he lifts the lid even before I've taken off my outdoor clothing. He recoils with disgust and screws his face.

'What's this?' He sounds as if he was about to cry. Nastusha looks over his shoulder then catches my gaze. Her heroically controlled disappointment is hard to bear. I wish she'd explode and scream, then I could rant with her.

'It's the fish soup,' I say, 'that's all they had. And some bread…' I take out the black brick from deep inside my coat pocket and attempt to cut it into thin slices. A saw would be more useful here. I skim the eyes and the tails off the surface of the broth and leave them aside. I demonstrate to Pavel how dipping the bread in the soup softens it and makes it edible. I chew it with a show of relish adding, 'Not bad… not bad…'

Pavel does not believe me, but his hunger is stronger than his disgust. Nastusha wakes up Tomek and Daniel and places thin slices in their hands. They are confused. Daniel's lip quivers then he notices the bread. He takes a bite and chews, struggling to keep his eyes open. Tomek, wide awake now, competes with Pavel, who finishes first.

'I could eat a loaf. Ten loaves!' Pavel declares, his eyes feverish with unsatisfied hunger.

'Me too! Me too!' Tomek shouts. They both smell of fish.

I cut them each another thin slice. 'We've got to keep some back for breakfast,' I explain. Pavel stuffs the whole slice in his mouth. He looks like a hamster. Tomek does the same. I haven't got the heart to discipline them. They are quiet for a long while as they struggle with chewing and softening the bread enough to swallow it. Pavel asks,

'When can we have normal food like my Mum's at home?'

'We'll just have to wait and see what's in the canteen tomorrow,' Natusha tells him with a hint of a promise of better things.

'Is there anything else left? Now?' Pavel asks hopefully.

She places our food sack on the table and looks through. Empty paper bags come out, which she has been storing. One does not throw anything away. There is a handful of rice left in one bag and about the same amount of wheat grains in another. There are some dried beans, peas and lentils.

'How long will it take to cook these?' Pavel asks.

'It's best to soak them first,' Nastusha explains, 'but we'll cook them just as they are. It'll take longer, though.'

'I'll wait,' Pavel says, his eyes brightening up.

I throw on my outdoor clothes and nip outside to look for undisturbed snow. I fill the pot and bring it indoors and place it on the central stove to boil. Nastusha empties the remnants of our provisions into the pot, gives them a stir, and then we set about getting the bunks ready for the night.

Tomek and Daniel fall asleep straight away. Pavel lies down beside his younger brothers, and fights sleep though his eyelids become visibly heavier by the minute.

'Close your eyes and go to sleep, Pavel,' Nastusha persuades him. It'll be some time before the lentils are cooked. I'll wake you up when the soup is ready.'

While the boys sleep, for the first time in a month we can empty all our bags and bundles and sort out in some order the possessions we've got left. I empty my old leather bag on the table and am pleased with its contents of nails and pins and all the handy small tools that were luckily stored all in one place on the night when we were so unexpectedly driven out of our home.

Nastusha folds the boys' clothes and ours into neat piles.

'We could do with a shelf,' she comments, putting them back into a card box. She sits down at the table with me. Even the dim paraffin lamp seems like a chandelier after the perpetual dusk on the train. I can see how tired she looks, her pallor accentuated by the dark circles under her eyes.

'I'll make some shelves at the first opportunity,' I promise her, 'maybe even a chest. God knows, one thing we'll never be short of here is wood.'

She gives me a penetrating look.

'You need a good shave, a good haircut, and I need to cut my hair too,' she says.

I like her long dark hair, that goes with her dark skin in the summer, and with her full defined lips, that make me think of red berries on the rowan tree.

'Don't cut your hair. Don't change anything about yourself,' I attempt a smile.

'We're already changed, Julian. Caricatures of ourselves.'

'Don't be so hard on yourself. Things can improve.'

'Can they?' There's a bitterness in her which upsets me.

'They already have, Nastusha. Isn't this better than the freezing stations?'

She is quiet for a while as if struggling with her thoughts.

'Julian, you heard what the man said. Here we'll live. Here we'll die. I can't bear the thought of being buried alive in this God-forsaken place.' Her eyes fill up and I place my palms over her tensely clasped hands.

'I don't accept for a moment that we'll stay here forever, Nastusha,' I tell her with conviction, 'we just need time to acquaint ourselves with this area. In this half of the cabin alone, we've got enough thinking heads to devise some plan of escape. Trust me. This is really going to happen.'

My heart flips when a sparkle of hope returns to her eyes and her mouth curves upwards.

'Really? Do you really mean it?'

'Absolutely! Without the tiniest doubt!'

She looks at the sleeping boys.

'And what about our little orphans?'

'Half-orphans,' I correct her, 'we'll wait until their father catches up with us.'

'And what if... what if something's happened to him?'

'Then we'll take them along with us.'

She nods and becomes thoughtful and her eyes fill again and I know she is thinking about our child. I sit next to her and cuddle her to me.

'Nastusha, it's the same for me,' I whisper, 'the pain never goes away. But we've still got each other. And now we've got these little boys.'

She dries her eyes and blows her nose.

'I can't forget their mother's pleading eyes,' she says, 'I'd never forgive myself, if I let her down. You're right, we've got a commitment. We've got no choice really, we've just got to get on with it, don't we?'

There's a squeal from Daniel.

'Mama! *Mrovki*! Ants!' He smacks himself on the head.

We rush to him. Nastusha picks him up and I run my fingers through his hair. Something crawls over my hands. Bed bugs. As large as woodlice. I ruffle his hair and shake out the creatures.

'It's like a plague!' Nastusha shudders. She cradles Daniel in her arms and sits on a chair away from both bunks. I examine the hay underneath the sheets, careful not to disturb the sleeping boys. Something like black dried raisins falls down past my head and shoulders onto the bunk. I look up and discover the walls crawling with the bugs. It appears that the moss that acts as insulation along the crevices is also a perfect habitat for them.

'Quick, Nastusha, cover up the boys and I'll burn this scum!'

While she throws sheets over our bunk and over the sleeping boys, I fetch a candle and matches from my bag. Careful not to set the moss on fire, I drag the lighted candle along the walls around our tiny room. Soon, the top sheets on both bunks are littered with hundreds of little charred bits. I stand on the table and repeat this process along the ceiling until I burn off the last visible bug. This is only a temporary measure, I realise with a sinking heart; the whole building needs a thorough fumigation, but it's not a job that can be carried out in mid winter. I envisage months of fighting with the bugs ahead of me.

We shake out the sheets outside, Nastusha sweeps up the floor with a communal broom (there are four such brooms in the hallway crudely made of branches and twigs), then she fetches the cooked lentils from the communal stove.

The boys are fast asleep.

'Poor mites,' she says, placing the pot on our cold clay stove, 'it was too much and too long for them to wait. Still, it'll be a nice surprise for them in the morning.' She turns to me and stifles a yawn. 'I'm so tired I can hardly stand any more. And look at this Julian! A bed all to ourselves! I can't wait!'

There's no coquetry in her words. It's just a statement. In fact, I had exactly the same thought the moment we entered our room. Such luxury! To be able to lie down, to stretch our limbs in comfort, to be unencumbered by others pressing against your back. Images of us flash through my mind, images of us, young and desiring and playful, enjoying each other's bodies, laughing inanely at each other's silly jokes. At twenty-nine I feel old. Dead. I feel no stirrings, no desire, no impulse to run my fingers through her hair, bring her face to mine, make her quiver in my arms.

I feel an overwhelming grief that I have no energy left to resurrect my vigour. I feel like a traitor to my young wife, whose pale, emaciated face, louse-ridden matted hair, and a persistent stale odour do not fire my mind with erotic fantasies. She must feel exactly the same about me, I realise. In my present state, I'm hardly a catch for even the least demanding.

Yet I love her. I love her so much it hurts. There's that other pain, constant, inescapable. It's become part of me. Like an incurable disease. I stop myself from thinking. I force a smile.

'Yes,' I tell Nastusha, 'we'll sleep like kings tonight. But first, I must check on Ryszard. See how he's coping with the bugs. Must be a nightmare for his girls.' I lower my voice and glance at the sleeping boys. 'We've still got to take Mr. Zastavny's body to the *kartzer* before bedtime.'

Nastusha kisses me on the cheek.

'I can't promise to stay ready and willing, waiting for you all night,' she says, and I swear that for the briefest moment there's a teasing twinkle in her eyes.

CHAPTER 10

The *kartzer,* a small wooden building, next to the large bulk of the smithy and the stables, from which indeed the smell of horse dung emanates strongly, is still locked at ten, when we arrive with Mr. Zastavny's body. The policeman makes clear his power and importance by making us wait.

We've wrapped Mr. Zastavny's body in a sheet and carried him over inside a thick blanket, Roman, Henryk, Ryszard and I holding each corner. In the faint glow of a paraffin light above us, we lay him gently on the frozen ground and wait. Before long another group arrives with a body on a make-shift stretcher.

'My mother,' a tearful woman explains. 'What has she ever done to them? I'll never forgive them! Sons of bitches! I'll curse them to my dying day!'

More bodies are brought along. People just like us. Alive yesterday. Gone today. It's all so senseless. So cruel.

A young couple, perhaps our age, arrive with a little white parcel and stop beside me without a word. Their silent grief wrenches my heart and in the dark I screw my eyes and blank out all images of Dorotka to stop myself howling.

At last, the policeman arrives with his partner in tow. They unlock the door, and one of them steps inside. Between them they direct and keep order, as each group carries a body indoors.

We place Mr. Zastavny's body by the wall and in the dark, I can just make out a shape of a man huddled in the corner, behind the bars in the other half of the hut. He's sitting on a pile of hay and is wrapped round with a blanket up to his eyes.

'What's he doing here?' I blurt out in astonishment.

'Lateness for work can't be tolerated,' the policeman answers in a flash. 'This is a good lesson for him and a warning to others.'

I experience something like an electric shock pass through my body, I am so incensed. Yet I can do nothing. Not even vent my frustration on the policeman with a single punch. The young couple with their dead child stand right beside us. Roman speaks to them,

'Leave your baby with my uncle. He's the kindest person I know. Your baby will be safe with him.'

It is all so bizarre, yet the couple go along with Roman's suggestion, place the little bundle on Mr. Zastavny's chest and Roman rearranges the covers. I find this infinitely poignant, the old and the very young, two strangers united in death.

'We'll give them a beautiful funeral tomorrow.' Roman keeps his voice steady.

Outside, with shouts of *Bistra*! the policeman jangles the keys to hurry people along. When the last body is laid down, and he locks the hut, I can't stop thinking about that one living man among all those dead bodies. Roman asks,

'What time tomorrow? We need to bury our people'. For a moment it looks as if the policeman is ignoring him, and then still without facing us he says,

'Midday is best, that's if the sun comes out at all. The ground's frozen solid. You'll need pickaxes.'

'Where can we get them?'

'You'll be issued some for work. When you come to the meeting at ten.'

Nastusha is asleep when I return to our room. The boys are motionless on their bunk, their arms flung over each other, their faces mercifully restful for once.

I undress to my vest and pants, slip in beside Nastusha and brush my cheek against her shoulder. The bunk is hard wood and the hay is lumpy and my whole body aches with tiredness and a torrent of the day's mixed impressions floods my mind and I wonder how am I going to fall asleep and get the much required rest. The next thing I'm aware of is Nastusha shaking me awake.

'It's seven o'clock, Julian. We've not slept this long for over a month!'

By ten o'clock, the time of our all-important, compulsory meeting, I feel as if we've done a week's work. But I'm in good spirits. It must be the long sleep. All the most pressing jobs are done.

Ryszard and Roman have been busy supplying the central stove with chopped wood, raising the temperature to tropical, excellent for drying. Henryk and I have been lugging buckets of snow and melting it and boiling for Nastusha and Eva, as they bathed the children before setting about the most needed washing. We've fixed some lines to the ceiling and now the washing hangs down like an upside-down forest of grey shapes.

The children are transformed. It's heart warming to watch their animated faces as they play out some imaginary games in the space around the stove. Little Stella's enamelled baby bath so fortuitously brought along, has proved priceless. The boys' cheeks shine, their washed and cut hair stands out fluffy around their pinched faces. Even the little Dorodny girls, who took some persuading to part with their plaits, now sport with self-conscious pride, the big white bows which Nastusha has tied in their hair, giving them the look of exotic butterflies.

All adults have taken turns to borrow Stella's bath and in the privacy of our rooms have given ourselves a good scrub. We men look human again, with clean-shaven faces and trimmed hair. Only Ryszard refuses to shave off his beard and moustache.

'There'll be time enough on our first day of freedom,' he declares defiantly.

'And may it arrive before you trip on your beard!' Henryk's wide smile reminds me of his old self, at home.

The sight of Nastusha and Eva in their clean dresses and white aprons stirs forgotten feelings within me, touches of normality, the warmth of simple pleasures of a good woman's presence. They look like page boys with their cropped hair, one dark, one like pale cream silk.

Nastusha's unsentimental practicality took me by surprise when she dropped the scissors in my hand with instructions to cut.

'Are you absolutely sure?' I hesitated, 'you can't stick it back on, once it's chopped off. It'll take ages to grow this long again'.

'I'm absolutely sure,' Nastusha insisted, 'cut it off! And with it all the bad things too!'

And when, with great reluctance and slightly shaky hands I cut through the long and matted plait, she threw it in the fire.

If only we could dispose of all our problems so simply and radically. And yet, I begin to feel a smidgen of hope and optimism and a fragile belief that today is better than yesterday. For a start, the foul-smelling soup was gone, when I went to the canteen to fetch breakfast for us and our boys. There was *kasha* instead, a kind of porridge made of buckwheat. On my way back to the cabin with the precious breakfast in the pot, I came across an Ukrainian woman. She stopped me and whispered,

'Have you got a rouble or two?'

'Why?' I was a little taken aback.

'Because I've got some goat's milk for sale.'

After weeks of cramped conditions on the train, *keepiatok* and whatever we could scrape together for meals, this morning's breakfast was indeed princely and civilised, eaten at the table, elegantly with our adopted family. Porridge, goat's milk and tea. And there's still lentil soup for later.

'Nastusha,' I deliberately lighten my tone as we pull on our outdoor clothing to brace ourselves for the cold outside, 'we've not done so badly, have we, so far? Look what we've packed into this morning, and it's not even ten yet. I think the secret to survive this place is to take each day as it comes. One day at a time. Not tormenting yourself in advance about what may come or not. In time, you'll see, and I hope to God I'm right, they'll ease off, loosen their vigilance, when they think we've been brainwashed and quashed down by their system. And that is when we'll escape. I'm totally determined that we shall do that.'

Nastusha stops tying the scarf around her face and looks at me with those luminous dark eyes of hers, that have the power to pull at my heart.

'Julian,' she says, 'I'll pray every day for your words to come true.'

The others are ready in the hallway and are calling out to us. We leave the children in Mrs. Zastavna's care, whose age and Roman's assurances to be responsible for her, have merited her dispensation from attending the meeting. Roman has pulled out a chair for her so she can supervise the playing children from her doorway. Her face looks almost transparent like wax and her eyes are swollen from crying, but she has to save her grief for later. For the moment she has to concentrate all her attention on sleeping Stella in her arms, on Daniel clutching her skirt and the children around her who are rediscovering their childhood with sudden subdued bursts of laughter.

The community hall is in the same block as the dispensary, the commandant's office, the canteen and the shop. This row of wooden buildings is directly opposite our quarters, across the wide square. As the newly arrived contingent of Poles troops into the hall, two policemen, with guns in their holsters, stand on each side of the entrance, and appear to make marks on their writing pads. In the daylight their features are visible, shocking in their appearance. Their battered faces speak of their time in the war. The smaller one has a deep scar across his brow and a dropped eyelid. In my mind I call him Boar, after the one-eyed wild boar that used to roam my part of the forest at home until one hunting season, that finished badly for him. The taller policeman I call Stork on account of his long legs. His chin is pockmarked with gun powder and his lower lip is deformed.

Inside the hall we make a formidable crowd and there's a rumble of muted voices. Nastusha and Eva stand right before me and Henryk, nestle against us, their fur hats brushing our faces with the slightest move. Roman and Ryszard stand right next to me, the crowd pushing us tightly together. None of us speak. Above the empty podium at one end, there are large portraits of Lenin and Stalin with the hammer and sickle emblem on a red flag hung between them. A hush falls on the crowd when two men come out of the door from the back of the stage, walk to the edge of the podium and stand still for a long time staring down at us. The silence is overbearing, creating unease. This is intensified when six armed policemen follow them onto the stage and form a line against the back wall. Nastusha shrinks back against me.

'*Ya bit* Borodin,' the first of the two prominent men speaks, a gold tooth flashing between his thick lips. He is a big, military man, with a purple face and bulging eyes, like a frog's. His uniform with a red stripe down the side of his trousers, and a red stripe around his hat signifies that he's from NKVD, the secret police. 'I'm the commandant of this *posholek*. You'll call me

Tovarish Borodin, because we're all equal here. However, don't presume to take my kindness for granted. I hold the supreme power here. Mine is the supreme judgement and the final decision. All for your own good and for the good of all people here.'

'Perfect equality,' Henryk mutters under his breath

'My right hand,' Borodin continues, 'is *Tovarish* Kursky.'

Tovarish Kursky throws him a nervous glance. He is a head shorter and looks like a padded rag doll, in his shabby grey *koofayka*, padded grey hat with ear flaps, padded grey trousers and oversize *valonki*.

'*Tovarish* Kursky,' Borodin raises his voice, 'is responsible for organising the work parties, for overseeing the integrity of the workers, for ascertaining and enforcing high standards of achievement, for meeting targets without fail. Any questions and requests will be addressed through him to me.'

Kursky's chest expands and he grows a few centimetres taller.

'You should consider yourselves extremely lucky,' Borodin states with force, his eyes bulging, his floating gaze nailing at random some unfortunate individual. 'Your working week is only six days. Some places work all seven…'

'In prisons,' Henryk whispers, and Eva gives his hand a tug.

'You have the option, of course, of working the full week,' Borodin makes this sound like a privilege, 'and you'll be duly rewarded for your loyalty to the state. There are just a few rules you must respect for the smooth running of this camp. Any leave from this place must have my permission. You may think you need to visit our neighbouring town Yugovo, but we do possess our very own shop on the premises, and there's really no need for you to leave this place except for work.'

'Wonderful!' Eva whispers, as a murmur of discontent pervades the crowd and is challenged by Borodin's raised eyebrow. Some brave person ventures with,

'And why are we forbidden to go outside this place? Is this a prison? Are we prisoners here?'

Borodin barks an imitation laugh.

'You're not forbidden. This rule is for a purpose. For your own safety. You wouldn't last very long alone on the taiga. What, with the wolves and the grizzly bears roaming the land?'

'That's told us,' Henryk mutters and my dream of an escape plunges with my sinking feeling.

Borodin's voice drones on,

'We need to know where you are at all times, so we know where to go looking for you if you don't come back. You can always rely on our friendly policemen for help.' His lips curl unpleasantly as his backward glance acknowledges his men, and I'm taken aback by his barefaced lies, delivered with such arrogance.

Kursky steps forward and shifts his weight from foot to foot.

'You're extremely fortunate,' he clears his throat, 'you've got the whole day free. Acquaint yourself well with our *posholek*, so you know where to assemble tomorrow morning for work.' He pauses and clears his throat. 'It'll be just outside the smithy and the stables where you'll be given out your working tools. Sort yourself out into working groups today, so we don't waste time tomorrow. Twelve in each group.' A pause and another throat clearing. 'The first bell will sound at five in the morning. This will give you an hour to get yourself ready and eat your breakfast. The second bell will sound at six. No delay can be tolerated. It will be punished severely. This rule is for the benefit of everyone. In fairness to the hard workers. I think I've told you everything you need to know.' A cough and, 'any questions?'

A great number of questions come from the crowd. What type of work? How far to work? What kind of transport? What kind of tools? But above all, what about the food? We are all hungry, one man calls out, we've got hungry families to feed!

Borodin's face turns a shade deeper purple.

'You parasites! You scroungers!' he yells, disregarding the women in the crowd, 'we'll soon teach you here to forget your bourgeois expectations! The first lesson you learn is this: *kto nie robotayet, ten nie kushayet*, who doesn't work, doesn't eat!'

There's another eruption of protests from the crowd. *We're hungry now! We've not started work yet, so what are we to do before our first pay? Let our families starve?*

A blast from the gun freezes the crowd. Nastusha stifles a cry and I hold her tight. It's only a blank, it appears, but my nerves are frayed. Borodin smirks in the silence that follows.

'Now we can talk again. You'll be apportioned daily rations from the canteen until your first pay. The cost of this will be deducted regularly in small amounts until full payment is completed. Now, what could be fairer than that?'

I want to believe him, but I know I can't. No one raises any more points and we're dismissed.

Outside, Roman looks anxious.

'What about pickaxes? No one's mentioned distribution of tools. I've got to dig the grave and bury my uncle before it gets dark. They said the smithy, last night, didn't they? I better go and find out and get on with it.'

'What, a matchstick like you?' Henryk teases, stretching himself and throwing his shoulders back, 'do you think we'll let you do this all by yourself?'

'Not such a matchstick,' Roman protests in his good-natured way, 'but I won't turn your offer down.'

Our girls leave us and hurry back to the children and Mrs. Zastavna, while we make our way across the square towards the smithy. I wonder about the poor soul locked up with all the dead bodies in the *kartzer* next door.

The four men busy around the four horses, emaciated pitiful creatures, are Russian. They stop to listen to Roman's request, and then without a comment, all except one, turn back to their cleaning and mending jobs. The one with the keys opens a side door for us to the store room, which is full of tools for outdoor jobs, pickaxes, axes, saws, hammers, ladders and ropes. The man motions to us to take what we need.

'It's my uncle,' Roman explains, 'didn't quite make it to this paradise. Can you direct us to where we're supposed to bury our dead?'

The man comes outside with us and points towards the forest beyond the exit road from our camp.

'You'll find a clearing there,' he says , 'it'll be hard to dig too deep. Just bury him deep enough to stop the wolves from getting to him. We rebury our dead in the Spring at the first signs of a thaw.'

Our astonishment must amuse the man.

'Don't worry,' he says, 'the frozen ground acts like a deep freezer. And you'll have time to make him a wooden box by then.'

CHAPTER 11

Even in the icy wind that freezes the bark on the trees and makes them crackle, my trained nostrils anticipate whiffs of smells that are inherent in the woodlands. Resin, mushroom, damp moss, the earthy odour of decaying leaves, trapped underneath the snow, surely there, waiting to explode in multiplied fragrances at the first sign of thaw.

Henryk, labouring his walk beside me with the pickaxe hooked over his shoulder and a large shovel acting as a walking stick, must feel this too.

'I can't stop thinking,' he says, 'how busy we'd be at home. Who'll be doing all the regular jobs when we're not there?'

I picture our forest at home, which we tended with deeply felt attachment, like our very own, at the foot of the mountains, with running streams, coppices and clearings and caves that shelter the bears or foxes or wild boar. In my mind I see and feel the sun filtering through the open spaces, left by the old felled trees to make room for young saplings. The warmed forest floor shimmers with rising warmth. It is rich with nutrients that sustain the forest life. I long to be back.

'I can't imagine ever doing anything else,' I reply.

Roman asks us about our work and we are both eager to tell him everything he wants to know and more. The forest is my favourite, inexhaustible subject. Ryszard walks quietly beside us. He is a man of a few words, poor soul, no doubt contemplating his future with his three, motherless girls.

Our meandering route among the trees brings us to the clearing. I'm surprised at the size of it, like a small meadow. The founders of this camp must have worked very hard indeed, to fell and remove this number of trees. I notice straight away in the snow the marks of animal visitation.

'The wolves,' I point to the paw marks, 'at least four of them'.

'And a bear here,' Henryk stops to examine the wide paw prints semi-circled with deep holes where the bear's claws have gripped for steady support.

'Are you trying to scare us?' Roman asks with pretend alarm in his eyes, but his nervous glances all round suggest he's not so totally indifferent to danger lurking behind the trees.

Henryk stops and rests his tools on the ground. He pulls himself to his full formidable height and flexes his shoulders.

'My friends, you've got nothing to fear, when Henryk is here.'

Roman and Ryszard look puzzled but they follow his example and lay down their tools.

'Now cover your ears with your hands,' he tells them, 'be prepared to be shocked.'

I know what is coming, so I do as he says. Roman and Ryszard do the same.

'Ready?' Henryk asks and shapes his hands around his mouth like a wide funnel. He emits an almighty, blood-curdling roar. An elk roar.

'Christ!' Roman recovers first, 'how did you learn to do that!'

Henryk's expression is smug.

'Years in the forest. You learn all kinds of tricks.'

This is my cue to go into the tale of the hapless starving wolf, which so disastrously chose Henryk's garden to scavenge around. Henryk's famous roar gave the wretched animal a heart attack, as the post mortem later revealed. The wolf died on the spot.

'And not only that,' Henryk can't help himself, 'the shock to the wolf was so strong that it squeezed all excrement out of him. It shot five metres across the garden to the other side.'

This little punch line never fails to amaze Henryk's audience. Roman and Ryszard contemplate his words, but neither of them show any amusement.

'You know,' Roman says, 'I know exactly what this poor animal felt. I feel like him now.'

We all do, I think, even Henryk, I guess.

We pick up our tools and walk on to the far side of the clearing. There is a section that is the cemetery. In place of tombstones there are wooden poles bearing names and dates. Mostly Ukrainian, some Russian too.

'I'll make a cross for my uncle,' Roman says. He marks out a rectangle in the snow, close to the last grave and we set about our task. The ground is indeed as hard as steel. Roman and Ryszard are unused to such labour. They tire easily and have to pause for rests. Henryk and I plod on, until we chip enough snow and earth to shovel it out in a heap.

In the two hours it takes us to dig the hole deep enough for Mr. Zastavny's body, we are joined by two supervising guards. They have arrived with other bereaved people who are digging graves for their dead. The guards stand on the edge and watch us with bored, indifferent eyes.

The young couple from last night come up to our side. Henryk and I help them to dig their baby's grave. It doesn't take long.

'What's your baby's name?' Roman asks in his soft, sympathetic voice.

The woman's eyes fill up.

'Yanusz. My little Yanuszek. Only ten months. Why? I just can't understand why?'

We are all quiet for a moment then Roman speaks gently again.

'He's in Heaven now. With little angels like himself.'

71

The woman shakes her head and looks away and I feel her grief and her anger and I shout to God in my mind. I don't want Dorotka in Heaven yet! I want her here on earth with us!

Before the four of us leave, Roman ignores the guards and raises his arms to attract attention.

People gladly stop for a rest, their faces red and steaming from the exertion.

'I'm Roman Zastavny,' he introduces himself. 'As we've not got a priest in this camp to conduct the funerals, I'll gladly step in, if you'll have me. I'm not yet ordained, but I hope to be, when we're freed from this place.'

There's a loud, derisive snigger from the guards. In the silence that follows, people nod or wave their consent. Roman ignores the guards and suggests,

'Shall we set a time then? About three? Before it starts getting dark?'

We return the tools to the smithy, then knock on the office door to lodge our request with Kursky. He comes out looking like an Easter *baba*, a yeast-risen globe of a cake, with all the padding on him. He has this stupid officious expression of people with a chip, but he doesn't intimidate me. Borodin is the man to beware. We explain we're ready with the graves.

'And no doubt,' Roman suggests, 'it's in your interest to clear the *kartzer* for its proper function, don't you think?'

Kursky appears to hesitate as if unsure whether to agree with Roman or not, his brow puckered, his eyes roaming the low, ice-laden sky, then he agrees. Three in the afternoon.

On the way back to our dwelling across the ash-blackened square, we meet Yurey, our supervisor from the *banya* last night. He remembers me.

'Kalinski, *zdrassfitye*! Good day! You've not forgotten your promise, have you?' He turns and points at the last wooden house in a row adjacent to ours. 'The first three are Russian. The second three are Ukrainian. We're in the one at the very end.'

I explain about the funerals but he insists.

'Come over later then. We'll be in all evening.'

When he walks away Henryk is suspicious.

'I wouldn't go. Why is he so keen? How can you be sure he's not one of them?'

'I'm not sure at all,' I reply, 'I've got exactly the same thoughts as you. But if he is indeed one of them, evading him will be seen like deliberate hostility. I can't chance it. But if I do go, who knows, it may turn out to our advantage. I'll be on guard. And I'll take Nastusha with me.'

At three in the afternoon, there's a crowd of us gathered at the cemetery, surrounded by a frozen forest, underneath a ceiling of grey frozen sky.

There's more snow on the way. I feel it in the penetrating cold that reaches the very marrow of my bones. We huddle together, Henryk and I, with Nastusha and Eva leaning close against us, their fur hats brushing our faces. Ryszard the Beard has stopped behind, to take Mrs. Zastavna's place in minding the children. I suspect this is all too much for him. The children, at least, keep one focused on some semblance of normality with their natural needs. Mrs. Zastavna stands next to Roman in the middle of this human circle, dressed in black, her white pained face like a medieval painting of the Mater Dolorosa. There is a murmur of sighs and stifled sobs.

Seven wrapped bodies rest on the ground beside their dug graves, waiting to be buried. I can't bear to look at the little white parcel close to Mr. Zastavny's body, yet my eyes keep straying towards it, despite all my efforts to look the other way.

Roman conducts this service like a fond farewell, rather than a depressing lament. He does not invoke prayers for the departed sinners, followed by traditional reminders of retribution and hell. This little dead body on the ground before me; a sinner? I find myself bristling even at the very thought of it.

I listen with fervour to Roman's uplifting words of God's love and of heaven and of eternal joy. In his eulogy our dear ones, so prematurely snatched from us, are compared to Polish saints and heroes. I want to believe everything he says, as I picture Dorotka cradled in an Angel's arms.

He intones, in his clear, melodious voice, God is Love, an uplifting hymn of promise and hope. Sobs and sighs gradually die down as we all join in, the women's sopranos rising above the baritones of men, and floating heavenwards. The two armed guards, standing back at the edge of the cemetery, make noisy comments and snort stupidly. We ignore them.

Afterwards, when Roman goes round to speak to individual people, the men set about filling the graves. We stamp hard on the surface to ensure the flattened mixture of soil and snow freezes back into a hard block, impenetrable to the wild animals.

Nastusha and Eva take Mrs. Zastavna with them, and leave with the crowd, men carrying the spades and shovels, relieving us of ours. Henryk and I hang around until the last few people are gone and Roman is free to walk back with us.

One of the guards steps forward and bars his way.

'Fancy yourself as a great leader, do you?' He looks like a school-boy, the insolent kid. I'd soon put him in his place at home. 'Just watch it,' he warns, 'so you don't get too big for this place. We have well-tried methods of dealing with upstarts like you.'

Roman gives him a long steady look and in his peaceful manner replies:

'You're mistaken if you think I consider myself anything at all, yet alone a leader, as you put it. All I'm trying to do is comfort these people the best way I can.'

'Really?' the other youth, callow and spotty, emboldened by his comrade's impudence, comes up too and stands so close to us, that I swear I can smell drink on his breath. 'And who's going to comfort you when we decide what to do with you? Are you going to cry out for help to your God?' His laugh is so repulsive I find myself bristling. I want to squeeze my hands around his neck and shake him so hard, he'll beg for mercy.

'Please let us pass' Roman asks politely, 'I've done what I came to do. I'm sure you want to get back too.'

'Please let us pass...' the guard mimics and, without warning, gives Roman a punch straight in the mouth. Roman loses his balance, reels backwards and we catch him in time, before he falls to the ground. The youth watches us with a leer that widens into a satisfied grin when Roman's hand goes automatically to his lips and blood appears on his scarf.

I'm shaking with rage and sense Henryk's frustration and catch a look in his screwed eyes: he'd love to bang the heads of the two morons together. We can't do a thing; not even shout obscenities at them. They have the guns; they have the power. And they know it. With amused expressions and a show of tiresome leniency they let us pass.

'Go and tell your people that no one messes with us!' one of them shouts after us.

It is only when we're a few metres ahead of them, that I give vent to my fury and call them all kinds of bastards under the sun. Henryk's familiar repertoire of expletives multiplies with impressive originality.

'Hushshsh.... you two,' Roman attempts to calm us down, 'nothing's happened. I've still got all my teeth. It's only a little cut on my mouth.'

'If I was God,' Henryk speaks hotly, 'I'd bloody strike the son of a bitch with a bolt. Right here! On this spot!'

'Henryk, shshsh...' Roman taps his friend's arm gently, 'you know the saying. *Bóg jest nie rychliwy ale sprawiedliwy*. God is slow but just. Trust Him.'

At this very moment there is a scream behind us, and I swear to God, I witness a real miracle for the first time in my life. When we turn around, the sight before our eyes is incredible. The youth who's just attacked Roman is lying on the ground, flat on his back, with one leg stretched out and the other bent at an unnatural angle. He is howling in pain.

'Well, don't just stand there! Help!' his companion shouts.

We are no doctors, Henryk and I, but we have witnessed a number of injuries in our work in the forests. We crouch over the injured youth and Henryk commands,

'Stop blubbering for a start! Are you a coward or a man?' I recognise his tone of quiet satisfaction in having the upper hand. The boy screws his face with the effort while Henryk questions him, running his fingers gently over the injured knee.

'I think it's dislocated, but only a doctor can diagnose it correctly. You've got to go to hospital and have it fixed properly.'

'No need,' the boy's comrade decides for him, 'there's a nurse at the dispensary. She'll know what to do.'

'Please yourself,' Henryk shrugs as if he couldn't care less. Nevertheless he and I help the youth to sit up and position him in the cradle of our hands that we have criss-crossed and gripped together, scout style, and lift him off the ground. He cries out in pain at the changed position of his leg. Roman rushes to lift it up and holds it to relieve the pressure on the knee cap. The other youth has sobered up. There's fear in his darting eyes. He appears to be struggling with carrying the two heavy guns.

'It's all your fault, you fucking *sobaki!*' he yells, 'you'll pay for leaving holes in the ground!'

'Holes? What holes?' Henryk asks, as the snow comes down in a thick flurry.

We make slow progress, bent and rapidly turning white, and I can't help reflecting how easy it is for God. Why can't He be always on *our* side?

CHAPTER 12

There is a curfew in our *posholek*, from 9pm. to 5am, another strange phenomenon in this camp called Svoboda. I'm not ready to visit Yurey till after seven, after we've eaten our meagre meal of gruel and black bread, after we've settled the boys for the night, with Roman ready to tell them a bed-time story. His lips are swollen, but he insists it's nothing. He'll be all right again in a day or two, unlike his attacker, who'll be out of action for a few weeks.

Nastusha and I pull on our outdoor clothing and muffle our faces up to our eyes. It's still snowing hard. Outside, I grasp her hand and hold it tight as we make our way close to the line of buildings in a snowstorm so thick that it obliterates all reference points around us. Even the paraffin lights under the eaves become invisible. We count the buildings, and when we reach the sixth one, we guess that must be the last in the line, Yurey's dwelling. It's only when we're right on the doorstep that we see the paraffin light in the window.

I knock hard on the door and it feels like a long time before a voice asks from within,

'Who is it?'

'Kalinski, to visit Yurey.'

The door is unlocked and we hurry inside to keep the snow out.

'*Dabro pazhalavat*! Welcome!' Yurey greets us, his grey eyes shining underneath his animated eyebrows, and I want to, really want to believe that he's genuine. He leads us across the central hallway, just like ours, with a hot stove in the middle. Four sets of doors indicate four rooms. They are all closed except Yurey's. His wife Meela stands just inside, beckoning to us, her smile guarded on her worn face, her white-grey hair pulled back and tied on the nape. I guess she is younger in years than her appearance suggests.

We step inside their room, they close the door hurriedly, and we shake hands and introduce ourselves officially, as good manners require, and it all appears so normal, so civilised. Except that I can't allow myself to relax my vigilance even for a moment.

They invite us to take off our coats and hats and to sit at the table, which is exactly like ours, with two chairs, the edge of the bunk acting as a bench.

Their clay stove in the corner is warm and there's a samovar standing on top. Meela pours tea into four glasses, places them on the table and joins us.

'How long did you say you've lived here?' I ask noting the green colour of the tea, also some shelves on the wall that act as storage space with a drawn curtain over them. There's a wooden chest in the corner, rough and chunky.

'Eight years,' Yurey replies.

'Eight long years,' Meela confirms with a sigh.

I wonder how careful they have to be with their answers. I wonder if anyone's listening at the door. But on a night like this with the snow coming down thick and heavy, and the wind whistling through the tiniest cracks in the walls, I guess they must feel safer too.

'Have you a family?' Nastusha makes polite conversation, 'I've not seen any children in this *posholek* yet. Only our own.'

Yurey rubs his forehead and his eyes take on a faraway look.

'There were children at the beginning,' he says, 'most of them died.'

'What happened?'

'Famine. There was nothing to eat. When they dumped us here in the summer, it was still bearable. There were mushrooms and all kinds of berries growing in the wild. We had to hurry to build some dwellings before the winter set in. But then, there was really nothing left to eat. No bread available anywhere. No flour, no grain, no seeds. All such things were taken by the state for equal distribution. We never got anything. People dug up roots, ate the bark off the trees. Some died of that. The children, especially babies, died like flies.'

We become quiet for a long while digesting his words, and I feel dread seeping into my soul like black oil.

'Did any survive?' I ask.

'Some of the older ones did,' Meela says, 'but they were taken away the following summer.'

'Where?' Nastusha is shocked.

'The children's homes. In big cities.'

I hear Nastusha's intake of breath.

'Why did they do that?' she asks, 'what did the parents say?'

A tear glistens in the corner of Meela's eye.

'The parents had very little choice. They feared their children would not survive another winter here. They did it to save their children's lives.'

'And are these children alive?' Nastusha wants to know, 'can the parents visit them?'

'Theoretically.' Yurey's voice hardens. 'But in practice it means travelling from one end of the country to the other. You must know something about the size of this land, by now. The cost of such travel. Getting permission to be off work for so long.' He sighs. 'They do everything to erode family life, to divide and disperse. Once you're on your own and uncertain and frightened, they've got you. People do all kinds of things to preserve themselves.'

I dare not ask about their family. Instead, I ask about Yana, their neighbour and their workmate.

'Poor woman,' Yurey says, 'she lives across the hall from us. She lost her mind. Never fully recovered. We keep an eye on her. So she can work and earn enough to keep herself going.'

'What happened to her?'

Again Yurey's hand brushes weariness off his face.

'What happened to her?' he repeats my question. 'She lost all her family. First her husband in a freak accident. When they were felling trees. Then her older children died, one by one, two boys and two girls. Children's diseases. But with no food, no medication, they had no chance, poor souls. When her youngest child died, a little boy of two, she went mad with grief. It was frightening to watch. She wouldn't part with him and would scratch and bite anyone who came near her. They had to hold her down and inject some stuff, to sedate her. They searched for the child and found him half eaten, buried in the covers on her bunk.'

A wave of sickness rises to my throat and I see Nastusha's hand shoot up to her mouth.

'Was it the rats?' I ask.

Yurey and Meela exchange glances before he speaks,

'No, not the rats…,' he allows a pause for our brains to register the horror of his account, 'but she wasn't the only one. There were others. Long term famine does strange things to you. The instinct to survive kills off all other finer feelings. Besides, when you reach that stage, it's a fight between you and the wolves. And why should the wild animals survive when you're starving to death?'

For the second time nausea fills my mouth with excess saliva and I take a hurried sip of tea. It is bitter, no doubt a brew from some dried leaves, but I swallow it and suppress the sickness. I feel a strong, demanding need to know the truth about Yurey and Meela. Were they like the others, losing their humanity in order to survive?

'And what about your family, where are they now?' I ask.

Meela leans forward, her body rocking gently.

'We have a son and a daughter. They were left behind when we were taken away. They were with my parents at the time. Yurey and I were distraught, as you can imagine, but now I praise God that they were saved from what we've been through.'

I don't know why, but I heave a sigh of relief.

'Yurey, tell me, why did you want to see me?'

His shoulders appear to relax and his face loses that tense look.

'Why do you think!' He allows himself a smile. 'Dear God! We're so cut off here! All we're ever told is how great Stalin is and how victorious his armies are, how together with Hitler they'll conquer all Europe. But tell me, what's really happening in Ukraine, in Poland, in Germany? What are the British doing? Will they withstand Hitler, or will they end up like France?'

'God no!' I deny vehemently, 'I can't even bear to have such thoughts. No, they are our allies. They'll go on until this war is won!'

I take turns with Nastusha to tell them about Poland, invaded from both sides, about our army's valour in the September campaign, about their defeat, the grief, the terrible aftermath.

'You can't trust anyone anymore,' Nastusha says, 'they've destroyed our communities. We led peaceful lives, where we lived near Dolina, Poles, Ukrainians, Armenians, Jews and so many others, accepting each other, tolerating each other's needs, traditions and religions. It's all in ruins now. The Russians promised your people to expand their land if they denounced the Poles and the Jews as the enemies of the State. There have been unspeakable atrocities and burning down of whole villages, even before our arrests.'

Yurey and Meela listen with grave expressions, then Meela's eyes fill up.

'Dear God,' her sigh is like a sob, 'what's it all for? I dream of home, of our children every night. I imagine our home-coming. Our house with the lace curtains in the windows, the hollyhocks by the fence. Deep red and pink. I wonder if anyone's living there now?'

I don't tell her of the large black patches on the ground and the cinders between the remaining fruit trees, where once stood the family homes. I force a smile and raise my tea glass.

'Here's to our home-coming!'

We all take a sip of the bitter brew then Yurey fills us in on all the gossip and the goings on in the camp, who is approachable, whom to avoid, whom to distrust at all times. I want to believe that he's our new friend, but caution holds me back. I can't get Demitrey out of my mind, Demitrey who was a trusted member of our working team, the same man who led the NKVD to our house on the night of our arrest.

CHAPTER 13

At six in the morning, after a blaring first reveille from the loudspeakers an hour earlier, a crowd of us is waiting ready for work in the square. The *buran* storm at night has added two or three feet of snow on the even ground, with drifts around the houses, some peaks touching the windows. The whiteness creates an illusion of dawn light, even though the sky is inky black.

Our group stands close together, Henryk and Eva, Roman and Ryszard, Nastusha and I. Two more men and four women from another barrack have been allotted to us. One girl looks like a child, but she must be fourteen to have been forced to work with us. Her mother's arm draws her close for warmth. I estimate twenty degrees below zero. My cheeks are stiff with cold. I press them against Nastusha's fur hat. She leans her back hard against my body inside the circle of my arms. I feel her shivering and wish the remnants of my warmth to penetrate her clothing. My legs, clad in two layers of trousers are tingling still from the exertion of panicky rushing to be on time. To avoid punishment for lateness in the *kartzer*.

The most demanding in terms of time is the *slavoyka*. There are two latrines at the back of our row of houses, and even with the four holes in the long wooden seat (a bizarre idea), it takes a long time to service so many people all at once. Having to be fully dressed and muffled against the freezing temperatures for each such visit, slows down the progress even more.

The least time is taken up with the breakfast. *Keepiatok* and *kasha*. We've left some for our boys with Mrs. Zastavna. We're extremely lucky that she's exempt from labour, on account of her age, and can be left to look after our children, Stella, the three Dorodny girls and our three boys. But then, if she doesn't work, it's as if she did not exist. She will not be allowed any food rations. *He who does not work, does not eat.* We'll all have to work harder. As my stomach rumbles with unsatisfied hunger I dream of bread and butter and eggs.

Guards with rifles come up to us, call out to their groups and we follow ours, who leads us behind a horse-drawn sleigh, laden with work tools around two large metal pots, our lunch, we've been told. We walk down the wide road out of the camp. This gradually narrows into a path through the forest. The first group, well ahead of us up the long snake of workers, sleighs and horses have the most difficult task of having to wade through the deep snow and make way for us. The relentless, intensive walk proves increasingly tiring for everyone. Sounds of laboured breathing are occasionally punctuated by a quiet word of desperation.

'Dear God,' Nastusha gasps beside me, 'how much longer are we going to walk?'

Eva is holding onto Henryk's hand for support. His mutterings sound like an animal alphabet: bloody dogs, fucking pigs, stinking skunks and so on until Roman can't stand it any longer.

'Hush my friend,' he chides him, 'save your energy for prayers and work. Ask God to give us strength!'

'And to strike the bastards with plagues!' Ryszard adds promptly.

We've been walking for an hour. The women are visibly exhausted, their pace slowing down, unable to keep up with the horse. I lengthen my step to catch up with our guide who leads our horse. If only he could stop, even for a minute or two. But just then we enter a clearing that is as wide and as long as the cemetery area close to our camp.

We are ordered to stop and wait till all the groups are assembled again.

'I'm all shaky,' Nastusha whispers against her scarf, 'I never imagined it would be like this.'

'Neither did I.' I want to think of something cheerful to say, to lift her spirit, but I can't think of one positive thing as I imagine miles of thick forests surrounding us.

The guards shout instructions again and lead their groups away in all directions.

'Where are we going?' I ask our guide.

'To the river Yuga. That's where you'll be felling the trees.'

Another half an hour of (laboured) walk through the deep snow, when the mother of the young girl behind me cries out,

'Please wait! My Hania can't walk any further!'

Henryk and I turn around. Hania, who looks like a ten-year-old, is hanging on to her mother's arm and they both have that feet dragging walk of someone about to collapse. Henryk and I make our 'scout' seat, criss-crossing and gripping our hands together.

'Sit down, Hania,' I tell her, 'just hold on tight around our shoulders.'

We make it to our place of work just after seven-thirty. It is a long and wide swathe of land close to the river Yuga. The river is frozen, its bank piled with long logs, that will float with the first thaw, when the current will send them to the timber yards in Ustyiug. So we're informed by our guide.

'Men in twos!' he shouts. 'Get saws and axes and start on the nearest trees. Women, get the brazier going! When the first tree is down, your task will be to clean the trunk of all branches and twigs and to stack them in neat piles. Now get going!'

'How about a drop of *keepiatok*?' Henryk requests.

'There's plenty of snow around you, if you're thirsty,' the armed guard steps in, 'don't waste time! You've got targets to meet. Requirements to fulfil. You'll be paid according to your performance. Now that's fair, isn't it? Why should the lazy stinkers be rewarded as well as the hard workers?'

His perfidious words reignite my anger. The sight of Nastusha's pained eyes, the women's weary faces, the young girl's white lips, make something snap inside me. I swear under my breath and feel Henryk's hand on my elbow.

'Come on, Julian, there'll be time for everything. Shall we show our boys how it's done?'

The work is familiar to us, but Roman and Ryszard and the other two look awkward even as they carry the heavy tools. Henryk pairs with Ryszard, I lead Roman to our tree and we tell the other two men to watch and copy us.

'You've got to chop out a cleft first at the side of the trunk, about a foot off the ground,' Henryk instructs. 'That is the side the tree will fall on, so you must stand back at all times.'

Henryk demonstrates with an axe. The tree is frozen solid. I help him and we take turns to strike the trunk. The boys get the idea and so our work begins, arm-breaking and relentless under the guard's watchful eyes, so that our pace does not slacken. He marches up and down, stamping his feet. He'd soon get hot helping us.

Our tree is down first, a magnificent giant spruce. Its heavy fall is absorbed by the snow. My whole body aches with the effort. And this is just the beginning.

Straight away the guard shouts for the women to come over. The axing and the cutting with saws are not the jobs for women, especially in this brutally fierce environment. My mind jumps ahead anticipating their stress at having to tackle something so unfamiliar. At home, as it was only a month ago, but feels like long decades from the past, they would have been baking in the warmth of the kitchen to the happy sounds of gurgling of their babies in their cradles.

I jump forward and pick up the axe which Hania is dragging along. Her face is crumpled with weariness and fear.

'Get back to your own work!' the guard reprimands me.

'She's only a child.' I want to shout the obvious, but I temper my tone. 'The axe weighs more than her!'

'She can do the stacking then! It doesn't mean she can get away with doing less!'

I lean the axe against the tree trunk, send Nastusha an encouraging glance, and then with a heavy heart I follow Henryk to the next tree.

We are allowed a drink of hot water at eleven, by which time the brazier is red with the burning logs. It is bliss to stand in the warmth around it, but dangerous too. Sweat and freezing temperatures are a lethal combination.

At one o'clock we get our bowl of *kasha* and another hot drink. We sit down on one of the long logs, but there's very little talk, even among the women. They warm their gloved hands around the aluminium mugs and look stunned. I can't bear the look of despair in Nastusha's eyes.

The sky lightens to a pale grey in the midday hours. By three o'clock it is dark again, but we carry on till five in dusky visibility made possible by the whiteness of snow.

I'm so weary I can't resurrect any feelings of relief when it is time to down the tools on the sledge. My friends are silenced with exhaustion. Little Hania walks about like a drunk, each swaying step threatening a total collapse. We beg the guide to let her sit on the sledge, wedged between the pots and the tools, as we begin our long trek back to the camp. She looks dead by the time we arrive. Henryk and I carry her indoors with her distraught mother close behind. There are three small children awaiting their return. They rush to their mother with cries of relief.

'Where have you been all day? Have you brought something back for us?'

Henryk and I rest Hania on her bunk and cover her up with blankets.

'She'll be better tomorrow,' I tell her mother with as much optimism as I can fake, 'the sleep and the warmth will do her good.'

The mother nods.

'I'll get permission for her to stay at home. I'll just have to work harder.'

Our own little brood, Pavel, Tomek and Daniel are waiting too.

'It's been such a long day,' Pavel complains, 'I worried all day that you weren't coming back.'

I want to weep, like Hania's mother. I pick him up, this 'big' skinny boy, and give him a heartfelt hug. Nastusha bends down and cuddles the little ones. She looks ill with tiredness.

'You can lie down next to me,' she tells them, 'I just need a few minutes rest.'

She takes off her outdoor clothing and curls down on the bunk, like a baby. Tomek and Daniel cling to her on both sides.

'My whole body aches as if someone has knocked it with a hammer,' she breathes the words with a shuddering sigh. Nevertheless she is asleep within seconds.

'When are we going home?' Pavel asks. 'It's so boring here.'

I avoid answering with a question.

'What did you do all day?'

He sits right next to me on the other bunk and holds me tight around the waist.

'Mrs. Zastavna gave us lessons. History. Geography and Religion. I enjoyed the Bible stories. She also told us the story of King Macius. But it was all talk. We've not got any reading or writing books. Or pencils even.'

I stroke his hair.

'It's only the first day, Pavel. As soon as I earn my first pay we'll go to the shops together and see what we can find.'

'Some apples?'

'And maybe some other things too.'

His face is small and pinched. There's doubt in his eyes.

'Is there anything left to eat?' he asks. My stomach feels like a hard ball.

'I'll go to the canteen and see what they've got.'

The same two women with flushed cheeks, greasy hair and broken teeth serve broth and black bread. It is a watery soup with a few diced potatoes and a handful of lentils, but I'm glad to take home whatever's on offer.

Back in our room I keep a portion aside for Nastusha and divide the rest between the boys and myself. There's no childlike excitement or banter over the meal. They chew their bread in silence, softening it first by dipping it in the soup.

'I'd love more,' Pavel licks the last trace of food off his bowl. I feel pain in my heart.

'My dear Pavelek,' I use the diminutive to persuade him, 'if we go to sleep soon, we won't be feeling hungry while we're asleep.'

Later, when the boys are asleep on their bed of hay and bugs, and I've covered them up as much as it's possible against the pests, I lie down beside my wife. It seems like a lifetime since we were man and wife. In the biblical sense. All I feel now is a numbing weariness in every fibre of my body, and a gnawing emptiness in my stomach.

Nastusha opens her eyes and whispers, 'Julian, I don't think I can face another day. If only I could go to sleep and never wake up again.'

A spurt of anger overrides my tiredness for a moment. I raise myself on my elbow and scold her, 'Nastusha, you must never, ever talk like that again! What about me? What about the boys? Aren't we worth your effort? Remember, as long as we're alive, there's always hope. One day we *will* escape from this hell!'

CHAPTER 14

SIBERIA – 1941

27th of June 1941. One year and three months later we're still here in this hell. But not for much longer. Our escape is planned in detail. We're all involved; Ryszard, Roman, Henryk and I, and of course our girls. The children will be told only at the last moment, when they're woken up in the middle of the night. Too dangerous for them to know, now that they attend compulsory classes, run by Comrade Borodinova, Borodin's wife. As ugly as her husband with thick features and large, bulbous hands. I pity the children. Something twists inside me when I have to listen to the idiotic verses that the children are forced to memorise about Stalin's ruby lips, as red and sweet as raspberries. I want to vomit.

First of September is the date we've set. This thoroughly considered decision is based on the necessity of harvesting and saving all available provisions for our journey. Summers here are short but kinder than the savage winters, despite the midges and the mosquitoes and the ensuing epidemics of typhoid and dysentery. The two seasons change virtually overnight. The sudden, intense heat and humidity bring out a burst of growth, ripening fruit and vegetables with surprising speed between May and August. The forest floor becomes overgrown with varieties of berries and a profusion of mushrooms. One has to be cautious though and check with the horticultural experts among us. A family of five died last summer from mushroom poisoning. As did another from their grandmother's well intentioned use of a tree bark to bulk up their soup when they had nothing else left at the end of winter.

In the summer months the evenings stay light until midnight. Despite aching all over with tiredness after the thirteen hours hard labour, we men, force ourselves to walk down to the nearby tributary of the river Yuga and catch some fish. Our method is simple: an old net curtain immersed in the water and held tight at both ends. We've had luck with perches, trout and carp. Nastusha and Eva have dried half of the fish for the journey, as well as half of our bread rations, and even some berries.

They've also dug a strip behind our barrack and planted carrot and turnip seeds, which Henryk and I obtained at the Yugovo market for an old petticoat. All our neighbours cultivate vegetable plots with anxious anticipation. Mrs.

Zastavna's silver chain has secured us a small bag of potatoes. It took all our willpower not to consume them all at once. With millimetre precision Nastusha and Eva cut off a third of each potato for planting. Every night when I close my eyes I dream of the taste of the new crop.

Today, as every day, we arrive at our place of work just after seven. The summer sun, up since three, shines strong through the trees, dappling the ground with bright spots. The warm air is heavy with the scents of moss and pine needles, a welcome escape from the stale fish smells trapped in the fabric of all the buildings at the camp. There's no escape from the midges and mosquitoes, already filling the air like grains of sand in a sand storm. We're well prepared this summer, having been bitten before till our skin was raw with hundreds of red, swollen and oozing spots all over our bodies. We have equipped ourselves with cheap net material from Yugovo market in exchange for Mr. Zastavny's smoking pipe. Our heads are totally veiled, our arms covered down to our wrists, our trouser legs pushed inside our boots, men and women alike.

The men get down to the task of felling trees. Last few weeks, I keep reminding myself. I couldn't bear another winter here; the daily trudge through the snow, the steely resistance of the frozen trees, the arm-breaking effort, the residual pain and the paralysing tiredness afterwards.

The women are busy with their handsaws, cleaning the felled logs, cutting off branches and twigs. Two are already standing knee-deep in the river, where the logs have been stacked all winter on the frozen surface, in preparation to be pushed out with the first thaw and directed with the current to the sawmill in Yugovo. Our girls hate this job. It is backbreaking and dangerous. One has to watch the moving logs with the awareness of a hundred eyes and jump out of the way in time. A young girl in our group was crushed to death last summer. We carried her broken body wrapped up in a blanket back to the camp, to the heart wrenching cries of her mother. This haunts me daily, every time my gaze falls upon the women wading through the water, with loose logs floating around them.

Nastusha and Eva suffer with chronic cramps in their legs and frequent bladder infections. There's no medication to relieve the pain. They treat themselves with camomile infusions and hot compresses, soaked in juniper or Siberian cedar extracts, a remedy learnt from the local people. They protect their feet with layers of rags against chafing inside their soaked then dried rock-hard boots. They also keep a strict watch that none of the women stand in the water longer than half an hour each time.

Soon we'll be free, I promise Nastusha every time she cries with sheer exhaustion, with barely sustained endurance of the inhuman situation we've been thrown into by force. There's not one centimetre of soft flesh anywhere on her body, her breasts and buttocks are as flat as a boy's, her skin is sallow and marked with mosquito bites, her dark eyes look too large for their sunken sockets, her hair, kept deliberately short, is nevertheless, regularly infested with lice. Like mine. Like everyone else's in this God-forsaken, Soviet Paradise.

At night time when fitful sleep brings her temporary relief beside me, I dream of the girl she once was, with abundant shiny hair, sparkling eyes and lips that made me think of rowan berries and I vow that I'll do everything to get her out of here and recapture our previous life so she can be that girl again. Deep down I know we are changed; our repair, if at all possible, can never be complete, but dreams are all we've got left, especially when the long, black, frozen nights mock our hopes of escape.

We stop for lunch at one o'clock and sit down on logs arranged around a fire, which is kept alive all day to keep the midges away. This and our smoking twigs have little effect on the black cloud that descends upon us the moment our food is uncovered. Our diet never changes; some kind of indiscriminate gruel and a slice of black bread. Our chronically empty stomachs don't fuss about the awful food or the midges settling on it like thickly ground pepper.

Today, only Ivan, our guide is supervising us. The two armed guards, just as on a few previous occasions, have mysteriously disappeared, but as they can reappear at any time without any warning, we carry on with our work for everyone's sake. Even the slightest misdemeanours are punished severely, the worst punishment being the withdrawal of food from the whole group for a day or two or longer, depending on Borodin's mood.

Just as I have predicted, he's totally confident that the harsh environment with its vast forests, with bogs and marshy grounds, with its wild and dangerous inhabitants, wolves and bears and wild boar, with freezing temperatures in the winter months, is in itself a deterrent to fanciful ideas of escape. He appears to have relaxed his grip of constant surveillance, by employing the armed guards elsewhere for parts of the day. He makes up for it with compulsory weekly meetings for the purpose of re-educating our deranged, west-contaminated rotten views and shouting at us Stalin's pronouncements on equality and justice.

We sit and eat in silence, chewing long and hard on every bite of bread. Ivan shares our diet with an extra slice of bread. He's an ex-prisoner. Twenty years inside for subversive activities against the State. His crime: possession of translations of foreign writers. Now that he's out, he's been sent to this camp to redeem himself through hard and honest work. He does not communicate much, but neither does he create tension when alone with us, and strangely, our bread rations are increased every time he records our daily output in the log book. The ruse of counting additional logs, felled the previous day, is made possible because the guards change daily. He's a good man, Ivan. And we've got nothing to give him to show our gratitude.

We all look up with surprise when he clears his throat as if ready to speak.

'*Vy slishat?*' his coal black eyes run rapidly around our faces, 'have you heard the news?'

The question is rhetorical; we're never informed of anything that happens outside of this place. It's as if the rest of the world did not exist. We shake our heads and wait for him to tell us.

He clears his throat again and looks at the ground.

'Five days ago, on the twenty-second of June, Hitler's armies crossed the Russian borders and attacked our armies.'

My hand with the precious bread stops in mid air as I exchange glances with Nastusha and my friends. It takes a moment to absorb the meaning of his words, then we all talk at once. Hitler? Attacking Stalin? Does it mean that Poland's defeated? Is it Russia next? The great, invincible continent? But how's that possible? What will happen to us? Will it get better? Or worse?

All afternoon, as we work, we speculate, with our hopes buoyed one minute, and sinking the next.

'We've got to ask bloody Kursky,' Henryk decides, 'once he knows that we know, maybe their tactics towards us will change.'

'He'll grill you to find out how you know,' Roman warns him

'Well I'm hardly going to snitch on Ivan, am I?'

'He can't hide this news for ever,' Roman reasons, 'perhaps it's safer to wait until it comes from him.'

'I'll go with Henryk,' I butt in, 'I want to know too.' So it's settled.

At six o'clock, the armed guards reappear, check our output against Ivan's notes and count all tools as we down them on the horse-driven cart. The pitiful animal, starved like us with a meagre diet all winter, is rebuilding its strength, grazing on the grassy patches while we work.

On the walk home, we keep our thoughts to ourselves. I strain my ears to catch the odd word from the chatter between the guards behind us, but it's only small talk. Nastusha waits for me to catch up with her, grabs my hand and gives it a squeeze. I feel excitement in that little gesture and catch light in her eyes.

'Everything could change yet,' she whispers.

We don't seek Kursky straight away. His mood is bound to improve after the evening meal. We have our evening routines too. We wash and change and eat the eagerly awaited supper: a slice of bread and *kasza*, obtained at the canteen. At the moment we're blessed with additional food from the forest: mushrooms and bilberries. Pavel's mouth is stained deep red with the juice and this sight lifts my spirits and the fact that he can eat all the berries there are, because tomorrow we can fill another bucket full. He wipes his mouth clean and recites a poem about Stalin, about the great man's kindness exceeding that of any parent's inadequate love.

Nastusha raises an eyebrow and throws a furious glance my way, though not at me. I understand. She wants me to say something.

'Pavel,' I ask quietly, 'what do *you* think about this verse?'

He leans towards me and whispers back,

'Don't worry, uncle Julian, it's all just a show. I know what they did to my Mum and my Dad. To my brothers and sisters. I hate them. Agata and I have a nickname for him. Stalin, *Sralin,* shitty Stalin.'

'Shshsh…' I place my hand over his mouth, 'don't ever get caught saying that.' I can't help a smirk of amusement though, and he sees it.

'Uncle Julian, it's only for the bread. We're the best in class, Agata and me.'

After supper our group gathers together, Henryk and Eva with their little Stella, Roman, Ryszard and his Agata, almost eleven now, and us two with Pavel. We carry our containers, but first we head towards the cemetery, just outside the camp. Now that daylight dominates virtually around the clock, with just a dusky dimming between midnight and two, the curfew hour has been moved to eleven. People make use of this extra time to tend their miniature vegetable plots or to venture out into the woods to collect anything edible they can find. We are permitted to do this, as well as the occasional shopping trip to Yugovo, with Borodin's signed pass. The twenty kilometres walk each way is in itself a deterrent.

Our group strolls together indulging in small talk until we're out of earshot. Once outside the *kolhoz* compound, our concerns return inevitably to the news we've heard from Ivan earlier in the day.

Roman repeats his reservation about confronting Kursky tonight.

'If the news is true and they don't want us to know, then our questions will just make them mad!'

'So what do you suggest?' Henryk is in a challenging mood. 'That we sit like bloody mice and let them continue to walk over us? No, I think our questions will make them sit up and maybe for once start them worrying about their own skin.'

'I wouldn't be surprised if they're already worrying,' I add. 'I'm with Henryk. We'll go together and ask him outright!'

Nastusha calls me rash, Eva calls Henryk inconsiderate of her fears. Pavel clings to me.

'Don't go, uncle Julian. I don't want anything bad happening to you!'

I hug his thin body to my side and reassure him.

'I'll only ask politely.'

'They'll want to know who told you.'

'A man at the market in Yugovo,' I improvise on the spot.

This answer appears to satisfy everyone, especially that in truth, we are all desperate for news of the war in Europe.

We reach the cemetery clearing and form a circle around the wooden crosses that mark the graves of our loved ones, whom we have buried close together.

There's not one family in our camp that has not suffered bereavement. The savage first winter decimated our numbers with pneumonia and tuberculosis. The summer that followed attacked us with plagues of mosquitoes and midges, then with epidemics of typhoid and dysentery. The camp dispensary with its single nurse and empty shelves is a sick joke. The nearest hospital is in Yugovo, not exactly on our doorstep to deal with emergencies. The few who attempted the long march died of fever and exhaustion. Some froze to death caught in the feared and ferocious *buran* storm, that is so thick with snow it robs its victims of all sense of direction before killing them with cold.

Everyone in our group has been ill at some time; mainly with severe symptoms of influenza and coughs that went on for weeks. The killer diseases got hold of our eldest and the very young. Mrs. Zastavna, Roman's aunt, died of pneumonia last winter. Ryszard's two younger daughters, eight and six, two small exotic butterflies with their white bows, died of typhoid last summer. Tomek and Daniel too. Just five and three. It breaks my heart thinking about them, seeing their thin little bodies, their sunken eyes as they begged for a bite of an apple, the fruit we've not seen since leaving Poland. Nastusha cried for weeks afterwards, the fresh pain compounding the old grief. As for Pavel, the only survivor of his family of seven, he follows us like a puppy, the moment we're back from work. I have dreams for him too, when we're out of this inhuman land, when he can officially become our own.

Hania, the young fourteen-year-old, who looked ten on her first day of work, is buried here too. She died of pneumonia in the third week of hard labour that was beyond her strength.

It is a miracle that Pavel and Agata survived their illnesses despite the continually poor diet. They are not unscathed, though. Their scalps are covered with recurring sores; their eyelids are purple-rimmed and dandruffy, the corners of their mouths look perpetually red, as if recovering from cuts. Nastusha and Eva do their best improvising treatment for them with infusions from any medicinal plants they can find, but what these children need is a good basic diet.

As for little Stella, her survival is a source of constant wonder. She looks like a miniature doll, with her matchstick fingers and feet that would fit inside match boxes. How is it possible that she has got away just with the winter colds and occasional runs ? Roman believes it's Providence. This makes me angry. Why doesn't Providence save us all? I often catch Nastusha watching Stella's wobbly walk and her attempts to communicate. I can guess her thoughts and feelings, but I don't ask. The pain is still raw inside me. Dorotka would have been two soon. In August. I comfort myself with the thought that we've been spared watching her die of starvation, had she survived the journey.

Of our other companions on the train, Mrs. Novitzka with her boys Artur and Aleks are still alive. Though they're only eleven and twelve, they go to work with their mother to earn larger portions of bread. This is irregular on account of their age, but Mrs. Novitzka has begged Kursky to allow them, as her worked norm alone would not have been enough to feed all three of them.

The three elderly Bogusz siblings and the Russian couple picked up at random at a station towards the end of our journey, are all resting together now, declared enemies by the Soviet State, united and equal in death.

We pray for them all for a few minutes in our thoughts, as public praying is forbidden, then we disperse in search of berries and mushrooms.

Later, when our half of the barrack is ready to settle for the night, Henryk and I venture out just one more time. Just five minutes, I tell Nastusha and Pavel. It's as light as midday outside.

At Kursky's door an armed sentry bars our way.

'*A vy po tzo?* What's your business?'

'Private information,' Henryk whispers. The sentry's hostile expression changes. They're always eager to recruit informers, beaten down men whose resolve has crumbled over the months, widowed mothers, who have offered their services for extra portions of food. We reserve our judgement; we just have to be more vigilant.

The guard knocks on Kursky's door, then, as we wait he studies us with an unrestrained stare.

Kursky's head pokes out from the half-open door. He looks none too pleased to see us.

'*A vy chego?* What do you want?' His voice is gruff.

'We've heard rumours,' Henryk drops his voice.

There's instant interest in Kursky's eyes. His gaze darts nervously round the deserted square, then he beckons for us to come inside. Out of his padded winter clothes, he looks a much smaller man. Henryk and I would have no difficulty tackling him to the ground, as we used to tackle poachers in our previous life. His shaved sides and stiff standing hair are no doubt intended to give an illusion of added height, but instead they give him the appearance of someone in a state of constant fright.

We follow him inside to his office, just right off the entrance door. It is a small room with a desk, a chair and portraits of Lenin and Stalin on the wall behind him. He sits down, we are left standing.

'What rumours?' he asks, clasping his hands hard. His nails are bitten, their length shorter than their width.

'Last Sunday,' Henryk's tone is confidential, 'at the market in Yugovo, people were talking about Hitler…'

Kursky's hand shoots up to his face, his fingers with their bitten nails rub hard on his cheek.

'What about Hitler?' his attempted nonchalance is pathetically transparent. I feel a moment of pleasure in delivering *the coup*.

'That he's crossed the Russian border and is heading for Moscow.'

There is a long pause, deathly silent, which makes his outburst all the more unnerving. He slaps the table with a mighty clout, jumps up and overturns the chair behind him at the same time.

'It's a lie!' he shouts. 'How dare you spread such lies! No one would dare cross our great leader Stalin. And you two, you need to be taught a lesson!'

Too late I realise that, indeed, Henryk and I are fools. We should have heeded Roman's advice, we should have been patient enough to wait.

'Comrade Kursky, these are just rumours.' I use my diplomatic tone, often employed at stale-mate points in our parish council meetings at home, when a decision on the most minor of points could waste an inordinate amount of precious time. 'Comrade Kursky, this is precisely why we've come to consult with you. All we want to know is the truth. What is happening in Europe? Is the war still on or over? Is Poland a free country? When can we go home?'

He actually does listen to my words, readjusts his chair, sits down and clasps his hands so hard that his fingers dig into his flesh. His voice is still edgy when he speaks.

'There's no need for you to know anything. You're under some misapprehension if you think you're going back. Back where? Your home is here now. Here you'll live, here you'll work and here you'll die. You owe your loyalty to one person alone, our great leader Stalin. As long as you remember that, and work hard, you'll always have bread on your table. Those rumours are lies! Our army is invincible. They sacrifice much for us. We can demonstrate our gratitude by supporting them, doubling our productivity, and sharing the benefit of our honest toil. Is that understood?'

He stares at us and we nod obligingly. But that's not enough.

'I want to hear,' he stresses each word, 'Perfectly understood Comrade Kursky!'

Like parrots we repeat his words, and I feel so stupid I can't bear to give Henryk even a sideways glance.

'I won't stop you from working tomorrow,' Kursky continues, 'we need all the workforce we can get, but perhaps a night inside the *kartzer* will help you to consider my words and make you think twice before repeating rumours next time.'

He rings a bell on his table, a small metal bell with a wooden handle, and immediately two armed guards walk in, no doubt having been eaves-dropping on the other side of the door.

'Take these two to the *kartzer* for the night!' he orders.

We're stunned, we're in a daze as we're led away, pushed inside the wooden hut and locked up with much chain clanging.

I'm filled with such rage I can hardly contain myself. I punch the air, stamp my feet and curse and swear until Henryk has had enough.

'Oh, for goodness sake, Kalinski! Have you gone bloody mad? Stop this drama and sit down!' he pats the hay beside him. 'Save your energy for when it's really needed!'

Reluctantly, exhausted with my fury, I drop down beside him. The hut is hot and stuffy, but infinitely more bearable than the freezing temperatures endured by some wretched innocents punished in the winter months. There are the bugs, of course, in the hay and on the walls, but it's best not to think about them.

'So we're bloody idiots!' Henryk states with some emphasis on the last word, 'but so what! We've got our answer, haven't we?'

'And a great help that's to us now!' I retort.

'Patience, Kalinski! We've got him rattled. We're only here so he can gain time. I bet this very minute he and Borodin are working out their next move. What to tell us, and how much and when?'

'If anything at all. They don't have to. Who's going to take our side against them in this place where we count for nothing?'

'Julian, just think. If Hitler's armies are heading for Leningrad, there are bound to be changes soon. Their silence in this matter will become unsustainable at some point. It'll all spill out, mark my words.'

'And what difference will this really make for us? It'll be just one tyrant replacing another.'

Henryk is quiet for a moment, but does not give in.

'It's just a feeling I've got, nothing more. Perhaps a premonition. But a good one. I think there's a change on the way. But if nothing happens before our escape, then we still stick to our plan. First of September, right?'

CHAPTER 15

There's no change in our routines in the weeks that follow. The news of the German attack has been confirmed many times over by casual contacts with people in Yugovo, but neither Borodin nor Kursky have made public announcements about the Red Army's retreat. We continue working thirteen hour days, but in the evenings and on Sundays we carefully prepare our food supplies for our escape. We have bags of dried bread, fish, mushrooms, even dried berries and some flour and grains. Nastusha and Eva have been saving beans and peas that they've grown themselves, but the root vegetables have had to be eaten fresh. It was a feast each time when our soup or *kasza* could be bulked up with diced carrots or turnips. New potatoes alone have been a long awaited delicacy. Slowly, the girls are clearing our little vegetable plot of all the things we can take with us, but not totally, so that a stripped garden does not arouse suspicion.

The time of our escape has to be between two and three in the morning, just before the midnight dusk changes to dawn. That is the time when the guards are least vigilant. We know, because Henryk and I have spent nights spying on them. They either play cards inside the doorway of the assembly barrack, or they take turns for a quick nap, no doubt confident that nobody in their right mind would wait through the twilight to make a run for it in the bright glare of dawn. We've also used the *slavoyka* at that time, Henryk and I, for a trial run. Successfully, though not without the feeling as if all the hounds of hell were after us. This means, we can leave through the side window unseen, make our way into the ditch past the *slavoyka*, crawl into the long grass on the other side and make our way into the forest.

Once we're out of sight, we'll have well over three hours to distance ourselves from the camp before our absence is discovered at six. We can only speculate that their search party will follow us naturally to Yugovo, the nearest town with a station. For this reason we've chosen to head the opposite way to Piniug, fifty or so kilometres away. It will be hard for Pavel and Agata, but later, we can slow down to their pace.

In Piniug, we're counting on luck; on staying hidden until a goods train arrives, whose hundred wagons' length will enable us to board the last truck unseen. We count on not being discovered until we're way down, hundreds of kilometres away from this place. Our bluff will be simple: we're on our way to a labour camp in the south. A place called Stalinin. Who could dispute that?

If we're discovered and detained earlier, we'll start planning our escape again. I cannot bear the thought of another Siberian winter here.

Today is Sunday, the last day of August. Tonight, so distant all summer, is now right upon us. I feel moments of great excitement and sharp twinges of fear, which for once supersede my constant feeling of hunger.

Everything we do today must look exactly the same as each Sunday, so there's not the slightest suspicion of change. In the morning, Nastusha and Eva do the weekly wash and change the children's clothes. The weather is on our side. Everything will be dry by the afternoon. Henryk and I tidy up our miniscule vegetable plot, leaving in a few carrots and peas. It feels almost sinful to be leaving them behind, but no doubt someone else will have the benefit, for nothing is ever wasted, not even a sorrel or a dandelion leaf.

Roman and Ryszard, his beard making him look like a monk, are going round our dwelling and smoking out the bugs from the crevices between the wood joints. Their smoking tools are dried leaves rolled inside a rug and lighted. This has to be done regularly to be effective, even if just for a short while, and is a much easier task in the summer with all the doors and windows open.

After lunch, enhanced these days with mushrooms and berries, our group gathers together to walk up to the cemetery. It is the end of the summer; the midges and the mosquitoes are gone. We have folded away our nets and can enjoy the balmy warmth on our uncovered arms. We all have scars of mosquito bites that became infected on our faces and arms. The forest and the land around us, with the abundance of colourful wild flowers contain so much beauty, yet I feel no attachment to this place, only a constantly live urge to get away. If only we could leave behind all our suffering and pain and start our new life recovered completely in body and soul.

I wish I could possess Nastusha's calm. She tells me she's scared too, yet quietly, methodically, she has been preparing for the journey. The baggage is not a huge problem; we've got just a few possessions left. Two changes of tatty old clothing, old leather hardened boots and a pair of worn shoes each. The rest is food provisions, all neatly packed in rag bags.

As every Sunday, in the absence of a chapel, we celebrate our Sunday service around the graves of our loved ones. Tonight, we'll be leaving them behind. I feel a pang of grief as I look down on the bowed heads of our young, Pavel and Agata. They still don't know they'll be leaving their dead siblings, never to return to this place again. But, I comfort myself that this is a tranquil, sun-dappled spot, in the shelter of tall, scented pines, a safe resting place. I like to imagine Dorotka's grave somewhere close to a church, if the good people, who took her away, had indeed kept their promise to Roman.

He whispers the prayers, then hums the melody of a hymn, which is an integral part of our collective Polish nature.

95

God who has safeguarded Poland for centuries, let us return to our free country.

We hum along with him, the sound rising strong above us, the words sung in our minds.

At the beginning there were angry protests from Borodin to stop this nonsense on Sundays.

He followed us on one occasion with armed guards and screamed at us, his purple face threatening to explode.

'There's no God! There's only Stalin. Where's your God? Why isn't he here to help you?'

He ranted on in this vein for a good few minutes, finishing, 'I forbid it! Do you hear? Anyone who disobeys my orders will be severely punished!'

We disobeyed. Our group was frogmarched to the *kartzer*. The frightened children cried and we men could hardly contain our impotent rage, but Roman calmed everyone with his soothing voice.

'Listen everyone, if we're forbidden to sing at the cemetery, we can certainly sing here.'

I thought he was mad, but no one opposed him when he intoned,

Kto się w opiekę poda Panu swemu...
He who submits himself into God's protection
Can say with certainty
God is my defender
No dreadful terror shall befall me...

Then something strange happened. We heard accompanying voices from outside the hut. And as the volume increased with every new hymn, we knew all our compatriots had gathered in our support. We heard shouts of the guards and the clanging of chains. We could not believe that Borodin had relented. But as we were let out onto the bright blinding snow, the guards lifted their guns at us.

Everyone froze. The crowd behind us became deathly quiet.

'A warning from commandant Borodin,' one of the guards shouted, 'he's got no time for your stupid games! One more religious song, and next time, it won't be just a short time in the *kartzer*!' He fired a shot in the air, making us all jump, making our children cry out.

We remained standing still after the guards were gone. No one said anything. Many of our compatriots came up to us and shook our hands before dispersing. Then when only our group was left alone, Roman said softly,

'They've not said anything about humming. And they can't erase words from our minds!'

After our short stop at the graves we disperse, keeping within visible distance of each other. It is easy to stray in this environment of tall trees, all looking alike, and to lose all sense of direction amidst the rampant growth of beckoning berry shrubs.

Henryk and I crouch down by a bilberry bush laden with fruit. As we fill our buckets I raise my eyes regularly to check on the presence of the rest of the group. Pavel and Agata are helping Nastusha and Eva while keeping little Stella amused with games. I find their childlike behaviour reassuring, their outbursts of giggles and their enjoyment of berries, like a flash of normality. Soon, God, how I hope it'll be soon, we'll reclaim normality for good.

A little further, Roman and Ryszard are down on their knees picking mushrooms. There must be a good find of them, because there are groups of other pickers close by.

Henryk is very quiet, but I can almost hear his thoughts rattling around his brain.

'I can hardly believe it's here. Tonight!' I whisper.

'The first bit scares me the most,' he whispers back. 'God, it'll be such a relief once we're all out of that side window.'

'And in the tall grass,' I add.

I don't tell him, but in the dead of night, when strange sounds reach us from the forest, I imagine all kinds of the worst scenes: being caught, being dragged back to the camp, being kept in the *kartzer,* put on trial, thrown into prison, forgotten for decades, like Ivan. I can't bear to think of Nastusha and Pavel being punished this way.

'We'll do it!' I tell him with emphasis, suppressing my own fear.

'Of course we will! Can you imagine another winter here?'

We look at each other and shake our heads.

'Once we're in the forest, out of sight,' he reassures me.

'It'll be child's play…' I add, and for no reason we laugh.

We're not aware at first, that our girls are running towards us, little Stella bobbing up and down in Eva's arms. Pavel and Agata are skipping beside them, their pinched little faces lit up with smiles. There's an air of uncontrollable excitement when they surround us. We get up.

'What's happening?' I ask. Before any of them can get their breath back, I see Roman and Ryszard coming our way with two strangers.

'We're free! Free to leave this camp!' the children squeal, jumping up and down as if on springs. Nastusha recovers first.

'It's true!' she gasps, 'Julian! God is merciful! At long last!' Her face is transformed. Her eyes shine, her smile is real, wide, engaging, reminding me of the good times, yet all I do is stare at her, speechless. Eva and Roman are laughing too and Ryszard's eyes have lost their preoccupied look and have come alive within all that growth of moustache and beard. The two strangers come close and shake hands with us.

'Father Norvid and Father Cybulski,' Roman introduces them, then raises his hands up to heaven, as if in prayer, 'Good God! You've not forsaken us!'

'For Christ's sake!' Henryk exclaims. 'Can anyone tell me what's going on?'

Father Norvid measures him with his penetrating gaze.

'Peace be with you, my brother,' he says. His voice is deep, commanding. He's in rags, like the rest of us, but he's shaved clean and his hair is neatly combed back, and lice free, I note. His whole appearance bears marks of prolonged starvation, the sunken cheeks, the tall thin frame with spindly limbs, the concave chest. But there's a glow in his dark eyes, something that revives my own hope and defiance. 'We bring you good news,' he says, 'you're no longer prisoners. It's hard to believe, but we're now declared friends and allies of the Russian people!' His mouth curls with wry amusement, revealing missing teeth, a mark of starvation or beatings.

'How can this be?!' Henryk pushes back his cotton cap and scratches his head.

Father Cybulski's tone is warm, he's like the true messenger of good tidings.

'Dry your tears,' he quotes words from an Easter hymn. He is smaller than his companion, and with his shaved head and wizened face, he looks very much in need of tender convalescence. 'My dear friends. You are all free. The commandant of this camp has no longer any authority to hold you back if you wish to leave!'

I don't know whether to laugh or to take him seriously.

'But do *they* know that?' I ask.

'Yes, they do!' he reassures with his warm smile that is attractive despite his greyed teeth. 'They've all been informed and directed to convey the news to all of us Poles, wherever we are in the Soviet Union. But it's in their very nature to hold back true information from their people, and to lie to them instead. There are times however, when even the professional liars cannot change facts that are too great to be twisted and ignored. And these are the facts: three weeks ago, on 12th August, Stalin signed a treaty with the West. He can no longer fend off Hitler's armies on his own.'

'So, it's all true!' we exclaim almost in unison. 'The attack on Soviet borders!'

'Not only true, but dire!' Father Norvid confirms, his dark eyes flashing. 'All northern borders have been crossed. Riga's been taken. Smolensk's been taken. The Germans are moving south with alarming speed. They've got Kiev and Odessa's under siege. Thousands of Russian soldiers have been taken prisoner. It seems Stalin's back is against the wall. One can only imagine his rage at having to join the West against Hitler. So much for all his rants against the rotten West.'

I hang on his every word.

'How does that change our fate?' I ask.

He looks at me with his penetrating gaze.

'Sikorski's government in exile has moved to London from Paris after the fall of France,' he explains. 'Sikorski's diplomatic skills have much to do with what's happening to us now. He's pointed out to Churchill the usefulness of the Polish army, once all the thousands of imprisoned Polish soldiers all over Russia were to be released. Stalin was given an ultimatum: yes, he could join the West but on condition of freeing the Poles to form an additional military force against Germany.'

We stand quiet for a while, contemplating his words, struggling to absorb this incredible news. Even the children listen with grave interest, Agata clinging to her father and Pavel holding me tight with his arm around my waist.

'And Stalin's agreed? To all that?' Henryk shakes his head in disbelief.

'He's been left no choice,' Father Cybulski's smile is like a magical wand, changing dreams to reality, 'look at us. We're proof of those changes. We've been held prisoner together with our soldiers in a camp near Konosza. They've already been released and are now on their way to Buzuluk near Kuybyshev, where a Polish army is already being formed under the leadership of General Anders.'

We remain quiet, mesmerised by this unexpected turn of events. Henryk scratches his head again, vigorously, before pulling on his cap. He chuckles to Ryszard.

'You can shave off all that jungle now, on your face and head.'

'When you show me the evidence,' Ryszard replies with a rare smile.

Father Norvid gives them both a long, understanding look. 'That's why we're here,' his voice is a fraction gentler, 'to tell and convince people of their changed circumstances. We've been to a few other camps already. Of course, nothing's been said to the people. But everything changed as soon as we confronted the commandants and showed them our papers. You see, they're so intimidated by their own system, that anything looking remotely official, especially with a seal, throws them into a panic. They fear for their own lives. They must already have had directives. But secrecy and delay are safer. People don't matter. They can be made to wait for action.'

'Not to mention the convenience of enforced labour,' Father Cybulski adds.

'Then let's go and find out,' I decide, with a sudden spurt of impatience.

'Let's go!' my friends agree, and I add quickly, 'I'll just round up all those people over there. Just imagine their shock when I tell them!'

'I'll come with you,' Henryk says. 'And me!' Pavel adds eagerly, clutching my hand. We rush off as our little party follow the two priests back to the camp.

Henryk forms his hands like a trumpet around his mouth and calls out to the people moving about with their containers at some distance between the trees. Pavel hops with excitement still holding onto my hand.

'Listen everyone! We're free to leave! Come back to the camp to hear the news!'

They stop and listen and take a moment to register his words then they start walking towards us. Like us before, they are stunned when we tell them of the two priests' mission.

When we arrive at the camp there's already a crowd gathering in the square outside the administration barrack. News travels like lightning.

'The priests are with Borodin,' Nastusha tells me. Stella holds up her matchstick hands to Henryk to be picked up from Eva's arms. There's a suppressed rumble of excitement around us, but I can't rid myself of apprehension. What if the priests receive the same treatment at Borodin's hands as Henryk and I received from Kursky? What if they end up in the *kartzer* and we end up here for ever? Except our group, I remind myself. We leave tonight no matter what! A shudder runs the length of my body.

A booming sound from the loudspeakers makes us all jump. And though the words that come through now are clearly and officially spoken, I find it hard to accept the announcement.

The Soviet Government has granted amnesty to all Polish prisoners and deportees. The amnesty document will serve as the family passport and as a one way travel permit to the destination of your choice.

I feel Nastusha's arms around my waist. She presses hard against me on one side and Pavel on the other. I look down into their faces. Pavel smiles. Nastusha's expression is full of uncertainty.

'Can this really be true?' she asks.

There's no shout of jubilation from the crowd. Like us, they're cautious with premature celebration. Our attention is caught by Kursky's appearance. Our friendly priests come out of the building with him and walk towards us, as he pins a large notice on the door of the assembly hall.

The crowd surges forward to see it close, we wait until there's a space to file past. It's the announcement in writing. The script. Black on white. We've all seen it now. Borodin can't hide the facts from us any longer.

Our group walks back to our barrack with our two visitors invited to tea. Everyone's animated, yet our voices are kept down. Old habits can't be wiped out in minutes.

Pavel and Agata are running round the square with other children and playing tig. I leave my bucket of berries by the door, relieve Nastusha of hers and pull her by the hand to the side of our barrack where the grass is mossy and soft. I ignore her questions of surprise, just hold her close in a dance pose then take her with me in an energetic polka, round and round in circles, until laughter bursts out of her, and she becomes the young and happy Nastusha, whom I love so much. I stop for her so she can catch her breath, hold her close and promise,

'Nastusha *kohana*, my dear, this is our new beginning!'

CHAPTER 16

We rejoin the others indoors. Nastusha and Eva prepare a meal for the two priests, seated in Roman's room; quick noodles made with a handful of flour, mixed with the left over mushrooms, and raspberry tea. Their eyes light up at the sight of such a sumptuous meal. We gather round them on the bunks, eager for news from the outside world. It seems there's no stopping Hitler's armies from marching across all borders to the north, as far as Finland, or south, to the African continent.

'They're everywhere!' Father Norvid says between quick nervous bites of Roman's toasted bread, 'In Norway, in Yugoslavia and Greece, and now they've even crossed the Mediterranean to Egypt!'

Father Cybulski's eyes are damp with the steam from the aluminium mug. 'Some friend Hitler's turned out to be! Stalin must be seething. And yet, in a strange, perverse way, we owe our freedom to Hitler's betrayal. Stalin would never let us go.'

'I can't believe it!' Henryk's expression of wonder is fixed to his raised brow and cheeks. 'Can this really be true? That we can just walk out of here? Free people. Any time?'

We give the priests an account of our planned escape. Father Norvid's angular face looks even sterner as he listens.

'Thank God! You've been saved from such madness!'

'It was desperation!' I correct him.

His dark broody eyes penetrate mine.

'Some of our boys got desperate. Beyond endurance. Beyond precaution. Too impatient for their own good. They were followed, shot, dragged back to the camp, and days later their corpses were still there, in the middle of the square, half eaten by the marauding wolves at night. We begged, then bribed the commandant with extra hours of work for permission to bury these poor souls.'

We fall silent. I feel a shiver down my spine. The tension is broken by Stella's squeals. Pavel and Agata have come indoors and entertain the toddler with ring games in the hallway.

Nastusha sighs with relief.

'Thank God for our children! What a blessing, that they're still so normal after all we've been through!'

And Ryszard adds,

'What wouldn't I give to recapture the past!'

I can't help a stab of intense sadness thinking about the wife and the two little daughters he's lost. Roman speaks to him gently,

'Ryszard, we've all got to look forward now. You've got Agata to think about and her future. Soon we'll be out of here.' Then turning to the priests he says, 'We're ready in fact. Ready to leave tomorrow'.

Father Norvid gives him a wry smile.

'Arm yourself in a lot of patience. You know their delaying tactics. They'll make you wait for your papers.' From his breast pocket he pulls out two folded sheets of paper. He flattens them on the table. One is the amnesty document, declaring him to be a free citizen, the other is a travel permit. He points to a space half way down the page.

'Here, you'll be asked to name your destination'.

'That's simple,' Eva says, 'we just want to go home.'

Father Cybulski shakes his shaved, shrunk-looking head.

'You musn't do that, on any account. You'd escape one enemy only to fall into the hands of the other. No, you must think of as far away as possible from both, the Germans and the Russians. Our released soldiers from our camp have already gone to Buzuluk. Anders has appointed two other initial destinations for gathering; Tatichevo and Totzkoye, I'd advice Buzuluk. It's the nearest to this area.'

'What'll happen to us and our children, when our boys join the army?' Nastusha asks linking her arm through mine.

Father Norvid's craggy features soften surprisingly when he replies,

'General Anders has thought of everything. He wants everyone to be released, and together with the army moved south. It'll be easier there to evacuate people across the southern borders to freedom.'

Father Cybulski leans forward, his shaved head and scrawny neck making me think of a featherless chick, and tells us,

'Give Tashkent as your destination on your form. This will permit you to travel the full length of this country.'

I contemplate his words and visualise another long journey, weeks on the trains, the hunger, the thirst, the cramped conditions, the dirt, the exhaustion, yet none of these things can blur the clear vision of leaving this land and stepping out on free soil. The very thought makes my chest expand with joy.

'We must go and tell everyone!' I say with unsuppressed enthusiasm.

'We will!' Father Cybulski smiles. 'After we've enjoyed this feast to the full!'

Roman invites them to share his room for the night, before they set off on the next leg of their mission.

'Excellent training for a marathon,' Father Cybulski smiles, 'but we've met some kind people with their carts and horses. Russians. God bless them!'

'And what about night time?' I ask.

'Providence,' he smiles again, 'you'd be surprised how even in these remote places a dwelling appears out of nowhere every single night. And when we explain who we are, they make sleeping room for us as if that was no trouble at all. Though they have so little themselves. How true it is; there are only two kinds of people; good or bad. Nothing else really matters. Colour or race or nationality or religion. Divisions made by people.'

I listen to his words with wonderment at our incredible luck against the miserable existence of the Russian people sentenced to spend their entire life in this oppressive regime.

Nastusha and Eva stay at home with the children when we go round with the priests to all the Polish barracks to advise the people about considering and naming their destinations on the travel permits. For the very first time, with no guards about, it feels like a peaceful, normal settlement, inhabited by a contented, close-knit community.

At six in the morning, there is a crowd of Poles outside the administration block. No one has presented themselves for work. We watch the two small groups of Russians and Ukrainians gathering by the smithy, collecting tools on their carts and being led away by their group leaders, the reformed ex-convicts.

'I almost feel guilty,' Nastusha whispers, 'God, how they must hate us!'

I have the same thoughts. All of us here are the victims of a madman's warped philosophy, yet we, Poles, by some unimaginable chance, have been spared from eking out this abominable existence, while the other two groups are sentenced to this undeserved punishment for the rest of their lives.

'It's inhuman, isn't it?' I agree, 'I wish we could take them away with us.'

An hour passes, then another, but Borodin's door remains firmly closed. It is the first of September, two years exactly since the German planes dropped the first bombs over Poland. This morning with its first hints of the coming winter in the nippy air, is bright and uplifting, and despite the long wait, a feeling of optimism and hope permeates the chatter of the groups within the crowd. I think of the two priests, who, like angels from heaven have brought us good tidings, and send my prayers after them, to guard them all the way to their next stop.

Little Stella sits quietly on Henryk's shoulders, mesmerised by the activity around her. Pavel and Agata exchange small talk, yet, for precaution, link their arms with ours, Pavel with mine, and Agata with her father's, who, true to his promise has shaved all of the growth off his face. His sunken cheeks and pallid skin give him an almost ghostly appearance. Roman's face is animated, his eyes sparkling like blue stones in the morning light. Our girls look different too; almost pretty, I would say, their freshly washed, fluffed hair, softening the sharp contours of their emaciated faces, the summer tan disguising the ravages of mosquito bites and the marks left by ensuing infections. Eva's white-gold hair stands out, perhaps too eye-catching in this land of dark haired people. But the girls have already vowed to stay together for safety at all times until the end of the war, until we return to them.

There's a commotion. Someone brave, or fool-hardy, goes up the three steps and bangs his fist on Borodin's door.

'Commandant Borodin! We need to speak to you!'

Astonishingly, we hear the door unlock, and as our spokesman stands down, Borodin and Kursky, both dressed in their NKVD uniforms, appear from within and stop on the step above us.

Borodin's face is purple and blotchy, Kursky's shoulders and arms twitch as if he's got bugs up his sleeves.

'*Vy Polaki* are free to leave!' Borodin declares, with a malevolent flash of his gold tooth. How he must hate us too! 'But not all at once! Forms need to be filled in. And that takes time! For that reason, we've listed your names on six sheets, one for each day of this working week. We'll expect you in our office only on the day allotted to you and your form filling. Otherwise, I'm advising you to return to your work. Now that we're allies, united against our common enemy, it is your duty to work in support of our noble army fighting so bravely at the front. And besides... I don't see any fat *bourjouye* here, indifferent to a few more handy roubles...' he gives us an ugly smirk.

I clench my fists. The man's cynicism has no boundaries. Allies, then *bourjouye*, all in one breath. Friends? Only in his twisted mind.

The crowd watches in silence as Kursky pins the sheets to the door. When he and Borodin retreat indoors, it takes a while for everyone to file past the lists of names. We discover they are not listed alphabetically, nor in the order our barracks are lined. This means that our exit from this camp will have to be delayed for four days, as everyone from our group, Roman, Ryszard with Agata, Henryk, Eva and their Stella and us two with Pavel, have all been allotted different days for dealing with formalities.

We are all annoyed as we walk back to our dwelling, but Roman runs a few steps ahead, turns round and claps his hands. 'Hey!' he calls out, 'what's four days in the scheme of things?' His eyes sparkle like blue flames.

Borodin's voice thunders regularly through the loudspeakers extolling the glory of joining the Red Army to fight the common enemy. To no effect. There are no volunteers. People are busy preparing to leave the camp. To follow Anders' men.

Our girls and children spend the last few days gathering the remnants of the forest fruits. The men in our group still go to work but only when not waiting for the amnesty and the travel documents to be finally handed to them. Just knowing that this is now our own free choice what we do with our time is infinitely satisfying, not to mention that even the few measly additional roubles could prove essential on our long journey.

In our free time Ryszard and Roman catch fish and smoke them over an open fire to keep for later. Henryk and I have constructed a simple, hand-pulled wooden cart on wooden wheels, as there's a shortage of metal. Even essentials such as nails and screws are hard to obtain. We got ours from my friend Yurey.

Nastusha and I visited them on Monday evening after the news of our amnesty had spread like wild-fire around the camp. Yurey and Meela received us with the same hospitality as always, betraying no rancour at our good fortune of being allowed to leave the camp.

We found Yana, the poor mad woman in their care, squatting on their bunk busy scooping the fluffy centre out of a baked potato. Her face was totally covered by her stringy hair and she appeared unaware of our presence.

We were seated at their small table and offered mint tea and flat-fried flour and milk cakes.

'So… it's amnesty for you..?' Yurey's large frame could look intimidating if one did not know his caring nature. 'I thought amnesty was only for the criminals.' He shrugged, allowing himself a wry, amused smile.

'We've never been in doubt how highly they rate us,' I replied, 'but hey, let's talk nice things on this occasion. Here, this is for you. For our friendship.' I placed my nickel cigarette holder on the table and pushed it towards him. He looked puzzled for a split second then his large hand closed over my gift and he pushed it back to me.

'Your need is greater than mine. You've got children in your group. God knows what you may have to buy with it yet.'

'Please,' I insisted, 'indulge me!'

He thought for a moment, picked it up, snapped it open and ran his finger around the shiny smooth surface.

'All right. Now tell me, what do *you* need?'

'Everything!' I laughed, adding, 'I bet you haven't got the one thing I really need!'

'Try me!'

'Ten nails would be a treasure.'

'Done!'

Nastusha gave Meela one of her own embroidered table runners; one of the last few things left in our 'bargaining' bag.

'This is beautiful! Such fine needlework!' Meela's eyes glistened.

'We shall miss you,' Nastusha said with feeling. 'We wish we could take you with us.'

'We have no Sikorski to stick up for us,' Yurey's tone was wistful.

'I pray your time will come too,' Nastusha assured him.

'Will you remember us?' Meela asked.

'Always!'

'Then promise me, promise me you'll write. Once you're out of here, out in the free world, please write and tell me what it's really like.'

We reminisced about the good old times, about our homes, our families we had been forced to leave behind, and when it was time to leave, my heart was like a weight in my chest.

CHAPTER 17

On Monday, our allotted day for obtaining amnesty and travel documents, Nastusha, Pavel and I stand outside Borodin's door with about twenty other people soon after the working parties leave the camp. The morning air is cool, but there's a promise of a warmer day later, when the sun has risen above the wall of the forest surrounding us.

Constant supervision over the last eighteen months has taught us to keep our thoughts to ourselves. There's a low-toned banter around us, yet I detect underneath it a quiver of excitement. People's worn, emaciated faces show signs of furtive animation. They catch your eye then look away, anxious not to betray their thoughts in front of the two NKVD men guarding Borodin's door.

The very sight of them makes me boil. We're supposed to be allies and free citizens, for God's sake! Getting away from this place is all I can think of now. This urgency inside me is stronger now even than my constant feeling of hunger.

By nine o'clock we've been waiting for almost three hours. The gravelly surface is dry, so we've found sitting spots on the ground. A little dust will make no difference to the appearance of our shabby clothes.

'Dear God, I hope they've not changed their minds,' Nastusha whispers. That is possible; anything is possible in their perfidious world. But I make light of it.

'They need us to fight Hitler. They'll let us go.'

There's a fleeting relief expressed in her sigh, in the drop of her skinny shoulders, in the lift of her mouth, dry and flaky and prone to frequent bleeds. The summer tan has camouflaged the marks left by mosquito bites and ensuing infections, but it cannot hide the skeletal thinness of her face. I force a smile and squeeze her twig-like hand.

'We'll be out of here soon,' I tell her and turning to Pavel, to that haunted expression of his, I add, 'and the very first thing we'll do is have a big feast of our favourite food!'

A dreamy look glazes their eyes and mine become moist.

'Pavel, want to play *Guess*?' I suggest. It's the simplest game of matching the number of fingers as we 'shoot' from our clenched fists at the same time. He's game, so we pass the time until the first couple is called out at about half past nine.

The process is puzzlingly slow. I cannot imagine why it takes forty-five minutes to fill and sign two slips of paper. I want to ask them when they come out, but the man gives me a discreet shake of his head and with his eyes indicates the two guards.

By twelve our small crowd has diminished by only a third.

'I'm so hungry,' Pavel says, his face puckering as if he were about to cry.

I see alarm in Nastusha's eyes.

'Pavel, my dear, if we leave this place, we could miss our slot. They could cross us off their list altogether!'

Pavel bows his head and hides his face in his hands. His shaved scalp is covered in sores in various stages of healing.

'I'll tell you what,' I speak with forced brightness, 'run to aunt Eva and ask her to bring us a slice of bread each'.

It takes only about three minutes for Pavel to run across the square and come back, but I see torment in Nastusha's face. She relaxes only when he is back with us. She hugs him to her side.

'I couldn't bear it if they held you back,' she says.

He returns her hug then we all three play a game of *I spy*.

Eva and Henryk are on tomorrow's list. Totally illogical as their surname comes before ours in the alphabet. She comes out to us with three aluminium mugs of watered down raspberry juice and three slices of black bread. She does not linger under the supervising gaze of the guards. I half expect them to comment, but they're too busy looking out for their colleagues who are supposed to relieve them and, judging by their swearing, are already five minutes late. We dip the black hard bread in our raspberry flavoured water and fool our stomachs again.

At about half past two our names are called out. Julian Kalinski. Anastazia Kalinska. Nothing about Pavel. We take him along with us anyway.

Indoors, Borodin is at his desk in his NKVD uniform and his side-kick Kursky, uniformed too, is shuffling through some papers at the end of the long desk. He motions to us with an impatient hand to stand before Borodin. For a long while neither speaks to us. Borodin studies the two forms before him, as if he's seeing them for the first time. This pose of ignoring us carries on for what seems like an hour, though it probably is only half of it. I feel my blood pressure building up.

Finally, Borodin's frog-like eyes roll upwards and his blotchy face looks as serious as a hangman's.

'So you want to leave? And why's that?' Again that menacing glint of his gold tooth.

This is surreal. I force myself to stay calm.

'Comrade Borodin, in view of the fact that we now have a common enemy, we can't sit back and do nothing. Hitler has devastated our country and now he's trying to do the same with yours.'

'Ours,' he corrects me, his thick lips curling unpleasantly. 'This country has saved you from him and given you shelter. Now it's your turn. It's your duty to join the ranks of the Red Army and fight our common enemy side by side!'

God, how do I persuade this blockhead to let us go? I sense Nastusha's anxiety, Pavel's unrest.

'Comrade Borodin, I'm not a military man. I can't pretend to know anything about military strategy. But one thing is clear. We Poles have got to assemble together if we are to form a force that will be strong enough to withstand Hitler's attack. We'll be the much needed additional army. That's in everyone's interest, isn't it?'

Even as I say these words I know he can't agree with me. They want the Poles in their army for the sole purpose of being used as buffers against the German attack.

To my surprise Borodin doesn't argue. He changes the subject. I can only suspect that something else is at stake. If only I knew what?

'And this boy?' he asks, throwing Pavel a glance. 'Is he yours?'

Please God, don't let him pick on Pavel.

'He is for the time being,' I state categorically, 'until he's reunited with his father.'

'So where's his father? Abandoned him? That speaks volumes, doesn't it?'

'Indeed, it does.' I want to punch his ugly mug, I want to grab him by the ears and shake him until that stupid brain of his is smashed to pulp inside his skull. Incredibly, he continues,

'We have places for abandoned children. Good education. Caring teachers. Excellent training in loyalty to our superior State. They grow up confident, with a sense of belonging that no family would be able to give them for life.'

It defies all belief that he can believe such drivel, unchallenged, parrot-fashion learnt. I count to five before replying.

'Comrade Borodin, I have every faith in your good intentions, but this child is not yet totally abandoned. He's got us. And my promise to his father must be kept.'

Borodin gets up abruptly and leaves the room. Nastusha sends me an anxious glance. I shake my head and touch her arm reassuringly. This stupid talk was all a show. To intimidate us. I sense there's something else Borodin wants from us. I wish he'd just come out with it, so we could conclude this crazy charade, get our documents and go.

Five minutes pass, then another ten. Kursky is ruffling some papers at the end of the desk as if totally unaware of our presence. Pavel is quiet but his limbs are getting restless. He rubs the back of his neck. He gives his shoulders a stretch.

'How long is it going to be?' he whispers.

I repeat his question to Kursky

He looks up and shows surprise as if seeing us for the first time.

'That depends on you, Kalinski.' He sidles up closer on the other side of the table.

'I don't understand,' I say, although I'm beginning to.

'You want everything for nothing, you rotten *bourjouye*!' He bangs the table with his fist. 'Those times have finished when you've exploited the poor. Now's your chance to give something back!'

Now I understand. Perfectly.

'Tell me Comrade Kursky, what is it exactly you want from us? The rags we wear? The remnants of our shoes? A slice of black bread, perhaps? A fag? Or the stash of *reds* that we've never got paid?'

Kursky's expression turns dark.

'Shut your gob! You impertinent son of a bitch! If you know what's good for you, you'll soon think of something!'

'Give me a clue.' I want to hear him say it, to witness his base act.

'How about some silver or gold!' With that he strides out dramatically, as if this was his last exit.

Pavel clings to me and Nastusha's eyes fill up. She wipes them with her sleeve.

'What are we going to do? We've got nothing valuable left to give away.'

I rage inside. I feel utterly helpless against such shameless cynicism of our captors. Our allies.

Then I think of something.

'We've still got our wedding rings, Nastusha!' Her expression is shocked, as if I uttered a sacrilege. 'Once we're out of here, in a normal world, once we start living and working and earning decent money... my dear Nastusha, I'll buy you twenty rings!'

She shakes her head,

'But these are special. Nothing can replace them.' Nevertheless, she unbuttons her breast pocket and pulls out a small lace handkerchief, an elegant reminder of our past, and inside its secure knot, our two wedding rings. She kisses them and places them on Borodin's desk. Two gold bands.

It must be another twenty minutes before Borodin returns alone. I watch his gaze skim the desk, note our rings then move swiftly to the papers. He sits down and without looking up at us asks all the official questions and writes our answers down on the forms. Name. Date of Birth. Place of Birth. Last address. When it comes to 'Destination' he knits his brow and remains silent for a long, unnerving pause. Then he asks,

'Why do you all want to go to Tashkent?'

It's tempting to vex him with a biting retort, but that would be madness.

'Comrade Borodin, it's a wonderful chance for us to travel the length of this beautiful country and feast our eyes on its unique landscape.'

He gives me a thoughtful look and for a second I fear I've gone too far. But then, without further comment, he signs our papers and hands them to us.

Outside, there's no way we can warn the remainder of the waiting group; the guards are within earshot. But we can warn everyone else in the camp before tomorrow to come prepared with backhanders.

'They'll mint a fortune by the end of the week,' Nastusha remarks when we're half-way across the square, where no one can hear us.

'It's an opportunity for them, Nastusha. Just think, they're stuck here for ever. Without any hope. I'm almost tempted to pity them.'

CHAPTER 18

5th of September. The impatiently awaited day of our departure. We don't hang around. As soon as the working parties leave the camp, and the square is quiet, we come out of our barrack, for the last time, and hurriedly fill the wooden cart with our few possessions. The rag bags are the vital ones, filled with our religiously stored groceries, and all the edibles that we have been able to dry or smoke for long keeping. We've bribed Igor from the smithy with some tobacco to let us have four tin cans, that had contained lubricating oil. We flushed the cans several times with boiling water, before filling them up with water for the journey. We've got supplies of blackberry and raspberry juices in bottles and jars we've managed to obtain through some clever bartering.

A woman runs out of the barrack next door, her uncovered arms as thin as twigs, and hurries to me and Henryk. There is a feverish, desperate look in her eyes.

'Which way are you going? Tell me. We'll catch up with you in a day or two.' Her loosened teeth wobble as she speaks.

We tell her. Eastwards all the way, until we hit the North-South railroad. Piniug, about fifty kilometres away is our nearest station. She wishes us a good journey. We wish her and her family a speedy exit from this place.

Out of habit we glance nervously towards the administration block across the square. People are already queuing up for their appointments with Borodin and Kursky, and out of habit, the armed guards loiter at Borodin's door, making a mockery of our alliance pact.

'Let's go!' Roman's voice is decisive. He and Ryszard march on first, Nastusha and Eva follow behind them holding Pavel and Agata firmly by their hands, and Henryk and I are the rear guard with the hand-pulled cart between us. Henryk has made a niche among the bags and the packages and lined it with a blanket for little Stella to sit in. Despite the early hour, her eyes, as crystal blue as her mother's, are wide awake and inquisitive.

No one speaks, as if by tacit agreement. We walk at a brisk pace, out of the camp, along the eastward track, Pavel and Agata having to keep up with us with frequent running steps. The track gradually blurs into a softer ground, a treeless swathe that cuts through the forest, as far as the eye can see into the grey distance. We relax our pace, but Henryk and I have to pull the cart harder against the friction of small bumps of moss or grass. This inconvenience feels infinitesimal against the growing elation of being free at last.

After a few kilometres we stop. Pavel and Agata flop on the ground and laugh. Nastusha and Eva wipe sweat off their faces, breathe out with relief and smile. Ryszard looks back, craning his neck and squinting his eyes.

'I don't trust the bastards! Even now. Or ever!'

Roman squeezes his shoulder affectionately.

'Relax! Others have left before us and have not been brought back.'

Ryszard shakes his head,

'I feel as if they're playing games with us.'

I have that feeling too. I expect the NKVD to jump out from behind the trees and march us back to the camp.

'There's no sign of them,' Henryk's tone reassures us, as he picks Stella from the cart and puts her down on the mossy ground for a little run. 'This land is too vast for them to patrol every corner. We must be vigilant but not paranoid. I suggest we walk as briskly as the children can manage and stop every two hours for a short break. Longer for our lunch. We should cover a fair distance by the evening.'

This sounds like a good proposition and that's what we do.

It is amazing how in a space of a week, as if nature knew the months by name, the length of the day has changed dramatically. It will be dark by eight o'clock. We need to leave ourselves enough daylight, to light the fire, to prepare the evening meal and to construct a shelter over our sleeping ground.

Henryk and I check our compasses regularly, fortuitous remnants from our working days in the forest at home. Once we hit the south-bound railroad, the final part of our march will become easier.

The September sky is clear above the forest. The air is close with accumulated warmth beneath the branches of the pines and firs. We're all sweating and undressed to our shirts. A prickly sweat covers my scalp which I've scrubbed with carbolic soap in the hope of ridding myself of lice. This is a constant, uncontainable plague, affecting us all. But soon... soon everything will be different.

Walking at the rear of our group with Henryk, we reminisce about all the things happening at this time of the year in our forest at home: the boar hunts, the duck shoots, beaver watching as they build their dams with cut branches strategically left in chosen sites for ecological balance, the tree felling in preparation for planting young saplings in Spring,

'They're bloody stupid,' Henryk remarks, 'denuding their forests like that. And not planting new trees.'

'They'll get their wake up call when they run out of trees. And timber. When the industry comes to a standstill.'

'They can't bloody think beyond their five-year plan.'

And indeed, as we march on, deeper into the forest, one gets the feeling as if the whole world is covered in trees. Twigs snap underneath our feet, their sounds mingling with distant echoes of bird cries. I recognise some, the ravens and the sparrows, and now and again a startled hare darts away from our path.

'It's so peaceful here,' I breathe in the scent of the pines and moss, 'takes me back to our forest.'

'Not a bear in sight,' Henryk remarks.

'Don't tempt fate.'

He laughs.

'We'll keep the fire going all night. And take turns to keep watch.'

'Certainly!'

By seven o'clock in the evening, we estimate we've walked about thirty kilometres. The railroad should be within reach, but the fact is we can't see it, so we have to stop for the children's sake. I'm astonished they've managed so well all day. However, their spirit of adventure is on the wane now and they throw themselves on the ground and curl up. Stella is fretful. She needs her feed and sleep.

We men collect the firewood, start a fire, and while Nastusha and Eva prepare the evening meal, we construct a shelter over a spot chosen for its mossy softness. We stretch a blanket over six poles dug into the ground.

'Perfect!' Roman rubs his hands.

'We'll be like sardines,' Ryszard smiles down to Agata.

'Well insulated,' Roman laughs.

'Safety in numbers,' Henryk adds.

'A juicy find for wandering wolves!' I make light of it, my mind conjuring up alarming images. Henryk slaps my shoulder,

'You worry too much!' he tells me off.

We sit round the fire and enjoy the long awaited meal of boiled oats and mushrooms, a slice of dried bread, softened in the raspberry tea. It's bliss! Pavel and Agata finish first and crawl away onto the blankets spread out underneath the shelter. They're too tired for banter. They're asleep within minutes.

Eva wipes Stella's hands and face and places her down close to the sleeping children. She and Nastusha pull hats over the children's heads and cover them all round up to their chins. There's already an evening chill in the air.

We tidy everything away, cover the cart, and draw lots for our two-hourly watches through the night. Roman is first, followed by Ryszard. Then I'm on from one to three, and Henryk is last till five.

We remain fully clothed and in addition pull on our hats too, before arranging ourselves around the children as comfortably as it's possible on the bumpy ground. I feel as if I've got a hundred bones and a hundred muscles in my body all aching at the same time.

'Still alive?' I ask Nastusha, her back curved against my chest.

'I'll tell you in the morning,' she heaves a big sigh.

It feels as if I've only just fallen asleep, or have slept for a week, when someone shakes my shoulder. For a second I've no idea where I am.

'Julian,' Ryszard whispers, 'it's one o'clock. Your turn.'

I sit up. I feel stiff and achey. The chill makes me shiver. Total blackness surrounds us. I'm glad of the glow from the fire.

'Everything all right?' I ask, scrambling up.

'Just some distant sounds. The fire must be kept going.'

'Of course!'

We swap places. He curls up on the ground underneath his blanket, close to the sleeping group huddling together. I draw my wrap tight around me and sit close to the fire. Two hours ahead seems like an eternity, but I distract myself with thoughts of the first light, of the next leg of our journey. Once we're in Piniug, once we're on the train... I daren't hope for too much too soon. But it's happening, it's really happening, I tell myself. The present discomfort is nothing against the reward of freedom.

The darkness around me is eerily quiet, so different from our forest at home that hums and murmurs and snaps with sounds of night animals. Time hangs heavy. I stare into the fire and conjure up scenes from home in the dancing flames.

Just before three the first hint of light appears in the space above the growth covering the forest floor. As the dawn spreads skywards, trees come into focus, the blackness around them paling into misty greys. By the time I shake Henryk awake, it's almost light, and I feel a flutter in my chest at the thought of the new day that will take us closer to freedom.

'It'll be morning soon,' I tell him, 'and we'll be on our way again. I wish I could hurry time.'

He sits up and stretches and shivers like a wild cat, then wraps his blanket around him and joins me by the fire.

'Go!' he says, 'go and lie down. You need more sleep. We've got another long day ahead of us.'

It is at that moment that our foresters' attention is alerted by a sound, very faint at first but recognisable by our trained ears. It gains volume as it heads in our direction.

'Bloody wild boar!' Henryk jumps to his feet.

'A herd,' I can tell, as I throw off my blanket in readiness for action. 'We must divert them!'

We sprint away from the fire and position ourselves on the outward side of the shelter. We stare hard into the distant growth between the trees. There's no doubt the sound of their hooves is getting closer. The trick is to frighten away the animals just at the right moment: they've got to be near enough for

Henryk's roar to make full impact, but yet not too close, so they can turn back before stampeding our little camp.

Henryk forms his hands into a trumpet around his mouth and I pull out a pot and a lid from a bag in the cart. We wait. I feel my heart pounding. Then in a split second the leader of the herd shoots out of the growth about twenty metres from us and at the same time Henryk emits a roar. An almighty elk roar. The boar, a formidable beast with strong pointed tusks, stops suddenly as if he's hit a solid wall, his hooves digging into the ground. Panicked, he turns and bumps into the oncoming herd. Henryk roars again and again. I create an additional din banging the pot and the lid together. There's a heaving jumble of animal bodies crashing into one another, falling over, jumping up in terror and disappearing back into the growth.

We stand still and listen. The sound of their hooves becomes distant then it dies down altogether.

Of course, everyone is awake by now and up on their feet. Pavel and Agata hop around us with excitement. Little Stella wants the pot and lid, and when I place it at her feet, she squeals with happiness as if I've given her an expensive toy. After we explain the cause of this commotion and everyone's been through a few 'what ifs', Nastusha suggests,

'It's light enough to start making breakfast. Not much point going to bed now. We may just as well get on with our journey.'

Everyone seems as eager as she is. We feed the fire to last us through breakfast, then we dismantle the shelter. The morning chill is fresh and penetrating, but the boiled oats and mint tea seem exquisite as we sit in the warm aura of the fire and warm our hands on the aluminium mugs. Talk is of wild boar at home, of the numerous occasions when a herd would run through the village at night and rummage through the stores of garden produce, leaving behind a trail of destruction.

Suddenly we're aware of yet another sound. Talk stops and we all listen. Our glances dart about each other's faces and our cheeks lift up in smiles. It's the whistling sound of a locomotive and the rhythmic thudding sound of the wagon wheels.

'We've made it!' Henryk shouts, 'it's no more than a kilometre away!'

We reach the railway line and turn southwards towards Piniug station. The weather is kind to us. The chill of the morning has gone underground giving way to the mild warmth of the September sun. The air is free of midges, fresh in our lungs, reminding me of the pine-infused air of our forests at home.

There's a continuous narrow strip of flattened land on both sides of the railway line, making our march easier than yesterday's trek over the rough ground through the forest. Nevertheless, Pavel and Agata tire more easily, their thin, malnourished bodies still affected by yesterday's exertion. We make frequent stops for them and as we rest on the ground we dream aloud of a month-long holiday, of being lazy like sloths, of being fed non-stop all our favourite food.

'*Pierogi* with cheese!' Pavel's face lights up as he chews a blade of grass.

'*Nalesniki* for me!' Agata clasps her hands in anticipation, 'pancakes with plums!'

'We'll have a feast. The best feast ever! As soon as we leave Russia!' Nastusha speaks with convincing certainty.

The very thought of food has the same effect on us all. Our stomachs rumble and I experience such a strong attack of hunger I'm prepared to give up all my possessions for just one square meal. Just once. To fill my stomach to satisfaction. As it used to be at home. Every meal. Every day.

Eva gets up first.

'We'll have something to eat at our next stop,' she says. 'Let's walk this time as far as we can get.'

CHAPTER 19

It is close to mid-day when we catch sight of the first buildings of Piniug. I guess it's similar to Yugovo, with wooden houses and pavements made of wooden decking, raised above the street level that becomes a mire after the winter months, with no drainage to suck up the thawing snow.

We stop, as we've promised the children, have a slice of black bread softened in the raspberry-flavoured water and a boiled egg each. This is a luxury provided for by Roman, thanks to his uncle's legacy of architect's drawing pens and pencils, compasses and rulers, sought-after curios in this part of the world, like valuable antiques at home.

'Last stop for wee-wees,' Nastusha reminds the children, when everything is tidied away and packed. We all take advantage of the space around us and the screening trees. After that it's only a short walk to Piniug. We walk along the railway line, passing the few wooden houses set back on the other side of the parallel-running mud-track, riddled with potholes. Close to the station, a crumbling brick building, we are stopped from further progress by a high wire fence, topped with barbed wire. The sight through the fence is alarming. Hundreds of people are standing on the platform, in every available centimetre of space, some balancing precariously on the edge of the platform.

'God Almighty! Bloody hell!' Henryk exclaims. 'What chance have we got?'

'Don't worry,' Roman speaks calmly, 'all it takes is just one train to take this crowd away.' I want to believe him.

We have no choice but to scramble up the embankment, Henryk and I pulling hard on the cart, onto the gravelly road that runs past the front of the station. Here the place is crowded so tightly there's no chance of getting through the main entrance.

'What shall we do?' Nastusha bites the dry skin on her thumb, her eyes darkening with anxiety.

'Just be very patient,' I tell her, my own fear niggling me. Dear God, we could be stuck here for days!

We move to the edge of the crowd as grey and shabby as we are. There's no indication of any order; there's no obvious formation of a queue or an end to it. Stressed faces turn our way and give us hostile looks. A small child wails in his mother's arms, wriggling out of its covers. She looks flustered with the effort of holding him still. An old man's cough sounds as if it's his last. Two big men with bulging bags thrown over their shoulders annoy the people squashed tight behind them. There's anger and swearing, there's much muttering rumbling through the crowd.

'Mama,' a small girl's request is to be taken to the toilet. Her mother looks frustrated. 'You can't! We'll lose our place!'

The child cries. Nastusha gives me a quick glance, then turns to the woman.

'Take your daughter. I'll hold your place.'

The woman yanks her child by the hand, exasperation twisting her face. They rush across the road, to the semi-circular lay-by used as a turning point for horses and carts. It is then I realise where the stench-polluted air is coming from. People are using that small piece of land at the intersection of roads, for their natural needs. Men relieve themselves, their backs to the crowd, and women hide behind the outstretched skirts of their companions. The ground is covered in wet patches and excrement. There's nowhere else for them to go.

'It's shocking!' Eva hugs Stella closer and turns away.

'What else can they bloody do?' Henryk asks. 'You can only hold it for so long. No one wants to lose their place. You may yet have to climb down from your high horse, your highness!'

'God forbid!' Eva shudders.

The angry woman comes back with her little daughter, whose tears are still wet on her cheeks. Nastusha steps back for her to slot into her waiting spot.

A uniformed man appears before our group, one of the station staff.

'If you want tickets,' he announces gruffly, 'I want to see your travel permits first.' Though he's smaller than Henryk and me, he gives the impression of looking down on us, by raising his head and eyeing us from underneath the brim of his cap.

Even before we unbutton our breast pockets, Roman performs a sleight of hand that any magician would be proud of. I see a quick movement, a touch of hands, the official pocketing a small package. We show him our amnesty documents and our travel permits.

'We've not been given any money for any tickets,' Henryk tells him, then he bluffs, 'all we've been told is that our amnesty documents entitle us to travel to the destination point named on the form.'

The official looks uncertain. He reads the document, again and again. Then to our suppressed relief he issues our tickets.

'How long before the next train?' Henryk asks him. He shrugs.

'Sometimes we get one, sometimes two trains in a day.'

My heart drops. I sense Nastusha's and Eva's spirits wilt. But Henryk perseveres,

'The next train, is it going north or south?'

'There's no timetable,' the man says, 'you'll know when you see which direction it came from.' One cannot ague with logic.

'One more thing,' Henryk adds, 'we can't take this cart with us.'
The man's eyes narrow with interest. He says,
'When you get close to the entrance, I'll come back'.

For the next three hours there's no movement forward through the main entrance. The crowd keeps on growing at the back of us. We take turns to rest our legs perching on the sides of the cart. The children are getting weary and impatient. Stella is restless, it's hard to keep any banter going with people pushing around us, the air getting hot and heavy with odours of sweat and bad breath.

Close to four o'clock a burst of excitement ripples through the crowd. We can hear it too, the distant sound of a train whistle. Even before the locomotive reaches the station in billowing steam, people begin to push forward. There are shouts of anger and panic from the ones crammed in the entrance. They can't move any further until the platform's been vacated, they yell. Our group sticks solidly around the cart. There's a sudden surge around us, as if a bottleneck's been unblocked. Everyone's pressing forward.

'We better go too!' Henryk shouts, grabbing the cart and pulling it alongside the crowd, the rest of us running after him.

The entrance gets blocked again. There are sounds of a fight going on, screaming and objects flying in the air. Two officials elbow their way through, grab the two offenders by the scruff of their necks and push them through the crowd that is reluctant to give way. They move them to the side of the building, out of sight.

'Poor idiots!' Nastusha reflects. 'They'll have to start their waiting all over again.'

This little incident upsets me too. 'It's hard to keep a cool head when everything and everyone conspires against you.' I share my thoughts with her. It's of little consolation that we've moved on and have found a spot right by the wall of the building and are now only a few metres away from the entrance. But it's progress nevertheless. Stella is inside the cart amidst all our bags, Pavel and Agata perch on the sides and we stand around. I feel overcome with dejection.

'Bloody hell, Kalinski! I know that look,' Henryk slaps me on the shoulder, 'stop fretting! We've come so far. We'll make it further'. He's right. I mustn't give in to moods.

'I hate this place!' I mutter. 'Look what they do to their own people!'

It is about another hour before we hear the train leave the station. Pavel and Agata get up and run along the building to the end, then along the railings to watch the locomotive hissing in clouds of steam.

'It was a passenger train,' he informs us when they get back, breathless

119

from running. 'I wish we were on it!' he kicks the ground. 'Those people are so lucky! And we're still stuck here!'

'We'd be squashed like sardines!' Agata tries to reason, 'they were all standing, Pavel. They were pushed flat against all windows and doors!'

'I'd still rather be there than here!' he argues.

I stroke his shaved head. 'Our turn will come, Pavel.'

'I'm sick of waiting!' He kicks the ground again.

We wait. It's like waiting for storks in the middle of winter. We kill time with small talk, my ears straining all the time for the sound of the train.

The official who has issued our tickets appears and walks towards us. He stops and says,

'I'll take your cart now. Just follow me.'

He leads us along the line of the building at the end of which there's a metal gate in the railings. He unlocks it and orders us through.

'Find a place at the end of the platform. The carriage that stops there is less likely to be overcrowded.' We pick up all our belongings and the water containers and leave him the wooden cart. He pulls it away, relocks the gate, and disappears.

'Bloody hell! What do you think of that!' The old Henryk smile hovers on his lips.

'Bzovski, sorry to disappoint you,' I feign great sorrow, 'but it's not our cart that clinched it.' I look at Roman. 'Now tell us, honestly, what did you give him?'

Roman raises his hand in a pose of innocence.

'Who me?'

'I saw you.'

He capitulates.

'All right. My aunt's silver ring.'

'What!' Nastusha and Eva exclaim together. He shrugs.

'It's hard to guess what it's bought us yet. But we'll soon find out.'

Soon? Nothing happens soon in this place. The platform is packed as before. We climb up the wooden steps on the side, and one by one, we work our way round the edge, sit down and wedge our bags between us. Pavel and Agata sit together, dangling their legs. They have regained their spirits as their excitement grows in anticipation of our imminent journey. Little Stella frets. When Henryk and Eva have run out of ideas to amuse her, Nastusha and I have a go. I sit her on my lap and we play baby games of peek-a-boo and palm tickling and finger counting. I feel a twit doing such silly things, and yet, every time Stella giggles I feel a warmth spread inside me. It gives me an unexpected pleasure to watch Nastusha's smile and I think of our past happy times at home and imagine happier times in the future. Once we're on that train... our first step to freedom.

We wait. Intermittently people rub along past us down the wooden steps to walk along the railings far enough for just a semblance of dignity. There's no shelter to give them privacy as they relieve themselves. The sparse tufts of grass sticking up from the shingle between the railing and the railway line cannot hide the old and the new spreading mess of excrement.

Roman gets up.

'This is terrible. I've got to see what's inside the building,' he says.

'I'll come with you,' Ryszard gets up too.

'No!' Agata grabs his hand, 'What if the train arrives and you're not here?'

'Don't worry, *moja mała,* my little one, we'll hear it coming. We'll be back in a minute.' He gives her a hug.

I share her concern. The crowd is solid. Impenetrable. Roman and Ryszard slink their way sideways along the wall and sink into the throng.

It's only ten minutes before they reappear, but it feels much longer and all the while Agata's worried glance darts upwards, her chat with Pavel drying up. Her face relaxes when she catches sight of her father.

'There *are* two toilets there,' Roman tells us, 'both broken and both full of crap!'

'But,' Ryszard adds, 'there's a tap with running water. Clean. We should fill our cans.'

We join them this time, Henryk and I with our canisters, to burrow our way through the mass of bodies. The inside of the station building is jam packed. Anyone with a hint of claustrophobia would be driven insane. Some probably are, judging by the simmering anger and uncontrolled expletives. We follow Richard to the tap in the wall outside the toilets. The doors have been left ajar. The stench is eye-stinging. The toilet bowls are heaped with excrement, layers of which cover the floor. I can't imagine anyone's desperation to exceed revulsion at even entering such a place.

We fill the cans as people push at us from all sides, we work our way back like moles to our place, we sit down on the edge of the platform, we wait.

At around eight in the evening we hear the sound we've been waiting for all day. There's a wave of movement through the crowd and panicky shouts from people at the front who fear being pushed off the platform into the path of the coming train. To my relief the crowd lists back as the train thunders through, seemingly unable to stop. It does slow down and comes to a halt. There may be about thirty carriages or more, a third at the front and a third at the back stretching out beyond the station on both sides. It is a goods train. Like the one that was our home for eight weeks on our way to Kotlas.

This time the doors are not padlocked. They are slid back on their metal runners by the impatient crowd, which like a river floods all the spaces inside the carriages. Our group is up and waiting, and like everyone else we scramble to the carriage in front of us. Henryk and I jump onto the wagon floor first and haul up everyone else together with all our possessions. Nastusha and Eva rush to the corner that's not yet occupied and secure the two bunks for us. The wagon fills up with feverish speed. There are far too many people. I have visions of us all suffocating when the doors are closed.

However, after the first wave of panic, the ones crowding the middle of the carriage realise that there may be more space in the wagons at the front and at the back of the train. When they leave and the air and light are allowed in, I estimate there may be fifty people occupying the eight bunks. There's a metal stove in the middle, a latrine in the corner. Familiar. We've managed before. We'll manage again. This time it's our journey to freedom.

Two hours later, our train is still stationary. The station has been emptied, the silence is eerie. Muted sounds reach us from wagons along the line. The girls organised a supper earlier, of dried bread dipped in watered down juice and a carrot each. My stomach never lets me forget how empty it is. Hunger never leaves me, it kills all other desires. I dream of being again that young virile man I was at home, when just a certain smile from my wife, her soft hand's touch would set me on fire, hold me erect all night, when I could pleasure us both again and again.

Pavel and Agata have worn themselves out with waiting for the moment of our departure. They are asleep with Stella on the upper bunk. Henryk and Eva are with them, the rest of us are here on the bunk underneath. Fully clothed we lie down next to each other on the hard boards, our bodies aching after the long and gruelling day.

There's a sudden jerk, metal clunking, wheels squeaking, I feel the pull of the train. Nastusha, next to me, exhales a long sigh.

'Julian, at long last! To freedom!' She takes my hand and places it against her cheek. Her touch and warm breath make my hairs stand on end.

Roman next to her, crosses his hands over his chest.

'*Chwała Bogu*! God be praised!' he says.

'Amen.' Ryszard concludes. He's got the tightest space against the wall.

I close my eyes and give in to the rocking of the carriage.

CHAPTER 20

Three weeks and two days, and over two thousand kilometres later, on the 29th of September we arrive in Orenburg, a vast place of concrete buildings and draughty passages with snow flurries drifting in. Winter has caught up with us, after all.

Our goods train has stopped at all the major stations on the way, Kirov, Perm, Sverdlovsk, Chelyabinsk and Orsk. It has stopped in smaller places and we have been abandoned to wait two or three days or sometimes longer in the sidings, with no explanation or indication when our journey was going to continue. Some people have been left behind when, without any warning, the train would move on. Some of them were Poles, eager like us to get away from their labour camps, and like us, bedraggled, grey, emaciated. We picked up increasing numbers of our compatriots on our journey south. Nastusha cried with the ones separated from their loved ones. Delaying their escape to freedom, perhaps indefinitely, they would leave the train at the next stop with the hope that their relatives would catch up with them. The saddest cases were the children, like Pavel, separated from their mothers. We kept them back on the train with promises that everyone would catch up eventually in Buzuluk, where we were all going.

Our journey, as we had expected, had all the repeat discomforts of our previous journey, only this time, although endured no less painfully, was withstood with the stubborn and uplifting hope of freedom within our reach. Stops for hot water, meagre food rations from our stores, the odd chance of a glass of milk, an egg, hot *kasha* or watery soup bartered for at the stops, kept us going, at times only barely, when stomach disorders left us prostrate on the hard boards, when the overused latrine in the corner polluted the air with stench.

Some elderly people and young children died on the way, as before. They were taken away on carts at each stop, after the NKVD had searched all wagons for dead bodies. Nastusha cried most days. The irony of their fate was unbearable; so close to freedom, only to be thrown into a mass grave, at some unidentified spot.

By some miracle, understood in a contorted way only by Roman, who takes his role seriously as the would-be priest and therefore the spiritual guardian of our group, we escaped the cruellest of fates, but we all had our share of fevers, stomach cramps, sickly headaches, dizziness and diarrhoea. Our only medications were herbal teas and hot water.

Pavel lay doubled up in pain, soiling his clothes till we had nothing left but rags to wrap round his abdomen and legs. He became weak and shaky and though we did not admit our concerns to ourselves, I saw the fear in Nastusha's face. I held him up so she could feed him some solid food for regaining his strength. Some *kasha* or some bread softened in water. I had to stop myself from blubbering with relief, the first time he sat up by himself. The soiled clothes had to be kept till the next stop, where people rushed out to the taps, to wash off the dirt. The smell remained and rose with the vapour as the wet garments dried in our confined space, stop after stop after stop.

The lice, our unconquerable enemy, are with us permanently. Pavel, Agata and Stella are checked daily for signs of lice eggs on their eyebrows and eyelashes. A mother with four children joined our wagon somewhere near Sverdlovsk on the vacated bunk across the passage from us. Her two boys and two girls (between four and ten in age) were so infested, she had to scrape the lice off their eyes and eyebrows. A painful task, leaving the skin raw and the children in tears. Nastusha and Eva dabbed the affected spots with camomile solution, giving them temporary relief in place of unavailable medication.

We are in Orenburg. Our goods train has disembarked its human cargo, before its return journey north. Russian soldiers, our allies, are managing the crowd, hundreds of groups like ours, with yelling and swearing and pushing us along passages to another platform. From here, we're told, trains leave to Buzuluk. What time? I ask an official looking man. He shakes his head. It depends. It all depends on the time the train leaves the previous station. It could be an hour. It could be a day. I understand. A wave of weariness sweeps over me at the thought of having to spend the night on the concrete floor.

The platform is crowded. Hundreds of Polish families.

'Near the wall!' Henryk shouts, leading us. 'It'll be less draughty by the wall!'

We follow him and squeeze ourselves into a tight spot by the wall, against the reluctance of others.

'Can't you see? We were here first!' A disgruntled man shouts at us. And who can blame him?

'As soon as I grow bloody wings,' Henryk tells him, 'I'll hover above you.'

The man looks angry. He's older than us, with sunken cheeks, sunken eyes, ill-looking, perhaps on the very last reserve of endurance.

'You're no better than them!' he shouts.

Roman gets in between him and Henryk.

'I'm Roman Zastavny. A priest,' he introduces himself. This always breaks the ice. With us, he straightens this little inaccuracy by prefixing it with 'almost'. It doesn't do any harm, he says, and it may just be of some comfort at times. The old man's expression loses that savage look.

'Tell me Father,' he says, 'tell me is there really a heaven after this purgatory. Tell me, what have we done to deserve it?' To our consternation his eyes fill up with tears. My throat feels tight.

Roman's tone is gentle.

'Have faith, my brother in Christ. Our fate is already changing.'

'Is that so? Pity then, that my family have been denied such luxury. What is my life without them?'

We are all silent. Any word sounds tawdry against his grief. Roman speaks first.

'Where are you from?'

The man looks up.

'In Poland? South of Lvov. They took us to Archangelsk. My wife died on the way. My daughter and my grandson died of malnutrition at the camp. My son-in-law was already in the army. He knows nothing of our fate. God only knows if he's still alive.'

Roman places a comforting hand on the man's elbow.

'While there's hope, we must never give up.'

The man gives him a look as if to say, what do you, young puppy know about life? But then he nods.

'There's one sister left, older than me, in our family home in Poland. I pray she's still there when I get back.'

I wish that too for him, wondering how he can possibly rebuild his future, from the pain, the loneliness, from the ruins of his life.

Our attention is distracted by a passing group. I've seen a lot in the last couple of years, but this sight is shocking. Small skeletal creatures, dressed in rags that allow glimpses of bone-thin limbs, shaved heads covered in sores, faces erupting with oozing boils, pus dripping from their ears. Their carers, emaciated women, cowering inside their shawls with weariness, guide them across the platform following a noisily commanding NKVD man.

Something breaks inside me and I want to call out to heaven for vengeance. Nastusha wipes her eyes. Pavel clings to me.

'Who are they?' he asks, his voice a frightened whisper.

'They're orphans, Pavel. They've no one else left to look after them.' He clings to me harder. 'We'll never give up looking for your dad and your sisters,' I tell him. What I don't tell him is that Nastusha and I have already decided to adopt him officially.

For lunch, we have a bite of black bread dipped in water. Afterwards we men go with our cans in search of the taps, and maybe, just the remotest chance of obtaining additional food. I have very little hope as we weave our way through the mass of people, tired, malnourished, dejected, some old women, surprising survivors of the Soviet paradise, sitting on the concrete floor, hugging their few possessions to them, their glazed eyes fixed on some invisible point.

Inside the building the canteen is like a swarming hive. No chance of pushing inside. The fishy, sickly smell hits my nostrils and I get an urge to eat a whole vat of the dish-water soup, the fish eyes, the fish tails, the whole rotten lot. My eyes sting with longing and revulsion.

We give the toilets a miss. The stench emitting from behind the half-open doors is enough for one's imagination. We proceed straight to the taps fixed to the wall beyond. And as the crowd pushes around us when we take turns to fill our cans, I witness a miracle.

A boy of about eleven slides up towards us along the wall and hugging a bundle wrapped in old yellow newspapers, leans his head between us.

'*Lepioshki* for sale. Do you want some?'

It takes a moment to register our luck.

'*Lepioshki*?' I'm first to recover, 'show me then.'

He obliges by dexterously ripping open the paper with his dirty fingers. The sight of the miniature buns makes me feel faint. This is a miracle, I swear to God, and this street urchin is a real angel in disguise.

'We'll have the whole lot,' I tell him. We manage to collect enough *roubles* between us and Roman gives him a stub of his old pencil into the bargain. The little pedlar's face remains serious as he pockets his earnings and sinks into the crowd.

'Probably stolen,' Henryk remarks. His wry smile cannot hide his glee.

My heart threatens to burst in anticipation of our girls' and children's joy when we show them our trophy. We make a tight-knit circle over this parcel of God-sent feast. There's enough to have two each, with the remainder to be kept for *czarna godzina*, an emergency. For a few minutes it's heaven in my mouth. The taste is so good, so very, very good, it makes me want to cry with happiness. The old angry man is bumped against Henryk in a sudden wave of movement through the crowd.

'Make room for me,' he grumbles, 'it's lonely out here by myself.'

We squeeze tighter against each other, let him in, and share our *lepioshki* with him.

Luck is on our side today, though it does not seem so at first. The first train to arrive is a goods train. The crowd rushes in, the sad little orphans are hoisted on board, the little old women are hurried along with their possessively guarded few belongings, but when our group reaches the edge of the platform, it is clear all space has been taken up in the tightly packed wagons. I can't help a twinge of bitter disappointment. It is late afternoon and only God knows in this godless place when the next train is likely to arrive. It is getting dark, the temperature is dropping all the while, I shudder at the thought of having to spend the night on this draughty, concrete floor.

Incredibly, two hours later, only two hours, another train arrives. It's a passenger train. Two miracles in one day!

We all get on. The train is already full, the passages and the metal link platforms between the carriages, packed with people sitting on the floor. We stagger around them and over them but it is clear our group has got to split up to find room wherever possible. Nastusha, Pavel and I fall into one of the compartments and find ourselves in a room of dead men, so it seems. The proverbial skin and bones has real meaning here. They sit on the two facing benches, reclining against the backrests, their legs stretched out in front of them, as thin as broom handles. Their shabby coats have been worn thin or right through. Some have hats with earflaps, some have *valonki* on their feet, some have neither, their feet and toes blue with cold. The two closest to the sliding door shout to their companions to move up a space. Nastusha and I sling our possessions onto the shelf above us and squeeze in beside the men. Pavel slides onto the floor between my legs. It's going to be hellishly tiring, but we're one step closer to freedom.

'A veritable miracle!' the man next to me remarks, 'I never imagined we'd come out alive.'

He tells me more. They are soldiers. Our soldiers. The freed prisoners of war. Employed until a few days ago in a quarry, digging and breaking rocks for hardcore. Roads and railways and such things. 'The winters were killers!' he tells me through his blackened lips. He has no teeth left. 'Pellagra,' he explains, 'thanks to malnutrition. Always feeling starved. It attacks the gums then your teeth fall out. And this…' he unravels the rag on his hand, showing three fingers with their tips missing. 'This was frost bite. So severe, I had to chop them off. Or the gangrene would eat me up. Some men lost all their toes.'

I nod in sympathy but I can barely endure his story of pain, on top of the old man's grief, on top of the orphans' suffering, on top of our own experiences. I look around the compartment. All of them, squashed against each other on the facing benches, look like bodies waiting to be buried. Anders' army. Good God! What chance have we got?

A bright morning welcomes us in Buzuluk. There's a surge of excitement throughout the train as it comes to a halt. Even as people spill out onto the platform and we wait our turn laden with bags and sacks, I hear voices outside, calling, directing, instructing in our native tongue. Polish soldiers.

A warm feeling fills my chest. Pavel pulls at my sleeve. His wide, toothy grin looks oversized in his thin face. Nastusha's eyes catch the light as she leans against me.

On the platform, amidst the milling crowd, we reassemble with our own group. It's been some time since I've seen joy on their faces. There's no need for words. We ignore the presence of the NKVD men. We've only got eyes for our boys.

One of them approaches us.

'This way. Follow me.' He wears the Russian winter padded uniform and high boots. Round his left arm there's a white and red band, our national flag colours, and pinned to his ear-flap padded hat, the Polish crowned eagle.

'We're here to join the army,' I make conversation as he leads us through the main passage outside.

'But of course,' he replies, his eyes following the freed prisoners of war just ahead of us, limping and coughing and pulling their rags tight around their shoulders. One man's frozen toes peep out of the frayed cotton strips that tie his feet to cardboard soles.

The square outside looks like a market place, deserted at this early hour, with roads leading into the town. The pavements are frozen over with blackened snow, the rooftops glisten white against the icy sky.

We are escorted, the entire train contingent, perhaps three hundred people, to a nearby vast hall, a warehouse of sorts. Our Polish boys partnered with the NKVD men divide us up into smaller, manageable groups. Our guide informs us,

'You'll be given some food soon, and after that we'll show you to your quarters.'

At the mention of food I become acutely aware of how hungry I am. Pavel and Agata's practised resignation breaks down and they start looking round with renewed impatience. It never fails to amaze me how undemanding little Stella is. She can chew a morsel of dried bread for hours. Henryk places her down on the blankets spread over our belongings, that Nastusha and Eva have pushed together to make a perching round seat for us all.

Before long, a truck drives in through the wide open door. Our guides rush towards it, unchain the tail gate and pull down sacks that bulge with their contents.

What happens next is like a fantasy. I stare intently and cannot believe my eyes. Our guide unties the sack and hands out, to each single one of us, even to little two-year-old Stella, a whole loaf of bread. White bread. Real.

'There's also tea for you,' the guide tells us. 'Bring your containers and I'll fill them up for you.'

While we men queue up for the tea, poured with aluminium mugs from large metal pots, Nastusha and Eva are busy dividing the bread and saving some for later.

Then we all sit down on top of our bundles to enjoy our breakfast of white bread and tea.

The tea is hot and sweet. Warming our hands, uplifting our spirits. I chew the bread slowly, stopping myself from devouring my portion all in one go. There's a hush around us, like the reverent silence in church. The men are pensive, the women watchful of their children, willing them to eat every last crumb. The steam from the mugs thaws their faces and releases tears from their eyes.

The prisoners of war group are addressed by one of their guides.

'Gentlemen, we'll take you to our military hospital first. We'll do everything in our power to get you back your strength. We need every single able-bodied man to join our ranks. Anders' army.'

The group is led outside to the waiting lorries.

Our guide addresses our group of about fifty people.

'All men willing to enrol will come with me to the camp. Unfortunately there's not enough room to accommodate civilians. At present, our emergency plan is to place families in lodgings with the people of this town. My companion here,' he indicates with a nod the NKVD man, 'will take you round to the people already notified of this necessity.' Notified? I pity the poor wretches. What say have they got in the matter?

I don't like the sound of this. The idea of separation from Nastusha and Pavel becomes a reality that fills me with unease. I had imagined we'd be together until we leave this accursed land, when I'd no longer have to be tormented with fears for their safety, on my way to the front.

Nastusha looks anxious, Pavel clings to me. Agata cries and grabs her father's hand. 'I don't want you to leave me!' Henryk hugs both his wife and his child to him.

The Polish soldier, a man of our age, perhaps a family man himself looks serious, but there's a hint of understanding in his tone,

'Gentlemen, you don't have to come with me right away. There will be a long enrolment queue waiting all morning. You've got plenty of time. You can go with your families, see them to their lodgings, then come back. Anyone will tell you the way to the camp.'

His suggestion makes sense. Still Nastusha needs reassurance.

'Will the families be far from the camp?'

'Within walking distance,' he tells her. 'The houses on the outskirts, closest to camp have been requisitioned already. We've got trainloads of people arriving every day. It's already becoming a problem. We haven't the resources to keep up with the demands. Our boys are already digging trenches for *lepianki* around the camp'.

I remember living in one when we were sent away from Svoboda for two months to build an extension road near Ustyug. It was a dwelling made in a dug-out hole and covered over with a wooden roof or tarpaulin. Cool in the summer, but unimaginably cold in sub-zero temperatures. I shudder at the thought of the unfortunates who will be assigned to such a dwelling.

'Listen my friends,' Roman says, 'I'll go ahead and save you a place in the queue.'

Suddenly, the whole idea does not appear so bad. He leaves with all the single men, the willing conscripts, and the rest of us, the families, the young and the few old people, tag on at the end.

We pass some formidable solid buildings. One of them has our Polish white and red flag hung high over the entrance.

'Polish Army Headquarters!' Our guide points it out with pride. It is a building of imposing beauty with its tall elegant windows and a semi-circular deep entrance, the roof above it held up with white columns. A fortunately saved relic from the pre-revolutionary architecture.

Away from the centre the houses become smaller, squat, increasing numbers built of timber.

Beyond them, the open space leads the eye over white fields. In the distance, against the blur of a forest, I detect rows of long wooden huts.

'The military camp,' our guide informs us.

The group of men, perhaps a hundred, carry on marching along the peripheral road, while the civilian group is directed and escorted by the NKVD men towards a small estate of dwellings, that look as if they had been thrown out of a toy box and got stuck in the snow without any plan. Bare fruit trees, ramshackle sheds, covered wells, sections of broken fences create a feeling of dereliction, compounded by the blackened footpaths sprinkled with ashes.

'*Poytee z minya*! Come with me!' Our NKVD guide orders.

The crowd gets fragmented as people are led away in all directions. Our man, ridiculously young, with a severe expression in his narrowed eyes, counts our little group.

'*Vosim ludi?*'

'*Niet*! Not eight,' Henryk corrects him, 'only two women and three children.'

He leads us to the nearest hut and bangs on the door with his gun. I find his act repulsive.

The door opens almost immediately to reveal an old woman totally wrapped in a thick woollen shawl, only her lined face showing, her arthritic hands gripping the folds together on her chest.

I guess she is shocked by the number of people and our appearance. She shakes her head. I recognise dejection and helplessness in her expression, against a lifetime of intimidation.

'I did not expect so many,' she tells our escort. He could be her great-grandson.

'Orders are orders!' he states curtly.

'We're not all stopping,' I reassure her, 'only the women and the children.'

She steps back to let us in. We crowd the one and only room of her timber hut. The Red one pushes in too and watches from the side. The room is sparsely furnished, a small table in the middle, a dresser, a bed, a tall and narrow wardrobe. The tiled stove creates a niche at the side, where a bare mattress has been placed directly on the wooden floor.

'That corner is for you,' she says. We drop our belongings on the mattress. Henryk kisses Stella and hands her over to Eva.

'It's not the Royal Hotel my sweetheart, but you'll be warm here.' He embraces them both.

Nastusha and Pavel hug me too.

'I'll be back later,' I promise.

Agata cries again and doesn't want Ryszard to go.

'You've got to be brave,' he tells her. 'In times of war, men go to fight and women have got to be brave.'

'I don't want to be brave.' Her face crumples and copious tears run down her cheeks. 'I just want to be with you.'

'And you will be, my little Agatka. I'll come later, I promise.'

Last hugs under the watchful eyes of our escort. I want to give the old woman something, but not with him watching. I dig in my pocket and feel for a paper note. As we leave the room, I take her hand in mine, shake it with a polite, *Do Widzenia* and transfer the note into her palm. For a split second her eyes widen, then she hides her hand inside the pocket of her thickly gathered skirt.

'We won't forget your kindness,' I assure her. She bows her head and looks away.

The military camp vacated by the Russian army, now fighting at the front, lies outside Buzuluk, close to the edge of a forest. We're marching along the rough frozen road, perhaps forty men, with the few, but ever present, NKVD minders. Our allies.

But our spirits are good. There's a surge of optimism in the low-key banter, in the reawakened energy of our thin emaciated bodies.

'Julian,' Henryk nudges me, 'I feel bloody pleased inside my head today. Perhaps I'm losing my mind?'

'I'm feeling like that too,' I say, 'perhaps they've put something in that tea. I can't wait for some action to get started. I wonder how long it'll take to get us ready?'

'The sooner the better,' Ryszard mutters flicking a sideways glance at our escort. 'We'll show them yet what stuff we're made of!'

Bravado words. I like them.

The future is a blur in my mind. I push away intrusive images of bombings and destruction. And death. Instead, I make myself think of the smart and warm uniform, of regular meals, of decent accommodation, of the pay that will make me the bread winner once again.

We march through the wide open gate, past the guard at his sentry post, towards a line of large brick buildings, some single, some two storeys high, that face an open square, the assembly and drill area, I guess. In the centre there is a sturdy ten metre mast with a white and red flag hanging in still folds. As before, an uplifting feeling of pride fills my chest.

On the other side of the square, rows of long wooden huts look almost picturesque amidst a pattern of sparkling snow and blue shadows. The woodland beyond them offers a protective screen against the north winds, unlike the claustrophobic taiga that hemmed in our labour camp with thick overgrowth and malevolent shadows.

There's much activity going on around the perimeter of the camp where men are digging trenches. I guess that's in preparation for the afore-mentioned *lepianki*.

We are ordered to stop at one of the large buildings where a group of men like us, are just leaving through the swing doors, following their commanding officer's instructions to find the warehouse. The officer then beckons to us to follow him indoors. The NKVD come in behind us.

The hall is buzzing with voices of at least a hundred men waiting in three queues to reach the desk at the far end. What can be glimpsed through the gaps in the crowd are the officers sitting at some trestle tables pushed together, with wire trays of papers before them. Dotted around the hall are the ubiquitous, undetachable NKVD men.

We spot Roman. He waves and comes to join us. The queues move up at a snail's pace, but nobody minds. Complete strangers exchange life stories and give accounts of recent horrors: imprisonment in cattle trucks, relentless hard labour, the famine, the diseases, the countless numbers of graves. There's not one person in the crowd who has been spared the far-reaching consequences of Stalin's evil plan.

'I shall curse him to my dying day,' one man says with so much hatred that his words send a shiver down my spine. 'He's destroyed my life. He's taken everything from me. My home. My wife. My three sons. May he rot in hell for all eternity! And now, we're supposed to be allies. Allies? I spit at the whole lot of them!'

A Polish officer comes up close to us.

'Not so loud my friend. We're not out of the woods yet. Walls have ears, as you can see for yourself.' He walks away, we lower our voices and continue to air our views.

The form filling is straightforward: personal details, family details, home address in Poland, present whereabouts of my wife, the name of our labour camp.

'Svoboda, near Piniug in the Archangelsk Oblastia.'

'Svoboda?' the officer looks up. 'This is no time for jokes.'

'It's the honest truth,' I tell him. I also explain about Pavel.

'There's an orphanage already set up and running in town,' he informs me. 'The child would get adequate clothing and food.' I think of the poor orphans we saw at Orenburg station, the walking skeletons with sores on their faces and oozing boils.

'My wife will continue taking care of him,' I confirm. 'We promised his father. I believe he and his daughters will catch up with us someday soon. Now that we're all free citizens.'

He glances up and with a curt 'Indeed' acknowledges my sarcasm, then adds, 'I wish you luck.' The unexpected part-advance payment issued with my papers is a treasure in my pocket. Nastusha and Pavel will no longer go hungry. 'Just one more thing,' he says, 'the medical. When you've scrubbed and changed you must visit the hospital. Here in the camp. There's a section designated specially for medical examinations.'

Our group sticks together. We've been allotted to barrack number 25. First, on the way, we visit another huge brick building which is a store for uniforms and equipment. A wall to wall barrier separates the waiting area from the rest, which is filled with rows of wooden racks and shelves packed with carton boxes and wooden chests.

One of the duty privates comes out to us with neatly folded bundles, our uniforms.

'You're lucky,' he says, 'the supplies are dwindling rapidly. We've been promised much more, but deliveries are being constantly delayed. My advice? Hang on to your good bits of clothing. You'll need them for the dirty jobs.'

'The whole of this bloody war is just one big dirty job,' Ryszard remarks bitterly.

'Come now,' the man tries to humour him, 'aren't you just a tad pleased to be the proud owner of this glorious *ruski* uniform?'

We all smirk quietly. There's always one of them outside the door.

We lose him, or he loses interest, when we cross the square on the way to our quarters. I'm happy. I clutch my bundle to my chest, the padded jacket and trousers, the new hat with ear flaps, the thick socks and the high boots. It's all new and warm. What luxury! It's Russian only for a while longer. A white and red arm band, and a badge of the Polish Eagle will soon bestow upon it a new identity.

Inside number 25 a warmth envelops our cold hands and faces, though not without its stale odours of sweat, smoke and rancid clothing. Our long barrack has two metal stoves, one in the middle of each half. There are twenty four-tier bunk beds. I calculate automatically. One hundred and sixty men, when the barrack is occupied to full capacity.

Heads lift, questions and greetings come our way and we exchange banter while looking round for the nearest column of empty bunks. All the ones closest to the stoves are already taken. We gather round ours and inspect the tiers; a mattress on each, a blanket and a pillow. Luxury again! We send Roman, the slightest in build among us, to the top. Ryszard is next, then myself, then Henryk on the floor level. As instructed, we leave our possessions 'at home', a metre by two of personal space, and take with us the washing kits and the newly issued uniforms.

The communal baths is another large brick building on our side of the square. In the ante-room we're instructed by the private on duty to leave our uniforms in the pigeon-holes built into the walls and to dispose of all unwanted clothing into a sack. There's another voluminous sack for clothes needing to be deloused.

Before I undress, I stand at one of the hand-basins, lined like soldiers against the far wall. I cannot believe such luxury again; white enamel (cracks and stains don't matter), hot running water and a small, browned-around-the-edges shaving mirror above each one.

'Civilisation at long last!' Henryk remarks tersely.

'It's their elite, after all,' Roman examines his pinched face in the mirror.

'Elite?' Ryszard smirks, 'that sounds dangerously like bourgeois.'

'My dear equal comrades,' I laugh, 'just forget everything for one moment, and enjoy what we've got!'

Inside my washing kit there's a towel, carbolic soap, a brush for lathering my face, a cut-throat razor, a solid tablet of tooth paste, and a toothbrush. I'm engulfed for a moment with a vivid memory of my previous life.

Later, I run my fingers with pleasure over my clean shaven face. In the mirror I see my protruding cheekbones, shadows around my eyes and a streak of grey in the lock falling across my forehead. I am thirty years old and eight months. I want to be young again. And I will be, I tell myself.

I feel it, I feel there's a good change on the way. Things are improving.

The shower room is spacious enough to contain at least a hundred men without overcrowding. Above us, a network of pipes is fitted with shower heads at the intersections. With streams of water hitting the tiled floor and the men's voices rising above the hissing sound, the room resounds like a school playtime confined to a classroom on a rainy day. The milky steam acts like a veil over our naked bodies, softening the contours of thin bony limbs, protruding ribcages, flat buttocks and sharply shaped shoulder blades. It is stunningly exhilarating, to stand underneath a strong jet of warm water, to feel its cleansing power. I lather my hair with carbolic soap, rub and rinse, rub and rinse, until I've rubbed off all traces of lice and their eggs. Now I can go for my medical with some dignity retained.

The day flies in a whirlwind of meetings, instructions and walks around the camp to acquaint ourselves with its geography and services. There's the administration block, an assembly hall, a kitchen and a canteen, a dispensary, a small hospital, and a small general store. The Red Cross office is run by the newly established Women's Corps, the PSK, who have also set up an orphanage in town and have organised additional help in running the surgeries, the kitchens, the laundries and sewing the much needed clothing to withstand the winter months. With daily arrivals of ever increasing numbers, the task is monumental. Everyone we meet talks about the dreamed-of journey south, to the warmer climate, as far away as possible from Siberia, and out of this accursed land, to freedom. But things cannot be arranged overnight, I remind myself, yet the first day in the army has the feel of a good omen.

In the evening Roman stays with our colleagues in the barrack, while Henryk, Ryszard and I go out to request passes to visit our families.

The issuing officer comments,

'Don't expect to get passes so easily in future. This is an army. Not a holiday camp.'

'Yes Sir! Thank you Sir!' We salute him and march out, our new boots rhythmically crunching the frozen snow.

Nastusha, Eva and the children greet us with open arms, as if we've been away for a whole year and not just a few hours. I notice they all look scrubbed and their clothes changed. As before, our presence fills the small hut. The old woman and her husband, absent earlier, as crinkled and as ancient-looking as her, are sitting on their bed, seemingly pushed out of their own space. I can't blame them for their sour expressions.

We gather round the small table and from within our padded jackets we produce the food that we have saved from our lunch and from the evening meal. It's a veritable feast: bread, boiled eggs, three tins of sardines, some potatoes and cooked beetroot. It gives me indescribable pleasure to watch our children's faces. I beckon to the old couple,

'Please come. Eat with us.'

They look at each other then at me. Their hostile expressions waver. They look uncertain.

'There's enough for everyone,' Henryk assures them.

'No need to press them if they don't want to,' Ryszard is simply practical.

But then something strange happens. The old woman smiles, all creases rearranging around her thin lips. There is a glimpse of rickety teeth and gaps, and her eyes shine like black beads.

'*Spaseeba*. Thank you.' She wriggles off the bed. 'I'll brew some good *chai.*'

Her small and wiry husband stands up too and extends his rough hand.

'Kalinski,' I introduce myself and my friends.

'Stepanovich.' His bushy eyebrows make him look severe, but he allows himself to be persuaded to join us at the table. 'We've been told you're released criminals,' he says, 'and that your poor families had nowhere else to go, but to tag along with you.'

The lie he's been told is too ridiculous to elicit a smile.

'Released, thank God. Yes,' Henryk tells him, 'but not criminals. We're just family people like you and your wife.'

When we get down to the serious business of tasting food and sipping the old woman's hot tea, we tell them of our life in Poland, of our families, of how this war destroyed our lives, but not yet our future, we hope. They listen and comment with surprise how alike we are, and tell us of their family. Their children, two sons and two daughters, in their fifties now, have been sent to work on collective farms, when young, hundreds of miles away from home. They see them, perhaps, once a year. Three of their grandsons are in the army. At the front. Somewhere in the north now.

'That's why we're here,' I explain, 'to prepare for fighting our common enemy.'

135

Ryszard sends me a wry look over Agata's head. Did I really say that? *Our* common enemy?

And yet, when the old woman brings out the photographs of her children and their families, and wipes a tearful eye, I can't help thinking how much her suffering is similar to ours.

It is time for us to go. Henryk and Eva sit down on the mattress with little Stella between them for the last few minutes together. Ryszard and Agata are invited to perch on the old couple's bed, and we remain at the table, Nastusha, Pavel and I. They both cling on to my hands.

'I rely on you, Pavel, to be the man of the house,' I tell him.

He rubs his head against my arm.

'I wish you didn't have to go, uncle Julian.'

Nastusha strokes his head. 'We've not done too badly today, have we?' she speaks brightly but I see sadness in her eyes. 'We've had food, we've had a good wash, our clothes have had a good scrub and are now drying in the shed. And, we've discovered four chickens there. Dear little chickens. We'll help look after them, won't we, Pavel?'

I give Nastusha the money.

'Some for your hosts. But make sure you have a meal every day. I'll come as often as I can. I'll do my best. We've already been told it's not a holiday camp. They've got a field kitchen there, Nastusha. In the camp. If I'm not back for a while, that's where you must go.'

I want to take her in my arms, to hold her close, to feel her body against mine, to kiss her. It's been so long since we've been husband and wife, since we've been able to enjoy each other's bodies. Persistent, relentless hunger has numbed our finer needs. Despite her thinness and pallor, Nastusha looks attractive in the halo of freshly washed hair. Her dark amber eyes still have the power to give me a jolt. I sense a stirring. A surprise. A joy. I'm not dead yet. I could make love to her right now and here.

Pavel rests his head against my chest, and throws his arm around my neck. I'm aware of everyone else around us. All I can do is caress Nastusha's hand in both mine, her thin hand with calloused palms and broken nails, and kiss it.

'*Moja kochana*. My dear Nastusha, it's been the first good day since we've left home. Things will get better from now on.'

She watches me with those dark serious eyes of hers.

'I want to believe you Julian, but what will happen now? And what next?'

'It's only for a short time, this place here. And I'll be close by. When the army moves, all our families will be taken along too.'

'And then what? What happens to us when you're sent to the front?'

The truth is nobody knows, but I improvise, to make her feel better, to make myself feel better.

'By then, Nastusha, we'll all be well out of here. Somewhere south. Where the sun shines. Where it's warm. Where you can wait in safety. Until our job is done. And then…' I pause, 'then we can all go back home.'

Pavel lifts up his head to look at me. Nastusha's gaze becomes distant then a smile lifts her cheeks.

'Oh Julian, my dear Julian, I'll pray hard that your words come true.'

'Soon?' Pavel asks.

'Who knows? Maybe even next year.' I want to believe that too.

We all three embrace hard and long, and then it's time for me to go.

VOLUME 2

ANASTAZIA

Khazakstan – Palestine
1941 – 1944

CHAPTER 21

I can't fall asleep tonight. I can't find a comfortable position to ease off the throbbing pain, like a jabbing dagger, under my arm. Third boil in the last six months, it's like a hard marble, under my skin with no flesh to cushion it. Chronic malnutrition and lack of vitamins have made physical wrecks of all of us.

I'm glad that the children at least, like pups snuggled together between Eva and me on the mattress, can find relief from their ailments in their sleep for a few hours. Pavel has patches of dry skin around his nose, his mouth, his ears, on his elbows and knees, that crack open and bleed daily. Poor Agata cries at every meal, every much awaited, longed-for meal, when her mouth ulcers prickle her ferociously like pins, she says. Little Stella, the tiny undernourished doll with distended belly, and as light as a sparrow, has never known what it's like to have a clear nose. The constant wiping away of oozing mucus has made it perpetually red and sore.

Eva suffers with night blindness, alarming when it first began last winter, a nightmarish obstacle to all her activities after dusk, and a source of constant stress when walking to work in the darkness before dawn to the shouts of *Bistra*! The unaffected amongst us partnered and helped the blind but this slowed us all down, resulting in lower output, resulting in smaller rations of bread, unless Ivan, God bless him, was left solely in charge and marked the log book in our favour.

The long summer days appeared to have cured Eva's condition, but now it's back again.

'It'll pass,' Mrs. Stepanovichova assures her, 'what you need is a good diet. Plenty of vegetables and fruit. Fresh meat and fish.' We all have dreams.

Mr. and Mrs. Stepanovich sleep on the one bed by the window. His hoarse snoring is so intrusive at times that it cuts through my sleep and grates on my nerves as I fight to ignore it. I'm used to peace at night, such that we enjoyed in our forest lodge at home, with the whispering woodland surrounding us, its stillness broken only by the odd bird song or a distant animal call.

Tonight unusually is peaceful. The whiteness of snow filters through the window and marks the outlines of objects in the room. The bulky forms of our sleeping hosts form a landscape of hills and valleys in their eiderdown. Eva, I and the children are tucked away in the corner between the warm wall of the tiled stove and the door leading to the shed. We're squashed, all five of us on two striped army mattresses pushed together, but infinitely more comfortable than the hard bunk in the cattle truck.

Eva's hand taps my shoulder.

'Nastusha...'

'It's all right. I'm awake.'

'I'm sorry...'

I know she is, but she can't help it. In addition to the night blindness she has recurring bladder problems. I see the halo of her pale bob lift from the pillow and I get up too and hold her hand. I open the shed door and lead her over the step towards the bucket that serves as the toilet in the night hours. The outdoor *slavoyka*, at the best of times, is like a refrigerator waiting to freeze your bum to the wooden seat.

'You're an angel,' she whispers over the sound of the urine hitting the side of the bucket.

There's a short outburst of chirping from the four hens cooped in the corner, then all is quiet.

'Me? An angel?' I whisper back over the rustle of her personal activity, 'when did you dream that?'

'I didn't. You're right here.'

'Pity then, I can't magic you back home. And myself. And the children.'

'One step at a time. Things are already improving, aren't they?'

Her optimism is irksome. The pain under my arm is becoming intolerable.

'Improving? So we're not freezing to death. Great! So we've got two miserly meals a day. Instead of one. I'm grateful for that. But do you know what?' bitterness creeps into my voice, 'most days I just want to scream and curse. At all those who have done this to us!'

'Are you cross with me?'

'Don't be silly.'

'Well then, Nastusha, what good will screaming and cursing do?' She stands up and lets the hem of her nightgown fall. She gropes for my hand in the dark, I give her mine. 'Nastusha, just think. the worst is behind us now. Just a little more time... more patience... and things will get even better. You'll see...'

She trips over the doorstep and my left arm shoots out to protect her from falling. A searing pain in my armpit stops me rigid, a stifled cry escapes my throat and tears flood my eyes. And there's relief. Instant, miraculous, and a sticky wetness under my arm. With my elbow I press the fabric of my nightgown against me to soak up the oozing mess.

'Nastusha... are you hurt?' Eva holds tight onto my hand.

'It's the boil... I think it's just burst.'

'Poor you! I'll bathe it for you in the morning and put some dressing on it. At least now it'll start healing.'

'Before the next one...'

'Don't think like that. '

I help her find her side of the mattress then in the darkness I rummage through my things to find a rag, which I stuff under my arm before I lie down. It feels very sore, but that unbearable throbbing is gone. I hear Eva sigh.

'We're so lucky, Nastusha, here in our warm corner…' she whispers.

Lucky? I haven't the energy for differences of opinion, but even in my disgruntled mood I have to agree that it is better to crowd on a mattress close to a warm stove than to rough it in a hole dug out in the frozen ground and covered only by tarpaulin.

'Sleep tight Eva.'

'I will. I won't bother you again tonight.'

I close my eyes and long for sleep to bring me relief from my own thoughts and the heaviness on my chest. I miss Julian. I miss my Mama and Papa. And Dorotka. That ache never leaves me. Soothed in the daytime by the demands of our group existence, it flares up every night and burns into my heart. I force myself to repeat Eva's words. We're lucky. In this tight warm corner. Unlike many of our countrymen who arrived later in this overcrowded town.

Buzuluk is close to explosion, its walls pushed out by thousands of Polish refugees, who have descended upon it in the last month, like a gigantic cloud of locusts. Every square metre of sheltered space is occupied, the market square, the warehouses, the alleys, the sheds in the back gardens. On the outskirts of the town, the hurriedly constructed tent-city is sprawling outwards daily as the numbers of new arrivals multiply.

At night, when we are cramped together on the mattress in the corner close to the burning stove, I can't stop thinking about the people out in the open snow-covered fields, with just a tent for cover. The fires kept going all night and day barely nudge up the temperature, but the biting smoke is a persistent irritant to their lungs and eyes. Dear God! What other cruel tests have been devised for us on our way to freedom?

There's a dire shortage of food. All local shops have been emptied of anything that's edible. I pity the citizens of Buzuluk. We, at least, have still got the military field kitchen as the last resort. The bread and the tins of corned beef and sardines from the British, are strictly rationed. It is all the more upsetting to hear rumours of theft. A young Polish soldier was found guilty of theft and shot by the NKVD as a deterrent to others. What was more shocking was the discovery of truth investigated by our own people. The young man was innocent, a hapless scapegoat for our cheating allies.

Eva and I are on good terms with old Mr. Stepanovich and his wife. The *roubles*, left us by Julian and Henryk, weave their magical way to his relatives and ensure a bag of flour or *kasza* or potatoes or cheese or milk on our table. Never more than one item at a time. On one rare occasion, when we saved flour and potatoes, Eva and I set about making *placki*. It felt almost like home. We bulked up the mixture of grated potatoes and one egg with extra flour and water.

We invited Mr. and Mrs. Stepanovich to join us in our little feast of miniature savoury pancakes, that were eaten with greedy delight, even by Agata through her tears of pain.

The old couple opened up with sentimental musings about their family and called us all their 'dears'.

'Anastazia, *maya lyoobeema*, and my dear Evanochka,' Mrs. Stepanovichova's bead-like eyes shone bright inside the folds of her face, 'don't leave us. Stay with us for good. You're like our daughters.'

I didn't have the heart to tell her that it's not my ambition to spend my life camping on a mattress, in two square metres of floor space.

'Gaspasha Stepanovichova,' I gave her the old fashioned title of respect, 'you're both very kind to us all. And we're truly grateful. But we've got families too. At home, in Poland. We miss them terribly. Every day. And as soon as the war is over, we must go back and find them.'

She nodded and wiped her eyes.

Some days she attempts to seduce us with gifts. In the shed that leans against the hut, where four little hens are kept for the eggs and are fed with a mixture of grains and seeds saved from the summer, she keeps treasures hidden in boxes on the shelves. One such box, brought down on her instructions, revealed a sheep's fleece, all in one piece, just as it had been shorn off.

'There's enough here to make a coat!' Eva exclaimed, excited.

'It's all yours if you stay,' Mrs. Stepanovichova's rubbery smile stretched all the creases around her mouth.

'Oh my dear Mrs. Stepanovichova,' Eva expressed regret, 'you know I can't promise that.' Nevertheless she plunged her hands into the mound of wool and kneaded it like dough. Pavel, Agata and Stella followed suit with giggles of delight.

Mr. Stepanovich, usually perched on the bed, smoking his pipe, cleared his throat and spoke out in his gravelly voice,

'Give the children some for their gloves.'

His wife nodded and without the slightest hesitation, separated six handfuls of wool from the bulk, enough to start crocheting six mittens.

Eva and I washed and dried the wool, then teased out tufts like 'angels's hair' and twisted them into a yarn between our fingers. Pavel and Agata were so fascinated by this activity, they skipped with impatience to take over from us, so we could start to crochet the mittens.

For Pavel and Agata the days are exceedingly boring in this cramped space. They look for things to do with a hawk-like alertness; they clean out the shed, feed the chickens and look for the eggs in the murky confines behind boxes and sacks, rearranging them with daily regularity. When Mr.

Stepanovich is in, they spend hours sitting at the table drawing with stubs of pencils on the wood shavings intended for burning in the stove.

Eva and I have managed to get rid of the lice with daily washing of the children's hair, which has now grown around their faces, softening their gaunt features. Little Stella's white blond hair makes me think of a little duckling. No wonder Mr. Stepanovich has taken a special liking to her. He calls her *maya malienka kookla*, my little doll, as he picks her up and settles her on his lap. Surprisingly she is not put off by his bushy eyebrows, droopy moustache and the perpetually smoking pipe. She examines these features with her matchstick fingers then pats him lovingly on his cheeks. He hugs her in return and tells her every time that she must stay to live with him.

Nevertheless we take the children out for long daily walks to give the old couple some respite from our constant presence, and ourselves, a gulp of bracing, head-clearing, fresh air. The streets are crowded with people like ourselves, looking like beggars in tatty greyed clothes, mostly women and children and the odd older man, hunched and hollow-eyed, unfit for army service.

We usually walk out of town, past the fields dotted with hundreds of tents, that exude smoke at both ends, a desperate exercise to catch even the faintest breath of warmth. The air is acrid here, filling our nostrils, irritating our throats. We make sure the children's faces are well covered. Eva and I take turns carrying Stella. I miss Julian, I miss all our boys and their ever practical support. Sometimes Pavel and Agata make a seat for Stella with their criss-crossed hands, like the scouts, and carry her happily part of the way.

The children like to stop at the gates of the military camp, though the view is obscured partly by the building behind the sentry post, and further by the administration blocks.

'Perhaps they're back,' Pavel and Agata repeat daily, straining their eyes to catch a lucky glimpse of one of our men.

'They'll come to see us as soon as they can,' I assure the children, and myself. Eva lifts little Stella higher and points at some imaginary spot in the distance.

'That's where your Daddy works,' she says, 'he'll come back as soon as his work is finished.'

We've had a message from our boys, shortly after our arrival, through a soldier on a day leave, that they were being sent out of the camp on an assignment: digging out more holes for *lepianki* and extending roads for transport. God only knows when they'll be back. We watch the lorries going in and out of the camp.

Pavel never gives up looking for his father and his sisters Aniela and little Marysia. Every time a newly arrived group of refugees is led from the station to the tents in the open field, he begs us to follow them and ask if they've seen or heard of the Yavorski family. I can hardly bear to watch the disappointment in his pinched little face. Sometimes he cries. I hold him close to me and Agata hugs him from the other side.

'You've got us,' she says. Her attachment to him is all too evident in the way she looks up to him, listens to his tales of his school escapades, laughs at his jokes, and shares with him all greedily sought activities in equal measures. She's only a few months younger than him, but her growth, unlike his, has been stunted by the poor diet.

One day, soon after our arrival, he begged me to take him to the orphanage.

'Auntie Nastusha, what if my Dad is already here, in the army, and my sisters are at the orphanage? Please, let's go and check. Then I'll know at least, one way or another.'

It made sense, yet I was filled with unease. Eva was concerned too.

'Pavelek dear,' she said, 'you realise, don't you, that if your sisters are indeed at the orphanage, then you'll have to join them. It's just easier for everyone when families are kept together.'

This puzzled him.

'But that won't be a problem,' he reasoned, 'we'll take them away. They'll come to live with us. Then we can all be together.'

Such touching innocent logic! Nothing would be a problem if only this situation was different, if we had food to spare, if we had room to live in comfort, if we were not governed by rules imposed upon us by others.

'Pavel, we have no official authority to make any decisions for you or your sisters. Only your Dad's agreement would allow us to take your sisters away.'

'But my Dad would agree! I know he would! We just need to find out if he and my sisters have arrived in Buzuluk.'

'What if it all goes wrong?' Agata worried, 'and they take you away from us?'

He thought and shook his head.

'We don't have to tell them who we are, do we? We can pretend to be distant relatives looking for lost people.'

It was hard to refuse him and so we tramped along the frozen, crunchy pavement, avoiding with frequent stops and sidestepping the relentless flow of people, until we found the old hotel, a solid, ornate building, that had been requisitioned for the purpose of sheltering the orphans.

The lofty oak portal was closed but not locked. We slipped inside the dark interior of the reception area, into the sound of hushed voices. It took a second or two for my eyes to adjust, for my brain to take in the scene. The floor and the walls were marble, the crystal chandeliers reflected light from the paraffin lamps lit around the edges of the room, and also at the far end, on the sides of the wide, massive staircase.

Children sat in groups supervised by adults, all dressed in outdoor clothes against the low temperatures throughout the building. Some huddled together, mute and motionless, some stood in the middle of their groups, encouraged by the adults to perform a song or a mime or recite a poem. One group appeared enlivened by a guessing game, and in another group a carer was organising little toddlers to hold hands in a ring. There was something infinitely sad about the appearance of these little waifs, and yet, at the same time, something uplifting and full of hope in their small gestures of normality. Little Stella clung to Eva's coat and watched mesmerised.

A woman detached herself from the group closest to the door, her worn thin face lost in the folds of her shawl.

'Are you newly arrived?' she asked.

'No, we're just here to make an enquiry. We're looking for two girls. Aniela and Marysia Yavorski.'

'Are you their family?' There was eagerness in the lift of her tone.

'Unfortunately not,' I replied, then explained, 'they've got left behind at one of the stations. They were with us. In our wagon.'

The woman went behind the reception desk and Pavel gave my hand a tug. She opened a folder with a thick wad of sheets covered in long lists of names.

'Yavorski, did you say?'

She searched down the alphabet while we waited, Pavel with abated breath.

'Yes, there's a Leszek Yavorski, but no girls.'

'Are you sure?' Pavel's hand became rigid in mine. I felt his grief. Guiltily I felt relief too. I wasn't going to lose him yet. Maybe not at all.

The woman's sad sympathetic gaze rested on him.

'Yes, I'm sure. But don't lose hope. Your friends may already be ahead of you. Some transports have been sent on. This place can't take any more. As you see, we're very crowded here. We pray every day for orders to move us on from here.'

Outside I gave Pavel another hug. Agata too.

'You heard what the lady said.'

He nodded and sighed.

'I'm fed up with waiting. We're always waiting for something or other. Why couldn't we have been left just where we were? At home. Then none of this would have happened.' Quite.

Today is another day. Wash and dress ourselves and the children, bathe and cover up my oozing boil, prepare breakfast of *kasza* and tea, lick every trace off the bowl with reverence, tidy up, feed the chickens, do the daily laundry, take the children out for a walk, hand-sew or crochet while there's still light, improvise the evening meal, keep busy at all times, to drown the boredom of waiting.

CHAPTER 22

First of November. All Saints Day. Family day in Poland. I can't stop thinking about my parents. I picture them at the table with my two sisters and their little children. Their husbands are absent, as is my brother, all traces of them lost after the disaster of the September campaign. My brother Voytek has not seen his first born yet, little Marek, who came into this world just as the German bombs fell on the railway station close by. The longing to be with them is like a constant ache. If only there was just one short note from them. In the last twenty months, since our arrest, it's as if they have ceased to exist.

In the evening Eva and I prepare a meal. Eva can only function close to the paraffin lamp. She insists on doing her bit on the lit table and prepares a mixture of flour, goat's milk, one egg, crumbled corned beef and a generous amount of water. I then fry the small savoury pancakes on the stove in the shady corner, where Eva does not trust her sight. Mrs. Stepanovichova brings out a jar of gherkins and we all sit down around the table moved close to the bed for additional seating. Little Stella climbs up next to her *dyedooshka*, her granddad, which transforms Mr. Stepanovich's thoughtful expression to that of beatific delight.

There's only just enough to quieten the hunger, my stomach never feels full. Every night I dream of a table laden with food, such as I prepared with my Mama for our family meals; home baked loaves of bread, large and round like the *babooshkas*, fresh butter and milk from our cows, eggs from our chickens, hardboiled and halved and served in mayonnaise, mixed diced vegetable salads, sweet beetroot in vinaigrette, shredded cabbage and carrot, ham and sausages and carp in aspic. Not to mention the cheese and the honey and the poppy seed cakes. The choices made me finicky. I can't forgive myself now.

A loud knock on the door makes us all sit up and listen in silence. Then the sound of the familiar voice does strange things to my heart.

'Nastusha! Eva! It's Julian!'

'And Henryk! And Ryszard!' the other two shout.

I rush to unlock the door and all three troop in, large in their padded uniforms, crowding our little room, and for the next few minutes there's one continuous outburst of joyous hugging and talk. They deposit their gifts of bread and tins of sardines and corned beef on the table and make a pile in the corner of their coats and hats. Eva and I clear everything away to make a little more space, if only illusory, and then we all settle wherever we can to sit or perch or stand to talk.

Julian sits beside me at the table and Pavel drapes himself over Julian's shoulder.

He covers my hands with his, bony and rough yet comfortingly warm and looks straight into my eyes. I feel an ache of all those weeks of missing him and long to hold his face against mine. His face is pinched and angular, but his dark eyes within their rims of thick eyelashes, have retained the same lively glow that I found so irresistible when I first met him.

'Nastusha, *moja kochana*,' he tightens his hands around mine, 'it's all beginning to happen now. Properly. Heavy military training. In Koltubyanka. We're being sent there tomorrow. Hundreds of us.' He looks so excited. My heart sinks.

'Julian, I wish…' No, I must stop this. No mawkishness allowed. 'Julian dearest, we'll pray for your safety every night. Won't we Pavel?'

Pavel's arm is around Julian's neck.

'I wish you didn't have to go,' he says. 'I wish you could stay so we could do things together.'

Julian lets go of my hands, and draws Pavel onto his lap.

'It won't be for long, Pavel. Soon we'll all be going south. We'll catch up with each other where it's warm and pleasant and free. We'll have as much food as we want. Bread and fresh fruit. There will be proper shops with everything you want to buy. There will be beautiful parks with water fountains and play areas for the children. There will be schools. Can you imagine? Going to lessons again?'

Pavel's eyes sparkle.

'You know uncle Julian, when I had to go to school at home, I always wanted to play truant. And now I'd give anything to be back in my class with my friends.'

'You will be,' Julian strokes Pavel's cheek with the back of his hand.

'I don't know where they all are.'

'There will be lots of other children. And you've got Agata. She's a truly good friend to you, isn't she? You'll always look after her, won't you? It's what decent men do. Look after others.'

Pavel leans across Julian's chest to look at Agata. She's sitting with Ryszard, glued to his side, listening to him, with Mr. Stepanovich on her other side, smoking his pipe. Pavel retracts and thinks for a moment.

'When I find Aniela,' he says, 'we'll both look after her, till her Dad comes back from the war.'

'That's my boy!' Julian praises him and elicits a shy smile on Pavel's pinched face.

We talk and dream of a wonderful future, yet all the while I feel like a character in a play, acting out a fantasy and pretending not to notice the heaviness on my chest, relentless.

Then all too soon it's time for the boys to return to base. There's no privacy for intimate kisses and words. Nevertheless Julian holds my face against his for a moment, and I run my hand over his dark hair, with a white streak combed back from his forehead. It's clean and lice-free and smelling of the fresh outdoors.

'When will I see you again?' I want it to sound casual.

'Nastusha dearest, don't think about it. Stick together with Eva and look after yourselves and the children. Time will take care of everything else.' He hands me a small leather purse. 'It should keep you going for a while.'

I give him one last hug, Pavel does too, then we watch them pull on their coats and hats and gloves, willing to prolong the time. And when they're gone, the little crammed hut feels very empty.

Later, in the dark, with the children asleep between us, and with Mr. Stepanovich's snoring cutting through the silence of the night, Eva whispers to me.

'They're like schoolboys with a new toy, aren't they?'

'What choice have they got? They may just as well be enthusiastic.' I play the sensible arbitrator.

'Well, I can't pretend I'm not scared!'

'You're not allowed, Eva!'

She sighs. 'I wish I could be like you. How do you stay so calm?'

I snort.

'What's so funny?'

'Eva, you know me. I'm not calm, nor brave nor strong. I'm a jittery wreck inside. I can't stop worrying about them. I can't stop thinking what if...We were so happy when we left Svoboda. But now...what's going to happen to us while we wait for the war to finish, for our boys to come home? And when will that be?'

I hear a movement and feel her touch on my shoulder.

'We've got each other,' she says, 'and the children. They'll keep us busy. And... have I ever told you? I bless the day when we first met.'

My mind is flooded with memories of our arrival at the forester's lodge called *Pianka*, to Julian's new job, to a new place, where we did not know anyone. Within half an hour, as we unpacked our belongings in the empty wooden house, echoing with our footsteps and voices, Henryk and Eva appeared on our doorstep with their offerings of food and drink and entertaining company.

'We were all lucky,' I answer, 'it's of great comfort to me now, knowing that Julian and Henryk are together.'

'They'll be living in those awful *lepianki*. I can't bear the thought of the freezing cold. And the choking moke.'

'If they survive this Eva, they'll be hardened to anything after that.' I do my best to sound positive.

150

She is quiet for a while before whispering again.

'Henryk's been telling me all sorts of wonderful fantasies about the south. Just one good thing would be enough to make me happy...'

Images race through my mind; the golden orb high in the blue sky, warm green earth, fragrant air shimmering with insect life, patches of light in deep shadows, long dream-like days of our Polish summers. And food. Lots of food.

'As long as there's food, Eva. God, how I'd love to, for once, stuff myself to bursting point.'

'No, not stuff yourself Nastusha. You must plump yourself up. Nice and slow. Get into shape again. And brown those arms and legs. So we look like those posh ladies, just back from their Italian holiday.'

She disarms my mood. I giggle.

'Eva, if I didn't know it's winter outside, I'd think you've had sunstroke. Me? A posh lady?'

'And why not?' Eva is undeterred. 'Neither Garbo nor Harlow were born film sirens. And look how they turned out. We're better than them. Dark and mysterious, blond and vivacious. Who could resist such a glamorous pair?'

'More like Laurel and Hardy,' I smirk. She ignores that and carries on,

'We'd turn heads, Nastusha!'

'What for?'

'For a bit of fun! Oh Nastusha!..' there's impatience in her hushed voice, 'ever heard of fun? It won't fall into your lap. We've got to make fun! If we're to stay sane!' she is quiet before adding, 'Seriously, it'll be fun to surprise our boys, when they come back from the war.'

I cannot imagine so far ahead.

'When will that be?' I sigh.

'Who knows? However long it takes,' she replies, 'we've got no choice, have we? But to wait. God knows what state they'll be in when they come back. They'll want angels to look after them. Not some neglected anaemic old frumps. As soon as we can, we'll invest in lipstick and powder. Hair's easy. We can curl it ourselves. Let's grow it long again. We'll look like models with that long fringe swept over one side.'

Her prattle is crazy but already I feel a lightness in my soul. I don't tell her of a sudden surge of a sisterly feeling for her. Instead I ask,

'Talking of sirens and all things glamorous, do you need a stroll to the shed before I fall asleep?'

'Thanks, but no. I hope to make it till the morning.'

'Then good night, Jean Harlow'.

'Sleep well,' she answers. Long silence, then, 'your hair's better than Garbo's, you know. See if it isn't, when you let it grow.'

On Sunday, the day before St. Nicholas Day on the 6th of December, Pavel and Agata worry whether St. Nicholas will find them so far away from home.

We're sitting round the table, little Stella between Mr. and Mrs. Stepanovich, over a supper of handmade noodles sprinkled with fried corned beef. Mrs. Stepanovichova cuts Stella's portions in mouth sized morsels and watches her like a guard, filling her spoon in advance, waiting for Stella to chew and swallow.

'*Yetz, yetz, maya malienka.* Eat my little one. So you grow big. Like Pavel and Agata.'

Pavel and Agata raise their thin shoulders and sit up.

'You know what, Stella?' Pavel's face becomes animated, 'St. Nicholas is coming tonight. With presents for us. But only when we're fast asleep.'

'And we've got to be good.' Agata adds. 'He'll only bring you a stick if you've been naughty. But we've been good, haven't we?' She looks from me to Eva. I'm overcome with a wave of feeling for her. It's a miracle she's so normal after everything that's happened to her.

'Your Dad would be proud of you,' Eva assures her.

'And uncle Julian of me, wouldn't he?' Pavel asks, his serious gaze fixing mine.

'Of course,' I stress, giving them both a pat on their shoulders. They smile shyly at each other.

The temporary rest in this cramped accommodation has already had a positive effect on them. Despite the limited variety of food, the meals are regular and they get plenty of sleep. Their hair is free of lice and has grown around their faces softening their gaunt appearance. Pavel's skin is slightly improved, with fewer cracked and bleeding patches, and Agata's recurring mouth ulcers are less frequent these days.

'You must realise one thing,' Eva tells them, 'these are hard times even for St. Nicholas. And he's got a long way to travel. He may not be able to bring you all the things you wish for.'

'I'd love a box of paints,' Agata looks up dreamily.

'I'd love some chocolate,' Pavel licks his cracked lips.

'And sweets...'

'And an apple...'

And pears, and honey cake, and jelly, and ice-cream... the list is endless. Stella's round eyes look from one to the other as she chews slowly on her first mouthful of noodles, struggling to breathe at the same time. Her little red nose is sore underneath the shine of the vaseline, which Mr. Stepanovich has managed to secure for her. His large gnarled hand is fascinatingly gentle as he strokes Stella's fluffy hair, pale yellow like a chick's down. Every now and again Mrs. Stepanovichova keeps repeating, '*Yetz, yetz, maya malienka...* eat, my little one.'

Later, when the children are fast asleep, having said their prayers and asked St. Nicholas not to forget them, Eva and I take out the treasures that we've been hiding from them in a suitcase. One can only hope that the children will be as pleased with our trophies as we have been in obtaining them, in great measure thanks to Mr. Stepanovich.

One day he came home with two tiny bags of sunflower seeds and dried wild strawberries. Another time he managed to find somewhere, two new pencils and two little notebooks. For Stella, since Eva's night blindness prevents her from doing finer things in the evenings, I've sewn her a miniature mouse out of some red felt, which had once been intended for flowers to decorate my hat. We've also got a soft embroidered handkerchief for her, to replace the one that has been reduced to shreds, which she rubs against her face every night before falling asleep.

We sit at the table, Eva and I, and in the dim light of the paraffin lamp, we divide the edible present into three equal parts and drop the seeds and the dried fruit into cone-shaped bags made of old newspapers. We keep the rustle to the minimum, as Mr. and Mrs. Stepanovich are already in bed. I can only imagine how disruptive our presence must be to their routines of going to bed at the same time as the hens, and rising at the crack of dawn.

We prop St. Nicholas' gifts against the wall close to the children's heads, so they can see them the moment they wake up. I wait for Eva to settle down, turn down the wick, snuff the flame and then I lie down too, beside the children.

'I wish St. Nicholas would magic our boys over tomorrow,' Eva whispers in the dark,' wouldn't that be the best ever present for everyone!'

'If only!' I wish it too with an ache of longing, 'and some good news would be welcome too. I'm so weary with all this waiting...'

'We must thank God for all the little mercies,' Eva reminds me.

I agree with a pang of guilt at my ingratitude. Her bladder problem has eased off, and my boil has healed too. There's just a crater in my skin the size of a small coin, but no one's going to look under my arm.

On our daily walks into town with its streets crowded to full capacity, despite large groups of constantly arriving people being moved into the tent city expanding around Buzuluk, we stop soldiers, our Polish soldiers with the white and red bands around their arms, and ask them for information. There's a slight hitch, they say. Stalin's moods. He had never expected such an immediate and vast migration of Poles out of the labour camps, and the impact this was going to have on the vacated places of work, on the transport and on the points of congregation. Nothing had been organised or prepared in advance.

'Surely,' I reason with the friendly soldier, 'the best thing would be to let us go south and leave this place and its people in peace.'

He lowers his tone and his head to mine.

'Stalin still wants our soldiers to join his army. We all know why. We can only hope that with Sikorski's negotiations, Anders can lead his army whole, out of here. In the meantime we're all left waiting while Stalin deliberates and procrastinates.'

We pray every night, Eva and I, that our boys don't end up in the Red Army. We call on all our Guardian Angels and Saints to help Anders lead out his men and us out of this land of fear and repression.

In the morning, I'm drawn out of my sleep by the children's excited chatter. They've discovered the edible presents and munch the seeds and the tiny red berries with much animation and joy. My instinct is to stop them, to save some for later, but then I hold back. It's St. Nicholas Day; let them be happy if a few seeds and dried berries can bring them happiness.

All day I have a feeling that Eva like myself, is on tenterhooks, glancing frequently at the window, listening for the sounds outside the door, quickening her pace on the way back from our daily walk. The evening passes uneventfully. There are no visitors, no news.

When our hosts have gone to bed in their dark corner by the window, and our children are asleep on the mattress with their presents close to them, and Stella's new handkerchief rises up and down over her face with her every breath, Eva and I pick up our crochet work and sit at the table, inside the dim circle of light from the paraffin lamp. Eva's movements are automatic, she does not have to rely on light. She sighs and puts her work down.

'All day I was so convinced our boys would come home tonight,' she whispers. 'I must have been a really bad girl for St. Nicholas to refuse my wish'.

I look up and notice her eyes glistening.

'Dear Eva,' I move close to her and throw my arm over her shoulder, 'then I've been a bad girl too. I've had the same hope all day. But it's not anyone's fault. I'm sure they're missing us just as much. They'll come as soon as they can. I'm certain of that!'

Eva gives a deep sigh and wipes her eyes.

'I know all that. I know. But I wish, I just wish… we could all be together. It's hard not knowing exactly where they are. If I could just see them for a moment, have a clear picture in my mind… I have this constant fear that they won't come back…'

'They will, Eva, they will come back,' I say emphatically to convince myself too. 'Once they complete their training. Do you know what I find helpful? Thinking about home. And our times together before any of this happened. Do you remember the Sunday afternoons? The food and the drinks. And when the others joined us, a jolly good sing-song. Now, that would really cheer us up!'

Eva becomes pensive, her gaze distant, then very softly she hums a folk song about a young girl Katie and her longing for her lover Johnny.

'Is this supposed to cheer you up?' I tease her, eager to elicit a smile.

She looks at me with those eyes of hers, clear blue even in the dim lamp light, and there's a reprimand in her words,

'You never sing these days. When will you sing again, Nastusha? I wish I had a voice like yours. I'd sing all day!'

I used to, I can't any more. Not since Dorotka's loss.

'I sometimes sing inside my head,' Eva continues. 'Strange how even pretending to sing, gives you a lift. Don't you think?'

I know that. I loved our church choir at home, the weekly rehearsals, the lingering melodies in my mind that gave bounce to my step on the way home.

'You know I can't sing here. Even if I had the inclination.'

'Then just hum. Anything. As long as it's cheerful.'

Hundreds of songs whirl in my mind. Anything too jolly would feel sacrilegious, diminishing my reverence for my child.

'I can't. It's because of Dorotka.'

Eva thinks for a long moment, sighs and says,

'Have you ever thought Nastusha, that she may be missing you? Wouldn't a happy song cheer her up too?'

This has never occurred to me, I've been so wrapped up in my own pain. I feel my heart filling up as if it's going to burst, then my eyes flood and I feel relief. Eva grabs my hands in hers and speaks fervently,

'Nastusha, for all you know, Dorotka may be right here beside us. Waiting for her mother to sing a lullaby. And all those other songs you used to sing to her.'

I want Eva to be right about this. I want it more than anything else at this moment, more than food, more than going home, more than seeing all the people I love. I just wish Julian could be with me. If only it were possible to see her just once more. For him and for me.

'Eva, I'd give up everything I possess for one last touch of her. Why doesn't God allow our loved ones to come back and tell us they are all right and happy?'

'Perhaps there's no need for that, if you believe that yourself?' Eva holds my hands tight in hers and looks straight into my eyes, 'it's not hard to imagine that she's a little angel, like a cherub. That she stays beside you at all times.'

I close my eyes and see Dorotka's little face, her smile, the soft down covering her head, and my nostrils pick up her baby smell.

'Hum something for her...' Eva whispers.

The words come automatically to my mind. *If I were the sun in the sky of blue, I'd shine all day only for you. If I were a bird in the month of May, Only for you I'd sing all day.* There's a humming in my head, a well loved melody, and somehow it feels right that I should be singing for my child again.

Later, when we're down on the mattress beside our sleeping children in the dark, Eva whispers,

'I've suddenly remembered lots of other songs. D'you remember that jolly one about *Auntie's Namesdsay Party*? With everyone there, family and friends and a magician and a trapeze artist and someone playing the opera on a comb and all sorts of other nonsense. The verse I liked the best was the one about food. The wine and the beer and the *pierogi* and the *gołąbki* and the doughnuts and the macaroons. And ... Nastusha, that reminds me, do you remember that midsummer party at Yan's? Those grilled sausages and the bread... mmmm... the best taste in the world!'

I have a clear sharp memory of the food we enjoyed that day. There's a spasm in my withered stomach and a sudden rush of saliva in my mouth. I close my eyes.

'Let's sleep, Eva.' I whisper back. 'Perhaps our dreams will bring us everything we need. And we'll be one day closer to freedom.'

24th December. *Vigilia* is upon us. There's still no news from our boys. Nevertheless, throughout the day, Eva and I make preparations for the special evening meal, for which we've been saving food in the last few weeks. Mr. Stepanovich has managed to ply his contacts with our roubles with a most fortunate result of obtaining a few potatoes, a couple of beetroot, a couple of carrots, and, unbelievable, one whole onion! We've made a rich *barszcz* soup, which we sweetened with a little honey from Mrs. Stepanovichova's emergency jar. For piquancy, we've added a little brine from her gherkins. We taste it, Eva and I, with miniature spoons to stave off temptation to eat more. The taste is perfect. The children want some too. We let them have a teaspoon each.

'You'll enjoy it all the more tonight,' Eva promises them, 'as soon as you spot the first star. Now, you'll have to play on the mattress. We need the table for making *pierogi*.'

They don't want to play on the mattress. Pavel and Agata stand glued to the sides of the table their eyes following avidly our every move. Stella watches us from the bed, rubbing her handkerchief and her felt mouse against her face.

I make the dough with flour and water and Eva rolls it out flat. We cut circles out with two drinking glasses, fill them with a mixture of mashed potatoes and cheese and make them into semi-circular dumplings, by sealing the edges together. Pavel and Agata count them as their numbers increase in neat rows.

'It's so long to wait till the evening, my stomach is rumbling now...' Pavel complains. 'Couldn't we taste just one?'

This is torture. 'My dear Pavelek,' I try to humour him, 'by the time we've been for a walk and come back, it'll already be dusk. We won't have to wait long after that.'

For lunch we have dried black bread dipped in tea. Enough to distract our hunger. We all dress up warm and go out for our regular walk, to kill time, to bring the evening forward. Pavel keeps looking up for the first star, but the fading rays of the sun are still lingering on the horizon. The air is brittle with frost. We walk along our familiar route, to the central square, and out of town towards the military camp, which is surrounded, as far as the eye can see, by hundreds of rows of tents. As usual, the tents are emitting smoke from both ends, a desperate struggle to generate warmth in this cruel climate. Here and there, groups like ours wander about, I guess in search of food or fuel, but the streets are less crowded, the people, no doubt eager to retreat to their dwellings before dusk.

'Can we go home now?' Pavel asks, 'it feels a hundred degrees colder than yesterday.'

'A hundred and one,' Agata adds with facetious accuracy.

It's neither, but indeed, as soon as the sky darkens behind the wall of the forest in the distance, the temperature drops with a breath-taking sharpness. We turn back and between us, Eva and I carry little Stella in the basket of our criss-crossed hands, while Pavel and Agata try to out-walk each other, while dodging other, none too pleased pedestrians on the pavement. We reach the door of our hut just as the night falls.

'Look!' Pavel exclaims, 'the first star!'

It is most probably Venus, glittering brighter than the sickle shape of the new moon.

'It's time for *Vigilia*!'Agata skips with excitement and when we deposit Stella on the frozen ground she emulates her older friend, looking like a bouncing ball in all her layers of clothing.

Indoors, the table is adorned with a flowery old curtain material. Mr. Stepanovich is smoking his pipe in his usual place at the foot of the bed. His thick wiry grey hair has been smoothed down with a wet comb and he's changed into his dark green thick cardigan. Mrs. Stepanovichova always wears black, and a headscarf even indoors. She is minding the pots on the stove and sends us a smile with a nod of her head.

'Will we ever have a Christmas tree again?' Pavel asks as we take off our outdoor clothing and fold it in a neat pile by the door.

'I'd love to make Christmas decorations,' Agata smooths down her dress and adjusts the collar with feminine self-consciousness.

'Perhaps next year,' I promise, 'who knows? We may be home by then.'

'We can still make this Christmas happy, can't we?' Eva suggests. 'We'll sing carols after *Vigilia*. And we can play games. As late as you like!' She gives Pavel a conspiratorial smile.

'Till midnight?' Pavel's face lights up.

'Can you last that long?' Eva teases.

He beams ready to reply, then his expression freezes. There's a loud knock on the door. The hut becomes quiet. Mr. Stepanovich holds his pipe with a still hand and his wife stands motionless by the stove.

'It's us! Your boys!'

The silence is broken with shouts of unrestrained joy. Pavel throws himself at the door to open it first. They walk in, big and bulky in their winter coats, Julian, Henryk, Ryszard, and Roman too, slip off their padded hats and drop their rucksacks by the door. The overwhelming euphoria, like a magnet, pulls everyone together. There's much embracing and kissing and laughter, even our hosts get their share of hugs, first a little surprised then giving in willingly, into the spirit of the moment.

I cling to Julian with all my might, and just feeling him, even through the thickness of his coat, and pressing my cheek to his, and having my breath squeezed in the tight ring of his arms, is the purest bliss. Pavel wants him too; his need calls on my generosity and I have to let Julian go. I make a fuss of Roman, as everyone else does too. We've not seen him for close to three months, since our arrival in Buzuluk. I hug him as if he were my brother.

'We've missed you, Roman. The army obviously suits you.' He's clean shaven, his short dark hair is beginning to curl above his forehead, his bluebell eyes could seduce any girl he chose. 'Which are you now?' I jest. 'A priest or a soldier?'

He smiles back and plants a kiss on my cheek. 'Neither has to exclude the other,' he says.

I hug Henryk, our good, faithful, always reliable friend, and note that his deloused fair hair has thickened around his temples, and that his wide smile is unchanged with that hint of a gap between his front teeth, giving him a look of constant jollity.

'Dear Henryk, perhaps next year we'll be celebrating at home. As it used to be. Remember?'

He returns my hug saying, 'Anastazia, it's a great relief for me knowing that Eva and you are together. Promise me, you'll always look out for each other, and stay together till we get back.'

'We'd never consider anything else. I need her too, you know. I couldn't exist without her!'

He clasps my hand in both his big hands and gives it a warm squeeze.

'Thank you. It's a relief just knowing that Eva's not struggling on her own.'

I turn to Ryszard, who is a prisoner in Agata's embrace. He's the thinnest of all our men, his greying hair covering his head like a fresh crop of thickly growing grass, his grey eyes reflecting the paleness of his skin, yet his expression transformed with the happiness of seeing and holding close his only remaining child.

'How can I ever thank you, Anastazia and Eva?' His eyes shine. 'I can hardly recognise my daughter. Look at her! Isn't she just turning into a princess!'

A beaming smile lights Agata's little face. I hug them both.

'Ryszard, for as long as you both need us… perhaps one day soon you'll have her back for good.'

'Perhaps,' Agata adds, 'we can all live together in one house, when we go to Poland.'

Ryszard and I laugh.

The men take off their coats and jackets and create another pile in the corner of our mattress. From their rucksacks they take out treasures that make my mouth water: a white loaf with a brown crusty top, four tins of corned beef and four tins of sardines. I leave the bread and the sardines on the table and put away the corned beef on our shelf of frugally stored groceries, behind the stove. Ryszard passes me another loaf as well as four boiled eggs.

'And something for tomorrow,' he says, 'we've saved these things from our last few meals.'

I feel deep gratitude. It's a well known fact that the unexpected numbers of civilians around Buzuluk have eaten into the food rations intended for the army. Stalin's promises of additional support have not materialised, and only the British aid keeps this nightmarish situation only just tenable, but for how much longer?

The men move the table closer to the chest that stands adjacent to the bed for additional seating, and with the two chairs and two stools, we can just about accommodate everyone around the table.

Before we settle down to our *Vigilia* feast of *barszcz* and *pierogi*, and the unexpected bread and sardines, Roman asks for a moment's silence. Out of his breast pocket he produces a folded sheet of paper, and out of it, gently, he shakes out onto his palm a flat square wafer. We are all impressed.

'Where did you get that!' Eva exclaims.

'Connections,' he smiles mysteriously, his eyes sparkling. He explains to Mr. and Mrs. Stepanovich that before our special family meal on the eve of Christmas, we share the wafer with everyone present as a symbol of sharing Christian love. 'And another thing,' he adds, 'at home at the *Vigilia* table, there's always a spare place for anyone who may knock on the door on that Holy Night.'

Not the NKVD, my mind panics, please God, not the NKVD!

Mrs. Stepanovichova bends over the wooden chest and lifts up the lid. It is filled with neatly folded linen. She pushes her hand down the side, right to the bottom and withdraws a flat wooden rectangle. It turns out to be an icon of the Mother and Child; rich blue and red hues on a golden background. Her old worn hands hold the painting with reverence for a moment, before placing it on the table.

'We're forbidden to worship in church,' she shakes her head sadly, 'but we're not pagans. Tonight we want to pray with you.'

Roman blesses the icon with the sign of the cross then leads a short prayer concluding with a quote from St. Luke's Gospel: *You shall find the Infant Jesus, born of the Virgin Mary, wrapped in swaddling clothes and laid in a manger.* He passes the wafer around our circle, so that everyone can break off a small piece. Little Stella standing on the chair with Henryk's protective arm around her is immobile with fascination, watching Pavel and Agata's every move, as they demonstrate to her the wafer on their tongues, 'just like communion.' When it comes to individual exchanges of best wishes and hugs, voices become choked and eyes moist.

'To be back home, next Christmas,' Roman sums up all our wishes in one. We settle down around the table and the magical evening begins.

Eva and I serve the beetroot soup in every available cup or mug, and later, the freshly boiled dumplings on Mrs. Stepanovichova's assortment of odd plates and saucers. We keep the same for portions of bread and equally divided sardines.

I feel drunk with sheer joy; so much pleasure all at once: food, warmth and Julian beside me. I'm aware of his every movement, of his every word, of the scents he's brought with him, soap smell on his skin, hints of smoke trapped in his uniform. Now and again, as we enjoy the meal, and I'm struggling with my instinct to gobble it fast, he looks at me with his dark luminous eyes, and smiles and hugs me to him. Pavel, on his other side, sits right up against him, and between the courses, grabs Julian's hand and rubs it against his cheek.

For the first time since leaving home my stomach feels satisfied. For the first time since Dorotka's death, I discover with a mixture of surprise and relief, that I'm capable of experiencing happiness again. For a while at least, maybe for longer, my ache is soothed by the sight of our children's contented faces and by the warmth of the strong bonds of friendship from the people I love.

After the meal is finished and every last crumb and trace of food is removed from the plates with the final morsel of bread, which is then chewed for a long time, like some exotic delicacy, Mrs. Stepanovichova treats us to tea, brewed in her prized silver-plated shapely samovar. The coarse brown sugar is hers too. With frugal restraint we all take a pinch of it from the small cup to sweeten our tea.

It is appropriate at this point to sing carols together, but the sound of a choir could draw the much feared NKVD men to our door. We encourage Pavel and Agata to sing a duet, but they decline shyly, not wanting to be the first to begin.

'I'll be first then,' Roman offers, and in his clear, melodious voice sings *Cicha Noc, Silent Night*. I swallow hard the gulp of tea together with a lump in my throat.

Ryszard and Agata sing next, a jolly carol, *The Shepherds came to Bethlehem*. The lively, bouncy tune brings smiles to all faces. It all feels so normal, so good.

'Now your turn Pavel,' Roman's gentle voice is encouraging. Pavel looks up at Julian and Julian laughs.

'All right, which carol shall we sing?'

Pavel thinks for a moment.

'I like that lullaby, *Sleep little Jesus, sleep*.'

Julian's voice is not the best in the world and he's not always tone perfect, but for me at this moment he is the great Caruso, charismatic and enchanting, and my eyes take in all his physical attributes that had attracted him to me when I was a young girl in love. His dark hair cut short is just softening the contours of his head, he has neat ears, (Dorotka's little ears were just like his), an elegant straight nose, dark eyes that still have the power to burn into mine and stir sensations at the pit of my stomach, and he's still got all his teeth. We have been lucky in our group; so many people and even young children have been robbed off theirs by the dreaded *pellagra.*

Eva and I sing another jolly carol to sustain the blissful atmosphere, then we ask our hosts to sing something too. Mr. Stepanovich declines with a self-deprecating smile and returns to smoking his pipe. Mrs. Stepanovichova says she knows many songs but they're all patriotic. We assure her that we don't mind.

She has a tinny voice that makes Pavel and Agata smirk shyly and look down. We listen to the sad, elegy-like tune and to the words that praise the River Volga, whose waters swell with pride at the sight of the loyal citizens of the Soviet Union, toiling in the fields in good and honest work.

We give Mrs. Stepanovichova a round of applause. Her small rubbery face creases in a hundred lines around her smile and she pushes an imaginary strand of hair underneath her black headscarf.

The children are reluctant to leave the table and stay with us listening without any show of boredom, as we spend the evening talking, reminiscing, speculating about the future. There's no room for intimate dialogues. Eva and I listen to our boys' accounts of their training and drills and the military manoeuvres in open, frozen fields, or in forests echoing with mysterious sounds. The Russian wooden replicas of guns did not exactly inspire confidence; the genuine training came only with the delivery of the British arms.

I don't like this talk of guns and fighting. I cannot imagine that any sane person does. But the impetus of this colossal war machine can only come to a grinding halt after it has run its full course. I shudder at the thought of the aftermath. I curse in my mind the two monsters who have unleashed such evil upon the world. Hitler and Stalin.

'Nastusha,' Julian tightens his embrace around my shoulders and looks into my eyes, 'why such a gloomy face?'

'Julian…' I respond with a quick smile and snuggle up to him, 'I just wish the war could end right now. I wish you didn't have to fight. I wish we could just go home in peace.'

'Dearest Nastusha,' his breath is warm on my neck, 'that'll happen soon, believe me. Any day now we'll start evacuating from Buzuluk and heading south. And once we're out in Persia, with all our units complete and prepared to fight, we'll go into action. We'll show the bastard what irrepressible stuff we Poles are made of!'

He misses my point completely, but speaks with such certainty, that I don't wish to spoil his good spirits with my reservations.

'Tell me about where you've been staying,' I ask instead.

He runs his hand over his hair wearily and his eyes widen as he tells me.

'It was hellishly cold in our tents. The only warm places were the refectory and the baths in the brick buildings. Once I got myself hot under a shower I'd wear all layers of clothing to retain this heat for as long as possible, especially at night time. The fire was hardly worth having, as it produced so much smoke. Some poor chaps had constant eye infections, or worse still, kidney problems from the cold.'

'Oh Julian...' I grab his hand in sympathy, 'how did you stand it all?'

'We stuck together, the four of us,' he says with a smile, 'literally like fox cubs. Huddling together, fully clothed, with all the covers around us. Never mind. It's all behind us now. We're back in our previous barrack here. At least it's a fraction more civilised. They've already sent some men on, to make room for us. Now, any day, it'll be our turn. Tashkent. They say it's so much warmer there. And we've been promised British uniforms.' His face lifts with anticipated pleasure.

'And us? Has anyone said anything about us?' I only want the good news.

Henryk nods in my direction saying,

'Civilians too. Any day now.'

The time flows too fast. I glance with nervous frequency at the wooden clock on the dresser, tightening my linking arm around Julian's. At half past eight, the boys raise themselves from their seats with obvious reluctance. Agata is like an appendage at her father's side.

'My dearest child,' Ryszard kisses the top of her head, 'the curfew is at nine. We can't be even a minute too late.'

'And what if you were?'

'It's the *kartzer,* absolute certainty, Agatka.'

We all get up and let go of our boys. They step into their roles of soldiers immediately, pull on their outdoor clothes in a fast and adept manner and leave with military punctuality, foregoing prolonged goodbyes. The room feels hollow without them.

In the morning, on Christmas Day at about eight, as we sit around our breakfast of small pancakes made with one egg, goats milk, a little flour and lots of water to bulk up the batter, and talk with much excitement about last night's *Vigilia*, there's a loud, commanding knock on the door. The children stop eating and look at us wide-eyed. Mr. and Mrs. Stepanovich exchange nervous glances, then he gets off his seat, and with a restrained gait, he moves towards the door. Two NKVD men enter, big and bulky in their padded uniforms, and crowd the space at our table. They're our friends, I tell myself, yet my mouth dries up.

They stand over us like a leaning rock face, then one of them produces a wad of sheets clipped to a board.

'We're checking names,' he announces, his tone dry, officious. 'We want yours.'

Eva gives hers and Stella's, I give mine.

'And whose are these children?' His cold gaze stops on Pavel then Agata.

'Their fathers are in the army.' I answer quickly. 'Now we look after them. Yavorski and Dorodny.'

He flicks through the sheets and runs his fingers up and down some pages.

'Dorodny. Yes. But no Yavorski here.'

'But there must be!' I say with absolute conviction thinking of the other Yavorski child at the orphanage. He continues to search in absolute silence, such that makes me hear the beat of my heart like a loud gong. Then suddenly, he pats the sheets into place and hides the wad inside his coat.

'These children should be in an orphanage,' he pronounces.

Fear like a cold trickle runs down my spine, but before I open my lips, Eva buts in,

'They are not orphans. They are children of our very close friends. They are like family. It is our duty to look after them. Doesn't Marshall Stalin say that the Soviet Union cultivates sentiments of friendship and fraternal cooperation among the people? We are just following his noble sentiments.'

I'm speechless with astonishment at her quick-thinking. I couldn't have thought of it like that on the spot. I wait for his reaction, squeezing my hands tight behind my back to stop them from trembling. He gives her a hard, long stare, then his expression changes. I notice a flicker of interest as his eyes travel over the pale blonde hair, that falls across her forehead.

'Repeat what you've just said,' he orders her.

Something flips over in my stomach. Eva brushes away the hair from her eyes. Her hand is shaky and there's a stiffness around her mouth. She licks her lips and complies with his order.

'They're like family. Like our own children. It is our duty to look after them.'

A leer spreads across his wide face.

'And could you extend this duty to us?' he sniggers. 'We wouldn't mind that at all, would we? When can you look after us?' He nudges his companion. Their jolly outburst is revolting.

Eva's expression becomes hard. The look of disdain in her eyes is unmistakeable. Even a blockhead like him must see it. Mr. Stepanovich draws in a breath of disgust. The NKVD man appears to only notice him now.

'Jealous? Do you still remember such things you calcified old fossil?'

I'm shaken with anger. At home I'd slap the bastard's face. Here, fear holds me back, yet my conscience urges me on. I clear my throat and with forced calm I speak to him,

'Comrade Stepanovich is an excellent host. He's like a grandfather to us. Have you a grandfather at home?'

I think I've surprised the NKVD man. He looks perplexed for a moment. Then annoyed.

'We're not here to discuss relatives with you,' he is terse, 'we're here to give orders. You've got to be at the station with all your bags in two hours. Promptly. Lateness will cost you!'

He is a nutcase! As if anyone would be stupid enough to stay in this place a minute longer.

We remain silent till the crunching sounds of their footsteps outside our window die down. Then all repressed excitement is let loose. Pavel and Agata can't stop talking and laughing and little Stella lets out sporadic squeals to be like them. Eva gives me a spontaneous hug and we hold each other with relief and renewed hope.

'At long last,' she says, 'at long last, we're a step closer to freedom.'

We finish breakfast and settle our account with our hosts. They are genuinely upset, Mrs. Stepanovichova wiping her eyes with the corner of her apron, and Mr. Stepanovich carrying Stella in his arms, stopping at the window to point out an abandoned stork nest on the top of a pole, at the far end of their garden.

'They come to nest every summer, you know,' he tells her, 'big white birds, with long red beaks. They'll miss you, my little doll.' Stella peers intently through the window, but there's nothing to see only the hard-frozen snow and black skeletons of the fruit trees.

We've got nothing much left to give our hosts. I find at the bottom of my suitcase an embroidered cushion cover and give it to Mrs. Stepanovichova. She runs her worn blackened finger over the raised poppies and daisies and smiles.

'Now it's always going to be summer in our home,' she says.

Eva scrapes a brown leather pouch from the bottom of her travel bag.

'For your tobacco,' she presents this to Mr. Stepanovich. He nods his approval and there's a shine in his deep-set eyes.

A short while later, hastened by bubbling excitement, we're packed and dressed in layers of clothing and ready to leave. Mr. Stepanovich brings out a large wooden box, places it on the floor and removes the lid so the children can look inside. There's a collection of wooden toys, hand-made and painted in colours that have once been bright: carved little dolls, animals, train locomotives, cars, boats and a set of cups and saucers.

'These are our children's toys. A keepsake. Our only link with them. A comfort when we've not seen them for a long time. Take one each. So you remember us.'

I'm deeply touched by his generosity but decline politely, so as not to upset him. Eva backs me up, but he insists. The children are bewitched.

164

There's no time for much thinking. We hurry them. Pavel chooses a boat of faded yellow and red, and Agata a black sleeping cat with white paws and a smug expression. Stella's choice is a miniature doll with moving arms and legs. She cries when the doll has to be packed away with the boat and the cat and has to be bribed with a morsel of bread dipped in sugar.

Last hugs with Mrs. Stepanovichova and we're off. Mr. Stepanovich has brought out his wooden sledge to transport our belongings and Stella amidst them to the station. Pavel and Agata help him to pull with much zeal. The temperature is minutely higher, releasing flurries of snow that float against our faces and settle on the ground covering our footprints.

CHAPTER 23

'Dear God! What have I done to be punished like this? Nastusha, it's driving me insane! I'll scalp myself if the pests don't leave me alone!'

'Then stop scratching, Eva. You're only making it worse!'

We can't stop the children scratching. Incredibly, they fall asleep, eventually, after we've bathed their raw, bleeding skin with the Siberian fir lotion, our very own product from the time in Svoboda camp. Stella usually wears herself out with crying, and it is a relief, especially to our less tolerant neighbours, when her whimpering subsides to even, somnolent breaths in Eva's rocking arms.

We then follow our own ritual: hats off, and working fast, for the cold is severe, we bathe our scalps and eyebrows against the lice. The temptation to scratch is irresistible, but once indulged, the itching intensifies into unbearable torment.

'Come on, then,' I tell Eva, 'sit up and I'll do your scalp again.'

It is totally dark in the stuffy cattle truck packed with sleeping bodies, the night thudding with the metallic rhythm of the wagon wheels, and punctuated with snores and sighs and sudden cries from dreams or nightmares. We keep the lotion bottle close to the pillow. My fingers find it automatically and remove the cork with care so it doesn't break. I moisten the corner of a small rag and find Eva's waiting hand to lead me to her uncovered head. She parts her hair in sections and I dab her scalp.

'Ooo... Ah... that's better. That's good. Oh, what a relief!' I sense her shivering with pleasure. Then we both hurry to put things away and to dive underneath the covers next to our sleeping children. We cuddle up close to generate and maintain body warmth through the freezing night.

Our transport is a cattle truck, just as twice before: four double bunk beds, a metre by two each, for eight families, an iron stove in the middle with a metal tube directing the smoke through a hole in the ceiling, and in one corner, an opening in the floor for toilet purposes. Florian and Dominik, two young brothers of fifteen and thirteen, have helped Eva and me to screen if off with an old blanket. All passenger trains have been requisitioned for military use.

Despite the now all too familiar discomforts, the numbing low temperatures requiring full dress at all times, the overcrowding, the dirt, the lice, the absence of washing facilities, the stench from the latrine corner, the constant self-restriction of food rations acquired back in Buzuluk, despite the nightmarish claustrophobia pressing down on us day and night, we keep reminding ourselves that this is the last leg of our journey to freedom.

Below our bunk, old Mrs. Severynova, doubled up under layers of clothing and a thick black shawl wound round her head and shoulders, ministers devotedly to her consumptive, constantly coughing daughter and a weakling of a grandson, shrunk like a yellow rubber doll inside all his clothes and covers. Every evening, with religious compulsion, she suggests that we all pray together. Most of us do, and then she intones a hymn. Singing soothes my nerves and lifts my spirit. We've been through all the repertoire of popular hymns several times over, but I never tire of *Wszystkie łąki umajone, góry doliny zielone*, that fills my mind with images of our green fields at home, of daisies and buttercups shining like precious stones, of poppies swaying in the Maytime breeze on their long, slender stalks.

Eva falters on the high notes at times and giggles, which in turn sets off Florian and Dominik chortling with amusement. Their mother, seemingly comatose with her back to the world, suddenly comes alive with a fiercely disciplinarian 'Behave yourselves!' For a while they sit very still dangling their legs over the edge of the bunk, but then their natural tendencies of youth take over. They tickle and pinch each other, or hide each other's things pretending it was someone else. Before the snorts and the shoves develop into a wrestling clinch, their mother lifts herself up and delivers each a slap on the back of the head. As soon as she is down again, they eye each other mischievously, rub the backs of their fur hats and whisper in practised unison: 'It didn't hurt at all!'

These snippets of normality keep my hopes alive.

Mr. Ostrovski lightens the boys' long, activity-deprived days with stories of legendary kings as well as lives of historical monarchs. The whole wagon becomes quiet when his hypnotic voice takes us into those other worlds of the Roman Empire or the Crusades or the French Revolution or Napoleon's exploits.

Florian's additional distraction is Helena, about his age, fourteen or so, I'd guess, who lives with her mother and two older sisters on the bunk below. Despite not even a centimetre of spare space for privacy, Florian and Helena manage to spend time together chatting about their schools and friends on the corner edge of Helena's bunk.

The remaining two bunks house a family of three elderly sisters with their three relatives, and two old couples with their relatives, who have all been strangers until fate forced them to become bed mates.

The three sisters' husbands have been imprisoned at their labour camp on some trumped up charge of conspiracy, when they disarmed a guard to stop him kicking a pregnant woman who lay helpless on the ground after collapsing from sheer exhaustion. The sisters have strong faith. Now, with the amnesty in action, they believe their husbands have already been freed and will catch up with them in Tashkent. I want to believe that too.

Mr. Ostrovski looks about sixty, but he may be much younger. He was a history teacher in Tarnopol before the Russians took him and his family away to some kolhoz near Archangelsk. He walks with a limp. His leg has been damaged in a tree-felling accident. He lives on the bunk opposite to ours, with his ill, hunched wife, his grey-faced daughter and two small grandsons, six and four, who remind me of Tomek and Daniel. Something twists inside me when I watch them, their eyes huge, oversized in their tiny, pinched faces, as they endure stoically the daily ritual of combing out the lice from their eyebrows and hair. Regularly our wagon becomes an animal cage, inside which we turn into monkeys, grooming each other, squeezing the lice dead between our blackened fingernails.

In his quiet manner Mr. Ostrovski commands respect and often diffuses potentially explosive situations. When tempers become frayed over ill-considered remarks, when quarrels erupt over a space on the stove, when the wait for the latrine corner is stretched to the limits of endurance, Mr. Ostrovski gets up from his bunk and stands close to the aggrieved adversaries.

'Patience, my dear people,' he speaks in his gentle mesmeric voice, 'soon, all this will be over. You've been through far worse and survived. What's another week or two?'

Strangely, no one challenges him. Only Mrs. Dubinska cries out sporadically against the prayers, against the singing, against Mr. Ostrovski's well-meant history lessons. The poor woman has been affected by the loss of her two sons at some labour camp beyond distant Omsk. Now she begs God several times every day to take her and her two little girls as well. She beats her chest or clutches her head in her hands and wails,

'End this torment, dear God! End their suffering and mine! Reunite our family in heaven!'

Her little daughters, perhaps five and seven, huddle together with their arms around each other and stare out of their grubby woollen wraps with eyes as blue as forget-me-nots.

Today, as every day, Mr. Ostrovski sits beside her and attempts to calm her down. He covers her hands with his and brings them down to her lap.

'Mrs. Dubinska, we're almost there. Soon we'll all be free. You'll feel better and your daughters will get everything they need. Any day now, it'll be all over. You'll see.'

Mrs. Dubinska frees her hands, beats her chest and there's a wild look in her eyes.

'You don't understand! No one understands! The pain, here, inside my chest. It won't go away. Day or night. I can't escape from it anywhere! Please God, hear me out! If you have any love for my children and me, take us! I beg you to take us!' She buries her face in her hands and rocks to and fro. Her daughters' eyes are wide with anxiety, their faces motionless like those of stone angels in a graveyard.

I feel her pain. We all carry pain in our hearts. Every single family in this carriage, in this whole train transporting hundreds, has lost a member, or several. It's the senselessness of Stalin's atrocious plan that hurts as much as the loss. Why? Why? The relentlessly burning question remains unanswered. And it will remain so. Together with the deepest and incurable feeling of this unforgiveable injustice.

At night, when for a few hours all ailments and sorrows are buried in all-soothing sleep around me, and only the beat of the wagon wheels is a reminder of the world outside our dark confined space, I open my mind and let sunshine in with my Dorotka's smiling face. The image is so clear, I feel the softness of her in my arms, the smell, the touch of her downy hair against my lips. My heart swells up as if it is going to burst. Then relief comes with unstoppable tears. And I thought I had cried them all. Compounding this grief is Julian's absence. There's a void beside me, shaped like him, that follows me around day and night.

I miss my Mama and Tato with the ache of a small child who pines after his parents all day when left in someone else's care. I'm a grown up woman, (am I really already twenty-eight ?!) but I long for the warmth of their arms around me, for the security of their firm embrace, for their soothing words.

My fingers wander gently to the forms of our sleeping children and Eva on the other side. Their presence is reassuring. They are my family now. I consider myself lucky, unlike Mrs. Dubinska who struggles on her own.

The iron-fortified sliding doors of our carriage are no longer locked. We can push them back ourselves whenever the train stops for water. Our Russian guards have dropped their aggressive manner towards us, but their armed, brooding presence does not inspire a rush of desire for a closer friendship. Now and again a Sergey or an Igor will rest against our open doorway when the train is stationary and with cigarette smoke screening his squinting eyes, he'll indulge in a nostalgic tale of his home town. We listen but no one initiates any conversation. Sometimes Mr. Ostrovski will point out the errors in a soldier's misguided concepts of our past.

'With respect, no, we're not criminals.'

'No, we're not *kulaks*, exploiting the working people. We are the working people ourselves.'

'We were just ordinary law-abiding citizens, just trying to make a decent living. For the sake of our families. For their future.' Mr. Ostrovski puts the record straight in his characteristic, gentle manner.

The soldier listens with astonishment at first, then shakes his head. His expression turns smug in his attempt to indoctrinate us.

'Aha! That's where you've got it all wrong! Allegiance to the State is paramount above everything else! To put yourself first is despicably self indulgent and contemptibly *bourgeois!'*

Occasionally we get glimpses of normality when a young soldier speaks of his mother and father, of the siblings left behind. He draws hard on his cigarette and exhales so long, as if his very soul is straining to return home.

I could never have imagined shedding tears for any of them, yet what happened at one of the stops shook deeply everyone of us, Russians and Poles alike.

The stops for water on this journey are usually longer though no less panicked. One cannot shake off fears accumulated over the last two years. For some strange reason, though nothing should surprise us in this country of weird anomalies, no warning is ever given of the train's imminent departure. As we stand in queues for whatever food is available, sometimes milk, or eggs, or *lepioszki,* or sunflower seeds, our trained ears always strain for the first hissing sound of the locomotive. There's a massive surge of movement, as the crowd rushes to climb aboard on time.

On this occasion in the second week of our journey, the train stopped at a small station past Orenburg. I was standing with our two buckets in the queue for the water, while Eva joined the queue for the milk and the flat bread. These are the left-overs from the bread dough, shaped into small balls, flattened and baked like pancakes. Suddenly, without any warning, the train jerked and began to move. My heart jumped to my throat, my throat screamed. Pavel. Agata. Stella. My screams drowned in the yelling and terror around me. Even the soldiers began to run along the platform with the train. Gun shots were fired in the air. The train stopped with a violent shudder, such that sent all the sliding doors back shut with deafening clangs. Eva, Mr. Ostrovski, Florian and Dominic, a few paces ahead of me, grabbed hold of the protruding iron handles and locks and struggling with all their might, pushed the door back. Inside our wagon, as I caught up with them with my two empty buckets, the children and the elderly were just picking themselves off the floor, where they were thrown down by the ferocious force of the sudden stop. There were cries of shock and pain, bumped heads and elbows, grazed knees and hands, but no broken bones. Amazing luck!

Pavel and Agata jumped down onto the platform and clung to me, their faces pale with terror. Eva picked up her crying Stella, cuddled her and rocked till the frightened little dot was appeased. Mr. Ostrovski jumped on inside the wagon and rushed to his family, miraculously still holding onto their bunk. His wife underneath her covers, had been pushed to the foot of their bunk bed, but the tight clump formed by his daughter and the two little boys stopped them all from falling off onto the floor. Even Mrs. Dubinska, so keen for her little girls to die along with her, embraced them and held them close to her with an expression on her haggard face that I read as relief.

Florian and Dominik's mother scolded them as if the incident had been their fault. Their faces, first frozen with shock now came to life with utter bewilderment, and something snapped inside me when Florian's lip quivered and tears welled up in his eyes.

'Mrs. Lekis!' I cried on impulse from the foot of the doorway. 'Be thankful that nothing's happened to your boys!'

Her head jerked in my direction. She looked surprised to be challenged. Perhaps no one ever did. Then a change came over her face, like sadness and loss of hope crumbling in defeat. She turned away her head to hide this, climbed back onto her bunk and lay down with her back to us.

In this short exchange and the general pandemonium still raging around us I wasn't aware at first of the commotion in the carriage next to ours. I felt Eva's tug at my sleeve,

'Nastusha, look! Something awful's happened!'

We moved along with our surrounding group and craned our necks to see better. The dreadful sight made me squirm with imagined pain.

On the edge of the open doorway in the neighbouring wagon a Russian soldier was lying down flat on his back, his legs pinned by the iron stove that had come loose and overturned with the train's powerful jerk. The lid had fallen off spilling the burning wood on top of the man's chest and head. He was screaming in agony.

'Shoot me! Shoot me! Somebody shoot me!'

Men and women closest to him were swiping off the burning debris as fast as they could with their gloved hands, while his comrades were wrestling with the weight of the hot iron stove. The moment his legs were released, they pulled him out and placed him on an army blanket spread out on the frozen platform. His screams died down, he lay limp and motionless. His clothes were burnt through, in places revealing raw flesh. His hands and face were blackened, but his hair was fortunately saved underneath his fur winter hat, now like a charcoal helmet..

The sight was unbearable. I shivered and turned Pavel and Agata away. We climbed back onto our carriage and from the open doorway, we watched his comrades carry him away in the blanket cradle. Soon after, the train driver, a tall stooping man with a dark expression, was escorted out of the station too.

'Where can they possibly take them, in this frozen desert?' I wondered aloud, turning to Eva, who climbed up beside me, with Stella in her arms. There was just a cluster of small buildings attached to the station.

'It all depends on how much they care for their own,' Eva said. 'He should be rushed to the nearest hospital.'

'On a horse and a sledge. If he's lucky,' I couldn't bear even to imagine his agony. And prayed he'd stay unconscious, unaware of his pain till he was given professional care.

'Will the driver get punished?' Pavel asked.

'He looked already condemned.' Eva said, 'It'll be the *kartzer* for him.'

'Did they punish the driver who left my Dad and my sisters behind?'

171

I hugged Pavel to me.

'Pavelek, those were stupid, cruel pranks. Lots of people got left behind. No one cared. Because they were our enemies then. Now, they're supposed to be our allies.' I didn't mention the numbers of women and girls crushed to death under the wagon wheels, as they crouched underneath the carriages to preserve just a little dignity when dealing with their natural needs.

'Now it's one of them,' Pavel said. 'How does that make them feel? Are they happy now?' Hints of anger and satisfaction modulated his voice.

'It's all so horrible! So sad!' Agata rubbed her eyes and leaned her head against my arm. I stroked her and Eva said,

'I think it's time for a story. A happy one. How about Pinocchio?'

There was time for a number of stories as we waited a few hours for the new driver to be brought from the nearest town, and for the stove to be fixed in the neighbouring wagon. There was time to replenish our buckets with fresh water, to buy *lepioszki* and a bag of sunflower seeds that kept the children busy all day, splitting them between their teeth to release the white, nutty kernels.

Undisputedly, the brightest day so far, like a white sail on a black ocean, is the morning we arrive in Aktyubinsk at the end of the second week of our journey. The concrete platform is lit with long shafts of white sunshine, blinding at first, when we push back the sliding door. The sight of the soldiers stops us in our tracks, but only for a moment. The soldiers are dressed in army-green British uniforms, long woollen overcoats and field-caps to match, each with a badge of the Polish crowned eagle. The white and red armbands make my heart soar and the greetings in our own Polish language confirm that we are among our own.

They stand along the platform in groups of three or four, with large, bulging sacks between them, and trolleys with steaming urns.

'Bring your mugs with you!' they call out, their faces beaming with the joy of heralding good news. 'There's coffee and bread for everyone!'

This is fantasy! My heart misses a beat, then it races like mad, and strange sounds squeak in my throat. Eva turns to me, a wide smile splitting her face, and there's a watery shine in her crystal blue eyes.

We're organised into queues, mugs are filled with steaming coffee and a whole loaf of white bread, real bread, is given out to every single passenger on our train. The Jewish and Ukrainian families travelling with us are treated alike.

We carry our precious drinks back to our bunk, Pavel and Agata theirs, and save our loaves of the real white bread in our bag of food provisions.

'One at a time,' Eva tells the children, as she divides the first loaf into five equal pieces.

The whole wagon becomes quiet in a dreamy kind of bliss, when people warm their hands around the aluminium mugs, inhale the intoxicating aroma and savour with deliberate restraint, the hot, dark, sweet, unexpected delight. Even little Stella smacks her lips with happiness at this newly discovered adult drink.

The bread is heavenly. My mind runs away with memories of my baking days at home.

We leave the children on the bunk to enjoy their breakfast then we climb down to join the groups on the platform talking to our soldiers. Excited voices, outbursts of laughter give the impression of festivity, as if we've already reached the end of our journey. Our Russian guards appear oblivious to the heightened spirits around them. In their usual brooding, muttering manner, they line the walls of the station buildings and inhale hard on their cigarettes between the gulps of coffee.

Eva and I corner a Polish soldier standing on his own.

'Please Sir,' she gives him a charming smile, 'I have a question for you. You haven't by any chance come across our husbands? Bzovski. That's mine. And my friend's is Kalinski. They're in the army too.'

The soldier is young and very thin, with a grey, pock-marked face, the skin under the protruding cheek bones sunken with the ravages of chronic hunger. His teeth are uneven, yet his smile is engaging when he looks into Eva's eyes. I note the flicker of interest and the prolonged gaze he gives her.

'I wish I could help,' he says, 'but I've not come across them. There's thousands of us now. Scattered all over this goddam country.' He smiles again. 'But don't worry. You'll all find each other in the end. We're all heading the same way. There's already a large military camp at Tashkent. And further in Guzar.' The names sound alien yet they fill me with hope of finding our boys.

'And when we get there, what's next?' I ask.

He shrugs.

'The ultimate destination is Persia. But getting out all the hundreds of thousands of our people is an enormous operation. Stalin's already digging his heels and going back on his promises of assisting with shelter and food. Never expected such a massive exodus. Must have been quite a shock to him that no one was eager to stay behind. There will be a lot of waiting around in the camps.'

'If we get coffee like this,' Eva grins, taking a gulp from her mug, 'I'd rather wait months in an army camp than a day in some *kolhoz* in Siberia.'

The look in the soldier's eyes becomes wistful.

'My father and my two brothers died in our *kolhoz* near Jarensk. They were made to build embankments for a railway track. It was back breaking work. Just a pickaxe and a wheelbarrow for tools. Nothing can be as bad as that again. I hope.' His gaze softens as he adds, 'I've seen things improve. We'll be moving out of here soon. Who knows, we may yet meet again in the south.'

I take a gulp of my precious coffee and nod.

'Perhaps in some exotic place?' I try to lighten the conversation.

He smiles and adds,

'And after that, when all our wanderings are over, when the war is finished and we all return home, I invite you girls to visit me in Pacykov, near Dolina.'

'Well, blow me down!' I exclaim, 'that's only a stone's throw away from where we live!'

'And where's that?'

'Old Mizun,' Eva laughs.

His moment of astonishment melts in a big grin. He embraces us both and holds us close.

'Then you're just like family!'

When he walks away, it feels indeed like letting my brother go.

In the third week of our journey, 15th January 1942, our train takes us through Aralsk port on the Aralsk Sea. We glimpse the water, navy dark near the docks, grading to shimmering light grey where it meets the horizon. Large cargo boats and steamers tower over the rectangular blocks of port offices and warehouses. We don't stop. Even the sidelines are busy with goods trains like ours, arriving, unloading, loading and departing locked and sealed.

Our doors are unlocked and left open in the daytime hours, for in the past few days there has been a remarkable change in the temperatures. The frozen plains have receded into the distance behind us, giving way to yellow grassy land, with scattered little shrubs appearing, then clumps of trees, more frequent and extensive as our train moved south into a green woodland belt. Rectangular houses, with small dark windows like closed eyes, indicated discreetly hidden lives going on, in this alien place, perhaps as normal as ours have been, it seems like centuries ago.

I delight in the pleasure of fresh air in my lungs, of warm breezes on my face and bared arms as I close my eyes against the fleeting sunrays and dream of the end of this journey, of the end of the war, of our reunion with all our loved ones. Our winter clothing is folded away, our stockings rolled down, our sleeves rolled up. The children feel happier and more agile now free of restraints and the weight of coats and furs and shawls and winter boots. In our confined space it is hard to devise imaginative physical tasks for them, but Pavel and Agata always find a way of making the ordinary exciting. They time each other standing on one leg, then on the other. Handstands are more demanding and require assistance to achieve a vertical position in the narrow passage between the bunks. Mr. Ostrovski's grandsons and our little Stella watch and want to copy. Pavel and Agata gladly assist them, much to their delight with cries of 'Again! And again!' Even Mrs. Severynova's sickly grandson, discards his covers and sits up to watch.

Florian and Dominik and Helena consider themselves too grown up for such games. They spend hours with Mr. Ostrovski devising crosswords or

174

number puzzles. Mrs. Dubinska's little girls prefer to stand by and watch, always holding hands, always with wary expressions, as if ready to retreat at any time. Their matted hair is crawling with lice. We all have them. The degree of infestation depends on the time spent grooming. Mrs. Dubinska appears oblivious to her daughters' plight, as she invokes God's mercy to take her and her little girls to heaven.

'What we need is a good soak and scrub, to drown the pests,' Eva repeats daily when we tend to our children's hair, then our own.

It seems that Providence is more kindly disposed to her prayers, than to Mrs. Dubinska's heart-rending cries.

Soon after leaving Kamyslybas station, where we've replenished our water supplies and bought an egg each, and, joy of joys, a marrow, our train enters a dense woodland area and slows down to a halt. It is mid-morning, the sunlight, filtered through the leafy canopy of oaks and elms and white ashes, falls in fragmented patches on the ground overgrown with ferns.

Our first reaction is that of puzzlement, then unease, reflected in the quick glances passed around. Deep forests, miles away from civilization, have retained their unpleasant connotations in our vigilant minds.

'I'll go and find out,' I tell Eva, as I climb down from our high bunk. I join Mr. Ostrovski at the open entrance to our wagon and we look out. Hundreds of heads poke out from the open doors. The soldiers spill out from their two carriages, at both ends of the train, and run along shouting something. When Igor, our guard reaches us, Mr. Ostrovski forestalls him with questions.

'What's happening? Why have we stopped?'

The guard's face remains officious.

'To have a wash. There's a lake on the other side of this line. You can't see it from here.'

It takes a moment to absorb this simple information. It's so bizarre. Is this genuine? Is this some cruel, cynical trick?

'I don't understand,' Mr. Ostrovski frowns, 'you've especially stopped this train for us?'

'For ourselves too,' the guard's serious expression relaxes, 'it's a good opportunity. We all need a wash.'

'For how long?' Mr. Ostrovski sounds terse. 'Can you promise the train won't suddenly move off leaving half of us behind in this jungle miles away from the nearest town?'

The young man shakes his head.

'You needn't worry. I promise. I keep an eye on you lot. Besides, the train driver needs to come with us. We'll be helping him to fill the engine's water tank.'

'So, how long exactly have we got?' Mr. Ostrovski perseveres.

'At least two hours. The train won't move off till we've checked everyone's on board.'

We should feel assured, but I'm still anxious when we repeat the soldier's message to the people in our wagon. Florian and Dominik's morose mother turns over to face the wall and does not want to leave her bunk. Mrs. Dubinska deep in her prayers remains oblivious to this incredibly fortunate opportunity to rid herself and her girls of lice. It is only when I approach her and offer to take them with us, that her motherly possessiveness wakes up and ignites her resolve.

'I'll bathe them myself!' she snaps.

Mr. Ostrovski stands in the middle of our confined central space and announces,

'Dear people! I think we should take this chance. I'll keep an eye on things. I shall stick around with the guards, and especially the train driver, to make sure there's no trickery!'

Florian and Dominic jump to his side, and before their mother can protest, Florian stops her with, 'Mama! You can't bathe with us anyway! We're going with the men!'

We collect what clean rags and worn towels we still posses, and our bundles to wash, and help each other to climb over and under the connecting metal buffers and chains between the wagons. Hundreds of people spill out and do the same thing.

The view on the other side is indeed wonderful. The lake curves close to the railway line with a wide shingly beach, overlooked by a dense forest of a variety of trees. In the distance, where the lake's shimmering surface touches the sky, it's like a gateway to a free world awaiting our arrival.

The crowd naturally forms itself into groups of men and women, symbolically maintaining their dignity. Women undress to their threadbare underwear, men to the wispy remnants of their underpants and young children to their knickers, if they still have any. When the first throes of splashing and plunging into water are satisfied amidst shouts of sheer joy, and our bodies get attuned to the cooling temperature, everyone gets down to the serious business of scrubbing lice off their bodies. The result is exhilarating: gleaming hair and freshness all over, especially in all the sweat prone nooks and crannies.

Before drying ourselves, Eva and I dry and dress the children first, and sit them down on the edge of the beach on a soft mound of ferns with instructions to wait till we've washed a few smalls. Their cheeks are shiny, their sores less apparent, their hair fluffing out as it dries, little Stella's, like a puff ball.

Eva and I have tied back our hair, hers sleek and shining and mine already escaping in drying tendrils around my face. Igor, our guard, walks up to us, himself now bathed and dressed in his stale smelling uniform and remarks,

'See? I told you there was nothing to worry about!'

That's disputable but, nevertheless, I treat him to a smile and to a word of praise.

'This was an excellent idea. Was it yours?'

'No,' he smiles for the first time ever, and I discover an acceptable young man underneath the usually worn mask of officialdom. 'Not me personally,' he explains, 'we all needed a good soak. Our uniforms are too heavy for this climate. It gets unbearable in the daytime.'

'Why don't you take them off then?'

'What?' He reacts as if I've blasphemed. 'We're only allowed that at night time.'

His eyes wander to Eva's hair, like pale gold in the sun. She is unaware of his interest, as she shakes out into shape the items we've just washed and wrung.

'Pity…' he says.

She stops and turns her crystal blue eyes at him.

'Pity what?'

'We could be friends…' he bends his head to one side.

She folds the wet garments into a pile, straightens and fixes him with a stare. He doesn't lower his gaze, which becomes serious, intense.

'We are allies,' she says with some emphasis, 'and that's a good thing. Isn't it?'

He nods, sighs and for a moment looks away, then brings his gaze back on to her.

'You see… I haven't got much time. We're only going with you as far as Kzyl-Orda. You'll get different guards from then on. When I go back, I'm due some leave. I'll go home. I've been watching you for a long time. I want you to come back with me, *gaspasha* Bzovska.'

We both stare at him. Is he serious? I glance at Eva. She licks her lips and swallows hard. Hundreds of responses must cross her mind, like mine. Friend? Ally? God, how does one get out of this hole? Without offending his pride. No one seeks to offend them now. Not when we're so close to freedom.

'Sir,' she puts up a barrier of formality, 'thank you sincerely for your kind invitation…'

He interrupts her, with sure victory in his smug expression.

'They'd love you, *gaspasha* Bzovska! I'm certain of that! No girl in our town has eyes like yours! Or hair that colour! I'd be the envy of all my chums!'

Eva lifts her hand in a sign to stop him,

'No Sir, please! Please, please, listen! I'm very honoured, but look! I've got a child, I've got a husband too!'

He throws little Stella a quick glance and smiles.

'No problem that! She's a very pretty child. Just like you. I'll take care of her too.'

His voice is persuasive, his eyes alive with expectation.

'My husband will never allow it!' There's anger and desperation in Eva's tone which he doesn't seem to notice.

'Allow it?' he snorts. 'And where is he now to have any say?'

I look around for someone to come to our rescue, but Mr. Ostrovski is a long way off keeping watch over the other guards and the train driver, and the groups closer to us are too engrossed in their own hurried activities of bathing and washing to take any notice of this little drama.

'Look Sir!' I exclaim, having no idea what to say next. Then miraculously words rush out of my lips, as if prompted from above. 'My friend is not as well as she looks. She has dormant tuberculosis that flares up when you least expect it!'

He takes an instinctive step back, stares at me then shakes his head.

'You're kidding me!'

Eva clutches her blouse at the neck, and with her other hand suppresses a cough. I rub her between her shoulder blades.

'You don't have to believe me,' I tell him, 'but it won't be much fun when you start coughing up blood!'

He remains a moment longer, unsure.

'I'll be watching you two,' he says, an unpleasant edge to his voice, 'I'll find out if you're telling lies.'

We keep up the pretence till he walks away towards his comrades.

'Well, I never! The cheeky sod!' Eva's words are like daggers chasing his retreating back. Then she looks at me. 'What's dormant tuberculosis?'

We both burst out laughing.

We carry the damp laundry towards our children, who are sitting obediently on the soft green edge of the ferns. They're talking to Mrs. Dubinska's little girls, standing over them. There's something inexplicably strange in their appearance. I'm suddenly filled with unease. Their wet hair is dripping and their saturated dresses appear to weigh down their skinny little frames.

'Where's your Mama?' I ask, depositing the laundry on the grass.

The older one's huge eyes look in the direction, opposite to where most of the bathers are grouped, to a part of the beach that curves away into the distance, with just clumps of grass like giant brushes growing out of the shingle.

'Show me,' I tell her, taking her hand. Her younger sister hangs onto her other side. Pavel and Agata get up to come with us, but Eva requests them to wait a little longer and mind little Stella and the clean laundry. They look disappointed.

'It'll be quicker, Pavel, than a whole army of us going. We'll be back in a tick.'

We rush, Eva and I with the little girls between us. I suppose it's become a habit, the surfacing anxiety the moment something's not right. The beach is deserted on this side, the rustling of the wind in the crowns of the pines has a menacing note to it, and even the tall reeds surrounding the wooden promontory, sway mysteriously as if pushed by a ghostly hand.

Then I see it. Eva sees it too.

'Looks like wet rags,' she tries to sound casual.

I know it's the girls' mother.

We leave them well back from the water's edge before we wade in. As fast as we can.

'Dear God! Sweet Jesus! Holy Mary! Have mercy!' Eva mutters feverishly. The water's only up to our armpits when we reach her, but shallow water can be lethal too. She lies face down, her arms floating, her grey dress forming flat pockets of air, like deflating balloons.

'Eva, take the girls back, and get help! I'll stay here!' Words fall from my lips.

She doesn't argue, just gives me a look that says, it's too late.

The moment their backs are turned I grab hold of Mrs. Dubinska, turn her over, so that her face is above the surface and pull her along, the buoyancy of the lapping water assisting me in this task. I brace myself against the last pull when we reach the edge. But she is as light as wood shavings, her flesh wasted to a thin layer over her bones. One strong tug and I lay her down on the pebbly ground. Her eyes are closed, her skin bluish-pale, her lips parted, with water spilling out. Without thinking, I turn her over onto her stomach and with all my strength I begin to press down on her back. The ejected water runs out to a trickle. Nothing happens. Not a cough. Not a twitch. What was I hoping for? A miracle?

I turn her over on her back, arrange and cross her hands on her chest, brush strands of hair away from her face, pull and smooth down the wet grey dress. She is still. Peaceful. She has outwitted God.

CHAPTER 24

We buried Mrs. Dubinska together with five elderly people, who ran out of time and strength to reach the next stop on our journey to freedom. We've had to part with them in a remote forest by the Aralsk Sea, marking their graves with roughly made crosses, carving their names with pen knives for posterity. Will anyone come this way again? Find them? Leave flowers on their graves? Say a prayer? My heart is heavy. I make myself think of a bright Spring day, of trees covered in pink and white blossom, of petals falling like pure snow. I imagine my Dorotka's resting place to be under a flowering cherry tree, not far away from caring people who remember to lay flowers on her grave.

Irenka and Terenia, Mrs. Dubinska's little daughters, have increased our assorted family. Pavel and Agata take their role of older siblings seriously, but all their attempts at eliciting the tiniest sparkle of response from the two girls fail disappointingly. Little Stella hugs them when we all sit together on our high bunk, but they shrug her off as if she were a pest. With changeless set expressions on their small thin faces they watch Pavel's dexterous tricks with his fingers and a piece of string. Agata tells them stories, humour-spiced versions of Snow-White or Cinderella to make them laugh. Pavel hoots on cue, my serious little boy, Stella squeals, but they remain quiet, holding hands inseparably, even when visiting the latrine corner.

Eva and I cut off their matted, lice infested curls on that fateful day, before scrubbing them clean. Their laundered dresses took a while to dry, and while they waited, wrapped in sheets, on our high bunk where the warmest air gathers close to the ceiling, I explained and showed them the tufts, as compounded as felt, with lice and dirt. Their stares were blank, their little bodies unnaturally still, as if indifference was the only safe place left them.

They live and sleep with us now on our bunk. Their vacated bunk has been eagerly requisitioned by the elderly sisters' relatives and those of the other two couples. At night time, after prayers, we settle our little brood to sleep, with cuddles and a story. I sense just an inkling of acceptance from Irenka and Terenia when they linger on my lap and don't fight off my arms from around their bodies. It's like embracing two fragile sparrows.

People are generous in our wagon. At each stop a rouble or two is donated to buy food for our little charges. Mr. Ostrovski believes there will be homes set up for orphans like Irenka and Terenia; God knows, there must be hundreds of them. I pray every night that their future will bring them better things than their short past has subjected them to.

We've not had a good wash since leaving the lake close to the Aralsk Sea. Just faces and hands at the taps on our stops. All the usual discomforts are our constant companions: the cramped space, the hard bunks, the disgusting latrine, the dirt, the lice, the hot stuffy air at night time. And hunger. Hunger never leaves us. The small provisions of whatever is available at the remote, third rate stations, just fool our stomachs and barely keep us going to the next meal, which is never a meal at all. Just another rationed piece of dry bread or a spoonful of *kasza* or a piece of hard cheese or the odd carrot or sometimes, when we're in luck, a potato.

Every night when I close my eyes, I travel home to my Mama and Tato, to the family table in their kitchen, laden with Mama's cooked food. My longing is so painful it brings tears to my eyes. It baffles me how the children in our wagon accept and bear this injustice meted out to them so senselessly, and can be appeased with a handful of sun-flower seeds. Every night, one of ours, or two, or sometimes all five, suffer with nightmares and wake up shouting for their Mamas. When they are soothed and settled and asleep again Eva whispers to me,

'I want my Mama too.' And I know by the way she extends her arm over the sleeping children to touch my hand, that her longing for her family is as overwhelming as mine.

She is dreading the arrival in Kzyl-Orda. The place is getting closer each day, the diminishing distance regularly calculated by Mr. Ostrovski, whom we've let in on the secret of Igor's infatuation with Eva's Nordic looks. Eva keeps well away from the open doorway at stops, but her undeterred suitor hangs around with a smoking cigarette and shoots impatient glances at our bunk. She gives regular performances of consumptive coughing, sometimes dashing behind the latrine screen to retch, sending waves of alarm throughout the wagon.

'It's not catching,' I appease the concerned who look out from their bunks, 'it's just something she gets now and again.'

'It seems like every stop. It's worrying and off-putting!' Florian and Dominik's mother complains.

'I promise,' I make my tone persuasive, 'once we get past Kzyl-Orda, the climate will change and this illness will pass.'

Florian and Dominik's mother grunts and mutters.

'It would be best if she changed wagons. We don't need an epidemic here!'

'No fear of that!' Mr. Ostrovski assures her, and later, when the train is on the move again and the thudding of the wheels muffles the sounds of voices, he warns Eva.

181

'Igor's no fool, Eva. Just stay in bed when we arrive in Kzyl-Orda. I'll think of an illness for you. Something simple. Like diarrhoea. Puts everyone off.' His brief smile is mischievous. 'Another deterrent is connections. Preferably with some high ranking official.'

We look at him with interest.

'How will you manage that?' Eva asks.

Mr. Ostrovski taps his nose.

'I've got an idea or two.'

I wish to share his optimism, but all I feel is deep unease.

We arrive in Kzyl-Orda on a bright morning. The long concrete platform stretches against a background of rectangular buildings, gangways, doors and tall dark windows. A line of Russian soldiers with their rucksacks at their feet is already waiting, our next lot of guards.

There is all the noise of the usual commotion, people leaving the train with their buckets for water, vendors running up with their goods and edibles for sale. They are Khazaks, their language is alien, their Mongolian features inscrutable to European eyes, so when they insist on bartering in the simple transaction of money for food, the whole thing becomes a nightmare. I feel frustrated and aggrieved at the thought of being constantly cheated out of the dwindling money we so carefully save.

This time the station is an even more clamorous place than usual with the two lots of guards changing and exchanging news, reports and instructions. I stand at the open wagon door and wait for Mr. Ostrovski to return with his buckets of water, before I go with mine. I look around. All our guards, with their rucksacks thrown over their shoulders are eagerly heading towards the exit. I spot Igor, with his comrade approaching our way. There's an air of insolent self-confidence in the way he swaggers and jokes loudly with his companion. They dump their rucksacks just inside our open threshold, jump up and, bypassing me, head straight for our bunk.

Old Mrs. Severynova, our choir leader, leans out from the bunk below ours, and with a pointedly disapproving expression asks them outright, what is their business here?

'Nothing to do with you,' Igor replies curtly and proceeds to shake Eva's shoulder at his face level. She's under covers with her back to him, surrounded by our children, who become quiet and very still, their eyes wide with a fixed gaze on his movements. Eva shakes off his hand and tightens her covers around her.

Igor looks at his friend as if to say, see what I have to deal with?

'Bad mistake, *gaspasha* Bzovska,' he says, and his expression becomes unpleasant, 'My patience's run out. Stop playing games and get up!'

The sharpness of his voice brings a sudden flashback. The night of our arrest. I feel a chill, though it's hot in our wagon. The children instinctively huddle together and there's fear in their eyes.

182

I've got to do something. I make a swift step towards them glancing back for a glimpse of Mr. Ostrovski in the crowd. I blurt out. 'She's ill!' They turn and look at me, like predators playing with their prey.

'Ill?' Igor laughs in my face, 'I know all your tricks!'

I look back. There's no one to help me. Only the sick and the young children left behind during the stop. Desperation drives me to more lies.

'She's been up all night with diarrhoea,' I cry, 'she's totally washed out. She can hardly stand up. What do you propose to do? Drag her out and pull her behind you? Like a sack? We're allies, for God's sake!' My voice is shaky with desperation.

His comrade gives me a smirky grin.

'There's no God,' he corrects me, 'and yes, we are allies, so what's the big problem? Your friend should feel honoured to be singled out and given the chance to remain in this country.'

God, give me strength! I sense a presence behind me and hear Mr. Ostrovski's steady but commanding voice.

'I suggest we settle this problem by calling the director of this station.'

Igor pulls himself up and stretches out his shoulders.

'He's got no authority over us.'

Mr. Ostrovski gives him a polite smile.

'But Colonel Zaborsky has.'

Igor and his comrade look at each other and shrug.

'Who's Colonel Zaborsky?' Igor asks.

'Don't you know?' Mr. Ostrovski's tone suggests his superior stance in this matter. 'He's one of the most senior commanders in Buzuluk. You should know him.'

They both shake their heads, but there's a change in their manner, suddenly less certain.

'So, what about him?' Igor challenges.

'I got to know him very well. I tutored his two boys before their exams. My voluntary work was very much appreciated.' Mr. Ostrovski pauses, for effect, I guess. 'He gave me his word he'd help if ever I had difficulties on my journey. I can ask the station director to get in touch with Colonel Zaborsky. You know how it is... do you really want a welcome party waiting for you when you arrive home on your leave..?' Mr. Ostrovski's hint is unambiguous.

Igor's face becomes purple at the audacity of this threat. In his country, any one at any time can be sent down on the flimsiest of charges. Any threat, gallingly even from a Pole, if well connected, cannot be ignored.

But he is not ready to give up. He yells at Mr. Ostrovski.

'Shut your gob, you puny old geezer! Look at you! And look at me! And tell me who is in charge here?' And he is our ally.

For a moment I get the plunging, drowning feeling that all is lost. Then something happens behind Igor's back. Eva lifts herself up in a fit of coughing. There's a pause, then her shoulders heave with another attack, as she presses a rag to her mouth. Igor turns to face her. Her whole body is shaken so violently, that her hand with the rag falls away from her mouth. We all gasp in horror. There's blood down the front of her dress and with every cough a spatter of blood is projected from her mouth. Igor, standing closest to her, gets the full impact on his face and his shoulders. He jumps back as if touched by a live wire. He yells at her,

'You bitch! You dirty bitch!' and frantically wipes his face with the sleeves of his uniform. He and his accomplice run with such haste, it's dizzying to watch. I turn my attention to Eva, fear for her filling me with panic. Stella lets out a wail.

'Pavel! Agata! Take care of her!'

I wipe Eva's mouth. 'Dear God Eva,' I mutter, 'what's happened to you? Serves us right for tempting Providence.'

Eva grasps my hands and makes me stop. Thank God, her coughing fit is gone.

'Nastusha! Calm down!' she holds me still, 'there's nothing wrong with me!'

'But the blood…?'

She unwraps the rag on her hand. There's a deep gash in her palm.

'What is this?' I exclaim in renewed horror.

'Sharp scissors. Needs must.'

All of a sudden I feel sick. Objects blur and fade away and darkness engulfs me.

When I open my eyes I'm sitting on the wagon floor, propped up against a bunk. Pavel and Agata are peering down into my eyes, fright and tears evident in theirs. Even Irenka and Terenia, forever holding hands, have placed themselves close to me, as if keeping guard. Things inside my head give me a floating feeling as I turn to Eva on one side, and then Mr. Ostrovski on the other.

'You've really got us worried,' Eva strokes my hand. Everything comes back. Vaguely at first, then clear. Her words are suddenly very funny.

'You're a fine one to talk!'

Mr. Ostrovski's voice is full of concern.

'You've nothing to worry about. I've organised Florian and Dominic to fetch you the water, and I can go back to get some food.'

Dear Mr. Ostrovski. He's like my own Tato. I choke back the urge to howl.

'Thank you,' I manage, then louder, 'you're very kind. But no, you've got your own family to worry about. Eva and I are as strong as horses, aren't we?' I cast her a glance and force a grin. 'After this little drama, bartering with the Kazakhs will be like child's play!'

CHAPTER 25

I feel it. We all feel it. The anticipation, the excitement of getting closer to Tashkent.

'Is it far yet?' Pavel and Agata keep asking with monotonous frequency.

'Oh, to leave this black hole!' Eva sighs, every time the door of our wagon is pulled shut for the night. The self-inflicted wound in her left palm has closed up, but I don't like the look of the red puffiness around it.

'Yes,' I exhale with longing, as we lie back on the bunk next to the children, and I stare up into the blackness and feel the sway of the rolling wheels, 'to get back to normal life! And you need to see a doctor with that hand of yours!'

'Nah! I won't die of it!' She pretends it's nothing, but I know it hurts her, the way she winces and pulls it away when Stella throws herself at her. She keeps it bandaged in a clean old rag and often rests it against her chest.

'I'll take you to the doctor myself!' I'm adamant. The truth is the thought of Eva becoming ill scares me. How would I cope without her support?

'Nastusha, you worry too much! Everything is going to be fine! Do you know what I'm dreaming of?' she pauses, 'A little tent all to ourselves. And fresh air. And decent food. Nastusha, can you imagine good, wholesome, decent food after all this time?'

'There's bound to be good food,' I assure her, touched by her optimism. 'We'll be safe. Close to the army camp. And just imagine if Julian and Henryk are there too!'

'And my Tato,' Agata adds.

'And your Tato too,' I stroke her head in the dark.

'Won't it be the greatest miracle if my Tato has caught up with the army by now!' Pavel's voice is excited, 'Aniela won't recognise me. And my little Marysia won't know me at all!'

I feel a stab in my heart. I want his wish to come true, but there are no miracles that bring dead people back. Only in the Bible. Only if you're Lazarus. Or Christ.

'Pavelek, we'll just have to wait and see,' I tell this poor child, who has endured more adversities than Job, 'but when we all meet together, I promise, it'll be like a party. Uncle Julian will be so proud of you! And you Agatka, I'll tell your Tato, he's got the best daughter in the world!'

They giggle in the dark, before settling down to sleep.

It seems like years since we've last seen our boys in Buzuluk, though it's only been five weeks, but even a few hours in these squalid conditions can seem like a life punishment.

We've spent nights in sidings of large city stations hidden from view; we've been left, as if forgotten, in remote little stops on the wide, open steppe, above which the star studded indigo sky was as vast as the universe, and the distant howling of hyenas was the only sign that life existed beyond our stationary train. Men would come out of the wagons and make fires with the *kolyuchki*, strange balls of tangled dried vegetation, that rolled eerily about the expanse of the empty land, as if propelled by some inexplicable energy of their own.

In the quiet of those nights, murmuring with subdued reminiscing voices recounting previous lives, the sight of hands warming over the open fires and the orange glow on the pensive faces, somehow filled me with hope and a feeling that freedom was almost within our reach.

The changing landscape of Kazakhstan, as we travelled south, buoyed my spirits even more, with sights reminiscent of our land at home: the greenery, sparse at first, expanding into woodland areas, then broken by arable land, rich with fields of sunflowers, pumpkins and linseed. We passed farm settlements and herds of cows and sheep shepherded to pastures. The cotton fields, like white blankets spread over the land were a novelty, as were the rice fields, with their surrounding irrigation trenches shining blue underneath the clear sky.

'It's like coming back to life,' Eva sounded happy.

'Real life, Eva. Soon we'll be really free.'

At the stations, the products for sale were more varied now: dried fruit, nuts, melons, packets of rice, lentils or wheat grain. However, our daily-shrinking shared purse made our choices ever more difficult. Often, the much awaited melon, our children's desire, had to be forsaken for the more nutritious grain.

1st February 1942. The day has arrived. We are approaching the city of Tashkent. The sprawling suburbs are a patchwork of orchards with orange, lemon and apricot trees, separated by copses of firs and cypresses and oases of palms. Further, we glimpse tall slender towers, minarets, blue and gold copulas crowning old ornate buildings, with arched gateways and elongated windows shaped like praying hands. It is all so different from our cities at home and I wonder what it would be like to explore the streets of this ancient city, but my only wish now is to be taken off this train, transported to the camp, given food and shelter and a cleansing bath.

There's no packing to do; we've lived out of bags for the past five weeks. Just our bedding to fold and leave the bunk clear.

The young ones, Florian, Dominik and Helena, have been standing at the open door for the last hour. Their talk is excited despite the boys' mother's disgruntled remarks being thrown their way. Pavel and Agata lean out of our bunk and point out to Stella buildings and bridges that float by with the unhurried rhythm of our train. Irenka and Terenia sit very still together, holding hands, as always.

Eva, with her bandaged hand, and I help old Mrs. Sverynova below us, to gather her few things together as she toils around her ailing daughter and grandson, both racked with a dry hacking cough and drained of all energy. We prop them up against their ready bundles and turn to Mr. Ostrovski's wife and daughter Ella. Her face is ashen with the effort of looking after her mother, whose every movement requires assistance. Mr. Ostrovski keeps the two little boys out of the way, at the end of their bunk, close to the open door, and tells them of all the wonderful things they'll be doing when they start school. They listen with parted lips, swallowing his every word.

In the other half of the wagon, the old sisters and the old couples and their assorted relatives are busy too, collecting their stuff together as they get ready to disembark.

Finally, the station comes to view, the platform, the buildings, the sights we've seen so many times before in their varying sizes and states. Soldiers are already waiting, mainly in Russian uniform, but Polish soldiers too, conspicuous in their British uniforms with the crowned eagle badges on their caps and white and red armbands. Some are accompanied by nuns. Their white starched cornettes look like dove wings spread protectively above them. The unexpected sight of them is comforting with its hidden promise of things being organised for our arrival. The youngsters wave to them while the train slows down to a halt.

The Russian soldiers run towards us with arms raised high and shouts of: '*Zhda*! Wait! Stop!'

There's a rumble of puzzlement throughout the wagon, as people are already up with their belongings and waiting to leave. I suppress rising anxiety.

'What is it this time?' Eva nudges me.

Mr. Ostrovski gets up and stands on the threshold of the open doorway. 'What's happening?' he asks.

By now, the Polish soldier and the nun closest to our carriage, manage to get through the groups of other travellers on the platform. The soldier looks up and explains.

'There's a change of plans. You've got to remain on the train. We're only here to collect the orphans'

It takes a moment to absorb his words. Pavel and Agata cling to me.

'We are not orphans, are we?' Two little bodies press on my other side. Irenka and Terenia.

'But we've been promised a break in Tashkent!' Mr. Ostrovski recovers first and remonstrates. 'We've spent five weeks on this train!'

'So have the others. Some longer than that.' The soldier spreads his hands helplessly. 'We've got thousands of people at the camp. Thousands too many. There's an epidemic of typhoid. We can barely cope. We've had to send away trainloads of people already. But you're all heading in the same direction. Krasnovodsk port. There will be other camps on the way, where room will be found for you.'

There are noises of anger and despair around me. I feel stunned.

'Please, Mr. Soldier,' Mr. Ostrovski pleads, 'have mercy on us!'

The soldier looks genuinely distressed.

'It's very hard for me to be the messenger of bad news. But I and Sister Franciszka have been given orders. We've got a duty to follow them.'

They climb up inside our wagon and look around, the nun with a clipboard in her hands.

'Listen,' the soldier says, 'it's not all bad news, I promise. You'll be safer in the next camp, before more crowds arrive.'

'And where will that be?' Mr. Ostrovski's face looks very tired.

'There will be several on the way. Samarkand, Guzar, Bukhara and others.'

'So why are you taking the orphans now?'

'Because,' the nun steps in, her emaciated face attesting to her own experiences, 'we've set up a separate home and hospital for the children who have lost their parents. There's hundreds of them. But they'll get the best that we can provide in our present circumstances. Everything will improve once we're out of this country.' She turns to the teenage boys and girls, 'There will be schools set up for young people like you. General Anders is working very hard to set all wheels in motion. But with thousands of us, refugees, it'll take a little while to organise and establish. I've got instructions to take names of all children present here, so we have a record.'

She speaks to the older children first, taking down their particulars; she writes down the names of Mr. Ostrovski's grandsons, then Mrs. Severynova's little boy, then it's our turn.

No problem with Eva and Stella. I explain about Pavel and Agata. She writes it all down then speaks to them.

'We can provide food and clothes for you. You'll be in a safe, clean place. And there's a lovely hospital for ill children with kind and caring people.'

Their response is to cling even harder to my arms.

'Please, Auntie Nastusha, don't let them take us away!' Pavel's on the brink of crying.

This is torture for me.

'Sister,' my voice is unsteady, 'your offer is tempting beyond endurance. But I made a promise to the fathers of these children, that I'd look after them, till they came back.'

The nun's gaze travels over Pavel and Agata. They shrink back and shake their heads and grip my arm harder. She nods then peers down at Irenka and Terenia, half hiding between me and the bunk.

It is hard to guess if they are aware of what's happening. They've not spoken a word since their mother's death. I give Sister Franciszka an account of the recent tragedy. She sighs in sympathy and bends down to them,

'Irenka and Terenia. What lovely names! Will you come with me?'

As expected they show no reaction, even when the nun's cornette threatens to poke Irenka's eye. I feel like a traitor, when I step aside to allow the nun to get closer. Terrible sadness grips me. I crouch down to their level and give them each a hug.

'You'll love the new place,' I explain, 'it won't be like this dirty, smelly train. You'll get good food, a bath and clean new clothes. Won't that be just wonderful?'

They stare at me with their wide eyes and when the nun takes Irenka by the hand, they allow themselves to be led away by complete strangers. The sight of them walking away, two little girls in shabby long dresses, their matted hair sticking out stiffly, their necks from the back like fragile stems of wine glasses, so vulnerable, is more than I can bear. Something breaks down inside me. I sit down on the edge of Mr. Ostrovski's bunk and bury my face in my hands. I stifle my sobs, but I can't stop the flow of tears. I feel Pavel and Agata lean against me, their cheeks pressing against my temples, their hands rubbing my shoulders.

'Please don't cry, Auntie Nastusha, please don't cry...' they plead. I hear Mr. Ostrovski's gentle voice.

'Your auntie will be all right in a minute. Just give her some time.'

The wave of grief recedes, I wipe my eyes and find Eva sitting beside me.

'Nastusha, don't distress yourself so!' She pushes a lock of my hair behind my ear, 'We've done everything we possibly could. We've filled the gap for them, the poor little chicks, between losing their Mama and now. They'll have a better life from now on. Don't be sad, Nastusha, be happy for them.'

I contemplate her words. She is right, of course. I just wish my heart wouldn't hurt so.

CHAPTER 26

The stop in Tashkent turns out to be no different from all the previous stops. We are all anxious to obtain some food and water before the train moves off.

We are warned against gangs of pickpockets, homeless children of all ages, whose existence depends on crime. This is Stalin's paradise: equality for all. As we make our way back between groups of travellers, with our buckets filled, Eva and I, two young lads, about fourteen, approach us and bar our way. They talk fast indicating their mouths and extending their hands for money, I guess. Their complexion is swarthy and already worn, their feet bare and dirty, their clothes in tatters.

'One lot of homeless preying on another,' Eva remarks under her breath. We spread our free hands before them to indicate we've got nothing to offer. But one of the boys taps his head that is covered in thick fuzzy hair, white with dust, and points to Eva's hair. All she has is a hair clip, not especially ornate, a black enamel with red and white flowers. She unclips it and gives it to him. I take out the rounded little comb that holds my hair in place and give it to the other boy. They run as if blown by a hurricane.

'We're such suckers,' Eva comments. 'What will we barter with when our money runs out? We'll be regretting this.'

We regret it almost immediately. Before we make a few paces forward, we are surrounded by half a dozen of these street urchins. They all shout at once and wave their arms and suddenly, my charitable disposition towards them turns to fear.

'Go away!' Eva cries, though they don't understand our language, 'Go away! No money! See? We're just like you!'

We attempt to break through their ring, but they are like a swarm of bees persistent around us.

'Help! Help!' I cry out with all my might. People part and a couple of Russian soldiers jump to our aid. I hate it the way they rain punches down on these youngsters. They scatter in all directions, but not before one yanks the bucket out of Eva's hand. His misjudgement of the weight makes him drop the bucket. Water splashes like a fountain over the feet of bystanders. There's much swearing and agitation as we cower away as quickly as possible and rush towards our carriage.

'Thank God, he's not taken my precious bucket!' Eva sounds out of breath and her face is twisted with pain.

'Eva! What's the matter?' My anger turns to concern.

'He's hurt my hand. When I struggled with him.' She holds up her bandaged hand. There's a patch of blood on the rag.

'Oh Eva!' I sigh. 'Just as your hand was getting better. Let's get you back to the wagon and I'll come out again for food and water.' She opens her mouth to protest but I pull her by the sleeve and amidst the growing crowd on the platform, she has no choice but to follow me.

Back in our wagon we unravel the rag. The wound has opened again and the flesh around it is swollen and fiery red. All three children are watching avidly, transfixed with fascination.

'Sweet Jesus, Eva, what you need is penicillin ointment. Or at least some iodine!'

'Yes, but from where and with what?'

'I'll ask one of the soldiers.'

'No! Don't go! I don't want you getting lost and the train moving off without you!'

One of the old sisters comes over.

'Don't worry, it won't be moving off yet. Let me bathe your hand. I've got some ointment left from home. It'll soothe the pain.'

While the good Samaritan takes care of Eva's hand, I run out for more water and some food.

During the night, as our train thunders through the next lap of our journey, Eva's delirious sleep talk wakes me up. I feel her forehead. It's very hot. In the dark, I rummage through my bag for the small jar of aspirins, which we keep for the *czarna godzina*, the emergency hour. I don't hesitate. I take two tablets out, save the rest like treasure, pour a little water from the canister into a mug and gently shake her awake.

'What is it?' she groans.

'Have some water,' I tell her, 'and some aspirins. You'll feel better in the morning.'

She doesn't argue. I can hear her drink greedily, the whole mug. She settles down with another groan. 'It's my hand,' she whispers, 'the pain just won't go away.'

'I know. It will now.'

In the morning, when the sun filters through the slits of the wagon windows and the first person up pushes back the sliding door and the fresh air rushes through our carriage blowing away all stale smells, Eva sits up and rests her hand in her lap. Her cheeks are flushed and her lips are flaky from the fever.

'It's better,' she says, but I can tell she's not feeling well.

'Stay in bed, Eva,' I advise her, 'I'll organise breakfast for us all.' I give her another dose of aspirins with a mug of water. For breakfast, we have *lepioszki*, the small bread pancakes bought yesterday, and some dried fruit. All the while I invoke the help of all our guardian angels to make Eva better.

At lunchtime, twenty-four hours after leaving Tashkent, our train slows down and comes to a halt at a small station on the outskirts of a minor town. Its sky line is flattish with rectangular, stone houses, the few scattered towers and minarets marking public and religious buildings. Crowns of palm trees rise above and between the horizontal lines of roof tops. There's only sparse greenery to break the bleak flatness of the surrounding land. On the other side of the railway track there is a slow running stream, its glinting surface camouflaging the muddy, undrinkable water underneath.

The guards jump down from their wagon and run along the length of the train banging their guns on the doors and shouting,

'*Vytieez!* Out! All get out!'

Mr. Ostrovski, close to the open door, stops one of the men and asks,

'Where are we?'

'Kermine.'

'What is this place? A Polish army camp?'

'It will be. No room for civilians yet.'

'So why are we stopping here?'

'You'll soon find out. Get all your things and assemble on that field.'

The field is a piece of waste land covered in dry yellowed grass. One's got to be thankful it's not snow, or slush or mud. There's a rough track sweeping through the field, one end leading towards the squatting town of Kermine, the other disappearing past the few isolated buildings in the distance, that blend with the hazy horizon, beyond which there is a faint outline of hills. The sun is high and warm. The children are eager to get out.

Before long the field is like an ants' nest, with people disembarking, unloading their bags and bundles, running to and fro, some losing their patience with children, some at the end of their endurance, having to assist and carry the old and the very ill. Voices are raised, frustration and disappointment visible in every face.

Eva and I find a spot on the grass amidst all this commotion, spread out an old blanket for our children and all our worldly goods; a sack of clothes each, two sacks of bedding, and two bags of provisions, with our possessively guarded cooking pots, water canisters, aluminium mugs, Stella's washing bowl and our two all-important buckets. We've still got some *kasha*, some rice and some lentils, but without cooking facilities, their use is limited to crunching them dry as a last resort. We lunch on sunflower and pumpkin seeds and some dried fruit.

Eva's hand gives her pain, though she does not complain. I make a sling for her out of an old pillow case, tie it round her neck and insist she rests her hand inside it. She does not resist.

When the goods train, our hovel for five weeks, has been emptied and checked, the older children shout *Hurra! Hurra!* as it moves off.

Eva remarks quietly,

'I wouldn't be too happy too soon. God only knows what's coming next.'

And indeed, there's no information from any of the guards as they stand around the edges of the crowd, easily six to seven hundred people.

'What are we waiting for?' Pavel asks, 'And how much longer have we got to wait?' He and Agata are up and looking around over the sprawling crowd, 'I wish we could go to play on the grass over there. Where there's lots of space.'

'Let's just wait and see,' I suggest, pretending calm and patience.

'Perhaps there's a Polish camp just near those hills,' Pavel says with eagerness.

'And that mist,' Agata adds, 'is the smoke from their fires?'

I want to share their optimism but I feel drained with the yo-yo jumping of my emotions. I expect everyone feels tired too. All the expectations, the hopes, the dreams that have kept our spirits up, have been deflated. It's as if fate was playing the cruellest joke on us.

'They've dumped us before,' I can't help remarking.

'But that was different, Nastusha,' Eva's crystal eyes flash in the sun. 'We're allies now. Families of Polish soldiers. They can't just dump us!' she reasons, giving Stella a hug for good measure. Stella raises her hands to Pavel and Agata. They pull her up and form a ring on the spot, and she taps her little feet to some imagined tune.

'Nastusha,' Eva squeezes my arm affectionately with her good hand, 'this is better than the smelly old train. We can breathe fresh air and enjoy the sun. Who knows, this could be a good omen. The beginning of a better time.' I want to believe her, but my anxiety is like smoke escaping a closed door, through every possible crack and crevice and I'm not able to push it back.

Mr. Ostrovski, close to us, gets up and limps his way between the sitting groups to the nearest guard. His ill wife, covered and curled up on the ground is being watched over by her daughter and her two little grandsons. I can only hope that there's a hospital for all our sick people in this new place assigned for us.

We watch him speak to the guard. When he comes back we are eager for news.

'Someone should be coming out soon, to meet us,' he says.

'Who? When?' Hope shoots up within me with images of Julian and Henryk.

He shrugs and spreads his hands.

'State secret,' he states drily, 'I couldn't get another word out of him.'

So we wait.

'At least it's warm. And it's not raining,' Eva says.

We lie back flat on our blanket and stretch our weary limbs. Eva rests her ailing hand on her chest. How does she remain so cheerful, when I'm tortured with the blackest thoughts? What if they send us away to the remotest part of Russia and I never see Julian again? The very thought is so painful I press my fist against my mouth to stop myself from crying.

'Nastusha, stop fretting,' Eva knows me so well, 'look up at the sky. It's like a pearly sheen up there. Close to heaven. You know that song with that lovely tune… *Let's go like children and nestle against Mother Mary's heart…*'

'Eva, I can't even hum the tune right now…'

'Then let's just say the words: *Her heart knows our voice. She'll turn away the painful blow…*'

I remain quiet and listen to Eva's recitation about Mary's kind heart, and God's grace, and Jesus' deliverance from life's cruel knocks and I wish they would hurry things along and help us leave behind this land of suffering and sorrow.

There's a sudden liveliness around us. Eva and I sit up, the children stop their game, and everyone's attention is focused on the cloud of dust approaching us from the town's direction. As it comes closer, two army trucks emerge and come to a halt nearby. The dust does not settle immediately. Following the lorries is a strange caravan of carts with very high wheels, drawn by oxen or camels.

'I've never seen real camels before!' Pavel exclaims, 'only in books!'

His spontaneous joy at something so trivial disarms me and suddenly I feel my spirit lift.

We watch with interest as Russian officials and soldiers climb down from the first truck, pull down a few trestle tables and folding chairs and set up office in the open field.

The second truck is the subject of much speculation at first, then the cause of growing joy. Six Polish soldiers in British uniforms set up additional tables and carry from their truck large metal vats, full and heavy judging by their effort of holding up the handles. An aroma of cooked food permeates the air. People start getting up for a better look, but our guards jump to attention and order us all to remain seated.

The long caravan of carts comes to a halt too, at the side of the field. The Uzbeks driving them jump down from their high seats and start feeding and watering their animals. It all seems so unreal, like a fragment of some film set in an exotic country. The men are dressed in long, loose kaftans, some like light cotton in pale colours, some made in heavier fabrics and dyed in rich blues and russets. Their faces are shaded with mushroom-shaped hats.

An NKVD man walks along the edge of the crowd, stops somewhere in the middle and makes an announcement through a trumpet–like speaker.

'You need to register first. After we've taken down all your particulars, you'll proceed to the field kitchen to receive your meal. When that is all done and finished, you'll be sent out into the country and installed with our people around the nearby *kolhozes*.'

I have a sinking feeling. Just what I feared most. I catch Eva's gaze. 'Dear God!' she exclaims. There's a rumble of discontent around us.

'Why?' someone shouts. 'We've been promised a passage to Persia!'

The official makes a step forward and pulls up his stocky frame to its full height. His knitted eyebrows make him look very angry.

'All in good time!' he shouts. 'What do you expect? Preferential treatment? There's thousands like you! A drain on our soldiers' time! They could be far better employed than wet-nursing you lot!'

'And whose fault is that?' Eva mutters.

'You should be thankful,' the man shouts, 'that we take care of you! As you can see, we've got eight officers ready and waiting to register you. The whole procedure won't take so long if you go immediately to your appropriate queues. We only need the heads of the families. All those with names beginning with A to C at the far end, then the next table D to F, then G to I and so on…' As he speaks, the officers at the tables display cards with the appropriate printed capital letters.

It takes only a few minutes for people, eager to obtain food, to position themselves in the correct queues. Eva and I have left the children on the blanket to mind our possessions. The woman in front of me in my queue is ancient, bent double, leaning on a crooked stick and holding a rag to her mouth as she coughs almost incessantly. Her face is half- hidden inside the folds of her wrap.

'Is there no one else to stand in for you?' I ask.

Slowly she turns round to look at me, with eyes so small and sunken, it's like looking at a skull. When she removes the rag from her mouth to speak, there's only a toothless rubbery hole.

'No. I'm the only one left,' she lisps. 'My husband died working in the quarry. Breaking big boulders. For building a new road. My daughter caught typhus. Never recovered. Her two boys caught scarlatina. There was no medication for them. And the hunger. That was the worst of all. Ay…' she gives a long sigh and a tear trickles down the side of her nose.

What can I tell her? That things will soon improve? That she'll feel better when she gets some food? I'm overwhelmed with the enormity of her suffering and the sure knowledge that nothing I say will lift even a fraction of the burden that she is now destined to carry for the rest of her miserable life.

'I have bad days and not so bad days,' she tells me. 'Today God is merciful.'

I can only nod in the face of such unshakeable faith.

The registration process goes unexpectedly smoothly, I guess it's because they want to get rid of us. Such concentration of numbers close to a small town can only be a recipe for disaster, as already experienced in Tashkent.

The military men sit behind their trestle desks and take down our particulars. They are Uzbeks, trained to speak Russian to us. They are a handsome race, slim, long-limbed, cream-coffee complexion, dark hair and eyes, precisely shaped eyebrows. Each one of them has an NKVD man looking over his shoulder.

Eva is ready first and joins me in my queue. I pray there will be no problems on account of Pavel and Agata. To my great relief the Uzbek soldier is civil in his manner, gives me the full attention of his attractive mahogany eyes when I explain about the children in my care and notes down everything I tell him. Predictably, he casts quick glances in Eva's direction, whose hair shines like cream satin in the afternoon sun.

Then it's time for our treat. My whole being tingles with anticipation. Our children join us in the food queue and carry their own aluminium mugs. We all receive a white loaf of bread each, which I store in our collective bag, and then the soldier ladles the soup into our mugs. It is thick and smells heavenly. He looks around Julian's age.

'Which place have you come from?' I ask him in Polish, 'before you arrived here?'

He carries on with his job as he replies,

'Buzuluk first. Then Tashkent. Now we're here in Kermine to set up another military camp.'

'You've not come across our husbands, by any chance?' Eva asks, 'Bzovski and Kalinski. They joined up in Buzuluk too.'

He shakes his head thoughtfully, concentrating on ladling the soup.

'No, but if I do, I'll tell them where you are.' I wonder if he says that to everyone.

'It's just that… we don't want to be forgotten and left behind…'

He gives me his attention and assures me,

'That won't happen. I promise you. We are here too to oversee things.'

There is no reason why I should believe him more than anyone else, but somehow his words lift the burden off my chest, and when we go back with our precious spoils to our old blanket on the ground, sit down and taste the soup, I experience a moment of pure bliss. I cut only one of the loaves into five pieces, saving the rest for later. I offer to feed Stella, but Eva insists on doing this herself with her one free hand. The soup is tasty, peppery, thick with diced potatoes, turnips, lentils and grains. I feel my whole being melt in the happiness of this moment. Little Stella's eyes are watery with pleasure. Agata eats slowly, weary of the mouth ulcers which beset her with regular recurrence. She dips a small chunk of bread in her soup to soften the crust before placing it in her mouth. Pavel eats fast.

'Slow down Pavelek,' I remind him, 'you'll get stomach ache.' But he can't help himself. He finishes first.

'Do you think they'll have more?' He gets up hopefully.

'Go and see' I encourage, praying he won't be disappointed. We watch him step around the sitting people and being joined by Florian and Dominik further along.

Eva eats slowly, as if in a trance, and when her soup is finished and she wipes her mug with the last morsel of bread and pops it into her mouth, she reflects,

'A portion of soup, just a portion of soup from an aluminium mug can be such heaven. See what they've done to us Nastusha? Reduced us to the level of animals.'

Her exaggeration makes me smile.

'Not at all Eva, if you can still think like that. And what's wrong with enjoying food? Remember all the trouble we went to at home to produce something special each time? All the additional ingredients, a pinch of this and a pinch of that just to make it a little different. Remember how we used to exchange recipes, then add something of our own to make it special?'

She nods,

'That's exactly my point Nastusha. Cooking became an expression of something more sublime than just the need to stuff our stomachs.'

I feel a warm touch of optimism, or maybe it's just the soup, when I promise her,

'Eva, when we get back to normal life, the first thing I'll make is a chocolate and coffee and cream gateau, from ground hazel nuts and beaten eggs and fresh butter and fine sugar...'

Her eyes become dreamy.

'I hope that God up there is listening to you,' she sighs.

The boys come back smiling. Pavel sits down beside me and shows me brown scratchings of burnt potatoes and turnips at the bottom of his mug.

'Want some?' he asks Agata. But she shakes her head.

Without hesitation and with one tablespoon he stuffs it all in his mouth.

'It's been a good day, so far, hasn't it?' he says.

By four in the afternoon, under the slanting warm sun, in the dust-hazy air around us, all registration is completed, all soup eaten, and the crowd is divided into smaller groups and directed to the waiting lorries. Packed to capacity ten lorries move off generating trailing clouds behind them like talcum powder. The remainder of us are relegated to the carts. Our *arba*, as these carts on very high wheels are called, accommodates our group on one side, and facing us, Mr. Ostrovski's family. Between us, able adults, and with the help of our Uzbek coachman, we lift Mr. Ostrovski's ill wife onto the cart, and make her as comfortable as it's possible among all the bundles and sacks.

Our motor engine is a harnessed camel, a not too pretty animal, with a hump, with a perpetually chewing muzzle showing off enormous yellow teeth, and with a swaying, unhurried gait. It appears that his master has brought all his worldly possessions with him, for thrown over the camel's back and dangling on his flanks are thick ropes with a variety of objects attached to them: leather sacks filled with water or oats, cooking pans, rolled-up blankets, soft bags stuffed with clothes, at a guess, shoes and sandals and some metal objects and tools.

When the long caravan of oxen- or camel-driven *arbas* move off, there are sounds of excitement among the younger people and children. Pavel and Agata giggle at each other, wave to no one in particular, and little Stella, wedged between them, copies them with a spurt of joy. This has an immediate effect on Mr. Ostrovski's little grandsons. They smile shyly and wave too. And in my mind I thank God for this moment of normality.

'They'll never believe us at school,' Pavel exclaims, his eyes lively in his thin face, 'when I tell them about this journey! Camels and a desert! It's like I'm *Stashu* and Agatka is *Nell*! Just like *The Desert and the Jungle!*'

I stroke his head, like a soft brush under my palm.

'You're right, Pavelek, no one will ever believe us!'

We arrive at the *Schastleeva Pteetsa*, The Happy Bird *kolhoz* at eight in the evening. We have passed on our slow-progressing journey isolated settlements of a few mud-huts scattered on this red earth, overgrown with yellow grass, where giant balls of dry vegetation roll about the plains unrestrained, the only free spirits in this land of restrictions and repression.

The land around *Schastleeva Pteetsa* village is different, having been tilled and shaped and cultivated, no doubt, by generations of native inhabitants. From the red dry soil there rise fields of cotton, refreshingly white, on either side of the dusty track. In the far distance beyond the *kolhoz*, patches of green indicate vegetation at the foothills of a mountain range. Closer, weaving its way across the land, there is a river, with a wide pebbly beach, shaded in places with spinneys of mulberry and apricot trees.

Our caravan rolls slowly along the one dirt-track through the village and stops somewhere in the middle in front of a long wooden building, like a huge barn or a warehouse. All other dwellings we've passed are mysteriously quiet behind their all-enclosing walls, with just a heavy wooden portal in each, firmly shut. There are trees leaning their branches over the enclosures or filling the gaps between the dwellings, softening the roughness of the clay and stone walls. Dusk is falling and with it a clinging chill. The only light now showing us the way is the dimming peach sky over the line of the distant mountains.

The wooden warehouse turns out to be the management block. The door is flung open and a large woman steps out. She is dressed in a puffed-out blouse, a gathered full skirt and boots. Her long black hair is plaited and wound around her head. Her features are coarse and don't inspire liking. I can only hope that inside that big frame of hers, there is a big heart.

She addresses us in Russian, her strong voice carrying far over the evening silence.

'My name is Babachka. You'll address me Comrade Babachka.' We later discover that her name means Butterfly. But for now we listen and memorise her instructions. 'I'm the *komandant* of this *kolhoz*. You'll be happy to know that there's plenty of work here. Each morning at six you'll be called but there are no penalties if you miss work. Only rewards if you show dedication to the common cause of our great country. If you don't work, you don't eat. It's simple, isn't it? At the end of each day the workers receive their rations of wheat grain. You'll come here to this *kantor*. At the end of each month, those with outstanding output will be rewarded financially. This kindness is the noble idea of our great leader Stalin.' She pauses, and though nothing should surprise me any more in this country, I'm stunned by such blatant, unashamed perfidy.

Eva nudges me.

'How can she listen to herself ?'

'Years of brainwashing,' I whisper back.

Babachka continues,

'That's all you need to know for now. It's getting late and dark. Tomorrow you'll need a day to sort yourself out, but after that I'd advise you to make the most of the opportunities offered you. Now your brigadiers will show you to your quarters.'

It turns out that the 'brigadiers' are our guides who have driven us here. Again, we later discover that their name derives from the working 'brigades' that they lead to work every morning.

Our Uzbek guide steers our camel around and takes us towards some dwellings at the far end of the village. He speaks a little Russian, and with much gesticulation and Mr. Ostrovski's linguistic intuition, we finally understand that we'll be neighbours in the two enclosures facing each other across the dirt track.

He gets down from the camel and stands at one of the heavy doors and hammers it with the attached iron knocker, sending echoes all around. The place looks deserted, but after a couple of minutes or so, half of the solid portal moves back and a head in a turban pokes out. It is that of an old man with a lined face and a grey droopy moustache. The two men exchange words, the door is pushed wide open and the old man is revealed in a long heavy *kaftan* over his baggy trousers.

The brigadier returns and with his limited Russian tells Mr. Ostrovski that this is his place. Together, as previously, he, myself and Mr. Ostrovski's daughter help him to carry his wife indoors. As we struggle along, for even emaciated bodies have a certain weight, I get a glimpse of the enclosed yard, a tree in the corner, the branches overhanging the wall, two goats tethered underneath it, some other objects stacked against the walls and the main building which is a mud hut. It has an arched opening and port-holes for windows, with lighted candles inside glass jars standing on the ledges.

There's just one room inside, with a clay stove in the corner, a stack of bedding on a low wide shelf and a table in the middle. The owner indicates a cleared corner lined with some string matting. The rest of the floor is bare dried clay. We lay Mrs. Ostrovska in that corner and cover her up warm before returning for the little boys and all their possessions contained in a few sacks and bags.

Then it is our turn. The evening has turned cold. We pile extra layers of clothing on our children and ourselves as we watch our Uzbek brigadier repeat the same procedure as before. This time when the heavy door opens and another old man comes out, there follows a long discussion, none too joyous judging by the old man's gestures; he shakes his head, shrugs his shoulders, spreads his hands, sends us hostile looks and makes it quite obvious he does not want us in his home.

'And who can blame him?' Eva reasons. 'Some strange tramps from God knows where. He didn't ask for us, as we haven't asked to be here.'

'But what will happen to us if nobody takes us in?' Pavel worries.

I cuddle Pavel and Agata to me. 'Don't worry, as long as we find some shelter, we'll just all huddle together, and keep ourselves warm.'

Nevertheless, the brigadier calls to us to climb down as he and the old man push back the creaky door to widen the entrance. Eva jumps down, I pass Stella to her, then Pavel and Agata help me to gather all our bags and bundles on the ground. We drag them with us inside the walled-in yard.

This abode is similar in plan to the other one; the mud hut, with its slanting roof covered thickly with dried twigs, reeds and some long stalks, leans against one side of the quadrangle, and consists of two halves, with two separate open entrances. There's a tree in one corner, its branches spreading over both sides of the wall, there's a wooden shed and next to it, a strange egg-shaped clay structure, stacks of clay bricks, and more piles of sticks.

'Where are they going to fit us all in?' Pavel wonders. I wonder that too.

Our brigadier and the old man stop at the opening to the smaller part of the hut. It smells of animals and the snorting noises from within confirm some animal presence there. After a short, less heated discussion, the brigadier explains in his halting Russian,

'This your room. Not now. Now goats there. Now you go Comrade Yakob.'

'Go where?' I ask. I'm suddenly overwhelmed with tiredness.

The brigadier just waves a farewell and leaves. He too has had a long day. Mr. Yakob (*comrade* does not suit him in his turban and a long *kaftan* dress) padlocks the door and turns towards us. The last of the faint light in the peachy sky colours his face deep amber. It is wizened and his eyes are like black raisins sunk in the folds of his skin. Suddenly, to my amazement he smiles to us, *us*, homeless people, huddled together over our few bundles. The lines on his face lift in wavy patterns and there is a welcome in the nod of his head. He gesticulates to us to follow him indoors and to leave our bags outside by the open entrance. I bring only the food bag in with us.

His room, like the previous one I saw, accommodates a clay stove in the corner, a wide shelf a foot above the floor, stacked with colourful bedding, a few shelves on the walls with pots and pans and other household objects, and sunk lower down in what seems like a trench in the clay floor, a wooden table. The room is surprisingly warm, despite the cold coming in through the open doorway and window holes.

An old woman is standing at the stove over a pot. She is dressed in a long russet *kaftan*, embroidered in wide bands round the neckline, the sleeves and the hemline. Her head is covered in a light muslin scarf, tied securely at the back. Her face is wrinkly but soft like an old yellowed apple.

The old man points to her and we guess his introduction; it is his wife Radvana.

There follows much talking from them both to us, but all we can do is smile and nod. Pavel and Agata giggle quietly at the craziness of the situation and Stella clings to them both, her eyes wide with curiosity. Mr. Yakob shows us to the table. We sit down on the floor to slide in around it and dangle our legs in the trench below. It is then we discover the source of the heat. In the middle of the trench underneath the table, there is a covered metal container with something slow burning inside. In addition, we are given covers to throw over our legs and knees. Before long, we are warmed up enough to take off our hats and coats, and place them rolled up behind us.

The whiteness of Eva's and Stella's hair catches Mrs. Radvana's attention. With a sudden, energetic move she comes over and runs her fingers through Eva's hair, talking excitedly to her husband.

'It's full of lice!' Eva laughs. Mrs. Radvana does not understand. She continues to stroke Eva's hair, then Stella's, with the stream of her words seemingly unstoppable.

Eva lifts her injured hand.

'Have you any ointment for this?' she asks. Mrs. Radvana stops talking, takes Eva's hand in hers and unravels the rag. She examines the wound with great concentration. Then she disappears for a moment behind a raffia screen at the side of the clay stove. She returns with a jar containing what looks like black treacle. Eva catches my eye, looking uncertain, but it would be churlish to refuse our hostess's kindness now.

'*Czary, mary*. Black Magic,' Eva mutters smiling, as she watches Mrs. Radvana apply the ointment to the wound and bandage her hand. 'I hope this doesn't make my hand drop off.'

'You'll soon find out,' I reply drily then add in haste, 'I'm sure she knows what she's doing. Look how long she's survived in this God-forsaken place.'

We continue sitting round the table with our legs dangling underneath, not knowing what to expect next, Stella's little head like a fluffy nest between Pavel and Agata.

Mrs. Radvana pours boiling water into a metal samovar and brings it over to the table. It has a miniature tap at the side. She demonstrates it's ready for pouring by placing a ceramic cup underneath it.

'I think she means us to have tea,' Eva suggests.

I stretch out to the food bag behind me, pull out our aluminium mugs, a loaf of bread and a knife. I slice the loaf into seven parts. Our hosts join us at the table, and though we understand nothing of their chatter, somehow the sharing of their tea and our bread brings us closer and banishes feelings of mistrust. I cannot stop marvelling at their good-natured acceptance of us, strangers, in their home.

'Where will we all sleep?' Pavel asks, chewing his bread hurriedly.

Agata sips her tea carefully, wincing now and again. She says,

'The man said that the shed is our new home. But how can that be, when it's full of goats? And where can we wash? Where can we go for a wee?'

'We'll have to leave the washing and the laundry till tomorrow,' I tell her, 'one more night won't make any difference now.'

Mrs. Radvana must be a mind reader. She gets up from the floor, takes one of the candle-lit jars and makes a sign for me to follow her outside. It is completely dark now in the little courtyard. The edge of the wall and the crown of the tree form black shapes against the navy blue sky pricked with thousands of glittering spots. The frosty air after the warm day is a shock as it pinches my face. She leads me along the side of the hut to where it forms a corner with the adjacent wall. There is a bucket there. The strong whiff of urine makes clear its purpose. I thank her. I think she understands the Russian *spaseeba balshoye*.

When our meal is finished Pavel and Agata take it in turn to use the toilet facility outside while I stand with the candle at a discreet distance. I assist little Stella, whose doll-like body would drown in a bucket this size. Back at the table the children snuggle together in the warmth. I then take Eva by the hand and lead her. Her night blindness is still a problem. She can pick out shapes in the gloomy interior but the darkness outside becomes a black sheet in front of her eyes.

Mrs. Radvana is perplexed. I try explaining and look to Mr. Yakob for support. I speak to him in Russian.

'Only at night. In the daytime fine.'

They talk a lot, Mrs. Radvana gesticulates then Mr. Yakob translates,

'Good food make right.'

We know that. Good food. It's been the object of our dreams and desires for the past two years.

Coming back from outside we both shiver. I catch Mrs. Radvana's glance and mimic sleeping on my joined hands. She nods and begins to take down the eiderdowns and blankets from the stack on the low bed. I assist her and begin to spread the bedding on the floor, but she stops me and laughs and makes a sign for me to watch her. She wraps an eiderdown around Agata, so that only her face is visible, and gently pushes her back to lie down on the floor, with her legs still in the warmth underneath the table. It becomes obvious that this is the way they sleep and keep warm through the night, against the cold drifting in freely through the open doorway and window holes.

Together with our hosts wrapped up to their eyeballs, we form a star of seven reclining bodies around the table.

'This is so crazy!' Eva yawns, 'These poor people are so oppressed by hardships, they can't invent comfort even for their sleep. I feel every bone in my body on this hard floor!'

I ache with tiredness too, and yet, as the warmth from that strange heater under the table travels up my legs to the covers cocooning me, I feel myself drifting into a blissful state of all-forgetting sleep.

CHAPTER 27

The first morning in the Happy Bird *kolhoz* is very busy for us. We feel under pressure to sort out our immediate personal needs, our living quarters and anything else that needs to be put in order before our first day of work tomorrow. I'm filled with joy that the sun shines, that the earth is warm, that the air is dry, and that nature is on our side when we do serious washing and laundry and drying and delousing our hair with Mrs. Radvana's secret but amazingly effective lotions.

All water has to be brought from the river in buckets. It snakes gently close to our end of the village which is slightly raised giving us a good view of all the area around us. We've done countless walks today, but I'm not complaining; it feels good to stretch my limbs which have been restrained from exercise for so long.

I insist that Eva saves her left hand for a day or two longer, especially that Mrs. Radvana's tar-like ointment has really helped. I've given the children as good a wash as possible in Stella's baby bath and scrubbed their hair clean of lice. Though their clothes are grey and shabby with use, it feels good to know they are clean. The children are ready to walk with Mr. Yakob and the two goats to a pasture on the other side of the village, where the river widens and nourishes wide belts of vegetation.

'Pavelek, Agatka, now you've got to mind little Stella at all times,' I admonish them, 'don't let her out of your sight for even one second.'

Eva bends down to kiss her little daughter, but Stella's already jumping with impatience to go. She does not resist her protectors' determined handgrips, and happily skips along with their longer steps. Pavel and Agata's thin little faces lighten up with anticipation, their clean hair shines in the sun. The vast land stretching before them with the river and the scattered groves of mulberry trees is irresistibly enticing.

'We'd never let her come to any harm,' Agata assures us.

As if feeling Eva's and my concern, Mr. Yakob places his old arthritic hand on Stella's white head and his face creases in a smile.

We watch them for a while, the children bobbing up and down alongside Mr. Yakob's slow and measured gait, as he guides and watches over his two precious goats that get distracted almost constantly with insignificant tufts of grass on the way.

Then we get down to the business of cleaning out the goat shed, the quarters allotted to us for our exclusive use. The floor area measures at a guess two metres by three. Mrs. Radvana brings us brooms made of bulrushes and twigs. As we sweep up all the trampled hay and goat droppings, she collects them with a shovel into a hessian sack and leaves the lot in a sunny spot in the yard to dry. She comes back with a bucket of water and douses the clay floor profusely. We sweep and brush with vigour, and when it begins to dry it appears convincingly clean.

She makes signs to us which we don't understand then she beckons to follow her into the yard. In a small shelter with just a bulrush roof above it, there hangs on the wall, among the stored gardening tools, a light aluminium bathtub, large enough for an adult to sit in. We understand and chuckle with joy and thank her in Polish and in Russian. We carry it indoors inside our little room and place it in the middle.

Before long, we enjoy in turn a soak in about a foot of water that has been warming in two buckets on the two clay stoves (indoors and outside). It feels good, after the bath, to plunge the whole head in the water and drown the lice and scrub them off our hair with the help of Mrs. Ravdana's camphor-smelling magic liquid.

Feeling clean, refreshed and changed, we then get down to the business of washing the backlog of all the dirty clothes. More walks to the river with buckets for water. It is red and muddy and needs to be stood for a good half an hour before the impurities settle on the bottom. For cooking, we have learnt from Mrs. Radvana, it has to be left to stand all night, filtered through muslin and boiled, before being used.

For this reason, I advise Eva to leave all the laundry to me, in case the impure water aggravates her hand. She unravels the rag to show me.

'Look, it's really healing fast with Mrs. Radvana's *czary mary*.'

I'm astonished. The wound has closed up, the swelling has gone down, there's only a pink blush around it.

'Amazing!' I exclaim with feeling. 'Thank God for nature! And thank God for Mrs. Radvana. But don't rush things! Leave the washing to me.'

'No reason why I can't help you with my good hand,' Eva insists.

It is quicker with three hands than two. When Mr. Yakob returns home at lunch time with our children in good spirits, their faces pink from the sun, and the goats' udders full, our washing is already drying out flat on the grass outside our enclosure.

We have also organised in our little shed a corner for sleeping, which we have covered with matting made of cleaned cotton stalks. We've spread out on it all the bedding we've got and in addition have been given a cottonwool-filled eiderdown from Mrs. Radvana. We've had to sacrifice one of our buckets for the toilet corner, which we've screened off with a sheet hung over a string attached and tied at both ends to the cane underlay of the clay roof.

Our bags and sacks are neatly lined by one wall and our garments neatly folded on top of an old bench, which Mrs. Radvana allowed us to bring in from the yard. She has also made it plain that we can use her stove for cooking. I've boiled some *kasza* and made tea and as we sit on top of our bedding in the sleeping corner and enjoy our lunch we all marvel at our luck. We have a place all to ourselves! What joy!

In the afternoon Mr. Yakob surprises us. He carries with him a square board, then fetches a few clay bricks and constructs a table for us. Mrs. Radvana beckons to Pavel and Agata. They return after a short while with five plump cushions made of hessian and filled with cotton wool. Our hosts invite us to sit around the table and when we oblige them, the pleasure on their lined faces is that of indulgent grandparents.

'We're like Turkish kings sitting on cushions,' Pavel comments and giggles. Something warms inside me at the sight of our children's smiling faces.

'I can't understand why they're being so kind to us,' Eva wonders.

Mr. Yakob pulls back the sleeve of his *kaftan* and shows us his large watch with bold digits, secured to his wrist with a wide black strap. He points to eight o'clock.

'*Czai*' he says then points to their part of the house.

I respond in Russian,

'Are you inviting us to your house for tea at eight o'clock?' He nods, and so does Mrs. Radvana.

'*Spaseeba balshoye*' we both thank them and the children join in. This appears to make the old couple happy.

When they're gone I express my reservation,

'I don't understand it either. Why are they so keen to be friends with us?'

'Perhaps they're just lonely,' Agata suggests. The faint glow on her skin makes it already look better just after one morning out in the fresh air.

'I'm sure you're right, Agatka. It's awful when you're afraid to trust people,' I reassure her, but I can't get rid of my own feeling of suspicion.

We visit Mr. Ostrovski and his family in the dwelling across the road from us, in an enclosure similar to ours with all kinds of objects in the yard and a shade-giving mulberry tree in the corner. Mr. Ostrovski comes out of the open doorway to greet us. There's something wistful about the angle of his grey head, about the stoop of his narrow angular shoulders. He's obviously had a wash and a shave and is wearing a clean shirt, streaked with unwashable old sweat and dirt marks. He runs his hand wearily over his hair.

'We won't stop,' I smile, 'we're just checking that you're all right.'

He leads us inside. They haven't the luxury of a room of their own. Their living space is the half on the other side of the sunken table.

'How thrilled they must be,' he says wryly, 'to have us foisted upon them.'

Old people like me. And all they probably wish for is peace and quiet in their lives.'

An old Uzbek woman is pottering at the stove. She stops and acknowledges our presence with a cheerless stare.

'All the young ones have gone to the war,' Mr. Ostrovski says, 'only old people, women and children are left to run this *kolhoz*.'

His wife is curled up on the floor bed and covered up to her chin. Her eyes are closed, deep down in her sunken sockets. Her daughter Ella, sallow as wax, gives us a smile of her pale lips and crouching on the floor sorts out the garments for washing. Her two little boys, Maks and Aleks, are sitting at the table drawing with stubs of pencils on some torn brown paper.

Like our children, like all children who have so far survived, they have that look of asymmetry and imbalance, their eyes too large for their emaciated faces, their heads appearing too heavy for their shrunken bony shoulders, their arms thin like sticks, their legs spindly like a spider's. Changed into a fresh set of clothes, discoloured with overuse, they nevertheless look clean with their washed and fluffy hair.

'We can take your little boys out in the fresh air,' I offer, 'we're going for a walk. Down to the village. To have a look around. Get to know this place.'

Agata comes up to the table and stretches out her hand.

'Will you come with us?' she smiles. They smile back shyly.

'An excellent idea!' Mr. Ostrovski says brightly. He helps the boys to scramble up and leads them with us to the main gate.

Pavel and Agata, like serious parents, organise the little ones to hold hands together and to walk five abreast. For no reason at all I find the sight before me infinitely touching: five heads bobbing up and down, five pairs of skipping feet causing the dust to rise from the stony track.

It is a warm afternoon with a soft hazy sun and white bright air that makes one squint. Colours are intense, the lines of the buildings sharp. From the top of the gentle gradient that takes the road into the village we have a clear view of the distant pale lilac hills that merge with the sky. Beneath them the vegetation shimmers with viridian and turquoise hues. Horizontal ribbons that look like water appear and disappear as if deliberately tricking the eye.

Closer, in the middle distance, the land is a patchwork of white cotton fields. Dark moving spots among them indicate work in progress.

'It's such a beautiful land, isn't it?' I think aloud. 'Pity then, that people here are so poor.'

'But, perhaps they are happy here,' Eva replies, 'perhaps they couldn't imagine living anywhere else. They're used to this place. It's the only thing that stays the same, that doesn't let them down.'

'Could you live here, Eva? Stay here forever?'

'I'm not from here,' she smiles evasively,' my home is near our mountains. Our very own Carpathians. That's where I belong.'

'If only those hills over there, were our mountains.' I sigh with longing, and my mind conjures up immediately memories of happy times with my dear Mama, my Tato, my family and Julian. Julian. Julian. Missing him is like a constant ache. 'Eva, I'd give anything for just an hour with our boys. God knows where they are now. I pray and dream every night that when they send for us, it will be Julian and Henryk coming to fetch us.'

'And I pray we won't have to wait too long.'

The village is a long line of dwellings on both sides of the wide dirt track, with mulberry and apricot trees between them, also clumps of tall grasses, patches of short coarse grass, narrow strips of vegetable plots with just a few onions, sweet corn or pumpkins on them, sections of uncultivated red soil and artificial ponds. The open gateways show courtyards in all their individual set-ups, yet similar to ours. Like our host, some people keep animals too, a sheep, a donkey, a goat, a couple of hens. There's even a cow in one enclosure, resting in the shade of the tree, chewing the cud. The bones in her haunches are sharply defined through her cream coffee skin.

'Poor thing, she doesn't look over fed, does she?' I remark.

'No, but where there are animals,' Eva's tone gets lively, 'there's hope of milk. Or cheese. And eggs!'

'Eva dear,' I point out, 'and how many people would these few animals feed in a village this size? We could do with hundreds more, but I bet there are restrictions. Like with everything else.'

An old Uzbek in his long kaftan and a mushroom hat goes by carrying a bucket and a shovel. Pavel and Agata pinch their noses and look back at us expressively. Indeed, there is a strong smell of manure trailing after him.

'Unpleasant as it is' I tell Pavel, 'it's like magic mud that you have to dig into the soil. To make things grow. Especially here in this dry and sandy land.'

As we walk past the open enclosures we recognize people whom we got to know on our long train journey. They are all busy sorting their things, washing, drying their laundry, sweeping the yard, some women cooking on the outdoor clay ovens. We come across Florian and Dominik helping their mother with the laundry. All three are bent over a wooden tub, stood on a wide bench. We call out to them, they stop and turn, and for once their dour mother appears pleased to see us.

'So where are you based?' she asks, squinting her eyes, frowning her forehead. We tell her. The frown deepens.

'Some people are born lucky!' she shakes her head. 'Just you and two old people? We've got to share with a family of six! All in one room! Can you imagine? Two women, one young, one old, and four boys. They've no idea how to discipline them. It's the cult of the male here, in this primitive country. I'd soon teach them!'

I notice Florian and Dominik roll their eyes.

'So where are they all?' Eva asks.

'Out in the cotton fields. Working. From six this morning. And their kids too.'

'Working!' I'm astonished, my mind somersaulting, thinking about our three.

'God knows,' Florian's mother shrugs, pursing her mouth, deepening the lines around it. 'They've got a goat which they've taken with them. I can only assume that the older boys mind it all day. What a life! Can you imagine? That's all they own! One goat! And a strip of garden behind this wall with a few puny pumpkins. Collectivisation in practice! Wonderful, isn't it? Everything for all, nothing for yourself! The brainchild of our dear benefactor Stalin.'

Florian sends Dominik a discreet smile. Dominik whispers,

'Stalin. *Sralin*...shitty Stalin.'

Pavel and Agata giggle as if this is the best joke ever. We bid them farewell.

'Till tomorrow morning!'

'Oh, I'm not going!' the boys' mother is emphatic. 'What have I reared these two for, if they can't support their mother now?'

We don't comment. We get back onto the road.

Past the *kantor,* the management block that looks like a sprawling barn, closer to the river where it bends in a wide sweep and irrigates the land, the enclosures are huge. It is clear that they are the state owned farms, for no one in this village of old people, women and children looks important enough to be the owner. Yet the herdsmen minding the cows, the oxen, the camels and the horses in separate herds are old men helped by women workers. A surprising sight are the children of all ages, like little mobile mushrooms in their round hats, playing in groups on the edges of the fields.

'Don't they go to school?' Pavel asks.

'We'll soon find out,' I promise, but he's not happy.

'If we're only here for a short while,' he reasons, 'then we don't have to go, do we?'

'We'll talk to Mr. Ostrovski.'

Before turning back, we stop by an open enclosure and watch from the distance horses grazing in a field. Just like the cow we saw before, the horses are thin and appear to move listlessly, as if in a trance. Mr. Ostrovski's little grandsons liven up as they demonstrate to Stella how horses should gallop and neigh. This amuses Pavel and Agata too.

'Wait till we go home,' Eva tells them, 'wait till you see our beautiful horses. How their skin shines, how they can gallop or stand up on their hind legs, like dancers, how their mane goes all wavy in the wind when they run, You've got to love horses. They become your best friends.'

The children listen to Eva's words, enchanted.

'Don't the people here love their horses?' the six-year-old grandson of Mr. Ostrovski asks.

I stroke his head.

'They do. But there isn't always enough food to feed all the animals.'

I don't tell him that in a world where human life is expendable, no one will shed their tears over horses.

At eight in the evening, after our supper of lentil soup and a slice of the saved, stale bread each, as arranged with Mr. Yakob, we troop inside his part of the house. All five of us.

Mrs. Radvana invites us with a sweep of her hand to sit at the table. She brings over the samovar and seven clay cups. Her slow elegant movements appear to bestow importance upon this occasion, which rubs off on the children, who sit very still and only their eyes follow her every gesture.

She fills the cups, places them in front of us, then disappears behind the raffia screen. All the while Mr. Yakob sits at the head of the table, as if presiding over a meeting. Except that no talk, small or serious, is exchanged. We show our appreciation by repeating a few words in Russian: 'Thank you. You're very kind.'

'This is bizarre,' I remark to Eva, 'why do they want to bother with us?'

Mrs. Radvana returns with a small saucer and a dish. The children's eyes nearly pop out. Eva strains to see. It is already dusk.

'What is it?' she asks me.

'Sugar cubes and small pancakes.'

Earlier on I saw Mrs. Radvana make them on the clay stove outside. The batter was thicker than the one I normally make at home. She made little balls, flattened them between her pressed hands then stuck them against the wall of the stove. The pancakes dropped off onto the waiting white cloth when they were cooked through.

We are all offered a sugar cube each and a pancake. It is a treat. A very special treat for us. I'm baffled.

'Eat slowly,' Eva tells the children, 'enjoy every little crumb.'

It is hard to string out a feast consisting of a small pancake and a cup of tea. We do our best. In total silence. To my relief, though I don't understand a word, Mr. Yakob and his wife suddenly liven up and begin to talk. The children begin to whisper and giggle among themselves.

Outside, like last night, the temperature has dropped right down. It feels just like a frosty night at home in Old Mizun. The goat shed offers us shelter, but its open draughty doorway only a numbing cold.

Nevertheless, when it gets to nine o'clock, we both feel it is time to go, to settle the children for the night, and ourselves too for an early start tomorrow.

Eva speaks to Mr. Yakob in Russian. He may be able to pick out the gist of her words.

'We've got to go now. Up at five for work in the morning. The children need to sleep.'

He shakes his head.

'No! Children no work! Children with *moya zhina*.' He nods towards Mrs. Radvana, busy over her pots on the stove.

I don't want to jump to conclusions, but if I understand right, he proposes we leave the children with his wife. That would be of enormous help. But how can we ever repay them?

We begin to withdraw our legs from underneath the table and the warm cover, but Mrs. Radvana comes over and stops us, placing her hands on our shoulders.

'*Zhdat!* Wait!'

Mr. Yakob taps his outsize watch and spreads five fingers like a fan. Does he mean us to wait another five minutes?

It would seem ungracious to disregard his request. So we wait. Mrs. Radvana talks over our heads, then Mr. Yakob tries in Russian,

'Wait. See Selim. Son.'

In a split second something dawns in my mind. But I don't share my moment of enlightenment with Eva. She's still suffering the effect of her self-harming rejection of Igor. All of a sudden everything makes sense: the welcome, the kindness, the offered friendship. Mrs. Radvana has found the perfect bride for her son. No one in this region has white-gold hair like Eva's nor her crystal-blue eyes. I daren't look at Eva in case I give my secret thoughts away. I don't wish to frighten her.

Little Stella has flopped into Eva's lap and given in to sleep. Pavel can't stop yawning and Agata's eyelids keep closing and opening with a start.

'Put your heads down on the table,' I suggest. 'No one will mind. We may have to wait a little while yet.' They rest their heads on their folded arms and close their eyes. They've had a long day and the early darkness in this region makes it appear later than it really is.

'I wonder how much longer?' Eva sighs. 'It feels a bit like being smothered with kindness.'

It feels to me like being held here against our wishes.

There is a discreet rattle on the outside gate, such that can only be heard if awaited. Mr. Yakob rushes out and there are sounds of the padlock being unlocked, of the heavy portal being pushed back with creaking, low male voices, snorting, neighing, horses, I guess.

I expect a younger version of Mr. Yakob to enter, in a long *kaftan* coat and a mushroom hat.

I'm taken aback by the sight of his two companions. For a split second fear grips my stomach, then lets go sending runny sensations through my bowels and down my legs. Military uniforms. Guns. Is this a trap? Have they come to arrest us? To take us away? Somewhere, where no one will ever find us?

'What is it?' Eva senses my fear.

'Soldiers.'

She peers hard through the candle-lit gloom. Then she squeezes my hand.

'Don't worry. Just watch our hosts. They appear happy. I don't think we're in danger.'

Her words have a soothing effect on my taut nerves, though I don't know what to think, whom to trust. But indeed, there's a look of joy in Mr. Yakob's eyes as he looks up to the young men. Mrs. Radvana turns from the stove and opens her arms wide. The men have to bend almost double to reach down her small stature and give her a hug.

Now that the initial rush of dread has passed, I can appraise the two men a little more calmly. They are slim, long-limbed, dark haired with regular features rendered somewhat menacing by the moustaches, drooping around their lips. Their stone-coloured uniforms consist of jackets with large breast and side pockets, and trousers tucked inside high boots. The bullet belts around their narrow hips are filled full of ammunition. They each carry a gun, hefty, with a long nozzle.

Mr. Yakob slips his arm confidently around the waist of the man close to him.

'*Moy sin.* Selim.' He tells us with open pride. Selim gives us a nod, his coal-black eyes momentarily catching the candle light, igniting afresh the unease inside me. He remains serious.

Mr. Yakob leans his head forward and looks at the other man.

'Nephew. Tariq. Boys very good. Selim and Tariq.'

We nod in polite agreement and I notice Tariq's eyes crease with a hint of a smile.

Mrs. Radvana comes behind us and shines a candle above Eva's head. Eva's hair glows like a halo in the semi-darkness of the room.

'Anastazia. Eva.' Her simple introduction is followed by a torrent of words, which the young men listen to without any change in their attentive expressions. She then goes back to her pots on the stove and they make themselves comfortable at the table opposite us.

An awkward silence descends. If they were gentlemen, they'd attempt to communicate with us. I can't wait to leave.

'Shall we go?' Eva feels obviously the same.

I address them in Russian, whether they understand or not.

'We have to go now. Work tomorrow. You need time to yourselves.'

Mr. Yakob nods and his wife does not try to stop us this time.

Before we begin to scramble up from our bench, Selim and Tariq jump up with feline grace and pick up sleeping Pavel and Agata, who appear as light as rag dolls in the men's strong arms. Eva picks up Stella.

With a lighted candle I lead Eva through the darkness to our shed, the men following us. I can't see them but I can hear the horses tethered to the tree. The shed is like an ice box. Eva lays Stella fully dressed on the bedding, covers her up and steps back for Selim and Tariq. I'm surprised at the gentleness with which they handle Pavel and Agata. I wait with a blanket to throw over them, and to preserve their body heat, before the biting cold sets in.

'*Spakoynoy notzi*,' Selim and Tariq wish us and disappear into the black night.

'Good night,' we reply.

Without losing another second we pile everything we've got, towels, coats, shawls, cardigans, scarves on top of the bed, and fully clothed, we slide underneath the pile, next to the sleeping children. I blow out the candle and pull the blanket over my head. The secret is to breathe into the covers and to trap all the warmth underneath.

'What did you make of it all, Eva?' I ask, my teeth chattering. 'They scared me at first, I have to admit.'

'But they're not in the Russian army,' Eva points out, 'that's a relief! I wonder who they are, then, and where they're based? And considering they are Uzbeks... they're not that bad looking...'

'Oh Eva...' I giggle, and like a shot of vodka this suddenly releases all my pent-up tension. 'You're so funny! Before long you'll be saying how handsome they are!'

'Well they are! You can't deny that! What's wrong with admitting something positive when it's the truth? Nastusha...' she yawns, tiredness catching up with her, 'all these people here are as much victims of this awful state repression as we are. They haven't asked for any of this. Neither them nor us like what's happening. But since we can't do anything about it, we may at least try to be civil to one another.'

'I have no problem with that,' I agree. I don't tell her that I find their fascination with her blond hair somewhat disquieting.

When I think she's asleep, she says,

'Just listen!'

'To what?'

'The silence! No thudding of the wheels, no shouting, no quarrels, no swearing. No horrible smells. No pressing bodies and bundles all around you. We are alone at last, Nastusha. All alone! Isn't this just the perfect bliss?'

I feel the warmth trapped underneath the layers of our covers spreading to my limbs.

'It is bliss.' I repeat. 'Who would have thought it? A goat shed and a clay floor. We just need a board across the doorway to make it perfect!'

CHAPTER 28

Eva wakes up first. She shakes me and we slide out from under the pile of covers, shivering in the chill of the morning air, though the bright slanting light of the sun is visible outside. We leave the children undisturbed, trusting Mrs. Radvana's presence next door.

In the courtyard the goats, like dark shapes in the purple shadow cast by the mulberry tree, are waiting to be watered and fed. There's no trace of Selim or Tariq or their horses; it's as if last night did not happen.

It does not take us long to get ready. We are fully dressed and bathed from yesterday. To save water, we use a mug each for a bracing, cold wash of our faces, then with the rest we brush our teeth. We've not enjoyed the luxury of toothpaste for a long time, but just to own a toothbrush is an immense good fortune to be cherished with ever-vigilant care against loss. They are the standard army issue toothbrushes acquired by our boys.

A scarf tied around the head, an extra cardigan, a slice each of stale bread and hard cheese in our pockets for lunch, water, three times boiled and cooled in the canister, and we're ready for work.

'I wonder, if they're up yet,' Eva says, hiding her hands in her armpits. Her left hand is still sore. 'I'm dying for a hot drink. I pour a little of the thrice boiled water into a small pot and come out into the yard. The outdoor stove won't be lit till later. I peer inside our landlords' dwelling expecting them to be still asleep at the table, but they startle me. They are up and dressed and call me inside. There's water already boiling on their stove. I make tea and take it back to Eva and we drink it for breakfast together with a small chunk of bread softened in our drink.

Just before six the distant sound of a brigadier calling the reveille to workers gets closer and it is time for us to go. I take a cup of *kasha* and a cup of lentils and with Mr. Yakob's help explain to his wife that these need to be cooked for our children's breakfast and lunch. She nods.

'*Dyeti. Da, da.* The children, yes.'

Before unlocking the outside portal for us, Mr. Yakob gives us a small hand-axe each.

'It's like a toy,' Eva remarks to me, 'it would hardly make a dent on a Siberian tree.'

Nevertheless we thank him with much nodding over our clasped hands, which seems to please him.

'Selim? Tariq? Where are they?' I ask.

He stands in the shadowed doorway and looks across the bright, sun-lit land, towards the distant mountains, pale lilac outlines against the pearly sky.

'Far. Very far.' He says. 'Selim, Tariq, good boys.'

Across the road, the pebbly dusty track, Mr. Ostrovski limps out in his worn grey suit with frayed cuffs and the trouser legs tucked inside his *valonki*. We hurry to him and show him our working tools.

'It looks that we've got to bring our own,' we inform him.

Mr. Ostrovski goes back, while the brigadier, the same man who has driven us here in his *arba*, dressed in a long thick *kaftan*, waits stamping his boot-clad feet and swaying, reminding me of his camel's rhythmic movements. Mr. Ostrovski's working tool is a kitchen knife.

'That's all they could give me,' he says. The blade is wide, with a heavy wooden handle, chunky and rough. 'Depends what we've got to cut today,' he says shrugging.

We walk together following the brigadier and ask Mr. Ostrovski about his family.

'My wife needs to be in a hospital. Ella does everything she can, poor girl, but she's not that strong herself. Skin and bones. I worry for them both.'

I don't know what to say. I do my best to sound optimistic.

'Let's hope our stay here is only a short one. The climate here is certainly better than the cold in Siberia. Perhaps the sun and the warmth will do them both good.'

'That's what I've told Ella. To get everyone out in the sun for a couple of hours.'

We walk down towards the village, and our procession grows as we pass each dwelling. The workers spill out and join us; the Poles and the Uzbek women and their children. There are old and young women, women with babies strapped to their backs, heavily pregnant women. The children's ages range from one to fifteen, I guess. The toddlers are warmly dressed in their fur hats and padded jackets, but their bottoms and legs are bare. I worry for their little bottoms getting cold, I worry about ailments and infections that can attack their exposed lower parts. I want to comfort myself with the thought that perhaps they possess innate protection in their bodies, evolved over generations.

All children, boys and girls, are unusually pretty, with large dark eyes, fringed with thick eye-lashes, the older ones slim and graceful. I assume school starts early for all these children of working women.

We tell Mr. Ostrovski about Selim and Tariq, and I ask,

'How did they avoid being conscripted into the Red Army?'

Mr. Ostrovski listens to our account thoughtfully.

'I can only guess,' he says,' that they belong to some rebel faction. A little while ago our papers at home were writing quite a bit about the Uzbek Freedom Fighters. They had no chance of resisting, let alone overthrowing the might of the Soviet power. They got fragmented all over the land. They're obviously still active in small hidden groups. But there's not much they can do. Perhaps just the odd subversive act. Smuggling people out. Or stealing from the state. Biding their time till their chance arrives.'

'This sounds right,' Eva says, 'this would fit in with what we saw and heard last night.'

'No wonder they are such good boys in Mr. Yakob's eyes. Patriots!' I add. ' No doubt they ensure adequate supplies of food as well. But isn't it dangerous for these two rebels to come into the village where they could be caught?'

Mr. Ostrovski shakes his head.

'And who would catch them? The women? The few old men? No, they know they've got the upper hand. It wouldn't surprise me if the village knows of their nightly visits. But it's always safest to keep quiet and not to know anything. Besides, secretly they must support the original cause that led to the formation of these rebel groups. Also, for anyone staying friendly with the old couple, who knows what favours this could buy them in the future?'

'Aren't we very lucky, then!' I joke.

'Who knows?' Mr. Ostrovski replies thoughtfully.

A crowd is gathered before the looming barn-like building of the *kantor*. I recognise familiar faces of people from the train. Babachka, the large, ungainly Butterfly in her open shirt tucked into her breeches, the legs of which are tucked into high boots, is standing on a chunky stump of a tree trunk and organising people into brigades, twelve people in each. The two men loitering in the background at the half open door look like NKVD men. She has back-up, after all.

Our brigadier calls our group, Florian and Dominik included, and leads us out of the camp in the direction of the river and the faraway mountains. We walk about forty minutes down a track through the cotton fields, all in different stages of readiness for harvesting, until we reach our allotted field.

The cane-like cotton stalks are high, reaching to our shoulders, heavy with bursting seed-cases that spill out the snow-white cotton wool. With a few Russian phrases and physical demonstration our brigadier explains the nature of our work. We are to work in twos, cut the stalks, pile them in neat stacks a metre apart. Two hundred stacks will secure our ration of wheat grain tonight.

It all appears simple. Until we tackle the job. Until we see how the Uzbek women work. As if in a trance, they become like automatons, cutting, gathering, stacking, oblivious to their surroundings, their whole attention concentrated on the row stretching before them. The field is about a kilometre square. Some have babies strapped to their backs. The babies must be well trained, for there's hardly any noise from them. The little toddlers pine for their mothers more. Minded by the older children, they spend their time on the edges of the field playing under the trees. The eldest of the children, both boys and girls, help their mothers in the field. Halfway through the morning, when people stop for a swig of water, the breast-feeding mothers run to the toddlers and spend a few rushed minutes comforting them. Their milk does not cost the state anything at all.

'Strange, there's nothing organised for the children here. No crèche, no schooling?' I think aloud when we stop for a drink of water.

'Speaks for itself, doesn't it?' Mr. Ostrovski says. 'Uneducated masses are easier to control.'

It is ten in the morning. The sun is strong, we're hot and sweaty with exertion. The earlier frosty chill seems improbable now. Eva and I work together, Florian and Dominik on the row next to ours, and Mr. Ostrovski, partnered by an Uzbek boy, on our other side. The air around us is impregnated with cotton-wool dust like pollen, getting into our noses, throats, ears and eyes, making us sneeze and our eyes water. The brittle stalks and the dry seed-cases are covered in tiny prickles that get into our fingers, making them increasingly sensitive and painful with pressure. Eva's bandaged hand tires easily. Stoically she carries on. What looked like a straightforward job has become a harrowing test of endurance. I shall never again look at anything made of cotton and not think about the human cost of pain and tears in the process of production.

There's also the question of output. Some of these small, bony, weightless women are already on their third row. Eva and I are still struggling with our first. We're three-quarters there, Mr. Ostrovski and his young companion close behind, but Florian and Dominik, the nifty little monkeys, have started on their second row.

'Your mother should be proud of you!' I tell them, later when we break for lunch, sit on the edge of the field and fortify ourselves with our meagre provisions. I'm so hungry, I feel as if my stomach has stuck to my backbone. The hardness of the bread forces me to chew it slowly. When it's soft enough to release some flavour together with the cheese, I have to stop myself from swallowing it all in one go.

'Mrs. Anastazia,' Florian looks at me shyly, 'then please tell my mother that.'

'I will, I promise!'

Florian and Dominik have a boiled egg each. The sight of this normal food overwhelms me with such a strong desire, I frighten myself with an impulse to snatch an egg from them. My eyes fill up and stream with tears of self pity, which I'm unable to stop.

'Nastusha,' Eva is alarmed, 'what's the matter?'

'Oh, nothing, nothing...' I blow my nose into a rag, 'it's just the dust. I never expected anything like it!'

'None of us did,' Mr. Ostrovski, the lecturer, the history man, the philosopher, now the cotton crops picker says, wiping his runny eyes, 'Ella wouldn't last five minutes here, with her lung problems.'

'Our mother is very sensitive too,' Florian says. His tone is ambiguous. He and his brother exchange glances from their red and swollen eyes.

'You're doing a very good job,' I tell them.

'Our mother would expect us to do half the field by now,' Dominik states simply.

'Good parents have high expectations of their children,' Eva remarks, 'it's only because they want their children to do well in life.'

'I would do, if only I could go to school.' Florian assures her, 'I actually like school. This work here is purgatory.'

'Where did you get the eggs?' I get onto the subject closest to my heart.

'Someone, two or three doors down from us, keeps chickens.' Dominik tells me, 'Mother had to part with her precious lace vest for ten eggs.'

I make a mental note. I don't mind what I part with. There's only one item in my possessions that's sacred, non-negotiable; Dorotka's baby bonnet.

The working day finishes at six. Before we leave the field, our day's output has to be noted on Babachka's notepaper clipped to a board. To make possible her duty of overseeing a number of fields, she rides about on a horse in a cloud of dust.

When she arrives at our field, we form a group around her and follow her along the finishing edge, so she can identify the rows of neat stacks with the corresponding workers. Eva and I have completed three rows. That's only a hundred and fifty stacks. Mr. Ostrovski and the young boy have done even less. She addresses us in Russian.

'This is below the required output,' she says, 'you've not qualified to obtain your rations of grain today.' She says it just like that, as if she was informing us about the weather. I feel as if she has punched me in the chest. I feel something break inside me. With all my willpower I stop the threatening, mortifying tears. I feel a sudden tide of anger sweep over me, consuming me, till I'm no longer able to hold it back.

'What!' I shout with such rage that the little women nearest to me jump back. Babachka too is taken aback. I doubt if anyone has dared to challenge her before. 'What! What did you say?!'

She licks her thick lips and clears her throat.

'I said, this is not enough. Not the agreed norm to entitle you to your reward.'

'Agreed? By whom? Certainly not by us! You talk of reward, as if this was some sort of a game. This is no game for us, hard-working, starving people who have families to feed!'

I don't lower my voice, but she appears to have recovered from her initial shock and pulls her shoulders up as if to shake me off. Her expression turns unpleasant.

'You can shout your mouth off as much as you want,' she tells me. 'But I warn you, this could finish badly for you. These are the rules. Who do you think you are to challenge them?'

Mr. Ostrovski clears his voice. His manner is gentle, appealing to reason.

'There's just one little issue that needs straightening out,' he says, 'we are free people. We are your allies. We did not ask to be brought here. Our requirements are minimal. Just food for our families at the end of a long working day. Surely that's not too much to ask for?'

'Ha!' she exclaims, pulling herself up even taller, looking down on us like the mighty mistress controlling her serfs. 'Look around you! All these people are free! Do you hear them complaining? They are all happy! They all think themselves privileged! They are all eager to work for the common good of all the people in our great *Soyouz*. Learn from them! And work harder!'

'But what about our food? Tonight? For our families?' Mr. Ostrovski looks ill with his reddened eyes and dark patches, like bruises around them. God forbid, if anything happened to him. He's the pillar of his family. Without him... I daren't even think.

'I said, work harder tomorrow!' The giant Butterfly turns on her heel and strides hurriedly towards her tethered horse.

Mr. Ostrovski slumps down onto a ridge of soil, his thin shoulders hunched in dejection. He buries his face in his hands.

'We shall all die here before long,' he says, 'and to think we were so full of hope...'

Eva and I crouch beside him.

'No Mr. Ostrovski, no!' Eva is vehement, 'we won't die! We won't allow them to win. We shall go to the *kantor* with everyone else and stay there and refuse to budge till we're given our rations!'

He looks up at her.

'We can try,' he says without conviction, 'but even in this remote place, their tentacles are hard at work, the accursed Bolsheviks!'

'I have a better idea!' I blurt out, my brain working overtime, 'I just hope it works. I shall appeal to Mr. Yakob for his intervention.'

Their expressions perk up. Mr. Ostrovski says,

'I wish you luck. It's our last resort.'

The walk back from the fields, after a whole day's toiling, takes longer than this morning. When we arrive at the *kantor* square, there's a crowd of tired, dusty, sunburnt workers, old people, women and children waiting for their day's pay: four hundred grams of grain per person, that's a cup each.

'It'll take ages before your turn comes,' I tell Eva and Mr. Ostrovski. 'I'll be back in good time.' I rush up the road to our dwelling at the end of the village.

The children have been looking out for us and run towards me, as if we've been parted for at least a year. *Where's auntie Eva?* they ask. *Mummy!* Stella keeps calling. I gather them in my arms and hug them and explain that I've got one more thing to do with Mr. Yakob and then we'll all be home.

He's been kind, they tell me, he took them to the river with the goats and Mrs. Radvana made them soup and gave them dried apricots and prunes. My soul gladdens. I hug them and kiss them again and take them inside the courtyard where Mr. Yakob is busy with some woodwork on a high bench. I speak to him in Russian and pray he'll understand.

'Problem with Babachka. We work all day. Work hard. Babachka says no. No grain for us.'

He stares at me with his penetrating black little eyes, listening hard.

'Babachka?'

I nod.

'Babachka *rooskee*. Babachka trouble,' he says, 'I go.'

He puts down his tools and calls out to his wife indoors, I guess to alert her that he's going with me.

'Stay here,' I tell the children, 'we'll be back soon.'

Eva and Mr. Ostrovski haven't moved much further since I've left them, mainly because there is general chaos, and queuing, it seems, is not a familiar concept to the people here. So we stand with the crowd that surges forward every time the few people that have been allowed through the half-open, guarded heavy door, are let out. The Poles are muttering their disgust; the Uzbek women stand stoically, like martyrs before an execution, hushing their children's whispering voices with stroking, calming hands.

Florian and Dominik, who have fulfilled their expected quota of work, have gone on ahead of us to the camp. They are now coming out of the building and stop to show us their prize. Two cups of grain tied up in a handkerchief, like a small rubber ball. This would have been a fraction of the chicken feed I served my birds at home. Florian carries it nervously in the well of his joined hands.

'Can't lose it now! God forbid!' he smiles with a hint of anticipation.

After about an hour, we're finally let inside. It is a very big room, the size of a dance hall, with the high ceiling blurred in the oppressive semi-darkness. In the middle there's a table with scales on it, and next to it on the floor, a wooden box, perhaps half a metre square, opened and full of corn. Stacks of similar boxes fill both ends of the room up to the ceiling, perhaps four to five deep. An armed guard at each end makes his presence felt. As if... I can't imagine for a second these subjugated, silent Uzbek women storming this corn store.

Babachka with her clipboard is assisted at the table by two old men, who weigh the corn and give out the appropriate rations as the workers come up. We move up, give Babachka our names, and she goes through the rigmarole of checking her list, as if she did not remember us. She does not look at us, just shakes her head, dismisses us with a wave of her hand and shouts ,

'Next!'

We stand aside for Mr. Yakob. The two old men suddenly move away and busy themselves with opening the lid of another box.

'Commandant Babachka,' is all I understand of Mr. Yakob's address to her. She darts a nervous glance sideways to one of the guards at the end of the hall, but Mr. Yakob's words appear persuasive, for after her expression changes from hostile to nervous to thoughtful, she shrugs her shoulders and spreads her hands as if explaining herself. She licks the pencil, deepening the stain on her already purple lips and makes a mark on her notes as if adjusting a detail. She then calls to her attendants to weigh our rations of corn.

To our amazement we all receive our portions as well as additional ones for all the members in our families. As we have no receptacles with us, we take off our headscarves and tie them into carrying bags, one for us and one for Mr. Ostrovski.

Outside, once we're back on the road, I take Mr. Yakob's hard old hand and give it a warm shake. Mr. Ostrovski does the same, with many words of thanks in Russian. Eva's blue eyes are lost somewhat today in the puffy redness surrounding them, but she treats Mr. Yakob to her most charming smile. All this seems to give him cause for merriment, for he is chuckling a lot.

'Tell me, Mr. Yakob,' Mr. Ostrovski speaks to him in Russian, 'how did you do it? What did you say to her to make her change her mind?'

'Babachka?' Mr. Yakob asks, then placing his finger on his lips, he lowers his head, so we make a small circle of eager and curious listeners around him.

'I tell her,' he whispers, 'Selim come. He kill her!'

We jump back from him as if scalded. He bursts out laughing, showing his brown, uneven teeth, and coughs and convulses with fun for so long that I begin to wonder if we have misunderstood him in the first place. He recovers, shakes his head, his mushroom hat swaying precariously around his head, and tells us:

'I joke. I tell her she make mistake. She must put right mistake.'

We express our thanks again. In my mind, I'm quite certain which method of persuasion has prevailed upon Babachka to change her mind.

I look up towards the lilac and pink sky, and though I'm aching all over with tiredness, I thank my Guardian Angel for placing me in Mr. Yakob's care.

CHAPTER 29

We wait every day for news from the Polish army. Every time a dust cloud appears on the horizon where the road narrows to a point, my heart beats faster and my eyes strain for the first sight of an army lorry or a jeep with our Polish soldiers driving and bearing the good news of evacuation.

And every time, when the emerging vehicle takes on the shape of an *arba* or a local truck, my heart sinks with disappointment and my fears return. What if we have been forgotten here, in this Happy Bird *kolhoz*, while the army is too busy moving everyone else along?

'Impossible,' Mr. Ostrovski is matter of fact, 'we're a big group here. They've taken our particulars. They've got a record of our whereabouts.'

'And everyone's got someone in the army. They'd be asking about their families,' Eva reasons. 'Can you imagine Henryk and Julian going on without us? Leaving this country without discovering where we are?'

'We mustn't panic,' Mr. Ostrovski reassures us, and I suspect, himself as well, 'of course it seems like a very long time for us stuck here, but the army have a monumental task on their hands. Training and setting up their own camps apart, they have to deal with thousands of people like us following close on their heels. I can't begin to imagine the scale of managing such crowds. The food, the shelter, the sanitation, the medical help. I believe it's just a question of time. As soon as everything moves forward, they'll come for us here.'

Of course that's what I want to hear, what I want to believe. If only there was some way of seeing into the future, of knowing the day and being able to lighten our existence with a daily countdown.

Marginally, infinitesimally, this camp is better than Svoboda. We are not prisoners here, and there is no punishment for missing work, but the constant fear of being denied food makes us all slaves to their rules. Compared to the harsh Siberian winters the climate here is kinder, cold nights and warm days, or so it appeared at first. Now that the spring is merging with the summer, the daytime sun has become scorching hot. We cover ourselves against burns and ensuing blisters as we work in the open fields with no shade. There's a proliferation of horrible black flies in the daytime, and the buzzing presence of mosquitoes at night. We've been warned against scorpions and snakes and with nervous care we shake out our bedding every night, after which we stuff rags in all holes and slits around our shed.

There's one good thing that alleviates the punishing demand of twelve hour working days, and that is the variety of work. No two consecutive days are ever the same.

After cutting down the cotton canes the first day, which were then transported in trucks to one of the large state enclosures, we spent the following day extricating woolly cotton balls from their seed cases and packing them into sacks. It was sitting work but hard on our hands and fingers, leaving them cut and hurting from hundreds of tiny splinters, in addition to the repeated eye, nose and throat irritation from the cotton dust polluting the air.

With our blistered hands bandaged in rags, we were sent another day into the field again to clear the soil of all residue cane roots and leave them in heaps to be taken away for fuel. Mr. Yakob's hoes came in very handy. We were allowed to take as much as we could carry of this dug out debris for our own fires.

This was an unexpected gift, as we now have a little tin stove of our own. Mr. Yakob has constructed it from a large empty oil container, by cutting out a vent at the bottom and attaching a tin pipe at the top. With a cleverly manipulated bend in the chimney he has managed to direct the exhaust end out of the porthole in the wall. He has also cut a door for us out of some old board, which we pull across the open doorway each night.

Fuel for heating can be found on the open land; dry bits of wood, rolling balls of dry vegetation, dry leaves, dry grass, all of which burns in a blink of an eye. But we've discovered another type of fuel, that burns for a long time, keeping the fire alive and the embers hot long into the night. We discovered this on the day we were sent out to pasture, Eva and I, with a herd of cows. The two shepherds, old men, were the herd leaders; we walked behind. Our task was to collect the cow dung into buckets and empty them into large containers dotted out on the grazing land, to be collected later and transported back to the camp.

Following our day out with the cows, we were employed in manufacturing dung bricks for burning. The dung is mixed thickly with hay, pressed into brick moulds and dried out in the sun. Eva and I were thankful, again, for Mr. Yakob's hoes. The unequipped workers were forced to employ their bare feet, as if they were stamping down grapes for wine, except that the revolting brown mess squelching through their toes, sent up gagging fumes of stench, rather than the intoxicating perfume of ripe fruit. Payment for this demeaning work was the prescribed number of dried bricks. I'm just thankful we've got some too.

On another day, the field that had been cleared of all cotton plants and roots, had to be reshaped and prepared for sowing the next crop. This was a shovel and bucket work, punishing on the arms and the back, as we dug a fresh network of trenches for irrigation and flattened down and levelled the hundreds of bucketfuls of dug out soil. Again, the expected output was beyond all our possible effort; the Uzbek women, quiet, uncomplaining, determined, produced eight hundred heaps each. Eva and I, working flat out and sweating like pigs, managed only half of that.

I've no idea how they do it, these undernourished, undersized women, who go home to their children after twelve hours of hard labour, to do all their daily chores of cooking, feeding, carrying water from the river, boiling it in advance, washing, grinding the corn for the next day, rushing all their own necessary housework in order to attend compulsory meetings at the *kantor,* where they have to stand through Babachka's oratory performances on the theme of happiness and privileges of life in the Soviet Union, under the kind and caring patronage of the great visionary Stalin.

Strangely, the Poles are not forced to attend these meetings. Babachka's contact with us is reduced to her distribution of labour tasks at the start of the day, then a hurried appearance at the end, so she can record our output on her clipboard. Her purple-stained lips suck on her pencil as her eyes scan the results of our day's work. There are no comments, positive or adverse, and no hitches later when we collect our rations of food.

Despite the general feeling of expectancy that our stay at the Happy Bird camp could end any time, the day to day existence has forced us to routines, in order to survive. One of the main problems is child care. After the first few days of having to leave the children behind, or taking them with us to the fields all day, Eva and I and Mr. Ostrovski's daughter Ella, went to see Florian and Dominik's mother. Her sourness is well known, but she is an educated woman, an officer's wife. We asked her to set up school together with Mr. Ostrovski.

She stared at us in surprise with those huge eyes of hers in her tired, bony face and for the first time since I've known her something like a hint of a smile lifted her usually pursed lips.

'A very good idea!' was all she said. 'When can we begin?'

And so, for the past six weeks a Polish school has been running daily in Mrs. Lekis' courtyard, more or less equidistant to all the parts of the village.

Eva and I have an arrangement with Mrs. Radvana to feed our children at breakfast and lunch with whatever provisions we have. In the evening we cook grain or lentil soup, varying the taste and the texture with a potato, a pumpkin or an onion, depending on their availability. We can only repay Mrs. Radvana's kindness with doing jobs for her, such that we would have done for the elderly in our families at home: we regularly tidy up the courtyard, wash down and sweep the clay floor, we fetch the buckets of water for her from the river, keep the goats clean, help her wring the washing and hang it out, and anything else we notice she is struggling with.

One evening we found Mrs. Radvana spinning the cotton wool. We have not seen the spinning wheel before and guessed it was borrowed and doing the round of the village. As the evenings are longer now, and the light stronger, Eva's night blindness is easing off. She fetched her crochet hook to demonstrate her creative ability, and before Mrs. Radvana's delighted eyes, a decorative flower grew fast in Eva's fast moving hands. Mrs. Radvana brought out a *kaftan* dress and pointing to the neckline, the sleeve edges and the hemline, asked for a chain of crocheted flowers. I demonstrated to her that I could do this just as well.

Our fame as crochet specialists has spread round the village. Uzbek women come with requests for socks, head caps, shawls or dress decorations, disappointingly small items. We'd love more orders and larger garments to make, but their stocks of cotton wool thread are limited, like everything else, in short supply, in this Happy Bird place. However, we have to be pleased with the extra milk or cheese or eggs that our little industry acquires for us. Our special treat some Sundays is the camel milk, thick like cream, sweetish and filling, which we obtain from a woman living on her own in her enclosure with just a small child and her camel. We often speculate on her means of self support, since she spends her days shepherding the camel to grazing land. Perhaps she too, like Mr. Yakob, has someone serving in the secret army and visiting her only at night.

We have no church here, and there's no mosque, no calling out to prayers. We have seen Mr. Yakob on odd occasions stop what he was doing, spread a mat on the ground and facing the east kneel and bend right down with his head touching the ground in prayer. Presumably this is what the other elders do in the privacy of their enclosures.

We Poles, there's about a hundred of us, meet every Sunday in the open field at the back of the *kantor*. There's no priest to say Mass for us, no sermon, no communion. We have asked Mr. Ostrovski to take the lead in prayers. We sing hymns to Mary, to Jesus, to God, finishing always with a heartfelt supplication to return us all safely to our free country.

It is late Sunday evening at the end of March. The day's been sunny and warm, but the night chill is setting in. We have lit our tin stove and threw in a couple of slow burning dung bricks into the fire, to maintain a bearable temperature at least halfway through the night.

The children are in bed, sleeping. Eva is keeping me company at the table where I'm crocheting by candle light. Her eyesight is still poor in the gloom.

We hear the outside portal creaking, male whispering voices, animal snorting, hoof stamping against the hard ground, the gate being padlocked again.

I rest my work on the table and look at her. She clasps my hand.

'They've come back!' There's alarm in her eyes.

'Shshsh… we just have to pretend we're already in bed.'

We sit very still, listening. The sound of footsteps comes close to the door, and there's a gentle tapping. Mr. Yakob's voice speaks through the narrow gap in the wall by the chimney.

'Anastazia! Eva! Come!'

We remain motionless, Eva gripping my hand harder.

'Anastazia! Eva!' Mr. Yakob's voice gets louder.

Eva stares into my eyes. 'He'll wake up the children,' she whispers.

When he repeats the knocking, I move swiftly to the doorway and move the screening board a fraction.

'*Kharasho!* One minute!' I tell him quietly. 'The children are asleep!'

'*Kharasho*,' he replies and withdrawing, he adds, 'come quick. I wait for you.'

We check the children, then while Eva holds the candle, I push back the board enough for us to slip through, then I slide it back into place.

We tiptoe to their open entrance and stop on the threshold. Their table is lit up with candles casting around an orange glow. Selim and Tariq are standing on the other side, in uniforms and armed as last time, their eyes alert and luminous, like refracting black glass.

'*Salam aleykum*,' they greet us in turn with a nod.

'*Aleykum a salam*,' we reply as politeness requires.

Mrs. Radvana invites us to the table with a sweep of her arm. We all sit down, Selim opposite Eva, Tariq opposite me, Mr. Yakob at the head of the table, while his wife busies herself at the stove. Selim looks at Eva long and hard. She lowers her gaze to her hands, resting and clasped before her, the cut fingers, the broken nails. In this soft light her hair, now grown longer and tied back, looks like pure gold. An unusual sight in a small Uzbekistan village. Whereas I could be easily mistaken for an Uzbek woman with my dark colouring and my skin burnt umber in the relentless southern sun.

'We've been hearing a lot about you,' Selim surprises me with his good Russian.

'Really?' I respond, perhaps too quickly. He gives me his full attention for a long moment. He is very good looking, that cannot be denied, yet there's something over-confident in his manner, something that unnerves me.

'Yes,' he says. He doesn't smile. 'You've proven yourselves to be like daughters to my father and to my mother.'

'Only in gratitude,' Eva lifts her blue eyes to him, 'they've been treating us very well.'

He nods, his expression serious.

'On my father's recommendation,' he says, 'I wish to offer you a proposition. My cousin Tariq and I are of marrying age. It is not good for a man to spend his life alone. Where we live the conditions are harsh, but not uncomfortable. You'd never be cold or hungry. You'd both be treated with respect, for I am the chief of my division, and Tariq is my second-in-command.'

He stops and for a second his expression relaxes, and for a second I'm looking at a pleasant young man, before his words hit me. Eva and I look at each other at exactly the same time. I see total astonishment in her eyes.

'I don't understand Mr. Selim,' she says politely, wedging a distance between them.

'It's simple,' he replies, 'we both need wives and my parents have found you.' Tariq nods in agreement.

Very romantic, not that it would make any difference to our decision, yet his plain speaking makes me smile inwardly. Eva clears her throat.

'Mr. Selim, this is a great honour to be asked by you. We thank your parents and we thank you. However, we're already married women. We have children.'

He shakes his head.

'That is no obstacle. You can divorce your husbands. And your children will come with us.'

I can't believe what I'm hearing. He is serious.

'Mr. Selim,' I can be very serious and businesslike too, 'in our country and in our religion there is no divorce. When you marry, you stay with your partner for life. We've made our vows. They are binding for ever. We would never choose to live apart.'

'So where are they now, your inseparable husbands?'

I detect irony in his tone, but I ignore it.

'At war. And you understand that, don't you?'

He gives me a long, thoughtful look. Tariq sits up lifting his shoulders, ready to have his say. He embraces both Eva and me in his relaxed gaze, and there's a lift to his droopy moustache when he says,

'You are two young women, too beautiful to waste in this village. We can give you and your children a far better life.'

'Thank you. I don't doubt you,' I reply, 'but we're here only for a short time. We're just waiting for transport. Any day now. To be rejoined with our husbands.'

There follows a silence, awkward, as they make no move to break it. Mrs. Radvana brings over the samovar to the table, then six clay cups and a plate of *lepioszki*. I would be ridden with guilt normally, eating someone else's rations, but tonight, I know, their rations will be replenished.

Tariq gets out a packet of cigarettes from his breast pocket, offers one to Mr. Yakob and one to Selim. While they light their cigarettes with a candle and exhale in an expansive, show-off manner, Mrs. Radvana fills the cups with *chai*. Eva and I sip quietly. The wavy haze of smoke allows me to observe the men discreetly. Tariq is as good looking as Selim, but altogether less intimidating, with his softer features and a gentler manner.

'Tell me about your country,' he suddenly says' drawing on his cigarette. Eva turns to him, watched broodily by Selim. She tells them briefly of our experiences in the last two years, of the German then the Russian invasion, of the eighteen months in the labour camp.

'They are certainly good at that, grinding people down with starvation and inhuman labour,' Selim remarks tersely, squinting through the smoke, 'but they'll get their come-uppance one day. We're working on that!'

My heart gladdens to hear his words.

'And may Allah be with you,' I state with strong feeling. His eyes widen in surprise. 'My best wishes go with you!' I add.

'But aren't you allies now? Your two nations?' He sounds provocative.

Eva and I chortle spontaneously.

'Allies? Never!' I stress, 'It's all just signatures on paper. And only because Stalin needs help from the West!'

Selim shrugs in a show of uncertainty.

'Signatures are proof ,' he says, 'and, right now, officially, you are our enemies…' he pauses, allowing his words to sink in.

'Mr. Selim,' Eva protests with fervour, 'the very idea! It's nonsense! We've just told you what we've been through.'

He fixes her with his intense stare.

'It's so simple for you to prove to me your good will,' he says. 'Just come with us. You'll always be safe in our protection.'

Eva shakes her head, her smooth hair catching the light in tiny glints.

'You know we can't do that!'

He shrugs. 'Mark my words,' he warns her, 'you'll regret rejecting my offer yet.'

Tariq buts in, his tone gentler.

'Just think it through, Miss Eva and Miss Anastazia. We are busy men. We'll be back in a month or two. Life is hard here. It'll help you to make the right decision. And when you're ready, just send word through my uncle. He knows how to contact us.'

In a month or two? In his dreams! In a month or two I hope to have left this country well behind me.

We finish our tea and our slowly savoured miniature pancakes, we thank our hosts for their hospitality and at the open doorway we bow our heads as we say our farewell,

'Salam aleykum.'

CHAPTER 30

Nothing changes in the next few weeks. Easter, which for no reason has raised my hopes, comes and goes without news. Eva and I with our children celebrate Easter with a boiled egg each. This was payment from the chicken woman for transforming her old grey shawl into a new one. We unravelled it, died the curly thread orange in some secret mixture of hers, and took it in turns to crochet a new wrap for her. She was pleased enough to add an extra egg in her payment.

On Easter Sunday the Polish community gathered together on the field at the back of the *kantor*, sang joyous hymns of the triumph of Good over Evil, of Life over Death, and prayed fervently for a speedy deliverance from this remote place and for the reunion of all our fragmented families.

A few days ago, while we were out at work a Polish delegation, two civilians and two military, arrived in a jeep to hold a meeting with us. The meeting was attended by Mr. Ostrovski with a few elderly and infirm people, while Mrs. Lekis held fort on her own at the school in her yard. The emissaries from the Polish *Delegatura* could give no assurances as to the definite date of our evacuation. They left with a message for us to stay patient and calm. They were doing everything possible to speed up the process of transportation of so many thousands of us. But Stalin's reluctance to honour his promises of transport assistance, medical aid and increasing the food rations, is continually delaying things. However, negotiations are in progress. We must not lose heart. We, in the Happy Bird *kolhoz* have not been forgotten. They'll come for us when dates to sail from Krasnovodsk have been set.

I'm deeply upset that we, the workers, have been denied the chance of having direct contact with the long awaited visitors because of some unfortunate mistiming. The anguish and the bitterness are embedded like thorns in my heart. I think constantly of Julian and, unable to imagine him in a familiar environment, I'm plagued by a recurring nightmare that he has disappeared irretrievably into a void.

I have to be carefully economical with expressing my fears to Eva. There's no point burdening her with my depressive moods. I hang on her every word for comfort, unbeknown to her. Our conversations sound often like this:

I: 'Why couldn't they have come at the end of the day? When we're back from work. It's so thoughtless! They must know how we're waiting for them every day!'

Eva: 'Of course they know, Nastusha! It wasn't deliberate. If they came in the evening, they'd have to travel back in total darkness across the desert.'

I: 'It wouldn't do them any harm to spend a night here in this *kolhoz*. They'd see what we have to put up with!'

Eva: 'They know, Nastusha, and that's exactly why they've come over to check.'

I: 'And what about our boys? Where are they? It's as if they've totally disappeared from our world!'

Eva: 'No they haven't! And you know it! They are setting up new camps and transporting people like us from place to place.'

I: 'I wish they'd come here to transport us!'

Eva: 'Who knows? We may be next!'

In my mind I cling to the image of a line of army lorries coming down the dusty track, and Julian's and Henryk's happy faces beaming at us through the windscreens. Every night, before I fall asleep I pull out this thought like a comforting blanket, to shield myself from the harrowing nightmares.

Tonight, before the sun sets, after a long day's work, we spend the remnants of the evening underneath the mulberry tree in the corner of our yard, making ordered crochet shawls. The air is warm, pungent with the goats' presence nearby, the sun's light is orange, its rays slicing through the branches and falling against the red clay walls of our shed. The children are lively, having devised a game of hopping over as many cracks in the ground as possible on one foot without stopping. Stella tries hard to emulate Pavel and Agata, making them laugh with her tiny skipping feet, that miss the point of the game. We've sewn sandals for her, Eva and I, out of the felt from the upper parts of Eva's *valonki*. Pavel and Agata's winter *valonki* were too loose on their skinny legs. We've shortened the upper parts, cut holes around the edges and threaded string to keep them tied snugly around their ankles.

Little Stella was three last week. We celebrated her birthday by adding a handful of raisins to the bread dough, so it could masquerade as cake. This brought back memories and longing. She's three. She's not known any other life, only primitive conditions, only hunger. I often wonder if she suffers hunger the way we do, or does her system accept hunger as the norm? She suffers with stomach cramps as Pavel and Agata do. All we can offer are warm drinks and gentle rubbing for comfort. When Eva or I apportion equally our meal of the day, Stella waits with her upturned face, her eyes following our movements, then she tucks in solemnly, with the same reverence as we all do.

Sometimes I allow myself to dream and imagine Dorotka sitting next to her, dark haired, dark eyed, like Julian and me. No longer a baby, feeding herself like Stella, talking like Stella, responding like Stella with giggles to the older children's humorous quips. I can imagine her now with Stella, like two little sparrows hopping over the cracks in the dry clay ground. The familiar ache returns to my heart as I ask God, why? Why couldn't He have spared both?

Eva clears her throat and pulls me back to the present.

'I've been thinking Nastusha, when we get out of here, we must find somewhere nice to live. Until the war is over. When Henryk and Julian come back for us. We must obtain somehow a sewing machine. Beg or borrow or work for the hire. If we could only make ourselves new clothes! Just imagine, looking normal again!'

My first reaction is to shrug off her impossible dream, but then I allow myself to be seduced by her optimism.

'Oh Eva, that would be heaven, wouldn't it! A new dress. New shoes. Hair pinned up. A necklace. Earrings. Our boys wouldn't recognize us!'

We laugh as if this was the funniest thing and I feel my spirit lift, above this lowly courtyard, above the sour odour of the goats.

Later that night, when we are all in bed, cocooned in inky blackness, and the children are asleep, and Eva is still whispering her dreams of the future, I hear familiar sounds of trotting hoofs. I hold my breath and lie very still.

'Good God! It's them again!' Eva's whispered exclamation cannot hide her alarm.

We listen. All the familiar sounds follow: the creaking gate, the horses' hooves, the men's hushed voices, the locking of the gate.

'Eva, we'll just pretend we are fast asleep,' I whisper. '*Ani mru mru*. Not a squeak!'

We lie very still. Only a few minutes later, there is a knock on the screening board that acts as our door.

'Miss Anastazia! Miss Eva!' Mr. Yakob's low voice is urgent.

We remain quiet. I sense Eva's body stiffen next to mine. I dare not breathe.

Mr. Yakob repeats the tapping and calling our names several times. We don't respond.

Then in this total darkness there is a scraping noise as the door screen is pushed aside. My eyes can just about discern a rectangle, a faint tone lighter. My heart seems to pound inside my head.

Mr. Yakob's shape pushes through. Eva grips my hand. I feel his presence, his breathing close beside us, then his hand searching along the covers till he finds my shoulder. He gives it a gentle shake.

'Wake up! Come! Selim here! And Tariq!'

All tension fizzles out of me. I cannot keep up the pretence any longer.

'*Jedna minuta*! One minute!' I say.

Carefully, not to disturb the children, we get up. Our nightdresses have long ago been worn down to useful rags. We have replaced them with daytime dresses. Nevertheless I don't feel fully dressed for this unexpected meeting, till I've wrapped my shawl around my shoulders. I find Eva's shawl and together we slip out, push back the screening board in place and stuff the rags around its lower edges against the nightly intrusion of snakes or scorpions. Then I take Eva's hand to guide her along the wall.

Our hosts' dwelling is lit with candles that spread a warm peachy glow, to which Eva's eyes adjust after a few moments. There is an aroma of burning wax, brewing tea, and vague hints of outdoor scents trapped in the men's clothing. All the rituals of polite greetings are observed, then Mr. Yakob sits at the head of the table, while his wife takes a seat by the stove. We are invited to sit opposite Selim and Tariq, as on the previous occasion. I send them a diplomatic smile as I make my complaint,

'We were already asleep. We have an early start tomorrow. And a long working day. We appreciate being invited here, but cannot this social occasion be postponed till some other time?'

'No.' Selim states plainly, his gaze fixed on Eva. 'No, because we can never tell in advance when we'll be free to visit my parents. Tomorrow we're going on an assignment to another part of the region. We could be away for a month or longer.'

A burden falls off my chest. My wish is sincere when I say,

'May Allah go with you!'

Selim and Tariq acknowledge my words with a solemn nod.

'He will come with us, the Great Allah,' Selim pronounces. 'We are His faithful followers.' He glances at Eva, his voice becoming tense, almost commanding. 'Wish me well, Miss Eva. Send me away with Allah's blessing.'

'Go with Allah's blessing!' Eva repeats fervently, her face animated, her eyes like crystals, reflecting the candle light. 'May Great Allah be with you, may good fortune be with you, I bid you all the best with my farewell!'

Selim's fascination with her is all too obvious in his mesmerized stare, in his slightly parted lips. He licks them and holds his head high.

'It's not a farewell, Miss Eva. No. We'll come back for you and for your children. We'll give you a comfortable life. You'll never have to work again in the fields. You'll be wives of high ranking leaders of our great rebellion movement. You'll be respected for the rest of your lives!'

I glance at Tariq. He grins and makes sheep's eyes at me as if there was already some agreement between us. Tariq, my husband? The idea is so preposterous I find it amusing rather than threatening. It is bizarre, it is as if our previous explanations about our husbands, our culture and our customs have never occurred.

'No, it is a misunderstanding,' Eva tells them firmly. 'Have you forgotten what we've told you before?'

Selim smiles. For the first time I see him smile and I'm annoyed with myself for finding him so attractive. Perfect white teeth, symmetrical features, dark eyes, fringed with thick eyelashes.

'Don't worry, Miss Eva, it's of no consequence,' he assures her.

'But I do worry!' Eva's tone becomes terse. 'We have never agreed to go anywhere with you. We're waiting for our husbands to take us away from this place.'

'All right!' he throws his head back in a cocky stance. 'So let's see who'll

232

get here first. Your husbands or us?' He exchanges a satisfied look with Tariq, who nods and smiles as if everything was settled.

'Mr. Selim,' I but in, 'no matter how long we have to wait, we will never change our minds.'

'We'll see.' His arrogant reply annoys me. I don't give up.

'One thing puzzles me,' I tell him, 'if you can offer us such a comfortable life, what are your parents still doing here?'

He shrugs.

'It's their choice. This is their life and here are their people. When the time comes for them to move on and seek fresh pastures and fertile land, they'll all move together. The whole village. Such are our traditions. I'm always within reach if they need me. But they don't need me now. Now, the need is mine. But, enough of that,' he changes the subject, 'let's have some refreshments.'

His parents have listened in silence to this exchange of words between us, but now, Mrs. Radvana gets up and busies herself at the stove. Eva scrambles up, pushing aside the leg covers.

'Thank you for your kind offer,' she says, 'but we really must go. It's very late.'

To my relief they don't try to stop us. Watched silently by Selim and my would-be husband Tariq, I follow Eva with haste and at the door we bid a polite *Salam aleykum.*

'*Aleykum salam,*' they reply, then Tariq reminds us, 'send word any time. We have loyal messengers.'

We bow our heads and escape, back to our goats' shed, which no longer holds the certainty of a safe refuge for us.

'What are we going to do?' Eva whispers when we're settled back beside our sleeping children. I'm anxious too, but I must not panic Eva, my ever optimistic, supportive companion.

'Eva, there's nothing to worry about in advance,' I state with a certainty which I don't feel. 'We shall be long gone before their next visit. But, even if we're still here, what can they actually do? Abduct us? All five of us? Not so easy. And besides, can you imagine the uproar? Babachka would be over like a shot. And our own people. They wouldn't let them get away with it.'

'They've got guns.'

'So have our guards.' I stop to consider my own words. 'Eva, I can't believe I've just said that. The notion of being rescued by the NKVD against the rebels. The rebels who are like us, oppressed and aggrieved people!'

'Oh please! Don't let's get sentimental about Selim and Tariq! They're crazy!' Eva cries. 'Our only salvation is God's mercy now!'

CHAPTER 31

It is the first week in June. The scorching heat is relentless. The once grassy plains around us have turned into a desert of clay dust and sand. The slow flowing river is getting browner every day, the water that we fetch requires filtering and boiling several times before it can be used for cooking. Dangers lie in wait on the flat bank littered with stones that have emerged from the receding water and created niches for snakes and scorpions. Eva and I have become paranoid about the children's safety and insist they follow behind us wherever we walk.

At school, which is Mrs. Lekis' dwelling, Florian and Dominic sweep up the yard every morning, before the children arrive, ensuring all the corners and holes between the walls and the huts are free of the pests. We do the same in our yard before setting off to work. The bites are not lethal, (only potentially if infected) but extremely painful and there have been a few instances of scorpion bites among our people.

With what's left of the green belt receding further away towards the distant mountains, the state owned herds of cattle, horses and camels have been removed to another place. It is strange to see the empty enclosures with the gates left wide open, as we return from work in the cotton fields tonight.

The Uzbek women walking along with us, some with babies strapped to their backs, some holding their toddlers' hands as the little ones totter along with them, seem unfazed by the long day's work and talk animatedly amongst themselves in high-pitched tones and with much gesticulation of hands.

We join the rest of the working force waiting at the *kantor* for their daily pay in the form of grain rations. The doors of the warehouse are closed and guarded by Babachka's armed auxiliaries. She is standing higher on a tree stump in her usual challenging pose of folded arms and high-booted legs apart. She doesn't say anything, just stares into the distance, and the prolonged waiting seems a deliberate act on her part to remind us of her authority. The babies begin to squeal, the toddlers cry with tiredness, the older children get restless; only their mothers and the old men endure stoically the senselessness of a regime that allows its minions inhuman behaviour towards their own people in the name of equality for all .

The Poles become impatient. An old man goes forward and demands an explanation.

'Let me remind you, Commandant,' he says to her in Russian, 'we're here on special terms. We've been pronounced your allies. Why are we not being treated as such?'

She looks down on him with undisguised disdain.

'Can you not see you're not being treated any worse than the Uzbek people?'

'That is indeed reassuring!' His tone is bitter. 'What I see, is that we're being made to wait for our ration of grain after a long day's work!'

She pulls herself up as if to inflate herself more. She looks past him at the crowd.

'I'm here to inform you that there's been no grain delivery this month.' She then speaks to the Uzbek people, presumably telling them the same thing. There is an outburst of gasps and exclamations. She raises her big arms for quiet.

'It is just a hiccup. Temporary difficulties. As soon as the grain arrives, you'll be given your due rations. In the meantime work will continue as normal.'

Normal? There is not one aspect of our existence here that is normal. Perhaps only one: the mutual sympathy between the Uzbeks and the Poles, both groups treated like slaves.

Someone shouts from the crowd,

'Open the doors! We want to see for ourselves!'

Anger shows in Babachka's flushed cheeks.

'Don't you trust my word?'

'Just let us see for ourselves!' the Poles insist.

'All right! See for yourselves!' she yells, jumping off the tree stump and striding towards her men, making a sign for them to open the heavy door. The crowd surges forward and I feel myself carried along until the group surrounding me stops at the open entrance to the warehouse. The hall is indeed empty. There's no sign even of the wooden chests. I guess they've been used for firewood. People stare for a long time at the space, then walk away dazed.

We walk together up the pebbly track trying to come to terms with the grim reality awaiting us. The evening is warm, the sky peachy in the west with a dusky lavender hue rising in the east, but even this beautiful sight tonight cannot lift my spirit.

Mr. Ostrovski and Eva go through a long list of possibilities and 'what ifs'. Then Eva suggests,

'Perhaps it's time to start planning how to leave this place.'

'But how Eva? On foot? Across the desert? With the children? And all our belongings? We'd need at least a small cart and a donkey. The donkey would need to be fed. His owner paid. How would we manage all that?' I want this to happen; more than anything else right now, but I can't see even the tiniest possibility of being able to arrange anything like that.

'It was just a thought, Nastusha…' Eva looks dejected and I feel a pang of guilt for my pessimistic nature.

'Anastazia, Eva,' Mr. Ostrovski is calm, 'panicking is not productive. What we need to do is take stock of all our existing provisions. We need to divide them up into the minimum daily rations that we can survive on till either the army or the corn arrive.'

'And what if they don't?' Anxiety is beginning to press on my chest.

'Anastazia dear, stop worrying so much. We'll be thinking up new strategies every day. You won't be alone. There's a big group of us. In the meantime, I think, we should start gathering everything edible off the land.'

Within a week all apricot and mulberry trees in and around our village are bare of fruit and leaves. The Uzbek people have gathered their meagre produce from their thin strips of allowable vegetable plots. Eva and I help Mrs. Radvana with this task, in the shade of the high wall surrounding our enclosure, after which she divides the harvest of a few vegetables of each kind – carrots, marrows, sweetcorn, onions and potatoes, equally between our two households. I'm infinitely grateful for her kindness, but I'm racked with a terrible guilt at the same time. Neither Eva nor I can ever fulfil her expectations.

'Do you think, Eva,' I say later, when we are inside our goat shed sorting out our daily portions to last us for as long as possible, 'do you think she's already thinking of us as her future family?'

Eva sighs and wearily rubs her forehead.

'I feel bad too,' she says,' about this whole thing. It bugs me being dishonest. But this isn't just about us, Nastusha, is it? We've got to think about our children.'

She's right. It's so easy to enjoy a clear conscience when everything is going your way. But when our children are threatened with starvation, the constraints of conscience have got to be adjusted to new circumstances. Would anyone blame us? I tell myself, no, yet no amount of reasoning makes me feel good about myself.

'And besides,' Eva adds, 'they've got Selim to look after them. They'll never starve.'

Two weeks later, the village is still waiting for the delivery of corn. The Uzbek women, programmed to follow blindly all orders from the state, go to the cotton fields religiously every day. The old men ride their donkeys out of the camp at dawn and return late at night with whatever food provisions they have managed to acquire. There are other settlements like ours, scattered in this vast desert, but I cannot imagine they have food to give away.

The Poles have stopped going to work, much to Babachka's annoyance. The first couple of days she visited our enclosures on horseback, her massive thighs gripping the skinny nag's back, and threatened us Poles with the withdrawal of our rations when the corn arrives.

'We want to work, Commandant Babachka,' I assured her, when she visited us, 'but who'll find food for our children, when we're in the fields all day?'

'You'll be sorry when the corn arrives,' she threatened and left. I was unnerved by her abrupt exit and voiced my concern to Mr. Ostrovski, who had come over to our yard.

'I think,' he said, 'she is not certain how far she can go in intimidating us. She knows we're on different terms from the people here, and she can't risk getting in trouble with higher authorities. We're a nuisance to her. Undermining her power. She'd be happy to see the back of us. But wouldn't we be happy too? To leave and never see this place again!'

The Poles spend their days searching for anything edible still left on the land along the river; dandelions, nettles, dock and wild garlic. Some recommend the wild tulip bulbs that flower profusely in the Spring, but Eva and I still manage with what's left of the flour and the lentils, seasoning the watery soups with Mrs. Radvana's vegetables, one at a time, to make them last longer.

Since Easter there have been seventeen funerals; mostly old people, but some children too. The Polish cemetery with its wooden crosses is spreading into the desert with worrying regularity, making us all fearful for each other. Eva and I spend all our time with the children, taking them with us in our search for edible vegetation, watching them, checking for any signs of change and praying for deliverance before any more deaths occur. The Polish school run by Mr. Ostrovski and Mrs. Lekis in her yard has ceased to exist; their families' survival is of prime importance now. She has done something so noble now, that I cannot believe she is the same morose person whose selfish moods we've had to suffer on our journey here.

When two older men in our Polish community decided to walk to Kermine to alert the Delegatura Management of our plight, she volunteered her sons to accompany them. Mr. Ostrovski called a meeting in her courtyard and a group of us Poles gathered there.

'Florian and Dominik will go with you,' she said firmly, 'it's safer in a group.'

I feared for the old men, I feared for the young boys, fifteen and thirteen now, their rags hanging off them as if off a clothes stand, to undertake such a journey on foot across the desert. But Florian and Dominik came forward, with the spirit of adventure brightening their emaciated faces and eagerness shining in their eyes. They worked it out, that if they left at dawn, they'd reach Kermine in the evening.

We sent them off with cans of water and provisions collected among ourselves. Mrs. Lekis, her cheek bones even more prominent with her hair pulled back, made a sign of the cross on her sons' foreheads.

'God be with you,' she said, 'you're young men now, and men have duties. Boys of your age died fighting the Bolsheviks. Now's your chance to show your bravery.'

They were gone three days. Eva and I were on tenterhooks awaiting their return; I can only imagine what it was like for their mother. We were walking back from the river with our buckets filled with water, Eva and I and our children unfailingly in tow these days, long shadows following us in the evening sun that bathed the desert in an orange glow, when Pavel exclaimed,

'Look! They're back! They're coming!'

They were four dots shimmering above the ground in the distance. My heart skipped and Eva exclaimed with a burst of relief,

'Thank God! Thank God they're safe!'

'Pavel, Agata, run along,' I said impetuously, allowing them out of my sight on this occasion, 'and tell Mrs. Lekis. Tell anyone else you see on the way. But don't be longer than half an hour!'

We deposited our buckets in our shed to stand overnight and hurried outside, Stella in my arms looking mesmerized by the sudden excitement. Mr. Ostrovski was outside his gate and more people began to appear outside their dwellings, as Pavel and Agata ran down the road spreading the good news.

Our heroes, the two old men, and Florian and Dominik looked tired and weighed down by the bulging sacks they were carrying, their flushed faces were smudged with sweat, but they were all smiling.

'Presents for you!' Florian announced as they reached us and we all followed them to Mrs. Lekis' dwelling. There was already a crowd outside, the courtyard being too small to hold everyone in. But space was made for our returning delegation in the middle, so that even those standing outside could hear the message they brought with them.

The Delegatura Management assured them, one of the old men said, that we have not been forgotten, and our evacuation would take place as soon as it was possible to arrange. In the meantime they were struggling with a Herculean task in Kermine: thousands of people to accommodate in tents, hundreds of them suffering with typhus and dysentery, the field hospital barely coping. The promised aid from Stalin was slow arriving, and the whole situation stayed only just tenable owing to the British and American supplies of medication and food.

This account was not what we had been waiting to hear; a weight of despondency descended on me.

'In the meantime,' the old man concluded, 'we've been sent back with loaves of bread for all us all here.'

Dear God, I thought, forgive me if I don't jump up and down with joy.

It is the end of June. We've been without grain supplies for four weeks. The countryside around our camp has been cleared of all edible vegetation. There's not a magpie in sight, nor the tiniest sparrow. The mornings are quiet without their screeching, without the chirping of the smaller birds in this Happy Bird camp. Occasionally, the fortunate amongst us finds a desert tortoise or a lizard. The Uzbeks go for snakes, but Eva and I hold out with our vegetarian food of dried dandelions and nettles added to the alarmingly diminished provisions of pulses.

Babachka's management team walk about at random and force the Uzbek women to part with their livestock. The chicken keeper had to give away two of her hens. She killed the other two to feed her family of four boys, thus eliminating all possibility of eggs. The old lady, whose cow has supplied us with occasional mugs of milk, cried and wrung her hands when they took her beloved animal away. The meat from the butchered cow was distributed round the village. We obtained a small piece which we chopped and boiled anew for the next few days with each fresh preparation of soup, until only pale little shavings remained in the last soup of rice and chopped grass.

Mr. Yakob was forced to give up one of his goats. He did not fuss. In fact feeding just the one is a big problem these days. He takes it out and is gone all day. It is just spiky bones, covered in loose hide, and the little milk that it yields has to be collected over a few days before it can be processed into a lump of cheese.

The children have lost weight and become listless. They are persuaded without any resistance to take afternoon naps. When they're asleep, Eva and I hurry down the dusty road to Shivana's dwelling and her camel. She is a young woman with a small child, whose absent husband is no doubt at war. Until recently, she's been taking her camel to work with her, where the animal could graze nearby while she worked. Our children like especially the camel milk, which is slightly sweetish, thick and satisfying. But we've not seen Shivana for over a week.

Today we knock hard on her heavy portal and wait.

'She couldn't have gone away, could she?' Eva wonders.

'Where would she have gone in this desert, with a small child and a camel?'

'Perhaps she's got relatives in another village?'

We knock harder and longer this time and wait again.

'Shivana!' Eva calls out. 'We've got something for you!' Just another of our token crocheted lengths of lace. We hope this will buy us a small cup of milk. But there's no sound behind the thick gate.

'Shall we go round the back and look over the wall?' Eva suggests.

At the back of Shivana's walled-in enclosure, there's an empty strip of sandy soil, where she once grew her few vegetables. The bare branches of the mulberry tree hang over the wall like dead arms. There's nothing to stand on.

'Climb on my back,' I suggest to Eva.

'I'll break your bones,' she hesitates,

'Don't be silly, give it a try'.

She kicks off her *valonki*, and I bend and press my hands against the wall to make a platform for her to stand on. She climbs on and exclaims,

'Holy Mother! Nastusha! Your back's like a cattle grid with all those ribs sticking out!'

239

'And you weigh like an elephant!' I shout back.

'I wish!'

She straightens herself up and I feel her stretching and peering over the wall. I sense her stiffen and go quiet as if she's stopped breathing. Then she screams, loses her balance and we both topple down onto the sandy ground.

'For god's sake, Eva! Have you gone mad?' I shout, picking myself up. She wallows about on the ground, hugging herself and muttering,

'Oh my God! My God! My God!'

I shake her by the shoulders.

'Stop it! You're scaring me!'

'Look for yourself!' she shouts back and before I can say any more she bends towards the wall, her hands pushing hard against it. 'Get up on my back! Quick!'

Her urgency is so compelling, I don't argue. I climb and feel her twig-like bones underneath my feet. I stretch and look over the wall.

The sight is shocking. I grab at the edge to stop myself from falling over. The big bulk of the camel lies on its side and next to him, the motionless bodies of a woman and her child. All three are covered in a black, seething mass: thousands of flies.

I jump off Eva's back, and with a hand over my mouth I stop myself from retching.

'We must inform them. At the *kantor!*' Eva shouts in panic.

The rest is a blur of urgent activity. We run down the road to the village office and alert the two guards who are playing cards in their tea room. Our news has immediate effect. They scramble up and shout orders to the old men in the back room. Within minutes a donkey is led out from the stable and harnessed to a cart. The two old men, in their long kaftans and mushroom hats, bring out a stretcher, white sheets, a leather bag of tools and throw the lot onto the cart. They give the donkey a prod with a stick and we're off. As our cortege moves up the road with the two guards leading, people come out of their enclosures to see what is happening. We tell them and many follow us, the Uzbeks and the Poles together.

We form a crowd at Shivana's gate. The guards waste no time. They break down the lock with heavy sledge-hammers and push back the portal's two halves. They direct the old men to lead the donkey with the cart inside the enclosure. I'm overcome with revulsion as I watch them approach the treacle-like thick mass bubbling over the two human forms and the camel. The men pull out a sheet from the cart, and holding it at both ends, they shake it vigorously. A burst of sound, like the amplified buzzing of a thousand bees, makes us all spring back, away from the gate. A black cloud whooshes up and fragments into hundreds of particles that disappear into the sky.

The Uzbek men throw the shroud over the bodies. They wrap up Shivana, then her child and shout something to the guards, who look around, point their fingers at some Uzbek boys and beckon to them. The four boys walk inside the yard and help the old men to lift the bodies onto the cart. The stench is gut wrenching when the cart is pulled past us. I can't believe that these bundles of rotting flesh are Shivana and her little boy, whom we visited just over a week ago; she, so pretty, so hardworking, so uncomplaining; she, who has never known anything else but hardship. I'm overcome with sadness as I wonder who will grieve for her.

One of the guards ties the two halves of the gate with a chain, as the other one raises his voice to the crowd.

'What's he saying?' a young Polish girl asks.

The guard shouts to us in Russian.

'Come back here tonight! There will be camel meat for everyone!'

Eva gasps and looks at me.

'Didn't he see the flies? God knows how long this animal has been lying dead in there.' She turns round to face the people behind her. 'Listen everyone! This meat has gone bad! Don't take it! Don't be tempted to eat it. It could poison you!'

She is hushed up by angry voices. A woman close to us is furious.

'And when have you eaten so well that you can refuse food?' she demands. 'Stop panic-mongering! We've all got starving children to feed. If he says there will be meat, then we're going to get it!'

Eva frets all the way home and imagines the worst scenarios, everyone dying from food poisoning. In the end, I override my own fears and tell her sternly,

'Eva, you've warned them. You can't do any more. They are adults. They are responsible for their own actions!'

Later in the evening, however, after we've finished our meal of a watery soup with lentils and dock leaves, and I glimpse Mrs. Radvana walk purposefully across the yard, I run out to stop her. I cannot bear to think of her obtaining a chunk of that rotting meat crawling with maggots.

'Mrs. Radvana! No! Stop!' I step in her way and call out to her husband, 'Mr. Yakob!'

She is perplexed, but waits for her husband to come out of his workshop.

'Please, Mr. Yakob, don't let your wife take that camel meat!' and I go on to explain. They have a short consultation after which he shakes his head and smiles.

'No worry Miss Anastazia. My wife go wash dead woman. Ready to bury. Tomorrow. Religion say must go clean to heaven.'

That's a relief! But not less of a worry that Mrs. Radvana's hands will be touching decomposing bodies.

CHAPTER 32

First week in July. There's an outbreak of typhoid fever. Muslim burials take place daily. Their cemetery is a walled-in piece of land, where graves are dug deep in this red soil and covered over with inscribed slabs of dried clay. The women wash their dead with reverence and wrap them in white shrouds. It is customary to lay them out on the floor of their dwelling and for all the neighbours to file by, pay their last respects, while the women hold an all-evening vigil with singing and prayers. In the morning the men carry the bodies to their graves followed by a long procession of mourners. A well attended send-off is of the utmost importance to demonstrate the dead person's worth in the eyes of Allah.

Our people are hit too. Yesterday we buried two elderly people and a small boy. A kindly Uzbek let us use his cart and donkey to transport the bodies, wrapped only in sheets, to our cemetery. The NKVD guard supervised the digging of the grave in this hard clay soil, to ensure the depth complied with their regulations. Shallow graves could attract packs of roaming hyenas.

All those still fit in our community came along to support the bereaved families. Mr. Ostrovski was asked to lead prayers and hymns in the short farewell service. My heart wept for the mother of the little boy. She was dazed with grief, her face streaming, her body trembling as her older children led her away.

'Mummy,' her daughter comforted her, 'our little Vitush won't be alone. Mr. and Mrs. Grocholski will always look after him.' All three were buried in the one deep grave.

This morning Mr. Ostrovski hobbles over as soon as our gate is unlocked. He looks so thin these days, like a skin-covered skeleton dressed in a baggy grey old suit.

'Anastazia! Eva!' he calls from the entrance. 'My wife's got it! Very high fever. She's barely conscious.' He comes closer, 'I'd like Mrs. Radvana to look at her. She knows about herbal medicine.'

We tell the children to stay at the table. Outside Mr. Yakob is already there too. We explain. He calls Mrs. Radvana. They have a short discussion after which she fetches a small muslin pouch filled with dried leaves. I take one out to examine it. It is a plantain leaf. Our meadows at home are overgrown with clumps of the flat, round, sinewy leaves, often used to treat boils and skin complaints.

Mr. Yakob repeats his wife's instructions to us in Russian:

'Six leaves. Mug boiling water. Twenty minutes wait. Drink. Good for stomach. Kill fever.'

'Dear God, I hope it will!' Mr. Ostrovski leaves with profuse thanks, and I feel like crying at his helplessness and my own, at not being able to relieve him of his burden. I offer to take his little grandsons off his hands.

We take them and our children out, along the river's edge, wide and pebbly where the water has receded over the last few weeks in the drying heat. Other people are already there searching for the smallest leaf or a blade of grass, overlooked yesterday. Sometimes, the odd, short-lived storm at night acts like magic on the roots hidden underground, and in the morning, it's like finding treasure in the sprouting vegetation.

But today, the sun is intense, beating down from a white sky, through a film of dust floating above the arid land. It is hard to believe that in this sweltering atmosphere, there are bright dots still moving about the distant cotton fields, the ever-working Uzbek women.

Our search is disappointing and we decide to take the children back into the cooler, safer environment of our shed. Eva goes to the Ostrovskis' for news, while Pavel and Agata seat the three little ones at the table and attempt to entertain them with stories. But they are hot and tired and fall asleep on their folded hands on the table.

'You're absolved,' I try to make light of it, 'you can go outside to play if you wish, but stay in the shade.'

When Eva comes back, she glances quickly at the younger sleeping children and shakes her head. 'It's not good,' she whispers.

'I'll go to see them after lunch,' I whisper back.

Later, for lunch, I prepare a meal of rice, which I have boiled before and boil again to make it swell so our small portions appear bulkier. The afternoon nap follows for all the children, and out of habit, Eva gets out her crochet work. I cannot imagine there's any surplus food in the village to bargain for, but this is like saving money for later.

Over at Ostrovski's, his wife's condition is all too clear. It is now just a matter of time. Perhaps only hours. He and his daughter Ella sit at the foot of the bedding, on which Mrs. Ostrovska is laid, her features dark and sunken, her hands crossed on her chest. Ella is haggard and old looking, despite the small difference in our age. She acknowledges me with a nod, and I join them. Their hosts, the old couple, are absent, perhaps tending to their only goat.

I pray for Mrs. Ostrovska, though I know there is no hope for her. I pray that her death is quick and light, it's the least she deserves, after everything that she has suffered.

We have kept Mr. Ostrovski's grandsons with our children overnight. As soon as Mr. Yakob unlocks the gate in the morning, I run across the road to the Ostrovskis'. He and Ella sit at Mrs. Ostrovska's side, just as I've left them yesterday.

'It's all over,' he whispers to me.

Ella looks as if she's made of stone. Her mother has a set expression on her grey face, peaceful yet strangely different from when she was just asleep.

Mr. Ostrovski gets up.

'I've no energy left even to think,' he says, 'but I've got to move. There's lots to do today.'

'We'll help all we can,' I try to comfort him.

And so we leave Ella with her dead mother, and all of our five children with kind Mrs. Radvana, to get ourselves ready for the jobs awaiting us. Unusually for her, Stella is fretting this morning, and it takes a while to persuade her to let Eva go. Mrs. Radvana bribes her with a dried apricot, and the other four gain in this situation by being presented with one each as well.

Mr. Yakob comes with us and Mr. Ostrovski, each one of us carrying a spade or a pickaxe on loan from the two households. We round up Florian and Dominik on the way, and wait at the *kantor* for Mr. Ostrovski to register his wife's death. One of the guards accompanies us to the site of the Polish cemetery, where other bereaved join us to dig two more graves. It is hard work, excruciating on the back, the shoulders and the arms. Just as well there is a group of us, all helping each other and providing rest breaks.

By mid-day the graves are dug, their specified depth passed by the overseeing guard. We agree with the other two families to assemble at three for the funerals.

Back in our dwelling the children are waiting. Mr. Ostrovski's little grandsons want to go home. I bribe them to stay a little longer with a promise of a finger-licking lunch. They don't know it's going to be only a mixture of boiled and cooled pulses, the very last remnants, seasoned with chopped grass and a few economical drops of oil. But Mrs. Radvana clinches the deal by producing another five dried apricots from her pocket. Before she leaves, she tells us in her sign language that Stella is not well. And indeed as we sit over our meagre lunch, she has no appetite. Her forehead is hot, she whimpers and clings to Eva's chest.

'Stay with her,' I tell Eva, 'there will be a crowd of us. No one would expect you to leave a sick child.' I know Eva's worried. I'm worried too. Dear God, don't let it be that dreaded typhoid fever.

'Perhaps she's just a little off colour,' Eva says, stroking Stella's fair hair.

'The afternoon nap will do her good,' I tell her. 'And everyone else.' I look around at the children. 'And you too Eva, have a rest.'

At a quarter to three the funeral cortege, the donkey and the cart, and a large group of Poles start at Mr. Ostrovski's dwelling, with his wife's body wrapped in a white sheet and laid with reverence on the cart. He is stooped and his face is ashen. Ella appears in a trance, her gaze fixed on the distant mountains, not seeing the surrounding crowd. We pick up the other two bodies on the way and then direct our slow shuffling steps towards the small piece of land, that has become a Polish cemetery in a remote corner of Uzbekhistan.

Later, without a word to me, Ella hurries back to her dwelling. Mr. Ostrovski accompanies me to ours, to fetch his grandsons.

'Please, forgive my daughter,' he apologises, 'this is all too much for her.'

'She's been a saint,' I tell him, 'the way she's looked after her mother. It must be an unimaginable void for her now.'

'It's hit her very hard,' he sighs. I can only imagine how anguished he must be too.

'She's still got her boys,' I say the obvious, for comfort, 'now they'll keep her very busy too.'

His grandsons are sitting at the table with Pavel and Agata when we arrive, scribbling on wood shavings from Mr. Yakob's workshop. Their faces light up at the sight of him, they scramble up and run up to him to embrace him round his thin thighs. He strokes their heads with both his hands.

'I hope you've been good boys,' he says and manages a smile despite his grief.

'They've been very good,' Eva assures him from her sitting position on the mattress. Stella is asleep, looks flushed and Eva has made a cooling compress for her forehead.

Mr. Ostrovski thanks her for minding his grandsons. 'It looks as if you've got a lot on your hands too,' he says, 'I'll take away my little rascals now, but do call me if you need my help in any way.'

When he leaves, Eva looks up at me, her expression crumbles and tears flood her eyes.

'Eva, my dear!' I exclaim and rush to her and sit down beside her and give her a hug. 'We'll do everything to make Stella better. You've made the compress. That's good. I'll make some camomile tea. It will be good for her tummy. And I'll go and ask Mrs. Radvana for her advice.'

When the camomile tea is cool enough, we attempt to spoon some between Stella's parted lips. Her cheeks are burning and she does not open her eyes, even when Eva pulls her up to a sitting position. My stomach twists with fear. Please God, please, don't let her get worse!

'Eva, I'll just leave for a minute to fetch Mrs. Radvana,' I keep my voice calm. She nods.

I rush out and stop at the entrance to our landlords' dwelling. I'm taken aback by what I see. Mrs. Radvana is lying back against the pillows on her bed of eiderdowns and Mr. Yakob is holding a cup to her lips. She takes a few sips and closes her eyes. Even though her skin is dark, I detect a deep flush in her cheeks.

'Mr. Yakob!' I remain at the entrance. 'So your wife is ill too? And I've come for her to help us! Little Stella is sick. We are very worried. Is there anything we should do to stop the illness getting worse? And do you need help with looking after your wife?'

Mr. Yakob moves in slow motion: puts the cup down on the table, adjusts his wife's covers around her, shuffles behind the screen in the corner and comes out with a small muslin pouch like the one Mr. Ostrovski was given.

'Medicine for Stella,' he hands it over to me. 'Six leaves make tea. Good for stomach. Make Stella better. No worry my wife. Cousin Haleela come. Cousin Haleela look after my wife.'

The rest of the day is spent indoors looking after Stella. We change the cold compresses and encourage her to swallow some of the brew made from Mrs. Radvana's dried plantain leaves. It is frustratingly difficult, as Stella is unable to stay awake long enough to receive anything. But I tell Eva,

'Her body needs the sleep. It's probably the best medicine for her at this stage.' I'm most probably talking nonsense, but I need reassurances too. Eva nods and wipes her eyes and watches Stella all the while, her hands clasped hard in desperate prayer.

Pavel and Agata sit quietly at the table and attempt a game of 'Hangman' on bits of brown paper. Their voices are hushed and they keep looking up at us anxiously, losing track of their letters and words.

Everything appears worse in the night hours. We've made a separate sleeping area for Pavel and Agata on the narrow strip of floor between the table and the wall. It's a relief that they are fast asleep. I take it in turns with Eva to keep vigil over Stella, but in reality Eva can't fall asleep for longer than half an hour. She sits up with a start and grips my shoulder.

'Eva, nothing's changed,' I tell her each time, and make her lie down again.

The cold compress on Stella's forehead is changed every half hour to keep her temperature down. At times she goes into peaceful sleep, at times she cries out and makes strange noises as her arms and legs thrash about. In the morning her eyes remain closed and the rhythm of her breathing is uneven.

Eva takes over while I cook some watery kasha and brew some herbal tea. Eva says she is not hungry, but I cajole her into swallowing her portion. Pavel and Agata eat theirs but not with the usual wolfish appetite. I try hard to ignore the niggling fear inside me. It comes to the surface with a jolt when Pavel announces,

'I feel a little dizzy today.'

'Pavelek dear,' I take a deep breath, 'you've had a tiring day yesterday. We all did. And none of us are that strong these days. But as soon as we're out of here and start eating normal food, we'll all regain our strength.'

'And when will that be?' he asks and puts his head down on his folded arms.

Agata massages her stomach, permanently distended these days. She never makes a fuss. 'It hurts a little,' she explains. I stroke her head and wish with all my heart that there was some way of getting us all out of here.

Eva looks up from where she's sitting on the mattress at Stella's side.

'I've been thinking,' she says, 'I've been thinking all night!'

'And...?'

'We've got to leave this place! The sooner the better!' She holds my gaze.

'But of course we do! But how do you make them come and take us away?'

'I'm not going to wait any longer!' Her tone is angry and determined. 'I'm going to hire a horse and cart and get us out of here!'

Hire? I wonder. We've got enough roubles left, but no one wants money. It would be easier if we had surplus food to barter with.

'And how are you going to do that?' I ask.

She sits up her thin shoulders erect, confident.

'I'll go searching through every dwelling in this village till I find a cart big enough to take us and our things. I'll bribe the Uzbek with promises of food when we get there, on top of what I pay him. Nastusha, think, once we get to Kermine, where they feed thousands, there will be food for him too. And I must get Stella to the hospital. I must! Before she gets worse.'

Her proposition sounds crazy, but the more I think about it, the more I find myself agreeing with her.

'Eva, it's not a bad idea! Not bad at all!' I feel a burst of energy.' Eva, you stay with Stella and I'll go! What about you, Pavel and Agatka? Do you want to come with me?'

Their eyes look blank, so I don't press. 'Would you rather go back to bed?' I suggest. It worries me when they do, it worries me how quiet they are today.

I visit Mr. Yakob and his wife before I leave. The old woman sitting beside her must be cousin Haleela. She is giving Mrs. Radvana a bed bath with a wet cloth, dampening her flushed face, wiping her arms that are covered in red blotches.

Mr. Yakob comes outside to me.

'My wife very sick,' he tells me, his sad expression deepening the creases in his face, his eyelids heavy over his eyes.

'You must take her to the hospital,' I tell him firmly.

'Hospital no. Haleela know medicine. Haleela make wife good.'

I haven't the strength to question his belief in Haleela's medical knowledge. 'But we must take Stella to the hospital,' I state categorically, 'we must get a cart and a horse to take us to Kermine!'

There's a flash of animation in his face and he stares at me for a long time. 'Make Selim sad. No go, Miss Anastazia!' Dear God, this is hard.

'Mr. Yakob, you are very kind. And we are grateful. But Stella could die. We must save her. When I find a horse and cart, will you be my interpreter?'

He is quiet for such a long while, just staring down on the ground, that I feel as if he's already dismissed me and my plea. But then he lifts his eyes and says,

'*Da*! I help you.'

I enter every enclosure and look around, first down one side of our road, then on the other. I find the odd goat, the odd sheep, the odd donkey here and there. There's even a camel close to the *kantor*, I guess one of theirs. The only carts that people possess are small, box-like, hand-made objects, with handles for the humans to pull, with room only for firewood or cans of water. Past the *kantor* in the spacious, state-owned enclosures, the carts are the size of large carriages, constructed to move big stuff, like stacks of cotton wool, containers with cow dung, sick animals and heavy farm tools. One of those would be perfect to transport our two families (we couldn't leave Mr. Ostrovski behind) and our baggage. I stand at one of the open gates and feel infinitely overwhelmed with helplessness. Here is just what I need, but I know that nothing, absolutely nothing could persuade Babachka to assist us. In this remote little village the power is absolutely hers; why would she endanger for us the only important thing in her life?

I'm filled with despondency at the thought of Eva's disappointment as I walk back from my unsuccessful mission. What can I tell her? I can't think of any solution, except deliverance by the Polish army.

She looks up eagerly when I walk in. I shake my head and give her an account of my fruitless search.

'Nastusha,' she sighs, 'we've got to do something! Mr. Ostrovski's just been. Now his grandsons have got it too.' She glances where Pavel and Agata are sleeping, 'I'm scared for them,' she says.

They look peaceful in their sleep, but their faces are flushed and their lips are dry and flaky. I feel their foreheads. They are burning. Somehow, that awful tension that I felt before fearing the worst, leaves me suddenly, now that I know the dreaded illness has caught up with us. I've got no choice but to tackle it the best way possible in our impossible circumstances.

'Right!' I say, 'Cold compresses first, then the plantain leaf brew!' As I busy myself I speak over my shoulder to Eva, 'I've even thought of stealing one of those large wagons at night.'

'Impossible without a horse!' she takes me seriously.

'Eva, the whole thing's impossible. Full stop! We have to shout to all our Guardian Angels together to take pity on us!'

Eva is thoughtful all the while when I soak small pieces of towelling in cold water and place them over the children's foreheads. They stir for a moment then fall back into a deep sleep, their eyes sunken, strange. I'm assailed with fears for our own health. What if Eva and I catch typhoid fever? Who will look after us? Who will mind our children?

I brew some camomile tea for us and sit down on the mattress beside Eva.

'I've even thought of walking it,' I tell her, 'leave everything behind and just take the children.' But even as I say it, I know that's not possible.

'I've been thinking too, Nastusha,' she says, 'there's only one possibility that maybe, just maybe, will save us.'

I look at her intrigued and alert. She holds my stare as she says,

'I never, ever imagined myself having to do it. But, if anything happened to one of our children, I'd never forgive myself for at least not having tried.'

'What?' my heart begins to pound for I already guess.

'I'll ask Mr. Yakob to get in touch with Selim.'

'But Eva, is that wise?' my mouth dries up, 'you know what they're expecting from us.'

She shrugs.

'We've got nothing else left. I'll appeal to his honourable side. It's our only chance. All I'll ask of him is to arrange a horse and cart for us. Shouldn't be difficult for such a mighty leader, as he claims to be.'

The idea is straightforward. At home, this would have been a natural request, which any of our friends would have been happy to oblige, but here... I feel a shiver of fear.

'Eva...'

'No Nastusha, don't stop me. I've got to try.' She gets up. 'Now I've made up my mind, I'll go to see Mr. Yakob now. We can't waste any time!'

As I wait for her to return, my feelings are a mixture of anxiety and hope. I check each child, touching their cheeks and their foreheads, feeling for their pulse, and all the while I pray that something good happens soon to deliver us from this nightmare.

When Eva gets back she appears more lively, but nervous too, the way she keeps biting her thumb nail.

'They've sent for him already,' she tells me, 'as soon as Mrs. Radvana became ill. But they can't say when he'll come. Dear God!' she paces up and down. 'Who would have thought that I'd be waiting for him like this? Praying for him to come as soon as possible?'

I keep quiet. I don't want to dampen her hope with my own doubts. For what guarantee have we got that he'll assist our escape from here?

We are on tenterhooks all night, barely able to sleep. On the second night when it gets past midnight, I feel as if all expectation has been sucked out of me. I am so tired, I don't even feel anxious any more. I just want to sleep and sleep, and when I wake up to discover that all this has been just a bad dream.

But this nightmare is reality. Eva and I tend to our children around the clock, making them as comfortable as possible with cold compresses and forced sips of Mrs. Radvana's prescribed brew. I'm no longer certain if their long, often comatose sleep, is a good or a dangerous thing. All I desperately want is to get them to the hospital, to deliver them into professional hands, so that their recovery has a better chance.

It's only been three days since the onset of their illness, but it feels like three months. We hang on to the tiniest positive change in their breathing, their sleep, their lowered temperature, even their ability to pass water, and tell ourselves that there are signs of improvement.

Tonight, as we sit in the darkness, Eva and I, the silence around us punctuated by the children's laboured breathing, we wait yet again for those other noises outside, of hooves on the beaten track, of the gate being unlocked. We hear that first distant sound at the same time. Eva grips my hand.

'He's come! Nastusha, he's come!'

I hold my breath. I'm glad, relieved, frightened all at once.

'Give him time,' I whisper, 'to see his parents first.'

In pitch dark senses become sharpened. We sit still through the gamut of sounds of his arrival, opening and locking of the gate, his horse's hooves stamping against the hard clay ground as he tethers it to the tree, then the muffled voices of our hosts through the dividing wall.

We wait for what seems like a very long time, but is perhaps only half an hour.

'I can't stand it any longer,' Eva whispers. 'I must go. I must do it.'

'I'll come with you.' I worry about her night blindness.

'No need. Stay with the children.' She sounds determined. 'I know every centimetre of this place like the back of my hand.' I don't argue. I help her move the board back from the entrance and the gap-filling rags, the so often repeated routine that can be done, indeed, blindfolded, and I let her out. Then I sit down and wait.

I expect old Mrs. Haleela has taken over the housework next door and has prepared a meal for the men. I expect Eva's mission may take a little while. I draw up my knees, rest on them my folded arms, then my head on top. I feel so weary, I'm overcome with self pity and feel aggrieved at all the injustices we've suffered: the abominable train journey, Siberia, the freezing, killing cold, the illnesses, the deaths, the inhuman conditions of further train journeys, and now this. Famine and typhoid. Will there never be an end to it all?

My ears pick out sounds, whispers and rustling and feet scraping the surface of the rough ground. I await Eva's knock. But all goes quiet. I strain my ears. Nothing. Only the strange mysterious creaks and thuds, and sighs like the breeze murmuring in the branches.

I slump down to my previous position and for a moment close my eyes. The sleep of tiredness creeps up on me in seconds. The tapping when it comes pulls me out of unconsciousness and I jump up startled and help Eva push aside the screening board.

'Eva, I'm sorry, I must have dozed off. How did it go? Was he agreeable? Did you manage to persuade him?' I throw questions at her. She brushes past me, and I catch a hint, just the tiniest whiff of a vague scent. Some distant memory stirs in my mind. Though I can't see her in the dark, I sense there's something wrong. 'Eva, is everything all right?'

'Everything's arranged and sorted,' her whisper assures me, but I'm not convinced. In silence we push the door screen back and secure the rags around it. I wait for her to say more, but she moves to the corner, where our water is kept. Living in a space so small, every object has to have its own, permanent place, especially for Eva's sake, who has to feel her way around in the dark.

'What are you doing?' I ask, impatient for her to tell me everything.

'I'm very thirsty. Lie down Nastusha, now that I'm back.'

I lie down on our bedding, separate from our sick children and wait. I hear Eva pour two mugs of water into our washing bowl. I hear the rustle of her undressing, and the squelching of the face cloth. She is having a wash.

I am about to grumble, 'Can't it wait till the morning?' but the words stick in my throat as a sudden flash of intuition hits me like a blow. My breath stops with the shock of it.

'I'm very hot,' Eva's whisper reaches me.

I was hot too, till a moment ago, in this stifling heat bearing down from the clay walls. Now I'm cold, numb, my mouth dry. God, oh dear God!

Eva settles beside me, her back curved against my side. I sense her shivering. What can I say to her? It is an effort to say something normal.

'What did he promise?'

Her answer comes after a pause.

'He'll arrange everything. He'll even escort us.'

'Really?'

'He wants me to come back with him.'

I don't believe it! 'But that's ridiculous! Eva, he can't force anything once we're inside the army camp!'

She gives a shuddering sigh.

'It could turn nasty. Him being armed. And them. And the sick children. God! It's such a nightmare!' She stifles a sob and weeps into the pillow.

I want to weep with her. I feel so utterly helpless and inadequate and sick with guilt. It happened so close and I didn't protect her. Such unspeakable evil! And infinite hurt! I can barely imagine her torment. Her lips are sealed. For voicing this crime inflicted on her would give it a name, make it real. This must never be. Her reputation and Henryk's honour must never be harmed.

251

In my feeble way I do my best to comfort her. I stroke her shoulder and whisper,

'Eva dear, tomorrow night it will all be over.'

Only for her, it never will.

Eva is very subdued in the morning. It scares me. She hardly speaks a word when we go through our usual routines of getting ourselves washed and dressed and our hair brushed, before we tend to the sleeping children.

'Eva, just a few more hours,' I tell her, when we wipe down the children's hot bodies with damp cloths. She picks up Stella, limp, her arms and legs dangling, and carries her around in the shade of the courtyard walls. She looks bereft, as if someone has already died.

I experience attacks of shivers every time my thoughts race ahead to the midnight hour and my stomach contracts every time I catch despair in Eva's eyes.

I'm glad to see Mr. Ostrovski when he comes over, but he has bad news. Now Ella has all the symptoms of the typhoid fever too. Eva livens up a little, to my relief, when she discloses our plan to him. We insist that he must get his family ready for the journey too. His eyes redden and his lips tremble.

'God bless you both,' he says quietly and withdraws.

We have a little *kasha* left, so I cook some for lunch and leave the rest for supper. All through the day we do what we can to force a little medication of the plantain leaves brew into the parched and blistered mouths of our children. In the afternoon, when Eva takes her much-needed nap alongside the children, I slip into the yard, where Mr. Yakob is planing some wood on the workbench. Passing by the open entrance of his dwelling, I get a glimpse of Mrs. Radvana, prostate on her bed, and Mrs. Haleela sitting beside her.

Mr. Yakob stops and wipes the sweat off his face with the back of his hand. He asks,

'You ready, Miss Anastazia?'

'Yes.' There's nothing much to pack. Most of our things are kept in our sacks anyway, as there's no wardrobe or even a chest. I'd like to say to him how much we are grateful for all his acts of kindness, and how much I'd like to come back one day and repay him. But that will never happen, once we leave this place. I choose my words carefully.

'Mr. Yakob, you and your wife have been very kind to us. We've got nothing to give you to express our thanks.'

He straightens himself and pushes back his mushroom hat. He studies me with his piercing dark eyes, like his son's.

'No need give,' he says, 'soon we family. Soon you Tariq wife.'

I cringe. I feel a prick of conscience. It gives me no joy to have to deceive him. What more can I say? Something about the children. That they'll miss him. No. That would sound like a farewell.

'The children are very fond of you,' I tell him, and watch, my stomach churning, when a smile lifts all those criss-cross lines on his face.

The night seems endless as we wait. Tiredness and heat overcome us and we doze on and off on top of our bedding, startling each other as we wake up, to resume our vigil.

Eva hardly speaks. I can only imagine her dread of having to see Selim again, of having to endure his presence all night, as he escorts us across the desert. And afterwards? I count on our soldiers' quick thinking and action.

At long last I hear them. The sound of hooves on the beaten track and the squeak of metal wheels. Eva grips my arm.

'He's kept his word!'

We jump up and feel our way to the door screen, slide it back, for the last time, and remove the rags. Moonlight falls inside our den illuminating all shapes and forms. Eva cowers behind the screen. I step outside. The sky is vast, sprinkled with a million stars. Everything is clearly outlined in the courtyard. Mr. Yakob comes out of his dwelling and like a shadow floats noiselessly towards the gate. I help him push back the halves of the massive door, then we both look out.

It is as if nature is in sympathy with Eva and me. I could not have imagined a clearer, brighter night for our journey. The desert on one side, with its softly rolling land visible as far as the starry horizon. The road descending to the village is white in the moonlight, the walls of every dwelling etched sharply against the shadows of the next. The river and the land beyond with its cotton fields are like a patchwork of soft greys, blending with the darker shades of the distant mountain range.

'Selim! No Selim?' Mr. Yakob's voice startles me. I notice that there's no escort to the horse and cart coming up towards us.

When they reach our gate, Mr. Yakob goes out to the coachman. They engage in a hurried conversation after which Mr. Yakob throws up his arms then clasps his head in both hands,

'Ay, ay, ay…!' is all I hear in his agitation.

'Mr. Yakob! What's wrong? What's happened?' I feel the grip of fear.

He drops his hands and in the bright moonlight I see his face twisted with pain.

'Selim no come! Enemy shoot him arm! Selim hide!'

I melt with relief. God is on our side! There's no time to waste. I turn but he catches me by the arm, his bony fingers digging into my flesh..

'Stop Miss Anastazia! Stop! No go! Must wait Selim!'

I'm horrified. This is our only chance.

'No Mr. Yakob,' I speak firmly, 'we cannot wait. Our children will die!'

And as I try to free myself from his grip I hear the sound of galloping hooves. Dear God, please! Not Selim after all! The horseman is getting close. All three of us have turned to stone statues. Then he is upon us, his horse panting as he reins him in to a stop. The man jumps down. He's armed with a rifle, he's one of Babachka's guards. Sokolov. He questions Mr. Yakob and the coachman in a salvo of staccato words, then he turns to me in Russian.

'Why have you arranged this in the middle of the night?'

I have no idea what they said to him. I have to think quickly.

'Comrade Sokolov, an emergency does not choose its time. Our children are very sick. We must get them to the hospital in Kermine. To the Polish military camp.'

I stress 'military' hoping for the right effect, favourable to us.

He hesitates. 'Have you got a travel permit from Commandant Babachka?'

Frustration overrides my fear. Words burst out of me.

'Comrade Sokolov, I have not the least doubt that you're well acquainted with the terms of our amnesty.' I'm not, but I bluff on. 'As the relatives of Polish soldiers, we're entitled to the same freedom of movement as they are. Are you going to stop us and risk breaking the rules of that agreement?'

I think I've got him stumped there. The faintest threat of repercussions from higher authorities has immediate effect on these wretched, brainwashed people, whose whole life is based on lies and uncertainties, who are afraid of their own shadows, of their own thoughts.

Sokolov thinks for a moment then turns to Mr. Yakob. As he listens, Mr. Yakob becomes visibly angry, stamps his foot and clenches his hands.

'You bad girl Anastazia! I kind, Selim kind, you bad!'

This is torture.

'Yes, I'm bad. But our sick children can't wait. We're going!'

We're ready in half an hour, all our belongings thrown onto the cart, and in the niches between them, our children and Mr. Ostrovski's daughter and grandsons curled up on the folded bedding. We three, thankfully still mobile, hurried on by adrenalin, climb on last, with Mr. Yakob's angry mutterings hurled at us like stones.

'He must be cursing us,' Eva says, when the cart jolts forward, and slowly distances us from him, waving his fists at us.

'His Allah is as omniscient as our God,' Mr. Ostrovski states, 'he'll comfort Mr. Yakob some other way. But now, I believe, now it's our turn to find refuge in Providence.'

I want to believe that too. The strange turn of events in the last half hour has left me unnerved, and uncertain of what to trust next. Sokolov is the big surprise: our unexpected guardian angel in the guise of an NKVD man. He

254

even helped us to carry our limp children to the cart, scolded all the while by Mr. Yakob.

Sokolov escorts us on horseback out of the village along the desert road that stretches before us and vanishes beyond the horizon. The land is bathed in white moonlight and could look magical were it not for the niggling fears inside me that this is all a trick which will be suddenly revealed when we are ordered to go back to the village, to Mr. Yakob, to Selim, to Tariq... I squeeze my eyes shut tight to push out these demons. Then Sokolov speaks,

'When did your children become ill?' He sounds human, concerned. We tell him.

'They need proper medication. Good hospital care,' he says. 'Don't worry. You'll still get them there in good time.'

'I pray hard that we do,' I tell him. 'Have you a family of your own?'

He looks at me, a little startled, I think, but then he replies.

'Yes. I have a wife and two sons. Misha nine and Sasha eleven. I see them every month.'

'Only once a month? I'd miss them terribly,' I say with feeling.

'Some people,' he tells me, 'live even further away from their families. I'm very lucky. And fortunate to be doing my duty for my country!'

Fortunate? I wonder how much he believes of that. Duty? At a remote, ramshackle settlement, forcing women and old men to work? What satisfaction is that? Especially on long lonely nights when all your being craves for the closeness and warmth of your loved ones.

'I wish you a really happy time together, next time you visit them.' I honestly want this for him. He is thoughtful, a little self conscious.

'Da... spaseeba... thank you. My sons never want to let me go,' he confesses with pride.

About two kilometres into the desert he bids us farewell.

'Time for me to turn back,' he says, 'it's a straightforward road. You should reach Kermine at dawn.'

We thank him. He'll never know the extent of our gratitude. As he gallops away, Mr. Ostrovski says,

'May God always have him in His care. I never imagined a *kind* NKVD man.'

CHAPTER 33

A severe stomach pain pulls me out of my slumber. I double up, embrace my stomach tight and look around. Eva and Mr. Ostrovski are slumped over the baggage asleep, as are the children and Ella, curled up on the bedding stuffed between the bags. Even our coachman is dozing, his body swaying in rhythm with the horse's trot.

I take in the scene with one glance in the apricot-coloured dawn. Another spasm. I want to cry out. I bite my lip and hug my stomach harder. Please God, not me as well! I can't let Eva down.

Then my eyes behold a most desired, wonderful sight: the rippling surface of hundreds of tents on the horizon. We have arrived!

No need to wake them up yet. I suppress another groan as a spasm grips my stomach. I feel prickly sweat all over my body, especially on the scalp, beneath my sticky hair. I take a swig of water from the canister and lay back for a moment closing my eyes against the brightening sky. We're there! We're nearly there! I keep telling myself, forcing myself to breathe deep and slow. Nothing brings me relief. I curl up and nurse my stomach and don't bother to look up when a short while later, an officious voice calls out in Polish,

'Who goes there?!'

The cart stops. Eva and Mr. Ostrovski are evidently awake. I feel their startled movements around me. Eva exclaims,

'We've got very sick children with us! We've got to take them to the hospital! It's an emergency!'

I wait for the duty patrol to ask more questions, but the two soldiers look over the side of the cart and one gives directions,

'Follow this track through the camp right to the end. The hospital tents are easy to see. They have red crosses on the flaps and are ten times as big as these here.'

The cart moves on and I feel Eva's hand on my shoulder,

'Nastusha! Wake up! We've arrived!' Then her tone changes. 'Nastusha!' I detect alarm in her voice. I try to open my eyes, but my eyelids feel like lead, my head begins to throb, and my body feels as if all the aches and pains of my whole life have multiplied and culminated in this moment. I open my mouth to tell her not to worry, but all I produce are uncontrollable groans. I feel myself floating away from her into a blackness that absorbs me and dissolves all my being into nothingness.

When I regain consciousness and open my eyes, the outlines of objects are fuzzy. Above me, the canvas of the tent roof is saturated with sunlight. There are soft sounds around me of busy activity and hushed voices. There is a smell of disinfectant. It is very hot, but I feel a blissful stillness and all the pain gone. I turn my head. It feels strange, prickly. I want to touch it but my arm refuses to move.

'They had to shave off your hair.' Eva's voice drifts towards me, and when I try really hard to focus my gaze, I see her sitting beside me, like an angel with a halo of white golden hair.

'Nastusha, you're awake!' Her voice breaks and her lips tremble. I want to touch her. She clasps my inert hand and attempts a smile. 'Nastusha! I feared the worst! I was so scared!'

Suddenly I know where I am and remember our sick children.

'Where are they?' A spurt of panic reactivates my brain.

'They are safe!' There's great relief in her voice. 'We got them here just in time! They're in the children's ward. Recovering well. Even beginning to eat. Nastusha, we were so lucky!'

I breathe deep and feel weak with gratitude. Then I'm puzzled.

'Did you say, recovering well?' I ask. 'So how long have we been here?'

Eva gives a wan smile.

'Nastusha, you've been like this for nine days!'

'What!' I'm astonished, 'I've slept for nine days?'

'You've been unconscious and feverish a lot of the time. They gave you daily injections and fluids to keep you going. You're over the worst, thank God!'

I contemplate this piece of information with a growing understanding of how worried she must have been, alone with us all sick and so close to dying.

'My dearest Eva...' I suddenly think of Mr. Ostrovski. 'And Ella? And her little boys? Are they over the worst too?'

There's hesitation in Eva's delayed reply.

'Maks and Aleks are recovering. But Ella... she died soon after we arrived here.'

This is a shock. I picture Mr. Ostrovski alone with his grandsons, the two women he loved the most in his life taken away from him, and my heart swells up with grief and I can't hold back the tears.

'I know...' Eva squeezes my hand, 'I can't believe it either! The cruelty, the senselessness of it all!'

My eyes and my nose need wiping. Eva slips a small white rag into my hand and helps me lift it to my face.

'Thank you,' I blow my nose, 'Eva, I'll be all right now. Don't worry any more. Together we'll get through this. Now tell me how you are. No symptoms, I hope, of this horrible disease!'

She shakes her head and her expression relaxes.

'No. I feel all right. It helps to have three meals a day. It is like heaven. I

257

started feeling stronger from day one. It's mainly soups for lunches and suppers. But thick, with lentils and vegetables. And we get bread every morning for breakfast and sweet tea.'

This sounds indeed like heaven, even though I feel no appetite at all.

'And how did you get rid of our coachman?' I ask.

Eva smiles.

'It was easy. I think he was so overwhelmed with all the panic around him, the soldiers, the nurses, and all the sick people on stretchers, he couldn't wait to get away. Mr. Ostrovski and I paid him what he asked for, I was surprised it was so little, and he turned round and was gone!'

'Do you really think that Selim would have been able to take you back with him? Amidst all that pandemonium?' I ask.

She looks away, a shadow puckering her brow.

'The whole thing has been so ghastly I never want to talk about it again! Ever!'

During my convalescing week, I'm transferred to another tent. I am weak and shaky on my legs, but regularly propped up against the pillows on my folding canvas bed, and encouraged to sit up, stand and take a few steps every few hours. I'm making good progress; I can't wait to get back with the others, to our allotted space in one of the tents in the civilian camp. I look awful! Quite a shock to see myself in the bathroom mirror (we've got a screened washroom area in our tent) when I stare back at myself with yellowed eyeballs and a bald head. Eva has cut a square of material from my old floral dress which I tie elaborately, like a turban around my head.

The women on either side of me are not as vain as I am; they examine their stubble on their scalps every morning and report to each other on the growth of their hair.

'It's not as if I'm out to catch anyone,' Vera laughs, exposing gaps between her uneven teeth, 'I've looked much worse, and did that save me? *Każda potwora…* as they say, every baboon finds a mate…' She speaks openly about the father of her one-year-old son, a veritable little Kazakh child, with Mongolian features and the Christian name of Joseph. He is brought daily to see her by his older sister Frania, blonde and blue-eyed and like a little mother to him. 'He's our little saviour, my darling little Joseph,' Vera often repeats, showering his dark hair with kisses. 'Without his father, Frania and I would have starved to death.'

Old Teofilia on my other side is less exuberant.

'I've experienced poverty and famine in the last war. It's all happened to us again. Now all I pray for is to be released from this place of suffering, so I can embrace freedom just once more before I die.'

'Mrs. Teofilia!' I reprimand her gently, 'Don't talk of dying! You've survived Siberia, you've survived Uzbekistan, you've survived typhoid. We're so close to freedom now, you'll survive anything. Think of your family at home, waiting for you to come back when all this is finished.'

Propped up on her pillows she sighs, and clasps her bony hands across her sunken chest.

'My life's finished,' she muses thoughtfully, 'my dreams of old age, *sielska – anielska*, happy and peaceful, can never be that with half of my family gone. What memories will fill my head at the close of my life? Their begging eyes? Their bloated stomachs? Their skeletal bodies? The trail of crosses we have left behind in every place we've been dumped to die?' She becomes quiet and tears slide down her wasted cheeks.

I sit down on the side of her bed beside her and think desperately of something comforting to say. Nothing comes to my mind. Her experiences have been multiplied thousands of times over.

'Mrs. Teofilia, when we get out of here, nothing can ever be as bad again.' She nods, but her gaze is distant.

On the day I'm released from the hospital, our children are allowed to be taken home too. Home is an eighth of the sandy floor space, in a tent shared with seven other families.

Eva collects me first. I say my farewells to the gap-toothed Vera and a slightly more optimistic Teofilia, now that her recovery is improving.

'Good luck! See you both in free Poland!' I wish them with a wave of my hand.

'I'll drink to that!' Vera raises her tin mug of tea.

Old Teofilia makes the sign of the cross in our direction. 'And may God help you find your husbands,' she calls to Eva and me.

Eva holds back the flap of the tent and as I walk into the bright sunlight, my eyes hurt. I pull my headscarf forward to form a shade over my face.

The children's ward is two tents away, a spacious, long marquee, with about forty beds at a first glance. The children appear at various stages of recovery, the very sick ones kept in a separate tent. Pavel and Agata spot us straight away standing at the entrance and wave enthusiastically their stick-thin arms. Little Stella, next to them, is too entranced watching them to look our way. All the children have shaved heads like me.

The duty nurse, in her pristine white uniform, amazing in this desert heat, comes up to her trestle-table desk and asks to see our identity papers. Mine have accompanied me hidden under my pillow where Eva had left them for me. I expect the nurse to question our authority as regards our guardianship of Pavel and Agata, and she does.

'They are our foster children,' I explain, 'till their fathers come back for them.'

She eyes us thoughtfully. 'It's a big undertaking,' she comments. 'We've got an orphanage set up in this camp. The children get all the care we can possibly give them. Food and clothes, activities and schooling.'

I shake my head, my shaved head with a funny turban wound around it.

'I can't do that. We've promised their fathers. We'll look after them for as long as it takes.'

She nods in understanding and walks away to fetch our little brood. They accompany her eagerly, dressed in their fresh Red Cross clothes, big and baggy preparing for their growth. Stella raises her little thin arms to be picked up and then clings to Eva with all the might of her frail doll-sized body. Pavel and Agata embrace me round my waist and push together so hard, I'm in danger of falling over.

'Steady, you two!' I laugh, but they hug me even more.

'Auntie Nastusha,' Pavel lifts up his large, luminous eyes, 'you must never be ill again!'

'You must never leave us!' Agata adds, pressing her head against my chest.

'So!' I tease them, 'It's all right for you to be ill and worry us to death, but not right for me to have a little rest?'

When we bid the nurse farewell with thanks, she turns to Pavel and Agata.

'I wish you every luck in finding your dads soon,' she says. 'They're probably in Persia already, waiting for you. Thousands of troops have already been evacuated there, in March.'

'In March?' I feel a pang of missed opportunity. 'In March? But we were already here! Not too far from this place. In the Happy Bird *kolhoz*. Why didn't they take us with them?'

'Hundreds of civilians went with them,' the nurse says, then she lowers her voice, 'but after that Stalin stalled the evacuation plan. That's why we've got such an enormous problem now. Not only here. In Samarkand. In Bukhara. In Guzar and hundreds of other places. But what does he care about people dying while he makes them wait?'

My euphoria at leaving the hospital fizzles out and my spirit dips. She must guess this for she quickly adds,

'Don't worry. This isn't for much longer. Rumours are rife that our departure to Persia is imminent any day now.'

'Dear God,' Eva sighs, 'let that be soon.'

We walk past rows of tents that make an orderly grid of paths between them, in the sandy soil, under the scorching sun. It is a relief to hide inside our tent, despite the overpowering heat. Our tent is full of people, seven families, the elderly, the mothers and their children, but as they are all seated on their blankets, their presence is not overwhelming. It is noisy and jolly as our group proceed to the corner bagged for us by Mr. Ostrovski, seated on his bedding together with his little grandsons. They were released from hospital yesterday and he has made them comfortable against plumped-up pillows, two small emaciated bodies with large eyes looking out of pinched faces.

I give him a hug, long and hard. What is there to say? His daughter has died. I have survived. The little boys are motherless. I'm bereft of my child. It is all so senseless, so infinitely cruel.

'It is good to have you back, Anastazia,' he pulls away from me and looks into my eyes. 'The more of us survive, the more hope there is for our nation.'

This tent city is like a giant waiting room. There is a feeling of restlessness, of impatient anticipation, and then a feeling of dashed hopes, as each day passes with no news of a change. Nevertheless, it is like an oasis of safety on our trek to freedom, with its mini-infrastructure: we've got a field kitchen, a field hospital, and a roof over our heads. The nearby river which, when we first saw it a few months ago, was just a muddy stream, has been cleansed and filled in the rainy weeks of April. Its waters provide washing and laundry facilities to the swarms of people that descend daily on its banks.

Those still in possession of a few roubles walk to Kermine, just five kilometres away. One day Eva and I ventured out, leaving the children with Mr. Ostrovski. Our purses have been recently topped up with a small allowance from our husbands' commission. We found the streets of Kermine dark and crowded with donkeys and camels. Pushing our way through the meandering crowd, we followed the streaks of light shining through the gaps between the tightly packed buildings into a small market square. The few stalls there offered only a limited variety and amount of miserable looking vegetables or melon seeds and dried fruit, or small hard cheese balls with *lepioszki*, the flatbread pancakes. We bought a little of everything, giving the marrows regrettably a miss, since we have no cooking facilities. I'm infinitely grateful that our life does not depend on such purchases and that we can go to sleep each night knowing there will be bread and tea for each one of us in the morning.

We take the children out on daily walks round the camp, a vast sprawling area, to build up their strength and to hurry on the long-stretched days. The military village of tents, separate from the civilian camp, has been set up on the field where our train contingent was deposited a few months ago, before being dispersed to the nearby *kolhozes*. A wide dirt track runs between them and us, and beyond the finishing line of our camp, there is a cemetery, with numbers of crosses increasing every day. In the distance, the road vanishes into the sandy, dry-grass-covered land that blends with the foothills of the mountain range. Somewhere there, we've left behind the Happy Bird, Mr. Yakob and his wife, and Selim. A name best forgotten.

Our children like to stop and watch the soldiers in training, their booted feet marching in unison, their sudden stops and turns, their rhythmic manoeuvring of their guns, their salutes and mechanical responses to booming commands. Sometimes, from a nearby tent, a soldier or two walks over to us to talk, and sometimes on very lucky occasions, the children are given a sweet; a hard-boiled marbled sweet, that can be sucked for a long time and leaves a sweet aftertaste.

The soldiers miss their families. We are always asked the same questions: where are we from? Have we, by any chance, come across their Magda or their Franek or their Yarek? We ask the same question: have they come across Julian or Henryk or Ryszard or Roman? We are given reassurances: our boys must have already crossed to Persia with the first evacuation in March. This makes our waiting all the more impatient, and my longing for Julian is like a chronic malaise.

On one of our walks, we step back to watch the long line of orphans, holding hands in pairs, and being led by the two minder nuns along the river's edge. Their little faces are as solemn as those of wise old men; there's not a smile in sight. Their Red Cross clothes are clean; the girls have white cotton scarves tied around their shaved heads, and the boys are wearing hand-sewn caps to protect their scalps from the sun. I admire the two nuns' pristine appearance with their white long habits and the stiff, winged coifs. The brightness of their attire seems to be a magnet for the flies and forces the nuns to shake their heads constantly to frighten the pests away. They must suffer from chronic neck ache, I reflect. I discover later, from one of the home helps at the orphanage, that the fly attraction is not the whiteness of the nuns' garments, but the sugar used to starch the coifs. Sugar? This leaves me speechless. But that comes later, when I reflect on the intransigence of drilled self-discipline over common sense.

Now I watch them walk by, the little orphans, clean, obedient and orderly, and I remark to Pavel,

'Pavelek see? You'd not have suffered the famine or the typhoid fever in the Happy Bird camp, if you'd gone with the nuns in Tashkent. You know, I often worry about what your Dad would have said.'

In response, he throws his arms around my waist and draws me close to him.

'Well, don't worry Auntie Nastusha. It was my choice. I didn't want to be anywhere else, but with you and Auntie Eva.'

'You were so ill you could have died,' I remind him.

'I could have been ill somewhere else. It would have been a hundred times worse without you.'

Agata squeezes my hand and plonks a kiss on my arm. I draw her close to my side. I love these children. Moments like this make me realise how much. I'm filled with gratitude to fate for having filled the emptiness in my life, after my little Dorotka. Stella stretches her little arms up to me. She looks like a miniature *babushka*, with her Red Cross dress a few sizes too big for her and a large white handkerchief covering her shaved head and tied under her chin. I pick her up and cuddle her sparrow-like body to my chest.

'What about me?' Eva jokes.

'There's room on my back,' I suggest. The children laugh and transfer their attention to her.

It's official. We are told the news by word of mouth as we stand in the breakfast queues. 28th of July. There's too many of us civilians to gather for one big meeting.

Yesterday, Stalin has relented and graciously agreed to restart the evacuation process of the Polish military and the civilians. Reluctantly he's had to abandon his plan of retaining the newly formed Polish army for the purpose of using it as a buffer against the unstoppable and pressing Werhmaht in Moscow and Leningrad and cities of the north. At long last, with Churchill's and Sikorski's patient diplomacy, he has been persuaded to see the sense of allowing the Polish forces to cross over to Iraq and Persia to guard the oil fields. There is a burst of euphoria throughout the camp.

Later, when we sit on our bedding in the corner of our tent, enjoying the breakfast of porridge, bread and sweetened tea, talk around us is of the next leg of our journey, of our final escape to freedom, of life afterwards, normal, ordered, perhaps with normal conditions of work and normal pay, all in preparation for our return home.

'I have a brother in Warsaw,' Mr. Ostrovski tells us, watching his two little grandsons eating their porridge from the one metal canteen, 'I'll go to him first. They've got a big family, with lots of grandchildren. It'll be good for Maks and Aleks to grow up with their cousins.'

I picture my Mama and my Tato, my sisters Hanna and Magda and my brother with all their families and I feel such a strong yearning to be with them again, it is like something tearing inside me. I swallow hard and suppress the pain. 'Yes,' I think aloud, 'the first thing I'll do is rush home to my family. And then,' I turn to Eva, 'do you think our former life will be still waiting for us in Old Mizun? Julian's and Henryk's old jobs in the forestry? And our houses with our gardens and trees, all our own work?'

Eva chews her bread thoughtfully.

'Whatever happens,' she says, 'let's all stay together. Wherever we're sent next.'

Pavel and Agata listen and look at us with large inquisitive eyes, as they eat their breakfast.

Then Agata says,

'I don't want us to be separated. Not ever!'

I give her a hug and suggest,

'Shall we find out first what your Daddy wants to do? You may like his plans better than ours.'

She nods, adding quickly,

'As long as we all stay in the same place!'

Every day we wait for our turn, watching large groups of people being escorted by our own Polish soldiers to the railway station in Kermine. In the scorching heat, the few kilometres walk is exhausting for everyone, but especially those considered more able, who have to shepherd young children and assist the ailing elderly. They are like overloaded donkeys carrying bulging bags, thrown over their shoulders. Their faces are worn with the effort, but the anticipated joy of the long awaited freedom appears to inject their wasted muscles with renewed energy and quickens their step along the hard dirt track.

One day, as a crowd gathers to leave the camp at one end, a plume of dust appears on the horizon. Before long, a caravan of horse-drawn carts and *arbas* come into view, more people being brought in from the scattered *kolhozes* in this vast area. Eva, the children and I wait and watch with interest the people disembark from their assorted carts and lug their few belongings as they follow the directing soldiers to the tents that have been vacated. My heart somersaults when I suddenly recognise faces from the Happy Bird *kolhoz*.

'Eva! They've not been forgotten! They've brought them here, at long last!' I exclaim, and at the same time catch sight of Florian and Dominik, their hair cut short sticking out in all directions, their jackets hanging loose off their spiky shoulders. Eva sees them too and calls out their names. They turn round and wave. Their mother, Mrs. Lekis, opens up her arms wide as if we were her long lost family. There is no substance to her, she looks like a broom pole, dressed in a limp rag. They each pick up a bag and head towards us, before following their leader. I cannot believe that the once grumpy Mrs. Lekis is so warm towards us and tearful with joy. She hugs us in turn and the children too, wiping her eyes.

'Come with us now, so I don't lose you again,' she says, grabbing my hand.

'All right,' I say, ' just so we know where you're placed. But you'll be getting your food first. We'll come back to see you later.'

Later is close to mid-day, when we get back to their tent, after they have been installed and given breakfast and had time to freshen themselves with the water brought from the river. Their tent is crowded like ours, but they make room on their blanket which delineates their living space. Florian and Dominik sit cross-legged, greet us with smiles and invite Pavel and Agata to sit close to them.

'Anastazia! Eva!' Mrs. Lekis exclaims, when we've wriggled in between their bags. 'Am I glad to see you! I was worried sick when you so suddenly disappeared from the camp. All kinds of rumours were going round. That you've escaped. That you've been abducted. But I didn't believe any of it. I asked Mr. Yakob but he just shrugged and pretended not to understand. I could not imagine how you'd venture out on foot, across the desert, with the children and your baggage. But with Mr. Ostrovski gone too, I guessed you were all together. And there's safety in numbers. Still, I couldn't help thinking what if..? People were dying every day at the camp…'

When she pauses for breath, Eva and I take it in turns to explain. In general. No details about Selim and Tariq. Her sunken eyes wander to me, to Eva, over the children as she listens.

'I can't believe it!' she exclaims, 'you mean to tell me that Mr. Yakob's son helped you? Then why was he so secretive about it?'

'Mrs. Lekis,' I speak in a pacifying tone, 'Mr. Yakob's son is in the rebel army. He couldn't very well shout about his son's involvement.'

She still looks bemused. 'Did he really do all that for you without wanting any payment?'

Eva nods. 'Thank God there are still some good people around,' she says. I don't trust myself to look at her.

'And how's Mr. Ostrovski?' Mrs. Lekis asks. We tell her of his loss. She tells us of some of the elderly people we knew at the Happy Bird.

'Poor souls,' she says, 'got so far, and never made it to freedom.'

'And here,' I add, 'graves are dug daily. There's a few hundred already.' We all fall silent contemplating the cruel fate of these people, but then Florian's cheerful voice breaks through the sad mood.

'I can't wait to join the Cadets Corps,' he says, 'General Anders is setting up centres alongside the army for all young people to join. So we can get back to school and also be trained like scouts.' He looks at Dominik, 'We've got a lot of catching up to do. We've lost two and a half years of education.'

'Only formal education,' Dominik corrects his brother with a wry smile. 'No one could have imagined the other kind of education we got absolutely free!'

The two brothers have had to grow up fast. Their extreme thinness makes them look like stick men, exaggerating the bumps of their knee joints.

'Yes! It's a wonderful idea!' Mrs. Lekis adds, 'The Cadets Corps. For all young people, but especially those with no families left.'

Pavel looks up at me and his face brightens up.

'Perhaps Aniela is already there!' he exclaims hopefully. 'Fancy that! A Girl Cadet! It'll be easier to find her. How old have you got to be to join?'

'Normally,' Mrs. Lekis replies, 'when you're fourteen. But now, they take them in at ten. To give all children a chance to get out of here.'

Pavel gets carried away with the idea. 'Agata! We could join too! We're both twelve!'

Agata sidles up to me and links her arm with mine.

'I don't want to join anything,' she says, 'I want us to stay together, just as we are now!'

'And we will,' I assure her. 'Nothing will split us up till we find your Dad.'

Friday morning, 7th of August is our lucky day. As we queue for breakfast, we are issued additionally with a loaf and a tin of corned beef each. We are advised to fill our canisters with water. Midmorning, the soldiers allotted to escort our section of the camp to the train, call on us, and the tents are vacated by the eager crowd. Our hand luggage has to be reduced to the bare essentials: food and a change of clothes. I save my personal papers and the family photographs, but everything else is so worn now, I leave it on the pile waiting to be burnt, when the camp is closed and the tents dismantled to be transported with the last platoon of the leaving army.

We each carry a bag, Pavel and Agata their smaller ones too. Eva and I take it in turns to carry Stella. The train is stationary two kilometres out of town in our direction, but the walk seems long and soon drains our energy in the heat, that comes down from a white sky and bounces back from the dry, sandy soil. With sweat dripping down my face, I'd give anything for our boys to be with us now. Florian and Dominik help Mr. Ostrovski to carry his few possessions, while he holds his grandsons by the hand, their little feet working hard to keep up with his limping gait.

The waiting train is a passenger train this time, with high metal wheels, massive carriages and steps leading up to every open doorway. The crowd fragments into numerous queues, and though there is the usual commotion of people shouting to each other in the excitement of the moment, calling for attention of one kind or another, children being fractious, mothers losing their patience, last minute decisions of what to take, what to leave behind, the embarkation proceeds surprisingly smoothly under the calm command of our soldiers.

Our group finds a carriage with a limited space for us all to fit in together, in addition to the people already there. We sit on a bench this time, squashed, with all our belongings piled and stuffed on the racks above us. Every centimetre around us and in the passages is occupied; the air soon becomes stale. It is impossible to avoid whiffs of rancid clothes and bodily odours, smells of infected teeth and gums, the oily fug of unwashed hair, the sourness of skin sores. I pray that we make a start soon, I long for fresh air, for a draught from the open windows to bring us all relief.

The banging of closing doors, when it comes, is a much awaited sound. The whistle and the first jolt of movement follows and the few shrubs and trees on this patch of wasteland come suddenly to life and run the opposite way to our destination. It is a moment of exquisite deliverance. Something soars inside me. Squashed together as we all are on the wooden benches, we exchange smiles nevertheless and raise our heads to the bliss of fresh air blowing in through open windows.

I'm suddenly aware of a humming melody that starts somewhere at the head of the train and grows in volume as it reaches our carriage. I recognise Psalm 117.

Boga naszego chwalcie wszystkie ziemie…
All earth praise our God…

Everyone in our compartment joins in, their eyes shining and their faces lifted with renewed faith. A pang of sadness and guilt overshadows this moment when I think of the hundreds of graves left behind on the outskirts of Kermine, with rough wooden crosses bearing Polish names.

CHAPTER 34

This journey is no more comfortable than our previous journeys in cattle trucks, but what makes it more bearable is the feeling that we are so close to freedom. Squashed tight, we rarely leave our places, except to visit the toilet cubicle. It is engaged most of the time, and when relinquished for a brief, opportune moment, it is found so soiled that one is overcome with fear of contracting dysentery, even before one's own pressing need has been satisfied.

Ill people lie doubled up in passages covering up their pain and mortification with old rags. Stepping over them is like a harrowing obstacle course.

The redeeming moments are the stops at stations to scrub thoroughly and to fill our canisters with fresh water. I still fear those senseless, few days' stops in sidings. That would surely wipe out half of our fellow travellers in these conditions. But the train runs fast and my anxieties abate with every city and town left behind us.

On the first day we pass Bukhara, an ancient walled city with slender towers and ornate minarets, surrounded by lush abundance of palm trees, a sight so picturesque it could have been taken out from Arabian tales of adventure and magic. Mr. Ostrovski informs us that it was totally destroyed by Ghengis Khan in 1220, and rebuilt with so much care and dedication to details that its architectural beauty has survived centuries and can still delight today.

On the second day we pass Ashkhabad, and on the third day, at around noon our train slows down on its approach to Krasnovodsk port. It is difficult to view anything from our tightly packed compartment, but we get a running commentary from some excited boys in the passage, close to the windows.

'Look! The sea! Can you see the water?'

'And the cranes!'

'And look at that boat! Ten times bigger than the buildings!'

'Twenty times bigger!'

Pavel and Agata stretch their necks to see out of the window, but we're on the side of the fields, a much greener land here, with mountains in the distance, and closer to the railway line, small farm holdings, wooden huts, timber houses, then larger concrete buildings and blocks, as we get closer to the port.

When the train bumps to a halt, there's a buzzing excitement among the people and impatience to get out. Our group remains seated till the compartment empties somewhat, so when we get up we can stretch our cramped limbs.

'I creak like an old door,' Mrs. Lekis complains, rubbing her back and pulling herself up, 'too soon for a young filly like me!'

Florian and Dominik exchange amused looks, pick up their mother's bag and Mr. Ostrovski's possessions and lead the way out of our carriage. Mr. Ostrovski takes his little boys by the hand, and we all get ready to disembark.

Outside, there's only a large field, with a few trees and shrubs and hundreds of refugees with their sparse belongings. I'm surprised how far we are from the port. The skyline of cranes and buildings must be at least two kilometres away.

'Another little surprise,' Mr. Ostrovski comments.

'Their inventiveness has no limits,' Mrs. Lekis adds sourly.

As we stand bemused, we see Polish soldiers accompanied by the NKVD men walking around and talking to groups. Two walk over to us and the Polish soldier greets us.

'Welcome. And bear with us. Your journey's almost finished. You'll be sailing tomorrow morning.'

There's a moment's silence while this information sinks in.

'Tomorrow morning?' someone exclaims. 'But we've still got the rest of today and all night to wait! Here? In this open field?'

The Polish soldier nods.

'Believe me, you're better off in this field than on the beach. We are instructed to inform you of a few things: firstly, no ill person will be allowed to board the ship. Secondly, you must leave everything behind, except for your personal things, so each person takes only one piece of hand luggage. There simply won't be enough room to take more on the boat. And thirdly, all roubles have to be left behind, in this country, where they belong.'

There is an outcry of protest. The Polish soldier, obviously aware of his NKVD companion, has little choice but to continue.

'Tomorrow morning, before you leave, there will be boxes for you to deposit all remaining money. Anyone caught in possession of roubles after leaving this field, will be sent back to where you came from.'

I feel a shiver in this heat, then a fiery but impotent rage. God, do they have to torment us right to the very end? All right, ALL RIGHT! Let them have my last few roubles! And all my rags! And the shreds of my shoes! All my rubbish, if that's what they want! As long as I get out of this hell!

'Bastards!' Eva mutters, so only I can hear.

'Oh well,' Mrs. Lekis shrugs her thin shoulders, and comments philosophically, 'it appears there must be some cause worthy of our support. There must be some people poorer than us, yet how is that possible in this wonderful country where everyone is equal and happy?'

I hold my breath and dare not look straight at the NKVD man. I wish I could repeat Mrs. Lekis' words and say much, much more, but now is not the time to endanger our still fragile position, now, when we're so close to freedom. To my relief, and I feel to other people's too, the NKVD man takes her words at face value.

'We don't have charity causes,' he instructs her, 'there is no need for charity in our great Soyouz. All people are cared for equally. The money you are ordered to leave behind is the property of the state. It's that simple!'

We remain quiet, for who's going to argue with him? The Polish soldier nods a farewell before they both move on. We look around for somewhere to settle for our overnight, open air stop. The shade around the row of maple trees is already crowded. We walk to the other side, now exposed to the sun, where later, we hope, the shade will favour us.

Our luggage is already reduced, but people around us are unpacking their bags and agonising over their choices of what to take and what to leave behind. Their battered possessions have become like old friends, companions in sickness and in health over the last two and a half years.

Our little group sticks together and we make use of three blankets spread out on the dry yellow grass, our temporary home, our bed for the night, and now our dining room as we sit down for our lunch. Eva and I have saved two loaves and two tins of corned beef, having used only one of each per day on our journey. Again, we eat sparingly, saving some for the evening meal and some for tomorrow. We've filled our canisters at the last stop, and I'm glad, as there is no such facility here in this open field. Mr. Ostrovski and Mrs. Lekis bring out frugal portions of bread, corned beef and water for their families, and one could almost delude oneself that this is just a pleasant picnic, were it not for the scarcity of food and the patrolling soldiers around us.

Another two come over to us, one of them the ubiquitous NKVD, the other, a Polish soldier addresses us,

'We've got orders to check that there are no sick people among you.' He looks at me, 'I guess you've had your head shaved, and the children too. Was it a hospital stay ? And what illness was it?'

Self-consciously I adjust my head scarf, my stomach contracting with fear.

'We've all had typhoid fever. That was some time ago. We've all recovered well,' I assure him.

He gives me an understanding look out of his grey eyes, and with the NKVD standing behind him, a hint of a smile.

'You all look well recovered to me,' he pats Pavel's shaved head, 'good appetite?'

'I could eat a horse!'Pavel tells him, rubbing his stomach.

'Good lad! Couldn't we all!' He smiles as they walk away.

Eva shakes her head and makes a face,

'They're not going to get one rouble from me! I'll make sure of that! I'd rather leave my money in town and at least get something for it!'

Pavel and Agata are alarmed.

'Please, Auntie Eva, please don't go!' Agata cries. 'I couldn't bear if you got lost!'

'My dear Agatka,' Eva laughs hugging her, 'nothing like that is going to happen! I won't go very far. As soon as I find some food to buy, and more water, I'll be back straight away.'

The boys come with us, Florian, Dominik and Pavel; Agata stays with the younger children in Mr. Ostrovski's and Mrs. Lekis' care. Soon there is an exodus from the field of like-minded people along the dirt track into town. The area we enter close to the docks is derelict, but we soon discover that the crumbling buildings hide small shops and service points, like bicycle and cart repairs next to a bakery, next to gardening tools, then a grocery and vegetable store next to household utensils and a jerkin and *valonki* centre.

The queue at the bakery grows straight away, snaking along the timber pavement, that is raised above the dirt track. We join the queue, but when we finally reach the counter, we find it empty with only some *lepioszki* left. Nevertheless we each come away with a paper cone filled with half a dozen small bread pancakes.

The grocery and vegetable emporium is marginally better equipped: there are some wrinkled potatoes, marrows, turnips and carrots. As we have no cooking facilities, we settle for carrots and a bag of melon seeds each. The young, thin girl of maybe fifteen, who is helping her mother has a friendly manner. I ask her,

'Have you any empty bottles for sale?' She looks perplexed, so I explain, 'If you have, we'll pay for them as well as the water.'

She nods in understanding.

'How many?'

'As many as you can spare.'

She disappears inside their ramshackle dwelling and after a while comes back with three filled and corked bottles. She does this several times, until we all get three bottles each. We pay her and come away heartened in spirit.

As we walk back along some obscure streets that merge with the dirt track which leads out of town onto the open wasteland, Pavel sounds chirpy, enlivened in the company of the older boys. Eva gives me a self-satisfied smile and remarks,

'I've still not spent all my money! Can you believe it Nastusha? I've got more money than I know what to do with! I wish it was like that when we get back to our normal life! As it is, we are two rotten *bourjouye* women, shamefully, filthy rich!'

She makes me laugh, as I look up and down our worn washed out dresses and note our dusty torn shoes, and as I adjust my head scarf that makes me feel as glamorous as a fishwife.

We spend the night underneath the stars. The earth and the air have retained the daytime heat and I feel thankful that nature is on our side. We are surrounded by hundreds of tired, reclining people but judging by the muted sounds of voices going late into the early hours, they cannot give in to sleep, perhaps afraid to miss the first light of dawn, that will herald a new chapter in our lives.

The rising sun, that colours the sky all hues of pink and peach, brings back memories of home and I wonder about all my family and where they are, marvelling at the thought that they too see the same sun thousands of miles away from me.

Eva and I take our little brood for a quick visit behind the bushes, but this promises to be a long wait, with everyone else queuing for the same purpose. We follow other women's example, who walk a fair distance away from the camp, where they can hide behind a screen of a blanket or a shawl. When our children are done, we send them back with Agata and Pavel, before assisting each other in retaining a vestige of dignity.

We breakfast on a slice of bread and a drink of water, and everyone's packed and ready to go by half past seven, when the soldiers arrive. The NKVD men bring carton boxes with them and watch each one of us, when we file past them following our guides. People empty their pockets, their handbags and purses, untie their handkerchiefs, shake out their paper bags. I've not got many roubles left, but I'm aggrieved that the little I've got is taken off me, after all the long months of starvation, when saving the last rouble for the *black hour*, was such a difficult discipline to keep.

'Don't worry, Nastusha,' Eva whispers when we move on, 'we've managed so far, we'll manage this last bit too.' We leave behind a field strewn with personal possessions, cherished like friends through the hardest times.

It is a long way to the port, across the wasteland, then through some ramshackle area which ends abruptly to reveal the long quay with cranes and moored freighters. We are led on for another kilometre along a wide timber promontory at the end of which stands our boat. As before, Eva and I take turns to carry Stella. Florian and Dominic help Mr. Ostrovski with his little boys. I am so exhausted I begin to see swirling black circles and taste blood on my tongue. Eva looks as exhausted as I feel; her limp damp hair clings to her forehead, and her face is streaked with sweat.

When at long last we are instructed by our guide to stop, I'm overwhelmed with relief. Eva sits Stella on top of our bags and breathes heavily, wiping her face with her sleeve. Pavel and Agata slump on the ground, looking hot and thirsty. Mr. Ostrovski's little grandsons sit on the ground too, looking up with squinting eyes against the sun at the strangeness of our surroundings.

'Well, what a morning run!' Mrs. Lekis remarks. 'Will keep me trim for the rest of this week!'

We are all too tired to respond. I notice behind us a mother with three children, Pavel's age and a little older. She is lying down on the ground doubled up with pain.

'Mum, we'll never leave you!' her older daughter sobs, her face puckered with crying.

'You must!' her mother tells her between the groans. 'Pomise me, you'll take Ania and Adam with you on the boat. It's your last chance!'

I feel sick with concern for them and impetuously but in. I crouch beside the woman and tell her firmly,

'You must get up when they call us. You must get up for your children's sake. Lean on me and limp. It's not your fault if you've had an accident felling trees!'

The woman can hardly keep her eyes open, but she nods. Our group quickly consults together and decides who's carrying what so we can help out in this situation.

'None of us must be ill now!' I admonish our children. 'Just follow their instructions, and do everything they say!'

I lean out to get a better look at our boat. It is a massive old freighter, its sides streaked with rust. On the land side of the promontory, the water becomes less deep as it gradually merges with the beach. It looks like oil sludge with rubbish of all kinds floating on the top. The beach is black with pollution, and on that beach there's a waiting crowd of hundreds of refugees like us. We certainly did get the longer straw last night, when we were relegated to the empty field.

There are shouts and movement ahead of us, and it looks as if the embarkation has begun.

We all grab our bags, our small children by the hand and begin our shuffle forward, with the queue surging behind us. I help the sick woman to sit up then I haul her up and hook her arm around my neck. Her oldest daughter picks up my bag.

Pavel and Agata look worried, but I tell them to walk ahead of me and follow Eva, with Stella in her arms. The sick woman's children follow me.

'We're doing well,' I tell them firmly, 'just a few more minutes and we'll be there!'

I pray frantically that she can last out and stay upright till we get inside the boat. It seems like the minutes turn into long excruciating days, but she is holding on to me, breathing hard, her face grey with the effort and myself straining like Hercules under her weight. And then, as the crowd in front of us thins down and I see the gang plank that connects the boat with the quay, I tell her again she must hold on with all her might. Just this last minute. For her children's sake.

There are NKVD men, one on each side of the plank. The Polish soldiers are at the other higher end, welcoming the people inside the boat. As we reach the plank, the sick woman detaches herself from me and shakily moves forward. Her children swarm round her, and in pairs, they make nervous progress up the plank that has no handrails but deep black water swirling below. Eva follows with Stella in her arms, then Pavel and Agata lugging their bags, then as I put my foot on the first tread, there's a shout from one of the NKVD men.

'Stop! No sick people on board!'

I freeze, then my heart pounds as if to break through my rib cage. I keep my gaze on the back of the sick woman's head, willing her not to look back, just to carry on. She moves up into the waiting, hauling arms of our soldiers and disappears inside the dark entrance of the hull. All this lasts only a few seconds and then I hear a commotion behind me.

'She's not sick!' I hear Mr. Ostrovski's voice, 'it's her age! Do I have to explain? The tiredness and the heat have caused her to faint!'

I look back and see Mr. Ostrovski supporting a young girl of about fourteen. He does not waste time. He drapes her arm over his shoulder, as I did with the sick woman, and rushes past me onto the plank. A woman with two young boys follow him with haste, I guess the girl's family, and a tight crowd forms around the two NKVD men. I guess some element of surprise slows down their reactions, for as they deal with the pressing people around them, the rest of our group mounts the plank with haste one after another: Mrs. Lekis with Mr. Ostrovski's grandsons, then I, then Florian and Dominik carrying all the rest of our luggage.

Halfway up the plank I experience a moment of panic. I get a sensation of being suspended over an abyss. I make myself look up and concentrate on the two soldiers helping people step over the threshold. Then I'm there too and feel their supporting hands leading me inside. I don't look back. I could not bear the sight of bodies left behind, of those who were robbed of life so close to freedom.

For a moment I feel blind. The contrast of the darkness in the lower deck to the white heat outside, is too much for my eyes to adjust to straight away.

'Eva!' I call out, 'Are you there? Can you see?'

'Not yet,' her voice comes back, 'but I'm holding onto the rail.'

I feel my way down the iron stairs and from the volume of voices around me, I guess there must be hundreds of people already there. Slowly my eyesight returns. This lower deck is the size of a hangar, normally for transporting industrial or military equipment or commercial cargo. Today it's our blessed bridge to freedom.

I spot Mr. Ostrovski in the crowd waving to catch our attention. When we join him he leads us to a spot close to the wall of the boat. It's a test of endurance having to weave your way amongst so many people and their bags, everyone trying to secure a little floor space for themselves. When our group reassembles and huddles together close to the wall, no one speaks a moment or two, overwhelmed by the last half hour's traumas. I spot my sick woman, not too far away, crouched and leaning against her bags, her children protectively close to her. On our other side, Mr. Ostrovski's little protégée lies curled on the floor, looking very ill. Her mother moistens her cracked lips and her pallid face with a damp cloth, as her younger brothers look on, their expressions stony. The mother catches my gaze.

'If I took her to the hospital,' she tries to explain, 'we'd all have to stay behind. Perhaps for ever.'

'I know,' I reassure her, 'you did the right thing. In Pahlevi she'll get proper care. And you'll all be able to stay together.'

'I pray she lasts that long.' Her eyes become moist and her mouth trembles. 'Do you know, if the worst were to happen, I'd still thank God for allowing her to leave that communist hell!'

'You mustn't think the worst,' I insist, 'we'll all get there tomorrow. And our lives will change.'

There is a constant flow of people descending into this lower deck. We are sitting squashed against the wall, against each other, against our belongings, till there's not a foot of space left anywhere.

'We'll all suffocate!' someone calls out to the soldiers standing by the iron staircase.

'There's even more people on the upper deck,' one of them replies. 'If you want fresh air you'll have to climb up again!'

The hot stuffy air intensifies our exhaustion. Eva is quiet, sitting beside me with Stella on her lap. The little doll is asleep, mercifully. I tell Pavel and Agata to close their eyes too.

'Sleeping will help you pass the time away. And before you know it, we'll be there!'

'But I must wait for the boat to start,' Pavel tells me.

Mr. Ostrovski has made a small niche between his bags with a blanket for his little boys. They call it their den and play an imaginary game of hiding from the witch, like Hansel and Gretel. Mrs. Lekis is resting her head on her drawn-up knees, and Florian and Dominik are content to quietly observe everything going on around them.

I doze off at some point in this stifling heat, for all of a sudden, Pavel pulls me awake and I feel the engines' reverberations through the floor.

'*Jedziemy*! We're off!' he cries, excited, and Agata claps her hands

Spontaneous invocations can be heard throughout this vast chamber. God be praised! Thanks be to God! Keep us safe o Lord! Then somebody intones,

Błogosław duszo moja Pana...
Praise the Lord my soul..
Let my song gladden you, my Lord...

We join in. I feel the slightest sway, when the boat detaches itself from the quay. We all feel it and exchange glances and smiles, while our hymn grows in volume. It is 10th of August, 1942, two years and six months exactly to the day, that we finally leave behind this land that has claimed thousands of Polish lives.

The voyage across the Caspian Sea from the port of Krasnovodsk to the

Persian port of Pahlevi is a nightmare of stifling heat, unrelenting thirst, lack of basic hygiene facilities, claustrophobic overcrowding and worrying metallic creaking as the boat negotiates the pounding waves of the roughening sea.

'There's too many of us on this boat,' Eva whispers with fear, 'I heard the soldiers talk. They said there were two thousand of us. The boat will sink under our weight!'

The woman with the sick daughter hears her.

'Better to drown free,' she says, 'than to be left behind as a slave.'

'No talk of drowning!' I command, 'we'll all get there! Safe and sound. This freighter is used to a far heavier cargo than weightless skeletons like us!'

I'm scared too. I don't like the creaking, the pounding, the sharp rise and fall of the boat. In my mind I pray hard and make deals with God, and promises of novenas and pilgrimages and additional Masses, if only He can see us safely through this last, punishing leg of our journey.

After our lunch of bread and water, pulled out and administered with much difficulty in our dire cramped conditions, I persuade the children to sleep. Eva and I close our eyes too, and miraculously, for a couple of hours I cut myself off from this surrounding purgatory. When the children wake up, they need to visit the toilet. Having scrambled up and pushed our way through hundreds of bent or stretched legs, and bags and sacks and bundles, we discover there are only two toilet areas, one at each end of the boat. This arrangement is adequate in normal circumstances for the crew of this freighter, but now, the never-ending queues kill all hopes of a quick visit.

I feel desperation deepening my mood of unease.

'Isn't there anywhere else I can take the children?' I ask a soldier standing nearby.

His expression of resigned helplessness says it all.

'Dear lady,' he says,' there's only *za burtę*, overboard on the upper deck.'

I can't believe he is serious, but I give him a polite nod and steer Pavel and Agata towards the iron stairs. These too are occupied by sitting people, who reluctantly squeeze tighter against the hand rail to allow us pass.

The upper open deck appears to be even more crowded than the chamber below. The overriding army green colour of uniforms creates a vision of a wide band around the periphery of the entire deck, while centrally placed are hundreds of civilians, crammed together, sitting or standing, some sick souls lying curled up among their belongings on the floor.

'Is there a toilet up here?' I ask another soldier, whose feet I've stepped on.

He chortles.

'Over there! Mind you hold on tight!'

'Over there' is at the far end, where some tarpaulin is stretched over a metal frame close to the edge of the deck, to resemble a cubicle. There is a long queue of women and children and older men. Young men urinate straight overboard into the sea. Stress and pain is etched on people's faces as they

275

struggle to control attacks of dysentery and diarrhoea, followed by their utter shame at their loss of dignity, when their illness overcomes their will. The floor along the edge of the deck, where they hang on to the rail for safety, is soiled with splashes of dirt and stains of blood.

Revulsion and panic overwhelm me. How do I resolve this problem?

'Where shall we go?' Pavel asks, his hand over his crotch, his face screwed with the effort of holding back.

My mind's made up. We've got to be practical.

'We'll just have to do it overboard,' I tell him, 'like the others.'

He doesn't protest, he is so desperate. We push through to the closest section of the railing on the edge of the deck. Agata and I screen him with our stretched skirts. When it's Agata's turn, I cannot risk letting her crouch on the edge, where the spray from the waves comes onto the deck and soaks our feet. The sea looks menacing so close, and the boat appears dangerously overloaded. I hold Agata's hand so tight, her thin wrist is red from the pressure, when she gets up and adjusts her skirt.

I tell the children to go back, then I request two women standing nearby to act as my screen. The people around us look the other way, but that makes no difference to my feeling of utter misery, when I have to address my most personal need surrounded by a crowd. Back in my place on the lower deck I warn Eva and Mr. Ostrovski of the dire conditions above us. Reluctantly we conclude that Stella's potty will have to serve us all. The idea is repulsive, but even more abhorrent is to be denuded of all dignity in front of an audience of hundreds, and also the fear of being pulled overboard by a rogue wave.

When night-time comes and with it total darkness in the hull, a blessed calm descends upon the sea. The boat's earlier alarming sway levels off to a smooth float, calming nerves and anxieties. Everyone makes attempts to find a space into which they can wedge or crouch or curl for a few hours of total oblivion. Voices die down and the wailing of small children, and only the odd whimper or groan testifies to the presence of others around us.

Eva and I and our children between us, all huddle together against our bags, against the wall.

'I feel as if all my bones have been thrown together in a sack,' Eva whispers to me, 'and Stella's dress stinks of wee.'

'Eva, what's a little wee in the scheme of things? Just one more day…' In my mind I pray, please God, let it be morning soon!

Despite the exhaustion, I keep waking up several times during the night. I'm drenched with the sweat of panic, then as my fear subsides, I calm myself down with the sameness of things: the pitch black darkness, the air-pervading stench, the moans of the sick. My instinct is to run up the metal stairs for a gulp of fresh air. Impossible with bodies and bags crammed around me. I adjust my position to relieve the ache in my neck and the deadness in my drawn-up legs, pull a scarf over my mouth and nose, and attempt to sleep again.

In the morning when the light filters through into the bowel of our chamber, a horrible sight is revealed. Many sick people are lying in their own vomit and dirt. Pavel clamps his hand over his mouth.

'I feel sick,' he says, 'can we get out of here for some fresh air?'

'It's even more crowded there,' I remind him, 'and dangerous, Pavel.'

We all stand up, however, in our three square feet of space, to stretch our legs, then to screen each other in turn, as Stella's potty is used. I offer to take it up to the upper deck and dispose of its contents over the rail, before handing it over to Mr Ostrovski. I throw a towel over it, and carefully make my way between the standing, crouching, prostrate people, tightly packed around me.

On the upper deck, I accomplish my mission with haste. It is heaven to breathe in the sea air. It has the sharpness of the early morning, and indeed, the people look frozen, having been exposed to the low temperatures all night. There's comfort in the rising sun, and as I catch sight of the glowing horizon, for a brief moment I forget all the misery around me.

Then my attention is drawn to an activity further up the edge of the deck. The soldiers are carrying bodies wrapped up in sheets and laying them down in a row. Perhaps a dozen, then a few more. Relatives, ashen faced, distraught, some expressionless in shock, follow the soldiers and watch, helpless, as the first body is pushed over the edge into the sea. There is no priest, no Requiem Mass, just quiet prayers and tearful farewells.

I cannot bear to watch. Besides, Mr. Ostrovski's little boys are waiting. I climb down the stairs, pushing through all the people barring my way and look around for the sick mother and the sick young girl. They are close to our group; they are both still alive. Relief makes me want to weep. The sick mother's three children are propping her up and giving her water to drink. The young girl is reclining against her mother's chest while her younger brothers cool and moisten her cracked lips with a wet handkerchief. I get an overwhelming feeling of wanting them to survive this journey, so their suffering is rewarded when their feet touch free land. Like mine. Like Eva's. Like all the lucky survivors.'

Close to mid-day, twenty-six hours after leaving Krasnovodsk port, the first sighting of land is reported from the upper deck. Soldiers stand guard on the iron stairs to prevent people from rushing upstairs.

'The boat will topple over,' they warn. 'We need ballast in the hull.'

So we all sit tight, feeling the sway of the ship, listening to the lashing of the waves against the sides, counting minutes, waiting for the first signs of slackening speed.

When it happens, the stillness of the boat seems unreal. We all exchange glances, afraid to smile prematurely. The children's eyes are round with expectation and with listening hard for orders.

'Praise be to God,' Eva whispers, wiping perspiration from her face, pressing Stella to her chest.

'Praise be to God,' I repeat, and like our children, hold my breath, willing the soldiers to give us the sign.

It is two hours before our turn comes to leave the ship. The reason for this waiting, we're told, is that the port water is not deep enough to accommodate the bulk of our freighter. It is anchored some distance away, while smaller boats are sent to fetch us in groups of about two hundred. Evacuating over two thousand people in this manner takes time, the soldier is apologetic. The adults don't complain, but the children get fractious in the heat. We've still got some water left. Frequent little sips keep our little lot distracted from the continual questions of 'will it be much longer yet?'

When our turn comes, and we emerge upon the open upper deck, the vastness of the freighter, now totally empty of its human cargo, is awesome. The shocking sight is the perimeter of the deck, that is blackened with excrement and blood all along the railing.

We have one more endurance test ahead of us, before reaching the safety of the land. Walking the plank again, over deep waters, between the freighter and the shuttle boat. I go through the same emotions of fear and panic and paranoid concern for our children, but we all get across and down to the outstretched and waiting arms of our soldiers.

As we sit in the open boat, tramp-like creatures with our shabby bundles, the sea breeze cools my hot face and soothes my frayed nerves, and I look around and feel my heart swelling with happiness. Everyone I love is safe: Eva and Stella, like my own family, Pavel and Agata, my dearest foster children, Mr. Ostrovski and his little boys, the noblest person I know. I love Florian and Dominik, and even Mrs. Lekis, at this moment too. The sick mother and the sick young girl have survived as well.

'Nastusha,' Eva dares to smile at last, 'we're almost there!'

I squeeze her hand in reply.

The boat takes us past the port works, beyond which, towers and domes and elegant white buildings and blocks shine white in the sun, offset by the greenery of palms and cypresses and exotic flowering trees and shrubs. It all looks unreal.

We sail past the periphery of the city, with houses becoming sparser and the green vegetation fizzling out into the desert. Here, where the wasteland blends with a wide beach of white sand, hundreds of tents are pitched, hundreds of tarpaulins stretched over poles to form shade giving shelters, hundreds of soldiers milling about with hundreds of people like us. Someone cares about us! I feel choked. After all that time, someone at long last really cares for us!

The boat moors in clear shallow waters and walking the plank this time is a matter of seconds, filled with utter joy. My feet wade through the water, touch the soft sand, Pavel and Agata run ahead of me and Pavel shouts,

'Auntie Nastusha! Are we in heaven now?'

Eva puts down little Stella and I throw down our bags. We embrace each other for a long time, then Mr. Ostrovski hugs us both in turn, then Mrs. Lekis too. No one speaks, no one hides the uncontrollable tears. People around us throw themselves on their knees, raise their arms to heaven and cry out their thanks to God.

I notice a delegation of soldiers standing back a little and watching us. The British and the Polish soldiers wear the same uniforms of khaki shirts and shorts; only their berets display different, identifying badges, and the markings on their sleeves. Among them, white turbans single out the Indian contingent among this reception party, but what I feel the most, is their genuine concern and sympathy, so infinitely reassuring after our years of banishment.

A Polish soldier and a woman in uniform approach our group. The woman's face is thin and bronzed by the sun. Her short hair is pinned back at the sides, her beret pulled forward at an angle, that adds a touch of panache to her professional appearance. I squirm with self-consciousness of my beggar-like appearance and experience an acute moment of longing to look normal again.

'Welcome,' she greets us with a kind smile, 'it's time for a good long rest.'

A poem by Martin Stepek

I lay down on the shores of Pahlevi – Soliloquy

I lay down on the shores of Pahlevi and wept
My body could not stop shaking from the dysentery
My emaciated frame of bones hugged the sand in gratitude
As my frail loose skin blew in the sea breeze
And the salt water flowed over my filthy remains.

How I shuddered with convulsive tears
And delight at the gentle warmth of the sun
and the coolness of the sea and the wind
And I didn't care if I lived or died
I was so very happy
To be no longer in the Soviet Union.

Free to die free, at last
If not to survive
As if that were possible
But no, to die was enough,
Free, in the caring hands
Of the British, the Persians,

And oh – how I'm crying again –
My Polish soldiers,
My own folk.

Look at them, in proud uniform
And health, their skin tight
And love on their faces
As they look to help me up.

I'm sorry I am crying so much,
To be helped by my people
And they so well
Who only weeks before must

Have been, like me, rags and bones
Fit only for the grave.

And yet, look, they positively shine health.
Perhaps, oh don't get excited,
It may be too much,
I may die of hope
That I might live yet

That I might live
And even feel again.
Look at me,
I'm in a state,
Beyond control.

 The irony.
For days I had no water
Now I'm pouring it out of my eyes.

And orange juice!
The British bring me orange juice
On a tray my God, on a tray.

I have not seen a tray for…
For, my, I don't know the years any more
Since Poland, since home
Since mama, since papa.

Oh mama.

CHAPTER 35

Happiness is a tarpaulin roof, soft sand underneath the matting, a cooling breeze, a wide beach as white as talcum powder, and the murmuring of lapping waves. I cannot get used to lazing about, to receiving regular meals, to spending my days resting and inhaling the sea air by order, watching our children discover their childhood, as they splash about in warm pools and make patterns in the sand with pebbles and sea-shells.

'Eva, is this real?' I keep asking incredulously, but most of the time, I'm blissfully soothed into silence in contemplation of this miracle of survival, my thoughts doing endless leaps, backwards and forwards, comparing then and now.

It is mid-morning. Soon the children will have to be called back into the safety of the shade against the scorching heat, that peaks between noon and four o'clock. We've tied scarves around Stella's and Agata's shaved heads; Pavel has a cloth cap and they all wear oversized Red Cross clothes, that protect their arms and legs.

Our tent, with its sides rolled up in the daytime, like hundreds of others lined in neat rows, has a square shape and a family in each corner. Our co-tenants are Mr. Ostrovski with his two grandsons, Mrs. Lekis with her teenage boys, and Mrs. Tokarska with her two boys of nine and eleven. Her daughter, who was so ill on the boat is now safe in the hospital. Thrown together into a limited space, yet again, we put up with our discomforts in good humour and respect each other's privacy, as much as it's possible in the circumstances.

'Eva,' I lower my tone out of habit, and squint my eyes against the glare from the sand, 'I sometimes think this is just a dream. And when I wake up, I'll be back on the other side of the sea.'

She lifts herself from her reclining position and adjusts her headscarf. Every single person has been through the process of delousing and having their hair shorn. She pulls her headscarf forward to shade her eyes.

'It's strange, isn't it?' she says, 'Nothing is ever quite as you've imagined it's going to be. It was like being drunk with happiness the first few days, wasn't it? And I still am. The relief... oh the relief... And yet... I get moments when I get the shivers... and the butterflies...'

She shades her eyes with her hand and we both look across to where the children are playing in the sand between excited romps in the water. There are hundreds of people like us, enjoying the beach and the sea; for many, like myself, a new experience. Our region at home was hundreds of miles south of the Baltic Sea. Mr. Ostrovski in his rolled-up trousers is splashing about with his grandsons along the water's edge. In the distance, Florian and Dominik are teaching the other two young boys to swim, no doubt, instructed by their mother to cultivate community spirit. Mrs. Lekis is out, and Mrs. Tokarska has gone to visit her daughter in hospital. We have the tent to ourselves.

'Why?' I ask Eva, 'what is it you're afraid of now? The worst is behind us now, and we'll be asking about our boys at the next stop. Who knows, we may even find them there. You heard what the soldiers said.'

We have spent the first few days in this transit camp going to the fence of the military camp nearby and asking any passing soldier about Julian and Henryk. We asked about Ryszard and Roman too, in case they got split up. No one had come across them, but they all said the same thing: our next stop would be another camp in Teheran. There's a formidable military base there, we were told, with thousands of soldiers, recovering from their varied ordeals and illnesses, and being trained and prepared for combat.

'I want nothing more,' Eva says, 'but to find them. We've been separated for so long!' She turns her crystal blue eyes at me, and there's anxiety in them. 'Eight long months! What if they've changed?'

'What do you mean? Changed… I hope they have. I hope they've put some weight on. I hope they are healthy and strong. Or how else will they be able to do their job?'

Hundreds of soldiers have been arriving in Pahlevi clinging to the last remnants of life, after prolonged attacks of typhoid, dysentery and malaria. Some did not survive. The Polish cemetery in the desert outside Pahlevi is spreading out daily as the numbers of graves multiply.

Eva nods, while her eyes scan the distant horizon, where the silver line of the sea runs across the gentian sky.

'I hope that too,' she says, 'I want them to be well. But what if the army life has changed them?'

'What they have now,' I remind her, 'must be a thousand times better than the hard labour camps they've all left behind. Daily drills? Training? Exercises? Terrain manoeuvres? It must be like child's play after what they've all been through.'

She is quiet for a moment. She is quiet a lot of the time. I didn't notice this change in her straight after my illness, but now, in the last fortnight of our own convalescing time, when I've had time to observe and contemplate her reticence, she has puzzled me many times.

'Eva dear,' I speak carefully, 'try not to worry any more. We've left all our nightmares behind. Far away. On the other side of the sea. They won't catch up with us now.'

'No,' she says, 'but things can haunt you wherever you are.'

I wince inwardly. What can I say? I try.

'Do you know what I do? Before sleeping, I squeeze my eyes tight till I see nothing but swirling circles. Then nothing. Next thing I know, I'm awake in the morning.'

'Lucky you!'

'Don't be like that!'

Strange, how it was always I who was the worrying one, and she would always find the bright side to any situation. Now, it's as if we've changed roles. She draws up her knees and hugs her legs and I observe an almost imperceptible shiver in her shoulders.

'I'm sorry,' she says, 'I know you mean well. It's just that... I sometimes have these terrifying thoughts... that after all that pining and waiting to be together with Henryk again, he may not want me any more... look at me, Nastusha, skin and bones and a bald head too!'

I guess her hidden fear but her words make me laugh.

'Oh Eva! How can you think that! We all look the same. Why would Henryk go after another bald girl, when he's got a perfectly bald one of his own!'

I elicit a smile from her. Then she adds,

'I hope you're right. Sometimes I don't know what to think any more!'

There is one little matter that bothers her. And that I can understand. Since our escape from Kermine camp and despite my illness, I've started to menstruate again, after over two years of total absence of this most natural monthly occurrence. I put it down to the reintroduction of regular meals, that our bodies have been denied for so long. But Eva's not had one period yet.

'It's a matter of time,' I try to comfort her, 'everyone's different.'

At the first thrilling show of blood, and my sharing this good news with her, she insisted on accompanying me to the Red Cross sanitary section for women. There was something reassuring at the sight of other women there: life was returning to normal. I felt uncomfortable though, when I received my package and Eva came away empty-handed.

'I worry,' she told me on the way, 'that all those times I had cystitis and other illnesses, they could have damaged something inside me.' I have no medical knowledge of such matters, so I didn't know what to tell her, but any little reassurance is better than nothing at all.

'Eva, it may be because you've had those illnesses that your body got weakened and simply requires more time to recover. Henryk will love you no matter what!'

'That's just it, Nastusha. I'd love to have more children when we get together. A boy for him would be perfect!'

'Just one?' I try to humour her. 'A team would be ideal for his work in the forest!'

Her smile is taut and her clasped hands are squeezed tight.

'If only! If only!' she sighs.

It is time for lunch. We call out to the children. Reluctantly they come away from their sand structures, making final adjustments. We pick up our aluminium mess tins, mugs and spoons and wait for Mr. Ostrovski and his grandsons. Together we make our way between the tents to the central path that leads to the communal and administration area. Here, everything is housed under large tents: the camp office and the Red Cross, the hospital, four giant marquees with a hundred beds in each, public baths and the laundry, with a temporary pipeline in place.

The dining area is a long, side-less, shed-like structure with a tarpaulin roof. There are rows of trestle tables with benches on each side. As we approach there is a queue already forming at the counter where soup is ladled out with bread. There is no panic; one can have as many helpings as one's shrunken stomach can hold. At the beginning some people got ill with over eating. The new diet of fatty mutton and rice proved too heavy for their shrunk stomachs. I want to think that they died happy, at long last, fully satisfied.

The kitchen staff are women in army uniform, the PSKs from the Women's Voluntary Service. Their army attire has not stiffened their manner towards the children, I'm pleased to note.

There's six of them with six large steaming pots and baskets with sliced bread. Ours leans over the counter to our children and remarks,

'You must have grown at least ten centimetres since this morning!' I guess she says this to all the children, but the effect is immediate. Pavel and Agata smile self-consciously and pull themselves up, their baggy clothes held up round their skinny frames with tie belts. Little Stella is swamped in her frilly dress, with a flower and butterfly print, the dress she loves so much she insists on keeping it on at night. The PSK gives her a wide approving smile as she ladles soup onto Stella's aluminium bowl and whispers secretly,

'There's a magic potato in your soup. It'll make you grow as big as your brother and sister!'

Stella is mesmerised. Pavel and Agata giggle quietly at the PSK's unwitting inaccuracy.

She chats with Mr. Ostrovski's little boys and adds some special magic peas to their portions.

We find a space at the long table, where we can all sit together. The soup is thick with mutton, rice and peas, and together with the bread, very nourishing. Every time, as I come away from the dining table I experience a moment of absolute happiness and wonder. My stomach is full and my next meal a certainty.

Later, after we have rested and the children have slept through the hottest part of the day, we walk out of the camp which is fenced with a mesh wire to keep out the pedlars. Nevertheless, they set up their makeshift stalls of hand-pulled carts, bicycle baskets, carton boxes, even battered old suitcases, just outside our camp. Again, as with our regular meals, I'm overcome with disbelief and wonder at the sight of such an abundance of fruit: water melons, mulberries, figs, bananas, dates, pomegranates, oranges and lemons. There are also stalls with pancakes and hard-boiled eggs and a variety of seeds.

On the first day of our arrival, after having been cleansed, given fresh clothes and food, everyone was also given some money and advised to buy fruit in order to supplement our staple diet of mutton and rice. This is the most readily available food in this part of Persia and also the most expedient for the inordinate numbers of refugees arriving daily at this camp.

In addition to this unexpected monetary gift, Eva surprised me. This was typical, old Eva, whom I loved and admired so much. Having divested myself of the few remaining roubles in Krasnovodsk, under the threats of the NKVD, I had not one single coin left in my purse when we arrived in this place. But when we made our first reconnaissance of the camp and outside the fence, and my eyes caught sight of all the wonderful, colourful, mouth-watering produce on the stalls, I almost cried with regret, especially as the vendors accepted any currency.

'Look Eva! Look what we could have bought with the roubles we were forced to throw away!'

And that was when she surprised me. With a defiant grin and a flash of victory in her eyes she announced,

'Not all roubles! I've still got most of mine!'

My mouth fell open and she laughed.

'Nastusha, they made me so angry, the bastards, I thought, I'd show them!'

'But how..?'

She laughs again.

'I stuffed them in my knickers!'

I'm speechless for a second.

'You mean?.. in your knickers?.. all that way?'

She chuckles.

'Don't worry. They are quite clean. I didn't sit on them. I wrapped them in a hanky and stuffed them inside the elastic around my thigh.'

It's the most amusing anecdote I've heard for a long time and we giggle all the while as we spend her Russian roubles in a Persian market.

Today, as we walk past the make-shift stalls, Pavel and Agata point to their favourite fruit: the red, sweet, juicy water melons. We promise to buy some on the way back, for first we plan to visit the cemetery.

It is a walled piece of land, on our side of the outskirts of the city. Here, on the pebbly, dusty ground, the vegetation is sparse and the trees have a stunted appearance. The grass, growing in scattered patches is short and yellow.

It is five in the afternoon. The land is coloured orange at this time of the day, and the intense, mid-day heat has cooled to a bearable temperature.

We are not the only pilgrims on our way to do homage to our unknown travel companions, whose journey ended in this place, so far away from home. People like us, in groups, pass us on the way. Most of them are strangers, but their pain is common to us all.

The wrought-iron gates of the cemetery are left wide open through the day. There is a gardener in charge of tending and watering the plants and shrubs inside the walls. There are flowers on most of the Persian graves. Flowers! Roses, lilies and dahlias! Just like our flowers in Poland, in the middle of this arid land!

We walk past the Persian graves to the far side that has a few hundred rough wooden crosses. We move slowly along the first row and read the carved names and dates. Anna Lozovska, 1880 – 1942, sixty two. She could have enjoyed her old age at home. Karol Zievny, 1868 – 1942, seventy four. It is a wonder he survived this far! The Siberian winter followed by the rigours of a Kazakh camp. Anetka Bilinska, 1938 – 1942. Bartek Bilinski, 1936 – 1942. Little siblings, four and six. My heart contracts with grief at the thought of their mother.

In a strange, paradoxical way, our group's illnesses in the Happy Bird appear to have hardened us against the epidemics of typhus and malaria that have decimated the refugee population in Pahlevi. We stop at the last incomplete row of crosses. Four more graves have been dug in preparation, now with the assistance of the army, who also provide wooden coffins. It's of great comfort to the bereaved to have their loved ones buried with dignity. Pavel and Agata say their short prayers in silence. The last two years have accelerated their maturity of understanding the pain of others.

I pray too over the graves of the innocent victims of one man's megalomaniac madness, and with a rush of rage I curse him. To the end of his days. To the end of eternity.

In the night we have a sandstorm, the third since our arrival here. The *hamsin* is a frequent occurrence in this part of the world; something to do with the hot climate and a sudden drop in temperatures. In this benign environment of sandy dunes, the force of the wind, when it comes, is frightening. We were warned about *hamsins* on our arrival, and every night, as a precaution, we secure the side tent flaps to the ground with additional hooks.

It is pitch black when the first gust of wind hits our tent. From then on the noise, like tons of dry rice being sprayed against the canvass, is relentless. We find our positions, (we know them blindfolded), Florian, Dominik, Mr. Ostrovski, Eva and I, and hold on with all our strength to the poles supporting our tent. Shouting from other tents can be heard, carried with the howling wind. The sand is blown in through every crack and crevice. I feel it beating against my ankles like an attack of a thousand needles.

The smaller children are awake and crying. The flimsy mosquito nets are no barrier against the sand. It is hard to shout instructions or words of comfort against the hissing and the screeching of the gale. I push against the pole with all my body, feeling the force of repeated attacks, that threaten to rip the tent off the ground. The children's squeals pull at my nerves. This merciless nightmare goes on for such a long time, that I feel close to collapse with the effort. My aching arms feel as if they are on fire.

Then just as suddenly as it came, the wind drops and everything becomes quiet. We stand in our positions for a minute longer, just to be certain the danger is over. It is with sighs of relief that we leave our posts and return to our bedding. My eyes and my mouth feel gritty. I just want to plunge my head in a bucket of water. I undo one of the tent flaps and tie it back. The sky is clear, and the bright moon, like a huge lamp floods our tent with light. Before we remove our covers from the mats on the ground to shake them outside, we bathe our children's faces and eyes; they squirm and sneeze, and their eyes cannot stop watering. The whole camp is awake doing the same.

When we're settled on our mats at last, to continue with sleep, Pavel asks,

'Why do we have to have sandstorms, when everything else is so perfect here?'

'It's so we don't get bored,' Eva chuckles then yawns tiredly.

In the morning, more shaking out is awaiting us; there will be sand inside our travel bags, in every little fold of cloth, in every sock and shoe, inside our mugs and plates; we'll be finding sand for the next few days in the most unexpected places.

'It's just another adventure,' I tell the children, thinking of the real horrors we have left behind.

After breakfast, a smart PSK visits our tent. She checks our names against a list on her clipboard. Her news is good.

'You'll be on the next transport to Teheran that leaves tomorrow. We need your tents. Hundreds more are arriving from Krasnovodsk. You'll be better off in Teheran. The camp is much bigger and better organised for a longer stay.'

'And after that?' Mr. Ostrovski asks. 'Any news from the home front?'

She raises her shoulders and her eyebrows, but then her wry expression turns to a friendly smile.

'We'd all want to know that. There's every hope that the war will finish soon. But in the meantime we've got an enormous task on our hands. No one had expected or was prepared for such numbers of refugees to descend on these shores. And Teheran won't be able to cope with this problem for ever. The British are suggesting sending our people to some of their colonies. There's nowhere in Europe that's safe at the moment.'

'British colonies?' Mr. Ostrovski repeats. 'But that could be anywhere in the world! Africa, India, Canada, even New Zealand! Half a world away from home!'

The PSK woman nods.

'That's right, but it wouldn't be forever.'

'But...' I come in, 'I thought we'd always be close to the army, somewhere just outside the war zone.'

'That's not possible,' she says, 'the Germans are everywhere in Europe. Believe me, you won't be forgotten, wherever you happen to be. You'll be sent for, as soon as our country is free.'

When the PSK walks away to the next tent, we sit down on our mats and discuss our future. In this place that has given us respite and the chance to replenish our physical strength and the will to fire our hopes anew, for the first time I sense a shadow falling over our bright horizon.

'Eva,' I find it difficult to hide my worry from her, 'if only we could find our boys before we're separated again.'

She nods looking distracted.

'If we don't find them now,' I add, 'it may be... God only knows when, before we see them again...'

Her eyes fill with tears.

'I can't stop feeling afraid,' she whispers.

Mr. Ostrovski clears his throat.

'Eva, Anastazia. Providence has kept us safe so far. Don't give in now to despair. Look at it as a new beginning.'

'And yet another journey.' Eva's thin shoulders give a shudder. 'It's as if we're destined to travel all our lives.'

CHAPTER 36

The buses leave about nine the next morning. There's about twenty of them lined along the wire fence. About twenty-five people are allocated to each one, so there's enough comfortable space on the wooden benches for us and our belongings. We have all been given enough food and water for the journey, which with an overnight stop, should terminate in Teheran camp before lunch tomorrow. There is a buzz of excitement around us: the children keen to take places close to the windows, their faces already pressed to the glass, adults settling down for the long trip ahead, speculating on the next stage of our unending odyssey; older women drawn inside their shawls, whispering prayers, their bony fingers moving along their rosary beads.

The driver is a young Iranian with thick black curls and lively eyes and a cigarette stuck in the corner of his mouth. He looks eighteen and I cannot help wondering about his driving experience. But he is partnered by one of our soldiers, a sensible looking man in his thirties. I have no choice but to trust them.

All benches face the front. Our group has taken two benches across the aisle, so that Agata can have a window seat on one side, and Pavel on the opposite end, close to Mr. Ostrovski's boys. Stella stands up between me and Eva, her oversize dress giving her the appearance of an umbrella. She points at people and objects, trying to make sense of yet another change in her short life.

'Soon, we'll be going soon,' Eva tells her, stroking her fluffy new growth. Then she turns to me. 'The Nomads, at least, choose the way they live. With us it's like being litter blown about by the wind.'

She puts into words my very own feelings. But I mustn't let such thoughts weigh down the buoyant expectancy of this moment.

'Eva, my dear, let's just enjoy the journey this time. We're travelling in style!' I try to humour her, but she still has that preoccupied look.

'Then tell me,' she says, 'why do I get those awful thoughts, that my life has come to an end, that there's nothing else left, that this is my lot now, to be sent from place to place, to the end of my days…'

'Oh Eva,' I give her a hug, 'I get such thoughts too. On my bad days. But there will be more good days than bad ones from now on.'

'Will there? How do you know?'

'I don't know. But I feel it. I make myself feel it. Just think, our boys must be as homesick as we are. When bad thoughts get me down, do you know what I imagine? Their faces, their joy when we finally find them.'

Eva's eyes fill up and she dabs at them with the sleeve of her dress.

We move off in a convoy. People stop talking and look out for the last glimpse of the Pahlevi camp, which was like a haven of peace and kindness after the gruelling, fear-filled years in the People's Paradise created by Stalin. Our buses go past the cleansing area, separated from the rest of the camp by a swathe of waste land. A new transport of people, as skeletal and tramp-like as we were, has just arrived, and like us, are being instructed by their guides to save only their most precious possessions, in the provided tin boxes, and leave everything else in a pile to be burnt later.

Like us, men and women will be separated for modesty, and asked to leave all their lice-infested clothes outside the baths tents, which are equipped with a network of overhead pipes and a number of shower heads to cleanse at least twenty people at a time. The ten-minute showers, with added chemicals, are compulsory to kill off all lice and bugs.

On the other side of the baths there are separate tents for men and women, with trestle tables displaying all manner of clothes and shoes donated by the Red Cross. I still experience the joy of finding clean dresses and underwear, fresh, clear colours, after the drabness of our rags worn for two years. Once we had dressed in our selected clothes, much oversized on our emaciated bodies, we were instructed by the supervising staff to pick another spare set and also a head-scarf.

Thus dressed and equipped, we were then sent to a hair-dresser's tent, where our heads were shaved. Those who were too ill to undergo this process were taken immediately to the quarantine hospital on this site, before their transfer to the main camp, where we have enjoyed our refuge for the past two weeks.

A thought crosses my mind, an anecdote told us by a PSK girl. When the first transport of Polish refugees arrived in Pahlevi, and people threw themselves on the sand with prayers of thanksgiving and cries of joy, the British soldiers overseeing this phenomenon, were surprised into thinking that they'd just rescued a religious sect, whose religion required them to kiss the ground on arrival.

The route out of the camp takes us across the dunes to a flat ground with sparse trees and vegetation. Here, there's one more place worthy of a stop, deserving a moment of respectful silence and contemplation. The buses do not stop, and only through the pane above Agata's head, I acknowledge in a silent prayer my countrymen buried in a walled cemetery. Hundreds of those who have made it only so far, and hundreds more to join them for all eternity, in an alien land so far away from home. The old praying women raise their sad, washed-out eyes and bid the departed farewell, with a sign of the cross.

291

Then this section of our journey is cut off and left behind. Before us, outlined against a clear blue sky lies the distant mountain range. By mid-day, the air becomes comfortably cooler as our road enters a green valley overshadowed by massive rocks and perpendicular mountainsides.

'Elburz Mountains,' Mr. Ostrovski informs.

The mountains are awesome in their majestic grandeur, and I'd be quite happy to remain in the valley, amongst the abundant greenery, and surprising colourful flowers, and the mountain streams gushing down the rocks, but our road rises to higher ground and becomes a track chiselled in the flank of the granite. It meanders and turns back on itself in hair-pin bends, while our bus struggles up the impossible gradient. I dare not look down. I notice most adults turn away from the sights outside the windows. The old women cower inside their shawls and frantically whisper their prayers.

'It's like hanging in space,' Agata informs me, straining to see the gorge below, 'and there are cars. And lorries. Smashed and rusting.'

My legs go numb. I lean towards Eva, towards the centre of the bus, towards the centre of gravity, as if my one weight made any difference.

'God save us, Eva!' I whisper, 'this is torture!'

'Close your eyes,' she replies, 'and pretend you're somewhere else.'

I screw my eyes tight, but it does not work. I grip the edge of my wooden seat till all my muscles hurt. The bus brakes suddenly, eliciting screams, excited from the children, frightened from the adults. The impossible is happening. There is a lorry coming towards us.

'What now?' My mouth is so dry my tongue feels like a piece of wood.

The young driver draws on his cigarette, then squinting through the smoke at the side mirror, he throws the gear stick into reverse. Slowly, the bus rolls backwards into a niche right against the rock face. The lorry passes by, foot by tortuous foot, its outside wheels seemingly hanging over the precipice, and it's like a miracle happening before our eyes when it continues its journey intact, and we continue ours.

I'm limp with relief, but not for long, as this mental torture resumes and is prolonged on our descent. Apart from occasional comments from the fearless children, all adult conversation has died down, the silence almost tangibly tautened with every new stop and turn and near miss with the on-coming traffic. When at long last, after about four hours, the bus wheels roll onto level ground, my muscles ache all over from the rigid gripping of the bench. There is no sight of other buses either ahead of us or behind.

Our Iranian driver stops at the first small village in the valley and our guide gives us half an hour to stretch our legs and visit the bushes, growing in plentiful abundance by the roadside. When these basic, most important needs are satisfied, we take the children for a quick walk to the village, five minutes from our stop. The houses here are solid, built of rock stone, their slate colour enhanced with climbing vines and lilac and white wisteria. The few people in the square look at us with interest; the women, in long, dark dresses, gathered at the waist; the men in grey baggy trousers and thick shirts, like smocks. A vendor of boiled eggs skips up to us with his basket, but we decline politely with repeated '*spaseebas*'.

Back at the bus after our much-needed exercise, we open our brown paper bags, with varied sandwiches of corned beef, boiled eggs, or cheese, and in addition some bananas, dried figs and dates.

I save most of mine; I've no appetite left after our adventure in the mountains. A number of the elderly people look ill, and sit back with their eyes closed. Most of us take cue from them and willingly lose ourselves in blissful sleep when the bus restarts the journey.

In late evening, with the sky like a vast inky dome stretching above the land, our bus stops on the outskirts of Qazvin city. Its orange glow can be seen from our place which looks like a hangar or a warehouse. Polish soldiers, about twenty, space themselves out along the line of buses that have now all materialized as if by magic.

Before we leave the bus, our guide informs us that this is just an overnight stay to give everyone a break, especially the driver. I bless him in my mind.

The building is lit with bare bulbs above the entrance of massive sliding doors, and inside with more bulbs that hang on a sagging cable around the vast hall. All along the sides, the concrete floor is covered with army blankets.

We make a bee-line to the nearest available space and save room for Mr. Ostrovski next to us. Even with the twenty buses emptied and over five hundred people sheltering indoors, there's room for more.

'What's it normally used for, this building?' I ask our guide, who is standing nearby, minding his charges, busy unpacking and making the floor bed more comfortable.

'For storing aircraft,' he replies. 'You'll see in the morning. We're in a military airfield. They test engines here.'

We unpack our sandwiches, and after satisfying our hunger (mine still much blunted), we go in search of the toilet before settling down for the night. We are directed to a long brick building outside the hangar. There is already a queue forming at the open door, which throws a long, rectangular shaft of light on the waiting men and women.

It is with some surprise, we discover that everyone can enjoy a moment of privacy, for facing the row of about twenty washbasins against one wall, there is a row of the same number of toilet cubicles with doors and locks.

'Such luxury!' I whisper to Eva.

'And a good clean wash at last!' She looks pleased too. I can only imagine the joy of those who have suffered stomach troubles throughout the journey.

Inside the hangar the guides stay with their groups, on their narrow mats that they have brought with them. For us, the floor is very hard and the blankets cannot soften the contact between the concrete and our bones. It takes me a long while to position myself, curled up on one side, in comfort long enough to fall asleep before my thin flesh starts protesting again. The conditions are harsh, but the discreet light left in the corners and the open gap between the sliding doors has a reassuring effect on me, that no one will come banging on the door in the middle of the night to take me away into the unknown.

The first impression of Teheran is a miniature cityscape in the far distance, with white buildings set against the greenery of rising hills on one side, and on the other, snow-covered peaks of mountains, shimmering against the backdrop of a sapphire blue sky.

Our buses do not go that far. Around mid-day we take a detour from the straight wide asphalt road onto a pebbly, beaten track, that takes us through a town of tents. Hundreds. In the passages between them, people are going about their business singly or in family groups. Our bus comes to a halt at what appears to be the centre of this buzzing place. Large wooden buildings surround the square, in the middle of which tall masts fly the British and the Polish flags. Our guide stands up and turns to face us.

'We've arrived,' his self-deprecating smile follows a sigh of relief. 'Just a few minutes more, and I'll show you to your quarters. A short visit to the office, to have the documents checked.' He lifts his wad of papers. 'This is Camp One. There are five such camps around Teheran, all a few kilometres apart.'

'And the soldiers?' someone asks. 'Where can we find our husbands?'

The guide nods in understanding.

'There are military bases all over the place. Some quite close, but some hundreds of kilometres away.'

'So how can we find our relatives?' the same woman asks.

'Word of mouth. The Red Cross,' our guide suggests. 'Once everyone is settled it'll be easier to establish contact through the army post.'

My heart sinks. I glance at Eva, She looks lost in her thoughts. I catch something in the guide's words that makes me concentrate.

'Excuse me,' I ask him, 'did you just say the camp authorities will help us?'

'They'll try to do what they can,' he confirms. 'Also, there's a temporary military base in the city itself. But again, this is just for passing units. They stay for a fortnight then they are moved on for further training elsewhere.'

His words are meant to be comforting, but all the time I feel as if we've reached a dead end.

'Eva…' I can't say any more. I feel beaten.

'Nastusha,' the strength in her voice takes me by surprise, 'we'll knock on every door. We'll leave no stone unturned! Until we find them!'

Compared to all our previous dwellings in the last two-and -a-half years, our present refuge is a luxury. We have been placed in one of the huts that form the other half of this gigantic camp, consisting predominantly of tents. Our hut, with its corrugated metal roof, has four separate partitions screened with raffia mats. More mats cover the clay floor, making our room look clean and civilised. We all have our own sleeping mattress, on the two facing bunk beds, which accommodate Pavel and Agata on the top, and Eva with Stella and myself sleeping below them. With donated bedding and pillows, they are comfortable and totally free of lice and bugs. In the daytime we use the lower bunks for our sitting area.

All basic facilities are in place: a huge field hospital with nearly a thousand beds in eight marquees; several field kitchens placed at convenient spots to facilitate distribution of food to thousands three times a day; there are bath houses with rows of shower heads and rows of sinks for washing and laundry; there is a number of latrines dug at intervals around the perimeter of the camp, screened by high boards.

The diet is basic, but regular: porridge, tea and bread with jam for breakfast; nourishing soup, thick with vegetables, lentils and mutton for lunch, and sandwiches with tea for supper. As it's impossible to contain the growing numbers of arriving people in the original dining huts, a system has been devised of collecting meals from the nearest kitchen points.

In addition, local vendors visit the camp daily with a variety of fruit, pancakes and flat bread and the ubiquitous hard-boiled eggs. Even this basic diet is too rich for some shrunken stomachs. Hundreds are ill with dysentery. Also, with typhus and malaria. As in the previous transit camp, the cemetery outside the camp spreads out with newly-dug graves, and the wooden crosses multiply each day.

After the first day of acclimatising in the camp, sorting out our few things for washing, visiting the Red Cross in the hope of acquiring another set of underwear, and returning joyful at the happily accomplished mission, Eva and I have spent the last week walking round the camps and enquiring about our boys. Camp Two, only a few kilometres away, we visited on foot, leaving the children in Mr. Ostrovski's care. Camps Three, Four and Five we visited by courtesy of jeeps and lorries, coursing frequently between the camps. We've spoken to every soldier we've met on the way, we went to all administration offices and gave details of our missing boys. We were promised each time, that our enquiries would be followed up, but with so many thousands of displaced persons constantly on the move, we're told, the result of our search could take a long time yet to reach us.

It is compulsory to shelter indoors from the scorching heat in the midday hours. We sit on the lower bunks and eat off our laps: a thick vegetable soup with bread. Little Stella's face is a picture of all-engrossing concentration as she tackles the task of lifting the spoon to her mouth without leaving spills outside her mess tin. So prematurely serious and grown up for her three years!

'First of September today. Did you realise that?' Mr. Ostrovski asks through the partitioning screen.

'Who could forget it?' Mrs. Lekis replies from behind her screen. 'Two-and-a-half long years of this homeless wandering!'

'I've heard that the bishop is coming on Sunday!' Mr. Ostrovski continues, 'there will be an open air Mass for everyone!'

My spirits soar.

'First Mass! After all that time!' I join in the conversation. 'It'll be like home!' My mind floods with visions of my 'Sunday best' from the past; the dress with the lace collar, the brooch, the cloche hat, the matching high heels. My scalp has grown a dark covering in the last few weeks, but I still wear a headscarf. 'Decisions, decisions! What shall I wear for this grand occasion?' Even as I joke, I cannot hide my excitement.

'What's it all for?' Mrs. Volska, our fourth co-tenant pipes up from her corner. She has three children, a girl of eight and two boys of nine and eleven, all suffering with skin complaints and gluey eyes. 'I mean,' she continues discordantly, 'what are we going to give thanks for? The starvation? The epidemics? The state of our dying people? The destruction of our families?'

Eva looks at me and raises her eyebrows. Mrs. Volska is not an easy co-tenant with her constant grievances, though everything she states is true. Mr. Ostrovski clears his throat.

'Mrs. Volska,' his tone is gentle, 'we've survived. Isn't that enough to be thankful for?'

'No!' hers is a vehement No. 'I've never asked for any of it!'

There are suppressed snorts from Florian and Dominik, followed by their mother's authoritarian 'Stop it!' Then she too speaks up,

'We are all angry, Mrs. Volska. But you mustn't let anger spoil the good things. The bishop's visit is just what the people need to boost their spirits.'

'You're welcome to all that! But count me out!' Mrs Volska insists. 'If God loves us so much why doesn't He strike Stalin with lightning, the son of a bitch! And don't give me that rubbish about God loving us so much He has to test us! I don't need testing! I don't ask for much! I just want peace and my old life back!'

Who can argue with that?

A shadow falls across our sunlit floor. I look up to the dark silhouette of a man etched against the brightness of the doorway.

'Dzień dobry,' he greets us, 'do Mrs. Kalinska or Mrs. Bzovska happen to live in this residence?'

His voice, after all the months of separation, has the power to send an electric shock through me.

CHAPTER 37

I jump off the bunk bed and throw my arms around his neck.

'Julian! Oh Julian! I don't believe it!'

He holds me tight against him and I breathe in his presence like an intoxicating balm. His face is against mine, and underneath the fabric of his uniform, I feel him tingling all over with our shared, overwhelming joy. This lasts only a second, for he is not alone. Two more soldiers, Henryk and Ryszard, are trying to squeeze into our small quarter. Eva cries out and Agata squeals and Pavel throws his arms around Julian's waist.

'Uncle Julian! Uncle Julian! We thought we'd never find you!'

When all the prolonged hugs are exhausted, and that first raw need of being close to the loved one is satisfied, we all sit down, and keep looking at each other in disbelief and wonder.

'But how?' I recover first. 'How did you know where to find us?'

Julian laughs softly. His happiness shows in his every move, in every expression. 'All shall be revealed soon,' he says mysteriously, with one hand over mine and the other on Pavel's shoulder, 'but first, there is one matter that cannot wait any longer.'

Henryk is sitting with his arm around Eva, and Stella between them. The thin gap between his two front teeth adds an air of jollity to his wide smile. Ryszard is holding Agata close to his side, brushing the top of her head with his lips. His gulag paleness has been replaced with a deep tan and his neat officer's moustache gives him a debonair appearance. They must already know what is about to happen, for they stop all talk and look our way.

Julian clears his throat. 'Pavelek, I've got some good news for you.'

Pavel is puzzled. 'What good news?'

Julian smiles. 'Who would you like to see the most in the world?'

Pavel returns his smile and hugs him. 'You of course! But you're here now!'

'And who else?'

Pavel moves his head back to look Julian in the eye. I watch as realisation dawns in the alertness of his face at the same time as I guess what is about to come.

'My Dad?'

As he says these words another person, a soldier, stands in the doorway. Slowly, Pavel detaches himself from Julian and shields his eyes against the glare from outside.

'Dad? Is that really you?'

Oleg Yavorski, missing for over two-and-a-half years from his son's life, gathers up the thin boy into his arms, buries his face in Pavel's shoulder and suppresses a sob. They cling together for a long while, watched by the rest of us in awed silence. I struggle with my emotions. This is all such a shock: the zenith of happiness followed so abruptly by a blow to my dreams. Of course I must be happy for Oleg and Pavel but the pain of my loss is too brutal to bear. I cannot stop the tears, which drip through my fingers as I cover my face. Julian hugs me to his chest, and I guess he believes my emotional state is brought on by great happiness. I cannot explain the truth to anyone, for who would have sympathy with my selfish mawkishness in the face of such a miraculous reunion?

When we settle on the lower bunks, pushed together but happy, and while everyone is talking all at once, I compose myself enough to ask Oleg,

'So, how did you all meet? And where?' His worn face lights up and he cuddles Pavel to him yet again as he explains,

'In Guzar. Uzbekistan. I got there in time for the March evacuation. But then Stalin stopped everything. Promised food rations. Nothing! It was dire, I tell you. We had to share food with the civilians. And they kept arriving in hundreds every day. Of course, I never stopped looking for Pavel,' he gives Pavel another hug. 'It was grim, I tell you. All those orphans! Sick and dying. And then, it was like a miracle! I came across Julian and Henryk!' His smile spreads across his face. 'After that we stuck together. We never stopped making enquiries. And here we are!'

'Here we are!' Julian's embrace is strong around my shoulders. I respond with my arm tightening round his waist. His closeness is soothing to my mixed emotions. I ask Oleg about his girls.

'Where are they? Aniela and little Marysia? Aniela must be about fourteen now? Quite grown up!'

His face takes on a serious look.

'Do you remember when we got left behind?' How could anyone forget! I nod. He continues. 'We waited till the next day on that freezing platform, before another train came by. Hellishly cold! I tell you. The station guard took pity on us and allowed us to wait inside his warm cubbyhole. The cold would have killed us otherwise. He gave us some hot *chai* and a slice of black bread each. Bless him! The train, that we got on, another cattle truck, went east, right up to Sosnogorsk. You know the rest. Backbreaking labour, dire cold, a hovel to sleep in and chronic lack of food. Marysia got pneumonia. There was nothing I could do to save her.' He pauses, containing the pain. Pavel catches his breath and looks up at his father with mournful eyes. Images of Dorotka and Tomek and Daniel flash through my mind, and I think of those other thousands of young lives that have been lost so senselessly, each one irreplaceable.

'And Aniela,' Pavel asks, 'is Aniela still alive?'

Oleg strokes his head.

'Yes, my dear Pavelek, she is alive. She has survived, poor little mite. She is well looked after. Better than I could have done now.'

'Where? Where is she?'

Oleg lowers his face to him.

'She is in an orphanage, in Isphahan.'

'Where's that?

'About two hours drive south. I know it sounds like a long way away, Pavelek, but,' he gives his son a reassuring smile, 'it's a really wonderful place. After everything these poor children have been through, it's like a fairy tale! The Shah was so moved by the plight of the Polish orphans, he's opened up one of his palaces for their use. Can you believe it? It's so beautiful there, Pavelek, I tell you, gardens, fountains, shaded courtyards, ornate rooms, but the best thing is, it's run like a proper school, with lessons and regular meals, and the children are dressed in proper uniforms and there are dormitories and everyone's got a proper bed of their own! And the teachers are like kind uncles and aunts...'

He looks at Pavel with excitement in his face and I guess what is about to come next. I guess right.

'Pavelek, I know we have to be separated again. But there you'll be together with Aniela. Safe. Till the war is over and I come to collect you both and we'll go home, back to Poland.'

Pavel is spellbound by his Father's tale, then he looks at me.

'So what's going to happen now? Where's everyone else going to go? I thought we were all going to live together in one big house.'

There's a moment of awkward silence, which Julian breaks.

'Pavel, your Dad is right. At the moment there is nowhere else that's as safe as there.'

Pavel's sad glance digs into my heart like a dagger.

'Auntie Nastusha, I wish you could come with me.'

'I wish that too,' I suppress my grief, 'but just look around, Pavelek. We've got nothing here to give you, and there... you'll have everything!'

'Pavel,' Ryszard buts in with a stir of his moustache as he composes his serious expression, 'I'm going to take Agatka there too.'

'Are you?' Agata clings harder to him. He kisses her on the top of her head.

'Yes, my dearest dove, because that's the most sensible thing to do. It won't be for long. Maybe just a few months. Everyone talks about the end of the war in the spring of next year.'

'But that's another six months!' Agata protests.

'Time flies quickly when you're busy,' he gives her another pacifying kiss, 'you won't be alone. You'll have your best friend with you and Aniela. All right?' She does not look convinced, and I feel for her, but he gives her another hug, then looks around and changes the subject. 'It looks as if all the time we weren't that far from you in distance and time. We crossed the Caspian Sea at the beginning of August.'

'That's only a fortnight before us!' Eva exclaims.

Henryk's arm tightens round her thin shoulders and he grins.

'God, am I happy I wasn't one of those unfortunate lads left behind in Pahlevi to recover. Dysentery, typhus, all sorts of other damned things!'

'We've had our share in Guzar,' Julian reminds him, 'will last me a life time! We've just returned from training in Rashit. Over the Elbuz mountains...' he lifts his eyebrows in mock horror, 'if your nerves can stand that, then you're ready for anything!'

'We know!' Eva laughs, and I want to feel as light-hearted as she is, but I cannot shake off the sadness. 'And where are you stationed now?' she asks.

'An old munitions factory,' Henryk says, with his perpetually wide grin, 'and do you know what? The bloody Germans built it. Some years before the war. Already with the plan of taking over this country. Bloody Hitler!'

'Hitler-shitler,' Eva mutters, then adds aloud, 'what I want to know, is how did you find us?'

Henryk plants a fond kiss on her white blond head.

'Like you,' he says, 'we kept making enquiries wherever we were. And here we are.'

It is very hot in our little quarter, even more so with our number doubled. I feel a trickle down the small of my back and stickiness in my armpits. I notice beads of sweat on the men's brows and forming stains on their shirts.

'Julian,' I suggest, 'there isn't really anywhere to go, but perhaps we could look for some shade under the trees?'

The others go along with my idea and will probably follow, but I don't wait. I pick up my folded blanket and leave with Julian. I get a strange feeling. I don't have to worry about Pavel or Agata any more.

The sun bears down with ferocious heat on the corrugated metal roofs, some ridges reflecting its brilliance like blinding searchlights. Julian and I walk in the shade between the huts, his head covered by his field cap and mine tied with a white scarf. We make our way towards the edge of the camp, where the last row of huts looks out onto a flat, desert-like terrain, with sparsely scattered shrubs and some cedars or palms. In the distance, like a mirage, the snow-covered peaks of mountains create a broken line against the pale blue sky.

'Reminds me of our mountains,' Julian comments, 'it seems like a hundred years ago. Every night when I close my eyes I think of our forests and hills.' He waits for me to join him, then he takes my hand and we walk on together. 'Perhaps it won't be so long now. Rommel's retreating. The British are giving him a damn good hiding by all accounts.'

'Oh Julian,' I breathe hard and long, 'I'm so tired of this unending journey. Like you, I dream of home every night. How much longer do we have to wander about like this?'

He squeezes my hand, looks at me and smiles, almost shyly, the way he used to when we were just a boy and a girl, attracted to each other, yet too self-conscious to speak our minds.

'All right. Tell me. What are you thinking?' I ask, as we go through a hole in the wire mesh, onto the open land. Groups of people shelter from the sun in the shade of scattered shrubs. His gaze scans the distance and he smiles again.

'I'm just happy,' he states simply, 'happy to be with you. It's been such a long time. I missed you. Especially at the end of a long day's training. Lugging the heavy equipment. The hot sand burning your feet. Then you collapse like a log on a camp bed, and sweat like a pig. And I ask myself what's it all for? So far away from home, from all the people you love?'

I lift his hand to my face and rub it against my cheek.

'I missed you too Julian. I wish we didn't have to part. Yet again!'

'*Nastusha, moja kochana*, let's enjoy the short time we have and not waste it on worrying about what's to come next.'

We walk across the dry dusty land covered in rough sun-bleached grass towards a mulberry tree, squat and wide, giving ample shade. We hasten our steps, then just as suddenly Julian stops, and pulls me to him. He winks at me with a wicked smile. The sounds reaching us from behind the tree are unmistakeable. We make a quick right-angle turn and hurry on to another clump of trees further away. I'm ashamed to admit, I cannot stop myself from a backward glance. The blanket covering the couple hiding underneath it is tossed up and down like waves on stormy water, and cannot silence the gasps and the moans.

I get a fit of giggles when we reach a lonely shady spot of our own. I spread out the blanket and we both collapse on top of it laughing. Then he takes me in his arms and holds me close and I feel the length of his body as we both tingle with happiness.

'Julian, we've not been alone like this since we left home,' I whisper into the crook of his neck, inhaling his scent, a hint of soap, tobacco and man sweat.

'I know.' He releases me and lifts himself up on his elbow. 'We've got a lot of catching up to do.' I sit up too and kiss his face.

'Here? Like them? Julian, I'd die of shame if anyone saw us!'

He laughs softly. 'Nastusha, what do you take me for? A barbarian? No, my dear. Today is like our first date, all right? We've got so much to tell each other. Let's just enjoy that.'

I am relieved. Much as I want to love him, kiss him, touch him, feel his nakedness covering mine, I don't want to do any of that here in the open rough ground.

'So when?' I ask.

He sits up and from his breast pocket he takes out a small flat card box. The corners of his mouth lift with self-conscious delight.

'For you!' he says.

I open the box and gasp. Resting on a fluff of cotton wool is a gold band.

'But how..?' I stare at it and remember the other wedding ring, robbed from me by Borodin.

Julian lights a cigarette and through the smoke grins at me broadly.

'Simple,' he says, 'I've been saving. Specially for this. Put it on!'

The ring is loose on my finger.

'I'll fix it,' I assure him, 'I'll wrap a little string on the inside. But how did you know you'd find me?'

'Like you, I kept looking. I never lost hope. And here we are. And that's not all!' He watches me for a moment as I hide the ring safe in its box and then inside my pocket, and his face is alive with what he wants to tell me. 'This coming Saturday, I'll ask for an overnight pass. This will give us two days together. On our own. It'll be like a holiday! I'll take you to the city. I've got enough saved to pay for a room!' He embraces me, but I wriggle out of his arms and laugh.

'Julian! Look at me! How can I show myself in the city, looking like this?'

He slips off my headscarf and strokes my growing hair, short like a boy's.

'Nastusha, the very first thing we'll do, is buy you a new dress, new shoes and a pretty straw hat!'

The picture his words conjure up is like a fantasy. 'And can you afford all that?'

'You're speaking to a wealthy bourgeois!' he teases. 'Don't worry Nastusha, I've thought of everything. Come,' he pats the ground beside him, 'come close to me and tell me everything you did when I was away.'

'How much time have you got?' I laugh. We lie back, holding hands, Julian exhaling the smoke, and I, squinting my eyes against the bright sky fragmented into hundreds of irregular shapes between the overhanging leaves.

He listens to my tale of the journey from Buzuluk right down to Teheran, with frequent questions about the people and places that Eva and I came across on the way. I don't dwell on details regarding Selim and Tariq. I conclude simply,

'We were lucky to have met some kind Uzbeks, Julian. Their help came just in the nick of time. Without them, there would have been a few more graves left behind in the Happy Bird.'

'Thank God for that!' he says, and draws on his cigarette. 'We had a few adventures of our own, our group,' he pauses as if gathering his thoughts. 'I wouldn't wish those on anyone. In Tashkent we all caught typhus. It was ghastly, Nastusha. Just as well I was knocked out most of the time. Every time I opened my eyes I was surprised I was still alive!'

I lift his hand to my lips and feel him shiver.

'Was Roman with you? Where is he now?'

'Here, with us. Appointed Junior Warrant Officer. Ryszard too. Made Senior Warrant Officer. There's a dire shortage of high ranking officers. Those taken prisoners of war by the Russians, after the September campaign, haven't been released yet.'

'Why ever not? It's over a year since the amnesty.'

'That's the answer that Anders is pressing for. Stalin pretends to know nothing about them. He jokes that they must have all escaped to China!'

I think of all those poor souls still slaving away in those dreadful labour camps.

Julian draws me close to him and assures me,

'Anders will not leave any stone unturned, till they are found. We all need them badly. To take up commanding positions and to lead their men.'

I contemplate his words with mixed feelings. There's only one purpose for forming an army.

'Julian, I wish there was no need for any of it, no need to fight, to die, to be injured, no need for you to go away and leave me again.'

Julian snuffs his cigarette butt against the soil, sits up and gives his sleeve a tug.

'Shame on you, wife of a Master Corporal! See these four stripes? Henryk's the same. We've got a platoon each under our command. And our forestry experience has gained us first position in doing reconnaissance on any new terrain!'

I sit up too and run my fingers down the stripes.

'Is that supposed to make me ecstatic? You being first in the line of fire?'

His smile is wry.

'You could show a little pride in your old man!'

'Oh Julian!' I sigh, 'I am proud of you. But I'm also afraid. A glorious inscription on a cross for bravery is no compensation for a lost life.'

There's seriousness in his eyes. 'I'm not always calm,' he says, 'I get my bad days too. Dark thoughts. Fears and uncertainties. But I've committed myself. I believe that's the right thing to do. And once our job is done, we'll go home, Nastusha.'

Not everyone, I reflect, but I don't want to quarrel in the little time that we've got left today.

Later, after our boys have gone with promises 'till Saturday', and the inhabitants of our hut are preparing for the night, Pavel and Agata climb down from their upper bunks and sit beside me, leaning against me on both sides. Pavel asks,

'Auntie Nastusha, will you be very sad when Agata and I go away to Isfahan?'

Eva, on the opposite bunk looks my way, as she rocks Stella to sleep. That gaunt expression is gone from her face, but there's sympathy in her eyes.

'I'll be very sad,' I reply honestly, 'you and Agata have become like my own children.'

He rests his head against my shoulder. 'Please, don't be sad. I want to be with Aniela again. If only you could come with us, then we can all stay together.'

Agata plants a kiss on my arm and adds, 'I want that too. Perhaps if we ask...?'

I draw them close to me, already imagining the void when they are gone.

'I want the same as you do,' I tell them, 'but for a while, just for a short time, things will be different. You have to be brave. Just like the soldiers going to the war. What we must do now, is make the next few days happy for us.' I kiss them both in turn on the top of their heads. 'Go to sleep now, and dream of our homecoming.'

They climb up onto their bunks and I'm left facing Eva. She adjusts the cover around her sleeping child, then comes over and sits down beside me. She links her arm with mine, leaning her head towards me. I open the little box and show off my gold band. Henryk has bought her one too.

'They must have planned it together,' she whispers, mindful of the thin partitions, yet even her whisper betrays her enlivened state. 'It's been quite a day! Such a surprise! I didn't have time to fret about my looks!' I know it's not her looks she's been worrying about. But her change of mood is infectious and I chuckle,

'Oh Eva! It's obvious Henryk's got eyes for no one else but you! And how he adores Stella!'

'He's taking us away for Saturday and Sunday. I can't imagine it!'

'Julian's taking me away too!' We hug each other and giggle like schoolgirls before their first date.

Pavel's head leans over the edge of his bunk.

'And my dad said, there will be buses on Saturday to take us and other kids to Isfahan!'

I look up to his lively face.

'It's all going to be so marvellous and exciting, isn't it, Pavelek?' I reply, as something squeezes my heart.

CHAPTER 38

Over the next few days my mood bounces between fizzing happiness in anticipation of being with Julian again, and utter sadness at losing Pavel. In my mind, for a long time, Pavel was already our child.

As I watch him play with Agata, I already anticipate the emptiness he'll leave behind. Little things, the turn of his head, the trusting look in his eyes, the spontaneous hug, the sudden smile, these things make me want to cry. I wish I could be unrestrained in my happiness for him as I am for Agata.

I keep my feelings to myself. Pavel and Agata's imagination has been fired by the fantasy of the orphanage at the Shah's palace and I keep up their enthusiasm with made-up stories of their future adventures together. Sometimes, when alone with Eva, I drop my guard.

'I shall miss them,' I tell her, 'I cannot imagine life without them now.'

'They'll be all right,' she smiles broadly. She smiles a lot these days. The brief reunion with Henryk has resurrected the real, optimistic Eva. 'Nastusha, it's all falling into place for us at long last. As it should. The children have found their fathers. We'll be seeing our boys again soon. I cannot believe such luck!'

Her effervescence is beguiling, but I am a realist.

'Luck? A day or two with our husbands, when we should be together at all times!'

'We will be,' she states with conviction, 'but better this for now, than nothing at all. You know what they say. All the best things come in small doses!'

'I've no objection to big doses of good things,' I retort, but she just laughs.

On the day of the children's departure, we don't prolong our goodbyes. A hug and a kiss and promises to write and I stand back to watch them queue for boarding the bus. We are gathered in the central square of the camp, Julian and I, Eva and Henryk with Stella in his arms. Ryszard and Oleg walk with their children right up to the bus, which is lined up with three more, each with room for about twenty-five children and their carers.

We wave them off and watch the buses follow each other out of the camp in a plume of dust. There is a lump in my throat, but I force myself to think of all the wonderful things awaiting them at the end of their journey. Oleg comes up to us and wipes his eyes.

'At least this time I know exactly where Pavel is going to be,' he says.

Ryszard slaps his shoulder amicably, his moustache twitching.

'Be happy chum! They'll be in good hands. And we've got a job to do. Let's go!'

We all pile into the jeep that Ryszard's higher rank has wrangled for a few hours, and as we drive off I repeat 'be happy!' in my mind and concentrate my gaze on the horizon and welcome the breeze on my face and feel Julian's hand resting on my thigh, squashed against his. When the dusty track merges with the wide tarmac highway to Teheran, Henryk bursts into a song:

Choć burza huczy w koło nas..
Though the storm is raging around us
Hold your head up high…

Julian and Ryszard join him heartily in the rousing, marching tune, the words of which extol the strong bonds of friendship that will carry us through the highs and lows of life. Only Oleg remains quiet and I hum along with Eva.

The Qazvin Road takes us along the main boulevard of the Shah right to the centre, to the old part of Teheran, with the tower of Eman Mosque overseeing the Bazaar Square. I'm overwhelmed by the sights we pass by: wide streets with green central sections, palms and scarlet bougainvilleas, modern white rectangular buildings, and as we get closer to the centre, crowded pavements with well-dressed people going about their business, coffee shops, restaurants, shop windows displaying a rich variety of goods, cars parked along with horse-carts and camels. I nudge Julian.

'I can't believe it! It's all so normal! It's as if there was no war!'

His laughter is happy.

Ryszard drops us off, Henryk and Eva too, at the end of Naser Street close to the Bazaar.

'Don't buy it all out at once!' he laughs, his moustache twitching. Oleg jumps down with us and kisses my hand and Eva's in farewell.

'I cannot thank you both enough,' he says with feeling, 'perhaps… one day… at home… we'll have a big party!'

We wave them off, then we part company with Eva and Henryk and Stella in his arms. Stella is distracted by the sights in the square and keeps pointing her finger at a number of things, as they walk away.

My eyes are assailed in a shock of wonder by the brightness and colours after the shadowy dimness of the side street. The crowd is a mixture of Eastern attire; embroidered kaftans and crochet caps of the men, dark long dresses and veiled faces of thewomen, as well as European suits and frocks and hats and army uniforms. All sides of the square are lined with shops overflowing onto the pavements with stalls displaying their goods. The middle of the vast market area is a network of stalls underneath their striped canvass covers. I can't wait to make a tour round all the passages so as not to miss anything on display. My eyes wonder already over the silks and cottons, rugs and kilims, trinkets and jewellery, florid patterned pottery, leather goods, shoes and handbags, countless stalls. I squeeze Julian's hand in anticipation, he smiles back and leads me through the crowd.

The air is pungent with odours and scents: coffee and cigarette smoke, sweet violets and stale sweat, ripe fruit on the stalls and things rotting in the gutter, a dead cat, I notice with revulsion.

There are donkeys and camels standing obediently in line with the pavement, the live transport waiting for its cargo. Their muzzles are chewing incessantly, their hind hoofs treading their own muck. Julian steers me away from it all.

We enter an emporium, like a deep cavern, its walls hung thickly with silky materials, eastern dresses and matching veils. There is a section with European clothes. The shopkeeper, hunched in his long grey *kaftan,* approaches us rubbing his hands. His knowing eyes appraise me and he leads us straight to the rail heavy with European women's frocks. Too many to choose from. I don't waste time. I go for a practical colour. Navy cotton with a delicate floral design in cherry red and pink.

I change behind the screen and when I reappear, Julian is pleased with my choice. The shopkeeper has lined an array of sandals on the counter. I choose navy canvas ones with high wedges. To finish the look, Julian suggests a white straw hat with an organdie navy rose. My attire completed I check myself in the full length mirror. The transformation is pleasing. I look normal again. Even a little pretty.

The shopkeeper looks at Julian and nods his approval. He then folds my Red Cross clothes and the heavy black lace-ups and the white headscarf into a brown bag and gives Julian his change.

We leave with thanks to his *Sob be kheir*! Good Day!

I cannot stop grinning when we step outside.

'I can walk proud now,' I tell Julian,' next to your smart uniform.'

He laughs. 'You worry too much about appearances!'

'Be honest,' I reply, ' wouldn't you rather strut around with a posh lady on your arm,' I give a mock curtsey, 'or slink around in the shadows with a tramp trailing behind you?'

He chuckles. 'Strutting around with a lady on your arm is not allowed here. See how all the women follow their men?'

'What are you suggesting?' I tease him.

'It's all symbolic, you know,' he explains, 'the man walking first, shielding his woman from danger.'

'Hmm, I rather like this idea, as long as I don't have to walk too far behind.'

Later, after I've rummaged through hundreds of trinkets and beads and come away with a string of white glass beads, we stop for coffee and cake. The wrought iron tables are set out on the wide pavement underneath a yellow and white striped awning. The tall palms on the green central section across the road are easy on the eyes in the white heat. The melting chocolate on my tongue, the taste of real ground coffee, give me shivers of delight.

'This is like a dream,' I tell Julian, 'I can't believe this is really happening.'

There's happiness in Julian's face.

'We've waited long enough for this day, Nastusha, haven't we?'

Later still, our lunch is a flat round bread like a thick pancake, its pocket filled with diced mutton and vegetables. We make a picnic of it on a park bench in the shade of palm trees and wash it down with vanilla flavoured soda water.

'Nothing has ever tasted as good as this in all my life,' I tell Julian. Again he laughs. With contentment. And later still, when our legs have tired of walking and we find a small ice-cream parlour, like a dark hole after the white brightness, till our eyes adjust, and we sit down and I lick the exquisite creamy vanilla and reminisce about the last time we enjoyed ice-cream at home, he munches his cone thoughtfully and says,

'You know, I've dreamed of this for such a long time...' he gives me a self conscious smile. 'I've booked a room with a Persian couple. Recommended to me. You won't believe it, but Mr. Rashid has already learnt a few words of Polish. We'll even get an evening meal there...'

I have a feeling of unreality, like being in a film.

'There's just one thing,' he adds.

'What's that?'

'I didn't have the chance to ask you before today. I've invited Roman. He's got no family to look for. Or find. Or visit. He's only got us.'

'Roman!' I feel a strong pang of yearning to see him again. Dear Roman, as dear as my brother Voytek to me.

'How is he?'

Julian thinks for a moment, his munching slowing down.

'He puts on a brave face, but he's younger than us. He still wants to finish his theological studies. He wants to be ordained. Eventually.'

'Really? After everything he's been through?'

'Especially because of that, he says. He says his faith is all the more strong now.'

I shake my head. 'You know, I'd really want to see him married to a good woman. He could do with a little support. Everyone needs a soul mate. Besides, he is too good-looking to be wasted on a celibate life!'

Julian laughs.

'Tell him that. We've tried. He is adamant about his mission in life.'

By four in the afternoon, we've had enough walking and sightseeing in the heat. Julian leads the way to Mr. Rashid's house in one of the smaller, narrower, shady streets away from the centre. The house, like all other residences, is screened from the street by a high wall. Julian pulls the bell rope at the tall sturdy ebony door and gives me a reassuring smile as we wait. Soon there are sounds of someone approaching and unlocking the door. Mr. Rashid is about forty with streaks of white in his neatly trimmed beard, his long slim body lost within the folds of his long baggy shirt. Julian shakes his bony hand and introduces me,

'*Moya zona.* My wife.'

Mr. Rashid gives a nod without looking at me, then beckons us to follow him inside the enclosed courtyard. It is shaded by a wide-crowned tree. He leads us across it to an exterior wooden staircase that takes us up to a balcony with two doors. He unlocks the first door and lets us in. The room is in darkness, shuttered against the heat and the light. He folds back one of the shutters to show us round. At a glance, there's a double bed, rugs on the tiled floor, a low table with two large cushions, a small wardrobe, and next to it a patterned curtain. He draws back the curtain to reveal a washstand with a washing bowl, a mirror above it, and two large buckets, one empty and one full of clean water.

'Toilet in the yard,' he says.

'*Mersi.* Thank you very much.' Julian looks pleased. 'Hot water ? To wash?'

Mr. Rashid nods. 'I bring now.'

'I'll come with you,' Julian offers. He drops his cork helmet and his rucksack on the table. I follow suit, and while I wait, I unpack our few provisions; two bottles of soda water, some dried figs and dates, tangerines and grapes. Mr. Rashid comes back with him, each carrying a bucket of warm water, which they place at the washstand. I long to wash all the sweat off me.

Julian stops Mr. Rashid at the door and points to his watch,

'*Hash*t. Eight o'clock. All right? My friend is coming too. *Shaam kaeye.* For a meal. Three of us, right?' He confirms his point by counting three fingers. Mr. Rashid nods solemnly, walks outside and closes the door behind him.

'Alone at last!' Julian gives a sigh of relief and we fall into each other's arms. We embrace long and hard. His whole body is alive, electrifying mine with tingling sensations and a spreading warmth from the pit of my stomach.

'I must wash first,' I tell him, when he releases me so I can catch my breath.

'It doesn't matter to me,' he chuckles, planting a kiss on my neck.

'But I must! I really must!' I insist.

He lets me go. I undress to my underwear, hang my precious new dress in the wardrobe, place my sandals neatly underneath and leave my hat safe on the shelf. Julian watches me as he reclines on the bed, but I wave him a mock goodbye when I step behind the curtain and draw it across the wash corner.

I pour the water into the bowl, mixing the hot with the cold, then I take the rest of my clothes off. I've brought with me a small saved piece of white soap (the carbolic I use for the laundry) and though very low in scent, it leaves a feel of freshness on the skin after use. I stir it around the bowl to make the water soapy, then I wash myself down with a wet piece of towelling. I use one of the provided towels to dry myself and to tie it around me above my breasts. I brush my teeth, enjoying the minty freshness in my mouth. I pour the used water into the empty bucket. I'm ready. I pull the curtain back.

Julian sits up and swings his legs off the bed. He's just wearing his underpants. His uniform is neatly folded on the low table. He is thin, but no longer skeletal looking. A layer of flesh is covering his once sharply pronounced ribcage.

While he washes behind the screen, I pull back the heavily patterned damask bed cover, fold it and place it underneath the shuttered window. I lie back on the bed and let my senses absorb everything around me: the warm semidarkness, the thin beams of light penetrating the tiny slits in the shutters, a hint of burnt sandalwood from the rooms below, the colourful designs on the rugs and the fabrics, the simple, functional furniture, the whitewashed walls and the central lamp, like metal lace hanging suspended on chains from the ceiling, it's all like a scene from a Persian fairy-tale. But what makes it all the more incredible in my mind at this moment is the fact that this has been here, timeless, untouched all the while, when the German planes bombed Poland, when we were snatched from our homes, when we froze in the gulags, when we slaved in the cotton fields, when hundreds died daily, it was here, just like this.

Julian pulls the curtain back in one sweep.

'Have you gone to sleep?' he beams. 'You're so quiet!'

In three long strides he comes over and throws himself on the bed beside me. He smells fresh, soapy and minty, a whisper of cigarette smoke in his hair.

'Julian,' I turn over towards him, 'I've just been thinking how unreal it all is. Such a short distance from Uzbekistan and it's another world!'

He raises himself on his elbow and looks down into my eyes, his own like shining black marbles in the half-light. 'My dear Nastusha, you are allowed to forget all other things just for today. This moment is real. Let's make the most of it.'

We make love. Just as we used to when we first got married, avidly, insatiably. All our desires deadened through long months by hunger, weariness and the constant crowding presence of others, resurrect themselves with a burst of unrestrained joy and pleasure. This morning, this afternoon, an hour ago, I could not have imagined such perfect attuning of our bodies, such fulfilling satiety, such blissful contentment in my soul.

When we lie limp with exhaustion in that relaxed post-coital state, Julian still holds me against him and takes me with him as he turns over on his back.

I rest on top of him, flesh against flesh, warm and sticky, and place my head in the crook of his neck. He kisses me, his arms strong around my back.

'I worried, you know,' he confesses, 'I worried that Russia had destroyed me. And then that infernal typhus... I was a total wreck... I couldn't imagine ever being able... but here we are...'

He hugs me again and I feel his vitality rippling through his muscles.

'Julian,' I tell him, 'everything will be all right again. When we return home. As long as we're together...'

'I know that now.'

He loosens his arms and I slip off his chest, our damp skin making amusing sucking noises. We lie back against the pillows with just a sheet across us. Julian lights a cigarette and the smoke forms gossamer wisps above us.

'You've missed that in Russia, haven't you?' I comment.

He shrugs. 'Smoking is very calming. It kills the tedium of our days. It enhances good moments. Like now...' he gives me a mischievous self-conscious grin.

'I wish I could stop time,' I sigh.

'So do I. But there are things that have got to be done first. It's on the cards we'll be moved around. Mosul and Kirkuk have the oil fields. The British want us in Palestine too. In reserve for Egypt. Things are hotting up there.'

'And where does that leave us? Women and children?'

He draws on his cigarette before replying, but I jump in first.

'Julian, have you any idea what's it like? Being left behind. First you, then Pavel. I've got nothing left. I thought Pavel and us...'

He kisses me on the cheek, his touch giving me a pleasant shiver.

'Nastusha, my dear, please don't be sad. Pavel's in good hands. Now is the time to think about yourself.'

'Meaning?' I look into his eyes, strangely luminous in the dusky light.

'Have you thought about joining the Women's Army. The PSKs? *Polska Służba Kobiet*?'

It is a surprise question. 'Frankly no. It never crossed my mind with having to look after two children.'

He smiles. 'Now you're free. Now's your chance. You'd be doing something for yourself, and a lot for others. What do you think?'

I don't need to think. I like the idea. Very much. Already I picture myself in a smart uniform, doing any of the jobs that I've already witnessed in action: nursing, catering, social care, addressing a variety of practical needs.

'Does it mean we'll be close to the army?'

'Part of the way. Maybe. But not at the front. Obviously.'

'They'll be needing nurses there, won't they?'

Julian looks at me as he draws on his cigarette.

'Nastusha, don't let's get carried away. Think it over before you decide. Nurse training cannot be achieved overnight. Even if they do run crash courses, it'll be hard work. Very different from nursing in peacetime. Do you understand what I'm trying to tell you? For your own good?'

I know he is trying to protect me.

'Julian, now's not the time for squeamishness. No one's asked the men if they are up to it. Are we women any worse? I'll ask about the nursing course. But equally I'll do anything else that I'm considered useful for. We'll see, Julian,' I feel a surge of excitement, 'but there's just one thing…'

'What's that?'

'How can I abandon Eva? We've been together through thick and thin.'

He sits up and places a comforting hand on my shoulder.

'Don't worry about Eva. She and Stella will be perfectly safe. There's talk of sending women and children to various places in the British colonies. Until the end of the war. Then we shall all get together again. And in the meantime you'll be doing something really worthwhile. Something patriotic for our country.' There's pride in his tone as he smiles at me.

At eight o'clock we come down the wooden stairs to a courtyard lit up with bare bulbs hung over the entrance gate and the doorway to the ground rooms. Simultaneously, there's the sound of the bell. I guess it is Roman. Mr. Rashid appears and strides hurriedly across the yard to unlock the gate. I get a rush of feeling seeing Roman after all those long months. We hug each other long and hard, then step back for a better look, his palms still on my shoulders. Mr. Rashid looks perplexed but Julian gives him a reassuring nod. Roman cries with excitement.

'Nastusha! God, it's so good to see you! You're all the family I've got!' I see admiration in his eyes and am all the more pleased with my new attire, hat included to cover my short hair. 'And,' he adds, 'for the first time I'm allowed to see how truly beautiful you are!' I know this is nothing more than Polish male charm. I laugh at his exaggeration.

'It's good, isn't it?' I reply, 'to have the taste of a normal life again. But I'm dying to know all your latest news, everything you've been doing since the last time I saw you. Everything! Promise!'

'A full confession!' he says with mock seriousness, his hand on his chest.

Like Julian, he is very thin, but the uniform gives him weight and stature. He is exceedingly handsome, with regular features, curly black hair and incongruously blue eyes. Wasted on priesthood, I decide, not for the first time. But for the moment I'm simply happy to be with him again.

We follow Mr. Rashid indoors. The whitewashed dining room has a bare tiled floor, bare walls, a metal oven in the corner with a good size range for several pots. The aroma emanating from them, sweetly pungent with herbs and spices, makes me aware of how empty my stomach feels. The worktop is a narrow high bench against the wall, and at the opposite end of the room, the long dining table can sit a dozen or so people. Above it, a filigree metal lamp hangs on decorative chains. The cooking corner is lit with oil lamps placed in niches inside the thick walls.

Mr. Rashid indicates for us to sit down. The table is covered in embroidered white cloth and set for six. I'm startled when he claps his hands. A woman in her thirties, chubby, smooth complexion, kholed eyes, enters through the curtained doorway from another room. She is followed by two girls of maybe twelve and fourteen. Their heads are covered in long scarves.

Julian and Roman stand up to attention and bow their heads in greeting, but Mr. Rashid gestures for them to sit down. In his unchangingly serious manner he mutters something which I can only guess is the introduction of his wife and daughters. They make themselves very busy and within minutes hot food is dished out into the serving bowls, and earlier prepared salads are brought from the other room. While all this activity is going on, two young men of perhaps sixteen and eighteen come through the curtained doorway and introduce themselves: Fikri and Isam. They shake hands with Julian and Roman, avoiding looking at me. Julian draws their attention to my presence, they nod and join us at the table.

The variety of food is overwhelming. 'Wonderful!' Roman exclaims, trying hard to catch Mrs. Rashid's attention, but she keeps her head bowed and like a shadow moves behind us. To my consternation, she and her daughters withdraw behind the curtain once their apparent duty is completed.

'No!'Roman protests to the head of the house, 'your wife and daughters must eat with us too! Family, yes? Family eat together!'

Mr. Rashid takes a while to understand, but seeing that none of us will touch the food, he shrugs in a great show of resignation and calls his wife and daughters. They come in timidly, their heads bowed and sit down close to their master.

The language barrier makes conversation difficult, but the three of us make it clear how much we are enjoying the food: Roman 'mmms' a lot raising his eyes heavenwards, Julian gives the thumbs up and I smile and praise with emphatic 'Excellent!' It is indeed excellent and a delicious treat after the years of starvation and I have to exert all my willpower to stop myself from gobbling too much all at once.

There are rice and lentil dishes, mutton kebabs, a mixture of finely chopped vegetables with red and green and yellow peppers, a salad with tomatoes and diced white cheese, a salad with boiled sliced eggs, not to mention the tasty flat bread. We are treated to red house wine, a little too sweet for the men, but just right for me, reminiscent of my own blackberry juice at home.

Mr. Rashid and his sons make an effort to engage in conversation with Julian and Roman. From their gestures and frequently repeated words we get the impression that they sympathise with the Poles and wish us victory and a free country to return to. I am unable to strike any kind of conversation with Mrs. Rashid and her daughters, as they eat in silence with their eyes cast down.

They come to life only after the men have finished eating, to clear the table. For dessert, they bring in pastries, fruit and seductively aromatic coffee.

I manage to catch Mrs. Rashid's hand. She looks down at me with her large dark eyes.

'*Mersi*! Big *mersi*!' I thank her and manage to elicit a shy smile.

'All food is excellent!' Julian adds and Roman kisses his fingers in a show of ecstasy. This causes the girls to giggle as they scuttle away behind the curtain. They don't come back, and Julian and Roman decide to leave it their way.

As we taste the sweetmeats, the young men and their father engage in their own animated discussion.

'I think they've given up on us,' Roman grins. 'Just as well. Now I can concentrate on serious gluttony instead of having to rack my brains on sign language.'

Our conversation turns inevitably to subjects close to our hearts: our families and our country torn by war. The last time Roman saw his older brother was when he left to fight in the September campaign.

'I live in hope,' Roman says, 'of finding him amongst us one day. I've made enquiries, but there's still thousands of them missing, when they should have been let out at the same time as us.'

'And I'm hoping all the while,' Julian says, 'that the Germans have treated my family better than the Russians have treated us. I can't imagine them being anywhere else than in our family home in Zolkiev.'

'Your brother will take care of your mother, Julian,' I comfort him, thinking of my own family and dreading the thought that they may have all been split up. Hanna's children would be eight and ten now, and Magda's twins, six. Both my brothers-in-law, army men, were lost in the turmoil of the first days of war. There was still no news of them at the time of our arrest. Every night when I close my eyes I think of them, but especially my dear Mama and Tato, whom I miss like a small child.

'I'd give anything for them all to be here with us now and enjoy this amazing feast,' my voice is heavy with emotion.

We drink our coffee in silence, sweet and silky smooth, against the unintelligible babble of the boys' talk. Julian is thoughtful, Roman has a faraway look, which he pulls back to focus on me with sudden animation.

'Nastusha,' he says, 'I've managed to persuade Julian to start writing his memoir. Dear God, we've all got a dramatic story to tell, haven't we?'

'And have you?' I ask Julian, 'Have you started recording our adventures?' I say the last word with a large doze of sarcasm.

He gives a self-deprecating smile. 'I'm no great writer, as you know. But Roman's right. If we don't write these things down, we may find it in time hard to believe that such things have really happened.'

'And I urge you to do the same,' Roman looks at me.

'Me?' I laugh, 'Roman, I can write a letter, but not a book!'

'Then write letters. As if you were writing to your sister. They'll become documents for historians of the future.' He is so earnest I have to keep a straight face.

'But when will I have the time to do it?'

'Right now,' Julian supports him, 'Nastusha, once you join the PSKs you'll have time between your duties.'

'Join the PSKs?' Roman's eyebrows shoot up. 'But that's wonderful! So patriotic! And practical!'

I'm touched by his enthusiasm.

'Now that my foster birds have flown the nest,' I can't keep out just a touch of bitterness, 'I suppose I'd better make use of myself some other way!'

The conversation turns naturally to the matters of war, with much speculation as to their next posting. Baghdad and Kirkuk and Mosul come up. The British. And the oil fields. And the German spy planes in these parts.

'I wish they'd hurry up and send us to where the real action is,' Roman sighs, 'I can only imagine what's going on in Europe.'

'So can I,' Julian says with a shudder, 'I can't wait to go and sort out the bastards!'

Later, when we bid Roman goodnight at the gate with his mates waiting in the open jeep, their drink-laced jollity all-embracing, he gives me a brotherly hug.

'Nastusha, it was good to catch up, wasn't it? Keep your promise with the writing. I'll see you at the Mass tomorrow.'

The Mass is celebrated in an open field, with just a canvas canopy over the altar, and a congregation of hundreds, military and civilians attending. The loudspeakers carry the bishop's voice clearly to the edges of the field, to the huts and tents within the camp, to the indisposed, too ill to attend, to the dissenters, too angry with God for His lack of an earlier intervention. But for the numerous faithful willingly assembled here, the bishop's words of thanks to God for the survival of the last two years, are uplifting and invigorating to the spirit for the next part of our odyssey.

It is the first Mass in two-and-a-half years. The familiarity of the ritual recaptures vividly a particle of our previous life and I experience the warmth of the promise of a great change. This feeling must be general, judging by the rapt expressions around me and the moist eyes.

Our little group, assembled before the Mass, have bagged a space close to the altar with a good view of the bishop and two assisting priests concelebrating with dignified seriousness. I follow their every move and join fervently with responses to their prayers and when it comes to 'Our Father', the air is filled with hundreds of voices, trembling with emotion.

The Communion is distributed to a few elderly people close to the altar, as the vast majority, who have endured close to death experiences, still feel unworthy of receiving the wafer without the preceding sacrament of confession.

I try to recall my sins but find them lost in a myriad of tragedies I've witnessed in the last two years. Can hell be any worse than that?

After the service people are reluctant to leave. The crowd fragments into groups who talk with animation about their vividly remembered recent past, about their families left behind or lost, about their immediate uncertain future, about later... If only there was a clairvoyant among them!

Our little group is complete again. We include Mr. Ostrovski and his little grandsons. He and Julian, Roman and Henryk appear to have an inexhaustible trove of subjects to discuss amidst much smoking and hand gesticulation, while Eva and I can't help acting like excited young girls as we recount to each other our experienced delights of the last two days. Like me, she and Stella have new clothes. The sky-blue dress offsets her eyes, startlingly clear in her thin tanned face, and fleetingly brings memories of us walking through the cornfields at home, in that other time, when we were young, unravaged by what was yet to come.

'The blue really suits you,' I tell her, wishing this pleasantly-meant preamble to lessen the blow of what I am about to say. 'Eva, there's no easy way of saying this,' her eyes widen with interest, 'Julian has suggested that I join the PSKs. With Pavel and Agata gone...' I need her so much to understand.

Her face breaks into a smile.

'Nastusha, that's wonderful! Believe me, I'd do the same. But with Stella...' she looks at her child playing happily with the little Ostrovski boys, 'Mr. Ostrovski is like a father to me. I'll stick with him. Henryk tells me that families with young children are already being sent out to safe places, until the end of the war. Who knows? It may not be so long now. And anyway, we'll be writing to each other, won't we?'

We hug spontaneously, my mind already projecting images of our reunion at home.

CHAPTER 39

It is the first half of November 1942. So much has happened since that Sunday of the First Mass in Freedom.

I've kept my promise to Roman and have started recording our journey from the very beginning, as well as keeping an up-to-date diary of events. The change in my circumstances has assisted me in this task. As well as having a job to do, I'm also provided with food, clothes and shelter, and allowed free time to myself. This normality still has the power to catch me unawares with awe, then with the never truly eliminated fear, that my present secure existence can be snatched away from me, just as my peace was destroyed two years ago.

On the Monday after the Mass, I went to the PSK Management quarters and joined. I was given a smart uniform, pale greenish-beige in colour, consisting of a brimmed hat, a field cap, a blouse and a jacket, a skirt, a belt and socks and brown lace-up shoes. I was sent for training to Camp Five, given a camp-bed in a tent for twelve women, and after an intensive fortnight of lectures, drills, a first-aid course, instructions on cleaning guns and keeping all equipment in pristine condition, night duties every third night, I was called before the regional Women's Corps Commandant, Chief Officer Novitzka.

'Private Kalinska,' her wise grey eyes looked at me straight, 'in the short time you've spent here, experiencing just a taste of what thorough military training should be, you've proved yourself ready for practical work, such that we have in mind for you. You've stated in your papers,' a pause as she glanced at the sheet in front of her, 'that your strengths are childcare, sewing and house or smallholding management. We've got just the job for you. There are schools being set up, wherever possible, wherever safe, for the thousands of our orphaned children. Tomorrow, a transport of our PSKs is leaving for Palestine. I've allocated you to a school in Bethany near Jerusalem. Young children mainly. I trust you'll do an excellent job there.'

I listen fascinated, my thoughts in a turmoil. Another long journey. Another separation from Julian. But Palestine! Jerusalem! Names from the Bible. And I'm going there! See the same sights, walk on the same soil as seen and touched by Jesus and Mary!

'Private Kalinska, you may leave.'

'Yes Ma'am. Thank you Ma'am, I'll not fail you Ma'am!'

A train journey, incredibly on a normal train with plush seats and refreshments, took a group of us PSKs to Baghdad, where after a night's rest in a comfortable tent camp, with meals and showers, we were added to a convoy of army lorries heading for Palestine. In the four-day journey, driven by expert Indian soldiers in turbans, their gentle manner charming, and overnight stops in military tent camps on the way, we crossed a yellow desert with not a tree in sight, and a black desert with strange looking scattered black stones and rocks. We experienced a *hamsin* sand storm, that blew the sand for hours into every crevice of every object inside the covered lorry. There were instances of *fata morgana*, an amazing illusion of water on the horizon together with palm trees and shady, cooling groves.

The last day of our journey, as we crossed the Transjordan, made up for all the previous discomforts; the fresh greenness of the land, the hills, the valleys with fast running streams, were like a soothing breath on our heat-tired eyes. The wild flowers shone in vivid colours, yellows, violets and reds; the orchards were like tapestries of oranges and lemons, the gleaming globes of water-melons sat in neat rows, the cornfields, the tobacco plantations, all those treasures of the land were reasons for the covering tarpaulin to be rolled back, so we could satisfy our eyes. The men in the lorry ahead of us burst into a song about the white blossom on an apple tree. In the song the man promises to kiss the girl who will help him pick the juicy red apples on the golden autumn days. The girls sang a song about the joys of diving into a cooling pool.

After crossing the border of Palestine, (a quick check by the British patrol) the lorries with the men went their separate ways to the established military bases in Gedera and Latrun and Jaffa. Our own first stop was Nazareth. I could not help marvelling at the charm of the white stone houses, the church spires, the olive groves, the tall cypresses. Our girls were dropped off at three other centres as we were driven south to Bethany, a suburb of Jerusalem.

It was evening time, with a fading light and a rising pale moon above the hillside, dotted with flat-roofed stone houses and fruit trees. There was just another girl, Yvona, and myself left, when we were dropped off outside the main entrance of a formidable three-storey building, with tall windows, all strengthened with metal bars.

I shook hands warmly with Amarjit, our excellent Indian driver and companion for the last few days and Yvona made sweet eyes at him.

'Never mind,' she sighed theatrically when he drove off, 'there will be others.'

We were met in the porch by Warrant Officer Kicinska, the head of the centre. She was a young woman of about thirty, dark hair, dark eyes, warm smile, pleasant voice, which yet immediately established respect. She led us straight down a corridor to a refectory at the back of the building, where we dropped our belongings by the door and washed our hands in the adjacent kitchen. A cook in uniform like ours, a mature motherly woman with grey hair, was busy heating our supper and made a greeting comment on the lines of 'the more the merrier'.

Officer Kicinska kept us company at the table as we were served *pierogi* with a cheese and potato filling together with a mixed vegetable salad. This was followed by tea and a home-made apple cake.

'This is delicious!' I could not help commenting. 'Just like home!'

'That is exactly what we are trying to create here,' Officer Kicinska said, clasping her hands, 'a home for our little orphans. When we first arrived here in August, most of them were ill and seriously undernourished. We hired this place to give them a convalescing holiday for a month. It was so successful we stayed. The kind Orthodox nuns have let us use their convent building until we find a bigger place. We've already got a hundred children and there are more on the way.'

'Where are they all?' Yvona asked. 'It's so still like a veritable convent here!'

Officer Kicinska laughed.

'It is a convent, after all! The little ones are all in bed, in the rooms upstairs. We've also got some annexed buildings round the courtyard at the back. Three rooms are being used as classrooms. I gather one of you is a seamstress?' she looked from Yvona to me.

I owned up and Yvona added with a cheeky grin, 'And I've been assigned to the kitchen. The best place to be!'

'The cook is very exacting,' Officer Kicinska warned good-humouredly.

'I've got high standards too!' Yvona assured her, a mischievous curl lingering on her lips.

'Good! That's settled then.' Officer Kicinska's light tone had a serious edge to it. 'I expect harmony and good relationship amongst my staff. The good of the children must always come first.' She then turned to me. 'There's an awful lot of sewing to do. Uniforms of all sizes, dresses and overalls for everyday use. Curtains, tablecloths, sheets and pillow-cases. We've been presented with bales of material. American Aid and *Polish Delegatura.*'

'Good. I'll start as early as you wish tomorrow. Normal work, at long last!' I already anticipated the feel of the new fabric, the cutting out, the pinning together, using the sewing machine again. I asked about that.

'Singer make. British,' she replied with a smile, 'but that's not all. In the evenings all the female staff are required to help with washing and putting the younger children to bed.'

'I've done worse!' Yvona exclaimed with a tone meant to be reassuring.

I laughed, then added seriously, 'I miss my two. Gone to Isfahan.' I explained about Pavel and Agata.

'Trust me,' Officer Kicinska said, 'here, you'll never be short of a shadow or two following you around. Even when you long for five minutes peace in the bathroom. There's always a little body hanging around outside. Which brings me to the question, do you prefer a cell of your own or a screened corner in a dormitory?'

'The cell, of course!' Yvona jumped in like lightning. 'God, I've had enough of crowding and being squashed and having to smell other people's farts!' Her primitive words nevertheless amused us.

'All right,' Officer Kicinska conceded, 'this leaves you Private Kalinska to share the dormitory with the little ones.'

'I'll be delighted!'

Yvona shook her head and rolled her eyes, and would never have believed that I spoke in earnest.

'And let me add,' Officer Kicinska continued, 'you'll have a comfortable bed, a locker and even a small wardrobe, all screened off in your corner. And... our little ones don't smell!'

The discomfort of sharing a dormitory with small girls, that Yvona was so afraid of, was no discomfort at all. They were always fast asleep by the time I went to bed, and still sleeping when I got up first to use the bathroom in pleasant privacy. This arrangement lasted only a month after my arrival. I'm now a contented tenant of a small, comfortable room, with a bed, a desk and a chair, a locker and a wardrobe. Four months ago I could not have imagined such bliss in my wildest dreams!

On the 10th of November, our new centre was opened in Ain-Karem, another suburb of Jerusalem, with great pomp and parade, with important dignitaries attending the ceremony, when our school was moved and renamed the Centre and School for Polish Girls.

The Polish Gazette in Jerusalem marked the event with an article praising enthusiastically the efforts of Warrant Officer Kicinska and her staff, and listing representatives from the Consulate, from the Polish *Delegatura*, from the Polish Army in Palestine, from the Ministry of Social Services, from the Red Cross, who graced the opening with their presence and were thereafter entertained warmly on the new premises.

This is a most charming place, a haven, a heaven, which of course it was before the White Fathers offered their monastery for the use of the Polish orphans for the duration of their stay.

The hilly land around us is dotted with patches of downy greens, a variety of trees, as well as fig and plum and orange trees in the orchards. It forms a natural niche for the monastery buildings, with its own church of St. John, its colonnaded courtyard and outbuildings, and gardens on the escarpment sloping gently towards the valley.

In the courtyard, the slender white stone statue of Our Lady greets the visitors amongst the fluffy acacias that throw dappled shade on the pebbly surface. The ground floor comprises a large refectory, a library that doubles up for cultural and recreational activities, Officer Kicinska's office and individual rooms of the teaching staff.

My room is upstairs close to the girls' dormitories, close to a room used as an infirmary, with a nurse at hand around the clock. All floors, waxed and polished daily, shine like mirrors.

In the basement, following on from the kitchen there is also a sizeable pantry, a storeroom and private rooms for the working staff.

'Suits me fine!' Yvona appeared pleased. 'A comfortable distance from the kids!'

The classrooms are spread out around the outbuildings, with the sewing room amongst them, but already there is talk of securing additional classrooms outside the monastery, as the number of girls arriving grows daily.

My days are filled with duties and activities. I love my job. I get myself ready to the expected military precision in my uniform for 7.30am in readiness to help the youngest girls, fives and sixes, ten in my charge, with washing and dressing. They are indeed well cared for, their small faces and limbs filling out, their hair gleaming, the white bows matching the white collars of their navy uniforms. Hugs and kisses are mandatory, this law vehemently imposed by them. I am constantly on guard to spread my attention evenly, as they clamour for a kiss, a hug, a stroke on the cheek, a blow on a poorly finger, a tug on my skirt.

The youngest ones are adjusting well to this new life, kindness and warmth and creature comforts replacing their deprivation and the loss of their parents. But the older girls' memories cannot be erased with this change. There's eight-year-old Hanka, who screams in her sleep every night. Nine-year-old Alina smuggles bread and cakes in her pockets and hides them under her pillow, only to find a mess of crumbs in the morning. This does not deter her and neither do we, if she can derive comfort and security from this compulsive behaviour. Another nine-year-old, Sabinka, does not speak at all. She has been rescued from some mortuary in Guzar, where she had been abandoned and left for dead between the bodies of her parents. Dr. Lisovska is reluctant to refer her for psychiatric treatment, when the child is only just beginning to settle here. Marcela and Zosia, two ten-year-olds, are known for their short tempers and constant fighting over the smallest things such as pencils, hairgrips, handkerchiefs and shoelaces. We have to be on constant alert to distract them.

'No one promised it was going to be easy,' Officer Kicinska reminds her staff at our nightly get-togethers in the library, 'but they are our treasures, the future pillars of our society, the future architects of our country after the war. Every good seed we plant in them will bear fruit many times over.' She is earnest, genuine, wanting for these children what she would wish for her own small child left behind in Poland with relatives, when she was arrested by the NKVD and sent to a Siberian gulag.

After breakfast, the girls are taken in groups by their teachers and the care staff get on with their appointed tasks. The sewing room is in one of the smaller outhouses. I'm the youngest among the four seamstresses, who have offered their services to various orphanages formed in Uzbekistan and were evacuated with them to Persia. Mrs. Paszkievicz, the most senior one, about fifty, is a widow with two sons in the army. She used to run sewing classes in her little town in Poland, and has plans to expand our sewing workshop to include older girls, as they mature towards the finishing Matura Class, before being transferred to the Liceum Higher Education in Nazareth. She is pleased with my work. So am I. Apart from the continuous navy of the uniforms, my eyes can feast on the colourful, patterned cottons intended for the girls' casual dresses. My shoulders and my neck ache daily from the monotonous sitting position at the sewing machine, but a brisk walk up and down the escarpment, usually in the company of one or two of my co-workers, relaxes me enough to forget this discomfort before the needy demands of my little charges.

This life, after all the traumas of the last three years, is an oasis of soothing peace. It would be perfect shared with Julian and Eva.

Since our time in Teheran two months ago, Julian has been sent to Kirkuk; more training and minding the oil fields.

'Dearest Nastusha,' he wrote, 'life is monotonous here, sometimes enlivened by monstrous *hamsins*, that leave you coughing, spluttering, with a runny nose and grit in your eyes. For a change we get flooding rainfalls. It's great fun! We dig lorries out of the mud, sleep in damp clothes on wet mattresses.

But life is not all light entertainment. We sometimes get down to the serious business of beating the Arab team in a game of football. Now and again the theatrically minded put on a show for us in the NAAFI Club. It's toe-curling bearable and no threat to the cinema, when you can get a pass. I've been to see 'Blood in the Sand' with a friend. It's great to lose yourself completely for an hour or two.

Our little group has all been dispersed. Henryk is in Mosul, Roman in Khanaquin, and the other two have been sent down to Aden. I live in hope of being gathered together again to be sent to Europe.

The other night, miracle of miracles! I came across an old teacher of mine from Rava Ruska school. He hasn't changed at all! It was like finding a good old uncle. I'm certain he had no idea who I was, but he still gave me a bear hug and I could swear his eyes went all misty!

Dearest Nastusha, please keep writing. It cheers me no end to hear all your good news.'

I received a letter from Eva too, courtesy of the good old Red Cross post. She was envious of my good fortune, but at the same time excited at the prospect of being transferred to Valivade in India.

'Don't worry about me,' she wrote, 'spending time with Henryk was the best thing ever! I'm well, in good spirits, filling out nicely on regular food. Mr. Ostrovski and I stick together like family and our children could be siblings. I'll write as soon as we are settled in our new place. I miss you Nastusha and pray for the day when we are together again.'

CHAPTER 40

It is Monday, the first week of April 1943. The last seven months have passed in a fast moving chain of days and weeks, replicating themselves in my appointed work and tasks. The school time-table has been enhanced with visits to Jerusalem, Nazareth, the Dead Sea for the older girls, and for the little ones, special shows have been put on at Christmas and special play days arranged with a variety of activities.

I've not taken any time off, saving my pass days for Julian's visit. He has been moved around to a number of places before being posted to the military base in Gedera, Palestine. It feels as if he's on the doorstep, after his long absence from my life.

Today I'm off duty, and wearing my navy floral frock, my navy high-wedged canvass sandals, and my white straw hat. My hair has grown. I have curled it round my face.

'You look good!' Yvona comments with some surprise in her voice, as she passes me in the entrance hall, where I'm waiting for Julian to arrive. Butterflies of anticipation tickle my stomach and my feet cannot stand still.

And then I see him. Tall and slim, his long strides traversing the forecourt in seconds, dappled light falling across his face and the rucksack on his shoulders. I run down the stone steps, he stops, drops his bag and I fall into his arms. So much time apart, yet it takes only a moment to fuse us together. I am breathless within his strong embrace, his hot face against mine.

'Julian, Julian!' is all I can say.

Reluctantly, we let go of each other and go inside the building. Officer Kicinska must have seen us from her office window, for she's already waiting in the entrance hall, her face beaming.

'Welcome Corporal Kalinski,' she offers her hand for a handshake, 'it is always a great pleasure to host Anders' people.'

Julian kisses her hand and I notice her appraising look. 'An army in waiting,' he remarks, 'I'd much rather be where the real action is!'

'It'll come. Soon enough,' she replies. 'I thank God every day for this breathing space. After Russia...' she says with feeling.

'Fair enough,' he concedes smiling, then he looks at me. 'It's reassuring to know that the families are out of danger. And thriving. Last summer my wife resembled a twig. Now she looks like the girl I married.'

I feel pleased and self-conscious at the same time, but Officer Kicinska gives me an approving look.

'We all scrub up well, don't we? Given the chance. Before you race off, refreshments first. I promise you, Corporal, you won't be able to resist our cook's delicious cakes!'

'I wouldn't even try!' Julian laughs.

She leads us to the refectory, now empty in mid-morning. The tables are gleaming like still water, the floor shines back with the squares of sunlight falling through the windows. Officer Kicinska sits down with us at the first table and soon the sound of crockery on a tray can be heard as it is carried in by Yvona. I introduce her to Julian. When she puts down the tray and he stands up to shake and kiss her hand, her eyes rove all over him with unhidden interest. Then, when she is ready to pour tea, standing behind him and Officer Kicinska, she gives me a nod and 'wow!' expression. I cannot help smiling. He sends me a questioning look.

'I'm just very happy,' I tell him and Officer Kicinska smiles too.

Yvona rushes off with a wink at me and we get down to tasting the plum and apple cakes cut into little squares. They are delicious. The conversation turns invariably to the subjects closest to our hearts: our families and the war. Fresh in our minds is the horror of the discovery of the Nazi death camps in Poland.

'And still they push on victorious,' I comment with disgust. 'It's as if they've made a pact with the devil himself.'

'No Nastusha,' Julian is vehement, 'no, the tide is definitely turning back. Look at Stalingrad. Devastated but reclaimed. And now Leningrad is making a real effort to fight back after all that time! I'm almost tempted to cheer them on. If only they weren't Russians!'

'But their people suffer as much as we did,' Officer Kicinska states wistfully.

'God, it's all so complicated,' I sigh, 'if the British and the Americans don't hurry up in Tunisia, Rommel will be knocking on our door next!'

'God forbid!' Officer Kicinska speaks in an awed stage whisper.

'That's exactly where we would willingly step in!' Julian speaks with impatience.

'Please, let's change the subject,' Officer Kicinska manages a smile. 'Please tell me of your life in Poland before the war.'

Our talk becomes light-hearted when Julian recounts some of his unplanned adventures with the bears and the boars and the wolves in his beloved forest at home. We finish our tea and cake and it is time to go.

Outside, I breathe in the warm air, fragrant with acacias and almond blossom as we walk down to the bus stop on the main road. Today I want to forget all the sad things. Today I want to be happy. I catch Julian glancing at me frequently, the back of his hand brushing my cheek or my arm, the creases round his eyes permanent with smiling.

'At home,' he says, 'our apple and cherry trees will be in full bloom, like these fig and plum trees here. And soon the linden trees will be covered in white and chestnut trees will become like enormous pink umbrellas.' I dream with him for a moment until we enter a built-up section of the street, with raised pavements and deep gutters and whiffs of urine and donkey droppings polluting the air. We walk close to the walls along the narrow strip of shade, for the sun is already high and hot.

Arab women, their faces sunburnt and lined, and with bulky baskets resting on their hips, sway and talk in high-pitched tones, as their children push noisily around them. A European dressed couple, possibly British or Jewish, stand silently on the side. We join them and the children stare at us unabashed and I expect them to beg *bakshish*. We are spared, for as the bus comes into view they begin to fight to be the first to get on. The bus arrives already crowded and there is a moment when I doubt there will be enough room for us. But the laconic driver waits and smokes and waits till everyone somehow squeezes inside.

The last ones to get on, we are closest to the door, a dubious blessing if there are more stops on the way. Julian looks amused, nevertheless, his face centimetres from mine, our bodies pressed together. When the bus moves on I lift my face to the draught from the open windows in this cauldron of heat and rowdy babble.

Twenty minutes later we arrive at the bus terminus in the vast square outside the Jaffa Gate. I step off the bus with buoyant anticipation. Julian throws his rucksack over his shoulder and picks up my overnight bag, but I stop him.

'Let me just take it all in!' I've been before on errands with Officer Kicinska, but every time I come the excitement for me is never diminished, it's like seeing this city for the first time. 'It's Jerusalem! The city of our bible stories. Can you believe it Julian?' He laughs.

I am overawed by the sense of occasion. Jesus was here. And before him David. Three thousand years ago! These walls have withstood centuries of invasions; the Romans, the Arabs, the Crusaders, the Egyptians, the Turks. And now, these very same walls are looking down at me, a mere speck in all of humanity.

The crowd milling about us consists of all nationalities. There is something incongruously modern about the sight of buses and taxis parked along the lines of waiting camels and donkeys. I smile at Julian. I cannot hide my wonder.

'Who would have thought it! When we were children. Reading about those faraway places at school!'

Inside the Gate, we find ourselves facing a maze of crowded narrow streets. Julian heads for the Polish Centre in Mushara Street and I follow close behind him, shielded from the oncoming throng. The air is pungent with sweet smells and odours, the stench of garbage , bursts of sandalwood and rose fragrance, cooking and tobacco smoke, rotting fruit, percolating coffee. Hundreds of open stalls display a variety of goods, and some energetic stall holders give a performance of mime dancing as they coerce you to buy their ready-cooked meats. The strange shrivelled appearance of the sizzling bits make me think of snails or chopped-up intestines.

It is a relief when we finally reach the wider, more spacious Mushara Street cast in the most welcome shade of adjoining buildings and ancient trees. The Polish Centre is a typically Eastern house, solid, square, with tall, barred windows, and a surrounding wall. We are met by an attractive PSK, in the reception hall.

'Just for your information,' she says, as she writes down our particulars in her register, 'if ever we are short of space there is a Polish YMCA not far from here. We provide breakfast, of course, and an evening meal if you order in advance.'

'Thank you,' Julian says. 'That will be most welcome after a day's sightseeing.'

Our room is reached from across the courtyard up the stone stairs and along an outside passage.

'We are very civilised here,' the PSK says with a touch of amusement, as she unlocks the door for us. 'No more holes in the floor, but actually real toilets! Inside your room, there is of course a bowl and a jug of water for your ablutions, but we've got proper bathrooms if you fancy a soak.'

We thank her and enter inside. The shuttered room is in semi-darkness, cool and surprisingly spacious. Two iron beds are made up with pristine white sheets and pillows, and a folded army blanket at the foot. A locker between the beds and a tall narrow wardrobe complete the furniture set. In the corner there is a wooden stand with the bowl and a large enamel jug filled with water.

We drop our bags on the floor and throw our arms around each other. No words are necessary. We feel each other's needs. We separate only to undress, we lie down on one of the beds and we make love. Afterwards, propped up against the pillows and squashed against each other under a sheet, we talk, Julian between puffs of smoke.

'All this is like a mirage, Nastusha. A *fata morgana*. An oasis of happiness in a desert of boredom, in this present existence of ours. You waiting here, me waiting in the army, being sent all over the place. What I crave is for us to be sent to Europe to finish off that son of a bitch once and for all. So we can all go back home.' He lifts himself up on his elbow, stubs out the cigarette and looks down at me. 'Nastusha, I think about you every night. God, how I long to have my old life back!'

My mind makes a leap backwards: our cosy little house, the surrounding woodland, the garden, the vegetable plot. Korek, our dear guardian. Gone. Dorotka. Her memory is a stab of pain. Every time. Hundreds of times.

'Can our life be the same? So much has happened. So much has changed...'
He looks thoughtful.

'I know you're thinking about Dorotka. I think about her too. Sometimes I have to stop myself or I'd go mad!' His eyes shine. He sits up, lights another cigarette and draws on it deeply. 'Nastusha, we can't forget the past, but we must not dwell on it. We can't change what's already happened, but we can make a new life for ourselves.' He glances at me and his mood lightens. 'In my dreams, Nastusha, I see us with a little boy…'

'And a little girl,' I add swiftly. 'Every woman deserves a daughter!'

He chuckles. 'When we have a boy,' he continues dreaming, 'we shall call him Vladislav. After Anders and Sikorski. It's like a good omen that they both have the same Christian names. What do you think?'

'I expect we'll have a generation of boys called Vladislav, but I don't mind.' I smile. 'Our little Vladislav will be our own little hero. But when we have a daughter, I shall call her Julia. After you.'

'I like that,' his face is relaxed with contentment, 'Julia. That's a lovely feminine name. I never thought of my own name as being anything special.'

'It's always special to me.'

He kisses me, then with mock seriousness admonishes,

'Now that we've done with sinning, perhaps we ought to visit all the holy places to sanctify ourselves.'

I laugh. 'Julian, this is the best place on earth for sinning. You can find immediate absolution virtually on your doorstep.'

'Just imagine,' he adds, 'if on your death bed it wasn't the sinning you were sorry for but for all your missed chances!' We both laugh.

Our pilgrimage around Jerusalem begins a street away from our lodgings; every part of the city bears a historical or a biblical footprint. Here a relief plaque on the wall depicts Veronica's meeting with the cross-bearing Christ, further a similar plaque is of Simon of Cyrenea relieving Christ of the cross. The trail of the twelve stations of the cross leads us to Golgotha, incorporated now into a basilica, resplendent with gilded mosaics, gilded statues and a golden star marking the entrance to the opening of the rock, the original place of Christ's tomb.

Out in the open again, we climb the wide stone steps to the viewing point above the Golden Gate, through which Christ rode triumphant on a donkey on the first Palm Sunday. The square below is symmetrically set out with green islands of spiry cypress trees around the mosque of Mohammed Omar. Beyond that, a fragment of the continuing city wall is named the Wailing Wall, where the Orthodox Jews, dressed in black, stand in a line to pray.

'A day in Jerusalem is just a lick.' Julian remarks. 'We need at least a month here. It would be great, wouldn't it?'

'If I could stand the heat,' I complain, feeling a burning on my neck between the rim of my hat and the neckline of my frock. Julian is wearing his cork helmet with a wide brim.

'Let's escape inside the churches,' he suggests.

We dash between churches and basilicas and mosques, grateful for their dark and cool interiors and ponder on the religions, the Jewish, the Muslim, the Catholic and the Orthodox, all claiming Jerusalem to be the true seat of their faith.

'Strange, isn't it?' Julian whispers when we sit in a niche at the back of The Holy Mother Church. 'In the end, we all pray to the same God, don't we?'

'We do. All these silly squabbles!' I shake my head. 'It makes us no better than kids squabbling in the playground. Who's going to please best their teacher! But look over there. Look how beautiful she is...' I point to the reclining sculpture of the Mother of God, her ivory face and hands finely chiselled and smoothed, her dress all painted in gold.

In the late afternoon, thirsty, our hot feet throbbing, we seek a more airy and leafy part of the town. We find a coffee place called *Imperial*, where we replenish our energy with coffee and cakes.

Afterwards, when I've cooled off and feel less sticky, to my surprise, Julian leads me to a jeweller's, by the name of Mundo Peysner, who turns out to be a Polish Jew, escaped from our country just after the German attack. He is pleased to speak with us in Polish and pleased to display an array of gold rings and chains.

'This is all my husband's idea,' I tell him in mock seriousness, 'I've never expected this, as I've already got a replacement for my wedding ring. My original one is lining the pocket of a certain Comrade Borodin.' I tell him briefly of our time in Russia. He tells us of his family's escape from Lvov, only days before the Germans reached the city and the Russians invaded from the East.

'Lvov! That's our city too!' I enthuse. 'There can't be another city as beautiful as Lvov!'

'I second that!' he says emphatically, his face creased with joy.

I make a show of studying the tray with the jewellery, for his and for Julian's sake, but twinges of insecurity hold me back.

'Julian, is this wise?'

'Let's not argue,' he says, 'not in front of this gentleman.'

Mr. Peysner's silent glance is encouraging.

I choose the least expensive ring, with a coral bead and tiny earrings to match.

'A good choice,' Mr. Peysner approves.

'Just like rowan berries at home,' Julian smiles, pleased.

In the evening we dine at the Polish Centre with some visiting soldiers, who are going back to Tel-Aviv the next day. We get up early for a lift with them on an army lorry and we take a room in a small hotel overlooking the sea.

Tel-Aviv is a modern and elegant city with a leafy wide promenade, open-canopied restaurants and a sandy beach. We take off our shoes and walk barefoot, the lapping water frothing at our feet, the breeze cooling our faces. It is bliss. I think of the Aralsk Sea, enticing but distant viewed from the cattle train, and later, I think with revulsion of the black oily water in Krasnovodsk Port.

'I have to pinch myself every day,' I tell Julian. 'It's hard to believe all this is true.'

'And I often wonder,' he replies, 'how is it, that some survive the most awful things, like the cat with nine lives, and some are cut down, just like that, as if they were just insects, as if their lives meant nothing.'

'It makes you fearful, doesn't it? Not knowing what's lying in wait for you.'

Julian places his arm on my shoulder and draws me close to him.

'Don't be fearful Nastusha. If we've been given days like today by Providence, they are meant to be enjoyed.'

In the evening Julian takes me dancing at the *Jargon* Hotel. 'For us plebs,' he jokes. 'The officers have their own dens.' Who cares? I love it here! It feels as if I'm in a scene in a romantic film: white covered tables, dimmed lights, drinks, laughter. Tangos and waltzes and some American boogie-woogies. It's intoxicating. Two of Julian's chums join us with their girls, but talk is superficial and bitsy, as everyone is eager to dance. I want him all to myself, my head on his chest, and his warm breath in my hair.

On the last day of our time together, we catch a morning bus back to Jerusalem, and after walking around the Christian Quarter and visiting the Church of the Holy Sepulchre and the Church of the Redeemer, we lunch in a nearby restaurant. It is run by another Polish Jew and provides a menu familiar to our palate. We order *pierogi* filled with savoury cheese and an array of salads: grated carrot, grated cabbage, diced beetroot and chopped vegetables in mayonnaise.

'It's like at home,' I comment.

When we enjoy the juicy cooling after-lunch drink, Julian tells me, 'In a few days, they are sending us to Aden. I'll be gone for at least two months.'

My heart drops, though I know this is his job at the moment.

'It sounds like the other side of the world!'

'I'll come and visit you as soon as we're back.'

'Why Aden?'

'The same old story. It's British. It needs protecting. Besides,' he smiles and covers my hand with his on the table, 'the British believe the change is as good as a rest. The two months will pass in a flash! I promise!'

Later he escorts me to the bus terminus and offers to go with me to Ain-Karem.

'Julian, there's really no need. I've done this hundreds of times. Whereas you have to get back to your base on time!'

'Unfortunately so!' he makes a face, and draws me close to him.

Buses arrive and leave in the square, vendors sell from their carts and vans, pressed orange juice, cooked corn on the cob, kebabs, toasted *nan* bread. Donkeys stand at the kerb, their heads stoically bowed in the heat, their ears twitching against the flies.

'I hate good-byes,' I tell Julian.

'It's not a good-bye. I'll be seeing you soon.'

When the bus arrives and the crowd pushes ahead of me, miraculously I manage to squeeze into a seat by the window. With a heavy heart I wave and maintain a smile, watching him to the last, a slim tall figure in his tropical uniform, etched dark against the brightness of the dusty ground around him.

A week later, when our attention and expectations are focused on the approaching Easter celebrations, our community in Ain-Karem is shaken to the core by the shocking news of the discovery of a mass grave containing bodies of Polish Officers in Katyn forest near Smolensk. The devout Russian peasant who came by chance across this grisly find was reported to say: 'The Poles are looking for their officers in Siberia, but they lie here in this forest.'

The occupying Germans have dug up over four thousand bodies, still in their uniforms, their identity papers on them, their hands tied behind their backs. All shot through the head. Other victims found nearby are Soviet civilians, killed in Stalin's purges, yet Stalin denies all knowledge of these crimes. He maintains this is deliberate German propaganda, when in fact the Germans themselves are responsible for this massacre.

In London, the Polish Government in exile, with General Sikorski at the helm, is demanding an investigation by the International Red Cross. This is to Stalin like a red rag to a bull.

Talk is of nothing else in the days that follow, in our sewing room and at the dining table. It is a relief to escape upstairs to the dormitories to my tasks with the little ones, who inundate me with questions about painting Easter eggs and doing colourful paper cut-outs. The aroma of advance baking permeates all levels of our building, reawakening comforting memories of Easters in Poland, yet I cannot eradicate from my mind the nightmarish image of bodies heaped in a trench, bodies of fathers, husbands and brothers. I cannot stop thinking about my sisters' husbands, about Florian and Dominik's father, and pray hard that they have escaped this horrific fate. How much longer is it going to be like this? I ask God every night. *You give us peace only to destroy it with yet another blow.*

CHAPTER 41

Julian keeps his promise. I receive fortnightly notes from him, post permitting. They bear exotic names: El Cantara, Suez, the Tropic of Cancer, Aden, Hisva. The boat is British. The daily relentless drills and mock alarms are lightened up with games of billiards, cards and chess in the evenings, as well as their own band, over a drink. Their days are unbearably hot, the nights cooler with painterly sunsets designed for artists. Dolphins are frequently seen somersaulting over the sapphire waters. The desert around Aden is an especially hostile place when you get a burst tyre or when you're caught up in a sandstorm.

He describes a sad story of a colleague, less enduring psychologically than most. 'Poor Joe, all his grief has caught up with him. The heat does not help the brain in this climate. One day he stood up against the raging *hamsin,* and started shouting that he was Jesus in the desert. He was commanding the devil to stop. He almost choked to death. Had to be restrained and kept in a safe place till the *hamsin* blew over. He is now in Aden, in a British hospital, poor soul!'

His other letters describe lighter moments: a dip in the sea, the finds on the sea-shore of pearly shells and red coral, the football matches with the British soldiers, the visits to various bars, the films he's seen, *Casablanca* and *Gone with the Wind*, and some with Garbo. For the presentation to the Sultan El Kerim they were all ordered to buy a new tropical uniform. 'What an extravagance! Still, a man can't be shown up by a sultan, can he?' His amusing tone keeps me comforted and reassured of his well-being.

In July I receive an unusual letter from Eva. Her letters travel a long time from India. So far, I have received only two since her arrival in the Valivade Camp near Kolhapur. It appears that she and Mr. Ostrovski have settled happily with thousands of other families in the little town of wooden houses.

'My dear Nastusha,' she wrote before, 'we still have to rough it a bit with the communal showers and latrines, but each family has its own furnished room. We can cook our own meals, we have food shops in the camp and a regular market outside. We have our own hospital and pharmacy, an organized school, a community hall for meetings, shows and of course our own church. It's like a microcosm of Poland. For the first time since leaving Russia, it feels as if I've recaptured some of my former life.'

Her next letter continued in much the same vein: she was happy for Stella to experience stability and routine at long last. Stella was growing well and filling out nicely on regular meals, on papayas and bananas. 'She is unafraid of being left in the playschool, and I have made friends with other mothers. But there's no one quite like you, Nastusha. I want to tell you things that I cannot put down on paper.'

This has left me intrigued and wishing she would not hold back things from me. I wrote to her and told her I would destroy her letter, if that was her wish. And now, I've just opened her third letter. I've read it several times, and though I'm astonished by the news, I'm still baffled why it was necessary to keep it from me.

'My dear Nastusha, I wanted this to be a surprise, but things don't always work out the way you plan. On the 4th of April I gave birth to a premature, still-born baby, a girl.' Her words are like physical blows. 'As you can imagine, I felt utterly devastated. On the same day, a young, unmarried girl died of complications giving birth to her little girl. The nurse, who brought this baby to me did not even ask about my feelings. She said, they were desperate to save the child, and would I consider feeding her. You don't refuse to feed a dog. How could I refuse to feed a helpless baby? A tiny innocent little crumb?

I love her, Nastusha. She is officially mine now. Her mother, a fifteen year old child had no family. Stella adores her. Henryk's been amazingly supportive and has signed, by post haste, the necessary papers for this process to be completed.

I've called her *Nadzieja*. Hope. Our little Nadia.'

I keep re-reading her letter with a sense of growing unreality. It sounds so simple on the surface of it, but my sixth sense picks up on things she is not telling me. Why hasn't she told me of her pregnancy before?

My first reaction is to pay her back with my own reticence, but that would be a childish tit for tat. So when I write to her and express joy and excitement at her good news, I also add mine. 'I'm pregnant too,' I tell her,' our baby is due at the beginning of January. I can hardly think that far ahead! 1944! Dearest Eva, perhaps in six months time we can celebrate my baby's christening in Poland!'

A few days later, our small community is stunned by the news of General Sikorski's tragic death. Our great leader in exile, our guardian of Anders' Army, and of civilians alike, our unbending buffer against Stalin's perfidious machinations, our beloved hero is dead.

A plane crash in Gibraltar. Just after the take-off. Just after his visit to the Polish troops in Egypt. No one has survived, except the pilot. He's been spirited away to a safe place, out of bounds to journalists. The British are discouraging suspicions of sabotage, but we Poles know better. The British have not experienced the Soviet Paradise. The questions over Katyn remain unsolved, even though the International Medical Team investigating the mass grave have come up with mounting evidence of Stalin's involvement. He still denies all knowledge of the crime and plays the role of an offended diva, perversely accusing the Polish government in exile of supporting a Hitlerite provocation. To the consternation of the British, he's severed diplomatic relations with the exiled Poles.

I cannot imagine the depth of her grief. The general's wife has lost her husband and their only daughter, her father's supportive companion, in one cruel stroke of fate. Julian constantly tells me in his letters to have faith and not to be afraid, but when such terrible things happen to generals, what chance have we got, lowly wives of lowly corporals?

Talk of war is the inevitable subject when Julian visits me in August and later in October between his training postings in Iraq and Lebanon.

'If Stalin does not retreat from Poland at the end of the war, there will have to be a third war. Surely, it's obvious to anyone observing him that he's just another Hitler!'

'It's obvious to us Poles, Julian. But who'd want to start yet another war?' It's not my intention to rail him, but I'm tired of this subject. I hate the waiting, I hate his constant absences, I hate living so far away from home, with our baby on the way. 'Julian, when this war is over, the whole world will want to get back to normal living. Who's going to fight your war with Stalin? Churchill? His people won't let him. The Americans? What importance is Poland to them? They've got enough on their plate with the Japanese, haven't they?'

We are sitting on a bench in the shaded courtyard of the school. With the girls in classes, there is a monastic hush around us, and the buzzing of insects in the hanging branches of acacia trees only adds to the somnolent air of the afternoon, heavy with heat.

Julian shades his eyes with his hand.

'No Nastusha, you're wrong. They are our allies. They won't let us down. And any way, haven't the Poles already proved themselves? In Tobruk? And what about the Polish pilots? Daredevils! Unstoppable. Showed the Germans a thing or two!' he chuckles. 'And what about us? We are raring to go. They only have to send word, and we'll be over like lightning!' He chuckles. His optimism is necessary, I know, but all I imagine are bloody battles and death.

'You'll need a host of guardian angels to shield you,' I remark tersely.

He takes my hand in his, smiles into my eyes and speaks softly,

'All I need to carry with me is an image of you. Like a photograph. Come on. Indulge me. A big happy smile. That's better. Now shall we go in search of an ice-cream parlour? Somewhere cool!'

The very thought of ice-cream or the taste of hot milk or the smell of cooking cabbage made me heave with revulsion in the first three months of my pregnancy, but now my appetite has returned, my flat shape is filling out,

I've got back my breasts and my hips again. My stomach has rounded but is not sticking out yet. I feel feminine, attractive.

'Yes, let's go Julian and let's do some nice, normal things. Let's not think about the war for a few minutes!'

CHAPTER 42

At the end of November, after brief formalities of standing down from my PSK post, I have to leave my beloved oasis of serenity at Ain-Karem School and move to Ramallah, to the Polish Home for Mothers and Children. My bulk has become cumbersome, slowing me down, making my legs ache, making me tired before I've tucked up in bed the ten little girls in my charge every night. My young assistant, a lively PSK is going to replace me, and I watch with mixed feelings my little charges' growing attachment to her. I've got to let go.

Officer Kicinska bids me farewell with a warm embrace and sincere words.

'We need babies. Lots of them. They are our future.'

My sewing companions have made me gifts of baby clothes and covers. Even Yvona came to my room after work one evening.

'I've made something for you,' she said, 'your baby will get enough things.' She crocheted a silky white shawl for me with a long delicate fringe all round. I was astonished. 'You need to look glamorous for your husband. Mind if I smoke?'

I did not object, as the window was wide open inside the bars. She sat on the chair facing me sitting on the bed and lit a cigarette. 'Anastazia, always remember this,' she blew the smoke, throwing back her head, letting her hair fall on her shoulders, 'men are weak creatures. Never allow their attention to wander elsewhere.'

'That's a bit difficult at present,' I remarked laughing, certain of Julian's love for me.

She gave me a long look. 'This is no good, to anyone,' she said, 'this constant separation. I've no idea where my husband is, or with whom. The last time I saw him was at our *kolhoz* in Siberia. He was taken away to build roads somewhere. A long way away. I've been looking for him ever since. Asking about him. To no avail. The Polish Soldier's Centre in Jerusalem is a mine of information. But still nothing...' she smiled wryly. 'What's a girl to do? No harm in a little recreation. The dances there are good, and the shows. Have you ever been?'

I know of the place, but I've not been tempted. Not on my own.

'Too late now,' she said nodding at my bump and tapping the cigarette ash against the windowsill. As if I cared. I joked,

'Perhaps you'll baby sit for us when Julian comes on leave?'

She threw her hands up in horror.

'Heaven forbid! I'd rather dance with your husband any time!' She paused, then added quickly, 'Don't get me wrong. I love our little rascals here. No nappies, no bibs to wash. They eat everything you put in front of them. And that's how I like it. My efforts appreciated.'

'I shall miss your cakes,' I humoured her.

The Home for Polish Mothers and Children is a three storey building of substantial size, with thick walls, four large rooms on each floor, each room housing four mothers and their children. Each corner is furnished with a bed, a cot and a locker. There is a bathroom and two toilets on each floor, and on the ground floor, an extension for the kitchen and the dining area. Laundry is done in the basement. The tree-shaded courtyard is a safe play area for toddlers, surrounded by a protective high wall. A shelter in the far corner forms ample cover for the prams and the pushchairs donated by the American Red Cross.

A PSK officer, Sergeant Turovicz is in charge. She is a mature, motherly figure with the patience of Job and the wisdom of Solomon, when petty squabbles erupt between the young mothers, tired and irritated by grizzly babies and sleepless nights. I miss the peaceful serenity of Ain-Karem, but here, for the mothers and their babies a feeling of security has been created, comforting after two years of wanderings to uncertain destinations. When babies have colic or teething problems, when mothers need advice on breastfeeding or prolonged post-natal bleeding, Nurse Volska is at hand with her round the clock dispensary, and Sergeant Turovicz with her common sense.

I'm given a corner in one of the rooms overlooking the road at the front of our home. My immediate neighbour is Marcella, about my age, late twenties, with a three-month-old boy. Her manner is calm and sensible, obviously beneficial to her good-natured baby. He feeds well, looks contented and only cries for a nappy change.

The two young girls in the other two corners of the room are awaiting their confinement, like me. Yolanta, a delicate blonde, cries a lot. The man she was expecting to marry stopped seeing her as soon as her pregnancy was confirmed. It turned out he was married already.

Sometimes I manage to persuade her to go with me to the nearby park. I suspect she may be glad to get away from Lisa, the fourth girl, who appears to consider herself an expert on every subject under discussion.

'I'd give him a good kick up his pants,' she advises Yolanta. 'Then chase him for child maintenance, give him such hell so that his wife would get fed up too and throw him out! Now that would teach him, wouldn't it?'

But that is not what Yolanta wants. She had dreams of a happy married life.

'You'll still have that,' my words of comfort sound inadequate, as we sit in the park away from wailing babies, away from Lisa's endless overbearing monologues.

'Who'll have me now?' Yolanta raises her tearful eyes. 'My father would kill me, if he knew. Just as well he is so far away in the army.' She has lost her mother in Siberia, two siblings in Uzbekistan. Her only remaining brother is with the Polish Cadets Corps north of Nazareth. 'He knows. But he won't snitch on me.'

'Then he'll be your support. You are not alone. Believe me Yolanta,' I wish I had a magic wand. 'Every situation can be resolved. Eventually. You're still very young. You've got your whole life ahead of you. You'll meet hundreds of people yet. Someone among those people will be the right person for you.'

'But what about my child?'

'If that person truly loves you, he'll also love your child. For all you know, your father may be delighted to have a grandchild. So many people died in the last three years. Every new life is precious. Try not to think the worst.'

She is thoughtful, then a pale smile crosses her face.

'You make it sound so simple.'

'You have to be brave and stand up for yourself. It is not a crime to have loved a man.'

Sometimes, the three of us, Marcella with her little Lucas in the pram, Yolanta and I go to the park together. Lisa is bored with our company; she needs a fresh audience every day. Unfortunately for her most of the inhabitants of our home have had a taste of her tireless monologues and suddenly remember some urgent matters that need attention immediately. Nevertheless, in the daytime we manage to get respite from her, but at night time, when the lights are out, and I toss in my bed in search of a comfortable repose for my big belly, Lisa's voice still drones on from her corner. Then suddenly it cuts out. The silence and the warm darkness are bliss.

Those of us still awaiting our babies, help Sergeant Turovicz make our Christmas special with colourful paper chains and tree decorations; crepe paper wrapped sweets and walnuts and shiny mandarins hung on twisted threads. Lisa knows the best methods of tackling any of our pleasant tasks and teaching us the obvious. I burst out laughing in the end, to her consternation.

'What?' She looks at me puzzled. Sergeant Turovicz steps in. She is diplomatic.

'Lisa, we have a sea of expertise here, from all over our country. Everyone's been making these things for years. Their own way. We can all learn from each other. In the end, it's the result that matters, doesn't it?'

Lisa is quiet for a minute or two then she turns to the girl sitting next to her and teaches her the quickest method ever of making *pierogi*. Our caretaker Aarif, a local man, installs in the corner of our dining room a potted conifer about a metre high. Dressed in our vivid paper creations, it becomes a fascinating attraction for older babies and toddlers.

Vigilia is prepared traditionally with all cooking ingredients available, still a source of wonder to us all. The cooks have made a special effort with the beetroot soup, the battered deep-fried fish, the *pierogi*, the *goląbki*, the variety of sweet cakes. There is much emotion, as always, when we share the wafer and wish each other the longed-for reunion with our families and a quick return journey home.

Yolanta sits between Marcella and me. She appears happier than usual.

'Do you know what I've wished for?' she asks. I can guess, but I'm wrong. 'I wished that you could be with me when I tell my father.' Her face brightens up . So does mine.

'Yolanta, I promise you, if it's at all possible, I'll be there to support you.'

Lisa is sitting opposite us. She emits sporadic shouts interrupting herself in her long-winded account of some distant relatives' adventure many *Vigilias* ago, when their sledge got stuck in a hollow in six feet of snow.

'Ouch! Ouch!' she presses her hand to her distended belly, 'I think it's started. I wish the little monkey would hurry up!'

'So do I!' Marcella winks at me.

It seems our prayers have been answered. Close to midnight, Lisa's ever more frequent contractions unmistakeably herald the imminent birth of her child. Sergeant Turovicz accompanies her in the van, driven by Aarif to the hospital. That Christmas night, Marcella, Yolanta and I experience true peace in our room. We shall be enjoying Lisa's absence for the next two weeks. Except that for me, my time comes before her return.

Our little Julia was born in the maternity unit of Tel-Aviv hospital on 4th January 1944. I missed Julian. I missed my mother, I missed my sisters. I had a deep need to show off my little daughter to them, my trophy. The assisting mid-wife, a beautiful Jewish girl with large dark eyes made up for their absence with her soothing chattiness and her real joy at delivering my baby, whole and healthy, just under three kilograms, all match-stick fingers with perfect nails in place, a dark down covering the tiny head, eyes shut tight, with a trace of minute arcs of eyebrows above them.

I lay back against the pristine white pillows, the hospital smell of cleanliness in the air, exhausted but infinitely relieved from the racking pain, the tiny warm bundle resting on my chest, and I cried. With sheer joy.

The nurse stood by and looked down at me, her face soft with understanding. But I had to explain.

'She looks just like her sister. She could be her twin!'

Later, Julian echoed my words, the first time he held Julia in his arms. 'It's like cuddling Dorotka again. It's as if she has come back to us!'

Saturday, 22nd January 1944. Only two and a half weeks since Julia's birth but we are going to have her christened tomorrow, so Julian can still make it in time before being sent to Europe.

Troops of the 2nd Polish Corps have been called from all over the Middle East, and have been assembling in Port Said and Alexandria in preparation for sailing to Italy. Julian's recent letters have been full of renewed fervour and impatience. I feel the coldness of fear, every time I read them.

But today I stubbornly banish all pessimistic thoughts from my mind and concentrate on the pleasures of caring for my baby; the intimacy of breast feeding, the softness of her when I bathe her, the sweet smell of her close to my chest, the changing expressions of her tiny features, the squealing, snorting sounds, like Korek's when he was a puppy. So much joy from one so little.

I want Julian to experience it all. I hold Julia in my arms as I sit at the window and look out into the street awaiting his arrival. I am well, but sitting is more restful while the post natal bleeding is running its course. I cannot imagine how the hard working women of Uzbekistan cope with it all. Perhaps some don't. Perhaps there are deaths that need not happen. But who will stand up for their suffering? I feel infinitely grateful to be in a safe and caring environment.

Quite randomly, it is a dry, calm day in this season of rains and winds. The tree outside our entrance yard makes me think of autumn days at home, with grey skies toning down the greens of nature. It is a mild day. There will be time for a walk in a nearby park when Julian arrives.

He's been given a special leave and I've been given the guest room for our use during his two-night stay. Pity, we can't all have our separate rooms to isolate our noisy, needy babies from each other. Night time is regularly fraught with broken sleep, yet as time goes on, it is quite extraordinary how the mothers develop sensors to pick out only their own baby's cries, like bats in a colony. Lisa's constant tiredness must have sapped all her physical energy and activeness of mind. She sleeps much of the time these days, waking up only to feed and change her baby boy. Sergeant Turovicz has given me instructions to take Julian into the dining room and give him his meal when he arrives. We've had ours. Everything is ready: the vegetable soup, the minced pork in mushroom sauce with rice, and our cook's special apple cake.

Waiting makes me jumpy, despite my resolution to stay calm. I watch the cars go by, not many in this suburb, Arab women balancing baskets on their swaying hips, with their children trailing behind, the odd European dressed couple, or a suit with a walking cane. It is almost three o'clock, but Julian will have travelled since the crack of dawn.

And then I see him, a tall slim figure in his thicker, winter uniform, his field cap at a precise, off the centre angle, a rucksack thrown over his shoulder, his strides long and full of purpose.

I rush out of my room down the corridor, with Julia asleep in my arms, and meet him inside the porch. He drops his rucksack down, and I feel his arms around us, his face against mine, then his lips brush our baby's forehead,

'How I've been waiting for this moment!' He sounds breathless, there's a tremor in his voice and his eyes shine. And that is when he says, 'It's like holding Dorotka again.'

Later, when I've warmed up his meal and we sit at the end of the long table, with Julia in her pram beside us, and other mothers come and go to make tea or heat the milk for their babies, we have eyes only for each other. Perhaps not exclusively. Julian can't stop glancing at our sleeping baby. While he is eating I tell him all my news, the hospital stay, snippets from Ain-Karem, surprisingly brought over by Yvona on her flying visits to a man friend in Ramallah, about Eva's letters from Valivade.

'Have you seen Henryk lately?' I ask Julian.

'Yes!' Julian replies with excitement, 'as it happens, we are all stationed in Cairo at the moment. Our little group. I see Henryk regularly. And Roman too. I've come across Ryszard and Oleg the other day.'

'Really?' I feel a rush of emotion. 'How are the children?'

'They are both well,' Julian assures me. 'And doing well at school. It helps with Aniela keeping an eye on them.'

'This is really good news, Julian. I think about Pavel and Agata every day. And how's Henryk?'

'What about him?' Julian raises a questioning eyebrow, as he stacks the empty soup bowl on top of the empty plate. I share the tea and the cake with him.

'I can't help wondering,' I confide, 'about this adoption business. It all seemed to happen so quickly. Did Eva really think it through? Did Henryk? I can't help feeling that there's something odd about it all.'

Julian thinks for a moment.

'Henryk doesn't say much. But he must have been really upset for Eva. Perhaps he felt guilty?'

'Guilty?'

Julian nods.

'Because he couldn't be there for her. Because, I don't know…' he shrugs, 'Nastusha, some men find it really hard to be away from their wives for so long…'

'What do you mean?' I challenge him, 'Henryk would never..!'

'I'm not saying he did. It's just that, it's happening all the time. Everywhere. Loneliness. Longing. Attractive PSKs. It's inevitable, Nastusha.'

'What about you?' I tease.

He takes my hand and kisses it.

'I don't need anyone else. The PSKs are good company. At the socials. But we always end up talking about our families.'

'And Henryk?'

'We are hardly ever stationed in the same place at the same time. But my guess is, that knowing what a softie Henryk is, I think he just gave in to Eva, you know, about the adoption. Just so she was happy. And he had peace.' He adds, 'and it's not hard to love other children, is it? We loved Pavel and Agata, and either could have been ours...'

'Yes... I suppose so,' I want to be persuaded against the niggling doubt, 'I just wish we did not have to lose them...'

'Nastusha, my dear, even with your own children, they are not our property to keep for ever, are they? They grow up and you have to let them go.'

'Of course, but not just yet...' I stretch out my arm and run my hand over Julia's sleeping little body. 'Have you asked Henryk yet to be the godfather? Eva's already replied. I think she was pleased to be asked.'

'So was Henryk,' Julian smiles and from his breast pocket he produces a passport-size photograph. It is of Henryk in his army uniform, the 'Poland' half moon on his arm, the white eagle badge on his field cap His posed serious look does not fool me; there's a hint of a grin lurking in the corners of his lips. Dear Henryk. I turn over the photograph and read the inscription: 'For my god-daughter with love. May we celebrate your Confirmation at home in our free Poland. Henryk Bzovski.'

'Pity they can't be with us,' I say with regret, 'but I've asked Sargeant Turovicz and our church warden, Mr. Dymski to act as their stand-ins.'

'And one more thing,' Julian says, 'I've brought all my notebooks to leave with you.'

I laugh.

'So you've succumbed to Roman's influence? Me too!'

Later, after I've fed our baby, changed her and wrapped her well against the outdoor temperature, Julian and I go for a walk in the nearby park. January here is grey, like an autumn day at home, without the blaze of the autumn colours. Julian pushes the pram with pride and I walk beside him with happiness inflating my chest. We find a bench and sit close together, our sides touching, his arm around me, his other hand resting on the handlebar of the pram. Excited children's voices drift over from the sand pit and the play area; mothers enjoy a respite from their lonely childcare in adult company; an old well dressed lady is led by her poodle on a meandering walk; two granddads, both with walking-sticks do their best to keep up with their lively grandsons. It is such a normal comforting sight.

'I wish we could stop time,' I tell Julian, 'I wish you didn't have to go on Monday.'

He lowers his face to mine and brushes my face with his lips.

'Nastusha, we've been waiting for action so long. I can't wait to get on with the job. Do it. Finish it. Get back home. The Germans are losing ground. The Russians are pushing hard from the east. The British and the Dutch are putting up a great fight in the north. Now it's our turn to attack from the south. It may all be over very soon.'

I nod. 'I understand all that. I just wish… when will I see you again?'

He hugs me to him.

'No one can tell you that. But Nastusha, think only of the good things now. Promise me, you'll do that. Every night before I go to sleep I think of you and of the day when I come back to collect you and Julia. I imagine our boat journey across the Mediterranean. A cabin all to ourselves. Lounging on the deck. The sea air in our lungs. And then the train journey. Plush seats and refreshments. For people, not animals. And then our homecoming…'

'Like scenes from a film..?' I don't mean to mock him

'No, that's going to be real. I promise!'

I study his face, his intense, persuasive eyes, his neatly cropped dark hair around his forehead and temples, his lips stilled in a smile with lingering shadows of his dreams. I want to remember him like that, as he is at this moment. I want to carry this image with me till his words come true.

CHAPTER 43

PALESTINE – ENGLAND
1947 – 1948

It was not meant to be like this. Our plans, constantly affirmed, constantly dreamed of, were simple. As soon as the war was over, Julian was going to come back for me and Julia, so we could return together to our home in free Poland.

The reality is different. There is no home for us. There is no free Poland. Our broken dreams, nurtured for seven long years in exile have fallen about us like leaves blown from the trees.

Our reality is this: our troops, the 2nd Polish Corps, sailed for Italy soon after Julia's christening. In January 1944 we, the families left behind, in this once safe land, lived for the daily news of action from the front. The news was encouraging. Italian cities were being relinquished by the Germans one by one, as the Allied forces pushed north. Monte Cassino. Ancona. Bologna. At the time of Rome's liberation, the Allies drove the Germans out of Normandy, then Paris. The end is near, we kept telling ourselves, revelling in our repeated mantra. Under the blue Palestinian sky we could not have imagined the scale of losses and devastation throughout Europe.

Our community of Poles in Jerusalem, Ramallah and Ain-Karem was hit hard by the news from Warsaw that September. The heroic uprising was crushed by the Germans, while our 'allies', the Russian troops, stood on the other bank of Vistula and watched thousands of civilians being slaughtered. Painful and galling as this news was, it was of no surprise to any Pole who had experienced the Soviet Paradise, in which human life is not valued. The Red Army walked in victorious to occupy Warsaw, before heading west for Berlin.

After that, the victory in the Netherlands, the liberation of Rome, the fall of Berlin and the deaths of Hitler and Mussolini came as a relief rather than reasons for great rejoicing. For Europe the end of the war was real: the nations could start rebuilding their future in the true spirit of freedom. For us, scattered Poles, nothing had changed except the name of our oppressor: Hitler was dead but Stalin was very much alive.

In February 1945, three months before the end of the war, two of the 'Big Three', Churchill and Roosevelt gave in to Stalin's demands. At their meeting in Yalta, deliberately excluding representatives of the Polish Government in Exile, they redesigned Polish territories, they set up a Soviet controlled communist government in Poland, and sanctioned the Red Army to remain.

Our utter dismay turned to bitter disappointment. How could this be? Two great powers, Britain and America selling us to Stalin. Afraid to stand up to him!

Our incredulity was further challenged when our Polish 2nd Corps of the British Army was excluded from the Victory Day celebrations, in London. It appeared that the British Government cared more for Stalin's volatile moods than for acknowledging the bravery and sacrifice of the Polish soldiers. Only some representatives of the Polish Airforce were symbolically singled out to attend this ceremony. They declined this dubious honour for the sake of their snubbed compatriots.

Two years have passed since then. We are still here in Palestine, families of Polish soldiers, waiting to be reunited with them in England. There has been an active campaign by the British Government at the instigation of the communist government in Poland, to persuade the soldiers and their families to return home. 'To rebuild Poland'.

Some did return. Out of sheer homesickness. Out of a deep need to find their lost families. Stories came back of arrests and mock trials and sentences to be served in Siberian gulags. What's new? This only strengthened our resolve to hold out until such time when Poland regained her freedom and independence.

Monday 17th November 1947. I am outside the Jaffa Gate in Jerusalem waiting for my bus to take me home to Ain-Karem to my little Julia. Since the first riots flared up between the Jews and the Arabs two years ago, tension has been mounting with ever more frequent fights and skirmishes between the two opponents. Every outing into Jerusalem fills me with dread, and I keep putting it off, until I cannot leave pressing matters any longer. Today, I've come to collect my travel papers and my last allowance, a portion of Julian's commission, before my departure.

The facade of the King David Hotel still bears visible marks of fire and destruction, where the Jewish Irgun terrorists planted a bomb last year. It was aimed at the British Army Command, but as always, civilians were killed and injured. There have been Arab attacks on Jewish shops; there have been Jewish bomb plants on Arab buses. Though the city endeavours to function as normally as possible, there is almost a tangible tautness in the hushed atmosphere in the narrow, stalls-crammed streets.

I should have taken a taxi, but taxi drivers refuse to drive to certain quarters. Earlier, I took a bus, and with strained nerves forced myself to walk to the Polish Delegatura Building, amongst the crowd of wary, distrustful-looking people, Orthodox Jews, European Jews, Arabs and Eurasians. I prayed hard that I should in no way attract attention and spark off an individual attack, as did the Polish consul who was shot by the Jews, convinced he was a spy; as did one of our male teachers, mistaken for a Jew and shot by the Arabs at the Damascus Gate. Not to mention a number of instances when Polish soldiers were targeted, despite the clear badges on their uniforms.

I was giddy with relief when I reached the Delegatura building and ran up the stone steps inside its wide entrance hall. I registered at the reception desk and was asked to take a seat in the waiting room.

Like most official buildings, it had a shiny tiled floor and whitewashed walls adorned with the Polish emblem of the white crowned eagle, portraits of our national heroes, Pilsudski and Sikorski, and on the entrance-facing wall, a gold-framed painting of Our Lady, Queen of Poland.

There were just two other people in the waiting room, an elderly couple. I was called out within minutes and followed the official, a uniformed man of about fifty, with greying hair and a neat moustache, to his room. The sturdy wood bureau in the middle was surrounded by walls lined with filing cabinets. He bade me to sit down.

'It all appears in order,' he said from the other side of his bureau, as he looked through the papers. He placed them before me. 'Please check yourself in case you have any questions.'

I turned the sheets over one by one, all officially signed and British-countersigned: my returned passport, a flimsy sheet and a photograph of me with shaved head taken in Teheran, Julia's particulars, my travel document stating my present address and my destination: England. I could not imagine it. All I could think of was Julian.

I nodded and thanked him.

'Now it's all so close, I can hardly believe it.'

He gave me a polite smile and placed a sealed envelope on top of the papers. My final monthly allowance. 'You'll find,' he said,' that half of it is in British currency. Anything you want to ask me?' I was just relieved that after all those years of waiting all final formalities were concluded.

'When are we likely to sail?' I asked.

'When a boat becomes available.' His eyebrows rose slightly. 'God knows, the British have had their hands full with having to evacuate their own.'

'So, next Monday, the set date, is that not certain yet?'

'It is. All is set for departures from Ain-Karem, Ramallah and Rehovot. You'll be taken to a transit camp near Tel-Aviv. Beit Jirja.'

I nodded thinking, another stretch of nomadic life before us. As if guessing my thoughts, he explained.

'Our soldiers are still there. They'll ensure safety for you as well as all possible comforts.'

'I don't doubt that,' I wished to sound gracious, 'after the Soviet experience, everything else is a luxury.' I thanked him again and he wished me and my child a safe journey to England.

346

Out in the narrow crowded streets I was beset with unease and only stopped briefly at a stall to get some fruit and vegetables.

I feel no less anxious now, as I stand at my bus stop in the square outside Jaffa Gate. I pray fervently that the bus will hurry. The square, a large expanse of pebbly, dusty ground, is no longer as busy as it used to be before the troubles began. Crowds have diminished to small groups waiting at their stops, mainly the elderly and Arab women with young children. In my calf-length coat, my felt cloche hat and with my European features, I could be mistaken for a Jewish woman, and perhaps because of this fear, I get a strange sense of expectancy in the air, as if something is about to happen.

Nervously, I look around. The thick ancient walls of Jerusalem city appear excluding rather than protective, with their back to the outside world. Two taxis are parked nearby, their Arab owners, wearing ordinary trousers and shirts, leaning on the bonnets and smoking , no doubt, putting the world to right. Further down, donkeys are tethered to their carts that sell boiled sweetcorn or juice from pressed oranges. A bus is just leaving, the tyres making indentations in the recently rained-over ground. I pray my bus will hurry. It is already fifteen minutes late. But lateness has to be accepted in these days of serious concerns.

Cars and trucks are parked at random in the middle of the square. I cannot explain why, but one particular lorry appears sinister, parked on its own. My fear is irrational. It reaches a level when I can no longer control my panic. I think of Julia left at home with my Arab family. They are kind people, she'll come to no harm, I tell myself, yet my need to be with her becomes so strong, I give into my instinct. I leave the queue at the bus stop and run with my bags to the nearest taxi.

'Ain-Karem!' I shout, '*Shybko!* Please hurry!'

If the Arab taxi driver is startled, he does not show it. Slowly, he stabs out his cigarette, says something to his companion and we both get into his taxi. My heart pounds when he circles the square and I cannot take my eyes off the lorry. Hurry! Hurry! My whole being wants to shout.

As we leave the square behind us, and the taxi accelerates on the widening route out of the city, there is a deafening explosion behind us.

'Almighty Allah!' the driver exclaims, his eyes round with horror reflecting in the mirror. I turn in the back seat and look through the window. Despite the recent rain, despite the wet ground, clouds of dust billow above the square where I stood only minutes ago. I cower in my seat, hugging myself, stilling my pounding heart, sending fervent thanks to God for saving me. For my child.

The shocked taxi driver cannot stop talking. Words tumble out of him which I don't understand, but I empathize with his evident emotional state. I recognize words such as Irgun and Haganah and Sterna, names of Jewish terrorist groups, ruthlessly intent on expelling the British and eliminating the Arabs from the territory they consider indigenously their own.

I'm not an enthusiast of crazy driving, but today the driving is still not fast enough for me, when we whizz along Ain-Karem road with much klaxon pounding, overtaking all other vehicles. Isolated roadside houses, trees, telegraph poles, become a continuous blur, and then at last, Mr. Ahmmed's, my landlord's house comes into view.

It stands on its own, on lower ground from the main road, about ten minutes walk from Ain-Karem centre. Like most houses in this area, it is built in white thick stone, solid square in shape, with outside stone steps leading up onto the roof, surrounded by a parapet, and in one corner, a tank for collecting rain water. The doors are strengthened with iron and the tall windows are protected with bars.

The terraced land around us, sloping down to the valley is beautiful in Spring with its flowering fruit orchards. Now, it's as colourless as the grey sky above us and as sombre looking as my mood feels.

The taxi leaves the road and pulls up in front of the house on the half-moon-shaped pebbly forecourt. I just wish to pay and run to Julia.

'*Ile*! How much?' I ask, money ready in my hand.

The taxi driver waves his hands, grabs hold of my shopping bag and runs ahead of me to the front door. Only Mrs. Mastura and her twelve-year-old daughter Ameena are at home. Their men are at work. I choke with emotion at the sight of my little Julia holding Ameena's hand. I pick her up and hold her close to me, my legs shaking. There is a very lively conversation going on between the taxi driver and Mrs. Mastura. Julia pulls back her face from mine and looking seriously into my eyes she asks,

'Mummy did you get the sweetcorn for me?'

'Sweetcorn and pomegranates and a sweet juicy melon,' my voice wants to sing as I put her down on the floor. She crouches to look inside the bag. I stretch out my hand to the taxi driver with the money in my palm.

'How much?'

He waves his hands and shakes his head.

'No! No pay! My life safe! Allah good!'

'Yes,' I reply in Polish, 'our God was good to us both. But take the money. Donation to mosque. To say thank you to Allah.'

He considers my meaning for a moment then the intensity in his dark eyes softens. He takes his fare from me and leaves with much talking to Mrs. Mastura. Ameena helps me with my bags and follows me and Julia outside. My room is entered from a side door, separate from the rest of the house. Its thick stone walls make it cold in the winter months and a paraffin heater is necessary.

Before I light it, I give Ameena sweets and pocket money for having looked after Julia in my absence. She has learnt enough Polish from us to be the best communicator in her family.

Her dark eyes look into mine with intense seriousness when she tells me, 'Man say what happen. Man say trouble at night. Man say we hide.'

'What trouble, Ameena?'

'Men fight.'

I feel frail and jittery. Her warning fuels my alarm. But no, I must not give in to panic. We've had such warnings before. The men got ready with their guns on the rooftops, exhausted themselves with tense waiting all night. Then nothing. A war of nerves.

I stroke Ameena's head.

'You're a good girl. And you mustn't worry about tonight. Your father and your brothers will be here to protect us.'

I returned to live in Ain-Karem when Julia was six months old. Much as I liked the secure atmosphere at the Home in Ramallah, the day-to-day existence amongst the wailing babies, overactive toddlers, squabbling mothers, and having to share the room with others, became less attractive as time went on.

Before I moved, I kept my promise to Yolanta. I stayed by her side when her father came to visit her for the first time. Expecting his wrath, she stood white-faced and rigid, while I braced myself for firm talking to him.

It was not necessary. The sight of his tiny grandson transformed this stern, self-disciplined soldier to an instantly proud grandfather. Tenderly he held the little bundle in his arms and hid his emotions behind his hooded eyes. When he trusted himself to speak, he raised his misty gaze to us and said, 'We've had enough deaths in our family. It is time now to celebrate life!'

My Arab landlords here are friendly family people. I feel safe with them, especially now, when most of our Polish community, thriving when I first arrived, has been evacuated in large numbers, mothers and children to join their soldier husbands and fathers in England.

The school, ten minutes walk away, my place of employment before Julia's birth, is virtually empty now. St. John's Church used to be crowded at Sunday Masses; now there's just a handful of school girls, with three remaining staff, a few families, a few older people, and a few mothers like myself, with their young children attending.

Till last July I've had a friend living nearby, Marcella and her little boy, my room-mates from Ramallah. I envy her allocation on an earlier transport to England. I envy her reunion with her husband. I've heard nothing from Julian for such a long time. Last January I received an official letter from a hospital in England. Lots of medical terms, but I want to believe that he is making progress.

For Julia and myself our room is of ample size. There is a tall iron bed in one corner, wide enough for us both; a wardrobe for my few belongings, a small table with two chairs, an iron stove with a few pots, and a washstand with a bowl and pitcher behind a screen. Water has to be brought in a pail from a nearby well. It is clean, but caution has taught me to always boil it first before using it for cooking purposes.

As I stand at the stove cooking our lunch of vegetable soup and lentils, I watch Julia play on the rug on the tiled floor. I have bought her a set of hand-carved animals for a few *mils* at the market. Her favourites are the donkey and the shepherd boy whom she calls Ameena. She likes her colouring book with simple shapes of everyday objects, and I like to watch her concentration with her pursed lips as her little fingers grip the wax crayon and lead it laboriously inside the lines.

I feel overwhelmed with love for her as I recover from the shock of my miraculous escape. A minute longer and Julia would have been motherless. I cannot bear to think of it. Would her father come to fetch her, as we have so often planned in our exchanged letters at the beginning? One more week, I remind myself, and we'll be on our way. To be with him for good.

In the afternoon I dress Julia and myself in coats and hats against the cooler temperatures of the winter season and we go out. I need to clear my head, I need to be with people, I need to talk to another adult.

I walk to the centre of Ain-Karem, with Julia in the pushchair, along a broken line of stone houses, stooping fig and olive trees, vertical cypresses, barren vegetable plots, pebbly, unused patches of land. The flat rooftops display drying washing on stretched lines or rugs airing over the parapets.

I visit St. John's Church first. Its lofty, colonnaded central nave is like a cloak of protection with its quiet, dusky, frankincense scented air. There is always someone about in one of the pews or revisiting the stations of the cross. Old Mr. Dertz, in his incongruous Arab head gear, and Mrs. Mrovka, hunched and clad in her perennial black, appear to be permanent residents here. I acknowledge them with a nod and walk up to the pew closest to the altar.

No words can express the relief and the gratitude I feel. Julia wriggles off the pushchair, climbs up beside me and throws her arm around my neck in a tight embrace. She presses her lips to my ear.

'Mama, the candle now.' Her stage whisper lifts my serious mood. She releases her vice-grip on my neck, clutches my hand and pulls me to the candle stand at the side of the altar. Her eyes sparkle when I help her to light a candle and slot it in place.

'For Daddy,' she says out of habit. She does not know Julian, except as the man who is holding her to his chest on the christening photograph. 'And now to Franio,' she reminds me, her upturned face, her outstretched arm and her pointing finger urging me to go.

'Now to Franio,' I repeat.

The Polish Centre in the Abu-Kebir House, the source of daily communications for the remaining Poles, is just off the square with its small grocery and hardware shops. There is a coffee house where the Arab men pass away hours smoking hookah pipes and playing dice games. Their women do all the chores. Dressed in long, some richly embroidered, dresses, and ample cotton scarves falling in folds about their shoulders, they move with rhythmic steps and practised grace, balancing on their heads water pitchers or baskets filled with fruit and vegetables from the market. In this sleepy square it is hard to imagine the violence that has occurred this morning just a few kilometres down the road.

I hurry to my place of refuge, a solid stone building with an arched entrance leading to a central courtyard. I follow the sound of voices to the meeting hall. It is a large whitewashed room, its walls adorned with the Polish white and red flags crossed over the emblem of the white eagle, a painting of our Polish Black Madonna, prints of watercolours depicting rural scenes in our country.

Among the milling lively children, Julia spots her friend Franio, a four-year-old like herself, and she skips up to him with unrestrained first love. There are cardboard boxes of toys for the children, a Red Cross gift, rag dolls, wooden cars and engines and colourful wooden ricks. Mothers sit around the room in groups watching their children and discussing the inevitable topics: who has already gone, who has written, and what to expect on the next lap of our journey when it starts next week.

I sit down next to Franio's mother, Adela, a small woman with a trim figure and prematurely greying hair. Her husband was killed at Monte Cassino. She has been given permission on compassionate grounds to seek refuge with the rest of us in England, but not without the initial attempts by the British officials to persuade her to return to her native Poland. Grieving and bewildered she asked me at the time, 'Would they go back and trust the very people who have destroyed their lives?'

Today, the first thing I tell her is of my escape from a sure disaster. A minute longer… and God knows! She watches my face with awe.

'It seems there is no longer a safe place for us!' she says.

'England is safe,' I comfort her and myself.

'But for how much longer? What if there is another war? With Stalin?' Her eyes look pained.

That is what many Poles hope for, those still in uniform. For how else are we going to recover our country? Free ourselves of the Soviet communism? My own feelings are very torn. More than anything else I want to be with Julian and return home. But another war? Another such cataclysmic upheaval? Who would want to start that again?

'Adela, I don't think there will be another war in the near future. Who would have the energy and the resources for that? I think we'll be quite safe in England for a long time.' I repeat my conversation with the man at the Polish *Delegatura* and we talk about the start of our journey next week. By the end of the afternoon my anxiety gives way to pleasant scenes of our imagined travels that fill my mind. We'll stick together throughout, we tell ourselves, and make it an exciting adventure.

My improved state of mind does not last long. In the evening things begin to happen around our dwellings. I'm filled with unease. Mr. Ahmmed and his two sons are on guard on the roof of our house, as are other men in the near vicinity, also lurking and skulking between houses, outbuildings and sheds, and behind the raised ridges of the terraced hillside. The houses on the other side of the main road are at a definite advantage, looking down at any approaching vehicles or individuals.

The women, myself included, have been warned to lock themselves in behind barred doors and barred windows. In my room it's pitch black and claustrophobic. I pray and hope with all my being that this is another false alarm.

Julia is asleep beside me, her warm little body against mine, her breath regular. It is a blessing she is too young to understand. In moments like this I want to be her, with my own mother protecting me, making all the decisions. The longing is so strong at times it's like a physical ache. It's seven years since my last contact with her and all my family. I've left their particulars with the Red Cross in Teheran, but despite my regular enquiries, there has yet not been any discovery of their whereabouts. And Julian's silence sits like a lead brick on my chest.

Soon after Julia's christening his battalion left Alexandria for Italy. At the beginning I received short notes from him from a number of places. San Vincenzo, San Michele, Nicola, Pizzone and others, as the Allied Forces fought their way north. Every letter listed his fallen or wounded colleagues. Some of the ill-fated were husbands of the girls I knew in Ramallah. The brown envelope was dreaded by everyone: an official notification of wounding or death.

Julian's white envelopes, even before I tore them open, were tangible proof that he was still alive. Even in times of intensive battles he managed to keep in touch with me. Monte Cassino, Piedimonte, Loretto and Ancona. And the longer his notes kept coming, the more fearful I became that our luck would run out. And what I dreaded the most caught up with me in the end. One day I received the brown envelope too. When the war was nearly over. When Bologna was one of the last battles won. I remember that day clearly; the little insignificant things, before and after the shock.

It was at the end of April, two years ago, the day Hitler killed himself in his bunker, only the news had not reached us yet. Here the air was fragrant with Spring, the sun warm in the clear sky, the orchards fluffy with white and pink blossom. Julia was fifteen months old, a quiet serious child, chewing and sucking the frilly hemline of her white dress, as she sat in her pushchair.

At the Polish Centre in Jerusalem (it was still a peaceful city then), the attractive, young Polish PSK checked the mail for me in the pigeon-holes behind her desk. I remember how her fingers hesitated over a brown envelope. Something stopped inside me and it seemed like a very long time and in slow motion that her hand came towards me.

'Just one letter for you, Mrs. Kalinska.' Her voice was low, apologetic.

I stared at the brown envelope. But it couldn't be! Not for me! My hand felt paralysed, unable to pick up the letter.

'He may be just wounded,' she prompted in a small voice.

Of course! That's all it is! I grasped at her words, and picked up the envelope. I stared hard at it. No mistake. My name on it.

'Mrs. Kalinska,' the girl spoke again, 'why don't you go into the day room. You won't be alone there.'

I shook my head.

'Thank you. I need to be alone.'

Here clarity fails me. I remember nothing of the short distance to the nearest church. Just a sense of blurred vision and my hands gripping the bar of Julia's pushchair. I slipped into a bench at the back of the church and as my eyes were adjusting to the half-light, I placed on Julia's lap a paper bag with a few dried apricots. Then I tore the envelope open.

Words jumped up at me. The standard official print. The type-written message. Battle of Bologna. Corporal Julian Kalinski. A head wound. Amnesia.

I read the letter several times trying hard to absorb the full meaning, reassuring myself that Julian was not dead. My body slumped with relief and I let copious tears flow down my face and drip down onto my chest.

A hand on my shoulder made me jump. I looked up and found the kindly face of a white-dressed monk peering down at me.

'Sad news?' he asked in Polish.

I wiped my face with a handkerchief and showed him the letter.

'Wounded. But alive! Thank God he is alive!'

For the next two months I sent weekly enquiries to the hospital in Bologna. It was relentless torture waiting for just one reply. For my child's sake and my own sanity, I imposed a strict routine on myself, a rigid timetable for meals, active play with her, walks to the park, visits to the community centre, Masses on Sundays. Talking to other women helped, but it did not stop my mental torment of imagining Julian imprisoned in bed, perhaps comatose, perhaps aware but suffering, and I separated from him by hundreds of miles and unable to help.

And then, at the end of July the much awaited letter came. Not from him. From the hospital secretary. Julian's *mild traumatic* injury was healing well, but the amnesia would require further treatment. Definite prognosis was not possible at this stage. He'd be shortly moved to convalesce in Cervia, near Rimini.

It was a kind of relief to know he was improving, but I felt no ecstatic joy. The next letter, a couple of months later, repeated a similar report. Physical recovery was good, but Julian's *post-concussional shock* had left him *vulnerable mentally and emotionally*. What did it all mean? Just a word from him, written by himself was all I craved for.

'I wish I could ask someone,' I poured out my concerns to Adela.

'Ask the doctor next time you go with Julia,' she said. So obvious! Visits to the doctor were frequent with young children. Inoculations, skin rashes, sore throats, ear infections, sudden fevers.

I took Julia to have her eye examined, the membrane on it swollen like pink jelly.

'Conjunctivitis,' the doctor declared. She squirmed against his touch and cried into my chest. He turned to his desk on his swivel chair and wrote out a prescription. 'These drops should clear it in a few days. Use them in both eyes.'

The doctor, a middle-aged, slight, neat man was a survivor, like the rest of us, of the Russian experience. One could always count on his sympathy and patience. Sporting an officer's uniform, he was also a representative of the authorities, British and Polish combined, who had set up surgeries for the scattered Polish communities in Palestine.

I took a deep breath and asked,

'May I ask you a question? I need your advice on a different matter.' I told him about Julian and I showed him the letters. 'What does it all mean? Is my husband not able to write to me himself?'

The doctor thought for a moment, his gaze skimming the letters again.

'They've mentioned amnesia. It's possible your husband has lost all memory of his past.'

'But... is he really not able to write?'

The doctor's expression remained discreet.

'Just imagine,' he said, 'being told to write to a stranger on the other side of the world. Where do you begin? What do you say? And that's assuming his concentration is not affected.'

I could not imagine Julian in that condition. 'But me? His wife? And his child. Is it possible he'd have forgotten us completely?'

The doctor's professional face softened.

'It's hard to imagine, I know. What you must also remember, is that it's not a deliberate act on his part. He has no awareness of being any different than before, because he does not remember 'before'. The brain is an extraordinary, complex organ. Sometimes this condition can last for a long time. Sometimes just an object, a word, a tune, a fragrance, like spring flowers, can trigger off something in the brain, and the memory returns.'

'Really?' I latched onto his every word. 'Then there's hope, that when he sees us, his memory will come back?'

The doctor remained serious but there was a well-meaning touch to his words when he replied,

'No one can give you an absolute assurance, but these things do happen and you must never lose hope.'

I hold onto this hope as I dream of our reunion in England. The soldiers of the Polish 2nd Corps, who have refused to return to the communist Poland, have been given refuge in Britain on the strength of General Anders' diplomatic insistence that the pre-war alliance pact between our two nations of being mutually supportive, should be honoured.

Henryk is already in England. I know this from Eva's sporadic letters. In her last note she wrote with some regret of the closing down of the Polish camp in Valivade, India.

'We had found peace here, Nastusha. This has been a small corner of Poland for us. A thriving community recreating life, such that we had enjoyed at home. It will be sad to leave. Though, of course, I can hardly wait to be with Henryk again after all the years!'

I cannot help wondering at Eva's true feelings. The memory of that night and of Selim haunts me still. I can barely imagine what effect that memory must have on her. How does she cope with it? I shall never know. She can never tell me.

'You'd not recognise Stella now. Eight and pretty, (though I say so myself). Cornflower blue eyes and pale blond hair. Turns heads when we go into town. She's a great help to me, like a little mother to Nadia.

Mr. Ostrovski is going back to Poland. He's got no one in the 2nd Corps. His brother near Warsaw has an extensive family. They've promised to help him bring up his little grandsons. Not so little anymore! Maks is eleven and Aleks nine!'

As I lie in the dark in my barred room, with only my small sleeping child for company, my mind is crowded with people I got to know on our long exile from home; names, faces, old, young, some newly-born. So many have died, the rest scattered all over the world, waiting for the big change, for a miracle to take them back to their old life. My musings are interrupted by a bang, like a distant thunder.

CHAPTER 44

Running feet thud on the rooftop, then there is silence. My heart misses a beat and I hold back my breath. Another sound like a clap of thunder, followed by a succession of crackles. Getting closer. Specific noise. Machine guns. Shouts from the roof. Blasts.

Julia stirs and clings to me. I know by her quickened breathing that she is awake.

'Mama, I'm scared!' she cries out.

So am I. Sheer instinct drives me to sit up, take her onto my lap, wrap a blanket around us, and in pitch blackness slide off the bed and crouch down on the floor underneath it. There's only my one suitcase. I stand it on its side to form a barricade. Behind it, I slide along the floor to the furthest corner against the wall.

Outside, there is a full-blown battle raging now; a cacophony of shooting, blasting, yelling, thudding. Julia is crying against my chest and I feel as if all my insides are turning to water. I squeeze my buttocks rigid and pray.

The all-piercing clamour is relentless. There are gunshots just outside our window, then a crashing of something heavy against the bars. Julia is shocked into silence and presses her face against my chest. I can hardly breathe with fear. There is an ear-splitting crack, then another, as the bar lock and the door lock are shot open. I freeze.

The door is pushed back with force, and my peeping eyes can just make out a black figure inside the moonlit door frame. My thoughts race. If he finds me I'll just shout, I'm Polish!

He yells something. It's not Arabic. He must be from the Irgun lot. Pointing his gun with one hand, he shines a torch around the room. I feel as if I'm dead already. Julia takes cue from me; she is as mute as a mouse pressing against me. The beam jumps over the objects in the room, slides along the floor, the length of the bed and away from my hiding corner. He shouts something again, jumps off the doorstep and disappears into the night.

My first instinct is to rush to the door, shut it and barricade it, but I dare not leave my hiding place. I pray with manic fervour that no one else will invade my room. The echoes of shooting resound in the valley, doubling the effect of this frenzy, that goes on and on, till I feel as if I'll go mad with terror.

It is hard to estimate time, but suddenly I'm aware of a change. The shooting becomes distant, and then as if by magic it fades away altogether. They've moved on. I wait a moment longer in this blessed silence, before crawling out from under the bed. I place resisting, crying Julia on the bed, rush to the door, close it, and feeling my way in the dark, I push our table against it. It is a small table, but made of heavy, solid wood, its legs scraping noisily along the tiled floor. Julia is bereft by now, her cries ever louder. I take her in my arms and hush her, sensing the pressure suddenly of my dire need to use the bucket.

'Mummy wants pooh,' I tell her, but she clings all the more to me, her little fingers digging into my flesh. Even in pitch black I can find my way to the bucket behind the canvas screen. I make it just in time, sit down with Julia in my lap and feel weighed down like a marmoset monkey. Nature takes its course. I feel hollow when I stand up. Julia is quiet now and amazingly uncritical of the stench.

'Mummy must wash now,' I tell her, and she does not protest this time when I put her down. I cover the bucket with a lid then I feel for the matches and the candle on the shelf above the stove. In the dim candle light, Julia is content to wait on the bed for me while I wash.

Later, secure beside me, she falls asleep. But I cannot sleep. The whole building is eerily quiet. I wonder about Mrs. Mastura and Ameena. I pray they got away in time. But I won't know till the morning. The creepy silence makes my nerves taut. I cannot go through a night like this again. My mind is made up. I'll leave tomorrow. I'll go to Ramallah. Anywhere. Where it's safe.

I must have slept a little after all, for the banging on the door wakes me up. I sit up with a start, all the fears returning with an overwhelming tension. I recognise Ameena's voice calling out. I feel faint with relief.

'Madam Kalinska! It is Ameena! It is my mother!'

I slide off the bed and rush to the door. 'One second!' I shout, struggling with the table.

The moment the daylight floods our room, and the fresh air fills my lungs, the sight of the two friendly figures on the doorstep reduces me to a weeping wreck. I control myself and hug Ameena. Mrs. Mastura wipes her eyes.

'You're safe!' I cry out. 'Where did you hide?'

Ameena points to the end of their garden where it drops down to the lower terrace.

'When they come close, we run. They break all door. They look for Aisa. Our leader.'

'And what about your father? Your brothers? Are they safe?'

'They go meeting.'

Julia has wriggled off the bed and is now standing barefoot close to Ameena, with her arms around her big friend's waist.

'Ameena,' I pause, choosing my words, 'can you explain to your mother that I shall be leaving soon.'

Ameena's expression drops and she hugs Julia to her side.

'When?'

'Maybe today. I don't know. I've got to go to the Polish Centre and find out what's happening.'

Mrs. Mastura nods to her daughter's translation, then talks very fast. It sounds like a long, high-pitched recitation. Ameena interprets,

'My mother say sad when you go.'

'It's sad for us too, dear Ameena.' I say this with true feeling. I've grown to like this family. Already I feel twinges, like the shame of betrayal, as I long to escape this place. Strange, how I'm the lucky one here, despite my statelessness. I've been assured refuge in a secure and civilised world. They have no such certainty of a safe tomorrow. 'You may get peace now for a long while,' I say lamely, 'now that they've gone to some other place.'

Ameena nods. 'Today it will be quiet. We must tidy and clean.'

'I must do that too,' I say, wishing I could give them more than just a reassuring smile.

Later, when I get to the Abu-Kebir Polish Centre at nine, it is already crowded with mothers and children. There are a few older people, including Mr. Dertz in his Arab head-gear and black-clothed Mrs. Mrovka, remnants of the once thriving Polish community. Mr. Zablotzki, a university lecturer in Poland, our now respected elder and spokesman, stands in the middle of the hall and raises his hand. A hush follows. His voice is loud and clear.

'In view of what's happened last night, I've already made telephone contact with our authorities in Jerusalem. They will try to organise buses for us for tomorrow.'

Questions are raised, fears are expressed.

'Tomorrow? What about tonight? Is it safe for us to stay another night? Our landlords haven't come back yet. Our doors have been broken down!' And so on…

Mr. Zablotzki listens then raises his hand again.

'If you don't mind crowding for one night,' he suggests, 'this place will take you in. There are also empty rooms at the school.'

The murmur of consent supports his idea.

'Well then, let's meet here tonight. Safety in numbers. Get ready for tomorrow.'

And that's what we do.

I spend the morning cleaning and tidying up my room, then I pack my suitcase. I tie together Julian's exercise books of assorted colours and varying in condition, filled with his neat handwriting, Roman's good influence. I must buy an elegant wooden container for them one day. I slip them underneath my folded clothes to the bottom of the suitcase.

When I'm ready, I walk around with Julia to the main door of the house on the other side. It is open. Mrs. Mastura is busy at the oven and Ameena is on her hands and knees wiping the floor with a wet rag. Seeing us she gets up and shows me the broken door lock, and the splinters hanging off the damaged wood. Julia rushes to her side and seeks to hold her hand. Ameena smiles happily.

'Father make door right,' she says, 'later.'

I explain my visit. It is time to say our farewells. Mrs. Mastura comes over and when I present her with a colourful soft cotton shawl from Jerusalem market, her eyes look moist. She bends down to Julia and gives her a hug.

'Please tell your mother, Ameena, many, many thanks for everything.'

Ameena translates, folds up the wet cloth over the side of the bucket and follows us back to our room. She helps me with my move, pushing Julia in the push chair, while I carry the suitcase. I stop now and again to change hands and to look around at this terraced land that has been my place of refuge for the last few years. Life here has been good, and I'll always be grateful, but this wasn't my home.

At the entrance to the *Polski Dom*, I drop the suitcase on the ground and embrace Ameena, holding her close to me for a moment.

'You are a good girl. We both love you.' Ameena smiles shyly then laughs when Julia raises her arms to her. Ameena picks her up and Julia showers her face with kisses.

'Come Julia, it is time for us to go,' I relieve Ameena of my child's weight. Then I give Ameena a carved miniature box. 'For you, but don't open it till you get home.' Inside, wrapped in tissue paper, I've placed a silver chain bracelet with rose-buds, interspaced with rose leaves. Her eyes shine like jet marbles and her teeth are brilliant white between her damson lips. This image of her stays like a photograph in my mind.

CHAPTER 45

This was six weeks ago: one night's cramped conditions, but no one complained. Three buses arrived in the morning and transported about seventy of us to Beit Jirja, a Polish military camp outside Tel-Aviv. The barracks with their iron beds, proper mattresses and bedding, the availability of food and water, the sanitised latrines and washrooms, the laundry facilities, were paradise compared to some conditions we had experienced before. People were happy, buoyed by the knowledge that this was just a temporary stop on our journey to better things.

The one week's stay was utilised for the final checking of papers and inoculations against cholera, rampant in Egypt at the moment. More civilians arrived from the suburbs of Tel-Aviv, from Ramallah and Rehovot. The military personnel were courteous, helpful, even entertaining in the evenings with their impromptu concerts of songs and accordion music at the mess.

On the 6th of December, the gift-giving St. Nicholas Day in Poland, all of us civilians, perhaps three hundred, and our soldier guides were taken on buses to the pre-booked train in Tel-Aviv. Our baggage allowance was one suitcase. I left behind Julia's push-chair to be passed on to the Red Cross. We were given sandwiches and bottled soda water for the journey. The seats on the train were wooden benches, but everyone had their own allotted space and the side passages outside our compartments ensured access to the toilets and the chance to stretch our legs.

The excited children quietened down as the train started and picked up speed. Running past the windows were countless miles of orchards with orange and lemon trees, the intense colours of the fruit gleaming like baubles on Christmas trees.

At mid-day we arrived in El Arish, the end of the railroad. Army lorries were already waiting for us. We were sat aboard on rather tightly arranged benches, with the tarpaulin roof protecting us, and a flap on each side, rolled up to give us light and fresh air. We were promised a break in the journey by the assisting, good-humoured officers.

Lulled by the droning of the engines and the mild breeze, most of the children slept in their mothers' laps through the next part of the journey, which took us across the desert. There were two short stops at some roadside settlements. The latrines were dire, but needs must. Easy for the little boys, but with the little girls, it took some persuading.

Our convoy of lorries arrived in El Quassassin late in the evening. I felt shaken, sweaty and tired, yet I could not ignore the magical beauty of our surroundings. The undulating sand dunes, pale and smooth like soft flesh, were bare of all vegetation. Not the tiniest tree or a blade of grass in sight. Shining down on us from a deep sapphire sky were brilliant stars, appearing so close as to be touchable with a stretch of the arm.

'Mama, look! Fairy lights!' Julia sat up in my lap and with a wide-eyed wonder pointed to the sky. Most children were awake now and looked round with curiosity, as our lorries drove up the central route of the Polish military camp that seemed to stretch for miles with its sprawling sections of tents and huts.

We were taken to a compound, vacated for us, I presumed, with its own administration and communal blocks. We were helped down from the lorries and led by our ever courteous escorts to a large hall, where tables had been prepared for us in long rows. It was too late for tired, fractious children, but the chicken and vegetable broth served promptly by a number of assisting soldiers, proved a soothing distraction. A slice of apple cake with tea for dessert improved everyone's mood further, and it was with happier children that the mothers were shown to their living quarters.

I was allocated to a wooden barrack with hardboard partitions to house eight mothers and their children. The night turned chilly, and without further fuss, I got into bed with Julia (rough thick army sheets and blankets), both fully dressed, and pulled the blanket over us. Within minutes our hut fell silent, its inhabitants exhausted by the long day.

Bright sunshine streaming through the bare windows woke me up the next morning and the stirrings of my companions, their every word penetrating the thin hardboard walls. Children's voices calling for drinks and wee-wees.

I took Julia with me to the nearby latrines screened off with wooden panels, then to the ablutions hut. There was a row of showers which I would make use of later, but for now I washed Julia's face and hands and mine.

And so, our month's stay at El Quassassin began, almost identical to our stay in Beit Jirja camp. With all the basic facilities available, one could create a semblance of normal living. The community hall proved the most popular place, serving as a play area in the daytime, drawing the adults in the evenings for social gatherings and concerts and acting as a chapel on Sundays.

The Holy Masses were celebrated by Father Oczko, the camp chaplain, who ruled his flock of soldiers with a rod of steel. His sermons were fiercely unambiguous in their message regarding the sins of the flesh. Yet the spectre of the compulsory confessions did not deter the boys from looking for delights in the nearby town of Ismail.

I went to confession once before Christmas, racking my brains what to confess. Father Oczko's sole preoccupation was whether I was seeing other men in my husband's absence. I was so incensed I found myself sinning with my anger against him. He gave me absolution and ten *Hail Marys* to recite and I never went back to him again.

In fairness, he redeemed himself with his sentimental homily at the Midnight Mass after our *Vigilia*. Our traditional meal was celebrated in the dining hall with three hundred women like myself and hundreds of soldiers, all longing to be reunited with their families. Our seventh Christmas in exile. Father Oczko spoke with a catch in his voice, his bushy eyebrows shading his eyes, but God willing, this may be our last. Next year, who knows? At home perhaps. With our loved ones. Please God. His eyebrows moved with each enunciated word, and the crowd exhaled an entreaty in their breath.

4th January 1948. A new year. Julia is four years old today. She is a slight, thin child, but will be tall like her father. She has his dark eyes and his dark hair that forms a shiny bob around her head. She likes bows, but to her frequent frustration, they never stay in place on her smooth, slippery hair.

She is happy today, dressed in her lightweight cream coat and a beret to match, sitting on my lap, looking out of the window and commenting with lively interest on the passing countryside. We are on our way to Port Said, with a large contingent of Polish mothers, their children and a group of older people who have survived all our journeys so far. Another journey, but we are close to the end. Perhaps one more after that.

My thoughts run ahead of me to Julian. I want to believe that all will be well, once we're together again. Our little daughter has never experienced a family home, has never enjoyed her father's presence. I want to believe that the start of the next phase of our journey on the day of her birthday is a good omen.

CHAPTER 46

We are on SS. Samaria sailing to England. I cannot imagine how much better the First Class and the Second Class accommodation could be, when our Third Class feels like a luxury. Especially when I think of that other sea voyage on the dark and oily waters of the Caspian Sea; the gnawing anxiety, the frightening sound of the rusty creaking vessel, the crushing overcrowding, the ill and the dying prostrate on the bare floor, the stench of human waste and blood soiling the perimeter of the upper deck.

Here, everything is clean and comfortable. The soldiers and the sailors, Polish and British make sure that all the public places maintain 'best hotel' standards. Three times a day, all civilian passengers descend the wide staircase into the dining hall. We are well catered for: a cereal and toasted bread for breakfast with varying additions of a boiled egg or ham or cheese or marmalade; a cooked lunch and a cooked supper. There's always a desert too. Ice-cream and jelly are Julia's favourite.

Cabins are shared. I'm with Adela. There is a narrow space between our bunk beds, but when we need to stretch our legs we go walking along the numerous corridors or out in the open on the upper decks. For Julia and Henio it is an adventure, giggling and whispering at bedtime on their upper bunks. They also enjoy with hordes of other children all the attractions of the playroom; roundabouts and see-saws and swings suited to their size. There are large open containers, like treasure chests, overflowing with small individual toys. Appointed child minders ensure safety and order, which gives us mothers a break and a chance for adult company.

Adela and I escape to the upper deck. I love the feel of the breeze on my face, of the fresh air filling my lungs. The sea is awesome in its vastness. I'm forever fascinated by its changing shades, that reflect the mood of the weather; the true blue on a peaceful day, the slate greyness of an imminent storm, the red horizon of the setting sun, the greens, the turquoises, the indigos in the folds of the waves.

My mirror flatters me more each day. There is a deepening colour in my cheeks, a honey tone to my skin. I cannot stop hoping with happy anticipation, that looking good for Julian will have a truly positive effect on his recovery.

Adela and I, and other girls too, get stopped constantly on our walks by the soldiers who have a need to talk to us. About their families. All histories are similar: deportations to Siberia, then Kazakstan, Uzbekistan, Persia. Then individual stories unravel: starvation, illnesses, deaths, grief. The same boys in the evenings put on shows for us with songs and comedy acts.

A certain Sergeant Czarek Bielski takes special interest in Adela. He sits with us most evenings at the concerts, treating us to soft drinks. His wife has been killed in the Warsaw uprising. His twelve-year-old son is with his brother's family in Krakow. Sergeant Bielski tells us often of his dream of being reunited with his son.

'I'd like to create a family home for him. I'd need the support of a good woman. But I could also be a good father to someone else's child.' He couldn't be more explicit than that.

When we are in bed at night, Adela whispers to me in the dark.

'It's not love, it's the necessity that drives him to say these things, Anastazia. I think that any woman would do for him. He is lonely. He wants to rebuild his life. Not necessarily with me.'

'I think he is sincere,' I tell her my honest observation. 'Why doesn't he court other women? Why does he always make a bee-line for you?'

She is silent for a while.

'You know,' she says, 'I never imagined I could warm to another man. There was never anyone else but Yanek. I think about him every single day. Yet I quite like Czarek too.'

'Is it surprising?' I ask, 'you've got a lot in common. You'd be good support for each other.'

'Then, do you think, I should..?'

'Adela, only you know how you really feel. Only you can make that decision. If Czarek really cares, he's not going to press, he'll wait for you.'

We sail past Gibraltar on a bright breezy day. We all want to see the rocks on which General Sikorski's plane crashed over four years ago. It is hard to imagine such tragedy on the white, sun-drenched shores, the rocks and the buildings so clear and precise in the distance, as if washed and polished. Later in the day, the ship's chaplain says Mass in the chapel for Sikorski's soul. The chapel and the extending hall are packed, the atmosphere is electric with reverence and pent-up emotions. The rousing sound of the male voices vibrates through every cell of my body when they sing:

Let us o Lord return to our free country!

For two days, as our boat negotiates the rough sea in the Bay of Biscay, people suffer with sea-sickness. I am one of the few lucky ones. Julia and Henio revel in the swaying of the boat and run up and down the passages to the playroom. Adela is badly affected and lies limp on her bed. I hold her up for regular sips of boiled water.

'My tongue is like a dry sponge,' she complains.

On the third day, the sea calms down, the boat regains its steady, serene pace and life returns to normal. Every time a landmark is announced on the loudspeaker, we make our way to the upper deck for viewing. It is hard to believe I'm so close to the shores of Portugal, then Lisbon, then the western flank of France and all those names of places I have only heard of before.

As our ship heads north the climate becomes chilly, then very cold. Each walk on the open deck requires a few more layers of clothing. It soon becomes clear that our lightweight garments are no match against the biting, piercing winds. Getting protective coats will be my priority on arriving in England.

Our boat SS.Samaria docks in Liverpool one freezing morning in the third week of January 1948. The damp, penetrating cold makes me shiver inside my two vests, a blouse, two cardigans and my light coat on top. I've pulled on my felt hat and wrapped a shawl round my shoulders. I've done the same for Julia, until she resembles a cabbage with all the layers on, but she is still trembling. She is holding onto my hand, her face pale, her eyes bewildered by the wall of bodies standing around us, waiting to descend the wide gangway.

We have already been divided into groups, each group instructed to follow their leader, an officer in uniform. There is a murkiness in the air hanging over us, blurring the outlines of the monumental red-brick buildings on the other side of the quay. There is a sudden surge and the crowd moves forward. Slowly we descend the wooden gangway that creaks and rumbles under the weight of hundreds of feet. A blast of cold air flows up underneath my coat making me flinch and shiver more. I cannot pick up Julia as my other hand is weighed down by my suitcase. Children whimper and cry with the cold, but soon we are down on the concrete quay, my first step on English soil, and we are hurriedly led by our guide inside a spacious building. The customs officers are ready at their desks. I fear that with hundreds of us arriving all at once, the checking process will take hours. But to my relief, each group is led to a waiting official, the group list is checked against our individual travel documents and we are passed through in a smoothly moving file.

The groups are kept together and led outside to a line of ready waiting coaches. There are mounds of dirty snow which has been swept from the pavements and has frozen solid. For a few minutes there is a commotion while our suitcases are packed into the side holds of the coaches. Finally we're on board. Our coach is unheated, as yet, but it is bliss to escape the biting cold and to sit down on a plush seat. I sit Julia on my lap and hug her to me, and soon we both feel as if we're thawing out.

I'm glad Adela is with me. She has her arms around Henio sitting on her lap, his nose and hands bright red. She tells me,

'Czarek's been directed to another coach. But he knows where we're going. Hertford Bridge. Near Morpeth. He said he'd get in touch with me.' She raises her eyebrows in question.

'I'm sure he will, Adela, I'm sure he will.'

She visibly shivers.

'I hope it's warmer where we're going. It's like being plunged into the Arctic after the tropics of Palestine.'

We leave in a convoy, perhaps a dozen coaches or so. The mist, becoming thick fog in places, ruins our chances of sight-seeing this sprawling city, and it is only after about an hour's drive that we are allowed a proper glimpse of this island, so much talked about in Eastern Europe, imagined, dreamed of. I cannot believe I am here.

We head north. The fog has disappeared completely. The undulating land is pristine white against an icy blue sky. Fields are neatly separated with unbroken lines of hedges or stone walls, the roads are cleared of snow, well-maintained, tar-black. Everything looks so well planned; post-card pretty. One thing surprises me though. Adela notices that too.

'How can they leave the livestock outside in this cold?'

Our farm animals are sheltered in barns through the winter months. I feel sorry for the herds of sheep huddling together close to the clumps of stark naked bushes.

The names of places we pass, announced by our guide, sound strange. Preston, Lancaster, Kendal. The children, apart from the odd squeal or cry, are surprisingly well behaved, pointing out things, intrigued by the snow which they have never seen before. Even the older ones, who were only babies in Siberia, have no recollection of snow. Julia keeps whispering questions to me, careful not to wake Henio, asleep on Adela's lap.

Around lunchtime, our guide makes an announcement.

'We are close to Penrith. We shall make a stop now at a camp called Lowther Park. The Guards Regiment has been stationed here through the war. Now it's one of the camps that has been vacated for the refugees. There's already a large group of our compatriots living here. You may even find some of your old friends!'

My heart races. Could Eva already be here? I wonder what happened to Mrs. Lekis and her boys? Has Mr. Ostrovski already gone to Poland with his grandsons? I wonder where Henryk may be stationed or Roman. Have Pavel and Agata been reunited with their fathers yet? And Julian. Does he know we're on our way? Will he be waiting for us?

We are taken down a narrow country road, flanked on both sides by a thick but totally bare hedge, then through a woodland area, where the trunks throw a pattern of shadows across the sparkling snow. Beyond that a sight emerges of black wooden barracks in neat rows on either side of the central road. Our coaches stop close to a cluster of brick and concrete buildings. I notice then that only two other coaches have arrived with us.

'Where are the others?' somebody asks.

'Sent to other refugee camps. In Wales and in the Midlands,' our guide replies. Adela gives me a questioning look.

366

'Czarek will find you,' I repeat my previous reassurance.

Our guide goes on to explain,

'We're stopping for a meal. And some hot tea!' he smiles. 'Toilet facilities are close to the canteen. Please be back in an hour. We'll assemble in the community hall for checking.'

On the square in front of the buildings a small crowd has gathered, people watching eagerly as we leave our coaches. I run my feverish gaze along their faces, but it is hard to see clearly anyone. They are all muffled up with shawls and scarves, hats pulled down, shading their eyes, and only the soldiers in their long winter coats, have their faces a little more exposed underneath their field caps. I can't help a twinge of disappointment when I don't recognize anyone.

Julia and I are both shivering, despite the shawls around our shoulders, and I steer her hurriedly towards the building. There are shouts of surprise and joy from the few people, who find each other after years of separation since that awful time in Russia.

I am astonished to hear my name called out.

'Anastazia! Mrs. Kalinska!' I stop and look around. A woman is running towards me with open arms, her face half hidden in the folds of her shawl. She embraces me and her greeting is a mixture of crying and laughter. Only when she pulls away the shawl from her face do I recognise Mrs. Lekis. I return her embrace with a sudden overwhelming feeling and we cling together, with Julia between us, like some long-lost sisters.

'Come, let's get inside, too cold to stand here,' the ever practical Mrs. Lekis hurries us indoors. There's already a queue at the food bar at the other end of the dining hall. The atmosphere is homely, warm, with a mixture of baking and frying aromas filling the air, promising a cooked meal.

We stand to the side. Mrs. Lekis can't take her eyes of me, as if she needed to memorise my face.

'Anastazia! After all those years! I can't believe it!' She looks down at Julia who is puzzled by all the activity around us. 'And your little daughter!' She strokes Julia's head. 'Go now, have something to eat first, and we'll meet in the community hall later.'

The NAAFI team, mainly uniformed women, are well organized. We are sat at the tables and given a hot meal of potatoes and stew, and to follow, a wedge of sponge cake and tea. For the first time in my life I drink tea with milk. I'm not sure about the taste yet, but it's hot and sweet and warms me up to the tips of my fingers and toes. Julia is a good eater, and at times like this, I am especially glad. Henio starts with all the zeal of a competitor, but then gets distracted by some siblings further down, arguing over the sizes of their portions.

Adela and I wait till our children have licked laboriously every last crumb off their plates, then we take them to the toilets. It is a brick building with twelve cubicles, proper toilet seats and cisterns for flushing, toilet paper and a row of hand basins. Luxury! Despite the freezing cold.

We rush back into the warmth of the community hall, busy and noisy with gathering people. Mrs. Lekis is already there, looking out for me. We sit down on the chairs lined along the walls.

'I'll keep an eye on them,' Adela says, when our children run off to join the others, who are letting off steam.

'Where are your boys?' I ask Mrs. Lekis, watching her face with fascination. Six years I've not seen her! Last time in Teheran when she joined the PSKs. She must be in her late forties now, but her face has a worn look, and the streak of hair escaping the pulled-on beret is grey. 'Florian and Dominik must be grown-up men now!'

She gives me a wide smile which takes years off her face.

'Indeed they are! Florian is twenty-one and Dominik nineteen. All the while when I served in the army, they attended the Young Cadets Schools. First in Palestine and then in England. They both did well. Managed to catch up with their interrupted schooling. Passed the matriculation exams and now they're both in Dublin. Florian studying medicine and Dominik engineering.'

I can hardly take it all in.

'You must be so proud of them! But why Dublin? Why so far? You must miss them terribly!'

She nods.

'It's not easy. They applied to a few places here, but Dublin was the only university inclined to show interest in them. I'm very happy for them, and I'm happy they can be together and look out for each other.'

'But how can you afford it all?' I ask the obvious question.

'Funds have been set up by the Polish authorities to help out young people. It's the most important thing to keep the education going. For us. For Poland. The Russians and the Germans have done their best to leave our society headless!' Her eyes fill up. 'No doubt everyone knows about Katyn.' I nod. She says, 'I lost my husband there. I've been sent official papers. This has made me all the more determined to do something worthwhile for our people. I've set up a temporary school in this camp for the younger children. While we wait to go back.'

I'm moved and overwhelmed by this woman's dedication to our country's cause. I cannot imagine how she lives with the horror of her husband's murder. I clasp her hand in both mine and all I can say is, 'I don't know how you do it, but you're doing a wonderful job!'

She shrugs as if this is nothing, and she asks what has been happening in my life. I tell her briefly, finishing,

'I pray hard every day that Julian is well when we finally get together. And after that, like everyone else, I just want to go home.'

We talk about the past, about the people we knew, about our future in fast, disjointed phrases, aware of the little time we've got. And when I have to go, Mrs. Lekis gives me a piece of paper with her address on it.

'Please write, Anastazia, as soon as you get settled in. And where is it, that place you're going to?'

'Hertford Bridge, we've been told. I've no idea where it is. Somewhere in the north of England. But of course, I'll write. We must never lose touch!'

We hug each other in a long, heart-felt embrace.

On this January day, dusk begins to fall in the mid afternoon. When our coaches arrive in Hertford Bridge camp before suppertime, it feels like midnight and most children are asleep. Someone asks our guide,

'Do our husbands know that we've arrived today? And how do we contact them?'

'Don't worry,' our guide assures her, 'the word soon gets round. There are three military camps nearby. One close by, one outside Morpeth and one in Felton Park. Every single day our boys send our their scouts for news of recent arrivals.'

And indeed, as we leave the coaches there are a few men in uniforms waiting, their faces lit up by the headlights. My heart beats faster as I peer and pray that one of them is Julian. There are shouts of recognition and joy. Men run to their wives and sweep them off their feet in strong and protective manly embraces. My heart sinks with disappointment and envy.

The whiteness of the snow is our guiding light, first to the dining hall for a hot meal and wonderful hot tea, and then along the paths between rows of wooden barracks to our allotted accommodation. Each barrack has four rooms, with a door at each end and a small shared entrance to access the two adjoining rooms. Adela and I take up rooms next to each other.

The most luxurious thing about my basically furnished room is the warmth generating from the iron stove in the corner. There is a bucket of coal and a box of chopped wood. Julia has a child's wooden cot next to my bed. There's also a small table with two chairs, and a tall narrow wardrobe in the corner. I'm overwhelmed with gratitude for all these objects of comfort that someone has prepared for us.

Julia is tired and sleepy. Her bath will have to wait till tomorrow. I unpack her pyjamas, get her ready for bed, cover her with the rough sheet and the army blanket, and she is asleep within seconds.

Our nearest washroom and toilets have been pointed out to us on the way. I take turns with Adela to mind our sleeping children, as we each make a dash to the icily cold brick building. Just face and hands and teeth for now, and then it's bliss to be back in the warmth of my room. Underneath the covers I stretch out my stiff limbs with a shiver of pleasure. I close my eyes and think about Julian. So near yet so far! Please God, let it be tomorrow.

CHAPTER 47

My body clock wakes me up at half-past seven the next morning. It is still dark outside, but the whiteness of the snow filtering through the bare windows gives enough light to see round the room. The window panes are covered in patterns of frost. I feel the cold on my exposed face and hands. My first priority is to relight the fire.

I get up and wrap my coat, my flimsy summer coat, around me. I check Julia, still sleeping, readjust the blanket around her and add a shawl on top. Some kind soul has left everything in place for lighting the fire in the stove: matches, some old newspapers, and a little shovel for removing the ashes into a pan.

As I crouch round the stove watching the fire spread through the layers of wood and coal, I realise that Julia and I will immediately need some warmer clothing. As soon as I get together with Julian, that'll be my priority.

Later, I find out the Red Cross Centre is here to assist. When we meet up with the seasoned inhabitants of the camp in the communal dining hall, with the warm damp fug of tea and toast hanging comfortably about us, they tell us also of a travelling pedlar, who visits the camp regularly with his suitcase, out of which he sells women's and children's underwear, socks and stockings and knitting wool.

'For less than three shillings you can knit yourself a cardigan,' one woman tells me, showing off her patchwork masterpiece. 'The only problem is he never has enough wool in the same colour. But who cares?' She smiles, pleased. 'As long as it's warm and it's not Siberia!'

After breakfast, Adela and I visit the Red Cross Centre, together with other mothers and their shivering children. It is a heated room, thank goodness, with a counter behind which two women in their Red Cross uniforms write down our requests on a piece of paper and disappear through the door into a back room, from where they bring out the needed items, as close as possible to given sizes. The queue is long; Julia and Henio amuse themselves with some imaginary games as they stand between Adela and me.

I am overjoyed when I get a warm coat for Julia. It is a boy's green tweed coat. There's also a jumper in her size. It is navy and rather severe in colour, but very practical, I tell myself. Henio's clothes are all grey and he looks like a little old man except for his child's pleased face.

There is no excess of warm coats for women, but we obtain long thick knitted cardigans, scarves and pull-on hats. Odd balls of wool are also available, so we take a few to knit mittens for us all.

Before we venture out to explore the camp, Adela and I resort to our well tried methods of keeping warm, learnt in Russia: layers of clothing and wrapping our feet in rags on top of stockings and socks.

The layout of the camp is similar to the ones we've experienced in recent months, except that the sand has been replaced with snow. Julia and Henio are irresistibly drawn to it, mimicking other children who appear drunk with the excitement. They throw themselves on it, roll about in it, taste it, make balls. Some older children have started making a snowman. Julia and Henio clamour to join them. We stand back and watch and soon, with their faces getting redder and their hands colder they give in and come back to us to have their hands rubbed warm.

We stroll along the central path flanked with neat rows of black-stained wooden barracks on each side, till we get to what used to be the sentry post at the entrance of the camp. It is abandoned now, but marching towards us is a group of soldiers in their long winter coats.

My heart flips and I hasten my pace. They come level with us and stop, their smiling faces welcoming, their eyes as searching as mine. Julian is not among them.

'Where are you from, ladies?' one of them asks. We tell them and then I add, 'Do you know my husband by any chance? Julian Kalinski.'

They exchange glances but then shake their heads. One of them explains, 'We're just from outside this place. But your husband may be in Morpeth or in Felton Park. Don't worry. Sooner or later he'll come looking for you.'

They move on, and I cannot hide my disappointment from Adela.

'It's only our first day here,' she says. 'All the other people will be waiting like you. Even I,' she adds with a little smile. 'I wonder if Czarek will keep his word?'

Her calm, uncomplaining remark makes me appreciate, that I at least have a husband to look forward to. I perk up for her sake.

'Adela dear, he won't let you go, if he's got any sense. And I think he has. And a lot of affection for Henio too.'

We don't venture out any further, we just look around. The view beyond the sloping field is of a sprawling farm with a wood in the background. The bare crowns of the trees are covered with frost and blend with the pale sky.

'It's beautiful,' Adela says shivering, 'but perhaps enough for one day.'

We return to the warmth of our rooms and start knitting, while Julia and Henio play on my bed with their few toys.

In the afternoon, after a warming cooked lunch of noodles and mince and tinned pears, we stop in the entrance where notices and newsletters are displayed. We discover there is a playschool held daily in the community hall.

Also in the adjoining building, classes for women in all manner of handiwork: sewing, knitting, embroidery, crocheting, 'in a pleasant atmosphere of sociability'.

The community hall is a spacious Nissen hut, with concave, corrugated iron walls, and chairs round the floor for mothers if they want to stay. Taking the lead in the ring games is Mrs. Czerska, a teacher from Poland, and her daughter Helenka, a pretty young girl with a plait down her back. Holding hands together, Julia and Henio skip off totally unconcerned to join in the games, while some children cling tearfully to their mothers.

Adela and I take this opportunity to slip out just across the passage to a twin Nissen hut, that acts as the adult common room, where the visiting soldier husbands play snooker or darts in breaks from an animated talk with their wives and companions, who sit at the coffee tables, enveloped in a haze of cigarette smoke.

Adela and I find a table, unbutton our coats and the three layers of cardigans and pull off our knitted berets. I loosen my squashed hair with my fingers and rub my itchy scalp. Adela has sensibly plaited her hair at the back. My eyes dart around the room with envious interest. All those lucky women! With their husbands already!

'Well, here we are Adela. I wonder what next?'

She shrugs and gives me a resigned smile.

'We can't do much else, but wait. You know what?' her glance goes around the room and comes back to me, 'I still get moments when I hope there's been some mistake, you know, about my Yanek. Even though I've got all his papers. I look around and hope against all hope that I'll see his face in the crowd.' Her eyes become moist. 'People mean well and they tell me how it'll pass. Give it time. You're still young. You've got to think about your child now. Etcetera... etcetera...'

Perhaps Czarek, Sergeant Bielski, will fill that void for her, but I keep that thought to myself.

'And of course, people are right,' she continues. 'I've got to consider Henio. It won't get me anywhere feeling sorry for myself. So I've been thinking, I'm a trained nurse, I shall look for a part-time job to begin with. Till Henio goes to school. And afterwards, who knows? It'll get easier when we return home in the end. My parents are living now in the Wroclaw region where they've been transferred from Lvov. I'm just thankful that they are still alive.'

I admire her spirit. I cannot boast professional skills. I was just a housewife at home. But I'm prepared to look for any work that will help Julian and me to rebuild our life together.

A uniformed man, an officer, judging by the white V on his sleeve, turns away from watching the snooker and comes over to us.

'On your own, ladies?' he asks. He is slim with hollow cheeks and a shock of blond hair, with the sides of his head shaved almost clean.

'Just waiting for our children,' I indicate with a nod towards the noise of the children's games in the adjacent hall.

'Care for a smoke?' He produces a silver looking cigarette holder from his pocket. I decline, but Adela takes one. He lights it for her asking,

'Mind if I join you?'

We don't mind. I sense straight away that all he needs is to talk about his family. I am right. As soon as he draws up his chair, he says,

'I'm waiting for my wife and my two boys. One eight and one nearly five.'

'Where from?' I ask.

'India. I thought your transport yesterday was theirs.'

'Sorry to disappoint you,' Adela breathes out the words with the smoke, but she sounds sincere.

'Not at all. We're all waiting for someone or something,' he says.

'India, did you say?' I ask. 'I've got a friend in India. In Valivade.'

His face brightens up with surprise.

'The same place!' he exclaims. 'Their transport should arrive any day now!'

My heart somersaults. Eva! My dear Eva. Is it possible that I'll be seeing her soon?

'But how do you know they'll be sent here?' I ask. 'Out of our transport only three coaches were sent up to this camp.'

'Frankly, I don't know,' he replies, 'but since I'm stationed near Morpeth, I count on some logic when sending out our families to their destinations. The whole purpose is to reunite us.'

I count on that too. I hope that Julian is stationed nearby, and that any day now he'll come looking for us.

We make polite conversation, always the same when strangers get together: that awful night of the arrests at home, then Siberia, Uzbekistan, Persia. Freedom.

'And still nothing much has changed,' the officer squints through the smoke. 'We've been given this time now to consider our options. But what's there to consider? We can't go back straight into the clutches of the communists. And Stalin will never willingly withdraw. And who's going to fight him? Poles on their own? The 2nd Corps? We're not that even more. The Polish Resettlement Corps. That's what we've been renamed. Only the accepting ones. Those who have opted out are kept apart in separate camps, like some pariahs!' He exhales a long ribbon of smoke. 'And do you know what else? They've actually allowed agents from the communist government in Poland to come over and infiltrate our camps and persuade people to return. Lecturing us that it is our duty to go back and rebuild our country! Our country that they've ruined!'

The officer speaks with passion and we listen politely to allow him the chance to vent his indignation.

'And another thing,' he adds, 'the unions here hate us. And is it a wonder?

Many of them are communists. But they've no idea what Soviet communism is really like. All they see is alien Poles coming over and wanting to steal their jobs!'

'Are you surprised?' I ask, 'It's not easy for them either. Being demobbed in their thousands, looking for jobs, struggling with all kinds of shortages. It must be pretty galling having to compete with all those refugees on top of everything else.'

The officer raises his eyebrows as if disapproving of my remark.

'We've never asked for it, have we?' he points out. 'All we ever wanted was to go back to our free country. And what did Churchill and Roosevelt do?'

There's no argument against that. Adela adds,

'This shouldn't be such a problem for the British. They've got colonies all over the world!'

'Oh please, not another journey!' I protest.

'Well actually,' the officer leans over the table,' there is talk of emigrating to Canada or Australia. America and Argentina have agreed to take in limited numbers too.'

My thoughts spin with these new ideas. Life on another continent? So far away from Poland? I look around to get rid of such images from my mind, and my glance stops on two soldiers at the door, long winter coats and field caps in their hands. My heart misses a beat, though in a split second I know that neither of them is Julian. One looks late thirties, good-looking, young face, but his hair is completely white. Distinguished. He says something to his companion, a younger man with black hair and those unmistakeable violet eyes.

I feel a rush of excitement and an overwhelming emotion. I run up to him and he opens his arms with a look of utter surprise, enfolds me in his brotherly embrace.

'Roman! All those years!' I gasp.

He releases me and stands back for a better look.

'Anastazia! This is incredible!' He turns to his companion, his eyes shining, his face creased with joy. 'Theo, this is my best friend from my worst times!'

The man called Theo shakes my hand and gives me a friendly smile. His grey eyes give me exclusive attention. I notice a beauty spot on his clean-shaven left cheek. 'So pleased to meet you.' His surname is Lutovski.

I return his smile and look back towards Adela. She and the officer watch us with interest.

'Please, join us at the table,' I invite Roman and his friend. Short introductions follow, after which our incidental companion, the officer, politely withdraws, and we sit down, the four of us.

My questions are burning.

'Roman, do you know where Julian is? Have you seen him? Is he all right? How can I contact him?'

Roman laughs, 'Nastusha dear, one question at a time!' He pats my shaking hand on the table, 'just hear me out.'

I sense constraint in his deceptively light-hearted tone. I'm aware of Theo's eyes on me, and of Adela's quiet as she draws on her cigarette.

'Is he all right?' I cannot help myself.

'He is getting better all the time...' Roman hesitates.

'Tell me! Tell me everything!' I cannot bear not knowing.

'All right,' Roman's shoulders sag as if he's giving in, 'it's good news on the whole, but Julian still gets his bad days.'

'Bad days?'

'He gets forgetful. Or easily upset. He cries...'

'Cries?'

'But we look after him. Theo and I. He lives with us in Felton Park. Just a few miles from here.'

'Then where is he? Why hasn't he come with you?' Disappointment and anxiety threaten to erupt in a burst of tears.

'Nastusha,' Roman pats my hand, 'he is all right. He is away. For a few days. In the Midlands. A place called Derby. A friend of his may be able to secure a job for him.' I breathe out with relief. But then Roman adds, 'in a warehouse.'

'A warehouse!' I cannot picture that at all. 'But that's not at all for Julian! He loves the forests. The wide open spaces!'

Roman nods with sympathy.

'We'd all like to return to what we did before. But this isn't Poland. And time has moved on. Eight years!'

Adela and Theo are passive listeners, their glances bouncing from Roman to me.

'So what now?' I ask, just to say anything in my utter defeat.

'Nastusha!' Roman sits up and sounds energetic. 'There are things going on all the time! So we've been disarmed, drawn into the Resettlement Corps. So what! We've got to make the most of every situation. We've been offered courses in all variety of subjects to prepare ourselves for work. Now, isn't that a positive thing? Julian's learning English together with Theo and me, and also doing a carpentry course.'

'Really?' I feel a sudden lift. Perhaps not everything is beyond hope. 'So he is well enough to do such things?'

'Yes,' Theo assures me,' we go together to the woodwork classes. He gets really absorbed in his work and I think that's very good for him.'

I feel a warm feeling towards this man, eternal gratitude.

'Julian's very lucky to have friends like you,' I say, 'and I cannot thank you enough.'

He makes a movement with his hand as if my thanks were not necessary. 'Please, don't mention it. What are friends for?' He turns to Adela and offers her another cigarette. And I ask Roman,

'Tell me, what have you been doing with yourself all those years? What about your theological studies?'

Roman gives a half-smile and sends Theo a quick glance. But Theo's talking to Adela. Roman's violet eyes give me a thoughtful look then he gazes down at his clasped hands on the table.

'All that is behind me now, Nastusha. Lots of things have happened. I've changed. But you can't live looking back all the time. So...' he sits up and his chest expands with a deep breath, ' I intend to do English at matriculation level to enable me to pass other exams. I want to teach mathematics at college level. It's a universal subject. I think I'll manage that.'

'Oh Roman, of course you will!' I'm filled with awe and admiration. Then I notice Theo looking at me. 'And you, Mr. Lutovski, what are your plans for the future? Where are your family now?'

He removes the cigarette from his mouth and his reply comes with short puffs of smoke.

'Before the war, I had a job in railway management. I cannot expect anything like that now. Perhaps a porter? If they'll let me.'

'And your family?'

He shakes his cigarette over the ash tray before replying. 'I'm on my own.'

Roman butts in,

'Theo's my sergeant. And my hero. He's saved my life. Pulled me out from underneath a mound of soil when a bomb exploded close to us. Even with a wounded thigh he dragged me to a safe place.'

I watch Theo through Roman's account. He shrugs and comments,

'No big deal if you do it for a friend!'

'But,' Roman continues, 'his bravery cost him. His hair turned white all in one night!'

Adela and I look at Theo with interest. He runs his fingers through his hair, releasing a faint scent of hair cream. Pleasant. Clean. He shrugs again.

'Sooner or later I'd turn white anyway. And it's not as if I need to be perfect for a beauty contest!'

We laugh and our talk turns light-hearted. They both chat to Adela for a while and then we reminisce about our friends.

'Ryszard and Oleg,' Roman tells me, 'have been reunited with their children and have both decided to emigrate to Canada. Montreal, I think.'

'For good?'

'Most probably.'

'But it's so far away! I'll never see them!' An ache, hidden deep, surfaces again.

'Nastusha, who knows? Once things settle, anything is possible.'

'Pavel will be quite a young man now. And Agatka grown up too. Eighteen! Can you imagine that? You've not told me about Henryk. Is he all right?'

'He's here too. In Morpeth camp. Waiting for Eva to arrive.'

'So that's certain then? She'll come here?' My heart leaps. Some good news at last! 'And is he well?'

Theo turns my way. 'Outwardly,' he says, 'Henryk's recovered well from his shrapnel wounds down his back. That shouldn't stop him from doing any work.'

Poor Henryk, I feel deeply for him. Always so proud of his healthy physique, so active, sport loving, competitive, have-a-go-at-anything-Henryk. 'But…?' I prompt.

Theo's expression becomes serious.

'When I first knew Henryk,' he says, ' back in Alexandria, and when we sailed to Italy, he was always that gregarious chap. The soul of any party. But the fact is, the war has affected us all. We've all seen dreadful things. Some things are impossible to forget. Some people manage better than others. But no one, if they honestly admit it, is free from their bad days…'

'Like a lot of men,' Roman adds, 'he is struggling with depression.'

'Depression?' I'm relieved it's nothing worse. 'But that's like feeling sad. I'm sure when Eva arrives he'll feel better straight away.'

Roman shakes his head. 'It will help a lot, no doubt, but depression is not just a mood. It's an illness, Nastusha. I don't think enough is understood about it. And because it's not a visible thing like a broken arm or a rash on your body, people expect you just to snap out of it. He can't, poor chap. I think he's still missing the family he was billeted with in Italy. They were like his own people. Paola, their oldest daughter was besotted with him.'

'But she knew he was married. Surely!' I'm a little surprised.

Roman gives an understated smile as if humouring a child.

'Things happen Nastusha. Not always to plan.'

God, don't I know it! I think about Henryk, his open, friendly nature, and I think about Eva. And her terrible secret. Why couldn't our lives have been allowed to go on in peace at home?

It is time for Adela and me to fetch our children. Roman and Theo get up too.

'How are you getting back?' I ask, 'Do you want to stay for the evening meal? Apparently guests can be fed too for a small standard price.'

'Yes, I know, and thanks,' Roman replies, 'but I've borrowed the jeep. We need to get back in time. But I promise, we'll come again. Soon.'

CHAPTER 48

The next day and the day after I'm on tenterhooks waiting and looking out for Julian. It's like a constant ache inside me. But life goes on and the days that follow become a routine of regular meals at the dining hall, keeping our quarters warm with provided coal and wood, walks in the morning, playschool for the children in the afternoons, while Adela and I take this opportunity to join the women's sewing or knitting groups.

We sometimes venture out, despite the biting winds, into Hertford Bridge village, with its attractive bridge over the River Blythe, now swollen and fast running, crashing noisily against the banks. There is a post office and a grocery shop where we sometimes step in to buy biscuits for our children. We certainly look like tramps in our assortment of layers and colours and all conversation stops and quiet looks are passed between other customers, usually ladies in warm tweed coats and felt hats. But they acknowledge us with a nod and a polite smile. The serving lady is always courteous and now that she knows our needs she anticipates our requests. She weighs two separate quarters of biscuits in two small brown bags, and smiles with thanks for our prepared exact amounts and coupons. That is something that is pleasantly noticeable about the few English people we have met here: they smile at us. Even in the street. Even though we are strangers.

Today, the weather has turned even colder. Flurries of snow keep coming down, blurring the shapes of the barracks on either side of ours, making everything else beyond invisible.

Adela and I sit by the stove in my room knitting, and the children are sitting on the bed playing with their toys. There are sounds outside my bare, snowed-over window, like stamping of feet to shake off the snow. Then a hard knock on the door. I still get that split second of fear at any banging noise. But this is England. This is friendly, safe noise.

I put down the knitting and walk over to the narrow little entrance, to our shared front door. As I open it, snow is blown in together with two uniformed figures in their long army coats covered white. Even before they remove their field caps, my legs turn weak and my whole body trembles. Julian and Roman. I throw myself at Julian, disregarding the layer of snow down his front. I don't want to cry, but sobs burst out of me as I press my face against his cold cheek. There is a moment's hesitation before his arms embrace me. It is Roman who speaks first.

'Nastusha, shall we get out of our coats first?'

'Of course!' I let go of Julian and step back and watch them take off their coats and hang them on the hooks by the door. Desperately I want Julian to look at me, but there is something distant in his manner. We come inside the room, the children look up from their play on the bed and Adela gets up. Polite introductions follow, Adela says, 'It's lovely to meet you Julian, after everything I've heard about you, and it's so nice to see you again, Roman, but I'll go to my room now and let you have some time to yourselves. Let's go Henio, you can come back later.'

Both children protest and that relaxes Julian's features and a small amused smile appears. I can't stop looking at him, noting every detail of his face. Everything's the same, and yet not. There is a reticence about him as if he was seeing us for the first time.

Julia cries when Henio is led away, and she hides her face in my skirt. I invite Julian and Roman to sit down on the two chairs close to the stove and I sit down on the edge of the bed, hoisting Julia up beside me. There is a brief moment of strained silence which I'm desperate to break.

'Look Julia, this is your Daddy!'

To my relief he leans forward towards her and stretches out his arms. But she looks away and presses her face against my side. Incredibly, he is undeterred and tries again,

'Look Julia, look! I've got something here for you!' He sounds like my old Julian and there's liveliness in his face. His dark hair shows signs of greying at the temples, and where he's been injured, his hair has re-grown all grey. I think that only adds to his good looks. To me he'll always be my handsome Julian.

He holds out a large paper bag to Julia.

'Look inside,' he coaxes her. The lure of the mystery is too strong. She turns towards him and stretches out her hand.

'How about a kiss first. Here on my cheek,' he leans further and points to the side of his face.

She withdraws shyly and hides her face against my arm.

'Just pick her up Julian,' I suggest. His eyes meet mine. I long for the warmth and longing in them, but there is no sign of a connection between us. He picks up Julia onto his lap, but she is stiff in his arms and his embrace is clumsy. He kisses her on top of her head, puts her down and gives her the paper bag. Eagerly, she brings out his present: a child's red leather bag.

'Look inside,' he invites, his voice gentle. She presses open the metal catch, and lifts up the flap. Her preoccupied expression melts in a wide smile.

'Look Mama! *Cukierki!* Sweets!' She lifts up her arms to show me. There are two paper bags stuffed inside, one filled with jelly sweets, the other with broken mint rock pieces. I'm impressed.

'How did you manage that!' I exclaim with exaggerated excitement. For the first time, as he looks at me, he gives me a smile, exclusively for me. I feel a burst of warmth inside me.

'Just been saving coupons,' he says simply.

'Mama!' Julia interrupts and looks straight into my eyes, her expression like a puppy's, all love and loyalty and begging. I understand her perfectly.

'All right, you may have one of each for now. Take one of each for Henio. And we'll save the rest for later.'

When she is gone next door, with her rag doll and handkerchiefs and the treasured offering for her best friend Henio, I can at long last concentrate solely on Julian. Roman's been a patient, passive observer all this while, and I appreciate that.

'Boys,' I address them both, 'I can't offer you anything except some dry biscuits, but later I'm treating you to a hot tea and cake. Agreed?'

Roman smiles, amused, but Julian peers at me with concentration. It is unnerving.

'Anastazia. I remember your name. You're the same person as on the photograph. From Jerusalem, I think.' A coldness creeps into my heart.

'Julian, it's me. Your wife. And Julia is your child.'

He nods but there is puzzlement in his eyes.

'I want to remember. I really do!'

I swallow hard the lump in my throat as he continues, 'I get your photograph out every day. Things flash through my mind. Scary. Horrible things. Things I want to forget.'

Tears gather in my eyes.

'Don't be afraid any more, Julian. I'm here now. I'll look after you. You'll never be alone again.'

He does not reply, just stares at the floor. Then his attention transfers to fumbling at his breast pocket. He pulls out a packet of cigarettes and offers one to Roman. I watch them lighting and exhaling, I watch Julian's closed countenance and his thin shaky hand. I long to hold him in my arms. I long to be held by him. He speaks suddenly,

'My friend is already demobbed… Edek. We were together in Italy… '

I interrupt,

'You remembered your friend? But not me? Not even your daughter?'

He looks stumped. Then he makes it clear.

'But he's always been with me!'

I feel ashamed of my question. It was petty, demeaning.

'Dear Julian,' I soften my voice, 'thank God, you've had good friends like him!'

Julian gives me a considered look,

'Yes, he's found me a job. In a warehouse. Packing motor parts. Stacking them on trucks.'

'Haven't you had enough of trains and trucks?' I want to lighten the mood, but he just gives me another puzzled look. I think of his love of the forests and open spaces. I keep these thoughts to myself. 'That's very good news, Julian,' I say, 'so when will you be starting? When will we be moving south?'

Another perplexed expression and a strained silence, skimmed faintly by his exhalation of smoke. I feel as if there is a chasm between us, but then his composure surprises me when he speaks,

'I'm waiting for my demob papers. I'll be moving to Derby for good.' His brow puckers in thought. 'I'll find lodgings for you too.'

His words summon up hope and uncertainty at the same time. I hang onto hope. At least he's actually planning for Julia and me.

'I'll look forward to that, Julian. I think it's time we started living normal lives again. Not like a pack of animals, forever in groups.'

Later, when we sit together in the dining hall, Julian and Roman facing me and Julia across the table, I watch Julian's fascination with his daughter. Roman and I make small talk over our rations of a sponge cake and tea, and Julian's eyes follow Julia's every move. She takes small careful sips of her cooled tea and breaks her piece of cake into crumbs which she then laboriously brings up to her mouth, one by one, multiple times. Her attention is wholly absorbed by some noisy children on the next table.

'She'll use up all her energy before she's finished eating her cake,' I remark to Julian for something to say. He nods and smiles and continues watching her with, (dare I say it, or am I just imagining?) a hint of pride. I continue chatting with Roman. At some point Julian leaves us to visit the toilet. When he is gone I drop my guard before Roman.

'Dear God! I never imagined it was going to be so hard! What am I going to do?'

Roman delays replying and speaks to Julia instead. He compliments her on her red bow. She pats her head self-consciously but then awards him with a happy smile. 'Like my new handbag,' she says. 'I've still got it,' she allows him a glimpse of her newly acquired possession before replacing it on the bench between us. 'Mummy says I mustn't spill tea on it.'

'That's very good advice,' he smiles at her and then looks at me. 'Anastazia, it's not going to be easy. There's no immediate cure for Julian's condition. I can't even give you any concrete advice that will bring sure results. I can only give you my thoughts. What Julian needs is a lot of patience, a lot of understanding and a lot of time.'

I listen to his words and I try to absorb their full implications and all the while I feel this bitterness inside me, as if I've been cheated by fate.

'I'll give him everything he needs. But all I ever wanted is just a normal life.'

'We all want that.'

'Then why?...Why are we being given these crosses to bear? As if what we've already been through was still not enough!'

Roman shakes his head and replies gently.

'Nastusha, God only gives you what you can bear.'

I don't want to argue with him, but what would he know, a young cleric that he was at the time, about losing a child, about a long term separation between a husband and wife, about the constant racking torment between hope and despair?

'Oh really? Now you speak like a priest!' I feel agitation rising within me and to calm myself, I stroke Julia's head. She looks up then carries on counting her crumbs. Roman's silence irritates me. I challenge him with my gaze. There is a sadness in his expression.

'I'm no longer a cleric, Nastusha. I lost my vocation. Over a girl. Then I lost her too.' His words and his tone pull me sharply together. I am all attention.

'Roman, what are you saying?' His eyes roam the crowded lively dining hall, then they come back to me. I notice little telling lines on his face, which I did not see before. All at once, I feel cross with myself, and contrite for my self-absorption. 'Roman, I'm so sorry!'

He gives Julia a praising smile then the pain returns to his eyes as he speaks to me.

'Her name was Claudia. She was beautiful. And not just because I say so. She came up to me in the crowded street on the day of celebrations in Bologna. The day the end of the war was declared. She said she'd been looking for me all her life...' a little smile hovers on his lips at the memory, 'and now that she'd found me, she said, I had to meet her family.'

His description creates a vivid scene in my imagination, a beautiful dark-haired girl, a handsome soldier, with eyes only for each other amongst a singing, dancing crowd in a sunlit square.

'But how did you communicate?'

'Knowing Latin helped,' he grins. 'They took me in like one of their own. I was billeted with them for over a year. Nastusha,' his sigh is deep, heart-felt, 'it was the happiest time of my life. And yet I was constantly racked with guilt.'

'Why?'

'This thing, about giving up my vocation, about putting myself first. As a priest I would have been serving the church and the people. That had been my passion and my dream for so long. And I so easily gave it all up.'

'Wasn't Claudia worth it?'

'Every cell of her body!'

'There you are! Accept it. God had other plans for you. So what happened next?'

Roman's eyes darken. 'Fate, Nastusha. The most cruel fate! Claudia survived all the bombings in all the war years only to be killed in peace time.'

I gasp and Julia looks up startled.

'Roman,' words fail me, 'dear Roman, how, when?'

He composes himself, his jaw clenching for a long moment, before he speaks.

'She was just standing at a bus-stop. A builder's truck went out of control and ploughed into the queue of these unfortunate people. A number were injured, only two were killed, and Claudia was one of them.'

I am so shocked I remain silent. The enormity of his loss and grief hits me like a boulder. How could I ever imagine that my suffering was superior to his? I cringe with mortification and contrition. I seek his hand across the table and press it between both mine.

'Roman, I'm so sorry, so very sorry.' My eyes begin to sting. He returns my touch with a manly handshake and attempts to lighten his tone.

'My dear Nastusha, save your confession for a real priest.'

His words break the tension, I smile and tell him about my experience with Father Oczko, but all the while I can't stop thinking about the girl Roman had loved and lost. I want to know so much more. One day I shall ask him.

When Julian returns we resume our small talk and it feels as if Julian is somebody else and not my husband that I had been yearning for all those years. And later, when it's time for them to go, I am overwhelmed with the sadness of our parting, and the fact that he is unable to offer to stay with me, because I am a stranger to him. His hug is perfunctory, because politeness demands that of him. He leaves with a promise to visit me soon, but he cannot say when.

CHAPTER 49

It is the first week in February. The frost-preserved snow is sparkling in the sharp sunlight that makes you squint. In the long shadows between the black barracks, the air is like a breath from the Arctic and it hurts your lungs. Every morning I wake up to frost patterns on the window panes and icicles like needles hanging from the frame. Bracing myself against leaving the warmth of my bed, I get up, pull on layers of cardigans and then attempt to light the fire. Once the fire gets going, I escape again to the comfort of my bed till the temperature in the room loses that acutely frigid feel.

I think about Julian. I think about him when I go to bed. I think about him in the early hours, when I regularly wake up and cannot get back to sleep again. I tell myself to be patient. Adela tells me the same, but I cannot stop my imaginings racing ahead of me and creating images that induce an anxious heart beat.

'Anastazia,' Adela reminds me, 'it's all in your mind. Nothing has happened yet.' But it's the uncertainty of our situation that torments me.

Today, when Adela and I leave the dining hall after lunch, Julia and Henio pulling our hands, there is excitement outside, in the central drive, which acts as a turning point for any visiting traffic. Three coaches have just arrived. Warmed up by the hot soup, we stop with the gathering crowd and watch.

The new arrivals descend the coach steps, visibly shiver and wrap their coats and shawls tightly around them, muffle their children with scarves and woollen hats. There's something startlingly incongruous about their summer shoes and sandals.

I focus my eyes hard, like a hawk, hope bubbling inside me for a glimpse of Eva. Dear God, please let her be on this transport! After all the years! As the crowd increases and the two sides mingle in a busy commotion, it is hard to recognize anyone in their all-covering wraps. Guiding soldiers call out for their groups to follow them into the dining hall.

'Adela,' I request, 'could you take Julia with you? I'll go back and look for Eva. Who knows? Perhaps she's arrived.'

I wait against the wall at the back of the hall and watch the long queue of the newly arrived make their way slowly up to the counter where hot food is dished out. As soon as they are seated at the rows of tables and their outdoor clothing is loosened and the head covers are taken off in the warm steaming atmosphere, I spot her. Unmistakeably Eva, with her sun-bleached hair, pulled back smooth and twisted into a knot at the back. It is as if my soul has grown wings. I float towards her and wrap my arms around her from the back. Surprised, she turns her head around. Astonishment stills her features for a split second then her face breaks into an animated smile.

'Anastazia! My dear Nastusha! Who would have thought it!' She scrambles up from the bench and holds me so tight I can hardly breathe. I laugh and my eyes fill up and I return her embrace and we hold each other for a long moment and then I laugh again at the jolly comments from her companions on the table.

'Eva dearest,' I'm able to talk at last, 'we'll have lots of time afterwards. Eat your lunch now, and come to me later. I'm in barrack 28.'

But she still holds on to me with one hand and with the other she points to the two little girls with her, now hungrily enjoying their meal.

'Look how grown up Stella is now!' She strokes the older girl's head, white-blond like her own. And when Stella looks up at us, her eyes are as crystal blue as her mother's. 'And this is our little Nadia. Our little *Nadzieja. Hope!*' The small child lifts up her face and I find what I have been expecting all along: dark dewy eyes, like black marbles, Selim's eyes. It is still a shock and for a moment I struggle not to show it. When I look at Eva, it is with great joy.

'Eva, this is the happiest day for me, for a long time! Enjoy your lunch now and come to see me later.'

It is about an hour later when Eva knocks on my door. All the while I've been waiting for her my mind has been doing countless reruns of our past experiences endured together. We hold each other for a long time, fighting back the urge to cry.

'Enough!' Eva says at last and loosens her embrace, as three pairs of eyes look on mesmerised.

'Coats off,' I suggest, laughter bubbling inside me while I help Stella and Nadia out of their coats and hats and scarves. Then we all sit down close to the stove, the girls in a row on the edge of the bed. Julia already holds Nadia's hand in a ready-to-be-your-friend manner, but Nadia leans away from her against Stella's side, uncertain yet of this new situation.

'Stella,' Eva's excitement is evident in her lively hand gestures, 'your auntie Anastazia has been my best friend through all the bad times in Russia.'

'I know Mama,' Stella's brilliant eyes sparkle, 'you've told me so many times!' She gives me a dimpled smile and I feel a rush of love for this child whom we've nurtured through starvation and illnesses.

'You cannot imagine,' I tell her, 'how happy you've made me to see you again. And this is your little sister! So beautiful too!'

Stella places a possessive arm over the small child's shoulders. Dark complexion, dark curly hair and snow-white teeth. Selim's parents would have doted on her.

'And this is your little Julia! Spitting image of her father!' Eva leans forward and drops a small bar of chocolate in Julia's lap. Julia's face lights up and she looks appealingly at me.

'All right,' I laugh and stand up. I break the chocolate on a plate into small sections for the girls to share, and add my offering of biscuits and jelly beans. They make themselves comfortable on the bed, with the plate in the middle and Julia's simple and few toys challenging imaginative play.

For about an hour Eva and I talk incessantly, remembering people and places, and all the while all I want to know is just one thing: the circumstances of Nadia's birth. Our little girls become restless, but then Adela appears in the guise of a rescuing angel.

'I'm just taking Henio to the playroom. Who wants to come with me?'

Stella jumps off the bed, Nadia follows clinging to her, and Julia runs up to Henio to give him a hug. Wrapped and swathed in layers of clothing and muffled up to their eyes, they follow Adela happily into the cold outside.

Eva and I sit down again and I come straight to the point.

'Eva, tell me everything. The whole truth. I think I've guessed most of it, but tell me, how did you arrange Nadia's birth registration. What did you tell Henryk? And what did he say?'

Her eyes are locked with mine for a long moment as if she is struggling with where to begin and I worry that perhaps my questions were too invasive and abrupt. I'm just about to correct myself, when she says,

'I suppose I'd better start at the beginning.' She rubs her forehead. 'It's still painful to remember those times, but Nadia makes up for all the pain. Isn't she beautiful?' Her eyes shine. 'I owe you an apology. I owe you an explanation. But at that time I could not bear it, the whole nightmare of it all. I could not bear to talk about it.'

'Dearest Eva, you don't owe me anything. I guessed what must have happened. And we were both so helpless. To this day I carry this awful burden, that I was there, and I didn't know and I didn't save you from Selim.'

She shakes her head.

'Don't blame yourself. He had it all planned out. And someone had to stay with the children. I knew it was me he wanted to see. I just did not think, that in his father's house he would...' She pauses and takes a deep breath. 'He agreed to take us out of the *kolhoz*, but he said he didn't believe a word of my promises to return to him afterwards. He said, I'd only do that if I was totally his, and my husband would not want me any more.' Her eyes fill up and her lip trembles.

'Eva...' I can barely stand her pain.

She dabs at her nose with a handkerchief.

'I want to tell you. I want to tell you everything. I want to get it off my chest. I've not been able to talk to anyone else about it before. Not even to the kind Mr. Ostrovski...' she composes herself and continues, 'Selim forced me into his father's shed. You know, the one he used for his woodwork. He

386

pushed me down on the floor. I needn't tell you the rest... I couldn't even shout for help. What would be the point? Our escape depended on it...' she pauses, her gaze resting on the clasped hands in her lap. 'I wanted to die. I felt so utterly defiled. I hated him and I hated myself...'

I remember vividly the look of desperation in Eva's eyes all the next day.

'And when he didn't turn up that night of our escape,' she says, ' it was like a sign from heaven. I had to be strong, I told myself. In the end, no one would ever know if I didn't say anything. So I didn't. I pretended to myself that it never happened.'

I hug her to me and stroke her smooth silky hair, as if she were my child needing to be comforted.

'And then you became so ill, just as we got the children to safety,' she says. I let go of her and look into her face, strained with painful memories. 'Nastusha, I prayed night and day that you wouldn't die. I couldn't imagine having to cope on my own with the children. But that took my mind off my own problems. I convinced myself that months of near starvation made it impossible for me to become pregnant.'

I too would have thought that, remembering how erratic and at times totally absent my menstruation had become. Eva lifts her shoulders in an expressive shrug.

'I've no idea how it happened. I can only think that the regular diet we received at the hospital on arrival must have kicked my system into action. I still did not want to think about it when we arrived in Teheran. All I wanted to do was to be with Henryk again, so if I was in fact pregnant, it would appear to be his child.' She lifts her clear eyes to mine and they are flooded with copious tears. She wipes them away and blows her nose. 'Nastusha, you'll be repulsed by me. I would never have believed it myself to what shameful lengths I was prepared to go to hide my dreadful secret!'

'Eva, don't be so hard on yourself. Any sensible person would understand that.'

'Every raped woman,' she corrects me. 'When there are consequences, it is the victim who becomes the pariah that everyone shuns.' Sadly, she is right. 'Nastusha, I had to invent yet another charade, when Nadia was born.'

'How did you feel about Selim's child?'

She does not take long to think.

'I prepared myself for that. I thought I'd hate her, the constant reminder of what Selim did to me. I was prepared to give her away for adoption. But when I saw her, Nastusha, it was like a miracle. I loved her so much I couldn't bear the thought of being parted from her.'

'You must have been sick with worry about Henryk's reaction.'

'That's when I invented this other story. I wrote to him. I told him our child was still-born, but there was an orphaned baby, whose very young mother died giving birth. I wanted to adopt this child, but I needed his signature of consent for the adoption papers.'

I'm speechless with astonishment.

'And Henryk agreed?'

Eva gives me a small pleased smile.

'God moves in mysterious ways,' she says. 'Our letters missed each other on the way. His was like a bolt out of the blue. He begged me to give him his freedom. Though there's no divorce in our church, of course.'

I'm confused. The Italian affair was later. So what was Henryk doing then? Eva continues,

'Some PSK woman. In Alexandria.'

Henryk? Twice? I can't believe it!

'Eva, it must have been a nightmare for you! On top of everything else!'

'I was very upset of course, at first. That sense of betrayal... you just can't take it in, and the person you have trusted the most, suddenly he is no longer who you believed he was... But then the more I thought about it all, the more I became aware of a strange relief inside me. . . I was released from ever having to disclose my secret to anyone. Ever!'

'You just did,' I give her another hug.

'You're like my twin,' her confidence in me seals our shared secret. I'll never let her down. She tells me more. 'I thought hard about Henryk's request. It was such a blow. It was as if he had become some other person, as if Stella and I did not matter to him any more. But then, I was changed too. In the end it was like an agreement. I got his consent for the adoption and he got my consent for the dissolution of our marriage.'

My mind struggles with all these strange facts.

'But how?.. Nadia was really yours... '

'Where I was in India Nastusha, everything was possible to arrange with a backhander behind the scenes.'

I try to understand that. All the lies she had to invent and all the anxiety she had been through only so that her good name could be preserved.

'And Henryk? What happened in the end?'

Eva makes a face.

'A flash in the pan. But then there was another one. An Italian woman. They split up in the end. He came to England and wrote to me and begged me to forgive him.' She shrugs and looks to me for understanding. 'Nastusha, what choice have I got? He's my husband. Till death do us part. And Stella needs her father. I've been given a chance by Providence. Now I must do the same for him.'

I'm overawed by her practical thinking. I tell her about Julian, and like myself before, she is shocked then sympathetic.

'Nastusha, I think we've all got our work cut out. It's a challenge. But we've survived worse. We'll manage this one, won't we?'

I hug her and feel I've got my old Eva back.

The first time Henryk comes to visit, Stella is sent to fetch me to their barrack. Muffled up to our eyeballs, Julia and I follow Stella, wading through the snow.

It is warm in their room and the heat colours our cheeks and makes my fingers tingle. Before I take off my coat, I hug Henryk to me. I feel his spiky thinness through his uniform. There are lines on his brow and vertical creases on each side of his mouth. He is only thirty-eight, but already there is that look about him of a worn middle-aged man. He greets me with that Henryk-smile of his, the once, recognized symbol of his cheerful nature, but now I detect a touch of effort in this happy pose of his.

'Dear Henryk! It's been quite some time!'

'Yes...' he detaches himself and helps me out of my coat. We three adults sit down by the stove, and the girls pile on the bed to play with their toys.

I listen eagerly to his accounts of the war years in Italy. With thoughtful pauses, inhaling or exhaling the cigarette smoke, he tells Eva and me of the ferocious battles, of the friends he has lost, of the near-death instances, of the many miracles. There's something lost about him, something vulnerable, something very sad. I want our old Henryk back. I want this room to resound with his jokes and laughter.

'What's the latest with Julian?' he asks. 'I've not seen him lately.'

'Nor have I,' I cannot help sounding bitter. 'He's got a job in Derby.' I don't add that he left without seeing me first. Henryk gives me a long thoughtful look.

'But that's good news, Nastusha. We must all make that move in the end. Leave PRC and look for proper jobs. I'm just on the lookout myself for work in Morpeth. Family duties,' he gives a ghost of a smile and glances towards the girls. I follow his gaze to Nadia. She is a beautiful child with dark curly hair and those large soft eyes. I cannot help reflecting that she will be forever a reminder of his own lost love. Will that make him accepting or resentful of this foundling child?

Eva's practical remark pulls me out to the present.

'We've got a lot to be thankful for. No banging on the door in the middle of the night. A roof over our heads, warmth and food. The rest is up to us. *Sursum Corda*! And soldier on!'

389

CHAPTER 50

The initial deep hurt at Julian's uncharacteristic lack of feeling towards me, not bothering to see me before he moved to Derby, is slowly being soothed, but not cured by his regular letters. It is quite extraordinary. It is as if he were two different people. He sends me weekly news and a pound for Julia each time. He likes his work, he tells me, he copes well with remembering instructions, and Edek is there, by his side to guide him like a guardian angel. He is sharing a room with his friend, but all the time he is on the lookout for larger accommodation.

My feelings alternate between a strong yearning to be with him and recurring unease about the state of his mind. But if Edek, his chum is able to cope with him, then I, his wife, will surely manage too.

It is the end of March. All snow has disappeared, revealing bright green thick grass in the fields. On breezy, dry days the children roll about in it amidst squeals of laughter.

'Mama! It's like the green sea!' Julia shouts making swimming actions on the soft ground.

I pick her up and admonish,

'Look what you've done! Your front is all green! What will you do when you ruin your clothes?'

'Wear my old ones!'

'But we must look good and clean for Easter. Daddy may come and take us away to another place.'

She studies me with her serious eyes.

'But I like it here, Mama. I want to stay with Stella and Nadia.'

Henio has disappeared from Julia's life. Almost overnight. She kept looking out for him for days afterwards.

Sergeant Bielski had written to Adela, simply proposing to marry her. He'd settled in a Polish community in Bradford, had found a job as a farm-hand, and was ready to fetch her and settle down, if she'd consider to be his wife. He gave her a week to think about it. She replied the next day.

'Do you think I'm rash?' she fretted, as we sat knitting by the stove.

'Rash? Haven't we had enough time wasted in our lives? I can only give you my observations. He was always the gentleman, wasn't he? I think he has that need to recapture something of his lost family life. He'll understand your needs, Adela, and he'll be good to Henio too.'

Her reservations finally dropped away when her Sergeant Bielski arrived in a hired car to collect her and her few belongings. He was still sporting his uniform and looked clean, well-groomed and distinguished, his back straight as a rod. He greeted her with a bouquet of red tulips and gathered her in his arms like a long lost love.

'I've missed you,' he said, unabashed by my presence, 'you've made me a very happy man.'

He bent down to little Henio, planted a kiss on the top of his head, and out of his pocket he produced a bar of chocolate and a miniature metal car. With doors and a boot that opened. Ecstatic Henio was his friend for life.

When they were ready to leave and we'd said our tearful goodbyes, Sergeant Bielski gave me a sheet of paper with his address on it.

'Mrs. Anastazia, wherever you settle eventually, you and your family will be always welcome to visit us.'

It felt strange without Adela for the first few days, but Eva has filled that void almost immediately by asking to be moved to the vacated room next to mine.

Henryk visits weekly. He's found a job in Morpeth as a hospital night porter. The night shifts are better paid, and Eva's allowance from the Assistance Board has had to be adjusted accordingly. Mine, so far, has stayed the same.

When Henryk comes to visit, I take Stella and Nadia into my room for the night. Julia loves their stay-overs, all squashed in one bed, myself on the edge. A small inconvenience for Eva and Henryk's sake. Anything that can help to mend their relationship. I try to imagine Julian and me, intimate in bed. I feel no yearning, no desire, only a cold unease. Can we ever mend what has been broken between us?

On rare occasions when we sit together in the dining hall, Henryk opens up a little, and the lines of sadness around his eyes melt in a tentative smile. He reminisces about his friends from the army, about the gregarious and helpful Italians. He does not mention *her*, but I can only imagine that Eva must be thinking about him, thinking about *her*.

One day he talked to me about Julian.

'Nastusha, it was heart breaking when I saw him for the first time, here, in England. You know, since his injury. Roman discovered he was in Penley hospital. We went to see him. Such a long way from here. We stayed for the weekend. He couldn't remember who we were. I tried to jolt his memory with anecdotes of our exploits in the forests at home. I think he enjoyed our visit, but beyond that... there seemed very little connection. It felt as if my old Julian was gone...'

A painful thought crossed my mind then, that everything that had happened to each of us individually, was everyone else's loss too. I made a feeble attempt at talking about our future at home, perhaps for him and Julian back in the forests, but he shook his head.

'Our lands have been taken from us, Nastusha. Having to settle in western Poland will be like settling in another country. Who'll give us our old jobs back? And will Julian be well enough? It would never be the same without him.'

His words flattened my fragile spirit, but Eva stepped in,

'Listen you two, enough of this depressing talk! Challenges crop up to be resolved. And that's what we are all going to do!'

It is only ten more days to Easter, but there's been no letter from Julian last week. In moments of fantasising, I'm willing him to pay us a surprise visit. I want him to go to Morpeth with Julia and me, to buy her a coat and new shoes. Her old ones are pinching her toes. I've been saving every possible penny and coupons, and hope there will be enough left to buy something new for myself. But, just in case I've not got enough, I count on his company and on his financial support.

On Friday night, Roman and Theo pull up in the jeep right in front of our barrack. Our girls run out excited to greet them. The boys do their 'favourite uncle' stuff, lift them up to the back seat and give them a short circular ride. Then accompanied by much skipping around them and tugging at their hands, Roman and Theo come in and announce they want to take us out.

'You've got to experience this very English institution,' Theo laughs, 'the English pub!'

It sounds very tempting; God we all need a break from the monotony of our days in this isolated existence.

'But what about the children?' I ask.

Stella jumps up and down before me.

'Auntie Nastusha, we'll go to Mrs. Czerska. She tells us at school we can go to her at any time!' Mrs. Czerska, now the head of the temporary school at the camp, is known for her kindness. Her activity table in her own home is a legend and draws the children from all over the camp.

'Stella, dear,' Eva points out, 'this is after school time, and Mrs. Czerska needs a rest too!'

'Please, Mama, please. Can I just go and see? I won't bother her, if she's already too busy.'

Stella's voice is like a warm treacle. Theo backs her up saying,

'I've got a small offering, that I think will please her.' His grey eyes smile.

While Stella is gone for a few minutes, Theo produces three bars of chocolate in front of Julia and Nadia. Their excited hopping stops and their eyes widen eagerly to the wonder of the goodies in his hands.

'You may eat them all at once,' Theo pronounces with mock seriousness,

392

'as long as you leave one for Stella!' They look at him with disbelief, and I think what a good man he is, and how he would make someone and himself happy, someone like Adela and Henio.

Later, when all is arranged, and we leave our girls in Mrs. Czerska's charge, and stand back from the entrance to her room, no bigger than ours, Theo presents her with a chocolate bar too, and a white envelope. He must have thought it all out before.

'Thank you very much, but there's no need! Really!' Mrs. Czerska protests, her cheeks pink with pleasure when Theo kisses her hand.

'We won't be very long,' Eva assures her.

'Take your time,' Mrs. Czerska replies, 'we'll be very busy here.'

I get a glimpse from the door of the table piled with colourful crepe paper. Our girls, their faces lively with anticipation, are already settled and trying out the small metal scissors, while Mrs. Czerska's daughter is mixing glue in a jar with flour and water.

Roman gives us a quick jolly sound from his klaxon and grins when we pile into the back seat of the jeep. We wrap ourselves in blankets, for although the days stretch now late into the evening, there's still a chill in the air.

The central camp road runs partly through Plessy Woods before joining the main route through Hertford Bridge. The air is pungent with the scents of Spring, damp earth, bursting foliage and blossom, and the green blanket of nascent bluebells that will flower later in May. Above us, in the canopy of criss-crossing branches, the piercing calls of the birds peak before nightfall.

I hold the blanket tight around me. It's only on films that the actress stays unruffled in her open sports car, as the wind blows softly through her flowing hair. I expect I'll end up with a bird's nest on my head before we reach Bedlington.

Roman turns left on the main road and we cross the picturesque stone bridge. We pass attractive stone houses, arched doorways, tall mullioned windows, neatly fenced front gardens, with roses that will climb and bloom in the summer. Clean pavements and smooth tarmac roads. Such order and neatness! Memories of Ain-Karem come back, with the weathered, crumbling buildings and pebbly pavements riddled with potholes.

It is fun in the back seat, behind Roman and Theo, who burst into a jaunty tune of *Poszła Karolinka*. Eva and I join in, Eva with a fit of giggles, like a young girl, and I, with a feeling of relief from the heaviness that sits on my chest relentlessly these days.

The English countryside in Spring is as breathtaking as ours at home, and yet so different! Our fields, unfettered by hedges and fences, sprawl out for miles into ponds and lakes and woodlands, the flowering shrubs dotting the landscape at random. The country roads, rather like dirt tracks, are lined with shade-giving willows, their branches shooting up straight from the gnarled old trunks. The horizons are distant, the sky, a gigantic dome, studded with millions of stars.

Here, everything is so orderly, the hedges marking out fields in neat rectangles, the tall elms and the wide chestnuts forming painterly little arbours against the perfect evening sky. The gently undulating land has the curves of a young body, as if waiting for its lover. I get a strange yearning to throw myself on the ground and become one with nature.

Bedlington is barely three miles up the road. Roman parks the jeep outside the Northumberland Arms in Front Street. The white-washed pub looks barely larger than a cottage, so unlike our sprawling inns at home. Across the little square, the open gates in the railing give a view of the criss-crossing pathways around St. Cuthbert's church, an ancient building in grey stone.

'St. Cuthbert was actually buried here first, in this very church,' Roman informs us, 'before his relics were moved to Durham Cathedral.'

It's all the same to me. All saints appear to have led similar lives, unwavering dedication to God, selfless sacrifice for others, their solitary time spent in prayer. I could never live up to such ideals.

Eva and I roll up our blankets and Roman locks them in the boot. My hair is a mess, I do my best to shape it into place with my fingers. Eva's smooth hair, tied neatly at the back, is subtly elegant. Our boys steer us gently across the yard, Roman's fingers light on Eva's elbow, and Theo's on mine. They both look so clean and polished and I'm aware of my two layers of hand-knitted cardigans, thankfully hidden underneath my light coat.

We enter through the small front door, the raised doorstep forcing us to stoop to avoid the beam above. Our eyes need to adjust to the dim lighting from the wall lights, dark wood fittings and floral little lampshades. All the noise stops and the collective gaze directed at us is almost tangible. There are four men, in tweed jackets, on the high stools by the bar, and a few couples at the little round tables in the corners. Cigarette smoke hovers in wisps above everyone.

'Good evening,' Roman looks around in greeting, takes off his field cap and leads us to a table by the far wall. One of the tweed men detaches himself from the bar and stands in Roman's way. A conversation ensues.

'What's he saying?' I ask Theo.

'Apparently, all tables are booked.' Theo's brow lifts expressively.

The man continues to talk, he jabs the air with his finger and points to the door. I don't need translating, I get a sinking feeling that they don't want us here. Then Roman says something. The man's confident haughty expression appears to slide into an uncertain, pale grin. Roman gesticulates further, the man nods, his stiffness dissolves in a genuine smile and he returns to the bar. All normal noise resumes as Roman leads us to a table. The barman comes across, wipes the already clean surface and says,

'Please, sit down.' That much I understand.

When we are seated in the warm cosy corner, we all look at Roman with just one obvious question. He smiles like a cat smacking his lips.

'Slavic charm! That's all!' But we want more. 'All right,' there's a wide grin across his face, 'the tweedy lord wasn't so pleasant to begin with. Told us to go back where we came from!'

I gasp inwardly. 'Why? Don't they know anything?'

Roman shakes his head. 'Apparently not. Only what they read in the press. And that's only a vague fraction of the full story. If you think about it, how could anyone possibly understand all the experiences we have survived? Do you remember Pahlevi? We arrived half dead on the shores, and the Russians were telling the British that they had saved us from the Germans in that state. We were forbidden to discuss our experiences openly, even though the British leaders knew the truth. So how would the people here know anything different, than what the government wants them to know?'

We are quiet for a moment contemplating his words, then Theo says,

'No serious talk this evening. Time to have a laugh. Who remembers a good joke? But first, tell us Roman, what did you say to that man?'

Roman shrugs,

'A little humility goes a long way. I said to him, all right, I'll go back, but only if he lets me buy him a drink first. For friendship's sake. Between our two countries.'

'I'm impressed!' Eva nods with an amused smile.

'And we'll show the tweed and his cronies,' Theo adds, 'what stuff we Poles are made off. We'll buy all four a drink! Right ladies, what's your order?'

Eva and I ask for soft drinks and watch our boys go to the bar and stand beside the four men. As the ordered beers appear one by one and are placed in front them, they turn around towards Roman and Theo, and give them a thumbs-up. Eva is sceptical.

'They could still be saying horrid things about us. How would we know?'

But she is proved wrong. As soon as we are settled with our drinks, the barman comes over with a tray: two froth-headed beers and two small ruby-coloured drinks.

'From the men,' he says pointing to the four at the bar. 'Sherry for the ladies.'

Eva and I take a sip. Sweet and warming. Now we send them the thumbs-up and they return our smiles.

'So...' Roman sits back and relaxes, 'what do you think?'

'After this little charade?' Eva's tone is dry. 'Do you always get that?'

'Sometimes,' Roman sounds resigned, 'some of them think we started the war. Some are resentful, naturally, that we've become a drain on the state. Not many understand that this is the fallout from Yalta.'

Theo clears his throat.

'Ahem... we were supposed to be telling jokes!'

Our talk turns to the latest news about and from our friends. Eva gives a humorous account of the goings on in the camp, the petty squabbles, the jealousies, the falling out over children and the casually dropped gossip, all inevitable by-products of an enclosed community life.

I'm only half attentive, my mind obsessed with Julian's long silence. At one point when Theo and Eva compare notes from their times in Teheran, I tell Roman about my worry.

'He hasn't written to me either,' Roman says, and the way he smiles at me reassuringly I detect he is trying hard to hold back any alarm. 'Nastusha,' he leans towards me, 'it may be that he is working long hours. Maybe overtime. And also, his state of mind is a constant struggle. It may be hard for him to get himself together. Perhaps he is planning to come over for Easter?'

'Do you think so?' I grab at this suggestion. 'That's exactly what I've been thinking. I wish it wasn't so faraway. I'd myself go to see him...'

'It is far, Nastusha. And it is expensive. I imagine he wants to save for the time when you move.'

'It's just that I had this stupid notion that he'd surprise us. I need to go to Morpeth to buy Julia new shoes. Before I'm forced to cut them open for her toes.'

'Do you need him for that?'

I feel myself colouring with embarrassment.

'Roman, do I really have to spell it out? My savings are nothing to brag about, though I try really hard. If he were to come with me, I'd get a few other things.'

Theo looks my way and his offer is spontaneous.

'I'll come with you!'

'Sorry?' I must have misheard him.

'I'll come with you,' he repeats. 'It's no big deal. I've got some savings and some coupons saved as well. It'll be a loan. Julian will repay me later.'

It seems like such a god-sent solution, too good to turn down, but it feels awkward to accept this offer from a man I hardly know.

'Theo, I'm really touched. It's so kind of you. But it's not so desperate that it can't wait.'

'Yes it is!' Eva butts in. 'You've been fretting about it for weeks. Theo, Anastazia will go with you,' she decides, ' and she thanks you very much for it!'

I give up and laugh and catch Theo's friendly gaze.

'In that case,' I say, 'I invite you and Roman to our Easter feast at the camp.'

Suddenly the future looks less bleak.

CHAPTER 51

We take the ten o'clock bus to Morpeth the next morning, having checked the timetable in the bus-shelter last night, and Theo, having stayed over in the camp. There's always a room available, and the boys travel ever ready, like the scouts, with their overnight kits.

I sit next to the window with the flowering hedges running past me in ribbons of white and pink. The sky is clear, the sun brilliant and I feel an uplifting expectancy in the air. I turn my gaze to Theo and catch his look of quiet pleasure, his smiling eyes indicating Julia sitting on his lap and counting the buttons on his uniform. She can be wary of men, having had just me round her till now, but with Theo, there's been an immediate rapport. It is said that animals and children possess a sixth sense about kindness. Not only the children. I feel that I can trust him too.

He pushes back a lock of Julia's hair from her forehead underneath her knitted beret. His manner is gentle. Then he looks at me.

'My little boy was about her age. He would have been thirteen now.'

I'm taken aback. 'I thought you were on your own.'

'I am. Now. It wasn't always like that.'

I don't know what to say. But my soul knows what to feel. Acute sadness for this kind man.

'That must have been awful,' I say with feeling.

He nods, a thoughtful, faraway look in his eyes.

'I didn't find out until later. When I was released from the POW camp in Siberia. It was in Teheran. I found out through the Red Cross. Both my wife and my son were killed in an air raid where we lived in Luck.'

I could weep for his loss. I ask him,

'Have you any family left in Poland?'

'Two sisters. Both widows now. Their husbands were killed in Katyn. I've another sister in Sweden. Maria. She survived Ravensbruck. Her husband was killed by the Germans.'

Hundreds upon hundreds of similar stories. One runs out of comforting words. What can I say to Theo?

'Are you thinking of getting together with them?' I ask.

'It'll all depend on what happens next in Poland.' The same old question unresolved. 'Veronika and Sabina are stuck in there, but neither Maria nor I can go back till the Russians withdraw.'

Julia provides a welcome break to this sad subject on this beautiful day.

'Mama,' her serious eyes burrow into mine, 'will there be enough pennies left for a sweet?'

Theo's face breaks into a smile. He strokes her head and promises,

'Yes, there will be. And maybe for something else too!'

Julia shifts her gaze to his face with a look of wonder. A warm feeling spreads inside me and I wish that one day soon she'll be looking up to Julian in the same way.

Morpeth is a charming town with its neat streets, clean pavements and spring-fresh growth hanging over the walls. Houses here look so different from ours at home: tall, gabled roofs, redbrick walls and white stone framing doors and windows. I imagine the elegant furnishings indoors and wonder when we'll live in a normal house again.

With Julia between us holding our hands, Theo leads us past shops that display merchandise of all sorts in the windows. I want to stop and stare and wallow in nostalgic echoes from home. Theo chuckles.

'Anastazia, we've got all day. We'll come back, I promise, but first things first.'

We walk along Bridge Street into the centre, to a store called Rutherford. Its smart facade of white stone carvings impresses me and warns me at the same time; my purse is too modest for the prices here. Theo, nevertheless, walks straight in and holds the swinging glass door open for me.

I find myself surrounded by an array of fashionable ladies' wear displayed on stands and clothes-rails and hung diagonally on walls that are lined with glass drawers. The whole place overwhelms me with its confident air of long-established opulence, the oak floor, shining with polish, the solid oak counter and the oak staircase inviting the customers to the upper floors.

'I don't know where to look first,' I cannot contain my delight.

The other customers appear confident in these surroundings, the men expansive, their gabardine coats thrown casually over their suits and white shirts and ties as they pander to their women's choices. The women exude expensive scents with every shake of their elegantly coiffed heads and every wave of their manicured hands. I feel like a tramp, though my hand-knitted cardigan from recycled grey wool is fortunately well hidden underneath my flimsy coat.

A sales lady, neat and slim in a navy pencil skirt approaches us, her polite expression giving nothing of her inner thoughts at the sight of us.

'Coat for child,' Theo explains, indicating Julia. The lady smiles and points to the staircase.

Upstairs we are treated with the same politeness by a sales assistant who could be the other one's twin, with her crimped hair and a black straight skirt. She listens to Theo's request, gives Julia her full attention, then she leads us to a clothes rail, packed with children's coats and jackets. She picks out three coats and arranges them over the top of the rail: grey, navy and red. They are woollen with black buttons and velvet collars. Julia's gaze goes straight to the red one and her face lights up.

'Try it on,' Theo says, smiling. She needs no encouragement, and though a little long, she hugs it round her and admires herself in the mirror. The lady says something to Theo, he nods, and she fetches out a matching bonnet with a velvet bow on the side. Julia is smitten. I look at the price. It's heart-stopping.

'Theo, I simply can't afford it.' I speak low, though the lady can't understand me any way.

'Anastazia, please let me. For Julia. I'm sure Julian would want the same. And there's no time limit on repayment.' He looks at me with such a burning appeal in his eyes, that I find it hard to refuse. It is rash, and I shall most probably regret it, but for the moment all my commonsense melts in his pleasure and Julia's.

'All right,' I agree, 'but only if you'll let me treat you to an iced bun later.'

'Perfect!' he chuckles. He tops up my savings and my coupons with his own, and I also buy a liberty bodice and woollen stockings for Julia. Despite the calendar Spring, Julia is shivering most of the time.

Before we leave the store, Theo stops in the ladies' section downstairs.

'Why not make the most of this opportunity while we're here?' he suggests.

I give a brittle laugh. 'Theo, really!'

He doesn't give up. 'No harm in just having a look.'

I catch a glimpse of myself in the long mirror. God knows, I could do with a touch of renovation! What would Julian see? Not the sensible, scrimping and saving woman that I've been forced for so long to be, but some waif-like creature with tired hair and a worn, shabby coat. Theo's right. I must make the most of this opportunity.

'You're a bad influence, Theo!' He smiles at that and steers me towards the counter.

I decide that all I can afford is a long, jacket-like cardigan, with softly padded shoulders and a tie belt. It is coffee-coloured, a shade that I know goes well with my eyes and my hair. There's an awkward moment when I want to try it on, but am desperate not to reveal the hideous secret underneath my coat. I needn't worry; the sales lady leads me naturally to the changing cubicle, while Julia waits with Theo. I emerge feeling a hundred times prettier already, the long line of the cardigan making me look taller, and its colour enhancing my complexion.

'Excellent!' Theo gives me an approving look, 'now just one more thing!'

The situation becomes surreal, and maybe because of that, I'm led, as if in a dream, to the ladies' coats rail. I choose a beige one, with a pinched waist held together by three buttons, and with the lower part cut generously in A-panels. For Julian, I tell myself, appeasing my unease against such extravagance, and reassure Theo of my prompt repayment for his generous loan, when we leave the store in search for Julia's shoes.

I cannot quite quash the torment of my misgivings later, when we wait for our bus home and sit on a nearby bench, Julia and our precious purchases squashed between us. Theo's needs are small: shaving bits and pieces, hair cream, toothpaste and cigarettes. We share the iced buns I've bought, Julia's leaving white sugary streaks around her mouth.

'I've never spent so much money all at once.' I can't help uttering my worries aloud, hoping, I suppose, for Theo to appease my mind. And he does.

'Anastazia! You're not still worrying, are you? We've come here for a purpose. We've accomplished our mission. Be pleased, and think how you'll outshine everyone else next Sunday!'

This makes me laugh, for indeed there's a constant competition between women to look their best in church on Sundays. I shake my head.

'That really doesn't matter to me, Theo. But if only Julian could come…'

Theo gives me a sympathetic look. 'He'll be very impressed,' he says, 'and besotted with Julia.'

I feel so much gratitude to this good man, I don't know how to express it without sounding mawkish.

'Theo,' I keep my tone matter of fact, 'when Julian and I are settled somewhere in the end, probably Derby, we shall invite you all over. Henryk and Eva and Roman and you. We shall have the best party ever!'

'Perfect!' he turns his smiling face towards me, and this one word sounds like an endearment.

CHAPTER 52

Easter Sunday. The camp chapel, a large and spacious version of the Nissen hut, is packed right up to its concave corrugated-iron sides, which vibrate with hundreds of voices singing the hymns of Resurrection at full volume.

I cannot sing. My heart is heavy. All yesterday afternoon I waited. When the evening came and it was time to get ready for the Resurrection procession, I had to accept that Julian was not coming.

I dressed Julia in her red coat and bonnet. I put on my new coat. Before that, I had washed and curled and fluffed out my hair. I touched up my face with powder and lipstick. All for Julian.

When Eva and Henryk stood at the door I burst into tears. This made Julia cry. Henryk took the girls with him and went ahead. Eva stopped with me. My body was racked with the grief bottled up for days. She sat on the bed with me, with her arm across my back and let me cry for a while. Her tone was kind but firm when she spoke.

'Nastusha, there must be a good reason why he wasn't able to come. If anything really serious happened to him, you'd be officially notified.'

'But he himself could get in touch. They've got a phone at the office building!'

'Well,' she sounded like a mother explaining to a child, 'I'm sure everything will be revealed in time. At this moment there's absolutely nothing you yourself can do. So, think about Julia. Remember how strong you always were for Pavel and Agata? Now it's your Julia's turn.'

I nodded, too choked to say any more. It was different then. Even in the worst conditions I was always absolutely certain of one thing: Julian's love.

'And another thing,' she said, 'have you ever thought about visiting him? In Derby?'

Her words threw me, making me forget my grief.

'Well, no. He's never suggested it. And besides, it would be so expensive!'

Eva sat up, and spoke with an energetic voice,

'Well, that's what you must do Nastusha! We'll all help you to get you on that train!'

'I'll drown in debt!'

'Nonsense!'

'But … how will I manage? I barely know a few words in English.'

'You've managed in far worse situations. Roman will write down for you in English everything you need to ask!'

And so my decision was made. I'm going on Tuesday, the day when the regular train service resumes after Easter.

The Mass, as always, is concluded with *Our Free Country return to us O Lord!* And then there is a slow exodus from the chapel, everyone eyeing everyone else's best Easter outfits, new jackets or hats or new shoes, the old ladies, frugal as always, simply airing their flowery shawls in place of their ubiquitous black.

Pity Julian can't see me today, but I catch Theo's friendly gaze and respond with a nod to his smile. He and Roman came over this morning from Felton Park.

We walk in our group towards the dining hall building, along with the fragmented crowd. It is a true Easter-Spring day, fresh and breezy, with the sun high in the sky, undisturbed by the few scattered cottonwool clouds. Between the black barracks, the grass is thick and emerald green, lifting the drabness out of the buildings.

Roman, beside me, takes a long ostentatious intake of the fresh air. 'A good omen for the rest of Spring,' he states, mocking the certainty of a weather specialist.

'About time too!' Theo agrees with a grin. His white hair shines like swandown in today's brightness.

Eva and Henryk behind us, remind us how often we used to have snow at Easter at home, and how the poor chap who used to re-enact half-naked Jesus on Good Friday, would virtually freeze to death before the crucifixion scene.

Our girls, excited, skip ahead of us and are first to enter the dining hall. Long white tables are set out, and the walls are decked with pussy willows and green branches. We sit down together, Henryk, Eva and their girls facing us four, and while we wait for everyone to find a place, the men's conversation turns inevitably to the subject of jobs and transfers and possible decisions to emigrate. I only half listen, my thoughts running ahead of me to Tuesday, to my trip to Derby. A shiver runs down my spine at the uncertainty of the unknown.

Our Easter feast, when it's brought out on platters and in bowls, is based on garden produce, so even in these coupon restrained times, there is an abundance of salads made with potatoes and chives, mixed cooked root vegetables, and diced sweetened beetroot. Hard-boiled eggs, halved with the bright yolks up, are served in mayonnaise. At home, there would have been arrays of cooked ham and gammon and varieties of sliced sausages. Here, the ham is rationed to a slice per person. We make up the bulk with the margarine-topped bread.

The atmosphere is jolly, everyone included in one big adopted family, that soothes the sadness of being far away from their own. Roman and Theo.

They'd have no one, today they have us. I chide myself for my self-absorption and make a decided effort to join in all the small talk. Henryk opens up today and regales us with anecdotes and jokes. Roman and Theo add their bits and I surprise myself with my spontaneous laughter.

Stella, Nadia and Julia are getting restless. They have finished eating and are eager to go for a walk in the woods where we have promised them an egg hunt. This has taken some undercover doing, when they were in bed at night: first the moulds made of wet soil and dried, then the gluing of *papier maché* around them, cutting them in half when dry, covering the empty egg shapes in colourful crepe paper, and finally inserting jellies and segments of chocolate, before sealing them up.

We give in to our girls' entreaties and stroll out of the camp down the hill to Plessy Woods, while the three of them treble the mileage walked, with their tireless skipping and running to and fro before us. New outfits are everywhere on display, bought with hard-saved money and coupons. Henryk has treated all his girls to new coats; Eva's, pastel blue brings out the colour of her eyes, Stella, and Nadia's are practical gabardine in navy blue. I feel a sudden pride in my people, in their efforts to lift themselves up in any situation.

Theo is walking beside me, hands clasped behind his back, his calm gaze often catching mine.

'If I may say so,' he says, 'this weather has brought everyone out of their shells. I've never seen so many beautiful women in one place!' His remark is so blatantly flirtatious, I laugh out loud.

'Oh Theo! You are so funny! We all just scrub up well!'

He laughs back and is not at all deterred.

'I must correct you,' he admonishes with pretend seriousness, 'some scrub up better than others. You and Eva certainly belong to the elite!'

He makes me laugh again. 'Eva, yes,' I agree, 'her hair never stopped turning heads.' And I think to myself, much good that did her.

Theo gives me a prolonged look as if preparing to say more, but then he asks politely, 'So have you heard from Julian?'

A shadow falls over my lightened mood. I tell Theo of my plan of a trip to Derby. Roman detaches himself from Henryk and Eva's company and catches the last of our conversation.

'Of course I'll help you with anything you need, Nastusha, but now I need your help. Keep the girls distracted so I can go ahead and hide the eggs.'

We call the girls to us to show them something in the grass. Immediately they run, expecting to find the first egg. But Henryk pulls out a wide blade of grass and keeping it taut between his fingers, he blows at it producing a squeaking sound.

'Like a bird sound,' he tells them. 'Now see if you can do that.' They practise for a few minutes, with very little effect, only their mouths getting green from the grass pigmentation. Stella is first to protest,

'Can we do that later? Or someone else will find all the eggs!'

403

Indeed, when we enter the woodland area, groups like ours can be seen strolling between the trees, their children searching clumps of grass, squirrel holes in tree trunks, burrow openings in the ground.

'Where shall we look?' Stella is all concern and excitement. Nadia and Julia take instinctive cue from her and jump up and down with impatience.

'Over here!' Roman materializes and points them in the right direction.

A little later, when all three eggs are discovered and are carried possessively like priceless treasures, Roman leads us further into the wood, where paths criss-cross the woodland floor, now thick with the growth of the bluebell stalks. The air is warm here, trapped under the canopy of branches high above us, alive with bird activity. The girls are constantly ahead of us, and Theo, strangely, close to me.

'It's so lovely here,' he says, 'a lovely day altogether. Brings back memories of other Easters. At home. Yet I don't feel sad today.'

'Yes,' I agree, 'it's good to be together like this.' I mean our little group. I don't tell him I feel a void because Julian is not here.

When we reach the stony path on the top of the ridge that runs along the bank of the River Blythe, Roman organises us in a line. The crashing sounds of the fast running water make Julia flinch. Theo picks her up and carries her in his arms. Eva holds Nadia's hand firmly and Henryk walks at the front with Stella.

We cross the wooden bridge that spans the river, and make our way out of the woods straight onto the main road which runs through the village. It is so quiet here, I wonder where everyone is on this Easter Sunday.

A little way up the hill we turn into a deserted country road. Here the girls can run ahead of us freely and safely. Easy talk flows about anything and everything. It feels good to be part of this group.

Roman must feel it too, for at one point he remarks,

'I wish we could stretch today and make it last longer. We're all waiting for something to happen, and when it does, what will it be? More transfers? New jobs? Or going back? Whatever it is, it will be a change which will separate us again. Today feels special because we're together, like the family we once were when we were forced to start our journey together. Seems such a long time ago!'

We contemplate his words as we stroll along the clean tarmac road, the girls skipping ahead of us, collecting different shaped leaves off the growth around us. Only Julian is missing.

'It's up to us,' Theo says, 'to keep in touch wherever we are.'

'And that we'll always do,' Eva states firmly, 'won't we Nastusha?'

Theo catches my eye and smiles.

'Do I qualify for membership of your exclusive club?'

I smile back. 'You can't get out now, even if you tried!'

On Tuesday at nearly six in the evening I arrive at Julian's address in Friar Gate in Derby. The start of this journey early in the morning feels like weeks ago. Dear Roman drove me in his borrowed jeep to Newcastle railway station, got me on the correct train, equipped me with bilingual notes written in a little notebook, and instructions to change trains in Nottingham for Derby.

For hours I sat in my corner, other passengers changing at every station and the scenery of the continuous landscape running past the window. I wished I had Eva with me, but I could not expect her to indulge me at such expense, especially as this journey was funded largely by the kindness of my friends.

The house before me is two floors high with an additional floor under the tall gabled roof. The double door is recessed inside an arched porch. My heart beats faster when I rattle the metal knocker. I feel comforted by the thought that I look presentable in my new coat. I'm aware of muffled sounds on the other side of the door, before it opens. A woman of about fifty comes forward to the threshold. I guess this is Mrs. Evans, Julian's landlady, referred to in his letters. Her hair is grey, loosely curled around her face, which wears an expression of confident efficiency.

'Can I help you?' she asks, wiping her hands on the flowery, sleeveless overall.

I understand that. I've been memorizing Roman's written phrases all the hours I've spent on the train. I introduce myself, then I point to the line in my notebook which says that I'm Julian's wife, and what time will he be home from work? A pleasant smell of cooking stew drifts over from the depths of the house.

Mrs. Evans reads Roman's notes several times, looks at me with interest, angles her head as if thinking, then beckons me to come inside. She shows me into the front room, which is furnished with a brown leather sofa, two armchairs to match and a dark wood coffee table.

'Please, sit down,' she invites. I understand that too. She takes a photograph from the mantelpiece. There's an array of them in frames of all sizes, signed, and I guess they are mementos from her past lodgers. She hands the photograph to me. I'm intrigued. I look at it. Then I look at it again. There's a message there, which I don't understand. Two faces look back at me, two smiles, the man's arm rests lightly on the woman's shoulders and the woman's arm encircles his waist. Julian and some unknown woman. In a field of daisies. Last summer?

Mrs. Evans speaks simply, so I understand.

'Julian. Irena. His wife.'

It's some mistake. She obviously doesn't know.

'No, Mrs. Evans, I, wife!'

She looks at me intently, then tries again.

'Julian. Irena. Gone to Poland.'

This really is a complete misunderstanding. How can I explain to her that we have no intention of going back to a state governed by the very people who had packed us off to Siberia in the first place? There's nothing in Roman's notes to help me out in this.

She looks thoughtful for a moment then she says,

'I'll make tea. All right?' She points to half-past six on the mantelpiece clock. 'Half-past six. Julian's friend will be here. From work.'

She leaves me on my own and my head buzzes. I read all kinds of interpretations into her words, but nothing makes sense. I have no choice but to wait for Julian's colleague.

Mrs. Evans brings me a cup of tea in a porcelain cup on a saucer, and a biscuit. I'm suddenly aware of how parched I am and I thank her profusely. She excuses herself, presumably to finish her cooking. I am amazed how trusting she is, I, a stranger, left alone in her elegant parlour. But come to think of it, there is nothing I could pocket if I were a thief; the clock would give me away with its ticking, the framed prints of hills and lakes landscapes would be too cumbersome to carry, as would be the spider plant with its long tentacles hanging from a tall heavy jardinière.

I sip the tea (delicious, sweet) and chew the biscuit slowly, bite by small bite. I've had my sandwiches on the train and the bottled water and I've been counting on Julian buying me the evening meal. I keep going over Mrs. Evans' words, the few words I understood. Why did she say that woman was his wife? And why would she think he has gone back to Poland? It is all so bizarre. I put it down to some breakdown in communication and the language barrier.

I pick up the photograph and look at the woman. Irena. She is pretty, no doubt. Light hair falling about her shoulders, the sides brushed upwards and caught at the top. Should I be jealous? Suspecting? Julian had never given me any reason to be. I have to be patient. Soon everything will be explained.

My nerves tighten when I hear the key in the lock. I rise and stand just inside the open door of the parlour. The man who walks in is about Julian's age, middle thirties, and like him, dark-haired, casually dressed, brushed cotton tartan shirt, grey jacket, black trousers and army boots. There is a whiff of industrial smell about him, like oil or petrol. I address him in Polish.

'*Przepraszam*. Excuse me,' I stop him in his tracks, 'are you Mr. Edek?'

He takes a moment to absorb my words.

'No, I'm Gracz. Frederyk Gracz. Edek's not here anymore.'

'And Julian? Julian Kalinski?'

'He's gone too!'

It's as if someone has snatched the rug from under my feet. I feel shaky and hold onto the door.

'Are you all right?' He steers me towards the chair, his fingers stained with some dark substance. 'Please sit down. Is there anything I can get for you? Shall I call Mrs. Evans?'

'No…' I shake my head, 'no, I just need to talk to someone who knows Julian. I'm Anastazia, his wife.'

He stares at me for a long time.

'I don't understand. Irena is his wife.'

'She's not!' I speak with a sudden spurt of self-assurance, 'please tell me what's been happening? Where is he?'

The man called Gracz looks a little uncertain now. He runs his fingers through his hair and sits down opposite me. His movement exudes another whiff of the chemical smell.

'I've no idea what this is all about,' his voice is apologetic, 'all I know is that Julian and Irena are a couple. Edek is her brother. Both the men were in the army together. And now, much against everyone's advice they decided to go back to Poland!'

My heart pounds with such force, I fear I'm going to have a heart attack. Die on the spot. Never see Julia again. That thought forces me to take a grip. Slowly, I breathe slowly and regain my composure, all the time aware of Mr. Gracz's worried look.

'When did they leave?'

'About three weeks ago.'

That explains Julian's long silence. I take a few slow breaths.

'Mr. Gracz,' I tell him, 'I am his wife. Always have been. Since our deportation to Russia. He's also got a child. Our little daughter. I've waited four years to be with him again! Four years!'

Mr. Gracz's gaze is intense. I guess I can see disbelief in his eyes, then pity, followed by more pity.

'I am sorry. I'm so sorry!' he looks uncertain, a little embarrassed, 'what are you going to do? What shall I tell Mrs. Evans?'

I shake my head. I feel dazed.

'I've no idea. I had it all planned out differently. With Julian in mind.'

'Then let me suggest that you stay here tonight. I'm sure Mrs. Evans can arrange that.'

I can't think straight but I feel grateful for someone else deciding for me.

'That would be very kind. I'll pay, of course. Even a sofa in a corner will do.'

As I wait for him, I lean against the back of the armchair and close my eyes. I feel totally wrecked, as if I'm not myself anymore.

When he comes back, there's liveliness in his voice, in his attempt to cheer me up,

'It's good news! Sorry,' he corrects himself, 'I didn't mean it like that, it's just that it's fortunate that Mrs. Evans' daughter is away for a few days. You can have her room. And also, you've been invited to supper.'

'Thank you,' I nod, too numb to burst with gratitude.

'Also, because obviously, we can communicate better, Mrs. Evans has asked me to show you to your room.'

I raise myself from the armchair in a kind of trance, pick up my overnight bag and follow him upstairs. There's a corridor with seven doors. He opens the first one closest to the stairs.

'Make yourself comfortable,' he says, 'supper's at seven. And the bathroom is over there.' I see sympathy in his eyes and a helplessness he cannot express, for what can anyone do in bereavement? Because that's how it feels.

I sit on the bed and feel very alone. I feel as bereft as I did when Dorotka died. I'm in a normal world in this pretty room with frilly curtains and frilly cushions and a soft chair and a long mirror and a wardrobe, but I don't feel normal at all. I hug myself and screw my eyes against the agonising pain. Why? Why? If only I could understand.

Before going down to supper, I visit the bathroom and splash my face with cold water. I touch it up with powder and lipstick, fluff out my hair and brace myself against facing the people downstairs.

The dining room is at the back of the house and Mr. Gracz is already there. He introduces me to his friend, another Pole and a young English couple, all lodgers in this house. They engage in small talk, paused, fragmented, while Mrs. Evans serves the meal; boiled potatoes, boiled cabbage and carrots, and mince stew. I find the food bland, but to be fair, I feel no hunger. I am relieved no one bothers me with questions. But when the pudding arrives, an apple crumble with custard, I discover with surprise how delicious it is.

The two Poles turn their attention to me. Polite, general questions. I give them polite answers. Their history is similar to mine. Deportation. Russia. But when they arrived in Teheran they were sent to the Polish air force base in Scotland. Now, since demob, they are engine mechanics at some car factory outside Derby.

'Not without a bit of a fuss from the Union man at the beginning,' Mr. Gracz says, 'but we've proved to them, that the four years we've spent fixing British bombers have not been in vain!'

Tea is served with plain biscuits, after which the young couple excuse themselves and leave. Mrs. Evans disappears too, and there are just us three Poles. Though it eats at me, the need to ask questions about Julian, I hold back from being too familiar with strangers. But over the course of the meal their sincere manner has won me over and I chance a question.

'I'd like to ask you something.' They both look attentively at me over the table. 'How long have they been together? My husband and that woman?'

They exchange uncertain glances then Mr. Gracz says,

'They were already married when Julian came to work here in Derby.'

'But how's that possible?' I question. 'He was still living in Morpeth when I arrived in January.'

Mr. Gracz raises his hands defensively,

'I honestly don't know. We never asked. There was no need to. We simply assumed. We just know that she was his nurse in Penley hospital all through his recovery. They could have married any time.'

'But they couldn't have,' I protest, 'he was married to me!'

Mr. Gracz and his friend look at each other. Mr. Gracz says,

'Now that explains a lot to us. We couldn't understand their haste to go back to Poland now. Against all common sense. But if he committed bigamy, which it appears he has, then that is the obvious reason. This wouldn't be treated leniently by the British courts.'

I am stunned again. Shock after shock.

'But it's not at all like Julian,' I defend him, 'he'd never do such a thing!' And then I remember his visit, all cold and stiff and distant. That wasn't like him either. He was like a stranger. 'It must have been all her doing!' I state with bitter certainty.

Mr. Gracz's friend, a fair-haired man with a thin face and bony hands clears his throat.

'Mrs. Kalinska, I can barely imagine what it must be like for you,' his voice is gentle, tentative. 'We are all victims in the aftermath of the war. No one has asked for this upheaval. We are all changed people. Often beyond our control...' he pauses. 'They were a nice couple. She was very protective of him. Even now, recently, when he was supposed to have recovered from the worst, he still got his bad days. Panic attacks. Depression. Days when his memory was playing him up...'

Something grips at my heart and squeezes hard. I press my handkerchief to my mouth to stop myself from crying loud. When I can speak again, I say,

'If only he'd let me look after him. I'd do everything for him... Why, why didn't he let me?'

Mr. Gracz takes a breath,

'It was probably too late when you arrived,' he says, 'through nobody's fault, I hasten to add. Because of the state of his mind he was probably so attached to her, that he feared he'd be lost without her. But I think, the final, most pressing reason why he married her, was that she was expecting his child.'

CHAPTER 53

Roman is waiting for me on the platform when I arrive at Newcastle station. His welcoming smile and his energetic stride towards me are too much. My resolute willpower which held me together through the ghastly evening, through the sleepless night, through the long train journey with just a vague awareness of other passengers, like shadows around me, breaks down and I fall into Roman's arms sobbing.

'He's gone! He's gone!'

'Gone?' Roman repeats, 'gone where?' He holds me tight as people mill around us, till my sobbing subsides.

'Shall we go for a coffee, somewhere?' he suggests.

I detach myself from him, wipe my eyes and blow my nose. 'Thanks, but no. I don't want to be stared at. Let's go. I'll tell you everything on the way home.'

Wrapped up in a blanket and a scarf around my head, I remain quiet till he's manoeuvred the jeep out of the parking area, till he's made his way out of the network of streets towards the north road to Morpeth. His eyes are screened by his protective goggles, but I feel him glancing my way several times, as he waits for me to start.

The Northumberland landscape unfolding before us, with its patchwork of fields, with its distant horizons, with the vast sky, with the strands of clouds floating weightlessly, remind me of Poland so much that it hurts. That is what Julian is seeing now. Without me.

'Roman,' my voice is terse with anger and grief, 'tell me, how much did you know about Julian and that other woman! Don't spare me anymore! I don't want any more lies!'

I can tell he is upset by the sharpness of my tone. He swallows a few times as he hesitates before asking,

'So what's happened?'

'You tell me first!' I insist, 'everything you know!'

He slows down behind a truck, which turns into a narrow country lane, and picks up speed again before speaking.

'Nastusha, you're wrong if you think anyone lied to you. I can only tell you what I know. Not what I suspected or what I guessed. How would you have reacted to my suggestions if they had turned out not to be true?' He allows a moment for his words to sink in, but I don't react, I want to hear more. 'All right, I'll start at the beginning. When Theo and I arrived in Felton Park from Italy, we started making enquiries about all our friends. I was overjoyed when I discovered that Henryk was stationed in Morpeth. So close! I went to visit him. I was shocked. Not the same man! Not the same old Henryk. No more fooling around and silly jokes. He was very depressed. We did our best to cheer him up. Theo and I. We visited him every Saturday and Sunday.'

Roman pauses as he concentrates on overtaking a couple on bicycles.

'He told me about this other woman in Italy, and before you say anything, please hear me out. He was racked with remorse. He felt he had let everyone down. He hadn't asked for it, he said, it just happened…'

'Roman,' I'm choked with bitterness, 'you don't let things just happen!'

'Didn't you ever?' He asks. He irritates me.

'I never went out looking for other men, if that's what you mean!'

'Neither did we, Nastusha, go out looking for amorous adventures. The conditions we were in… hard to imagine, hard to understand. Daily battles, your friends being injured, blown to pieces, left, right and centre, yourself living on the edge, never knowing from one second to the next if this was your last. Believe me, a helping hand, a kind word, just the very presence of a sympathetic woman… we all yearned for a scrap of normality before it was too late…'

I understand what he is saying but it does not diminish my own grief.

'Anyway,' Roman continues, 'when we discovered that Julian was at Penley hospital, Theo and I took Henryk with us to visit him. We imagined it would do them both good to find each other after such a long time. Bosom pals that they had been all those years before.'

Roman takes a deep breath. The air is cool and fresh.

'It was terribly sad. Julian was very withdrawn and did not remember either of us. Henryk was very upset. We stayed at a nearby camp for three days and over the weekend we managed to establish some connection with him. It was obvious he was very attached to his nurse, Irena, and her brother Edek, who was an orderly at the hospital.'

'But didn't they know he was married?'

'We certainly did not keep it a secret! All last year we went every month to visit him. He recovered to the stage where he could live independently in one of the rooms annexed to the hospital. Last November, he was released and Theo and I went to collect him. I arranged a room for him next to mine in Felton Park. When it came to part with Irena and Edek he cried like a child. It was heartbreaking. They were upset too. They were just about to move to Derby. They promised to get in touch with him, as soon as they were settled in their new place that a friend had secured for them.'

The image of him so needy and desperate is like a knife-twist in my heart. I hold back the urge to cry. I blow my nose and reprimand Roman.

'Why didn't you tell me any of this before?'

'Nastusha,' Roman's voice is tired, 'I lived in hope all the time, that once he saw you, everything would change. I enrolled him on a course of English and woodwork, under Theo's care. They went together every day, and every night he cried and pined for Irena and Edek. He wrote to them daily. He stayed with them at Christmas. They got him a job in Derby and he couldn't wait to join them! The rest you know.'

'But all those letters he wrote me? And the money for Julia he sent? I just don't get it. Why keep up this charade?'

Roman throws me a goggled glance.

'He's not heartless, Nastusha. Perhaps, in his confused and troubled mind, there had been some kind of a plan. For you to get together.'

Of course, he doesn't know the full story. I tell him. The deception. Irena's pregnancy. The bigamous marriage. Their escape to Poland from the consequences of their actions.

Roman is so shocked he stops the jeep by the roadside.

'God almighty! I don't believe it! Julian? Married Irena? And gone to Poland?'

He removes the goggles, rubs his puckered forehead and utters disjointed phrases.

'It must have been... God, I see it now... last Christmas! It must have happened then! She must have told him... she was already... and he just agreed... in his state of mind.. to marry her. And then... you arrived.'

He rests his arms on the-steering wheel and his head on them. And I feel bitterness ferment inside me against the people I trusted the most.

'Roman, if only you had warned me. I would still have gone after him straight away. Did you really have no suspicions when he stopped writing? And all the while I waited and waited. Everyone knew about his dependency on that woman! You and Theo and Henryk! Even Eva must have heard more than I did. And I trusted you all. You must all think I'm an idiot!' I almost shout the last word.

He straightens himself up, turns on the engine and we drive away in silence. The beautiful countryside with its patches of shadows from the passing clouds cannot lift my spirits. I feel utterly betrayed. I break the unbearable silence after many miles only to tell him,

'I can never forgive you! Any of you! Ever!'

His voice is barely audible against the hissing wind on the windscreen.

'It's a matter for you, Nastusha. Our intentions were to protect you from unnecessary suspicions. For that was all they were. Believe me, I had every hope, and I prayed hard that your trip to Derby would resolve your worries and help to bring you and Julian together.'

'And much good that did!'I lash out. I'm angry, so very angry with everything and everyone. I'm angry with myself for being so horrible to Roman. I long for someone to protect me in their arms, to comfort me, to tell me, that this is just a passing nightmare, that when I wake up in the morning, Julian's smiling eyes will be peering down at me.

I look sideways at Roman. From underneath his goggles, a wet streak runs down his cheek.

For the next few weeks I live in a torture chamber, racked by alternating feelings of anger and grief. Eva does her best to get me engaged in all the activities organised in the camp, handicraft classes, choir singing, social meetings, sport afternoons for the children and rotas for cleaning the church and keeping the green bouquets fresh, but I push her away with curt replies. I see the hurt in her eyes and I show her that I don't care and that shocks me the most, yet my resolve is unbending to punish her and those I loved and trusted.

I realise my present state is unfair to Julia. It irritates me that she is so full of child's delight in Stella's and Nadia's company, yet becomes withdrawn around me. With a puzzled look in her large brown eyes and that vulnerable earnestness which makes me want to cry, she asks every day,

'Where is Mr. Roman? And Mr. Theo? When are they coming back?'

I don't know and I don't care! The traitors!

Neither have been to see us since my visit to Derby. Only Henryk comes at the weekends. I still have the girls to sleep over on my bed, more for Julia's delight than Eva's, and though I tell myself I no longer care if they make a go of their marriage or not, I find myself wondering, what's it like for them in bed, after all those other things that have happened.

It's the end of May, colourful and fragrant with wild flowers in the meadows, and a carpet of bluebells in Plessy Woods. Bright sunshine streams into my room as I sit on my own, hand-sewing a dress for Julia. I got this piece of white cotton with a print of pink rosebuds from the travelling salesman just for two shillings!

I hear excited voices outside the window, then Stella, Nadia and Julia, holding hands together burst into my room, jump up and down and announce in broken phrases,.

'Mama!.. Mrs. Czerska said…we'll be flower girls! In the procession! On Corpus Christi!'

Their joy is infectious. Despite my self-imposed introvert mood, I surprise myself by smiling. I put my sewing down and quieten Nadia and Julia.

'Shshsh… let Stella tell me what it's all about.'

'Well,' Stella's smile is ear-to-ear and her blue eyes shine, 'Mrs. Czerska said, it's the Corpus Christi soon. And we've got to make baskets and have white dresses and flowers in our hair and petals in our baskets to throw before the monstrance when the priest carries it to all the four altars!' She is breathless yet still jumps up and down.

Eva, in her room, must have listened to this bubbly recitation, for she appears in the doorway and catches my eye with a plaintive glance.

413

'Nastusha, this sounds like the Corpus Christi processions at home. We must show our girls how it's really done. What do you think?' She could not have begged me more if she got down on her knees and raised her clasped hands.

Our girls look from me to her, their excitement like a taut string ready to burst. Three sweet innocent faces. Something snaps inside me and I'm overwhelmed with a tide of remorse.

I walk over to Eva but am unable to say anything at first, just hold her close in a sisterly hug.

I feel her relaxing in the curve of my arm, and I turn to our children,

'You'll be the most beautiful flower girls in our camp!' They squeal, make a ring and dance.

On the next market day in Morpeth, Eva and I look for rolls of the cheapest material. We find some white stuff with a hint of sheen emulating silk, at a fraction of the price of the real thing. We spend the next few days measuring our girls, cutting out patterns, tacking the pieces together, trying them on our three willing, obliging mannequins. The hand sewing is worth all the effort, the result being three beautiful dresses with flounces and frills. For the flower baskets we cover shoe boxes with remnants of the same material and finish them off with lace and ribbons. The girls are beside themselves with waiting for the big day.

These days Eva and I spend all our time together, as it used to be before that fateful trip to Derby. I broke the ice first, on the subject of Julian, so it could be discussed, put away and not brought up again.

'I feel absolutely wretched,' I confessed one day when we sat sewing together, 'I cannot forgive myself for hurting all the people I love the most. You must all hate me. Theo and Roman haven't been around for ages!'

She looked up from her sewing, her clear eyes wistful.

'Nobody hates you Nastusha.'

'But I've been beastly to Roman. The sweetest man I know. My own brother wouldn't have had that much patience with me. If only I could take back all the horrible things I said!'

'Now listen Nastusha!' Eva was her usual practical self, 'what's done is done. Those who care for you will understand. And those who don't understand are not worth worrying about. But from now on, you can do something positive, right?'

I looked at her with woken curiosity. 'Right. Just tell me.'

She hooked a strand of her white blond hair behind her ear.

'There's talk of transfers to other DP camps. Further south. Where there's more work. More chance for us to do something.'

'You mean to settle there? For how long?'

'Nobody knows that. But we can't spend all our time waiting. It'll be good to take control of our lives again.'

Having been so entrapped with my own grief, I had no practical ideas for my immediate future, only the unchanging notion of returning home to Poland.

'So what are you and Henryk going to do?'

'We've put our names down for *Hasbend Bosford*. Near *Leycester*. Middle England.'

'And Roman?'

'Yes, he wants to go there too. And Theo's coming with us. Lots of factories there. And building work. And employment for women. So, what do you think? I didn't dare mention this to you before... you were so touchy Nastusha... I feared you'd just flatly refuse...' Her expression is apologetic, making me realise how trying my behaviour must have been for her. I cringe with shame.

'I'm so sorry Eva. But what would I do here, on my own, with my friends gone? Of course I want to come with you.'

She laughs a happy laugh, and puts her sewing down.

'Come on then. Don't let's waste any time. Let's get your name down on that list!'

On Corpus Christi Sunday, Stella, Nadia and Julia, and all the other little girls at the camp, look like angels and cherubs descended from heaven. In their white, ephemeral dresses they shiver against the northerly wind, for although it is half-way through June, and the sun is gracing this special day with its luminous presence, its warmth is far behind.

The girls seem unaware of the goose pimples on their bare arms and legs as, with rapt attention, they walk in two orderly lines ahead of the monstrance carried by the gold and white be -robed priest and scatter flower-heads in his path.

All the population of the camp is out; old women wrapped in their flowery shawls, with rosaries wound round their clasped hands, younger women in their Sunday-best home- made dresses, their styled hair bearing testimony to an all night discomfort of sleeping with curlers, old men in worn suits smartened up with white shirts and ties, and all younger men relentlessly sporting their uniforms, until such time when their savings allow them the extravagance of civilian clothes.

We follow the priest in a long procession, singing hymns and reciting prayers at each of the four specially constructed altars, in four corners of the camp, altars that are covered in white sheets and decorated with garlands of leaves and flowers gathered in the meadows. My sentimental thoughts take me back to all those other processions at home, amidst the scents and the warmth of mid-summer. I miss it all with a pang of longing, but seeing our children's enchanted faces, gives me hope that what they'll remember in years to come is the magic created amidst the black barracks.

I walk with Eva close behind our girls, replenishing their baskets with flower-heads, but I constantly look around for a glimpse of our boys. I spot them in the crowd, Henryk, Roman and Theo, elegant as ever in their uniforms. My heart leaps with joy, then shrinks back at the thought of Roman's justified rejection. I've got no choice but to endure this tormenting uncertainty till the end of the service.

At last, the concluding prayers are said at the fourth altar and the final laud is sung:

O Jezu w Hostii białej
O Jesus in the White Host
Disguised amongst us
With the kindness of your heart
You have won our hearts.

The English countryside resounds with the words of a Polish hymn sung by hundreds of voices.

The crowd disperses in slow-moving groups. Our girls resist our attempts at pulling on cardigans over their bare arms, but then all resistance is forgotten when they spot our boys coming towards us and they run ahead to meet them. I repeat mentally my rehearsed speech to Roman, cringing at the thought of his reaction, but for a moment I get distracted. I watch Julia run up to Theo and raise her arms to him. His face lights up with pure happiness as he bends down and picks her up. She plants a kiss on his cheek and gabbles away. God forgive me, in my blind anger, I've also deprived her.

I can barely stand it as I watch Roman coming towards me. My mind works overtime trying to remember all the suitable words I have been memorising. I open my mouth to blurt out something, anything, but he is first, with a warm, brotherly embrace.

I get my breath back. 'Roman, can you ever forgive me?'

He steps back and looks at me as if he has no idea what I'm referring to.

'Forgive you what?' Then his feigned forgetfulness dissolves in a wide smile. He taps his head. 'Senility. I can't remember what I did yesterday.'

'But I can guess!' I laugh with relief, my whole being suddenly as light as a sunbeam, 'Roman, happy birthday for yesterday. Did you do anything? It's quite a milestone, getting to the ripe old age of thirty!'

Theo chuckles, his grey eyes radiating joy. Julia's arm stays firmly draped around his neck. He tells me,

'Some dubious mixture that someone brought along. It's only best when mixed with plum juice. Homemade, of course.'

'You don't taste the stuff,' Roman laughs, 'you take a lightning swig. Or it burns your throat like hell-fire!'

'It's got its uses' Henryk adds, 'makes you sing like a lark in the clouds!'

'But how did you remember, Nastusha?' Roman asks.

'It's a woman thing…' I tease. I take out from my handbag a scarf I have knitted for him in navy and air-force-blue vertical stripes. 'Not quite the season for it, but it will do for next winter.'

'Oh, I don't know,' he rubs his hands together in a mock gesture of warming them, 'it will be perfect for today.' He throws the scarf around his neck in an exaggerated dandy fashion that makes our little girls laugh.

'And a little something from Henryk and me,' Eva says giving him a small package of coffee, a luxury these days, enjoyed only on Sundays. Roman is genuinely touched.

'Let's go and all have a taste of it,' he suggests, but Eva protests that he must keep it for himself.

We rejoin the crowd, now less compact, small groups in lively discussions, and make our way slowly down the central path towards the dining hall. The tables have been set out in long rows for afternoon tea with jam sandwiches cut in triangles and Swiss rolls cut in thin circles.

The hot drinks and the presence of so many people warms up the air and for the first time this afternoon I feel comfortably snug in my coat. Our girls have stopped shivering and are enjoying the sweet bread and the cake. I save mine for Julia, for later, wrap it in a paper bag (always tucked in my handbag) and warm my hands around the tea cup. Theo sits opposite. He leans towards me.

'I've missed our visits to the camp,' he says.

I feel the colour rise in my face. 'I'm sorry Theo. I've not been good company lately.'

'No, I'm sorry. Really sorry about what's happened.' The look of genuine sympathy in his eyes makes me look down. He says, 'Anastazia, I know that words are inadequate at the moment, but I just want to reassure you that you're not alone. You've got friends. Really good friends.'

I look at him. 'I know that Theo. I should have known it all along.'

'We all react differently to shock.' He tries to absolve me, good, earnest Theo. He adds, 'you've still got something that I envy you. You've got Julia.' His gaze falls tenderly on her, sitting next to me, her mouth sticky with jam. I know, I know how lucky I am to have 'family'. Theo's got no one. But having Julia does not ease the pain of Julian's betrayal.

I stroke her head and I say to him, to please him, 'I know you've made an impression on her. She's been constantly asking about you.'

'Really?' his smile reflects his delight, 'then that makes me feel as if I belong to your group.'

'Of course you do, Theo.' I want to tell him more, that he has impressed me too, with his kindness and his easy manner, that he's made me feel comfortable and safe in his presence and that I wish for him to find a good woman, deserving of his qualities so that he can find peace and contentment in his new rebuilt life after all the losses he has endured. As all these thoughts chase around in my mind, all I can say is,

'Tell me, what masterpieces have you been creating in your carpentry classes?'

Later, we all go together for a stroll in the Plessy Woods. The girls run ahead and play hide and seek in between the trees. Roman walks with Eva and Henryk, deep in discussion about all the possibilities of work in the Midlands, after our transfer.

Theo walks with me. There's always an aura of cleanliness about him, pleasant whiffs of soap and mint and hair cream.

'And what will you do?' I ask him.

'Whatever comes along. It's time to start living the real life.'

'They say there's not much choice for foreigners like us.' I repeat what I've heard in the common room.

'No. Most probably some farm work or digging roads. But whatever...' he shrugs, 'you've got to make a start somewhere. What about you, Anastazia?

I give him a sideways glance. I never imagined it was going to be like this, without Julian. I wish to sound practical.

'I too will be looking for work. Both Eva and I are good at sewing. It would be so lucky to get something like that...' I look up to where the blackbirds are chasing each other in the branches setting off other birds screeching. For a moment it's not possible to talk and he gives me an amused smile. Then the noise settles down and I carry on.

'It's hard to imagine the future, isn't it Theo? We've all had such a set goal. To return home.'

He nods, then walks silently for a while, before speaking.

'But it's up to us now Anastazia, to create a home wherever we are. Otherwise we could remain loners and aimless wanderers for the rest of our lives.'

I guess he is thinking about his own situation, robbed of his family and now completely alone. There is a good chance for him yet. As for Roman. Young and with his good looks and natural charm, he won't be single for too long. Henryk and Eva, despite their frequent 'quiet' days, are doing their best at patching up cracks in their marriage, for their girls' sake. And also because once you've promised to stick together through thick and thin *till death us do part*, that's what you do. And that's what I would have done, even now, if Julian returned to me. It would have been my duty.

'You've got to be free, Theo, to make those decisions. My hands are tied. I'm single yet still bound by marriage.'

'And do you intend to remain in this state for the rest of your life?'

'I don't know, Theo,' I tell him honestly and take a deep breath. 'I've no idea what to think any more. I even have this fantasy now and again, that when we all return to Poland, I'll find Julian yet...'

'And then what?' he gives me a withering look, and I shrug, knowing how stupid this sounds.

'But what else can I do? There's no divorce in our church'.

'No, but you'd have no problem getting a legal divorce on the grounds of desertion.'

Theo's words, though only words of information, have such a final ring to them they send a shiver down my spine.

'Anastazia...' he looks at me with pity, and his tone is like a father's tone admonishing a silly child, 'I had a proposition for you. But I can see you are not ready yet for it.'

'What?' I want to know.

But he just smiles, his ever patient smile and says, 'It can wait.'

Late in the evening, after our boys have gone, and the girls are asleep, exhausted by today's exciting events, Eva and I, with shawls around our shoulders, sit outside our door warming our hands round our tea mugs.

The air is very still and surprisingly milder than it's been in the daytime. The sky is still light with the moon rising above the woods surrounding our camp. I tell Eva about my talk with Theo.

'Nastusha,' her brisk tone suggests she's going to come straight to the point, 'it is quite obvious to anyone but you, that Theo's in love with you.'

'What!' she could have wacked me with a stick, 'bbbut... what are you saying?'

Eva rolls her eyes. 'Look! There's nothing shameful in that!'

'But I'm a married woman!'

She gives me another of her expressive looks. 'Nastusha! Listen to yourself! A married woman. Yes! On paper. Why do you think that no one else would fancy you except Julian? Theo's a lonely man. You've been nice to him...Da?'

'But only as a friend, a friend Eva!'

'That may be so, but when you're needy you appreciate everything. And look how he is with Julia... he's so attached to her. And she to him! Her favourite man! There's no doubt about that!'

What Eva says is true, and of course I was aware of it, but suddenly it all feels out of control.

'Eva, believe me, I've never led him on. God, I don't want him to be wasting his feelings on me!'

Eva's patience turns to chiding me. 'Nastusha, what I've got to say to you will be blunt. We've always been straight with each other. Hear me out and give yourself time to think about it. Do you honestly think there is a hope for you and Julian? When? In two years? In four or ten? Where will you go looking for him? And even if you were to find him? Then what? He's made his choice. Nastusha, he's abandoned you!'

Her brutal words make the truth clear and final.

'Eva, at this moment I still don't know what I want. I only know that my Catholic duty is to my marriage vows. Look at yourself and Henryk. You haven't given up!'

'Nastusha, if only you knew...' Eva's eyes become moist, 'sometimes I can't bear to be with him in the same room, let alone together in bed. We haven't yet... you know... but then I remind myself that he wouldn't want to touch me either if he knew... Sometimes the two days he is here we barely exchange a few words. Only in front of the girls we pretend that all is well.'

'But the important thing is that you're trying Eva. You're making a big effort. And it will pay off in the end!'

'Will it?' she sounds dejected and looks up into the darkening sky. 'I envy you sometimes, and before you protest, let me tell you what hard work it is trying so hard to patch up things between us, always on our guard what we say and how we say it. You've got a clean slate, Nastusha, you can start afresh with a clear conscience. You're an innocent victim of Julian's less than noble deeds. Don't waste a good chance now. Theo loves you. I don't think it would be so hard to love him in return. He is a good man. He'll look after you and Julia.'

In the week that follows I go over her words hundreds of times. I think back to all the times I've been in Theo's company. It felt good and calm and safe. I felt happy, I have to admit, and it was his kindness that I tried to reciprocate, with no intention of leading him on. And it is also true that my affection grew for him every time he showed a fatherly interest in my little Julia. Now that I've admitted to myself that I could be drawn to a serious relationship with him, I am torn with guilt at my betrayal of sworn loyalty to Julian.

In mid-week I pay our camp chaplain a visit. His vicarage is a small self-contained Nissen hut next to our camp chapel.

Father Mroz is a man of about sixty, with grey hair and black bushy eyebrows and a feudal manner, reminiscent of our village priests at home. He bids me to sit down on the other side of his desk, folds his arms, tilts his head back so as to look down on me.

I give him an account of Julian's injury, the ensuing condition and the outcome of all that for me.

'What do I do now, Father? For the rest of my life?'

He does not change his position, only his eyes wonder to the window, then back at me. There's no sympathy in them, just cold authority in his tone.

'As you well know,' he says, 'there's no divorce in our Catholic Church. An annulment can be granted,' he pauses, making my hope leap for a split second, 'but only in very unusual circumstances. If there's no consummation of marriage. If one of the partners is set against having children. If one of the partners is not a Catholic and undermines the faith of the Catholic partner. And in case of madness.'

None of these reasons apply in our case. 'So what am I to do?'

He sits up, business-like, and pronounces,

'Just get on with life and carry the cross you've been given.'

I swallow hard this bitter pill. 'What about my child? Isn't she entitled to a father figure in her life?'

'You'll have to be both for her.' That goes without saying, his raised eyebrows suggest.

I give him a long stare, anger and bitterness welling up inside me.

'Father, let me get this straight: my husband has left me, ran off with another woman, to another country, and I have to be punished for the rest of my life, for his sin? You call that justice?'

He shrugs.

'A lot of things in life are not fair. Was Christ's crucifixion fair? Was the persecution of Christians fair? The terrible deaths of our martyr saints? Be thankful to God for surviving the war. Your duty now is to your child. You're healthy. You're young. What else do you want?'

'Yes, I'm young. I'm thirty-four. And not quite ready yet to live like a nun!' I surprise myself with my outspokenness. I think I surprise him too. He looks annoyed.

'Don't you dare cheek me, young woman! I warn you! You'll be barred from all sacraments if you choose to live in sin!'

His words leave me livid. It takes all my willpower to control my fury. I stand up and with strained politeness I bid him farewell.

'Thank you Father, thank you for making it so clear to me!'

What is clear in my mind as I walk back to my place on this sunny June day, the air shimmering with floating pollen and the grasses between the black barracks swaying on long stalks, what is clear is that I'm done with grieving and tormenting myself with guilt over some rules of the church that has no compassion. I have no quarrel with God, and I shall continue to visit His house. The priest cannot bar me from praying. From now on I shall rely on my own conscience and let it be the judge of my deeds.

Eva is out and our little girls are at the playschool when I return to my room. I pull the suitcase out from under my bed and empty its contents on the bed, for repacking with a few additions from the wardrobe. Rumours are rife of an imminent transfer to Husbands Bosworth camp.

I unwrap Dorotka's little bonnet, that has travelled with me on all my unplanned voyages. I've washed it regularly to preserve its whiteness, but when I press it to my mouth and nose I still remember the sweet baby smell of her. I wrap it again and slide it inside a large envelope that holds all my saved photographs.

Then there are Julian's notebooks. The suddenness of my anguish takes me unawares. I clench my teeth and screw my eyes tight till the attack subsides. My reaction is to throw them away, but something stops me. This is Julia's only legacy. And the little red handbag. The only tangible link between her and her father.

I fit his notebooks, together with mine, inside a shoe box and tie it with string. Several times over. I place the box at the bottom of the suitcase. It will be covered over with layers of folded garments. That part of my life is over.

On Saturday afternoon, when the expected sound of the jeep is heard, Stella, Nadia and Julia run out to meet our boys, with squeals of delight. Even with Henryk sitting at the back, they pile into the vacant space and push and squash, till they are wedged tight inside. As always, they are taken for a spin along the main camp road and back.

Eva and I wait on the doorstep. She looks especially pretty with her smooth silky hair caught at the back, and her eyes reflecting the pastel turquoise of her cotton dress. She has made an effort for Henryk.

I've made an effort too. For my own sake. Somehow my shampooed fluffy hair and a touch of lipstick do something for my self-esteem.

The jeep reappears, the boys jump down, followed by our little girls, who skip around them gaily. Stella grabs Henryk's hand, Nadia clings to Roman, but Julia lifts her arms up to Theo. He picks her up and strides towards me, a wide smile across his face.

My heart beats fast, and somehow it feels natural to greet him with a hug and to feel his strong comforting arm around me.

'I've missed you, Theo,' I tell him simply, 'that proposition, you mentioned last Sunday, you've not changed your mind?'

His laugh is soft against my hair and his breath warm as his lips touch my face.

'I've waited so long to hear these words from you!' he says.

VOLUME 3

JULIA

12 Years later, 1960

CHAPTER 54

Last word. Full stop. Julia's stiff shoulders dropped with relief. She sat back and rested her clasped hands on top of her completed paper. Three more minutes and Sister Vespera would officially announce the end of the final exam.

Julia could hardly believe it. This very moment marked the end of an era. No fanfares, just a bubbling, bursting sensation inside her, threatening to explode.

In the strained silence, there was just the frantic scratching of pens, last minute amendments to the testing piece of French prose. The classroom was hot and stuffy despite the open windows. Not a whisper of breeze on this scorching first day of July. Long rectangles of sunlight reflected off the polished floor, making one squint against the brightness. Hints of musky smells and sweaty hands. Julia felt stifled in her uniform. She loosened the tie around her neck. She wished she could throw it all off and plunge herself into a cool bath.

Sister Vespera cleared her throat and rang the miniature brass bell on her table.

'Time's up! Pens down!' Her expression remained severe, as always. There was a collective exhalation of relief. Heads turned, cheeks burned, tired smiles hovered on parched lips. Julia caught Lidia's gaze. She gave a nod to say all was well. Streaks of sweat glistened below her hairline, below the mass of curls, too thick on this hot day. On the other side of the class, Yagoda gave a discreet thumbs-up sign. She looked like a twelve-year-old with her small thin frame and her fair hair in plaits. Julia's best friends throughout the school years, her soul-mates, the sisters she wished she'd had, statuesque Lidia and sparrow-like Yagoda.

Sister Vespera cleared her throat.

'No talking, till you leave this room. Kalinska, collect the papers and stay behind!' Sister Vespera gave Julia a piercing look with her blackcurrant eyes.

Whatever now! Bitterness welled up inside Julia over her elation. On this last day! There was no pleasing Sister Vespera, only if you were like Iza or Vanda with *regular* parents, or if your father was a *director*.

Julia collected the papers, placed them neatly on Sister Vespera's desk, and cringed, waiting, while all the other girls filed out of the classroom. Lidia was deliberately last. She mouthed from the door, 'I'll wait for you outside.'

Sister Vespera appeared oblivious to Julia's presence for a long time, writing notes in a hard-back exercise book. The brightness reflecting from the surface of the table made her round spectacles shine like the strange eyes of some alien. Julia felt sweat prickling her scalp and her armpits.

'Please Sister,' she dared herself to speak, 'may I go now?'

Sister Vespera did not reply. She carried on writing, then slowly read her notes, closed the book, meticulously screwed the cap on the fountain pen, placed it next to the notebook, clasped her hands, and only then did she look up at Julia.

'Kalinska,' she said, 'there's been a telephone message from your step-father.' She pronounced the prefix 'step' as if the word displeased her. Julia was surprised.

'From my Father? Alone?' They always rang together from the public telephone box, her Mama and her Tato. 'Why? What did my Father say?'

Another penetrating look from Sister Vespera. 'Your mother's been admitted to hospital.'

A moment to register. Then that shrinking feeling, at the pit of her stomach. That dreaded sensation. A relic from her childhood.

'My Mum? In hospital?' her mouth felt dry. 'What's happened to her? Was it an accident? Is she ill?'

Sister Vespera arched her thick dark eyebrows.

'If you let me speak, I'll tell you!' she pursed her lips, making the little hairs round them stand on end. 'No, there's not been an accident. Your mother is in for observation. In a psychiatric unit.'

Julia did not understand. 'In a psychiatric unit?' she repeated, the words racing around her mind. It made no sense, it was not possible! Her Mama? Like Mr. Rochester's wife, mad and dangerous? Like old and wrinkled Mrs. Vilczkova, whose fiercely guarded collection of empty food tins covered her entire floor.

'I can't believe it...' her voice faltered. Nervously she pulled out a handkerchief from inside her sleeve and dabbed at her eyes.

Sister Vespera looked at her severely as if somehow, Julia was at fault.

'People bring disasters upon themselves, you know,' she said. 'You make your bed, you lie in it.' It was like a stab. Julia felt helpless. She tucked away her handkerchief and straightened her shoulders.

'When did it happen?' she asked.

'Three weeks ago.'

'Three weeks! And I didn't know?' She was close to tears again. Sister Vespera's cold stare stopped her.

'And what good would it do? Telling you? When you needed all your concentration for your exams?' There was no arguing about that.

'So... did my Father say anything else?' Julia asked meekly.

'Yes, he did.' A pause. 'Tomorrow you're to wait for your step-father to fetch you. There'll be no train journey for you with your friends, I'm afraid.'

There was some relief in this piece of information. This meant that her Tato would be coming by car with her uncle Roman, the only one among their friends with such an enviable possession.

'You may leave now, Kalinska.' Sister Vespera's glasses flashed and her hand flicked dismissively.

Lidia and Yagoda were waiting for her outside. They detached themselves from the shade of the linden tree and ran up the path to meet her. Yagoda began to cough. She was always coughing.

'What did Vespa want from you?' Lidia asked, her huge brown eyes eager for news. She was half-Italian and had nick-named the nun *Vespa*, for wasp.

Julia told them, omitting to mention the dreaded word *psychiatric*, and was immediately niggled by guilt for holding back the truth from her friends.

'So, what's actually wrong with your Mum? Does she need an operation?' Yagoda's dry cough accompanied her questions.

'All I've been told,' Julia replied cautiously, 'is that she's in for observation. I'll know more when I go to see her tomorrow.'

'You must write and tell us,' Lidia's tone was decisive. She had always been like an older sibling, taking the lead and expecting to be followed.

'I'll write every week,' Julia promised. 'Can you believe it? It'll never be like this ever again. Our last day in this place! I'll expect letters from you both.'

They walked behind groups of girls from other classes up the tree-lined sun-dappled walk that linked the school buildings with the main house. Pitsford Hall had been their home in term time for many years. Today, Julia surprised herself with a stir of nostalgia already present in her mind, as she cast her glance over the familiar surroundings. The orchard at the back of the Hall, the well-tended gardens and lawns, the shady lanes, Mercury's statue in the middle of the algae-thick swimming pool, the white stone statue of the Virgin Mary at the end of the honeysuckle walk, all these things she would surely miss.

The nuns had been like an extended family, the wise Sister Benedicta, the motherly Sister Yadviga, the patient Sister Alicya, the entertaining Sister Michaela. Only Sister Vespera was different. Julia would not miss her.

'It will be strange not coming back in September,' she remarked to her friends.

'I can't wait to get outside the convent walls,' Lidia stated, throwing back her head, loosening her abundant curls, pushing forward her ample chest, smiling mischievously.

Yagoda, walking between them, threw her arms around their shoulders and brought them together.

'I shall miss you both. I dread to imagine what it'll be like without you two in my new school.'

'You'll make new friends,' Lidia said, wriggling out of Yagoda's embrace, clasping her hand and leading her like a child.

At the back of the main building there were wrought iron steps that led down to the basement, to a warren of rooms; the kitchen, pantries, storerooms, cloakrooms. There was a grand oak staircase that rose vertically, parallel to a pulley lift, used in the past by the servants to deliver hot food to the upper floors. The three girls climbed up to their dormitory on the second floor.

All twelve beds were in great disarray, as their friends chattered and laughed while packing their suitcases and bags. Julia, Lidia and Yagoda's beds stood close together at the far end of the room. The girls threw off their heavy pinafores and changed into summery blouses and skirts. Julia began to sort her clothes, roll them and pack them inside her suitcase.

Yagoda's cough was a preamble to her words.

'Pity we don't live closer...' she sucked on a cough sweet, 'we could all go to visit your mother.'

'Yes... she would love that,' Julia agreed, infinitely relieved that it was not possible. She would rather have died than have her Mama's suspected condition revealed.

Lidia was folding her clothes in perfect squares, humming to herself, a secretive smile playing on her lips. Julia could guess that Lidia was already thinking about Patrick, the young lodger at her parents' house.

'Planning anything exciting?' Julia asked.

'It's all excitement from now on, and I can't wait!' Lidia gave her a wide smile. Yagoda looked up from the pile of books she was sorting on her bed, her two long plaits hanging down her front.

'My Mama says,' she coughed, 'don't wish your life away. You're young for a very short time, and old for the rest of your life!'

Lidia laughed and hugged herself.

'If old means doing the things I want to do, then I want to be old! What about you, Julia, will you be seeing Miro?'

Julia gave her a suspicious sideways glance. 'Of course I'll be seeing Miro. He's my friend! As old as the hills!'

'Is that all?' Lidia laughed and the teasing edge of her tone irritated Julia.

'Yes! That's all! We played in the Infants, for goodness sake!'

'OK! Calm down! I believe you! Hey, how about getting together in the Summer? Going to a dance?' Julia's mind panicked at the thought of her friends arriving to discover the truth about her Mama's illness, but Lidia's next words dispelled her fears. 'Come down on the train with Miro,' Lidia invited, 'and you too, Yagoda. Goes without saying. Your Mum won't object, will she?'

Yagoda flung her plaits over her shoulders. There was excitement in her thin face.

'Of course she won't object. But how will your parents cope with this invasion?'

'No problem! I assure you!' Lidia tossed back her abundant curls with the confidence of a doted-on daughter. And Julia envied her. She envied Yagoda. Tomorrow they'd be enjoying all the comforts of home, their parents pampering them with treats, outings, extra pocket money, new clothes, to mark their homecoming for good. Julia had no idea what was awaiting her.

These last few weeks, packed with frantic swotting and daily exams, she had longed for her homecoming with increasing impatience. Each night, before she fell asleep, her mind transported her home, always sunny and warm in her dreams, and her Mama standing at the cooker, stirring something good in the pot, and singing, always singing or humming, her voice mellow, tone-perfect, her eyes smiling at Julia, through her uninterrupted song.

'Are you ready, Julia?' Lidia's voice pulled her out of her day-dreaming. 'Let's go and say our goodbyes!'

The teaching staff lived in the quadrangle across the main road, that once had been a stable block. It was converted into living rooms on the ground floor and girls' dormitories in the spacious attic. A tarmac lane led from the main house to this part of the estate, with lush growth overhanging on both sides. Lidia linked her arm through Julia's and they walked in bouncy unison, Lidia's controlled excitement all too evident. Julia's mind was preoccupied with her Mama.

Yagoda hurried on ahead and stopped at Our Lady's shrine, high in the hollow of the tree trunk, with daily picked field flowers, laid at the foot. A constant reminder for a moment's prayer.

'What's your wish then, Yagoda?' Lidia asked.

Yagoda shrugged her thin shoulders and coughed. 'The trouble is I want so many things. But that's being greedy, isn't it?'

'No! That's being ambitious!' Lidia spoke in her Big Sister tone. 'And you've got to be ambitious to achieve things in life!'

'I want to,' Yagoda spoke in earnest, 'but... I don't want to push my luck.' She'd had polio as a child. 'I just want to be well.'

'That, and much more!' Lidia corrected. 'Come on! The world is our oyster!'

'For ever!' Julia added for good measure. The three of them linked arms and walked on.

Professor Koscialkowski and his wife lived in a two-room ground flat. Julia had enjoyed tutorials in his study, the walls lined with books, like a miniature library, the smell of old paper and wood polish, the fascinating, colourful small objects, souvenirs of their enforced travels in the war years. They had been university professors in Poland before the war, now they endeavoured to educate pubescent girls.

Madame Koscialkowska opened the door, a small woman in her sixties, her grey hair caught in a net. Her cheeks lifted in a smile of expectation.

'*Comment, l'examen, est-il allé*? How did it go?' She always addressed her pupils in French.

'*Très bien, Madame, très bien!*' Julia and her friends assured her.

'*Je m'attends a de meilleurs resultats.* I'm expecting the best results.'

'*Mais bien sûr, Madame*! But of course!'

'*Promettez-moi pour lire les livres francais*! Promise me to read lots of French books!'

'*Toujours, Madame.* Always!'

Julia smiled inwardly. How could she possibly live up to those expectations when there were hundreds of other things she wanted to do!

They were invited in and perched together on the edge of a small sofa. The professor turned round from his writing desk, his grey eyes smiling behind his half-moons. His white hair and white beard gave him a gentle avuncular appearance. Julia had liked him instantly from the beginning. His patience was saintly, often challenged by his pupils' imaginative distortion of historical facts. Yet his corrective remarks were always humorous, never crushing.

'So,' he clasped his hands, 'the day you've been waiting for has arrived. Come back and tell us of your successes. A-levels. Then university. Choose your subjects well. Which one of you will go for Medicine? Which one for the Law? Education? Physics? Research?'

It all seemed so remote to Julia. They giggled shyly, gave all the polite, expected answers, expressed their thanks and said their goodbyes.

Mrs. Brzozowska's room was diagonally across the quadrangle, the white pebbly ground bright in the scorching sun. It was sparsely furnished, but she had softened the spartan appearance with an embroidered table-cloth, a rug on the linoleum floor, and cushions on the neat, flat bed in the corner. Her room always smelled fragrant, like the dressed-up ladies at the dances at home.

The door was wide open when Julia and her friends approached. Mrs. Brzozowska was sitting over some paperwork work at the table, but seeing them she got up to greet them, her beige cotton dress crisp and unruffled by the heat. Her fair hair was cut short and styled with a wave across her forehead, her makeup was discreet, she was the epitome of elegance amidst the sea of uniforms and black habits. Her smile widened as she listened to the girls prepared words of thanks and farewells.

'So,' she said, 'you're all keen to become Latin scholars now. Right?' Julia and Lidia giggled. Yagoda looked at them and rolled her eyes.

'I'd love to do that,' she said to her Latin teacher, swallowing a cough, 'I'd love to study ancient history, and Greek too!'

'Swot!' Lidia mouthed, but Mrs. Brzozowska's eyes shone.

'A girl after my own heart!' she said, 'I wish you all the best for the future. And keep reminding yourself: *ad astra per ardua*! Achievement through hard work!'

Julia wondered, as they walked away, if Mrs. Brzozowska got lonely.

Rumour had it that she had lost her husband and her son in the war. 'She is so pretty,' she expressed her thoughts aloud, 'I wonder if she'll ever marry again?'

'Julia!' Yagoda sounded indignant 'If they were like Romeo and Juliet, or Heathcliff and Catherine, then she'd never be able to marry again! For me, there will only be the one person, ever!'

'Yagoda!' now Lidia showed impatience. 'Life isn't always a fairy tale! What if you can't find that perfect person? Would you never love anyone else?' A cheeky grin crept to her lips. 'Me? I want to have fun. With lots of boys. Then, I'll decide!'

'Good luck to you, then,' Yagoda replied, 'I worry for you sometimes.'

'Only sometimes?' Lidia laughed. 'You sound just like my Mama, my dear little sparrow!'

Yagoda shrugged, her wide-eyed look expressive. 'I've got big shoulders. You may need them yet.'

Julia laughed too.

Next, the girls went to visit Mrs. Kulczycka and Mrs. Kuksz. They lived in a cottage outside the stables block, at the end of a path edged with thick shrubs on both sides, beyond which lay wide open fields stretching to the village of Moulton. Julia knocked on their door a few times, but it appeared that they were out.

Lidia strutted theatrically to the fence, overhung with crab apples, leaned her elbow on it, and with a pinched expression emulating Mrs. Kuksz she quoted,

'Under my tree, near my fence, in the grass, close to my house, there sits a moorhen on the ground. She has sixteen eggs.'

Mrs. Kuksz's Polish literature lessons were frequently enhanced with amusing non-sequiturs. Julia would miss her gentle manner, her softly spoken voice, her love of Polish poetry, which her mesmeric readings transferred onto her listeners. She made a mental note to write to her, as indeed, she would write to Mrs. Kulczycka too.

She always enjoyed the evenings when Mrs. Kulczycka was on duty in recreation time. The girls would sit spell-bound listening to her imaginative recounting of legends, novels or film themes, to her descriptions of memorable events and of great heroes in the free, pre-war Poland.

'Pity they are out,' she said with regret. 'After tomorrow nothing will ever be the same again.' Her Mama came to her mind, alone and far away in a strange place. Something heavy pressed on her heart.

'And I shall never know the end of that last story!' Yagoda remarked. Lidia laughed.

'Yagoda, you'll be reading thousands of stories! Adult novels!' A teasing smile curled her lips. 'Shall we pay our other teachers a visit?'

The male maths and geography teachers had rooms in the annexe of the main house together with the much loved and revered elderly Father Dallinger.

'You know we're not allowed there,' Yagoda pointed out, 'and anyway, do you think we're really their favourite class?' Yagoda was always so earnest.

Lidia had the grace to look sheepish for a moment, then she burst out laughing. 'Do you remember the furry spiders?' Julia remembered it all: the chalk dust on the teacher's chair, and Lidia hiding in the store room through the entire maths lesson and Mr. Łojewski's puzzled expression at the intermittent mice scratching and squeaks, and the leaping frog let loose in Mr. Jankowski's geography lesson. Lidia's imagination had had no bounds. It all seemed so silly now, yet all three were still laughing.

That night, in the dormitory, excited whispers went on till very late. Sister Alicya, their night time carer, did not come back to reprimand them this time.

CHAPTER 55

The next morning, by half-past nine, Julia was ready with her suitcase at the steps of the main entrance. Other girls, like her, waiting for their transport, stood in twos or threes with Sister Alicya supervising. The green expanse before them, punctuated at random with solitary cedars, shone vivid in the morning sun, yet, Julia felt, there was a touch of emptiness about the place with everyone gone.

Sister Alicya stood on the highest step and chatted to anyone close by and reminisced about her time in Africa, in an orphanage that catered for Polish children, bereft of their parents during the war.

'From shelters in the jungle to this grand mansion,' Sister Alicya said fervently. 'God works in mysterious ways!'

It was indeed paradoxical, Julia had thought that many times in the past, that her real home had been a Nissen hut made of corrugated iron, while in term time she lived in the splendour of elegant, pastel-coloured rooms, with high ceilings and richly decorated cornices.

'And,' Sister Alicya continued, 'we're standing on the exact spot where Queen Elizabeth, when she was a little girl, stood with the adults for a group photograph.'

This was indeed a fact, that Pitsford Hall had once belonged to the Drummond family, who had connections with the royals. The two little princesses, Lilibet and Margaret could be glimpsed horse riding, when the grownups came down for the hunts. Prince Edward and Mrs. Simpson had been frequent visitors, mentors or pupils of Captain Drummond's fascist tendencies that made him unpopular with the village people, then worse still, with the establishment. He and his family were forced into exile after the war, just as the Polish nuns arrived looking for a place to open a school for the daughters of Polish immigrants. Transforming Pitsford Hall into a convent school was planned as a temporary measure until such time when Poland's difficult situation was resolved. This summer, in 1960, Poland was still under Soviet rule.

Julia could not imagine living anywhere else but England. Besides, since her parents had been moved to the long- awaited council house, and since she had a room of her own, she could boast proudly now, that her family were living in a proper house.

It was hot in her uniform, the blazer and the felt hat. She willed her Tato and Roman to hurry up. Every time there was a crunch of tyres on the gravel beyond the screen of laurel trees, she gripped the handle of her suitcase in readiness.

Then at last, the familiar old car came into view, a grey and maroon Hillman, and swept round the wide curve of the drive, before stopping beside her. Roman greeted her from behind the steering wheel, with a friendly, avuncular smile, while her Tato got out of the car and hurried to hug her briefly. Theo Lutovski, her step-father, whom she had always called her Tato, her Dad. He wore his grey suit for this occasion and Julia caught a whiff of mothballs, which even the eau de cologne could not disguise. His hair was flattened with Brylcream for neatness, his stiff white hair, which had gone white all in one night, from the shock of exploding bombs, when he was only thirty-five.

He stooped to pick up her suitcase and Julia noticed how crumpled his trousers were, and how a fan of creases radiated from his collar down his back. Julia noticed Sister Alicya's discreetly bemused gaze registering these details and wished she could explain things. About her Mama's absence. About his distracted state.

Tato lugged the suitcase and lifted it inside the boot. He came back with a bouquet of pink and white carnations.

'For the chapel,' he said to Sister Alicya, 'with our sincere thanks for everything you did.'

Julia was pleased to note surprise then pleasure in Sister Alicya's face, and when she added her own thanks and farewells, the need to explain was gone.

The moment they were off, Julia took off her hat and her blazer, shook her hair loose and leaned forward against Tato's back-rest. He was lighting a cigarette for Roman and one for himself.

'So, what's happened to Mama?' She slipped automatically into Polish. He half-turned his face, his brow puckered, his eyes squinting against the smoke.

'She's in hospital, Julia. In Warwick. We're going there first.'

'Why? Why Warwick?'

He glanced at Roman. 'It's a special hospital,' he said, 'for people with nervous disorders.'

So, it was true. Her stomach tightened painfully.

'But why, Tato, why? How has this come about?'

He drew on his cigarette.

'These things creep up on you, Julia, unclear at first, so you don't react as you would to a broken arm or appendicitis. And when you realise there is something wrong, you still have no idea what to do.'

'But there is a cure, isn't there? They can make Mama recover from this… condition?' Not *madness,* please don't let it be *madness!*

Roman cleared his throat. Her adopted Uncle Roman.

'Your Mama is in good hands,' he said. 'She'll get special treatment. She'll need time. These things don't get cured overnight.'

'But what's actually wrong with her? Tato!'

He turned his head towards her.

'Her nerves, Julia. She's obviously not as strong as she appeared to have been all those years.'

Julia was bewildered. She had never perceived her Mama as weak, in any sense. Outspoken. Assertive. Passionately indignant about any injustice. Mildly didactic when sorting out Julia's childhood squabbles with her friends.

Julia wound down the window and let her face cool in the pollen-scented breeze. Ripe fields of corn and bright yellow rape-seed fields shone through the foliage of the hedges that passed by. She knew about Mama's past. She grew up with stories of starving children in Russia. She knew of her father Julian, who had walked out on them both. But that was years ago! Almost her entire lifetime. No big deal. She never knew him. She did not miss him. They had Theo, her dear Tato. Why was Mama still fretting?

'So what did she actually do?' she asked.

Tato stubbed out his cigarette.

'It was gradual,' he said. 'She started acting strangely. Stopped going to work. Stayed in her dressing-gown all day.'

Her Mama? So unlike her. Always so busy all evening after work: cooking, baking in advance, gardening, always some knitting or embroidery on the go.

'Then one night,' Tato continued, 'she lit a bonfire in the middle of the night.'

This was scary. 'A bonfire? Outside?'

'She said she had newspapers to burn. She said they had printed lies about her...'

The prodding fingers attacked Julia's stomach again. She held her breath for a moment.

'What did you do?'

'I put out the fire and managed to persuade her to go to bed. It was like being caught in a nightmare. Keeping an eye on her. Dreading to fall asleep. In the morning I called Dr. Hemmings. He assessed her and called hospital transport to take her away. It was just a little old car. The driver was friendly and helpful. The strange thing was, Nastusha did not resist going. She appeared quite lucid and agreed with me that a rest would be like a holiday for her.'

This at least was a comforting thought.

'And how is she now? How is she coping?'

'You'll see for yourself.'

'Julia,' Roman caught her gaze in the mirror, 'she'll get through this. Just give her time. Trust her. And don't worry so!'

The hospital was situated on the outskirts of Warwick. It was a red-brick Victorian building, solid and sprawling, with towers rising above the rooftops, grand and self-important, yet filling Julia with unease, as if she were about to descend into prison.

They pulled up at the row of marked parking spaces along the edge of a lawn and got out of the car. The hospital was surrounded by well-tended lawns and a variety of trees.

'Will you come with us, uncle Roman?' Julia asked.

'Only two people allowed,' Tato said, 'and only family.'

'It's all right,' Roman said, 'I'll go for a stroll. Take your time. Don't rush back.'

'See you in an hour,' Tato said.

'Only an hour?' Julia was indignant. She wanted to stay with her Mama all day.

'She gets tired,' Tato said.

They went in through an arched open doorway and followed signs down long corridors, painted brown and green, oppressive in their gloom, despite the glints of shine on well-scrubbed walls and floors. The place was so quiet it felt as if they were the only two people there.

Then at last they walked into sunshine streaming through some tall windows and arrived at her Mama's ward, spacious and white, its end jutting out into hospital grounds. With a surge of anticipation Julia looked around the ward, the two rows of ship-shape beds, the patients in their armchairs and the visiting relatives just arriving. She spotted her Mama at the far end, looking at the window, her back to the ward.

The ward sister at her desk by the door asked their names.

'Theo Lutovski, Anastazia's husband.'

'And I'm her daughter,' Julia added pointing in her Mama's direction.

They came up quite close, but still she did not see them. There was something infinitely wistful about the angle of her head, about her drooped shoulders.

'Mama! We're here!' Julia crouched beside her and embraced her long and hard. It was like embracing a rock. Like a shove of rejection. Something recoiled inside her and she got up, a tight feeling in her throat.

Tato bent down, kissed Mama on both cheeks and hugged her to him.

'We've missed you, Nastusha. Look, I've brought you black grapes. Really juicy and sweet. Your favourites.' He placed them on top of the locker, next to the jug of water and the orange juice.

There was still no reaction from her. It was hard to watch. Mama's fluffy hair, more grey than the original dark brown, had a freshly washed looked about it and was pinned up on the sides with hair grips. Tomorrow, Julia decided, she would style it for her with rollers and hairspray. Also, her nails needed cutting. They made her thin fingers look all the more scrawny.

She noticed other patients going outside with their visitors.

'Mama, shall we go outside?' she suggested. 'It's so warm today. You can show me the garden.'

To her relief, Mama's stiff features relaxed, as if she had just woken up. She nodded and got up and allowed Julia to help her with the cardigan. Surprisingly, her hands were cold. Outside, they both held her hands in theirs and warmed them and led her as if she were a small child.

The hospital grounds were extensive, with wide swathes of green, trees, shrubs and flower beds awash with summer colours of fiery marigolds, bright daisies and sky blue lobelias. They found a bench under a willow tree, with its soft hanging branches forming a curtain round it. Before they sat down, Mama let go of their protective hands and knelt down at the edge of a flower bed. She picked up a handful of soil and let it crumble through her fingers.

'Good soil,' she said, 'but not as good as mine at home. Are my flowers surviving?'

Her amber brown eyes sought Julia's for news and it felt for a moment as if everything was normal, as always before.

'Nastusha,' Tato patted the space next to him on the bench, 'come and sit down beside me and I'll tell you everything. Do you know what the neighbours are saying about your garden?...' They moved up to her when she sat in the middle between them, and it felt good having Mama so close. 'Nastusha,' Tato continued, 'your garden is bursting with busy lizzies and pansies. I have to wear sunglasses to water the marigolds. They're so bright! People stop and ask what miracle powder I use for the roses. They're like giant bouquets now! I tell them to ask the expert...' he chuckled softly encouraging her to smile. Her gaze remained fixed on the ground.

'Mama,' Julia clasped her hand and stroked it gently, 'I did my last exam yesterday. The school's finished for the summer now, but I'm home for good. Can you believe it? After all the years? Now, I've got to start looking for my next school. With a sixth form.'

To her relief, Mama lifted her eyes to hers. But there was a puzzled expression in them, as if it was a struggle to understand Julia's words.

'Tomorrow's Sunday,' she said, 'you must go to church.'

This was her Mama, all right. She never missed church. Julia's childhood had been filled with countless visits to the church: twice each Sunday, Mass and the vespers, stations of the cross in Lent, devotions to Mary in May, devotions to Jesus in June, Corpus Christi processions, rosaries in October, matins at dawn throughout Advent, then at last, her only truly enjoyable service of the year, the Christmas Eve Mass when she had sung carols to her heart's content.

She knew what to say to please Mama.

'Of course we'll go to church. And we'll pray for you. We want you home as soon as possible.'

Mama looked down on her hands, shaking in her lap.

'The pills make me sleepy,' she said, 'I feel worn out after the electric shocks...'

Electric shocks? Julia sent Tato a look of alarm. He nodded reassuringly.

437

'Part of the treatment,' he said, 'don't worry. They give the patient an anaesthetic first. The electric shocks are meant to erase from the memory the very things that have triggered off the mental illness in the first place.'

'And do they?' The thought of her poor Mama all wired up... Julia shuddered.

'We'll soon find out.' Tato went on to tell Mama about all the friends who have been asking about her and Julia added best wishes from Yagoda and Lidia, squirming with shame at the memory of how careful she had been not to disclose the true nature of her Mama's illness.

'Eva asks about you all the time,' Tato said. 'She said she'd come to see you as soon as you're home.'

Mama hugged herself and began to rock, her features setting, her gaze distant. Julia felt a growing unease.

'Mama, she must be very worried about you. Just as we all are,' she suggested gently.

Mama stopped rocking and looked at her. There was something strange in her gaze, though her eyes were the same familiar amber brown.

'Tell her,' she said, 'tell her not to worry... tell her that even when I'm mad, I'll never let her down...'

The intensity of her tone made Julia shiver.

'Nastusha,' Tato said, 'she was just asking about your health.' He hugged her. 'Things will be so much better when you come home.'

She was quiet for a long time, but when she spoke Julia was surprised by the clarity of her argument.

'But things won't be all right, will they? Theo, you know that very well. Not until we're married in church. And that's not possible, is it?'

There was hurt in his voice when he replied.

'But we are married, Nastusha. Perfectly legally. Why do you keep upsetting yourself over this?'

Mama hid her face in her hands and rocked. It pained Julia to watch her like this, in utter despair. Ever since Julia was old enough to understand *adult* matters, she had listened to her Mama's outpourings of grief over her deeply felt injustice. She herself had agonised countless times over her helplessness to solve her Mama's dilemma and to be able to make her happy.

'Mama, listen,' she prised gently Mama's hands from her face and lay them in her lap, 'listen to Tato. He is right. You two are married. We are constantly told how loving God is. And how He knows everything. Then He understands. Perfectly. You don't need anyone else to be telling you how you must live, when they don't know the whole truth.'

'Then why am I treated like a pariah? In my own church?' Mama's face was strained. 'The priest won't give me communion. He's told me many times what I've got to do. Renounce my life of sin. There's no salvation for me, except to live alone...' She stood up and started walking across the lawn, a sorry figure, with fly-away hair, stained dress and bare legs, startlingly white in the sun.

'Shouldn't we go after her?' Julia half got up, but Tato stopped her.

'Give her time.'

How did he remain so patient? So understanding?

'Tato, she didn't mean that, did she? About living on her own?'

He sighed. 'At this moment, she probably does. But she wouldn't do it. So don't worry. She'd only exchange one feeling of guilt for another.' He kept his eyes on Mama's back as she proceeded towards the quadrangle between the buildings. Did he feel rejection as strongly as she did?

'How do you cope with it all?' she asked.

'Not terribly well,' he shrugged, 'but she's been through a lot.'

'So have you.'

'We all have. Our generation. Some are stronger than others. At this moment, she is the one who needs support.' He looked at his watch. 'Shall we go to find her? It's nearly time to leave.'

Julia's earlier desire to spend the whole day with her Mama was replaced with a pang of guilt, as she suddenly longed to get away from this place.

They found Mama indoors, back in her armchair, her gaze fixed on some distant object beyond the window. Julia picked up the bag with washing, promising to bring fresh clothes the next day, a manicure set, hair rollers and a spray.

'You'll look like a film star, Mama, I promise, when I've done everything for you,' Julia chuckled softly, desperate to draw a smile from her mother. That was all she desired. And just a hug. But her Mama's expression remained set and her attention elsewhere. Her hands were trembling in her lap.

In the car park Uncle Roman stood by his car having a smoke.

'How is Anastazia?' he asked, stubbing out his cigarette. Julia had always liked him, though he was not a real uncle. He had saved her Tato from death at the battle of Monte Cassino, when he had dragged him from underneath a mound of soil after a bomb explosion. He had the eyes of clearest blue, and most of his hair was still dark, unlike her Tato's, which had gone white with shock.

Julia described her Mama's condition. 'It's like talking to a stranger. It's like she is not my Mama any more.'

'Roman, perhaps you could talk to her?' Tato suggested as they were getting into the car.

Roman steered the car down the drive and onto the main road to Warwick before replying.

'I will,' he said, 'when she comes home. Perhaps now's not the time. I'd hate to be a reminder of things she'd rather forget from her past.'

He and her Mama had been in the same labour camp in Siberia during the war, long before either of them had met Theo. That much Julia knew.

'What things?' she caught his glance in the mirror.

'Julia, my dear,' his tone had a touch of weariness, 'years of deprivation. Terrible things happened. Things, you can never forget. Anastazia's too sensitive for her own good. She's probably still haunted by those memories.'

Her poor Mama! 'Can they stop her tormenting herself like that?'

'That's what I hope and wish for,' her Tato said. 'A cure for her guilt about things she was not responsible for!'

A silence descended, which Julia found oppressive. She longed for the carefree times of the past when returning home at the end of each term was a time of joy. As if sensing her mood, Roman said,

'Julia, I know it's hard for you. Tomorrow will be better. I'll bring Joyce and Andrew along with us for the ride. They'll be pleased to see you.'

Julia was also pleased at the thought. Joyce was Roman's English wife and Andrew her ten-year-old son, two of Julia's most favourite people.

CHAPTER 56

Her Mama's absence hung heavy around the house. There was an eerie stillness in the objects in Julia's room, as if they too were waiting, breathless, for Mama's return.

Julia stood at her bedroom window tense and alert, listening, looking out for Miro. Earlier she had slipped a note through his letter-box. 'I'm back. Fancy a walk? 8pm tonight?' she had suggested.

She could hear Tato and Roman playing chess in the front room. He had come back for their regular Saturday night session.

How could her Tato stay so calm? He had appeared totally absorbed earlier in painting the shed, and later, when she had rushed around the house like a disorientated ant, tidying up and cleaning, he had sat with his ear glued to the radio, in his stubborn attempt to catch the odd word or phrase that escaped the screech of jamming. Even now, fifteen years after the war, the communists in Poland made every attempt to gag the Radio Free Europe. The noise alone was enough to make one go mad.

She wished her Mama could have seen her then. She would have made her proud. She had worked so hard.

The house had not been cleaned for weeks; dusty surfaces, hanging cobwebs, stained tablecloths, sticky floors. Julia could not do it all in one day, but she had made a start with the bathroom and the kitchen. She scrubbed and washed and wiped and dried and removed all the wilting plants outdoors and stood them in a tub of water.

Then she had set about the fridge.

'Tato! This is disgusting! I wouldn't feed Muszka with this green ham!' Muszka, her black and white cat, had shared a Spam sandwich with her.

Her Tato had just shrugged, his working clothes marked with spatters of green paint, his head covered against the sun with a white handkerchief, its four corners tied in knots for a snug fit. Why couldn't he wear his straw hat and look perfectly normal?

'You know your Mama best, Julia,' he had said. 'She won't throw anything away.'

No food was ever wasted, but used up the next day and the day after that. In memory of all the Polish children, hundreds, who had died of starvation in Russia. With an uncomfortable feeling of guilt, Julia had thrown away all the moulding remnants of cheese, sausage, paté and pigs' trotters in aspic.

Julia's thoughts dispersed at the sight of Miro. Her heart leapt, the weight fell away. For a split second he looked like someone else, tall, manly, his confident strides barely touching the pavement. He saw her and waved. His direct smile had a strange melting effect on her.

She moved away from the window, across her bedroom, across the hallway to the half-open door of the front room.

'I'm going for a walk with Miro,' she announced from the door, before Tato could say it was not appropriate for a girl to chase after the boys. Miro was not just any boy, he had been Julia's friend since their infant days.

Roman looked up,

'I've not seen him for a while,' he said.

'Well, he's here now,' Julia replied, rushing to open the front door.

He stood there, beaming at her, his dark, freshly-washed hair curling around his forehead.

'Is this the right time? Right day?' he asked.

She giggled.

'Come in. Tato and Roman are playing chess.'

Handshakes and small talk followed. Miro described his holiday job at the quarry and spread out his hands, roughened and scratched, like a mark of his strength and manliness. Julia remained by the door, impatient to get away.

'Good luck with your exam results,' Roman said, his blue gaze appraising Miro. 'Did you say the Law School in London? I'll be waiting for an invitation to visit you.' He said it with pride, as if Miro were his son.

Miro gave a short laugh.

'I've got to get the grades first.'

'You will, young man,' Tato said with conviction, 'I have no doubts about that.' Tato was alluding, no doubt, to Miro's regular successes and prizes at their primary school, and for some strange reason, it pleased Julia that he had remembered.

'Thank you,' Miro acknowledged her Tato's comment with a nod, his expression suddenly self-deprecating, 'you've set me a hard task. I can only hope I can live up to your expectations.'

'Go, enjoy your walk,' Tato's tone was indulgent. 'Back at ten Julia. Your Mama's rules.'

At last they were alone walking down the street, their strides bouncy, eager, their swinging arms almost touching, but not quite.

'Shall we walk by the canal?' Miro suggested.

Julia did not mind where their walk took them. It was bliss to be outdoors. Her inner turmoil was already subsiding, soothed by the peace of the warm, fragrant evening. Even her street, with the squat, prefabricated bungalows looked attractive, its harsh, concrete lines softened by the lush-crowned trees and leafy shrubs.

Julia was pleasantly self-conscious of her transformation from a schoolgirl into a young woman. She had bathed and taken care with her appearance, fluffing out her hair and shaping it into the fashionable bob, dabbing her mother's 'Paris Nights' on her neck and wrists, applying a little lipstick and powder. Her navy and white polka-dot dress, pinched at the waist, flared out at the knees with each energetic step.

Brownsover estate lay on the outskirts of Rugby, where the peripheral line of houses ended by the canal. Julia and Miro went over the hump-back bridge and along the path that cut across the open fields. There were other walkers; people exercising their dogs, elderly couples making the most of the good weather, taking their 'constitutional'.

'How does it feel?' Miro asked with a sideways glance. 'To be home for good now?'

She returned his quick glance. She had always been at ease with him. She could not understand the sudden feeling of shyness between them.

'I couldn't wait to be home,' she replied, 'but now... I just wish none of this had happened.' The weight was back in her chest.

'Julia,' his tone was soft with well-meaning, 'your mother's going to be all right. She's in good hands. My mother's been in hospital twice already. Appendicitis. Then some weird cyst. These things happen all the time. But they pass.'

Julia willed herself to draw comfort from his words, but her mother's illness was not something visible, something that people could understand.

'You know how people make fun of the mentally ill,' her voice was quiet, instinctively discreet.

He turned his gaze on her, his dark eyes sympathetic.

'Only the stupid ones do,' he said, 'and does it really matter what they think?'

He brushed his hand against hers. Her arm tingled. The ache inside her began to fade, like a shadow dissolving in sunlight.

'I wish I was a magician,' she said, 'I wish I could magic back all the happy times.'

'Your mother will be home sooner than you think.' It sounded like a promise. Then unexpectedly he grasped her hand saying, 'Shall we run?' and before she had time to think they were running at speed down the green expanse of the field and up the escarpment towards the little village of Old Brownsover. It was exhilarating. When they stopped to catch breath, and he let go of her hand, she could not control her laughter.

'See? You can laugh!' he said, taking deep breaths, and laughing with her.

They crossed the Leicester road and continued to walk along the narrow quiet street of Old Brownsover, where little cottages stood at random angles to each other.

'Where are we going?' Julia asked.

'Brownsover Hall,' Miro was enigmatic.

'Sounds grand! Frightening!'

Miro laughed.

'Not in the least! English Electric have taken over the building for their offices. I know the night watchman. Mr. Strachan.'

'A Pole?'

'Yes. A lonely man. Lost all his family in the war'.

Like Tato, like so many people she knew. Their stories retold often and regularly throughout her childhood had little more impact than Andersen's tales. Now, with an ache so fresh in her heart, a sudden flash of understanding made these people's suffering come alive with unbearable clarity. Julia shut her eyes tight and with great effort emptied her mind. She could not allow herself to think about such things now.

'Are you all right?' She was aware of Miro's hand on hers, of the cuts and scratches brushing against her skin. She opened her eyes wide.

'Just too many thoughts,' she said, and let herself be led, her hand comfortably in his.

Brownsover Hall was totally screened off the main Leicester road by a dense growth of bushes and trees. A tarmac drive, now cast in descending dusk, widened like a delta where it flowed into the open space in front of the main entrance. The mansion, a Victorian Gothic edifice, with its steep-roofed tower and tall mullioned windows, looked dark and mysterious against the paling sky.

Julia held onto Miro's hand and followed him round the side of the building, where an extension, as big as a family house, with its own porch, yielded a glow through an unshuttered window. Miro crept right up and tapped. Julia peered over his shoulder. There was a man sitting at the table reading a paper. His face was craggy, his thick greying hair cut like a brush. The sleeves of his chequered shirt were rolled up, exposing his arms. Just above his wrist there was a tattoo: bold, black, indelible digits.

'Those numbers on his arm. Auswitz?' she whispered.

'Some camp in Germany,' Miro whispered back.

Mr. Strachan looked up, nodded in recognition and a smile deepened the creases on his face. He got up with a jangle of keys at his belt and soon the unlocking of the porch door came with the creaking of un-oiled hinges.

'Prosze. Come in.' He locked the door again and led them down a corridor to his room. 'Find a chair, please, and make yourself at home.'

They sat down at the small square table while he boiled the kettle on the gas cooker in the corner. He made three mugs of coffee and joined them, lighting a cigarette and inhaling deep and long.

'You're very brave,' Julia said pleasantly to make conversation, 'I'd be scared here all by myself in this enormous building.'

'I don't scare easily,' he chuckled while Julia forced herself with great effort not to stare at his tattoo. He continued, 'This place is supposed to be haunted. A headless man driving a coach every night at midnight. Every country house has a resident ghost. But all I ever hear are owls, screeching foxes and fighting cats. The occasional intruder has no chance against the wail of the house alarm. Could pierce your ear drums if you hang around for too long.' Mr. Strachan squinted against the cigarette smoke. 'So what's the news in the outside world?'

Miro told him of his holiday job, of his plan to visit his cousins in France at the end of the summer, of his conditional place in London.

'The uncertainty gives me nightmares every night,' he said, wiping imaginary sweat off his forehead.

Mr. Strachan's craggy face creased in a wise old man's smile.

'Miro, my boy, what on earth are you fretting about? At your age you've got your whole life ahead of you. You can try out all sort of things as many times as you like, if you don't succeed at first. You've got the time. Now, I haven't got such luxury any more. I'm about twenty years behind. That's why I've decided to stop dreaming and to visit my brother in Poland later this year.'

Julia's interest was aroused.

'But how's that possible? Is it safe?' It was common knowledge that many Poles, returning to their homeland after the war, had been rearrested by the Soviet communists, denounced as traitors and sent back to Siberia to some remote hard labour camps.

Mr. Strachan stubbed out his cigarette and shrugged.

'I've taken on British citizenship for this very reason. So I can travel safely.'

Julia looked at Miro. She felt a sudden burst of excitement. 'Could we do that too? Is this really possible? I can't imagine it. All those places in Poland my parents always talk about... it all sounds so remote... I never thought... and now...'

Miro's eyes shone. He appeared amused.

'Of course we can go too, Julia. There's just one little problem of cost. And you've got to be eighteen before you can apply for a British passport.'

'I can wait two years. I'll work. I'll save up!' Julia's mind whirled with ideas.

'You realise,' Mr. Strachan said, 'that this is not a popular idea with our hot-headed patriots. To take on a different nationality. To visit our country while it's still in enemy hands. Some of my pals are calling me a traitor.' He paused thoughtfully, inclining his head to one side, 'But life has taught me many things. Sometimes, necessity has to overcome reservations. This is a necessity for me. I've got to see my brother. He's the only one left. Besides, whatever you sign on paper, it is just paper and ink. No one can truly take away what's in your mind and in your heart. I was born a Pole. I shall die a Pole. Nothing can change that'.

This was all new to Julia. Her parents had never discussed such a possibility.

'Still keen?' Miro asked, raising a quizzing eyebrow.

'What about you? Will you become British? Will you still be a Pole? What will British citizenship make you?'

'A hybrid,' Miro teased, 'seriously Julia, it's just a formality. To me it's straightforward common sense.'

It was dark when Miro and Julia came outside. He clasped her hand and she stayed close to him as they made their way, step by careful step, along the pitch black path, like a long tunnel with a faint glow at the end.

Once back in the village, on the illuminated street, they walked with long unhindered strides, but Miro continued to hold Julia's hand. Firm, protective. And she liked that.

'Miro,' she said, 'I can't stop thinking about Mr. Strachan and his plans to visit Poland. It's really fired my imagination. I had never imagined it to be possible. And now, suddenly...' she hesitated. All those years... the very little she knew about her father had been from her mother's censored stories and the few photographs she had of him in a soldier's uniform. 'When I go to Poland, and I hope I don't have to wait too long, when I go... I must go looking for my father.'

Miro stopped and turned to her, his eye sockets just dark shadows on his face.

'Is that wise? Don't forget, it was your father who left you and your mother. He's never made any attempt to get in touch with you. What about your Mum's feelings? What about your Dad?'

They resumed their walk. Julia did not know what to think. She had no intention of hurting anyone, but her need to find out more about her father had been resurrected again.

'I can't argue with you,' she said, wanting to sound reasonable, 'but have I no rights of my own? I'm not asking for much. I'd just like to see my father. Just once.'

They crossed the Leicester road and stopped on the top of the embankment with the fields stretching before them pearly in the moonlight.

'Only it wouldn't be just once. Would it?' Miro spoke gently. 'Are you truly prepared for what you could discover? Have you thought about his other wife? His other family? What if you didn't like them? What if they don't know anything about you? Your curiosity could open a can of worms. For everyone. For you too...' Miro paused, his eyes glinting in the moonlight. 'Besides, what's the hurry, Julia? You can't do much anyway in the next couple of years. Haven't you got enough on your plate right now?'

Julia resented his wisdom, his practical commonsense, yet begrudgingly she had to admit he was right. There was the new school to sort out. And her course, the A-level subjects. And most important of all was her Mama's recovery.

'But I'm not giving up,' she said, 'I'll just postpone my search. If that meets your approval, Mr. Know-all.'

He laughed off her barb, grasped her hand and they ran as before, down the escarpment, across the field to the bridge over the canal. They stopped there to get their breath back. There was no sound, no movement in the reeds, only the surface of the canal rippled, breaking the moonlight into sinuous silver ribbons. It was magical, like a set from a Hollywood musical, and for a moment all Julia's worries fell away and she enjoyed the inconsequential chatter with Miro, as he walked her home.

Roman's Hillman was gone. The curtained front window was lit from within and when they stopped at the front door, scratchy noises of the radio could be faintly heard.

'My Tato's still listening to the news from Poland,' Julia smiled.

'He'd enjoy television.' Miro suggested.

'So would I,' Julia said, 'that's the first thing I'll be saving for.'

'Are you going to the hospital tomorrow?' Miro asked, 'I'd like to come with you any time I've got a day off work.'

'I'd like that very much,' Julia replied, panicking. Not just yet, she thought. She did not want Miro to see her mother in her present state, a neglected, dishevelled woman, who was like a stranger and not the attractive, warm and friendly person they had always known.

'I'll catch up with you in the week,' Miro said. 'Tomorrow, as it happens I've been invited to a friend's eighteenth birthday party. A girl from my class. Rosemary.'

'Oh...?' something strange was happening to her lips. They remained smiling, yet felt stiff, not like her own. 'I mean, how lovely for you. Is she nice? Rosemary?'

'She is, actually,' Miro ran his fingers through his tangled curls. 'We were on the same History course. It helped to share notes and halve the research reading. She's quite smart too. Got a place in Oxford.'

Miro's words had a strange effect. It felt as if something had been dimmed inside her, though the moon was still shining bright, and the garden was fragrant around them and Miro was smiling and his eyes were looking straight into hers. The churning in her stomach returned.

'Will I see you in church tomorrow?' she asked.

'Yes, I'll be there. And next time we go out, we could go to the cinema. OK?' Was this a genuine proposition or was this his attempt to make up for something else that she was not a part of?

'OK' she replied, 'and enjoy the party tomorrow.' She did not really mean that, and at the same time felt annoyed with herself for feeling the way she did.

She did not watch him walk away, but turned her head and blinked hard to stop her eyes prickling. Muszka appeared from around the side of the house, waving her upright tail and mewling to be picked up. Strangely, her soft body was comforting against Julia's chest.

She let herself in to the blast from the radio.

'Good walk?' she heard Tato call out above the noise. She stopped at the door to the living room. Her Tato's brow was creased in concentration as he listened hard for the odd intelligible word or phrase. Why was he doing this, this mad assault on his eardrums? A television set would have been so much better!

'We went to see Mr. Strachan. At Brownsover Hall.' She had to raise her voice too. She knew this information would please him. Their walk had not been an aimless waste of time, but a kind deed in visiting a lonely man. A Pole. One of their own.

She had guessed right. Tato's gaze pulled back from the radio and focused on her. 'Good,' he said, nodding approval. 'Is he all right? I must invite him over, one day, when Nastusha's back and well.'

Julia wished he would turn the radio down. She wished…it had been so easy when she was five to climb on his lap and demand attention and receive abundant cuddles. He looked just the same as then, tanned face, tired looking but still too young for the white hair, kindness in his grey eyes that never disapproved of anything she did. He was her real Tato. With a pang of guilt she was relieved that he could not read her thoughts, know of her self-indulgent musings of what her natural father could have been. Instant remorse made her want to go up to him, hug him and make up for her disloyal thoughts. But she was not five any more.

'I'm going to bed, Tato. To read,' she said.

He looked up and gave her a pale smile. It occurred to her that he was aching too, for her mother's embrace, for her reassurance that everything was going to be all right. She opened her lips to offer a few words of comfort, but he looked away to the radio and turned up the volume.

The hands of her bedside clock had moved past midnight, but Julia could not sleep. She had tried to read but could not concentrate on the dialogue between Miss Marples and Superintendent Harper. She had switched off the light and watched the moonbeam slide across the bed and slip to the floor. It was quiet in the street, the branches of the beech outside her window so still, they could have been cut out of paper. She listened with envy to Muszka's contented purring floating from the cushion on the chair, as her mind went over the events of the day. Was it really only just one day? The morning seemed like a distant dot in time; the journey to the hospital, the shock of seeing her mother in that disturbing state, the homecoming to neglect and dirt, the vacuum around the house echoing her mother's absence.

It had been such a thrill, after all that, to be with Miro in the evening. But even their time together had lost its magic now. Her best childhood friend, her very own, was no longer hers. During her boarding school years away from home, he had grown up into another, separate life of his own.

Then there were questions about her father. Her natural father. The conversation with Mr. Strachan had given her an unexpected spurt of hope. But was it right to cultivate such hopes, to dream about looking for a person who had hurt her Mama?

If only she could share her burden with Lidia and Yagoda. How she missed them now! Only the night before, their last night at the convent school, awake with excitement, they had whispered their future plans and dreams long into the night. And now she had no one to talk to. An intense feeling of loneliness swept over her. Was her adulthood going to be nothing more than a solitary struggle? And to think she had spent years dreaming of this day!

There was still Nadia, like Miro, Julia's childhood friend. A year older, she was already in training to be a nurse. Julia's spirit lifted as she thought about her. Tomorrow she'd see her in church. Tomorrow, she and Nadia would make plans for their cycling outings on their free summer days.

CHAPTER 57

On Sunday afternoon, Julia was pleased with the result of their visit at the hospital. They had gone to the same bench under the willow tree as the day before, and while Tato did his best to keep his monologue alive in the hope of teasing some response out of Mama, Julia had styled and sprayed her hair, applied a little lipstick to her pale mouth, cut and filed and varnished her fingernails, and before they left, waited for Mama indoors to change into a freshly laundered dress.

The ward sister came over and complimented Anastazia on her appearance. Julia willed her Mama for a word of praise, for a look of pride. There was a moment of anticipation. Then nothing happened. Mama's gaze was distant, focused on some spot beyond the window, as she remained stone-like in her armchair.

'When will my mother start getting better?' Julia asked.

The sister's quick smile was businesslike.

'Anastazia's progress could be more satisfactory if her English were not so limited.'

Julia squirmed at the reprimand, feeling as if it were directed at her.

'Much of the therapy,' the sister continued, 'is based on the questions posed by the doctor and on the spontaneous answers provided by the patient, allowing the doctor to analyse her past and any possible traumas. This will help him to establish correct diagnosis and appropriate treatment.'

'I tell you,' Tato offered ,'what doctor want know.'

The sister looked serious.

'It has to come from the patient,' she said. 'We gather Anastazia has travelled quite a lot. This much she was able to tell us. Except that the places she's mentioned are flung so far apart we've wondered if she may have been confused.'

'No,' Julia said firmly, 'my mother's never confused about these things. She's got an amazing memory for places and dates.'

'Is that so?' a touch of disbelief showed in the sister's raised eyebrows. 'She said she'd been to Russia.'

'Is correct,' Tato said.

'As far north as Arkhangelsk?'

'Yes,' Tato confirmed, 'north and south. Tashkent, Persia, Iraque, Palestine. Then England.'

Julia detected a change in the sister's expression, interest in the forward angle of her head.

'I envy you Anastazia,' she said, her stiff smile returning briefly, 'I don't know anyone who has travelled so much. Promise to tell the doctor everything.' She bent down and gazed into Anastazia's eyes. 'Promise?'

Incredibly, Mama nodded, then, as the sister walked away she looked up at Julia and Tato.

'And where would I begin?' she asked.

In the carpark Roman, Joyce and Andrew were already waiting. Andrew ran up to Julia, his light silky hair bouncing, his face excited and eager.

'Julia! We had such fun in Warwick. There's a funfair by the river. All this week!'

'Lucky you!' Julia replied smiling, seduced by his joy.

'If ever you have to hang around Warwick, Julia,' Joyce said, when they joined her by the car, 'go inside Saint Mary's church. So much history there.'

'Thank you. I will,' Julia replied graciously. She could not think about anything else but her Mama for the moment, but she guessed this was Joyce's discreet attempt to distract her. She liked Joyce. Everyone liked her. Everyone had said how lucky Roman had been when he met and married her, even if she was a widow with a small child. Her genteel charm and her growing knowledge of Polish affairs had made her a most welcome member of the Polish community. Her valiant attempts at learning Polish, not an easy language, had made eager teachers of everyone who met her.

She gave Julia a reassuring pat on her hand after they climbed onto the back seat with Andrew.

'Everything will turn out all right, Julia,' she said, leaning forward, her mellow voice persuasive, 'try not to worry so.' Julia's chest felt tight but she forced a smile and Joyce continued. 'Life can present you with good surprises too, you know.'

Julia caught Roman's grin in the mirror.

'I can vouch for that,' he said.

They drove off, her Tato subdued, Roman sustaining a cheerful monologue and Andrew describing with lively animation the rides he'd had at the fun fair. When he paused for breath, Joyce said,

'What helped me when I was down, Julia, was to force my mind to think of the happy times. Maybe just one moment, or one event. An expression, a funny saying. A song. Anything, to push out the gloomy thoughts. Your mother's present illness is just a temporary hiccup. It'll pass. You must have hundreds of happy thoughts when you think about her. Perhaps funny incidents when you were little?'

Julia thought for a moment, studying Joyce's carefully groomed, pretty features.

451

'Yes.' she said, feeling her spirit rise unexpectedly, 'I can think of lots of happy times. Are you listening Tato? And taking note? I love it when Mama sings. I know then that she's happy.'

Joyce looked pleased. 'Then you know what you must do next time you see her,' she said.

Julia had asked to be dropped off by Nadia's house. She had seen her friend briefly after the church service that morning, at St. Marie's church that was the Sunday meeting place for the Poles in Rugby. Miro had been there too, with his parents and his two younger brothers, all in their best suits. He came up to her briefly, touched her hand discreetly, then withdrew to walk back with his family, when she and Tato got surrounded by her Mama's friends, eager for news. Finally, when everyone had dispersed and Tato had hurried to join Roman for a smoke by the car, Nadia had walked down the church path with her to the main road.

'Come round later,' Nadia had said, 'when you get back from the hospital. I'm going to London tonight for a week. Stella and Jack will be there to pick me up.'

'Lucky you!' Julia had replied, feeling a strange plummeting sensation inside her. She wished she had an older sister like Stella, beautiful, glamorous, living in London, and being driven around in a sports car by her adoring boyfriend.

His car was parked outside Nadia's house, a lilac and grey Triumph with a soft, convertible top. Julia fancied having a ride in it, her hair blowing in the wind, just like Grace Kelly's in *To catch a Thief*.

The front garden, all Aunt Eva's work, was a replica of her Mama's garden, bursting with summer flowers, red and maroon hollyhocks, fiery dahlias, giant daisies, sapphire delphiniums, white and cream lupins and violet lobelias fluffy round the borders. The Bzovski's house, though council owned, was like a proper house, with a living room and a kitchen downstairs, and three bedrooms and a bathroom upstairs. Julia liked stairs; a staircase (especially with a sweeping balustrade, such that she had only seen on films) added grandeur to a house, she thought dreamily.

Julia knocked and the door was opened by Marek, Nadia's eleven-year-old brother, his short trousers baggy around his thin legs. Zloty, his golden retriever was at his side and at the sight of Julia began to pant and shiver and produce happy little squeaks. Julia laughed with delight. She patted Zloty on the head, 'Clever boy! I'm happy to see you too! Hi Marek!'

Marek's mouth curled with pride, his hand resting possessively on his pet's back. He was blue-eyed and almost white-blond, like everyone else in his family; his father Henryk, his mother Eva and his older sister Stella. Only Nadia was different.

She appeared right behind him, her dark, almond-shaped eyes shining with excitement, her wide smile startlingly white against her coffee-cream complexion.

'Julia! You've made it! Come upstairs with me. I'm just finishing packing.' Her black hair, tied in a high pony tail, flicked from side to side with her every movement.

In the living room there was much high-spirited banter exchanged across the table, around which Nadia's family were enjoying after-dinner tea and cakes. Her father was not part of the group. He sat alone by the window, looking out, turned away from everyone. As a child, Julia had found his broody reticence a little scary, even though she had been brought up to call him 'uncle'. He looked at her now and Julia experienced a jolt of recognition: the same deadness in his eyes as in her Mama's. He gave her a nod then resumed his watch.

Aunt Eva, Mama's closest friend, got up from the table and drew Julia to her bosom in a maternal embrace. She smelled faintly of roses and baking and all things comfortable. Julia returned the hug, reluctant to let go.

'*Co nowego*? How's Nastusha? How's Theo? How are you all coping?' Aunt Eva asked in Polish, though up till then they had been speaking in English, for Jack's sake.

Julia replied in English, choosing her words carefully.

'Mama's having a lot of rest. A lot of sleep. She gets medication and therapy. She'll be all right. She just needs more time.'

Aunt Eva's brow puckered over her clear blue eyes, legendary blue, like forget-me-nots, according to Mama's stories of their wartime adventures endured together. Her ash-blonde hair had once been the envy of Uzbek women. Now it was combed back flat and twisted into an elegant French roll.

'Sit down Julia and have some tea with us,' Aunt Eva invited, but Julia sensed Nadia's impatience to get away upstairs, to her bedroom, for the longed-for natter.

'Thank you, I will,' she said, 'after Nadia has finished packing.' She stepped closer to say hallo to Stella and Jack. Their glamour reduced her to a self-sense of an ugly duckling, despite her Sunday best dress, a pale pink organdie with embossed white flowers, despite her fluffed out, teased and sprayed hair. It was like being at an audience with film stars; platinum-blonde Marilyn Monroe and sleek, dark-haired Tony Curtis.

'Hi Julia,' Stella's voice was warm, her red, glossy lips exposing pearly teeth. Julia could well believe Nadia's accounts of Stella's imminent big break. Stardom in London. Then Hollywood.

'Julia, there's enough room in the car if you want to come with us,' Stella said.

Was she serious?

'Stella, I'd love nothing more... but...' This was torment, such short notice, her Mama, Tato, they both needed her. If only none of that had happened. She forced a smile.

Jack's handsome face was all understanding and charm.

'When you come, Julia, another time, I'll show you round the film sets,' he promised. He was an electrician at Pinewood Studios.

Such an opportunity and she was not free to go. Julia's eyes prickled.

'Julia,' Aunt Eva stroked her bare arm, 'there will be other times, you'll see.'

Nadia clasped Julia's hand and gave her a tug. 'Let's go upstairs.'

Nadia's bedroom was furnished in light wood, patiently scoured from second-hand shops, the walls painted white and peach, and the window softened with a pale rose print from the market. The small television set on the dressing table provided entertainment late into the night, when Julia stayed over and shared secrets with her best friend, in Nadia's double bed.

'Julia,' Nadia patted the space beside her on the edge of the bed, 'sit down and tell me what's been happening.' Julia told her briefly. She could see Nadia had other things on her mind.

'I'm so glad,' Nadia's face was animated, 'that you've come home for good. We can start having some grown-up fun together. Mama will be happy now to have you for my chaperone. That'll stop her nagging. Maybe. But listen, you'll never guess!'

Julia was used to this preamble.

'Go on, tell me then.'

Nadia's face shone. 'I'm going out with Leon,' she grinned with self-satisfaction.

'Leon Tarnovski?' The question was unnecessary. There was only one Leon. Nadia was staring at her intensely, expectantly, seeking approval, and envy.

'Some people have all the luck!' Julia replied with mock peevishness to please her friend. Images of Leon filled her mind; tall, slim, exceedingly good-looking, an apprentice draughtsman, already earning his keep, though still living with his parents. He had a habit of descending noisily at the Polish Club on his Silver Shadow, in his sleek, tight-fitting black leather gear, chat up all the girls before whisking one off for a gravity defying ride. No girl ever refused him.

'How are you going to tame him?' Julia teased.

'I already have,' Nadia replied with smug confidence.

'And what's he going to do all week without you?'

'Pine after me, of course,' Nadia laughed, 'it'll do him good. I love it when we're together. He takes me home sometimes. His father is OK. Treats me like one of his friends and can't stop telling me his wartime stories,' Nadia rolled her eyes with ennui, 'but his mother...' Nadia shook her head, 'I just know that she doesn't like me at all. Her Leon is the best in the world and deserves the best. A blue-eyed princess, no less. Me, with my dark skin and my charcoal eyes… I don't quite fit into her scheme of things…'

'Oh, Nadia!' Julia rushed to contradict her friend with fierce loyalty, 'don't talk like that. That's nonsense!' Deep down she knew Nadia was right. She had clear memories of the taunts of other children that had followed them around the playground, because Nadia did not look like the rest of them.

'Look at me,' she said, 'I'm dark too. Dark eyes like yours. Dark hair. We can't all be blonde.'

Nadia shook her head, unconvinced.

'It's not the same for you, Julia. You're your parents' child. I'm just a foundling. No doubt, she holds that against me too.'

Nadia's adoption had never been a big issue for her; she had been brought up in the knowledge that she had been chosen to be loved, but occasionally thoughtless people took perverse pleasure in reminding her of her origins.

'Nadia,' Julia said decisively, 'if Leon really loves you then nothing will come between you.'

'I know he does,' Nadia's confident smile returned.

'Then let's take your suitcase downstairs. It sounds as if they're ready to go.'

Stella and Jack were leaving, saying goodbyes, bestowing hugs. Uncle Henryk got up briefly to embrace his daughter and to shake Jack's hand. Aunt Eva brought out a large card box filled with food for them to take away: *pierogi. bigos*, *kotlety* and a round *babka* cake that she had baked. Jack led the way to his car, where she deposited her gifts in the boot.

Nadia gave Julia a prolonged hug.

'I'll be back soon,' she said, then they were off, Nadia waving enthusiastically from the back seat her beaming face unable to hide her excitement.

The street was quiet after they had gone, the late afternoon sun strong in the July sky, but the long hours still ahead of Julia sounding already hollow.

Marek had Zloty on the leash.

'Mama,' he reverted to their native Polish, 'I'll take Zloty for a run round the park.' He skipped off on his thin legs, his shiny hair bouncing with every move.

'I suppose it's time for me to go too,' Julia said, checking her watch.

'Come inside with me for a few minutes,' Aunt Eva invited, 'you can borrow Nadia's bicycle.'

Uncle Henryk was still sitting by the window, with the Polish Daily spread out on his lap and appeared oblivious to their presence in the kitchen. Aunt Eva washed up, Julia dried the plates and the cutlery.

'Does Nastusha talk much?' Aunt Eva asked over her shoulder, 'I mean, does she say anything about the past?'

There was no point pretending with Aunt Eva. She had been and still was her Mama's best friend.

'The truth is,' Julia said, 'Mama says hardly anything at all. Tato and I do all the talking when we visit her. I can't even be certain that she listens to anything that we say'.

Aunt Eva turned from the sink and fixed her eyes on Julia. Her stillness appeared to hide a whirlwind of thoughts behind that blue gaze.

'When she starts talking,' she spoke slowly as if trying to convince Julia, 'you mustn't worry, if things she says don't make sense at first. It'll take time before the medication and the treatment begin to show some good effects. Don't get upset and don't believe everything she says.'

Julia was touched by Aunt Eva's concern.

'Anyone who knows Mama would realize that,' she assured her, 'and besides, I can tell fact from fiction. Mama's usually so precise.'

Aunt Eva turned back to the sink and remained quiet. There were only the sounds of splashing water, of the plates and cutlery being put away in their proper places, only the ticking of the clock in the living room, only the whisper of the newspaper pages being turned over on Uncle Henryk's lap.

'The thing is,' Aunt Eva said after a long while, 'we've been through such a lot together, Nastusha and I. I'm worried about the state of her mind. I'm worried her mind could play tricks on her and make her remember things that never actually happened.' Her shoulders heaved and drooped in a sigh. 'Pity, they can't cut out a part of your brain, like an appendix, and rid you forever of the things you want to forget.'

Julia's hands stopped wiping, the plate held still inside the tea towel. She was suddenly aware of a complete silence. There was no crackling of the newspaper pages from the other room.

'Auntie,' she said to break her own unease, 'you can come with me one day, when you've got the time. I'm sure Mama would be delighted.' She was not sure of that at all, and to describe her Mama as 'delighted' was a far cry from her present uncommunicative state. 'Yes... perhaps I should...' Aunt Eva agreed unconvincingly. 'Dear God... does this have to go on forever?... will our troubles never end?'

Julia pondered Aunt Eva's curious comments as she cycled home on Nadia's borrowed bicycle. She was puzzled. Was Aunt Eva worried about something else? In addition to her Mama's illness? Julia had a feeling like a hunch. Like when she unravelled an Agatha Christie mystery and predicted the identity of the culprit before Poirot's final denouement. Was there more to her Mama's and Aunt Eva's past, than was revealed in the stories recounted through her childhood years? Or perhaps, she should have listened more attentively and taken notes?

Now that Aunt Eva's words got her thinking, she felt a sudden strong urge to find out more. She would ask Tato, she decided, this time with a pencil and a notebook at hand. Or... she just remembered. Her Mama's old suitcase, discoloured brown and battered, no bigger than a grocery box, stuffed with yellowed, dog-eared exercise books and an assortment of old photographs.

'These are my diaries,' her Mama had explained, once when she was a small child, 'I've kept them for you, Julia, for when you grow up.' It had meant nothing then, but now... a horrible thought occurred to her. She could only hope that the papers that her mother had burnt had not been her diaries. She'd have to check as soon as she got home.

Julia cycled past Miro's house in a street adjacent to hers. The narrow front, one in a row of a long terrace, had a bay window with red roses trained to climb around it and a hanging fuchsia adorning the door. Julia felt a pang of longing, a desire to stop, to knock on the door, to speak to Miro, to see him, if only briefly. But pride prevented her. She was an adult now; she could not be seen to behave like a child.

All day long, whether tackling her duties or presenting a cheerful image in the company of others, she had been assailed by thoughts of Miro and Rosemary together, enjoying themselves at her eighteenth birthday party. She should have been glad for him, she told herself. Wasn't it what you were supposed to do, to wish your friends luck and joy and happiness? Yet no amount of rationalising could remove that sick feeling at the pit of her stomach. He'd said that Rosemary was nice. Nice as in beautiful? Blonde? Tall? He'd said Rosemary was very clever. How could she, Julia, compete with her? Last night seemed like a dream, when Miro had clasped her hand and held it tight and made it tingle and made her feel special. Perhaps he had not felt the same way at all, perhaps the wonder of the evening had been just her own misguided perception?

She had no choice. She could not be seen to be chasing after him, as her Tato would have put it. She had to wait till Miro made the first move.

For their evening meal, Julia fried sausages and sliced potatoes and made a salad with her mother's freshly-grown lettuce and with tomatoes bought at the corner shop. As they tucked into their meal, facing each other across the table, she and Tato discussed their earlier visit to the hospital, reassuring each other about a definitely visible improvement in Mama's condition. Julia mentioned Nadia and the much envied whole week in London, then she asked casually,

'Tato, you know Mama's old suitcase, the one she keeps some old photos in? She's not burnt any of the stuff from it, has she?'

Tato raised his eyes with a slow, guarded look and shook his head.

'I don't think so. Why?'

This was a relief.

'Do you know where she keeps the key?'

Tato thought for a moment as if trying to remember.

'She's probably got it with her. In her handbag. Why do you need to know?'

Julia chewed slowly before swallowing. She did not want to appear eager.

'No reason. It's just that I suddenly remembered that when I was little she told me about her diaries. She said I could read them when I was grown up. Well…here I am. I'd like to read them now.'

Tato cut his sausage with a show of concentration.

'Yes, I'm sure she meant you to have them. Eventually.'

'Eventually? When's that? When I'm fifty!'

'Maybe,' Tato's smile was indulgent. 'Be patient Julia. She'll open the suitcase herself for you when she comes home.'

'It's just that,' Julia pressed the point, 'I've suddenly realised I know so very little. All those years she's been telling me things and I've not listened hard enough. I want to find out more. I'd like to know everything. Have you read Mama's diaries?'

He shook his head.

'I don't need to. She told me everything she wanted me to know.'

'But aren't you curious?'

'Curious? No!' Tato said emphatically. 'I've had enough experiences of my own. I need no reminders.' His tone dropped yet it sounded like a reprimand. He resumed eating, his eyes cast down, fixed on the embroidered daisy on the tablecloth.

Julia fell silent, regretting her questions that so unwittingly had hit a raw nerve. Poor Tato! He never spoke about his past before the battle of Monte Cassino. She knew only from her Mama, that Tato's wife and his small son had been killed in a German air raid, while he was being detained in a Russian prisoner-of-war camp.

Looking at him now, his expression composed, closed to any further questions, she could not imagine him as this other man, with a wife and a child. He had always been *her* Tato. And for a moment her heart ached that she could not find in herself the capacity to grieve for his people, the people she had never known.

CHAPTER 58

Julia's heart skipped at the sight of Lidia's handwriting on the envelope. Her sender address stated boldly NR. WINDSOR underneath the humble Slough.

'I miss you,' she wrote, 'I'm in SHOCK! Patrick's GONE! In his place we've got Papa's old friend from the army, all hairy arms and bushy eyebrows. UGH! They play cards every night and talk about the war. YAWN! Nonna, (granny in English) is not very well. I do all the housework and keep an eye on Alberto. Mama treats him like a baby. Papa says when he was Alberto's age (12) he did all the hard work on the farm in Poland. The good news is that my cousin Vittorio is coming over from Italy, to improve his English. It's always SWELL when he is around. His friend Marcello (from last time) has already been round a few times.'

Julia felt a pang of yearning for her old friend. They had lived together for so many years, and now in their adult world, they were miles apart.

Yagoda's letter came two days later; chirpy and optimistic, typically hers. Her sender address stated simply, Braunstone Estate, Leicester.

'Dear Julia, It feels strange not seeing you every day. I've got good news! The persistent cough I've had is nothing serious. My brother's fiancée Sheila works in a surgery and arranged an examination for me. There was some fluid on my lungs, but with the antibiotics I'm already feeling better. You'll never guess what else the doctor said! That I should get a lot of fresh sea air and exercise. And guess what! Voytek and Sheila are taking me to Skegness! For two whole weeks! I fear I'll explode with excitement before I get there!'

This was indeed good news. With Yagoda's past history of polio, there was always the fear that her weakened system could easily succumb to ill health. Julia's passing wish, and just the tiniest twinge of envy, was that she could have gone with her friend.

In the evening she cycled to Roman and Joyce's. She needed their advice.

'So, how are things?' Joyce asked, her doe eyes soft, her voice sympathetic. She had brought in a tray laden with dainty porcelain cups, tea and biscuits and set them out on the coffee table, on heavy white lace.

Roman was busy with the record player. It was encased in highly polished dark wood, matching the elegant furniture in this subtly colour co-ordinated room of sage green and cream. The curtains were velvet, the armchairs velour. Julia could only marvel at such splendour.

Sitting next to her on the settee was Andrew, all twitching arms and legs in his eagerness to tell her about his holiday.

"We're going to Great Yarmouth soon. I can't wait to go to the fun fair. On the big wheel!' His fringe bounced about his forehead with his every excited movement.

The soft notes of the *Moonlight Sonata* drifted across the room. Roman joined them at the coffee table, picked up his cup and sat back in his deep armchair.

'Are there signs of improvement?' He meant her Mama, of course.

Julia sat on the edge of the settee, her hands protecting her cup and saucer, resting on her lap. She had been to see her Mama every afternoon this week.

'It's hard to say,' she answered, 'some days Mama looks so much better. It really feels that she's on the brink of recovery. Then the next time I go to see her, she's withdrawn again. I end up doing all the talking. Like an old rattle.'

Andrew laughed.

'I wish I could come on the bus with you,' he said.

Julia smiled back at him.

'I'd like that too. But you'd have to stick on a moustache and wear an old man's cap.'

He laughed again.

'Why?'

'Because they only allow adults.'

She did not mind the bus journeys so much; she read or simply watched the landscape float by. But lonely wanderings around Warwick, while waiting for her bus connections, were not much fun.

'Your Mum will be fine,' Joyce stated with a well-meant emphasis. 'It's just a pity that her recovery is taking so long. It would be marvellous,' her eyes shone, 'if you could go, all three of you, on a holiday. I believe your mother, even in her present state, would do so much better by the sea. The fresh air, the walks on the sand, the total rest would do wonders for her!'

Julia laughed softly. She did not mean to. She placed the cup and saucer carefully on the low table.

'Mrs. Joyce, that would be a miracle! My Mum and Dad never go anywhere. I mean holidays. They say their wartime travels will last them a lifetime. They're done with travelling. They like nothing better than to spend their July fortnight at home. Gardening and decorating.' She did not add that it would have been a financial strain for them. Their meagre earnings provided the basics, but did not stretch to buy luxuries.

Roman nodded.

'Most of my friends feel the same way. I did too. Till I met Joyce.' His features softened as he looked at his wife.

His situation had been totally different. He was younger than Julia's parents. He had studied hard on his arrival in Britain and had secured himself a position as maths teacher. Now, as the head of the maths department at the Technical College, he had done better than any other Pole she knew. His wife's inherited house was a bonus, but not a necessity for him to rely on.

'I still think,' Joyce persisted gently, her pretty features earnest, 'that it would be possible to arrange something for your parents, Julia. A friend of mine owns a caravan by the sea. Near Cromer. I'll ask him…' She was truly serious.

Julia smiled politely.

'You're very kind,' she said, 'perhaps next year?' An image of a golden, sandy beach and blue, lapping sea took shape in her mind. Would that ever happen for her? Perhaps one day… One thing she was certain about, absolutely sure, was that her Mama and Tato would never be persuaded to leave their home.

They enjoyed their tea and biscuits and small talk with Andrew's lively contributions on the subjects of his football team and activities at the Scouts meetings. Roman, his features relaxing in an indulgent smile, would ruffle Andrew's hair now and again and remind him to expand on his successes in swimming and cross country running.

'That's enough bragging for today,' Joyce said at length, 'I want to talk to Julia.'

Andrew got up, his bouncy step betraying his impatience to go outside.

'I'll practise tennis against the wall,' he said, then mouthed his mother's words aloud, 'but don't kill my flowers!'

They all laughed, he skipped out, and Joyce turned to Julia.

'Right, let's talk about your new school. I don't suppose you've had time to think much about it with everything else going on.'

'It has been a little busy,' Julia agreed with a wry understatement, 'but I wouldn't really know where to begin.' That's why she was here. On Roman's insistence. Joyce was a secretary at the Technical College and knew all the necessary contacts.

'Nothing to worry about,' she waved her delicate hand, 'I'll give you the address of the Grammar School for Girls. They're moving this holiday to their new site in Bilton.'

The grand name sent a shiver of anxiety down Julia's spine.

'Will I fit in? It all sounds so posh…'

Joyce laughed. She had a lovely smile. No wonder Roman had fallen for her. He gave Julia an encouraging nod.

'Of course you'll fit in,' he assured her. 'You've done well so far. I'm sure your exam results will be as good as the other girls'. Have you thought about your A-level subjects yet?' All through her childhood he had been her kind uncle taking an interest in her education. He had been instrumental in securing her a grant from some Polish fund, to enable her to attend the convent school at Pitsford. She owed him a lot.

'Yes, I've got those sorted out in my mind,' she replied. 'Do you know the headmistress? Is she nice?' The memory of Sister Vespera was still very fresh in Julia's mind. Her severe expression, her rigid demands of high standards, her scathing disgust at poor results.

'Miss Ogden is the headmistress,' Joyce said, 'I don't know her personally, but from all accounts, she's an excellent head. Doesn't put up with nonsense. Doesn't suffer fools. Prides herself in only the best at her school.'

Another run of shivers down Julia's spine.

'It all sounds so scary...'

'It'll be a piece of cake after the first day, believe me,' Joyce leaned forward as if to give weight to her assurance. 'Write to her, list the subjects you've taken and she'll give you a date for an interview.'

'An interview?' Another hurdle! Was there no end to it? And this was only the beginning.

'Just a formality,' Roman said, his face crinkling around his eyes, 'you don't have to go on your own. Your Tato can go with you.' The thought would have been comforting if only her Tato could speak English perfectly. To impress the excellent Miss Ogden.

'Good...' Julia spoke slowly, her mind racing, going through the list of her adult acquaintances with a good command of the English language. Roman would have been the best choice. But that would have upset her Tato. She pushed her thoughts aside. She would sort it all out, somehow, after receiving a letter from Miss Ogden.

'There's one more thing I want to ask. Nothing to do with the school,' she said. 'How do I go about getting a holiday job?'

They both gave her advice, using words like Labour Exchange and National Insurance Number and Taxation and other strange terms, that she had heard her parents talk about but that had never been of much interest to her before. It all sounded so complicated.

'Can't I just get a job, any job, without too much hassle?'

Joyce's soft brown eyes gave her a thoughtful look.

'I'm just thinking about all the possible places. Would you like to work in Woolworth's?'

'Woolworth's? That would be great! I love shopping there. It's like an Aladdin's cave!' Julia felt a sudden spurt of excitement.

'Then, all you have to do Julia, is go up there, ask to see the manager and if there's a vacancy, he'll do the rest,' Mrs. Joyce said.

'That's a relief!' Julia exhaled and chuckled. 'Of course,' she added, 'I can't do much yet until my Mum comes home.'

It was time to leave. Roman helped her with the bicycle down the stone steps from the elevated front onto the pavement. Julia had had reservations earlier about leaving her dusty old bicycle propped against the embossed papered

462

walls of the lofty spacious hall. The floor tiles were rich in patterns. Original Victorian. Outside, the street was flanked on both sides with lime trees that threw shade on the tall, mullioned bay windows. So superior to her street of grey prefabricated bungalows.

'Julia…' Roman said, as she climbed onto her bicycle, ready to move off, 'don't worry so much. Things pass. Believe me. And new things soon become familiar…' his expression was fatherly. She was touched by his concern. 'There was a time,' he continued, 'when your mother and the others in our little group were all the family I had left. She was like a sister to me. And Theo…we've been through a lot together too…' He paused and looked up at the evening sky, his eyes reflecting the streak of light before the dusk. 'You don't have to struggle on your own, you know. Joyce and I are here… for you both.' He brought his gaze down on her. He looked serious and kind at the same time.

His unexpected openness took her by surprise. She did not know what to say. A thought struck her suddenly, an uncomfortable awareness, that she had always taken his unfailing benevolence for granted, simply because he had been around like a fixture in her childhood. Here he was again, offering his support, generously, freely.

'I'm sorry,' she said, meaning she was sorry for her past immature thoughtlessness. He would have been right to think her totally devoid of gratitude.

'Sorry?' he asked.

'Uncle Roman…' she took a deep breath, 'I just want to say… I do appreciate all the things you do for us…'

He shook his head, giving a quick embarrassed smile.

'Remember what I've always told you, Julia? Doing well at school is the best reward you can give your parents. For all their troubles. For their expectations of you.' He looked up at the sky again, as if pausing to think. 'We've had everything taken away from us. Our lands, our homes… they destroyed our lives. But they could not take from us what was inside our minds. Knowledge, Julia, is the most secure treasure you can possess. Once you've got it, it's yours for ever. But I suppose,' he looked at her, his face breaking into a smile, 'the nuns have drummed that into you from day one!'

'They have, indeed,' Julia returned his smile, 'and it's been jolly hard work.'

'Then I won't say any more,' he raised his hands up in mock defeat. 'My regards to Theo. Tell him from me to leave all the fighting with the windmills to Don Quixote!' This had been their shared joke, ever since Roman introduced her to European writers and she had read Cervantes and skipped all the boring long paragraphs to pick out the plot and the humour of Don Quixote and Sancho Panza's adventures.

Julia laughed.

'I think Tato enjoys his rants.'

She found her Tato, for once not twiddling with the blaring radio, but sitting in his armchair with the Polish Daily spread on his lap. He looked up as she walked in, disgust threatening to explode his face.

'The bloody communists!' He slapped the paper as if it was responsible in some way. 'Do you know what they're doing now? They won't allow people to erect a cross! On the site that has been cleared for building a church. First church in Nova Huta. People have been collecting for years! Scrimping, saving, God knows how with chronic shortages all round. And now, they won't let them, the godless bastards! Twenty-one years! Can you believe it, it's twenty-one years since the Red Army walked in so graciously and liberated Poland! Some freedom!'

Julia listened and nodded and when Tato returned to his reading she went into the kitchen and made lemon tea. In jam jars. Her Mama's and Tato's quirky residue of their thrifty past. The first thing she'd buy with her first pay packet would be a set of decent porcelain cups.

She sat down beside him, and with Muszka suddenly materialising on her lap, she held her hot drink at a safe distance from the cat, and told her Tato about Joyce's and Roman's advice. He was very pleased.

'You must write to the school straight away, Julia.'

'I'll do it tonight.' Then she told him about her proposed holiday job. His reaction was an adamant NO.

'My sisters never had to work in their student days and I don't want you to be working either. Believe me, you'll be working plenty yet in your life...' His grey eyes widened with emphasis.

'But Tato,' she kept a serious expression though his outburst amused her, 'Tato,' she pleaded gently, 'these are different times. A lot of students work these days. Christmas post, summer work in the fields, strawberry picking, beans, peas. I'm not planning on going away. I hope to get a job right here. In Woolworths, if they'll have me.'

Tato's eyes widened even more, as if he'd seen a ghost.

'Woolworths! But everyone will see you there! They'll all be talking. Saying old Lutovski can't afford to keep his daughter!'

Julia patted his arm.

'Tato, they won't. All they'll see is that I've grown up. There's no shame in work. Whatever it is. You should know that better than anyone.'

He shook his head.

'Julia, do you think it's really my choice to work in a factory? Checking empty tins all day, packing, my neck and my arms stiff with the piece-work. I'd be in railway management back home.'

Julia did not know what to say. There was no comparison. Her holiday job would be just that; temporary, not binding. Her Tato was stuck with his.

'Tato,' she was thinking fast, 'I'm not starting tomorrow. Nothing's happened yet. I'll wait first till Mama comes home.'

'That's right,' he latched on readily, 'don't rush into anything. Nastusha

464

will need you here.' He looked around, and for the first time, appeared to notice the transformation. 'You've done a great job. She'll be so pleased!'

Julia had fantasized about the look of astonishment and pleasure on her Mama's face, while she continued cleaning the house on her days at home. Every flat surface had been dusted and washed, the lino floors scrubbed and polished, the tablecloths and lace covers laundered and ironed, the net curtains soaked in bicarbonate solution to restore their whiteness. She had done everything as she had seen her Mama do over the years.

In her parents' bedroom she had found her Mama's old suitcase by chance, when she removed the cover for washing. It was on top of three other suitcases, stacked and covered with an embroidered cloth to form a kind of a stand by her Mama's bedside. The flat top displayed an array of objects: a statuette of the Virgin Mary with a candle on each side, an olive wood jewellery box with the Jerusalem Cross carved on the lid, and two framed photographs of her sisters, Magda and Hanna.

Julia had pressed the springs on the rusty locks, but they did not budge. Her momentary disappointment gave way to relief. If she'd had the key, she knew what would have happened. She'd not have been able to resist the temptation. She'd have looked inside and broken her Mama's trust.

She pushed away those niggling thoughts for now. She gathered up Muszka in her arms and put her down on the floor. The cat yelped her protest, stretched uncertainly then made a reluctant retreat to her blanket in the corner.

Julia stood up saying,

'Let's hope the news is better, when we see Mama tomorrow. I'll go now, and write that letter.'

On Saturday, there was a note waiting for her from Miro when they returned from the hospital in the late afternoon. 'Can you come round tonight? I'll be home by six. Fancy going to the cinema?'

Julia's heart leapt. Then she was irritated with herself for feeling so eager. Miro had kept her waiting all week. Perhaps she should do the same? No contact. Not a word. All week. Two weeks. Make him feel the way she did.

She looked at her watch. She had an hour to get ready, if she decided to go at all. She made scrambled eggs on toast with a green salad for Tato and herself, fed Muszka and washed up, all the while whipping up her determination to resist Miro's invite.

She stood before the mirror in her room and looked at her own reflection. The window behind her framed the copper beech outside that shimmered with the bright sky shining through the branches. It was a beautiful day, what was left of it, too good to waste. And it was hard work sulking. She checked the time. She had seventeen minutes.

At six, she was washed and changed (her ubiquitous polka-dot dress), her hair fluffed out, her mouth touched with lipstick. Tato was already sitting by his radio, twiddling the knobs. The screeching and the squeaking and the sudden outbursts of deafening fanfares made it impossible to talk.

'Tato…' He did not hear her. 'Tato…' she touched his shoulder and he looked up. She waited till he turned the volume down. 'Tato, I may be back late tonight. We're going to the cinema.'

'With Miro?'

'Yes.'

'Then why isn't he coming here to fetch you?' The question hung heavy between them.

'Because I'm going round to their house. To see his parents. As well as him. Nothing wrong with that, is there?'

He gave her a long look. His sigh was weary.

'I suppose it's all right. Everything's changed. Customs. Manners.' A thoughtful pause. 'Give them my regards.'

She stopped herself from skipping down the pavement. There was a gentle breeze blowing, soothing her face, carrying scents of freshly-mown grass and strong-fragranced jasmine, from the open front gardens along her street. She must not appear keen. Turning the corner of her road, she slowed down her steps, in case Miro was watching. But his house betrayed no presence indoors, the gathered net curtains forming a white opaque screen.

Only when Julia knocked, there were sounds of a scuffle and squabbling on the other side of the door. It was yanked open, to reveal two perky faces beaming at her. Lukasz and Piotr, Miro's younger brothers. They were fourteen and twelve, very alike with their dark hair and their brown eyes emphasised with thick eyelashes.

'Hi, Julia,' Lukasz was gripped by a fit of giggles. 'You'll run a mile when you see Miro.'

'Why?' Julia found herself laughing with him, all previous peevishness gone. Piotr suppressed a squeal, clamping his hand over his mouth

Their father's voice came from within. 'Well, don't just stand there on the doorstep! Let Julia in!' As always, Miro's house was lively. Julia envied him

In the kitchen Mrs. Anna was baking, her cheeks rosy from the heat, her dark hair curling around her face. Mr. Michal was sitting at the table chiselling at some wooden box. Most of the wooden objects around their house, stools, bedside tables, large and small containers, shelves with ornate edges were the products of his carpentry skills.

Julia greeted Miro's parents in Polish first before saying 'Hi!' to him. He was covered in thick dust and standing at the sink scrubbing his hands. His hair looked like a mop that had been dipped in flour. He hadn't got ready for her.

'Hi!' he replied, his smile shining white in his smeared face, 'just got back. I didn't know they'd want me to stay this long today. Give me five minutes and I'll be as clean as a new pin!'

'More like five hours, with a bottle of bleach,' Lukasz snorted.

Going past him Miro flicked dust off his hair at his brother. 'Back in a tick,' he said to Julia.

She was requested to sit down at the table, but it was obvious that they had just finished their meal and the table hadn't been cleared.

'*Pomoge*. I'll wash up for you, Mrs. Anna,' she offered, reverting to Polish, 'and the boys can dry.'

'Ooo… the boys can dry…' Lukasz mimicked in a girlish voice, then catching his father's meaningful look, he added quickly, 'your servants, Julia!'

Mrs. Anna's concentration was centred exclusively on getting out of the oven two apple cakes and replacing them with two tins full of honey cake mixture. That done, she straightened herself, wiping her brow with the back of her hand.

'I could really do with a daughter,' she said, her gaze, nevertheless, following proudly her boys as they cleared the table.

Throughout the buzz and activity of washing up and drying the boys vied with each other in their eagerness to recount to Julia all their latest escapades.

'Now hush, you two for a minute!' Mr. Michal raised his head from his work and brushed back his hair with his fingers. 'Allow Julia to say a word or two. How's your mother? Is she getting better? When is she coming home?'

Julia squirmed, despite Mr. Michal's genuine concern. It was hard talking about her Mama's illness, it was almost like a betrayal. If only her Mama's condition could have been something else, like a broken leg. She'd have got unreserved sympathy. Julia remembered from her childhood the cruel nicknames shouted with self-inflating superiority at those who were considered mad.

'My Mama's doing all right,' she said with a lightness she did not feel. She was prepared. She had practised her little speeches for her mother's friends at the church. 'The medication makes her sleepy, but that's good for her. It forces her to rest. She loves talking about her garden and her flowers when we visit her…'

'Really?' Mrs. Anna turned round from clearing her baking things. 'But that's a very good sign. You forget all your troubles when you're down on your hands and knees, close to the soil, planting, watching things grow. I'd say that gardening is the best cure for everything!'

'Not for your back!' Mr. Michal corrected, rubbing his sides and rolling his eyes like a martyr.

Mrs. Anna gave him a pitiful look.

'And whoever asked you to dig the whole garden in five minutes? You're supposed to enjoy it, not kill yourself!' And not waiting for a reply she said to Julia, 'Come Julia, sit down. I'll make fresh tea.'

Lukasz and Piotr made a hurried exit and planted themselves in front of the television at the far end, the lounge part of the one through room. Julia sat down at the table with Miro's parents. Strangely, she found comfort in their light-hearted banter and felt her tension easing off. It did not seem to matter any more that Miro had not been ready and waiting for her.

'Your cake is excellent,' she said in honest praise, licking crumbs off her fingers. Mrs. Anna looked pleased.

'Take the recipe, Julia,' she replied, 'and surprise your Mama when she comes home.'

'Thank you, I will.' Of course, that's what she must do! Julia imagined her Mama's smiling face, the pride in her eyes, as she, Julia, placed a perfectly baked cake in front of her.

Miro came down with his hair still damp, glistening and curling over his white collar. The rolled-up sleeves exposed his tanned arms. There was something eye-catching, attractive about them, that caught Julia unawares. He sat down beside her and spread his hands, like fans on the table. They were grazed and scratched, with chipped fingernails.

'You need a good manicure,' Julia teased. He smelled clean, soap and after shave.

'Hard work won't harm him,' Mr. Michal remarked, a playful smile in his eyes. 'It sorts the men from the boys.'

Miro's mother placed his belated supper in front of him: a piece of chicken with green vegetables and potatoes, a princely meal compared to Julia's effort of scrambled eggs earlier on. While Miro ate his meal, she spoke to his father, asking him questions about his woodwork, knowing this would please him. He told her of the wartime years, of how one had to be inventive and enterprising to survive, of how necessity had taught him many things he would not have had the chance to learn in normal circumstances.

'But woodwork is in my blood,' he said, 'it was our family business. We'd have done well if it hadn't been for the war.'

'It's hard to imagine,' Mrs. Anna turned round from her tidying up, 'that our lives could have been so different. Still, we've got a lot to be thankful for. A roof over our heads, a cover over our backs and food to put on the table.'

'Oh please, not the war again…' Miro puckered his brow in mock pain. Then he gave his parents an engaging smile. 'Let's talk about normal things, shall we? Forget the bad times. Be happy!'

His father was not so easily charmed. 'You've no idea what you're talking about, Miro. I can only excuse you because of your ignorance.'

Miro looked suitably contrite. 'Tato, I only mean that life goes on… It's not good for you to dwell on the past… too much.'

'And no doubt you think we've turned into boring old folk!' his mother's tone was accusing.

Miro laughed. 'Mama, how can you say such things? You could never be old. Or boring!' That seemed to satisfy her. She gave him an indulgent look then turned back to her chores. Miro finished his meal and took the empty plate to wash up at the sink. He drank a glass of cold water.

'Right,' he said, coming back to Julia, 'shall we go?'

Julia half-expected tedious questions from his parents, but they appeared content and involved in their own activities and stopped only long enough to wish them an enjoyable evening at the cinema.

'Can we come too?' Lukasz called out, snorting mischievously.

'Next time. When they show Mickey Mouse,' Miro answered back.

Julia was still laughing to herself when she and Miro stepped outside.

They walked briskly, the energy of their pace barely controlled, past the long terrace of houses, cut abruptly by a narrow side street, past a separate block with a post office, a greengrocer's, a haberdashery shop and a barber's, that marked the invisible boundary of the Brownsover estate. In the open fields, across which the road swerved towards the town, the soft breeze was cooling and pleasant, like delicate fingers running through Julia's hair.

'So, how was your week?' she asked Miro. She had meant Sunday. Rosemary. The party.

He glanced at her, a smile touching his eyes.

'A slog. But it's well paid.'

'And the evenings? Were you busy too?' This sounded like a whinge. Too late. She could not retract her words.

'I worked overtime,' he explained, 'didn't get back till nine most days. They need people badly at the moment. It's some big contract. The M1, I think. Just outside Rugby. We can cycle over one evening, if you wish.'

Julia only half listened. She wanted to know about Sunday.

'And the party? Was that good?'

He gave her a blank look.

'Party...?'

'Rosemary's party.' She studied his expression. It suddenly came to life.

'Oh, that party! Goodness, it seems like ages ago!' He smoothed back his hair, pausing as if struggling to remember. 'It was all right. A lot of people I didn't know.'

'And..?' Julia prompted, 'where was it?'

He shrugged,

'At their house. In the garden. Lucky we had good weather. It was mainly family. Uncles, aunts, cousins. And just three friends from school. Her best friend, her boyfriend and me. Me!?' He repeated the last word with a question mark and laughed.

Julia laughed too. With relief. Uncles. Aunts. A boyfriend! Then realizing how Miro might misinterpret her mirth, she rushed to oppose him.

'Miro, don't be silly, it just shows how highly Rosemary thinks of you.' Was she really saying these words? 'And,' she added generously 'I don't suppose she'll find anyone again to share notes with her so willingly.'

'It was nothing more than a simple practicality,' Miro was dismissive with a good natured laugh, 'but she's put me in a spot now. I've been thinking, I suppose I ought to invite her and some of my friends before we all go our own ways in the autumn. When I think of their garden... like a park, Julia,' he shook his head, 'and our little stamp of green at the back... Our house is like a doll's house compared to theirs...'

'So what!' Julia's loyalty flared up in defence. 'Does it really matter what Rosemary might think?'

Miro smiled and looked at her in a strange soft way that made something melt inside her.

'No, it doesn't matter,' he said, 'your true friends remain your friends, no matter what. But tell me, what have you been doing all week?'

They had walked over the bridge that spanned a minor outflow of the Avon, its banks overgrown with brambles and shaded by weeping willows, and were now walking towards the town past the industrial estate of factories and warehouses.

Julia told him. Hospital visits every afternoon. On her own. Because her Dad was at work. And cleaning the house in between. Such a chore!

'I managed one visit to the library!'

'Must be my good influence,' he joked. 'Do you remember the library at the camp?'

Julia giggled. She remembered it as if it were yesterday.

'When we walked across the field in the dark? In the winter months? And you whistled all the way, to keep the wolves at bay?'

Miro laughed.

'Did I really?' then he added seriously, 'I'll come with you to the hospital, just let me know when.'

'Even on a weekday?' she tested.

'I'm owed a day off. At least one. For all the extra hours I've been putting in.'

'That would be nice,' she replied, not having much hope of this actually happening.

They walked inside the tunnel underneath the railway station, an anachronism from the inudustrial revolution era, a bottleneck for the modern traffic and for the thousands of factory workers who used this underpass every day. But it was quiet on Saturday night. Only the echo of their footsteps bounced off the brick walls and their faces lit up red, amber and green as the traffic lights changed continually in the murky gloom.

The light at the other end, the balmy warmth in the air were like reflections of Julia's feelings. She was happy just to be with Miro. She felt that the comfortable ease of their long friendship had been recaptured. Their talk became spontaneous, inconsequential, with frequent outbursts of laughter. In Park Road they slipped through the gates of the park and strolled among the flower beds that spilled with a profusion of colours and varieties, at their best in the summer.

'My Mum would love it here,' Julia said, inhaling deeply the scent of the honeysuckle and lilies, 'we'll come every evening when she's home.'

The wide steps of the Odeon drew them invitingly towards the glass doors of the main entrance. The posters showed Audrey Hepburn in a nun's habit, tropical white, her huge, beguiling eyes looking up into Peter Finch's face, the angle of his head telling, as he leaned towards her.

'Great!' Julia felt excitement bubbling inside her, 'I missed it when it first came out. Do you mind?' She referred to his preference of the westerns.

'Mind? Goodness, no! It's supposed to be good. The Belgian Congo, and all the problems there.'

The foyer, all red carpet and red walls and a hint of stale cigarette smoke, was quiet with just the odd couple going in or coming out, no fear of missing out any feature, as the showing ran continuously from two o'clock in the afternoon till midnight. Besides, Julia was not bothered much about the newsreel or the B movie, as long as she saw *The Nun's Story* complete.

They bought their tickets and walked towards the staircase, wide and carpeted, like the one in Rhett Butler's grand mansion, and for a second Julia imagined herself to be Scarlett, with men falling over themselves, fighting for her attention. She wanted Miro to be like Rhett. She certainly wouldn't have wasted her time on a whimp like Ashley.

She looked up and stopped. Taken aback. Speechless.

Coming down the stairs was Leon, tall, lean, as always, perfectly dressed, his crisp-looking jacket and trousers refusing to crease. His arm was resting lightly around the shoulders of his companion, a slim blonde, with a flamboyant bob and heavily made-up eyes.

'Leon, Hi! What a surprise!' She felt her cheeks turning pink. Oh bother! Why was she being embarrassed for him?

Leon looked down at the sound of her voice and his face broke into a wide smile, as if she had been his best friend, and he'd not seen her for years. She waited till he and the girl joined them at base of the stairs.

'Hi! Julia! Miro! Not seen you at the club for ages. And Julia, how are things at home?'

As if he really cared! Did he imagine she was going to discuss her mother with him? And in front of a total stranger?

'Everything's fine. Thank you. Could have been even better. I've missed going to London with Nadia just by a whisker.' She watched his face intently for his reaction.

'That's a pity,' he said, then added with a grin, 'I'm sure Nadia's having a whale of a time!' He looked at his companion. 'This is Alison, my friend from work.'

Alison nodded, her eyes darting towards the entrance doors. 'I won't keep you,' Leon concluded, his charm sweetening his voice. 'The film's really good. Enjoy it!' He winked at Miro before guiding Alison away, with his hand on her elbow.

'Well!' was all Julia could say in her indignation.

'Why? What's up?' Miro looked amused as they made their way up the red-carpeted stairs.

'I'll tell you everything. Later. You'll never guess!'

They entered the dark auditorium and stood inside the door for a moment until their eyes got used to the dark. The flickering light of the black-and-white newsreel illuminated the audience, making them look like cobblestones. The back row was full with couples busy with each other. Julia and Miro settled in seats closest to the aisle.

Princess Margaret's radiant smile filled the screen. The B feature was a repeat showing of her wedding in May. To a commoner. Mr. Anthony Armstrong-Jones. It was so romantic! Sister Alicya had praised her, the princess who had so nobly renounced her first love, the divorced Captain Townsend, in a sacrifice for the greater good of her country. That was true self-discipline, Sister Alicya had said. Now the princess could enjoy her well-deserved reward! Julia loved it all, the grandeur, the ceremony, the beautiful dresses, the diamonds. Her eyes were still starry when the lights came on.

The usherettes appeared by all the exits around the auditorium, their trays hung on wide ribbons from their necks and filled with confectionery. The whole place became alive with the rasping sounds of torn paper packets, opened crisp bags, general murmur and unrestrained giggles as smoke from the freshly lit cigarettes floated in swirls above the audience. Miro joined one of the queues and came back with ice-creams.

'Thanks,' Julia said, 'it's a real treat. Ages since I've had an ice-cream. My treat next time. As soon as I get a job.'

'Don't be silly,' he laughed, 'no tit for tatting between us, OK? Now tell me, what was all that about? In the foyer'.

Julia told him, recalling her last meeting with Nadia. She concluded, 'Nadia believes that Leon is her boyfriend. From what I've seen tonight, I think he is a cheat. A liar. Now, what do I do? Tell her the truth and upset her? Or keep it to myself and let him think that I'm colluding with him?'

'Julia, hold on a second!' Miro raised his hand as if to fend off an attack. 'Aren't you jumping to conclusions before finding out all the facts? What if... and it's only a supposition, what if Nadia thinks there's more to her friendship with Leon than there really is? If he's not made her definite promises, then in his mind he's still free to go out with anyone he likes. And there's nothing wrong with that, is there? What if this girl... Alison... is only, as he says, a friend from work? Hmmm?'

Julia was suddenly irritated that he did not share her indignation.

'But Miro,' she insisted hotly, 'he's been spending so much time with her lately. Taking her on days out. On his motorbike. Even home to his mother. He's even kissed her! Now, that surely tells you something!'

Miro bit a smile curling on his lips and his dark eyes remained fixed as if he struggled to look serious. Julia knew that look.

'What's so funny? I really thought that you'd see it my way. Leon's a cheat, and there's no doubt about it!'

'Julia, please,' Miro was all soft voice and sympathy, 'let it rest, OK? It'll all sort itself out. Does Nadia really need busybodies like us? Let's just enjoy the film, shall we? I don't want to be falling out with you over this.'

'Neither do I,' Julia answered begrudgingly. Nevertheless she could not stop herself from adding, 'I shall never allow anyone to treat me the way Leon treats Nadia!' And to prove the point, when she had scraped the last drop of the ice-cream from the bottom of the paper tub and crushed it and disposed of it, she folded her arms across her chest and hid her hands under her arm pits, so Miro would not get ideas about touching her in the dark. If his intentions were honourable towards her, then he'd have to prove that first!

CHAPTER 59

There were those twinges again, like something prodding her stomach, when Julia got off the bus at the main hospital gates. What was it going to be? Cold silence? Indifference? Dismissive distance in Mama's gaze that did not register Julia's presence?

She made herself walk fast to stifle the rising unease. There was a line of cars parked on one side of the drive. Just in front of her a car drove off leaving an oily stain on the dark tarmac. Its circular edge shone like a miniature rainbow though the sky was overcast. A distant memory stirred in Julia's mind: fragmented rainbow colours running through a network of cracks in a window pane. She must have been only three at the time but she remembered clearly sitting on her Mama's lap and listening to her songs and thinking that the magic of the colours in the fractured glass and the sweetness of her Mama's voice were one and the same thing. If only she would sing again!

Julia found her asleep in the armchair by the bed. Her clothes were clean but her hair needed brushing. Even in repose her face looked troubled and Julia wished she had the power to smooth out the lines. She placed her hand over her Mama's and kissed her cheek gently.

Her eyelids quivered. She appeared to struggle opening them.

'*Pigułki.* It's the pills,' she said, 'they make me so sleepy. I've got no strength left…' She spoke! Julia's heart quickened. Her Mama spoke to her!

Her eyelids closed and she began to droop forward. Julia caught her by the shoulders and held her against the back rest.

'Mama, let's go outside. The fresh air will do you good.'

To her relief, Mama did not object and allowed Julia to assist her with her cardigan and shoes. Then, arm in arm, they walked outside to the bench under the willow tree. She moved up right against her, their sides touching, and it felt like old times.

'Oh Mama!' Julia hugged her. 'We can't wait to have you home!'

Her Mama closed her eyes and tilted her head back as if sunbathing. There was no sun, but the air was warm under the soft grey sky. Julia picked up Mama's hand, placed it on her lap and stroked it gently. The silence between them was long, but not oppressive.

'Mama,' Julia said, her tone caressing, 'Eva's been asking about you. She's worried. Like everyone else. She wants you to be well and back home.'

Her Mama opened her eyes and turned them on Julia. There was a surprising sharpness in her look. Julia held her breath.

'Tell Eva not to worry. She'll understand.'

'Understand what?'

'She'll know.' Her Mama closed her eyes again. 'Sing me about Bernadette,' she requested. It was a well-liked song about Bernadette's vision of the Holy Mary and the message for the world. Julia's heart leapt.

'Mama, you sing better than me.'

'But I need to rest today,' her Mama replied not opening her eyes.

Julia stroked her hand and intoned softly, careful not to disturb the quiet of the hospital grounds around which other patients strolled with their visitors. Every time she sang the refrain, 'Ave Maria,' she saw her Mama's lips moving. She sang the song again, all six verses, just to hear her Mama hum.

'Your mother is making good progress,' the staff nurse told Julia, all crisp and businesslike, smart navy and white presence. 'Another week or so, and she may be ready to be discharged.'

Julia's heart skipped. She squeezed her mother's hand.

'Did you hear that, Mama?' She nodded, like a child willing to please.

They were indoors, back by Mama's bed. It was soon time for Julia to leave.

'Just a few more days of therapy and observation. We'll review things at the weekend,' the nurse promised. She retreated towards an anxious looking couple by their daughter's bed.

Mama said thoughtfully, 'It feels as if I've been here forever, I feel ready to go home now. There's so much to do in the garden.'

Julia felt another burst of joy. Her Mama was speaking normally, about everyday things. There was a fresh softness around her eyes, around her mouth.

'I'd love to take you home with me now,' Julia gave her a hug and her Mama held her close to her chest.

'You can take all these old Polish papers home,' her mother said, releasing her, 'I've almost learnt them all by heart'. Her subtle attempt at humour pleased Julia. 'You can bring me my favourite book with you, next time you come. The Book of Miracles. I like to remind myself how miracles can happen to ordinary people like me.' She smiled. Julia felt a wave of warmth pass through her.

'But you're not ordinary, Mama,' she protested, chuckling to herself, 'you could never be ordinary. I'll bring your book on Saturday. But who knows, you may be allowed to go home.'

Julia's good spirits were heightened at the sight of two letters, when she returned home. Her dear friends, Lidia and Yagoda.

Lidia wrote: 'Vittorio is HERE! Mama and Nonna are besotted with him, but all his charms and his sweet nothings don't fool ME! Papa says it wouldn't hurt him to help around the house and the garden, a big strappy lad that he is, but Mama says he needs to spend time with his friends to improve his English. Papa doesn't care for his friends. Alberto LOVES them. They congregate on the pavement outside our house, all black leather and motorbikes. All James Dean! And every pillion ride is HEAVEN!'

Julia was still chuckling to herself when she opened Yagoda's letter.

'Dear Julia, You'd never recognize me now! I've had my plaits chopped off. Sheila took me to the hairdressers and now I look like Deanna Durbin with an Alice band. Pity the face doesn't match! And Voytek has arranged dancing classes for me to strengthen my thinner leg. Margot Fonteyn better watch out!'

It seemed, Julia reflected with contentment, that the adult life the three of them had dreamed of for so long, was beginning to unroll with a promise of better things to come.

Saturday started badly. Julia woke up to pounding rain at her window, and dimness, like November dusk, hanging around the curtains. The anxious feeling returned. She suppressed it with exaggerated energy of jumping out of bed and pulling back the curtains. The scene outside was like a waterfall, distorting everything beyond it, making wavy lines of buildings and street lamps, and reducing her mother's bright flowers to pale runny stains in the overwhelming greyness.

She threw on her dressing-gown and tying it, went to check if Tato was up. Muszka woke up on the armchair, stretched, jumped off and following Julia, rubbed herself against Julia's ankles.

Tato was sitting at the kitchen table, in his navy and white plaid dressing gown, his white hair sticking out at all angles, his eyes moist over the steaming jar of lemon tea.

'Are you all right, Tato?' Julia felt a twinge of concern. 'It's like a deluge outside. What are we going to do?'

His lip quivered.

'I must have caught a germ. Bad stomach all night. And a hellish headache.'

She stopped filling Muszka's bowl and looked up. God, *please*! First her Mama, now her Tato!

'What are we going to do?' she repeated.

His face crumpled, but his tone was firm.

'Nothing, my dear. Typhus didn't kill me and this won't either. A day or two of hot drinks and I'll be all right on Monday.'

'And what about today?' The rain sounded torrential on the side of the house.

His rheumy eyes were thoughtful.

476

'You don't have to go. Nastusha will understand…'

The thought of her mother waiting, looking out all day tugged at Julia's heart.

'Rain won't put me off,' she said with forced brightness, 'I'll wear wellingtons. And my mac, and take your large umbrella.'

Tato's umbrella sheltered her shoulders, but within minutes of leaving the house, the hemline of her raincoat felt like cold soggy washing beating against her legs. The walk up Murray Road was like a test of endurance against the rain and wind. Giant raindrops bubbled on the pavement, streams swirled round her feet. There was a queue already waiting inside the bus shelter, as rain beaten and bedraggled as herself, and she could well imagine the steaming, stifling air on the bus once it picked up the passengers.

The bus to Warwick was late. Five minutes stretched to half an hour, as other buses came and went, wading through the puddles, throwing splashes of dirty water onto the pavement. Julia's unease turned to disappointment. She swallowed back threatening tears of utter helplessness. She heard a man, his face screwed up against the beating rain, enquire of the driver of a parked bus, about the bus to Warwick. The bus driver's answer came back muffled, but Julia picked up something about a breakdown and 'them working on it'.

She had a sudden feeling as if something dropped inside her, and to her horror, tears filled her eyes. She moved fast out of the bus shelter before anyone could notice.

No visit today. Her mother's troubled expression filled her mind, and as she stood on the kerb waiting to cross the road, she lifted her face to the cleansing rain.

'Julia! Julia!' She heard someone calling. She opened her eyes and peered hard through the rain, and listened through the noise of the traffic. After a moment she just made out a figure, clad in black leather, sitting astride his motorbike on the other side of the road. It was Leon. Panic gripped her. God, she did not want to be seen like this, hair hanging in wet strings, soggy clothes, ungainly wellingtons, but before her brain could think of an escape, he had turned his motorbike around and stopped right beside her.

'Jump on the back,' he commanded. 'I'll take you home.'

There was no point protesting, no time to explain. She pushed all reservations aside. She climbed onto the passenger seat and with her bag wedged between herself and Leon, and her arms tight around his waist, they were off.

It was like a ride on a roller coaster, frightening and exhilarating at the same time. She held on to him, glad of the shield of his back, and wondered how long it would take before her face and her hands froze dead in the cold.

He got her home in less than ten minutes, but her stiff lips made it hard to talk. Shivering, she forced herself to shout above the pounding rain.

'Come inside!' She wanted him to decline, wanted him to go. Because of Nadia. She did not want complications. God, she had enough worries already.

He dismounted and pushed his Silver Shadow down the side of the house. She ran to open the door and when he followed her inside, she put on a welcoming smile, as she wiped the rain off her face and pushed back her dripping hair.

'How can I thank you, Leon?' she said, and despite herself, added, 'The least I can do is offer you some hot tea.'

He took off his leather helmet and ruffled his hair loose. Before he could reply, Tato came out of his room, dishevelled and crumpled, his face puckered, his eyes runny. Julia cringed, but Leon smiled politely.

'*Dzień dobry*. Good morning, Mr. Lutovski. I'm sorry you're not well.'

'I thought I heard voices,' Theo's voice disintegrated in a rasping smoker's cough.

Julia explained what had happened. 'Now Mama will be waiting for nothing, all day,' she concluded with a heavy heart.

Leon listened.

'Why didn't you say anything?' he asked. 'I could have taken you there.'

Julia shook her head, for a second forgetting her wet hair and sending a spray of drops against the mirror.

'What, in this deluge? Thanks Leon. But look at me... we'd get soaked all over again...'

Leon would not give up.

'What time do you have to be there?'

'At two..., but Leon, there's no point even thinking about it.'

'Why not? I'll bring you a waterproof cloak. Specially for the motor.'

Julia was torn. This idea presenting itself out of the blue was not especially attractive, but it offered her the chance to see Mama.

'It's settled,' Leon decided, 'I'll come back for you at one. You've got two hours to get dry and ready.'

Her Tato looked worried.

'Is it safe? In this rain? The road surface will be slippery.'

'Safer than riding round the town in the traffic.' Leon assured him.

'Leon, let's not be hasty,' Julia tried to reason, 'let's leave it for today, if this heavy rain persists. But if it stops, then I'll be very glad of your offer.' Would Nadia have been glad?

He inclined his head and smiled.

'Agreed'.

It stopped raining by lunchtime, but the sun remained hidden behind the grey mass of clouds and clammy, misty air. The freshly washed trees shone like torches in incongruous bright green. Julia had changed into slacks, dried her hair, touched up her face, fed Muszka, made herself a sandwich and took her Tato a hot lemon and honey drink.

His room was stuffy. She placed the drink by his bedside and opened the little top window.

'I won't disturb you, Tato, when Leon arrives,' she stood at the foot of his bed, 'I'll just lock the door when we leave.'

He was totally covered with his eiderdown pulled up to his chin. He spoke over his shoulder,

'Come straight home afterwards, Julia, or I'll be worrying.'

'No need, Tato. I've no plans to go anywhere else.'

She felt weary, tired of the whole situation, of the chores, of the bus journeys, of the disruption to her own personal time. Her dream of a carefree holiday bore no resemblance to this dismal reality. She wished it had been Miro fetching her and not Leon. She was uneasy imagining Nadia's reaction, though none of this was of her making. Nothing was working out right for her. A feeling of dejection pressed down on her like a weight.

But her spirits lifted at the sight of Leon. There was no denying his good looks and his charm. She could well understand Nadia's infatuation. He greeted her with the wide smile of a winner and gave her a long appraising look, as if she were the only person worth his full attention.

'I've brought you the cloak,' he said, draping it over her shoulders, for her to button up, 'and the leather helmet to keep your hair in place.'

'You've thought of everything!' she said in mock admiration, fastening the strap under her chin, but then added seriously, 'I can't imagine why you're doing this, Leon.'

'Put on some gloves as well,' he advised before answering in a self-mocking tone. 'It's my mother. Questions me like the father confessor every day. About all my misdeeds.'

'All of them?'

He shrugged.

'A man is allowed to keep a secret or two.'

Only two? Julia wondered, but she could hardly question him when he was offering her his assistance.

'So, am I one of your secrets?'

He laughed.

'No, my mother was astonished that her prodigal son is showing at long last signs of redemption. I'm the emissary of her wholehearted approval.'

'Then I must thank your mother for your good deed today.' She gave him a mischievous grin, and immediately felt a prod of guilt. She must not appear over friendly, for Nadia's sake.

Julia was still thinking about Leon's mother, when she had settled to an exciting ride, warm inside her protective clothing, shielded behind his back, her arms tight around his waist.

She remembered clearly her unexpected encounter with Mrs. Tarnovska at a social event the previous Easter, where Leon's mother had been one of the tea ladies, selling their home-made cakes, to raise funds for the building of the Polish Club.

'Is this really our little Julia Kalinska?' Mrs. Tarnovska trilled, her eyes quick, assessing. 'My goodness, how you've grown! And beautiful too! And to think, it seems like only yesterday, you were only this high,' her hand wavered three feet above the ground. She was formidable, with her tall, solid figure, her abundant hair rinsed deep chestnut and twisted into a French roll. She had leaned forward over the counter, lowering her voice, as if to share secrets with Julia.

'So when are you finishing school?'

Julia had shrunk back at this sudden attention, but good manners demanded a polite reply. 'In the summer.'

'Really?' Mrs. Tarnovska's pencilled eyebrows shot up with interest.

'But not altogether,' Julia added.

'No?' The eyebrows formed arcs of disappointment.

'A-levels still to do. Then university'.

Leon's mother gave her a long, penetrating look.

'I think there's room for only one clever person in a marriage. And that should be the man!' She had married her daughter Marta to a nice Polish boy the previous summer, and now, Julia guessed it was Leon's turn. To find him a nice Polish girl.

She had felt too shy to argue the point, to tell Mrs. Tarnovska she had no intention of getting married just yet. She said,

'Your cakes look delicious. Please, may I have three, and three teas, please,' and as soon as she had paid, she made a hasty retreat with the tray to her parents' table, feeling lucky Mrs. Tarnovska was not her mother.

Her thoughts turned now to the imminent visit at the hospital, as the trees and the hedges whizzed by, the miles swallowed up by Leon's Silver Shadow, that tilted precariously overtaking the slower moving traffic. Her initial excitement was giving way to apprehension. What state would they find her Mama in? It was not supposed to matter what Leon might think, but it did.

Mama was sitting by her bed, a *Woman's Own* open on her lap. She looked absorbed. It was a good sign. Her hair was neat, her lips outlined with lipstick. She looked up as they approached, with initial surprise at the sight of Leon, then a warm smile spread across her face. Julia was overwhelmed with relief.

'Mama, oh Mama!' Hugs were long and strong. Leon fetched two chairs and they sat down close to her and told her about Theo's indisposition and the dreadful morning and Leon's fortunate appearance and his assistance in making this visit possible.

Mama listened, her eyes moving from Julia to Leon, her mouth relaxed.

'It rained here too,' she spoke slowly, as if the choice of each word was a mental effort, 'I didn't think anyone would be coming. But now you're here, I'm very happy,' she smiled and looked like her old, normal self and Julia felt happiness spread warmly inside her.

'Tell me about your family, Leon,' her Mama inclined her head forward with interest, 'is everyone all right?' He answered all her questions and told her about his work as an engineering draughtsman, and about his sister Marta and her little terrace house in Craven Road.

'It was totally dilapidated when they bought it last year. But she and Yurek are working on it. Every weekend. And evenings too.'

'I'm so pleased for Marta,' Mama's amber eyes glowed suddenly, 'I remember her when she was just a toddler. As round as a ball in all the layers of clothing, only her little face peering out. God, how cold it was! It's a miracle that any children survived at all those Siberian winters! I still feel a shiver down my spine just thinking about it!'

'My mother,' Leon gave Mama a beguiling smile, 'never stops reminding me how lucky I am!'

'You are Leon, you are,' her Mama confirmed, 'you were a summer baby. You were toughened up, with whatever feed your mother could get for you before the big cold came. The winter babies had very little chance of survival'.

They talked about the old times for a while, Mama reminiscing about her post-Siberian journey, about her arrival with thousands of mothers and children in Pahlevi, the first, longed-for place of freedom.

'The saddest thing was…' she became thoughtful, lethargic, 'that after all the horrors of the previous two years, hundreds of them died… of exhaustion. There's a cemetery in Pahlevi, hundreds of crosses with Polish names on them. Small children…young mothers…' She became quiet and Julia noticed how her eyes glistened.

'Mama, please don't upset yourself,' she clasped her hand. 'Let's talk about happy things. We're all lucky, not just Leon,' she sent him a sideways glance. 'Let's talk about all the things we're going to do when you come home.'

Leon stood up and bowed in mock Polish custom.

'Mrs. Lutowska,' he said, 'I'll just go outside for a smoke. Then Julia can have you all to herself.' Another charming smile.

Her Mama's gaze lingered on his retreating figure.

'He's nice,' she said.

'He is,' Julia agreed, keeping her thoughts of him and Alison to herself. 'He and Nadia… they've started going out together.'

'Really?' there was a sudden liveliness in her Mama's tone. 'As you know, I'm very fond of Nadia. I hope he'll be good to her.'

Julia stroked her mother's hand.

'Nadia's a sensible girl… we both are,' she said. She had to speak to Leon, she decided. Bluntly. She would ask about Alison.

'Who's Alison? Truly?' she asked, after the visit was over and they had walked back to his motorbike.

'What?' He stopped to look at her. There was the faintest trace of surprise on his face before it broke into a seductive smile.

'My, oh my! What's this interrogation?'

481

'Don't play games, Leon. You know exactly what I mean. Alison, the other day.'

'And you today,' he teased.

'You know today is totally different. Have you told her?'

'Have you?' he looked unruffled.

'It's not my habit to snitch, but I'll tell her about today. Might even put in a good word for you. Are you seeing her tonight?'

'Nadia's on duty tonight, and tomorrow I've got to go to Leicester with my old folk to visit their friends.'

'Really?' Julia's tone made it clear she did not believe him.

'Cross my heart,' he made a mock gesture, his expression comically serious.

This made her smile despite herself.

'Get me home first, before a lightning bolt strikes you,' she said.

Her Tato was still in his dressing-gown when she got home, but he had washed, shaved and brushed his hair. He was reading the Polish Daily in a cloud of smoke and coughing on his cigarette. He wanted to know everything. Julia sat down beside him.

'Mama says don't worry about visiting tomorrow. She just wants me to go to church and for you to get better. I'll be going on Monday anyway. We may even get some good news then. She's looking so much better, Tato. It's... such a relief!'

It pleased her to see his cheeks lift and a smile of anticipation hover about his lips. 'It'll be good to have her home,' he said, 'especially in the holiday fortnight when I'll be at home with her.'

'I don't think she'll need looking after. She appears eager to get down to some jobs around the house. She's still lethargic when she talks, but it may be just the medication.'

'She may have to stay on it for a while,' Theo said, 'but if it's good for her...' He tapped his forehead as if suddenly remembering something. 'Miro's been round.'

'Miro?' that was a surprise, 'I thought he was working today.'

'He was, to begin with. But only till lunchtime. The weather was too atrocious to work outdoors.'

'Did he say anything?' A flicker of hope sprung up inside her. She'd see him tonight after all.

'He left you a note. There, on the mantel piece.'

Julia stood up, picked up the sealed envelope and went to her room.

'Hi Julia,' Miro wrote, 'I anticipated an evening of fun. But since you've gone off gallivanting with Leon, I'm off to drown my sorrows. Seeing Stefan in Birmingham and staying overnight. Hope to catch up with you soon.'

His light-hearted tone did nothing to dispel her deep disappointment. She had been hoping to see him at some point over the weekend. His birthday was fast approaching on Monday, and though he had not mentioned anything about it, she had prepared a card and a present for him. With her pocket money she had bought him *The Catcher in the Rye* and packed it together with Sienkiewicz's *Hania*. It was the story of thwarted love and rivalry between two best friends. Miro, she was certain, would enjoy as much as she did, the nineteenth-century setting and the duelling scenes.

She had no choice but to resign herself to waiting till Monday night. It felt like such a very long time. The familiar weight settled on her chest and her face was blurred when she caught sight of herself in the mirror.

CHAPTER 60

'You'll never guess!' Nadia's almond eyes sparkled, her shiny jet-black pony-tail bounced.

It was fun to be with Nadia, after a long-drawn-out Sunday afternoon, with its indifferent weather of sharp showers and lingering clouds; after the tediously long hours of trying to fill time reading or writing letters, when it was hard to concentrate because her mind had been on other things. Earlier, the packed church felt empty without Miro there. She had made a quick exit to avoid questioning by her mother's friends. The solitary march home had only added to her sense of desolation.

Her mood was happier now as she watched Nadia step out of her formal navy skirt and put on a crimson dress with puffed out sleeves that gave shape to her slight frame and emphasised her dark complexion.

Julia had cycled over earlier, having left her Tato thankfully much recovered, just as Nadia was finishing her belated meal. Aunt Eva had offered her food as well, but Julia declined, feeling totally contented to be simply with her friend.

'*Co nowego?* How are things then?' Aunt Eva had asked, joining the girls at the table, clasping together her work-worn hands.

Julia had felt a thrust of pleasure in being the bearer of good news.

'*Dobrze.* Mama's much better. You can see the improvement. She may be allowed to go home soon. She asked me to tell you, Auntie, not to worry about anything. Ever. She said you'd know.'

'Know what?' Nadia raised her eyes, chewing with haste.

'*Nitz.* Nothing... nothing important,' her mother flicked a dismissive hand. 'Tell us about your day, Nadia.'

Nadia swallowed and took a sip of water.

'Nothing much to tell. It's quiet on Sundays. Just routine. Just making sure the patients get their medication and that they're reasonably comfortable.'

'And tomorrow?' Julia asked.

'Going round with the matron.' Nadia cut the meat on her plate into bite-size portions. 'And following doctors' instructions. Of course, I'm watched and questioned all the time. It's like doing exams every day.'

'Do you do injections?'

'Under supervision.'

'Aren't you scared?'

Nadia laughed, showing her white even teeth.

'I wouldn't be much good, if I were.'

Julia found it hard to imagine, that this slip of a girl, with her thin shoulders and arms, with her bouncing ponytail, with the fun-loving nature that had charmed Julia since the age of four, was capable of doing such a responsible job.

'She's amazing, isn't she?' Julia turned to Nadia's mother, knowing her words would please her.

Aunt Eva's smile was restrained.

'Pride comes before a fall. It doesn't do to be too cocky about anything that you do.'

Nadia shrugged, sending Julia the 'I told you so' look. This was not lost on her mother. 'Nadia my dear,' she added, in a softer, pacifying tone, 'there will be time for praise and celebration when you qualify.'

Later, when Julia was following her friend upstairs, she caught sight of Uncle Henryk. As always, he was sitting by the window in the living room looking out, the 'Polish Daily' open on his lap. Marek sat on the floor and waved to them automatically, his eyes fixed on the television screen as the music rose to a crescendo in a dramatic moment of *Dragnet*.

In Nadia's room it felt like a refuge, snug and comfortable. Nadia hung her navy suit inside the wardrobe and sprawled herself across the bed next to Julia.

'Well, aren't you going to guess?' her eyes were at once excited and challenging.

'Better if you tell me. Or I'll be guessing till this time next year.' Julia laughed knowing how hard it was for her friend to keep secrets from her.

A self-pleased grin curled Nadia's lips.

'Leon has asked me… to go with him to the sea-side.'

'Wow!' Julia gave the expected response, widening her eyes for greater effect.

'For the weekend. Overnight!' Nadia's gaze remained fixed, her lips smiling all the while, as the implication of her words crystallised in Julia's mind. Her heart leapt with alarm.

'Nadia! Is that wise?'

Her friend shrugged and laughed.

'Who cares, when it's going to be such fun!'

Now was the time to warn her, to tell her about Leon and Alison.

She opened her mouth, but strangely some other words came out.

'I saw Leon yesterday. When you were at work. He saved my day.' Julia went on to give an account of her litany of disasters before Leon came to the rescue and had made it possible to visit her mother, after all.

'He's such a dish, don't you think?' Nadia said, her eyes dreamy. 'And so kind too!'

It would have smacked of malice if Julia contradicted her friend. She asked instead,

'When are you planning to go? And what will your parents say?'

Nadia's smile was mischievous, secretive.

'I won't tell them the whole truth. But I won't be lying either. Just a little bit of discretion here and there. There's no harm in that, is there? I'll just say that I'll be visiting a friend. I know a few girls at work who live out of Rugby'.

Julia could not help but be impressed by Nadia's boldness. She would have died of sheer fright of being found out. At the same time she felt unease and distaste at her friend's guile. She was fond of Aunt Eva and felt like a traitor having to collude with Nadia.

'What if...' she could not bear thinking about the worst, 'Nadia, what if things go badly wrong? What if you get found out? What if... you know what I mean... you and Leon... and afterwards...'

Nadia descended with a bounce on the bed beside Julia and threw her arms around her.

'You're such a worry-guts!' she laughed. 'Trust me, I'm not a nurse for nothing. I can look after myself!'

The next morning, as Julia was getting ready to catch the Warwick bus, thoughts of Nadia and Leon together, doing things that she could barely bring herself to imagine, crowded her mind. All the while that she went through the actions of washing, dressing, making toast for herself and feeding Muszka, worrying thoughts pestered her. She was so preoccupied that it was only after a few firm knocks that she became aware there was someone at the door. She rushed to open it, expecting the morning post. Bright sunshine flooded the entrance and outside the earth appeared to be steaming after so much rain. Framed in this light stood Miro, his eyes lively in his smiling face.

Her breath stopped in astonishment, her chest heaved with the sudden joy.

'Miro! What a surprise!'

'Do you want a companion on your travels today?' he asked, laughter in his voice.

'Do I?... Oh Miro...' she replied with open delight, 'give me a minute or two.'

While he waited at the door, all spruced up in his white shirt and a light sports jacket, the folds of his black hair glinting in the sun, Julia went into her bedroom and fetched his birthday card and the small package wrapped up in blue crepe paper.

'Happy Birthday!' she said, presenting him with the gift, eager for his reaction. 'I never expected to see you before the evening.'

His smile was suddenly self-conscious.

'I didn't think you'd remember, Julia, with everything else going on. Thanks! Thanks very much!'

There was something very warm in the look he gave her. It felt as if he wanted to say more, and suddenly she felt shy too, and melting inside, then he clutched her gift to his chest and spoke with vigour,

'Let's go, Julia. I'll save opening your present till we get on the bus.' He relieved her of the canvass bag that she had prepared with her mother's things and slipped the package on top.

Julia had to stop herself from skipping as she kept up with his long strides. She could not believe her luck. The sky was clear blue, the sun warm, the trees and the flowers fresh and bright after the cleansing rain. Miro looked happy and every time their glances met he smiled.

'How come you're not working today?' she asked.

'I'll make up for it next weekend. The boss didn't seem to mind. In any case, I've done enough overtime to impress him.'

'And tonight? Have you planned anything special?'

'I'm doing it already,' another wide grin, 'I've been meaning to come with you for a long time.'

'My Mama will be pleased,' Julia said with feeling. 'She's so much better now. She was pleased to see Leon…' It was suddenly very important to her that Miro knew the full story of Saturday's disasters, that he did not misconstrue her time spent in Leon's company. He looked at her with interest, not a trace of rancour in his expression, while she gave him a brief account of Leon's timely assistance. She did not tell him about Leon's proposed escapade with Nadia. 'You may have been right about him, you know, the other evening at the cinema… perhaps Alison is only just a friend from work, as he said, perhaps he's not all bad.'

'Nobody is,' Miro laughed, 'we've all got traces of Jekyll and Hyde.'

'Surely not you,' she teased, then added, 'I was sorry I missed you. Did you have a good time at Stefan's?'

By now they had walked past the row of little shops on the edge of Brownsover, and crossed the bridge over a narrow section of the Avon, where the willows and shrubs hung in unrestrained profusion over the rippling water.

'Stefan's a good laugh. Any time. We went to the cinema. Good film. *Anatomy of Murder*. James Stuart played the lawyer. Stefan's still deluding himself that he can persuade me to join him at the medical school.' Miro gave a short amused laugh.

'You'd be good company for each other,' Julia pointed out.

'Sure, and that would be great. But blood and injections are definitely not for me,' he shuddered. 'We went on a long walk around the centre on Sunday after church. Window shopping.'

'I'd love to do that!' this came so spontaneously, Julia cringed at herself and at how she may appear so unsophisticated. But Miro looked at her, smiling.

'Then we'll have to do it! Sometime soon,' he said.

They talked all the way up Murray Road. They had so much to tell each other. The trees lined up at intervals on both sides of the road threw dappled shadows at them and the gaps in between reflected the sun from the white pavement and made them squint, but they were only aware of each other, fuelling their laughter with inconsequential anecdotes.

The bus was on time. They settled in the back seat, behind other passengers and as soon as the bus conductor had been round with the tickets, Miro pulled out his present. Julia watched with bubbly anticipation, and was pleased to see his cheeks lift while he examined both books with interest.

'Thanks,' he said, and when he looked at her, she had that melting feeling again, 'I'll enjoy reading these. I've heard about *The Catcher*. It's supposed to be good. And Sienkiewicz. My favourite Polish author. Do you remember the library at the camp?' he asked.

'And how we used to go together across the big field?' Julia reminded him with a giggle, 'I would pretend it was a green sea in the summer. I wanted to throw myself into the grass and swim. And in the winter, I'd imagine it was the north pole, all frozen up.'

'It certainly felt like that, even indoors,' Miro added, 'with the corrugated iron walls like solid ice and icicles hanging from the windows.'

'And in the summer it was like living inside an oven,' Julia mused. It all seemed such a long time ago now, their childhood spent in an ex-army camp at Husbands Bosworth, in the years after the war. 'But it was such fun. They were such happy times for us kids, weren't they? Do you remember playing ball games till dusk? And all our parents had to do was to call out to us to come home. They didn't have to worry about any strangers or us straying off. I wonder if they were as happy as us, kids? Thinking about it now, I wonder how hard or easy it was for them to adjust to those primitive conditions.'

'Julia, remember they'd had much worse. I think the camp was a sort of haven for them too. They didn't have to live in fear of banging on the door in the middle of the night and being arrested by the Gestapo or the NKVD and being sent away to 'disappear'. Just living a normal life, even in a corrugated iron hut must have been such a relief after years of being pushed around.'

They talked about their childhood friends, wondering what they were all doing now. Some, like themselves were living in Rugby, their parents having qualified, after years of waiting, to apply for a council house. Some people had managed over the years to save up for a deposit for a small terraced house.

'It was so easy to see each other at the camp,' Julia said, 'just a two minute run and I was at Nadia's or at Yagoda's. Now I have to cycle from one side of town to the other if I want to visit anyone. And those who went to live in Leicester or Northampton, it's an all day trip on the bus to see them for a couple of hours.'

Miro inclined his head towards her and smiled. 'One day,' he said, 'I'll have a car. I'll take you wherever you wish.' His smile alone was like a caress.

The journey passed so quickly that Julia wished it could have continued further. But soon the usually tiresome midday wait in Warwick town centre turned out to be an enjoyable adventure in Miro's company. He led her down to the park past St. Nicholas church, where they sat down on the grass by the river to share her sandwich and apple, and the iced buns and crisps and a bottle of lemonade that Miro had bought on the way.

There was a dreamlike air about their surroundings: mothers picnicking with their small children, older people in their straw hats, resting on benches in the sun, the sporadic sounds of longboats chugging along the river, the bright green patches of grass contrasting with the deep dark shadows underneath the trees.

They ate in silence for a while, looking out onto the river as they enjoyed the calm of the day. Every time Julia turned her head and met Miro's eyes, he smiled and something fluttered in her chest.

'We're so lucky with the weather,' she said, wanting to say how happy he'd made her, just being here with her. 'I'm keeping my fingers crossed that the news is good when we see my Mum today.'

Miro's glance and his tone were earnest when he replied,

'I hope so too. For your sake and hers. But Julia...' he placed his hand over hers on the grass and gave it a gentle squeeze, 'whatever happens, you've got me, OK?'

'OK.' she answered lightly to cover up the effect his touch had on her. Like an electric current shooting up her arm. 'Thanks!'

After the picnic, they walked up Castle Hill towards a network of narrow streets with medieval and Elizabethan houses. They stopped in Northgate to admire the lofty portals of the Church of St. Mary's.

'Looks like a cathedral,' Julia remarked lifting her eyes to the top of the tower, where a cluster of spires, ornate with stonework like black lace, stood out etched against the clear sky.

'Let's go inside,' Miro said. For a split second she had that feeling of apprehension, the fear of the unknown, but as Miro proceeded with confidence through the open side panel of the arched, thick oak door, she followed him. It was quiet inside, and dark, until their eyes adjusted from the brightness outdoors. No one else was there. The light fell in rainbow beams from the stained-glass windows across the central nave. The black and white flagstone floor made Julia think of Vermeer paintings.

'It's beautiful,' she whispered, her eyes noting the massive pillars and the pointed arches of the vaulted ceiling, high above them.

They tiptoed down one long side, round the altar to the side chapel with intricate stonework, elaborately carved wood panels, statues of saints, effigies of the Beauchamp family members. Julia's interest was even more excited by Robert Dudley's tomb.

'Miro, look! He was a real person! Not just a name in history books. I've just been writing about him in my history exam. Him and Queen Elizabeth. Amazing!' She went over to his wife's tomb. 'Lettice Knollys' she read. 'Why haven't they been buried together? It's so cruel. They're so close, yet so apart. For all eternity. I couldn't bear that!'

'What couldn't you bear?' Miro asked, stepping beside her.

'To be separated from someone I loved...' She was aware of his body warmth, of his breathing.

'We live in peaceful times,' Miro was practical, reassuring, 'don't worry about things that'll not happen.'

'I wish,' she said, 'they had candles here to light. As they have in Catholic churches. I'd light a candle for my Mama's health.'

Miro smiled. 'God doesn't need candles, Julia. You can pray wherever you like. We've got the whole church to ourselves. You can pray at the main altar if you so wish.'

They sat down in the front pew at the central altar. Julia prayed for her Mama to be well, for life to get back to normal, for her holiday to start resembling the fantasy of a carefree break that had kept her going through the weeks of exams.

Miro beside her was very still. She would have liked to know what he was thinking.

'What did you pray for?' she asked him when they came outside into the blinding brightness. As her eyes adjusted she saw him smiling.

'Some wishes you have to keep secret till they come true,' he teased.

Even with Miro at her side, Julia had that feeling again, the tightening in her stomach, the niggling unease that hastened her pace as they walked down the long corridors closer to her mother's ward.

They stopped at the wide door left open for the visitors. Julia scanned the two rows of beds, the patients sitting in their armchairs, some already receiving their visitors.

The sight of her Mama brought instant relief. She was looking good. She was sitting by her bed, neat in her navy dress, her hair brushed and pinned back, her face touched up with powder and lipstick. At her feet was the overnight bag, packed and zipped.

Julia rushed to her, embraced her and was held long and hard to her Mama's chest.

'Mama! Does this mean you're going home?'

A short pause. A hesitation. Her Mama spoke slowly.

'Yes. The doctor came round this morning. Asked me lots of questions. Some questions I did not understand. But I explained to him, the best way I could that I must go home. There's work to be done. I mustn't miss my summer break when I catch up with all the jobs.'

'Mrs. Lutovska,' Miro shook her hand, 'this is excellent news!'

She returned his smile, appraising him thoughtfully.

'It's good of you to come, Miro. I'm very glad that Julia's got such good friends. You and Nadia...I often watched you three playing together when you were little. You were like siblings.'

490

'I prefer best friends,' Miro replied with a laugh, 'I've got brothers of my own. They can be such a pain!'

A smile appeared on Mama's lips.

'You'll be glad you've got them Miro. In years to come. There's not a day that I don't wish my sisters lived close to me.' A wistful look crept into her eyes.

'Mama,' Julia hugged her, 'when you're well, perhaps next summer, we'll go to Germany to visit them.'

She thought for a moment.

'Yes. We must do that. That would be very nice.'

'Tato will be so happy tonight, when he comes home from work,' Julia said brightly, willing her Mama to be happy too.

She nodded.

'I've been a worry to him, I know. He is the one who needs looking after.'

The ward sister came over to them with a small brown paper bag in her hand.

'Medication for you to take home, Anastazia. You must take it every day as instructed. When you need more, just go to see your own doctor.' She turned to Julia.

'Are you taking your mother home?'

'Yes.' Julia was so overwhelmed with happiness, she did not explain that she had not expected her mother to be discharged this very day, in case the sister changed her mind.

'And have you come in a car?' the sister looked at Miro.

'I haven't got one,' a polite smile dimpled his cheeks, 'but please, be assured, we'll get Mrs. Lutovska home safely on the bus.'

The sister's eyes scrutinised him seriously. She then turned her attention to Anastazia.

'Are you happy with that?'

'Veri heppy!' Her Mama replied without hesitation.

'Very well then,' the sister shook her hand, 'goodbye, and I wish you a good and complete recovery.'

'Tenk you. Tenk you for everyting.' Mama's face became suddenly animated, and to her surprise Julia found Mama's imperfect pronunciation rather endearing.

They decided not to hang around the hospital grounds but to take the first local bus that came along and do their waiting in Warwick for the Rugby bus connection. As soon as the bus was off, her Mama fell asleep, wedged between them on the back seat. Julia leaned across her mother's lap and whispered to Miro,

'This is the happiest day of my holiday.'

Gently, he stroked her cheek with the back of his hand.

'Mine too.' The way he said it with a lingering look in his dark, intense eyes, made her feel special. She just wished she could quash completely and eliminate for good the nagging worry at the back of her mind. What if her Mama never recovered fully? What if her illness came back?

CHAPTER 61

It was sublime happiness waking up to the familiar comforting sounds around the house in the morning; her Mama's humming floating from the kitchen together with the aromas of coffee and fried bacon, her Tato's sporadic chatter as he busied himself preparing for his tasks, painting and decorating, checking the bicycles for cleaning and repairs, clearing out the fireplace, though no fire was required in this welcome heatwave. Halfway through their annual fortnight's break, her parents appeared to be happy with just pottering about the house, catching up with the backlog of unfinished jobs.

Her Mama had been lethargic in the first few days after her return from the hospital. She would wake up early, do whatever required attention, but after lunch, the drugs would affect her the moment she sat down and she would drift into deep sleep.

Then one afternoon she suggested a walk in the meadows by the canal.

'I can't sleep my life away,' she had said, 'especially now, in this beautiful weather.'

After that, she and Julia did things together, her Mama in a slowed-down manner. They shared the housework chores, they cooked and baked together, they weeded the garden and went for walks. Each evening Theo would return from work eager for good news about his wife's progress towards complete recovery. Julia noted how often her Mama's hands would shake, how she retreated into her inner self and remained quiet for long periods of time, but she did not mention her observations to Theo. Like him, she only wanted to see the positive signs. Every night he came home to a cooked meal, to an ambience of home-baking, to an agreeable wife, subdued by her medication. He appeared contented.

'Soon, I'll be on holiday, with you all the time,' he would say, his grey eyes lighting up with promise and with his own anticipation.

Julia did not tell him of one particular incident that had frightened her with its threat of ruining her mother's delicate equilibrium. That morning, on waking up, she could not hear her Mama's humming, as usual. The panic returned, gripping and twisting her stomach. She jumped out of bed and rushed out to look for her. She was by the window in the front room, sitting very still, looking out. Her eyes were red, her cheeks wet.

'Mama! What's happened?' Julia threw her arms around her mother's shoulders. Anastazia shook her head and fresh tears flowed down her face.

'Tell me, please tell me,' Julia pleaded, dabbing Mama's face with a handkerchief.

Mama composed herself after a while. She spoke in a hoarse whisper, as if not trusting her voice.

'It's the second of August today. Dorotka would have been twenty-one.' The pain in her eyes made Julia flinch, as her mother repeated, 'Twenty one! We'd be celebrating today. Having a party. I try to imagine what she would be like. More like her father, or like me? But all I see is this little baby. Starved and cold and ill…' another flow of tears, 'and I couldn't even give her a decent burial. I was too ill, too delirious to get out of bed.'

'Mama please, don't upset yourself,' Julia hugged and rocked her gently.

'It hurts… it hurts so much even after all the years…' Mama stifled her sobs.

Julia felt helpless in the face of her mother's grief. She had been told this story many times before, of how her baby sister, long before she, Julia, was born, died on the train to Siberia, with hundreds of other children, while her Mama lay unconscious with a high temperature, close to death herself.

'Mama,' she said, racking her brains for words of comfort, 'Mama, our little Dorotka is an angel in heaven now. She's looking down even as we talk about her. (Sister Alicya would have most probably used similar words). She loved you too in her own baby way. She would not want you to be unhappy for the rest of your life…'

Her mother remained quiet for a long time.

'Mama, please say something…'

'If only I could have had her buried nearby. I'd at least be able to place some flowers on her grave…' Her body shuddered.

Julia had no idea what else to say. Then a thought occurred to her. She could only hope that her attempt to bring her mother even a small degree of comfort would not have the opposite effect.

'I've got something to show you, Mama,' she said. She went back to her bedroom and from underneath the bed, she retrieved her treasure box, a large, square card box, that she had covered with silver paper.

Her cherished treasures consisted of an assortment of handmade birthday cards, miniature porcelain dolls and cats and dogs, a small notebook with messages from and signatures of her friends and teachers, and a tiny silver box that opened like a book to reveal a pearl-beaded rosary inside. On top lay a white porcelain angel with gilded wings and a golden halo. She had received it as a prize from Sister Alicya for consistently top marks in her exams in Religious Studies.

She came back to her mother and explained about the angel, rounding up her account with a touch of imagination.

'You know, Mama, I always fancied that this little angel was Dorotka really. Strange, isn't it? But the moment I opened the box, there she was, my little sister looking up at me. Only, she wouldn't be my little sister now. She

493

would be my big sister, like Stella, wouldn't she? I kept her with me always. Inside my desk and by my bedside at night-time. I'll leave her by your bed now. With some flowers.'

Julia watched with relief her Mama examining the figurine, then to her surprise, she kissed it.

'Did you really think that, Julia?' she asked, her face lifting, her eyes brightening up, and Julia felt terribly guilty at her own ruse, especially when her Mama said, 'That was such a beautiful thought. That's exactly what I have always wanted Julia, for you to feel a special connection with her.'

Julia squirmed, but as the day wore on and her Mama's mood improved, she convinced herself that the importance of her mother's wellbeing far outweighed her own discomfort at having been too inventive with her little white lies.

This morning she was aware of a happy mood in the house. The curtains, usually adequate on dull mornings, were too thin for the piercing brightness of another sunny day. It was Monday. Julia and her mother had already planned the evening before to go to the market. Julia looked forward to browsing through the long lines of stalls that provided endless varieties of goods. She enjoyed it as much as going to the cinema. She loved the fabric and the haberdashery stalls and the jewellery. She had already imagined the material she was going to look for: large red poppies on a white background, exactly like Stella's dress. And it would please her Mama, she knew, to instruct her daughter in the skills of dressmaking, the daughter whose nose was always stuck in a book.

Julia threw on her dressing gown, worn greyish pink, a relic of her six years at the convent school, splashed her face with cold water and brushed her teeth. In the kitchen, her Mama was already kneading the dough for baking later, while her Tato was sitting on the step of the wide-open door, sanding down a wooden stool in preparation for varnishing. Muszka was blissfully asleep, curled up into a furry ball on the chair.

Julia gave her Mama a hug, her Tato a peck on the cheek.

'There's a letter for you Julia, in a brown envelope. Looks important.' Her Mama turned around. Her face was smudged with flour. She gave Julia a scrutinising look. 'Time you had a new dressing-gown. We'll look for some nice material at the market.'

Julia sat down at the kitchen table and opened the letter. It was from Miss Ogden, the headmistress of the girls' school.

'It's this Friday,' Julia said, 'I've got an interview at my new school!' A feeling of nervousness crept in. She wished Roman was not away. She wished he was her real uncle, so he could go to the school with her and impress Miss Ogden with his perfect English and his vast knowledge on every subject under the sun.

494

Her Mama divided the dough between two baking tins and covered it for rising.

'I'll go with you,' she said, 'I want the headmistress to know that you come from a good family. That you have parents who care.'

Julia's conscience pricked her at her disloyal thoughts. She smiled to show her gratitude but inwardly she worried. What would Miss Ogden make of them? How could she assess her mother fairly when her pidgin English gave a distorted impression of her?

'I could cycle over on my own,' she said, 'if you're busy, Mama.'

'This is important,' Theo turned his head, 'everything else can wait. And anyway, we need to know exactly where your school is. We need to know where you are all day.'

For a split second Julia feared he may offer to accompany her as well. She loved him and appreciated deeply his kindness to her, but she would have died with embarrassment if he tried to foist his political passions onto Miss Ogden. Often, his English acquaintances, caught unawares in one of his tirades against the treachery of the Allies, could only listen bewildered, and express their apologies, as if in some way they had been responsible for the fate of the Poles after the war.

'I'll come with you,' her Mama decided. 'Once I've seen your new school I'll be able to picture you in your surroundings and not worry.'

Reluctantly Julia accepted this solution. At least her Mama would allow her to do all the talking.

Julia spoke of her worries to Nadia, when her friend and Aunt Eva had cycled over in the evening. They left their mothers talking over coffee and cake in the kitchen, and went for a walk by the canal. It was a warm, calm evening with a lilac sky. Young families played games out in the open fields, and dogs, taken out to be exercised chased balls and fetched sticks to the delight of their proud owners.

'I just don't like it when people stare at my Mum the moment she starts to speak. They have no idea how clever and wise she is. She could teach many a thing or two. But all they see is this woman with her funny English and get a totally wrong impression of her.'

'You worry too much!' Nadia said. 'We're all in the same boat. My Mum and Dad do their best to speak English, but they only know enough to get by. And don't forget how many languages they were forced to learn in just a few years. During the war. German and Russian was forced on them. But after that, all those other countries they were sent to! They still had to manage. It's a wonder they kept up with the changes as well as they did! Look at me! Five years at school learning French. Does that make me a linguist?'

Julia smiled, touched at the same time by Nadia's rare moment of seriousness.

Her friend continued, 'Don't waste your time worrying about that. You can't change what other people think. But anyway, give the headmistress a chance to make up her own mind.'

Nadia's words struck a chord. Julia looked at her friend with interest. 'You're so…'

'Amazing?' Nadia laughed at herself.

'Well, yes,' Julia said seriously, 'I needed someone to talk sense into me.'

'Sensibility. That's my first name!' A mischievous smile banished all seriousness from her face. 'Now ask me a question about Leon!'

'OK. I'm asking.'

They came up to a section of the canal where two longboats were moored one behind another, with cooking smells wafting from the open doors and windows. Two women were busy inside one of the boats, while two men sat out on the open deck enjoying their beer.

'What a life!' Julia whispered when they passed the boats, 'I think I could enjoy that too!'

'You'll do heaps and heaps better, when Stella invites us to Hollywood!' It was hard to tell if Nadia was serious or joking.

'And we'll put on our tap dancing shoes and outshine Ginger Rogers,' Julia laughed, falling into their childhood chatter. Nadia laughed too, but then added soberly.

'Who knows? Everything's possible if you really put your mind to it. We did. Leon and I.'

Julia stopped to look at her friend.

'What do you mean?'

'We went to Skegness. Last weekend.'

'Overnight?' An avalanche of images tumbled into Julia's mind.

'No…' Nadia sighed, 'I couldn't tell my parents lies. Not even white lies, in the end. No, we just went out for the day, but…' her eyes became mysterious, 'we found a secluded spot on the way back…' She held Julia's gaze as if trying to convey the meaning of her words without actually having to say any more. Julia felt her cheeks going hot, her throat dry. Nadia and Leon. Like that. Even the very thought of it was like a sin.

'I don't know what to say,' she said truthfully, 'Nadia, I just don't want you to come to any harm'.

Nadia's laugh was like a tinkling bell.

'As if I would! Julia, I told you. I know how to look after myself!'

'But…' Julia knew this sounded very naïve, even as she spoke, yet she had to ask, 'what about keeping yourself for your husband?'

'But Leon will be my husband, Julia, so there's no problem about any of it, is there?'

Julia was not convinced. Years of brainwashing about sins and purity and consequences of intimate acts reserved exclusively for marriage made her feel uneasy about Nadia's rashness.

'You're brave,' she said honestly, 'I'd be too much of a coward to do anything like that. But I do worry about you.'

'Well, don't!' Nadia ordered with a smile, 'I know how to protect myself. I'll be happy to give you advice. Any time you need.'

Julia could not imagine herself needing advice in these matters for a long time. She and Miro were the best of friends. And that was how she liked it.

When they came back from their walk, Aunt Eva was just getting ready to leave. She and Mama were at the front gate chatting, remembering just one more thing to tell each other, prolonging their parting, reluctant to let each other go. Theo was busy watering the flowers, a cigarette in his free hand, wisps of smoke following behind.

'I was just going to send a search party for you, Nadia,' Aunt Eva sounded in a good mood, her blue eyes sparkling. 'Time for us to go.'

'When will you come again?' Julia asked, pleased with her Mama's animated face.

'And persuade Henryk to come as well,' Mama added.

'You know Henryk,' Aunt Eva inclined her head, 'a bit of a loner these days. No, it's your turn to come over to our house. How about after church, on Sunday? You too, Theo. It'll do Henryk good to have company.'

Julia and her mother waved them off and stood at the gate watching till Nadia and her mother disappeared round the corner at the end of the road.

'You know,' her Mama said thoughtfully, 'I'm so pleased that Eva's life is shaping well at long last. She nearly lost Stella in Russia. But now, she's doing so well in London. And Nadia seems so grown up for her age. Nursing is a good profession. She'll do well. And little Marek is growing fast. A joy for his father. Henryk needed that. Things will improve with Marek's age. He'll be a good support for his father.'

Julia nodded in agreement, praying inwardly for Nadia to come to her senses, before a disaster occurred.

Miss Ogden looked forbidding with her sharp features, flat yellow hair, caught in a bun at the back, sage green suit, cream blouse, sensible brown shoes. She was about fifty.

She greeted Julia and her Mama with a quick, practised smile, such that did not put one at ease.

Julia smiled back, her stomach churning.

'My mother wished to come with me,' she said.

Miss Ogden gave a gracious nod and indicated two chairs facing her desk.

'Do take a seat.' She shook hands with Mama, then with Julia, before they all sat down.

Julia had been nervous all morning. It was touching that her Mama wished to accompany her, yet at the same time Julia worried that traces of Anastazia's illness would show through: the intermittent detachment from her surroundings, the shaking of her hands. On the other hand she could be proud of her Mama's appearance. She had made a conscious effort with her hair and face and looked smart in her light-grey suit and high heels that elongated her shapely legs. Would she be able to understand Miss Ogden's questions? What about herself? Would she, Julia, pass the test of Miss Ogden's scrutiny with her European accent and dictionary vocabulary, that sounded stilted at times.

She, too, had dressed with planned care; she had put on her navy suit, the newest and the best, and a white blouse with a lace edged collar, that Tato had bought her last Easter. Sister Alicya's words were indelibly ingrained in her mind: 'Never let your standards down. The way you dress shows the level of your respect for other people. They are the ones who have to look at you. Make it at least pleasant for them!' Would Miss Ogden find her pleasant enough?

The new school in Bilton, when she and Mama arrived at the gates after two bus journeys, was a modern building; red brick and gabled roofs, not unlike a residential dwelling, in contrast to the solid edifice of the old school, with its heavy stonework and rows of tall windows, Julia remembered, that reflected the sky with its continuous changes, like a glass wall, every time Julia had cycled by.

Miss Ogden's office was painted in palest cream and pastel green. Her desk was light wood, the matching chairs had soft hessian-covered seats, and the wall-to-wall carpet smelled new. Julia was very much aware of wearing outdoor shoes. She was glad that they were clean and dry and not likely to leave any marks on the pristine floor.

'We're in a bit of an upheaval,' Miss Ogden's thin lips stretched in a momentary smile, 'the end of a long era for our school in Clifton Road. It'll be further for some girls to travel now, but here, the open space on the outskirts of the town cannot be appree-cee-iated enough.' She pronounced the 'c' with emphasis. 'A new exciting year lies ahead of us. You're joining us just at the right time. Julia, isn't it? Ka…?' she looked up with a question mark in her tone.

'Kalinska,' Julia supplied promptly.

'What nationality is that?'

'Polish.' Julia's smile trembled.

The headmistress gave her a piercing look.

'How well do you think you've done in your exams?'

God only knows, Julia thought, saying,

'I hope, well enough to be admitted to your school.'

'I hope so too,' Miss Ogden treated them to another lightning smile, before turning her attention to Mama. She was holding her hands together in a tight clasp, resting them on her lap. Her eyes were focused with concentration on Miss Ogden's face as she spoke. 'We are very proud here of our tradition of high standards in achievement and in behaviour. Our rules are set to be cherished, not broken. As long as we observe this mutual understanding, Julia will be welcome here.'

She talked at length about what was permitted and what was not in her school, using words such as 'perspicacity' and 'preternaturally' and other words that Julia noted mentally to look up in the dictionary later.

'Are you in agreement with me, Mrs. Kalinska?' she asked Julia's Mum.

Mama's shoulders tensed, but she nodded and smiled.

'Tenk you,' she said, 'I em heppy wen Julia start here.'

'My mother,' Julia rushed to explain, feeling embarrassment colouring her cheeks, 'understands more English than she can speak. And... her surname is different from mine. It's Lutovska, after my step-father.'

'I see,' Miss Ogden gave them a slow scrutinising look then wrote something down. 'So how long have you been residents in this country?'

'Reseedents?' Mama asked.

'Miss Ogden means how long we've lived here.' Julia spoke softly to her Mama, then louder to the headmistress, 'since 1948. We came as refugees. After the war.'

Miss Ogden looked thoughtful for a moment.

'Twelve years is a long time to assimilate,' she said.

Julia squirmed at this veiled criticism. 'We didn't know at the beginning that we'd be here this long,' she said. To her surprise her Mama spoke.

'Every year,' she said, 'we hope Poland is free. End we go beck. But Poland is not free. Not safe. I afraid of Soviets.'

Miss Ogden's expression puckered with puzzlement. Julia stepped in. 'My parents were deported to Siberia during the war. Having escaped the Russian experience once, they're afraid to go back till their country is free of the Soviet rule.'

She could tell from Miss Ogden's expression that her attention was already on other matters.

'Thank goodness it's all in the past now,' Miss Ogden nodded politely, then her tone became brisk with purpose. 'Now, tell me Julia, which subjects do you want to take in the sixth form?'

Julia did not have to think.

'Art is my favourite. I'd like to go on to a school of Art and Design. I love literature, so English is my next best choice. And History is a must.'

'Right,' the headmistress thought for a second, 'I think these subjects will be compatible.' She stood up and passed Julia a printed sheet of paper. 'A few items for you to acquire before the start of the Autumn term. Your uniform is most important. We adhere exactly and strictly to the requirements. Never forget Julia, you'll be representing our school outside the school gates. Your dress and behaviour will be a true reflection of our expectations. Come to my office on the first day. I shall appoint someone from your class to look after you. Good bye, until then.'

Miss Ogden nodded to indicate the interview was over. Julia and her Mama left with profuse thanks.

'Phew!' Julia wiped her brow in a mock gesture as they walked outside into the sunshine, the bright pavement shining like a torch into their eyes. She felt a pang of longing for her old school. She spoke in Polish to her Mama *'Wszystko jest takie inne'*! Everything's so different here! Miss Ogden's quite scary. A little like Sister Vespera, but none of my other teachers were like that!'

Mama linked her arm with Julia's.

'Any new place is forbidding at first,' she said, 'do you know what the Russians used to say? You either get used to it or you die. No one wanted to die. We forced ourselves to get used to all kinds of conditions. Here Julia, you're the privileged one. I couldn't have imagined a better school for you.' She gave Julia a motherly squeeze on her arm. 'I'm very pleased for you.'

Julia's feeling was more like relief than happiness. One hurdle was over. There was the first day at school to look forward to. Life seemed to consist of continual hurdles. But she would not think about any of it now. She returned her Mama's hug.

'Shall we do something nice?' she asked, thinking of the summer dress sale at the Co-op.

'Yes, Julia, let's clear out the lettuce and radish patch and plant some fresh seeds. They grow so fast in this warm weather.'

At home, there was a letter from Lidia.

'DISASTER! Vittorio's crashed his friend's motorbike and broke his leg. BIG headache for Papa and Mama. Now I'm everything! A charwoman and a nurse! Dearest Julia, this is to say, with GREAT REGRET, I've been so looking forward to our summer dance, which now, will not be possible. I'm so SORRY! Can you forgive me?'

Lidia's first mention of the dance on the last day at their old school was so remote now, that Julia had stopped thinking about it. She felt only relief now, that she did not have to refuse her friend, for somehow, a dance without Miro, even close to the ROYAL WINDSOR, held no attraction for her.

'Dear Lidia,' she wrote back, 'don't worry! There will be hundreds of other chances to get together again.' And now that her Mama was so much better, she could invite Lidia to come over one weekend in the not too distant future.

CHAPTER 62

'Did anyone see you?' Her Dad looked up from his Polish Daily at the kitchen table. Julia was helping Mama prepare the evening meal.

'Hundreds of people, Tato.'

'You know perfectly well who I mean. Our people.'

'Old Mr. Bilinski came into the store. I saw him in the distance. He didn't see me. He was after some nails and screws. Not ribbons and sequins.'

A look of hurt came into her Dad's eyes.

'You're jesting, Julia. Making fun of me.'

'Tato, how can I persuade you that it doesn't matter who sees me and what they think. I'll only be there for a few weeks.'

'But there'll be talk. You know how they like to gossip.'

'Theo, for goodness sake!' Mama turned from the cooker, with a whiff of a chemical factory smell in her overall. 'There's nothing shameful in Julia wanting to earn a few pennies. In our village girls of sixteen got married. And boys of fourteen were already helping their fathers in the fields.'

'And I tell you,' Tato's tone was emphatic, 'that child labour is nothing to be proud of. In my family, when my sisters were students, they were just that. They were expected to concentrate entirely on their studies. No one expected them to go out to work as well.'

'Theo,' Mama's voice softened, 'those were totally different times. You must accept that. Besides, it's good experience for Julia to work. To meet lots of English people. To perfect her English. Surely, you must see that.'

Tato shrugged, lit a cigarette and went into the front room. The blaring sounds from his radio vibrated through the thin walls. Mama closed the kitchen door.

Julia could not understand her Tato. Their frugal existence could hardly be compared to his comfortable lifestyle in Poland before the war. It was not as if they ever had money in excess. The old furniture, the soft furnishings made from cheap materials bought at the market, the jam jars used for drinking tea, the old cracked plates, the haphazard assortment of cooking pans, every part of their second-rate house told its own clear story. She had thought Tato would be pleased with her enterprise, with her willingness to help out financially, even if it were only with her own expenses. It seemed his pride was stronger than his practical sense.

Similar conversations took place most evenings, since she started work at

Woolworths. Her first day had been full of trepidation, compounded by anxiety over Mama's return to work on the same day after nearly two months' absence. To her relief, life soon fell into a regular, comfortable pattern. Mama had reduced her intake of pills, wisely or not, only the future could tell, resorting to them only at night time. She still had her quiet days, and her hands would twitch when she was resting, making Julia watchful of any changes in her. But when they did things together, when Mama hummed, when she laughed and remembered amusing little incidents from her youth, life was good and Mama was the best mother in the world.

As for Julia, her tasks on the haberdashery counter were like child's play compared to the recent pressures of exams and lonely bus journeys to the hospital. She liked the girls, her co-workers, whose chatter was carefree and entertaining in a robust kind of way, opening her mind to all the goings on, whom to avoid and whom to please. After the initial questions of where she was from and when she was going back 'home' had been answered, she was quietly heartened, that her being different and foreign, which she herself was very much aware of, did not seem to put them off drawing her into their confidence.

Mr. Jones, the manager, who wore thick glasses and wide trousers that flapped about his thin legs, had given Julia a brief, informal interview, and thereafter could only be glimpsed through the glass partition of his office. But Mrs. Smith, a big lady with frizzy hair, took her position of second- in-command very seriously and patrolled the store with her hawk's eyes looking out for the slightest misdemeanours. 'You're not paid to stand around,' was her constant refrain, 'I expect the counters to shine and all the items you're responsible for to be spotlessly clean!'

So, when not serving the customers, Julia dusted and rearranged boxes of cotton reels, needles, pins, buttons, ribbons and lace and hundreds of other things indispensable in dressmaking. She liked the feel of the silk or velvet corsage flowers. They were a shilling each. She bought herself one, red, anemone-like, with a black centre, to match the large print of poppies on the dress that her mother had helped her to make, out of the material they had found at the market. Like Stella's dress from London.

This evening, when Tato asked her if she had seen any of their Polish acquaintances in Woolworths, she replied with a wide, mollifying smile.

'Yes. Leon came in. Briefly. In his lunchtime break. He actually needed something from my counter.'

Tato looked up from the Polish Daily spread out before him on the kitchen table. Even through the haze of cigarette smoke she could see disquiet in his eyes. Just as well he could not see her inner turmoil.

'Now it'll be all over the town. You know what his mother's like.' Sarcasm crept into his voice. 'Old Lutovski can't afford to keep his daughter!'

'Tato!' Julia feigned a light-hearted laughter and bent down to give him a peck on the cheek, a half-peeled potato in her hand. 'Let them talk. It's better to be talked about than to be forgotten.'

He gave a deep sigh.

'Julia, all I want in my life now is a quiet, peaceful existence.'

Julia had heard this before. Hundreds of times. So boring!

She returned to the sink, to washing the potatoes, while her mother stirred soup that simmered on the cooker.

'Is Leon into dress-making then?' Mama asked.

Julia laughed. 'No, he was after some silk flowers for corsage.'

'Really? For Nadia?'

'I suppose so.'

'Didn't you ask?'

'There wasn't time. He was in a hurry and there were people waiting.'

Julia did not tell her Mama that Leon had been astonished to see her, gob-smacked for a split second, then just as fast recovering his composure, his normal ebullient self, as he steered Alison towards Julia's counter.

'Hi Julia, fancy meeting you here!' Alison's large, blue painted eyes expressed genuine surprise, her voice was light with remnants of laughter.

Julia was struck dumb. Something boiled inside her. Nadia, oh Nadia… One…two…three… she forced herself to count. She forced a smile on her lips. She was aware of Leon talking.

'Just a quick lunch break from work. Alison needs a silk flower. Some party at the weekend. And I needed some fresh air…' a beautiful persuasive smile, so perfect, his eyes so seductive. Julia wanted to hit him. She gave him a hard stare. She mouthed 'Na…dee…ia' while Alison's attention was wholly absorbed in browsing through the array of silk flowers spread out before her on the counter. He grinned back. Amused.

'Right,' Alison decided, her eyes still examining the white camellia, 'this one please, Julia.'

Leon paid and Alison accepted, her manner naturally proprietorial. She linked her arm through his as they were walking away. Leon turned and mouthed to Julia,

'*Zapomniała portmonetkę.* She forgot her purse.'

It was a burden carrying this knowledge on her own. Julia knew what she had to do, but she could not bear the thought of being the messenger of bad news, and even worse, watch Nadia's pain. She had a few days for reflection; she did not usually see Nadia during the week, this would have to wait, but the weekend ahead turned out unexpectedly different.

Julia had half expected her Tato to say NO, no, it was not proper for a young girl to go off on her own with a boy and to stay overnight in someone else's house. She had expected her Mama to back him up and say Julia could wait to do such things till she was much, MUCH older and at least engaged to be married.

But when Miro explained that Stefan's parents had invited them both to stay overnight so that they could attend the Youth Summer Dance at the Polish Club in Birmingham, Julia was astonished by their reaction.

'It's very nice of them,' Mama had said. 'Work is important, of course Julia, but you're sixteen. You won't be young forever. You need to have some fun too.' Did Mama really say that?

'And you young man,' Tato's eyebrows had knitted in a serious look, 'you look after our daughter well. I put my trust in you. I trust that in your care, she'll come to no harm!'

After this none too subtle directive, when Julia and Miro were out walking alone, they had giggled at their old folks' preoccupation with propriety and their horror at the slightest whiff of 'shame' upon their family.

Julia had counted the days. It was her first real dance. She had accompanied her parents in the past to a few social occasions organised at the parish centre, where one could dance to the sound of records, if one so wished, and she had wished, desperately, together with Nadia, to escape the cigarette smoke and the heat of political discussions hanging heavy over the tables. Then there were the annual 'dances' at her school, which were nothing more than all-girl parties, as no boys were ever invited inside the convent walls. But she had learnt to dance. She was ready.

To make this weekend possible, she had swapped Saturdays with Sheila, her work companion, a friendly, accommodating girl. Now, as the train was slowing down, entering the long dark arrival platform of Birmingham station, Julia experienced pure joy and excitement at the prospect of spending the weekend in Miro's company. He stood next to her, their sides touching, his eyes soft and smiling every time he looked at her. She guessed he felt happy too. If only he'd say something. She often fantasised about his declarations of love. He did not need to say much. Only that she was special. To him. Thoughts of Nadia and Leon had become faint shadows at the back of her mind.

Stefan was already waiting, as the train came to a stop, his blond head visible above the crowd, his wide smile welcoming, his hand waving for their attention.

'Here, let me carry this for you,' he strode up to her and took the overnight bag the moment she stepped down onto the platform. The crowd, milling around them, dispersed with alacrity, some people rushing to get on the train, others hurrying towards the exit.

'That's better!' Stefan breathed out and smiled, when they were left with a comfortable space around them. He had an immaculately clean-cut appearance. He was wearing a pale blue shirt and a matching light-weight sports jacket. He kissed Julia on the cheek and shook Miro's hand. 'Welcome! Had a good journey? Nothing compared to what awaits you!' he said with mock seriousness and led them out of the station to his step-father's black Morris Minor, parked outside. There was an aura of bursting energy around him that Julia found fascinating. Miro appeared to be drawn into it too; his manner became lively, his face animated as they exchanged the latest news.

'That's my next item on the list of things to do. I must learn to drive. Soon,' he said, slipping into the passenger seat next to Stefan, watching his friend's every manoeuvre, as he started the car and they drove off. Julia was happy sitting in the back, the cityscape rushing past her with its gigantic redbrick buildings and sand-coloured stonework.

The boys had a lot to tell each other. Julia listened. They were no different from the opposite chin-wagging sex, which the girls were supposed to be. They talked about the opening ceremony of the Olympics in Rome. Not for the first time Julia wished her parents would buy a television. She felt she was missing out on all the latest news around the world, for although her Tato listened regularly to the free Polish radio, it was hard to pick out coherent information through the relentless jamming of programmes by the communists in Poland.

Stefan was excited about the Polish team. He turned his head a fraction, his eyes steady on the road, 'Isn't it simply great to hear Polish names mentioned? Good luck to them! Pity their supporters can't follow them to Rome to see and enjoy a little of the decadent West.'

'You need money for that,' Julia thought aloud. 'They wouldn't get far with their *grosze*. It's not as if we're rolling in it either or enjoying this wonderful decadence, supposedly around us. Where is it, anyway?'

'Ah, but there's one big difference, Julia,' Stefan remarked. 'Our only restriction is our lack of funds. And it's only temporary. We can be certain it will change in time. They have no such certainty. But let's not talk politics now. Tell me Julia, how are things with you? Have you got your sixth form fixed yet?'

Julia told him and the mood lightened as he and Miro reverted to telling entertaining anecdotes and laugh a lot. Miro would catch her glance in the mirror and make funny, amused faces. Julia felt buoyant. She wished all life could be as carefree as this moment.

Erdington, where Stefan's family lived, was criss-crossed with tree-lined avenues, that cast welcome shadows upon the rows of Edwardian houses, with their neat gabled roofs and arched, ornate windows. Stefan's house was one in a long terrace and looked royal compared to Julia's squat, prefabricated bungalow. Indoors, the hall was cool, painted all in glossy cream, the walls reflecting with a flat sheen, the tiled floor shiny with the patina of regular polishing. There was no trace of the usual clutter of shoes and coats and umbrellas; it was, Julia guessed, Stefan's mother's Austrian influence, her obsession with tidiness.

Mrs. Lilli emerged from the back of the house and came towards them, her arms outstretched in greeting. She was a beautiful woman of about thirty-eight, slim, blonde, with her straight hair like threads of silk kept long enough to brush over her left side, to cover her cheek. Like Lauren Bacall. When her hair swung in rhythm with her step, her cheek was exposed with its disfiguring scar. Julia avoided looking at it by focusing on Mrs. Lilli's eyes, true blue, like forget-me-nots.

'Welcome, Miro, Julia,' she hugged them in turn, then standing back at arm's length she said to Julia, 'it's been a long time. Last time I saw you, you were still a schoolgirl. And look at you now!' Her inferred compliment made Julia turn pink with pleasure and shyness at the same time.

Victoria and Leszek, Stefan's younger siblings, came up close behind their mother. Leszek was eleven, his square adult teeth funny in his child's thin face. He was blond like his mother and Stefan. Victoria was dark, with a thick plait hanging down her back, her thirteen-year-old body still as thin as a boy's.

'Victoria,' her mother said, 'show Julia to your room. And Miro, there's a camp bed for you in the boys' room. Come down for something to eat when you've unpacked.'

Julia followed Victoria up the wooden stairs with the boys coming up behind, their carefree laughter echoing round the house. The middle section of each step had a nailed down rectangle of carpet, unmatched, saved from some offcuts, that would have been otherwise thrown away. Stefan's step-father, Mr. Franek, had good contacts, no doubt, working as a car mechanic.

The furniture in Victoria's little backroom was dark and second-hand, the walls had been painted white to make the room feel bigger, but the lacy nets and the pale cream curtains with pink roses created a soft and feminine atmosphere. On the bed, covered by a pink candlewick bedspread, sat a doll dressed in a frilly dress and a teddy bear, his once yellow coat withered and grey with age.

'What a lovely room!' Julia put her bag down and moved to the window. It looked out on a small square of a neatly cut lawn, surrounded by flowers, beyond which was a high wall that screened off all the back gardens from the access alley. She turned round and smiled at Victoria, who was still standing at the door, as if a little uncertain, her cheeks dimpled, her lips curling self-consciously.

'It's so nice of you Visia,' Julia used the dimunitive to put Victoria at ease, ' to let me share your room. It's like a holiday for me. All thanks to you. Can I hang up my dress? It's probably all creased in the bag.'

Victoria came to life and moved swiftly towards the tall narrow wardrobe. She got out a hanger.

'Here, hang it up on the door,' she said, and when Julia did, all her own handiwork, Victoria's face lit up. 'It's very pretty. I like the red flowers. That's just the kind of dress I'll have for my first dance. My Mum still makes all my clothes, but one day, I'd love to go in a shop and choose the most beautiful dress.' She smoothed down her blue pique cotton skirt with embroidered pockets.

'I think your Mum's sewing is perfect', Julia said, and in a coaxing tone added, 'I bet all your friends are envious of all the lovely clothes you've got. They can't have as many. Clothes are so expensive!'

'You sound just like my Mum,' Victoria laughed, 'but one day, when I have bags of money, I'll do it anyway!'

'OK. Let's do it in style, then, let's go to London!' Julia's challenge brought a dreamy expression to Victoria's eyes.

'Agreed!' she said.

In perfect harmony, they went downstairs to the dining room. It was a large room extending spaciously into an open kitchen area. The white walls were decorated with photographs of Mrs. Lilli's Austrian family, and of Mr. Franek's relatives from Poland. There was the traditional holy picture of the Black Madonna, a print of a painting of the Tatra mountains and another print of the green hills of Austria. The dresser and the side-board were old wood, shining like polished chestnuts.

The boys were already sitting at the table, Leszek listening to their animated talk with rapt attention and parted lips.

Victoria helped her mother to bring in the food; cold meats, cheeses, sliced tomatoes and a mixed vegetable salad in mayonnaise. There was also a large plate laden with slices of apple cake, honey cake and cheese cake, home-made and smelling delicious.

' Uchta! It's a feast!' Miro exclaimed. It came naturally to break into Polish in the presence of adults. 'Mrs. Lilli, yours is the best restaurant in the whole of the town! Znakomite! Excellent!'

'I helped Mum to bake the cakes,' Victoria boasted.

'And I licked all the bowls clean!' Leszek laughed.

'And I never get the chance these days,' Stefan shook his head with mock sadness. Mrs. Lilli looked around smiling indulgently. There was a short hush as they all enjoyed their food, then Julia broke the silence.

'This is truly delicious, Mrs. Lilli. Pity Mr. Franek has to work today.'

'He'll join us later,' she replied with a smile, her platinum hair falling over her left cheek. 'He's just glad that they get so much work in. People seem to be able to afford cars. Amazing! Mind you, a lot of them are second-hand. There's never a shortage of repair work. He could be working around the clock, non-stop.'

'I suppose you're forever rushed off your feet too,' Julia remarked, 'but yours must be such a satisfying job.'

'It is, very rewarding.' Mrs. Lilli gave them another beautiful smile, 'I couldn't imagine doing anything else now.'

'You could Mama,' Victoria said in earnest, 'you could become a famous clothes designer.'

'Or the best cook,' Leszek added, smacking his lips with exaggeration.

Mrs. Lilli laughed then shook her head saying seriously,

'New mums need me. And their babies…'

Julia imagined the wonder of delivering babies, and she agreed, this was one of the best jobs, but all that blood… she shuddered inwardly, no, she couldn't picture herself in that kind of work.

She would have asked Mrs. Lilli more, but such talk was inappropriate at the dinner table, and certainly not in front of the boys. She changed the subject,

'Mrs. Lilli, are you planning to visit Austria again? Sometime soon?'

Stefan's mother put down her knife and fork for a moment.

'I'd love nothing more,' she said, 'but it's the cost. And all the form filling and waiting months for applications to be considered. They make it so difficult. On both sides. My parents made themselves ill worrying they might not see us again. We've only managed to see them twice since we arrived in this country in 'forty-seven. That's one visit, each side, in thirteen years!'

'Mama,' Stefan said gently, his blue eyes steady, 'it's just a matter of time. You'll see. Things are improving all the while. And when I start working… I'll help out of course…'

Julia glanced at Stefan's mother, curious for her reaction. She was struck by the look that passed between her and her son. Quiet pride on her side, reassurance in his expression. Julia wondered if he'd ever be free of his need to prove himself to her, of his compulsion to keep compensating, if only in small measure, for what had happened to her in the past.

Julia knew Mrs. Lilli's story from Miro's mother. Miro's parents and Stefan's father had been slave workers of the Nazis on an Austrian farm during the war. No personal contact was allowed between the slaves and the indigenous population. Stefan's father fell in love with Lilli, the daughter of an Austrian farmer. When their relationship was discovered, Stefan's father was publicly executed, as a warning to other Poles, and Lilli's left cheek was branded with a 'P', to shame her for having had indulged a Pole, as his 'whore'.

Julia could barely allow herself to imagine such atrocity; she preferred to think of the later, happier times, when Mr. Franek, a friend of Stefan's father, married Lilli and brought up Stefan as his own son.

'Mrs. Lilli,' she said, 'I like to think like Stefan. I hope too that travelling will be made easier for us as time goes on. I want to apply for a British passport as soon as I'm eighteen. I dream of visiting Poland.'

'Your parents' home town?' Mrs. Lilli asked, passing her the bread.

'I'd love to, but their home, if it still exists at all was in a little town near Dolina. That's now in Russian Ukraine. I'd be scared to go there. My parents would never allow it. They've already had a taste of the Soviet paradise. No, I simply want to see Poland. Warsaw would be lovely to visit. The old city…' Julia felt unable to reveal her true reason for wanting to go to Poland. How would she explain her curiosity about a man who had abandoned her as a small child, and the hope of finding him?

'We could start with Krakow,' Miro's voice cut through her thoughts, 'that is, if you want a companion on your travels. My parents came from that area.'

'And my Tato Franek,' Stefan said, adding less seriously, 'we should organise a party and go all together.'

'Yes, let's!' Leszek exclaimed, 'I'm coming too!'

'And me!' Victoria's hand shot up.

After that, the conversation disintegrated in a gabble, everyone talking, no one listening. Julia laughed. She loved the crazy liveliness around her. Stefan caught her eye.

'You must think you've fallen into a mad house. You're right!'

She shook her head, still laughing. He and Miro had no idea how lucky they were to have siblings.

'Believe me,' she said, 'it's no fun talking to the walls.'

'It must be bliss,' he replied, 'to have all the peace and quiet you want.'

After lunch, they all helped Stefan's mother to clear the table, and to wash and dry and put things away. Leszek disappeared and came back with a football, his unspoken request written all over his excited face.

'*Dobra! Dobra*! All right!' Stefan laughed. 'We'll play with you, if we must!' He turned to Julia, 'Not exactly the exciting weekend you had in mind, is it?'

'It's only just the beginning,' she replied with a mock-mysterious air, for Leszek's sake, 'who knows what adventures lie ahead of us yet!'

'What?' Leszek's curiosity perked up.

'Football. And more football.' Miro teased, catching Julia's eye.

'That's perfect for me!' Leszek cheered.

And Julia laughed. They all had their own expectations, no doubt, but she was simply happy.

Victoria linked her arm through hers saying,

'Let's go to the park, shall we?'

Julia was drawn into Leszek's excitement. She found him amusing and delightful at the same time as he skipped and ran up and down and trebled his mileage around their unhurried stroll across the park. She felt a lightness in her chest and calm in her mind, emptied of all worrying thoughts. Victoria walking beside her, their arms still linked, opened up and talked of her school and her friends.

'Amanda says she prefers women,' Victoria gazed hard into Julia's eyes, for her reaction. Julia wanted to laugh but responded with all the seriousness of a wiser older friend.

'It may be just talk, Visia, to draw attention to herself. At thirteen, do you think she's had enough experience to make such serious decisions?'

She caught Miro's glance and he smiled through the lively discussion with Stefan.

'And have you heard about *Lady Chatterley's Lover*?' Victoria continued undaunted. 'Penguin want to publish this book! I saw it on the news. Why would anyone want to read such stuff?'

'It's one of D.H.Lawrence's works,' Julia pointed out. 'And you can't judge it until you've read it yourself. He's a respected writer. No one's forced to read it.'

'Visia,' Miro came in, 'that's called democracy. And democracy is freedom.'

'But why then choose to publish something horrible when you can publish lovely things?' Victoria reasoned.

'Because Visia,' Stefan put on his older brother tone, 'lovely things alone, if imposed on us through repression, would not reflect the truth in our society.'

'Can you speak *normal*?' Victoria said, 'I don't understand what you're saying.'

'All it means,' Miro explained, 'is that you can have pretend order. Things made to look lovely that are not true. As in Poland now. Everything is dictated by the communists. Not by a real government chosen by the people. Yes, they organise beautiful, grand occasions. Everyone forced to go out on the streets and cheer crowds of workers, marching with their banners, singing rousing songs. All in praise of socialism and the wonderful wise leaders.' Miro gave a short laugh. 'Do you see what I mean? Where would you rather be?'

She was thoughtful for a moment before she replied, 'I still won't read Lawrence even if they pay me!'

'Your free choice,' Stefan said, 'And that is the point. Agreed?'

Victoria shrugged. 'If you say so!'

The park was a vast green field surrounded by a belt of trees and shrubs. Scattered groups of children were playing ball games, the cricket enthusiasts distancing themselves from the rest and keeping a watch on anyone encroaching upon their territory. There was a cool-looking spot in the shade of a large chestnut tree. Julia and Victoria made themselves comfortable on the grass, while the boys hurried to the pavilion at the far end to buy cold drinks and ice-creams. The pavilion was a wooden building, painted white, and overlooking a paddling pool, crowded with splashing toddlers, their mothers sitting languorously around the edge and soaking up the sun.

There was something dreamlike about the whole scene with the hazy sky, the shimmering pool, the stillness of the trees, heavy with heat, the distant shouts of children, all of which made the act of being so effortless.

'When we get bored with watching the boys play football,' Victoria suggested, her earnest brown eyes seeking Julia's, 'we can go for a walk around the park.'

Julia smiled. She wished Victoria was hers. Her sister.

'I won't get bored,' she said, 'it's so pleasant just to be sitting here. But yes, a walk round the park would be lovely.'

Victoria's quiet appraisal made Julia warm to her even more. She followed Julia's every move in getting herself ready for the dance. She sat at her small writing desk which served also as a dressing table with the mirror placed on it and propped up against the window sill. Julia's dress, white with red poppies, fitted snugly round her waist, and the petticoat, with its scalloped lace edge, was allowed to peep out a fraction from underneath the hemline.

'It's perfect,' Victoria declared, watching with avid interest Julia applying make-up. This was not an involved job. Julia's eyebrows were naturally well defined. She just accentuated her eyelashes with mascara. The lipstick was strong red to match the poppies and the beads around her neck. She brushed and fluffed out her hair and shaped it into a neat bob.

She examined herself in the mirror. The result was not bad, she thought, satisfied, considering that everything on her had come from Woolworths or the market. Except one thing. The little red handbag. Which looked like a child's. It had been bought for her when she was four. The only gift she had ever received from her father.

She dabbed a little scent on her wrists and behind her ears and did the same for Victoria. 'Mmm... smells like real roses,' Victoria approved with all the self assurance of a perfume expert. Julia's lip curled but she did not disillusion her.

'You look like Audrey Hepburn,' Victoria said.

' I wish...' Julia laughed. Would Miro think that?

'And I wish I was coming with you...'

Julia hugged her. It was easy to dispense love when one was happy. She had a buoyant, expectant feeling of an adventure awaiting.

'Visia, your time will come. Sooner than you think. Believe me.'

'Three years? That's like waiting for ever!'

Downstairs, in the hallway, the boys were already waiting, their hair combed and shiny, their shirts crisp white, their only, ubiquitous suits, refreshed and pressed.

'Very nice, Julia. Ve...ry nice!' Stefan gave her an approving, all-over look, accenting his words.

'If there was a contest for the Queen of the Ball,' Leszek said in all seriousness, 'I'd vote for you!'

Everyone laughed, but Miro did not comment. He just stared at her, hard, with a hint of surprise.

'Have I grown two heads?' she joked.

'Nno... no...' he stammered, then, as if coming out of a trance, he uttered one word. 'Wow!'

Julia giggled to cover up her self-consciousness.

Mr. Franek was home from work and came out of the kitchen. He was about forty, tall and thin, with abundant wavy hair, greying at the temples. Mrs. Lilli came too. She gave Julia a lace handkerchief with the letter J embroidered in one corner.

'I made it for you Julia, when I knew you were coming,' she said. 'Tuck it inside your handbag.'

Julia was overwhelmed. 'Mrs. Lilli... I... thank you...'

Mr. Franek's face creased in a good-natured smile.

'Have a good time, kids. And Stefan, I trust you to be sensible with the car!'

Stefan raised his hands in a show of indignation.

'Tato! How could you ever doubt me!'

The Polish Club, a rectangular fifties building, with steps leading up from a sloping pavement, stood in an area that was a mixture of residential and industrial quarters, where the price of land had been within affordable reach of the hard saving post-war Polish community. The foyer was brightly lit, looking into a bar, which had a comfortable feel about it, with plush red seats all round. A number of doors down the corridor indicated further rooms as well as the steps leading down to the basement.

The dance was in full swing when they arrived. Stefan had insisted that they should come later and make an entrance. And indeed, as they crossed from the foyer into the dimmed atmosphere of the dance floor, they were immediately surrounded by Stefan's friends. It took a moment for Julia's eyes to adjust. The size of the hall was imposing, with grouped lights, like baubles, lowered from the high ceiling, the tall windows draped in dark red, the raised stage discreetly lit, the spotlights sending rainbow beams over the dancing crowd and over the tables arranged round the edge of the hall.

A band, called 'Tango-Jazz' was playing *La Cumparsita*, the tall blond violin player teasing out a most romantic tune from his instrument, while his two companions, like twins, with the their dark sleek hair, played a bewitching rhythm on their accordions. Julia's feet twitched to have a go as she watched all the showing off on the dance floor with elaborate steps and moves.

This was pure fantasy! If only Lidia and Yagoda could have seen her now. If only Nadia was here and not with Leon, being led astray.

She felt herself kidnapped by Stefan's friends and seated at a table in the corner. She was relieved to find herself next to Miro. He was laughing and joking, obviously not a stranger to Stefan's companions. Lemonade was poured into their glasses and a large bowl of crisps moved towards them. A boy called Radek on Julia's other side, stood up, bowed and asked her to dance.

'Pity to waste such a good dance,' he said, already leading her by the hand onto the dance floor. Everything was happening fast, too fast for Julia to think.

He was a good dancer, steering her towards all the right moves, anticipating her steps, avoiding her toes. She had no illusion that it was his expertise that made her ability appear better than it was. It was strange dancing with someone she did not know, but he was attractive in a clean, modest kind of way, and did not harangue her with questions. As they wove their dance in and out of the crowd, she caught a glimpse of Miro. He was dancing with a petite blonde girl from their table, her huge dark painted eyes looking up naturally to him. Julia felt a stab of unease. Why hadn't Miro asked her first, before this stranger butted in? And where did he learn to dance?

When the music stopped with a loud, final chord, Radek escorted her back to their table and sat down beside the little blonde.

'Enjoyed yourself?' Julia asked Miro. God, she did not want to sound sarcastic. She did not want to be teased in return. In a lighter tone she added quickly, 'Where did you learn to dance? So well?'

Miro laughed heartily. He looked totally relaxed. 'Mila's Radek's sister,' he explained the blonde. 'As for my dancing, I've had a few lessons. All Rosemary's doing. She and her boyfriend wouldn't leave me alone till I agreed to go with them.'

He leaned closer to Julia, 'Forget all your worries Julia. Just enjoy the evening. We're all friends here. It'll be fun. You'll see!' His eyes went round the table as he named the girls, Mila, Ella, Danka and Teresa. The boys were Radek, Konrad and Yanusz. 'You'll be rushed of your feet,' he laughed, 'but the next dance is mine!'

It was a Polka. They whirled around the floor, everything spinning round them, becoming a continuous line, while they both laughed with exhilaration. Miro's arm was tight around her waist, she felt his body against hers, his warmth, his energy, his hot breath on her neck. They had never been so close before. She did not want this dance to end, though her feet ached as if about to drop off.

The next dance was rock-n-roll. As soon as they all got their breath back after the previous dance, Stefan stood up and gently pulled her up to her feet.

'Let's show them what we can do!' he shouted over the sound of music. They did the lot; the twists and turns and short and long steps, the skipping and the flinging out of arms and legs. 'Now the high jump!' Leon challenged. 'OK! You first!' Julia laughed back.

And so it went till break. The lights came on, the musicians left the stage, a soft, background record of Viennese waltzes was put on. Stefan's group collapsed round their table, their high spirits undiminished by their dire need to catch breath.

'Do you like it, Julia?' Miro's face was hot and shiny. He took his jacket off and hung it over the back of his chair. She caught a whiff of Old Spice and fresh sweat. She found the scent attractive, intimate. The other boys took off their jackets too. The protocol had been observed in the first half; now they could make themselves more comfortable.

'It's great,' she said, 'Better, heaps better than I imagined it!'

He smiled, held her gaze, looked happy too. 'We'll get some refreshments,' he said. The boys clubbed together and went out, while the girls moved up closer and talked and joked and laughed, just like her old friends, Lidia, Yagoda and Nadia. Miro had been right; they were all friends here.

The boys came back with a plateful of sandwiches. They needed to recharge their stamina for the second half of the evening.

A man, heavily overdressed with a long trench coat over his suit, approached their table and stood over them swaying, as he drew on the cigarette in one hand, then washed down the smoke with a swig from the beer glass in his other hand. He was about thirty, with black oily hair and a dark stubble, repulsive on his pale face.

'*Hej chłopcy!* Hey lads! How about sharing some of these beauties with me?'

Miro and Stefan stood up. They were taller than him. Stefan spoke in a polite tone,

'Sir, we're just enjoying our break. We don't want trouble, do we?'

The man made a step back and swayed.

'I just want a dance… no harm in a dance…' he reasoned, his eyes having a problem to focus.

'The music's too soft,' Miro pointed out.

'I've got music in my head… I just need a partner…'

'Not from our table,' Stefan said firmly.

'All right… please yourselves,' the man moved off with his unsteady gait.

They watched him as he made his rambling way among the tables, finishing in the middle of the floor. Still holding his beer and his cigarette and drawing amused glances from his captive audience, he began to dance on his own, his open trench coat flying like a dervish's skirt. Two older men, probably the organisers, approached him, gripped his arms and led him out without any regard for his protestations.

'Pity!' someone called from the adjoining table, 'It was just hotting up!' But Julia did not find any of it amusing.

'He's probably just a lonely man,' she said to Miro.

'He should know better then, not to get drunk,' Miro replied, matter-of-fact.

'I'm just thinking…' she said, 'how different things are when you've got friends…'

'Of course,' Miro agreed, 'do you want to invite him to our table?' he joked.

She shook her head, and thought how difficult it was sometimes to do the right thing. Though she felt pity for the man, she had found him revolting.

When the sandwiches were eaten, the girls got up to refresh themselves and powder their noses. There was a queue in the corridor outside the ladies' toilets.

'Let's go outside for a little fresh air,' Teresa suggested.

Julia followed them out of the back entrance onto the parking court. It was dark, but the daytime heat still lingered in the air feeling like soft gossamer on Julia's bare arms. Two spotlights attached to the corners of the building threw enough light over the car park.

'Want a ciggy, anyone?' Teresa asked, getting out a packet of Woodbines, a lighter and a cigarette holder from her handbag. Only Ella joined her in this clandestine activity. They puffed high and long, their heads thrown back, as Julia had seen Marilyn Monroe do, in an air of imagined sophistication, and with their arms bent, their hands pointing upwards, held their long cigarette holders, between two fingers above their shoulder level. Mila and Danka linked arms and giggled.

'Sure you won't have one?' Teresa asked.

Julia gave a short nervous laugh.

'One smoker in our family is enough.'

'Your Dad? That doesn't count. You don't know what you're missing!'

A red dot glowed in the shadows. Someone else was having a smoke. Then he came out and walked towards them. The man in the trench coat. The girls turned away from him and formed a closed circle, but he stood so close to Julia she could smell his beery breath.

'What's your name, young filly? I've not seen you before.' Good manners dictated that Julia should answer him politely, but she had no wish to talk to him at all.

'Please go away and leave us alone,' Teresa spoke firmly and blew smoke in his face. Julia winced. Yet the man was undeterred.

'What spirit! I like that! Here, give us a kiss!'

'Right, that's enough!' Teresa cried. 'Girls, time to get reinforcements!'

The man spread out his arms as if threatening to catch her, but she slid past him and they all ran towards the door. Inside, as they waited in the queue for the toilet, they could not stop laughing. But Julia felt uneasy.

'Shouldn't we tell someone he's still hanging around?' she asked.

Teresa wrinkled her nose.

'Don't worry, they won't let him in onto the dance floor again.'

In the ladies' room Julia freshened up. Her hair had become damp round the hairline with all the exertion on the dance floor. She fluffed it out with her fingers, smoothing the top layer with a comb. She dabbed perfume behind her ears and reapplied lipstick and powder. The other girls waited for her in the foyer, lively and giggling. She saw the object of their mirth. He was standing at the entrance to the dance hall, still sporting his trench coat and accosting anyone who went by.

515

'Ignore him!' Teresa instructed. 'Let's move fast!' Julia kept close to Mila and looked straight ahead. Now they were level with him.

'Hey you! Good looking!' she heard his voice.

'Quick, push the door Teresa,' she almost shouted. The door was swung open. Their way. A group of boys and girls spilled out into the foyer forming an immediate bottleneck by the entrance. Julia stepped back, out of their way. She felt a heavy arm on her shoulder. It pulled her back. She lost balance. Found herself falling backwards. Against the man. His grip was like a vice. She felt the roughness of his coat, of the buttons against her skin. His hot, acid breath was blowing down her neck, then something wet and rubbery touched the side of her face. His lips. She screamed.

Everything that followed happened very fast. Heads turned. Faces showed surprise then shock. The man was grabbed from all sides. His grip loosened. Then with one last move he tugged hard on Julia's string of beads. For a split second she had the horrific sensation of being strangled. The string broke, the beads cascaded down her chest and scattered on the floor between the feet of the onlookers.

She felt herself almost being carried by the girls, soft arms protecting, supporting, leading her back to their table in the corner, where the boys were engaged in a high-spirited discussion. She watched, like someone slowly waking up from a nightmare, Miro's expression changing, his laughter dying out, a puzzled look darkening his eyes.

'Julia! What's happened?' He jumped out of his chair and came towards her.

She had no chance to answer. The girls did all the talking, all four of them at once. She lowered herself onto her chair and gently rubbed her neck. It felt tender at the back.

'The man needs a good beating!' Radek exclaimed. 'Come on boys, let's show him!' The boys stood up with frightening readiness.

'No, no! Please!' Julia's voice rose. She grabbed Miro's hand to hold him back, to make her point. 'Please... I don't want any fuss. He's already been dealt with. He's not going to come back. Please sit down...'

They remained standing, looking uncertain.

'Please,' she repeated, 'it's a good evening. Why spoil it?' She forced a wide smile. 'Really, I'm all right!' They shrugged and sat down and slowly the carefree spirit of the evening began to return.

Miro pulled up his chair close to hers and picking up a sparkling drink from the tray in the middle, placed it in front of her.

'Drink some. Tastes like champagne. But it's harmless.'

Her hand shook a little as she brought it up to her lips. It was sweet, bubbly and warm inside her. She exhaled, feeling herself relax.

He was watching her closely, a brooding look in his eyes.

'I'm so angry,' he said, 'this wouldn't have happened if I was there with you!'

'Don't be silly,' she made light of it, 'you can't escort me to the ladies' toilets.'

'I promised your Dad!'

'I won't tell him, if you don't!'

'That's not the point! *I* know! And I can't turn the clock back!'

A lady came up to their table and asked,

'Which of you girls has lost a string of red beads?'

'I did,' Julia said, feeling all eyes on her.

The lady opened her cupped hand and exposed a broken necklace and about a dozen loose beads. 'I picked up as many as I could find,' she said with an-eager-to please smile. Julia thanked her profusely and wrapped up the beads in Mrs. Lilli's lace handkerchief, which she then tucked inside her red handbag. A child's small handbag. To her horror, her lip began to tremble and her eyes filled up. She bent her head to hide this and pretended to rummage through her bag. She became aware of Miro's hand resting on hers, comforting, holding her steady, while his other hand lifted up her chin till their eyes met.

'Don't upset yourself,' he said. 'The disgusting drunk is not worth it. I'll make it up to you, Julia. Somehow. Some way. I promise.'

It was strange, how just a few words from him were like a caress. Her lips, still shaky, formed themselves into a smile.

'It's just that,' she made herself sound practical, 'it's a waste of my well-earned money. From my very first pay packet.'

He was looking at her with so much tenderness, she could not mistake his unspoken feeling for anything else. She felt a warmth spread throughout her being. He enclosed her hand between both his and held it, warm and safe, saying,

'I shall replace that red necklace. With real coral. No less!'

CHAPTER 63

There was an atmosphere in the house. Julia could feel it, the moment she and Miro came in. Her Tato was reading at the kitchen table, apparently oblivious to Muszka asleep on his lap, the smoke from his cigarette weaving its sinuous course through the tense stillness.

She had been expecting an avalanche of questions. She had come prepared: a wonderful weekend, fantastic dance, and yes, she had been to church in the morning with the Dobosz family.

But Tato's expression was preoccupied when he looked up from the paper.

'Where's Mama?' she asked, her stomach doing strange things.

He shrugged. 'Gone for a walk.'

'On her own?'

'Her choice.'

Julia suppressed her unease. Her Mama was a grown up. Free to do as she pleased. She did not need supervision.

'Has she been out long?' she asked.

'A while. But don't worry. It's a lovely evening. The walk and the fresh air will do her good.' Then his expression changed as if suddenly remembering that they had been away. 'Good weekend?' he asked.

'Very good,' Miro replied with firm assurance. 'The dance was well organised. Mr. Franek and Mrs. Lilli made us very welcome. And we are back on time, as agreed.' His smile conveyed their proper behaviour throughout the weekend.

'Ah… yes… good…' Tato's mind seemed to wander for a moment. 'You understand it's for Anastazia's sake. You know Julia how she worries. Too much. Even when it's not necessary.'

'Well, we're back safe and sound,' Miro assured again, then turning to Julia he said, 'I better be off. I'll see you in the week.'

Tato stood up and shook hands with him. Julia followed Miro to the door. Outside he lingered, his gaze stopping long on her face, his manner hesitant as if he was formulating words in his mind.

'What?' she asked running her hand across her face, checking, adjusting her hair above her forehead.

'It was good, wasn't it? The weekend, I mean.' His tone was earnest, as if he needed her approval. 'We'll do it again, won't we? The dance, I mean… and everything?'

'Yes, of course...' Couldn't he see how much she had enjoyed it too? Couldn't he guess how she felt? She didn't want it to end. She wanted his arms around her. She wanted to be held close. If only for a moment. She certainly couldn't kiss him first, could she? A well-brought up girl like her. 'It was great, Miro. I loved all of it!'

He smiled with a hint of disbelief.

'And the drunkard too?'

'Who?'

'OK.' he laughed then, looking relaxed. 'Shall I see you soon? One evening this week?'

'Of course. Goes without saying.'

She watched him walk away with a smile, a wave of his hand and a spring in his step.

Turning indoors she felt that twinge again. Unease. In the kitchen, she sat at the table opposite Theo.

'Tato, has anything happened?' she asked.

He folded the paper, his face looking weary, resigned.

'It's the same old thing, Julia. Your mother went to confession. No prizes for guessing what happened next. She got upset. I keep telling her not to bother. But will she listen?'

Julia's heart sank. Frustration assailed her. She felt angry. She felt her Mama's hurt. Why was the priest, this man of God, so devoid of compassion?

From the age of six, through her child's interpretation of her surrounding world, she had been vaguely aware of some injustice upsetting her Mama. She heard strange words, like *divorce* and *civil marriage* and *living in sin*, but although the priest had explained the meaning of 'sin' to her class, she had been certain that had nothing to do with her mother. Her Mama was the kindest person on earth. Then why had she been barred from receiving communion?

When Julia was seven, all dressed in white and overwhelmed by the solemnity of her first communion day, she watched with envy as other parents followed their children to the altar to receive the wafer. But not hers.

She had it all explained to her by the priest. In the eyes of the Church, her mother's divorce from Julia's father did not count. Her civil marriage to Tato did not count. So what she was doing was wrong. And there was punishment for sinners who did not repent. Who did not amend their ways. Hell.

Julia had nightmares about hell. Visions of people burning for ever in flames as high as the house. She could not imagine her dear Mama and Tato being sent to a place like that. Her tormented mind began to invent ways of persuading God to relent. What if she were especially nice to Him and His family of Angels and Saints, then He might treat her family the same way.

From then on, whether at home, at school or at the church, she would stop by every holy picture or a statue of the Virgin, the saints or angels or Jesus on the cross, smile to them politely and bow with reverence. At times, when alone and unseen by anyone at home, she would recite poems for their entertainment or choreograph a dance. At times she would catch a worried look in Mama's eyes and get a feeling from the odd overheard word, that Mama was discussing her with Aunt Eva.

Then one evening Uncle Roman came to supper with them, his eyes smiling as always, his face kind, his jokes making Julia laugh. Afterwards, when the table had been cleared and Julia's parents were busy in the kitchen, he produced a new book for Julia to read with him. It was '*Misiu Puchatek*', 'Winnie the Pooh.' Roman read the story but Julia had to follow him carefully so as not to miss her cues for Winnie and Eeyore and Kanga and Roo's little speeches. At one point Julia's gaze wandered and stopped on the picture of Baby Jesus and his Mother on the opposite wall. Her compulsion was too strong for her to resist. She put her hands together, smiled and bowed her head. She prayed hard in her mind. *Please save Mama and Tato from hell.*

'Julia... Julia, are you all right?' Roman's hand lay gently on her shoulder. She opened her eyes, and suddenly felt very silly and shy. But he was not laughing at her.

'Is anything troubling you? You know you can tell me anything and I shall keep it a secret forever.' He made a twist with his hand over his mouth as if he was turning a key. This usually amused her, but this time her burden was too heavy to shift with a laugh. She looked furtively towards the kitchen door. It was slightly ajar with noises of splashing water, pots being washed, cutlery and plates being put away and her parents' talk coming from behind it. They wouldn't have been able to hear. Julia trusted Uncle Roman. He was her Tato's best friend. Like a second Dad to her. Perhaps he'd know what she had to do to save her Mama and Tato from hell.

She whispered to Roman, 'The priest says my Mama will go to hell because she's living in sin.' She looked hard into his eyes to see if he'd be shocked. 'I'm trying really hard to be good for God. I don't know what else to do to save my Mama.'

Uncle Roman did not look shocked. There was a soft smile on his lips, and his eyes were as blue as her doll's, when he patted her hand.

'Julia,' he said in a tone that made her feel as if he really knew that what he was saying was right, 'you must never, ever worry about this again. God loves you. He knows everything. He loves your Mama and your Tato too. Hell is only for very bad people. I've seen your Mama do a lot of good deeds for a lot of people. Long before you were born.'

Julia could not imagine such a long time ago. She felt something very warm inside her chest, like the hot milk at school on a cold winter's day. She liked Uncle Roman so much! If only he could have been the priest at their church!

'Then why is the priest saying all those things?' she asked.

Uncle Roman thought for a moment.

'It's like this, Julia,' he said. 'You know in your school there are rules that have to be obeyed. In another school the rules may be different. But it doesn't mean that the children from either school are bad, simply because they obey different rules. It's the same with the church and the priest. He has to preach the rules of his church, but some people may not be able to follow what he preaches. It does not mean that they'll be punished for that.'

'And they won't be sent to hell?' Just one last reassurance.

'Definitely not!'

A big boulder, a mountain fell off Julia's shoulders.

'How do you know all this?'

He smiled as if she had said something funny, but his tone was gentle when he replied. 'A long time ago, before the war, when I was young and a student, I studied theology. That's learning about all kinds of religions. I'll tell you something I've learnt, Julia, and I want you to remember it. Before God, whether you're a queen or a princess or a famous person or just yourself, you are all equal. He cares about every person in exactly the same way. And as long as, in your mind you know that what you're doing is right, you must not allow anyone else to frighten you with hell. All right?'

This was some nine years ago. Why hadn't her Mama listened to Roman? Why hadn't his wise words stopped her worrying? Sporadically she would approach the priest through confession with the hope of obtaining absolution and the longed-for permission to receive communion. But the laws of the Church did not change.

'Tato, why does she insist on tormenting herself like that? Is there really nothing else that can be done?' Julia's clasped hands on the table tightened tensely, the knuckles showing white through her tanned skin .

Tato shrugged and drew hard on the cigarette. His words came through exhaled smoke.

'There's one thing that, maybe, could bring her some peace. At least in her mind it would make her feel that she was again a rightful and accepted member of the congregation.'

'And what's that?' Julia's interest was alert.

'An annulment.'

'What, an annulment of her marriage to my father?'

'Don't get excited. An annulment is only for the kings and generals. Not for ordinary folk like us. Too difficult. Made easy and it could send out the wrong signals. Besides, in your parents' case there would be no grounds for that. They had a happy marriage, they had you and they are both Catholics.'

'But he deserted my mother. Doesn't that count?'

'No. If he's still alive, then she's still his wife. In the eyes of the Church.'

'So... in effect, she's being punished for something that he did?'

'Yes.'

Julia felt a rush of anger.

'But… that's… preposterous!' Thoughts raced around her mind. Suddenly the idea of going to Poland, to look for him, to find out if he was still alive, became urgent. If only she could accelerate time, and not have to wait another two years! 'Hasn't Mama ever tried to find out his whereabouts in Poland?'

'No,' Tato said simply, 'after what had happened, she never wanted any more contact with him. Besides, this would be only to check if he was still alive. A horrible idea! He's only forty-nine, wherever he is. Hardly a candidate for dying.'

Julia could not imagine her father as a living person. She had a photograph of him, a young man in a soldier's uniform. A sepia image of a stranger.

'What about you, Tato?' she asked. 'You wouldn't have to cope with any of this bother if Mama was free to marry you in church.' He was a widower, a free person after all.

Tato exhaled, forming a white haze above them.

'You know Julia, I've had worse adversaries than the priest. Even if he banned me from going to church, so what? I've been in situations when there were no intermediaries between me and God. I survived. God must have listened to a mere mortal like myself. Best not to rely too much on anyone.' He smiled through the smoke, his grey eyes lighting up.

'Tell Mama that.' Julia said.

'I have. Hundreds of times. She says I'm blasphemous!' He smiled again.

There was a sound from Muszka as she perked up her head, yawned, then jumped off Tato's lap. She arched her back before lazily proceeding to her bowl.

Julia stood up and got a tin out of the fridge. While she filled the cat's bowl, Muszka kept pushing against her hand as if telling her to hurry. This seemed to amuse her Tato. Julia warmed to his simple joy.

'I'd better go and look for Mama,' she said.

She found her on the humpback bridge, resting her elbows on the arched wall, looking down on the canal below. Julia's heart quickened. In exactly the same way as it used to when she was six and Mama met her out of school. Her mother was safe.

She approached her, taking in the sight, the comforting familiarity. A navy and white summer dress followed the line of her slim body, falling in soft folds around her legs. Her hair was held in place by a thin voile scarf, tied like an Alice band. Mama was not a stickler for fashion and would only succumb on occasions to Julia's persuasion to style her hair in a bouffant bob. Julia had yet to persuade her to cover the grey streaks with a colour wash. 'Forget the hairdresser's, Julia,' had been Mama's practical reply, 'I've not got the money to throw away. I can live quite happily with the hair I've got.'

She turned her head at the sound of Julia's footsteps on the gravel. Her dark amber eyes, thoughtful and distant, turned lively in a flash and her face broke into a happy smile. What a difference from only a few weeks ago!

Julia flung her arm around Mama's shoulders and held her close.

'I missed you, Mama. I was worried when you weren't home!'

Julia inhaled her scent; clean hair, fresh skin. Mama returned her embrace and chuckled.

'You're away all weekend, yet you expect me to remain like a fixture when you come home.'

'No, Mama, not at all!' Julia assured her, 'It's just that... it's so empty at home when you're not there... It doesn't matter now. I've found you...'

'Funny girl!' Mama gave her another hug. 'Tell me, how was it in Birmingham?'

'Shall we go for a walk? And I'll tell you all about it.'

It was a still evening with not a hint of movement in the long branches of the willows overhanging the water's edge. The clear sky reflected in the lazily rippling surface with broken ribbons of lilac and peach. A couple of ducks sat motionless in the reeds, oblivious to the walkers on the side footpath.

Julia and her Mama, arms linked, followed the track that cut across the field towards old Brownsover. Julia thought of Mr. Strachan, no doubt doing his night watchman's shift at the hall. All alone, and perhaps lonely. It was time she and Miro visited him again. But tonight, she just wanted time with Mama.

Mama listened with interest to Julia's account of her weekend with the Dobosz family in Brmingham and to her admiring description of their house and how well they were doing. She said,

'It's good that they're so enterprising. And good luck to them. Once I would have wished to be like them. But now...' her voice trailed off.

'But now, what Mama?' Julia coaxed. 'Wouldn't you like a bigger house? With a staircase? And a big garden, where you could grow flowers and vegetables to your heart's content?'

Mama shook her head. Her smile was a little wistful.

'No, Julia. I don't have such dreams any more. When you've lost all your possessions twice in your life, your desire for material things becomes somewhat blunted. First, my parents lost everything in the first war. Then, just as things started improving after long years of hardship, the German planes came and bombed everything again. We, of course, your father and I were taken away by force from our house. God knows if it still exists at all.'

Please Mama, Julia thought, not the war again. If only they could talk about normal things.

'I like to imagine things all the time,' she said brightly. 'One day, when I get a good job and earn lots of money I'll have a pretty house with bedrooms upstairs, with a staircase and a balustrade, with a lovely garden at the back and a drive in the front where I can park my car. It'll be a sports car. Like the one I've seen in the showroom in Railway Terrace.'

Mama's look had a touch of pity in her eyes.

'When I was your age,' she said, 'I imagined this perfect life ahead of me.

Marriage. Children. A house that I'd make into this perfect home. A happy life in our community. Then the war came. And nothing worked out the way I had imagined.'

'But Mama, it's all in the past now. There's not going to be another war. We're safe in this country.'

'And I'm quite happy with what I've got, Julia,' Mama added. 'You know, there's so little one needs to satisfy the basic comforts.' Julia was satisfied, for the time being, but she wanted better things in the future.

They were halfway up the grassy embankment that levelled off with the Leicester road. There was much twittering going on in the bushes at the side of the track.

'Sounds like sparrows having a fight,' Mama remarked, chuckling. 'Shall we turn towards the canal and walk back that way?'

The water was now in the evening shadow of the thick growth flanking it from the opposite side, with just a pattern of light, escaping through the branches and bouncing off the surface.

'I love it here,' Mama said, breathing in the soft air, 'I can't get enough of the peace and the quiet.' She closed her eyes for a moment as if savouring pure pleasure. Julia loved to see her Mama relaxed, so she refrained from adding that she loved company and friends, and that she'd had enough of the peace and quiet, all the weeks her mother was in hospital. She wanted to ask about her Mama's disagreement with the priest at the church earlier in the day, but decided against raising this delicate matter. As they started walking home along the path by the water's edge, her Mama brought up the subject herself.

'Did Tato say anything when you came back? About the church, I mean'

'Yes. He said you were upset. Mama...' gently now, persuasive tone, 'please, don't let that man upset you again. Believe me, he's no more important than you are. You know in your mind that you haven't done anything wrong...'

Mama did not answer straight away and Julia had a moment's panic that her words may have ruined her mother's emotional balance. She followed her gaze to the peachy sky where half a dozen geese, sharp like dark cut-outs, flew in a straight line.

'I know,' Mama said, 'both Roman and Eva keep telling me to develop a thicker skin. I wish I could. I agree with everything they say. And Theo. But I've always liked things to be right. And approved, I suppose. And they aren't. The priest makes me feel like a leper.' She gave a heart-felt sigh. 'I came from a good family, Julia. Well liked, well regarded in our community in Poland. It's all gone now. I'd love to retain just a little bit of the past. All I want is to receive communion.'

Julia had no idea what to say to that. She wished she could share her wafer with her mother on Sundays. She could receive communion every day, if she so wished. Did her Mama resent that?

'Things make me so angry!' Mama was saying, 'It's when I see those bigots surrounding the priest. Sakovska, so full of herself, she'll explode one of these days! She considers herself now his bodyguard. Can you believe it? Won't let people approach him without her vetting first. And old Cepelski. Everyone knows what a tyrant he is. To his wife and his kids. And Torkievich. Boasts blatantly about his cheating at work. Sleeps through most of his night shifts. The priest must know all this. Yet they go to confession, receive absolution and communion each week, then it's back to the same old tricks on Monday...' her voice rose in indignation.

'Mama...' Julia patted her arm. 'Don't upset yourself. They're not worth it...'

Mama became quiet and they walked for a while, with just the slightest whisper from the reeds, the odd splash of water from the moorhens hastening towards the opposite bank, the faint echoes of birdsongs in the distance, discreet breaths in the calm harmony of the evening.

'I can't help wondering,' Mama said, 'if things will ever be right for me again. I sometimes feel as if I'm somebody else, and not me at all. When I was in Russia, I thought once we get out of that hell, life will get back to normal again. I thought the same when I was in the Women's Army, and then in Palestine. All that had to happen then, I thought, was for the war to be over, for us to join your father in Britain and then our life would become happy and steady again. But nothing worked out the way I had imagined...'

Julia felt suddenly very tired. All the residual euphoria from the excitement-packed weekend was quashed in an instant. Was there nothing she could do to make her Mama happy? And what about Tato? Was he not worth more than some duty-bound gratitude for coming to the rescue when her Mama had needed support?

'You've got me and Tato,' she said, her voice a little more terse than she had intended. 'We both love you. Isn't that enough?'

Her Mama stopped and peered at her, surprise arching her eyebrows.

'Julia, my dear, of course I know that. No, what I'm trying to say is that life can be really hard and cruel at times. The church tells you that you're only sent experiences that you're able to cope with. They're meant to make you a better and a stronger person. And I'm saying that I could have well done without some of my experiences. They leave scars, Julia. Deep scars that never heal completely. . . When you've had something really good in your life and it's been snatched away from you, how can you ever stop mourning? How can you remain the same person?'

Julia's hurt at the moment was too deep for her to empathise with her mother's words. God, all she longed for was for her Mama to show some real interest in her and in all her present affairs. She was weary of Mama's chronic preoccupation with the past.

'Mama, what good does it do, living in the past?'

Her mother sighed.

'Julia, do you think I'm doing it on purpose? It is the past that keeps hounding me!'

Julia's exam results arrived in the post in the middle of the week. She had been hoping with all her might to pass in all the subjects, but when she saw written proof of her success, her relief was so great, it was like being a kite, buoyed upwards in warm streams of air. She could not wait to share her good news with her parents.

On Wednesdays, Woolworths closed at one, so she spent the free afternoon doing jobs around the house that would impress her Mama. When her parents arrived home from work at half past six, she waited with impatience for them to change out of their work clothes, that carried factory smells. She surveyed with pride the polished surfaces and the clean floors. She had also prepared the meal all ready to cook. She re-read the letter several times, even though it had made a permanent imprint on her mind the first time.

'Here, Tato, good news,' she waved the letter at him when he entered the room. He wore a fresh shirt and a scent of soap. His brow knitted in concentration as he read.

'Why didn't you get better marks in mathematics?' his grey eyes peered over the rim of the page.

Julia was instantly piqued by his remark. God, was nothing she did ever good enough? Did he have any idea what it was like to work under pressure of limited time, when your mind blanked out, when you panicked, when the algebraic equations or velocity problems became a blur of insolvable calculations?

'Tato, aren't you pleased that I didn't fail?' she retorted.

'Julia, I'd be very disappointed if you did. Mediocrity is simply not good enough. You've got to rise above that. You've always got to aim for the top!'

Easy for him to talk! She sighed inwardly, taking the paper from him. She followed her Mama to the kitchen, where she was already tying an apron around her waist and peering inside the pots.

'Look Mama, these are good results, aren't they? Look what I've got in English and Latin and History.'

Mama glanced over the list.

'Not bad,' she said, 'but your Tato is right. You've got to do your best when you start your new school. Show your teachers that a foreign, Polish girl can do as well as anyone else in your class. But above all, Julia, you're doing it for yourself. No one can rob you of what you've got in your head.'

That had been exactly Sister Alicya's mantra at her old school. How many times had she heard that? Cram and memorise and keep your knowledge for ever within you. It was now a part of her nature, like opening her eyes on waking up or responding with a start to a sudden bang.

'I know all that, Mama. God, we've been brainwashed enough all those years! But tell me, did you notice anything?'

Mama lit the gas rings underneath the pots and turned round, her glance searching Julia's face.

'The vegetables,' Julia prompted, 'I prepared them and I've also cleaned the house for you.'

'That's very commendable my dear,' Mama replied with a sweet smile, 'I'd expect nothing less from a grown-up daughter of mine.'

Today was different. When Julia returned from work just after six, there was a calm in the house pervaded with her Mama's gentle humming and aromas of baking. Her Tato was keeping Mama company in the kitchen, reading at the table, all scrubbed and spruced up after a day of catching up on the odd jobs. That was how Julia loved it best; the comforting, cushioning harmony that allowed her to concentrate on her own things.

It was the last Saturday for her at Woolworths before starting her new school on Tuesday. Mr. Jones, her boss had asked, would she consider coming back at Christmas, their busiest time of the year. Would she consider? She had to stop herself from hugging him, this taciturn man with his distant manner. She had already saved up enough to buy her mother the china set of cups and saucers from the market stall, the set with the painted shepherds in their velvet suits and shepherdesses dressed up like Marie Antoinette. On another stall she had seen a sturdy torch for her Tato with two settings; a continuous beam or a flashing light. He would like that. He had a battered old thing from his days in the army that he kept resurrecting with unfailing optimism with ever-new batteries.

For herself, she had seen a pair of black patent shoes in a little corner shop, costing one third of the prices in town. The first thing she would do on Monday, would be to buy these things while her parents were at work. Tonight she was happy to wear the white sandals she had worn all summer together with her favourite dress with the red poppies print.

Miro had organised a belated birthday party for his closest friends. Stefan would be there. Also Rosemary and her boyfriend Roger. Rosemary. Why did she still evoke feelings of unease, when it was obvious she had no interest in Miro beside their common subjects at college? Julia would have to force herself to act naturally and not make a fool of herself. She shuddered at the very thought of such mortification. She would rather die! What a pity Nadia was not able to come. She had already had a day planned with Leon. Another pang of guilt. Julia should have warned her. Or should she? God, life was so complicated. She had enough worries of her own without other people's problems. But Nadia was not other people. She sighed. She would do it, as soon as the right moment showed itself.

Miro's party was also a kind of symbolic farewell to his school days before

527

starting a new phase in his life. Tomorrow he was off to his cousins in France for the remaining three weeks of his holiday. He was keen on improving his French. As she combed and styled her hair and applied a touch of makeup, Julia let her mind wander into a fantasy about herself and Miro, going on a tour around Europe one day, perhaps in a little car of their own, sightseeing, stopping to admire some breathtaking views, taking long lazy breaks on a beach to soak in the sun. She shivered with pleasure. There was no harm in dreaming.

She would miss him. Would he miss her too? Would tonight be special? Would he declare his love for her and tell her she was the one and only for him and he could not imagine his life without her at his side. Like Mr. Darcy and Elizabeth?

She heard voices outside, her Tato greeting the Bzovskis. Through the net curtains she saw Aunt Eva and Uncle Henryk coming down the front path. And Nadia! Julia's heart skipped. Her friend had come after all!

Julia ran out of the house.

'I'm so glad you've changed your mind!' she hugged Nadia, then Aunt Eva, warm and motherly, then Uncle Henryk, bony and stiff. 'And what have you done with Marek?'

'He's escaped us, oldies,' Mrs. Eva's eyes smiled. They were startlingly blue in her bronzed face. 'Gone round to his friend's.'

In the front room Mama was waiting, readjusting things on the table covered with her embroidered white linen. There was an assortment of small plates and cutlery, and thick sturdy glasses from Woolworths, for the lemon tea. The cracks in the old platters were deftly made invisible underneath the sandwiches on one, and slices of home baked, sliced cakes on the other. Despite the imperfections the table looked sumptuous and welcoming.

Julia and Nadia excused themselves and escaped to Julia's bedroom.

'You look good,' Julia praised her friend scrutinising her from top to bottom. The pale, pastel pink dress, pinched at the waist and flaring at the knees, and the gauze scarf tied round Nadia's pony tail, accentuated her striking dark looks. 'What made you decide to come after all? Miro will be pleased.'

'Will he?' Nadia sat heavily on Julia's bed, 'I should have said Yes in the first place.'

'Has anything happened?' The question was rhetorical. Julia was used to reading her friend's expressions.

Nadia sighed dramatically.

'I'm so cross with Leon! But I'm even crosser with myself! Mad! I'm so stupid!' She slapped her forehead with the heel of her palm. 'I wasted all day waiting for him! And as if this wasn't enough, what else did I do? I only cycled to his house to make sure he was all right! And what did I find? Nothing! No one there! Just as well I did, or I'd still be waiting. Instead of being here with you!' Her eyes looked suddenly moist.

'Nadia,' Julia sat down beside her and patted her hand, 'there must be some good explanation to all this.' God, she squirmed with her own duplicity, she was such a liar, but now was not the time for revelations. 'Listen Nadia, I'm sure Leon will get back to you as soon as he can. If, as you say, there was no one in the house, he was obviously out with his parents. They must have needed him. You know how it is, how they rely on us to translate for them. Perhaps they've gone out to sort something important? Perhaps new furniture? Or even a car? Or maybe they put pressure on him to help out with the decorating at his sister's?'

Hope sprang in Nadia's eyes for a brief moment then she shook her head.

'Then why didn't he tell me? He knew very well that I'd be waiting. It's as if I... and my time did not matter...at all.'

Julia wished she knew what to say.

'Nadia, please,' she coaxed her friend, 'please don't be sad. I want you to enjoy this evening. Miro's friends will be there. You know Stefan. And I'm sure the others are good fun too.'

Nadia stood up, leaned towards the mirror and checked her face.

'It'll do,' she forced a smile, 'and I'll be nice, if I have to.'

At Miro's front door there were sounds of a shuffle on the other side. When it opened, Lukasz and Piotr greeted them with wide grins and devilment in their eyes, as they staggered outside crab-like, their arms entangled around a football.

'Hi Julia! Hi Nadia!' they called out, then chased each other down the pavement towards the playing fields.

'Be back before dark!' their father called after them, coming to the door. He wore a white shirt and a tie, for Miro's English guests, Julia guessed. 'Come in girls,' he invited them in his usual welcoming manner, traces of indulgence for his boys, playing in his expression. 'Now that we're rid of the mob, we can enjoy the evening in peace. There's a feast waiting for you on the lawn.' He pronounced the words 'feast' and 'lawn' in mock awe, as if he were a butler announcing a banquet.

He led Julia and Nadia through the dining area into the kitchen, where Miro's mother was busy tidying up. She stopped to greet them. She wore a flowery blue and lilac dress and matching beads and had teased her difficult wiry hair into the fashionable short bob.

'So lovely outside,' she said, 'we must make the most of what's still left of the summer. And there's so much more space.'

The space she referred to was in fact a small rectangular back garden, with a path and a flower border around a patch of lawn, virtually covered now with the table and six folding chairs, remnants of the camp furniture, after it had closed down. Red roses and honeysuckle climbed over the wire fences, creating a natural screen on both sides of the garden, against other people's back yards.

Miro and Stefan sounded in high spirits as they and the couple, whom Julia had guessed to be Rosemary and Roger, stood around with drinks in their hands. Shandy or lemonade.

Miro put down his drink on the table and strode in long eager steps towards them, his hair bouncing around his forehead, a wide smile reflecting his mood. Like his father, he wore a white shirt and a tie.

'Hi! Julia! Nadia! So good you could come! Let me introduce my friends. Stefan you know, of course…'

Stefan came forward, tall and neat in his light suit, and shook hands with them in turn, his appraising gaze interested and warm.

'Nadia! How long has it been? Seems like years! I want to know everything you've been doing all that time!'

'Everything?' Nadia teased, her previous mood melting in a smile. 'How many hours have you got?' The smile still lingered as she turned her attention to Rosemary and Roger.

They stood very close, Roger's arm draped over Rosemary's shoulder. Unmistakably bonded. Something lifted inside Julia's chest. Why had she been tormenting herself so? With untainted interest she gave them her full attention.

The initial, momentary impression was that Rosemary was plain. But that was not so. The eyes that peered at Julia through the lenses of the thick-rimmed glasses were as luminous as brown berries and the unpainted mouth showed even white teeth when it smiled. The dark golden hair was pulled back and tied in an elaborate knot on the nape. Rosemary was no slave to fashion. Her dress was a pale grey silky fabric in the twenties' style with a dropped waist and her matching shoes had shapely heels and ankle straps. Roger obviously approved, judging by his proud, proprietorial glances, that slid like caresses down her face.

His manner and appearance spoke of breeding and money. Crisp, stylish navy jacket, knife sharp creases in his cream trousers, abundant hair cleverly cut in layers and tapering behind his ears and a smile that was charming but politely restrained.

'Pleased to meet you, Julia, Nadia,' they spoke almost in unison.

'Let's sit down, shall we?' Miro invited. 'Make yourselves comfortable.' He pulled the chairs out and they all settled round the table, Julia and Nadia facing Rosemary and Roger, and Miro and Stefan at each end of the table.

'Your mother's gone to a lot of trouble,' Rosemary remarked, leaning forward and studying the sandwiches through her thick lenses. 'They look delicious. Each one like a little island.'

They were open sandwiches, each with a base of ham, decorated with slices of cheese, tomato, cucumber and egg and sprinkled with dill and finely-chopped chives.

'Please, help yourselves,' Miro encouraged.

'And the cakes?' Rosemary enquired, looking at the four distinctive rows of slices. 'They look exotic.'

'The usual array, traditional, Polish,' Nadia explained. 'This one's baked cheese cake, this is spicy honey cake, this is apple cake and the filling in this one is made of poppy seed, walnuts and raisins.'

'Poppy seed? How interesting!' Roger chuckled. 'Invite me again! Any time!'

'Totally harmless, I'm afraid,' Stefan said, 'it's the sap from the poppy seed head that would liven things up. But that's not on the Polish menu.'

What were they talking about? Julia wondered. She turned to Miro to enlighten her, but he was busy holding out the platter with sandwiches for everyone. Roger placed one on Rosemary's plate before serving himself. When they all had their first bite of Mrs. Anna's delicious food, Roger returned to the subject of poppies.

'I read an article recently, about the poppy fields in Italy. Near Avilla. Apparently the visions St. Teresa was experiencing may not have been entirely the result of her dialogues with the angels.'

'Then what?' Julia's question came spontaneously, before she could stop it.

They all laughed. Except Miro.

'The sap from the poppy seed-heads can give you hallucinations,' he explained simply.

'The sap?' she repeated, 'The white milky stuff? But that's so bitter. I tasted it once. Do you remember Nadia? In the camp. Everyone grew poppies. For the seeds. But why would anyone want to eat that awful stuff? And why would anyone want to have hallucinations?'

They all laughed again, but she did not mind. Strangely, it gave her a pleasant sensation to be able to entertain them, even if she did not understand why they found her amusing. Even Nadia. What did she know that Julia didn't?

'What's so funny?' she asked her.

Nadia shrugged evasively.

'Ask the experts,' she said.

'Julia,' Stefan stepped in, 'it's the latest craze. Apparently, in London. Smoking dope.'

'Dope?'

'Cannabis. Marihuana. That sort of thing.'

'What are they?'

'They're like tobacco. Only stronger. Give you pleasant sensations. Help you to relax.'

'I see.' She did not see at all. She could not imagine how filling your lungs and your brain with smoke could make you feel good. She changed the subject.

'Rosemary,' she leaned forward, taking another sandwich from the platter, 'I heard from Miro that congratulations are in order. Well done for getting a place at Oxford.'

'Thanks!' Rosemary nodded, 'Magdalen College. I'll be reading English and Classics.' Her statement was matter of fact. As if these things had been eternally pre-ordained.

Roger smiled and inclined his head so close to Rosemary's, Julia had a feeling that he would have kissed her if they were alone.

'We'll be just a few streets apart,' he said. 'I'm at St. John's. Economics. Pity this will be my final year.'

'And then what?' Julia enquired to show interest.

He chewed thoughtfully on his sandwich for a moment. 'Then I'll be back to help my father. With the family business. He's expecting that. As his father did of him. My older brother's already a partner.'

'And what business is that?'

'Estate agents. We specialise in farming land and country estates.' Like Rosemary before him, he stated a simple fact. Julia wanted to ask what it was exactly that their services involved, but did not wish to betray her ignorance about such matters.

Miro came to the rescue.

'That's indeed impressive,' he said, 'I mean this continuity through generations. Wouldn't I just love to step into a waiting job! You're so lucky, Roger! We're like nomads here. We've got to start from scratch!'

'But it's even more impressive, being a self-made man!' Rosemary said, as if already picturing Miro conquering all adversity. Julia was sure the English girl's encouragement was meant in all good faith, she did not even try to explain the differences between them. She could only imagine what a wonderful springboard to life it must have been to come from an economically well established family, with parents doing important jobs and being noticed and listened to when supporting their offspring as opposed to being a child of impoverished wartime immigrants, forever struggling to make ends meet.

She was contented to listen to small talk evolve, to enjoy slowly the morsels of her sandwich, to allow her eyes wander from Miro's animated expressions to Roger's gaze glued on Rosemary's lips, to Rosemary's calm face as they exchanged accounts of their colleagues' latest news. Rosemary interspersed her musings with strange little phrases that were new to Julia, something about a windfall and living on a shoestring and going to the wall. There was so much she still had to learn. A good dictionary with idioms and colloquial expressions was what she would need to get soon and study with speed.

Julia observed Nadia with Stefan. Their flowing conversation was punctuated with her frequent giggles, so different from her earlier mood. If only things could stay as light-hearted and carefree as this, if only her misgivings about Leon's suspicious behaviour would stop niggling her.

She concentrated her attention on Miro. She was aware of his every movement, of his shoulder and his elbow brushing against her, of the energy inside him invigorating his words, his restless hands, as he discussed things with Rosemary and Roger.

The moon rose golden in the dusky lilac sky, drawing out fragrances around them; honeysuckle, climbing rose, night-scented stock. Miro lit a candle in the middle of the table. The glow shaped the objects, giving them depth and solidity. This was like still life in a Murillo painting. Magical. Julia wished she could stop time.

When the sandwiches were eaten and each of the cakes tasted, Julia played 'mother' and dished out the dessert. A bowl of mixed tinned fruit in jelly.

Miro rose to his feet.

'Coffee anyone?' he asked.

'I'll help you,' she volunteered eagerly.

Indoors, Lukasz and Piotr were back from their outdoor games, following with rapt interest the adventures of Robin Hood on the television. Their parents were sitting at the table, Mr. Michal chiselling a piece of wood and Mrs. Anna hand-finishing the hemline on her new skirt.

'More food?' she asked, looking up from her sewing.

'Only if you want us all to burst!' Julia laughed. 'No, thank you. There was plenty! And all delicious, as always!'

'Just making coffee now.' Miro said.

Julia helped him get out six cups and saucers, china, like the ones she'd already planned to buy for her mother at the market, and she stood close to him as they waited for the water to boil.

'I wish...' his voice was muffled by the hissing sound inside the kettle, 'I wish I wasn't going tomorrow. I never thought I'd be saying that,' his smile was self-conscious, 'I wish we'd have more time together now, before I start in London.'

His words took her unawares. Her stomach fluttered.

'You can't mean that Miro!' she chided him gently, her heart doing funny little hops. 'I'd give anything to be going to France. So exciting! Just the travel alone! I'll expect you to polish up my French when you get back. And think of me on Tuesday, in my new school, when you're having fun!'

He smiled again and inclined his head.

'I'd be having more fun if you could come with me. They've got a little toddler, Jean-Pierre. I'll be his nanny, I expect, as I was last year. I could just picture us two taking him out for walks by the river, to the park, enjoying things together.'

'So could I,' Julia said in a tone that implied this was just a dream. She had to be practical. 'It's just three weeks, Miro, they'll go in a flash. Though not for some...' she raised her hands in mock horror.

'You'll be fine, Julia,' he assured her, passing his hand lightly over her bare arm.

'Miro!' his mother's voice came from the dining room. 'Can't you hear the kettle whistling? It's ready to explode!'

His eyes sparkled as he grinned, amused, and turned off the gas. He poured the boiling water on the instant coffee in the cups. Julia picked up the tray and he followed her with milk and sugar.

Outside in near darkness, the white cloth on the table reflected the candlelight and the moon's radiance. Lively conversation was still in full swing as Roger recounted his numerous holiday adventures in Brighton and Torquay.

'In January it's Aviemore,' he was saying, 'with my brother. For a long time Ralph was stronger and faster than me. Now, when the boot's on the other foot, he's not so smug any more. Fiercely competitive. Hates to lose. But I'll make no apologies for the excellent skills of his kid brother...' Roger made a mock bow.

'All that is too much effort for me...' Rosemary dismissed Roger's words with a wave of her hand. 'Give me the apres-ski any time!'

None of what she heard had any meaning to Julia; it was like a language from another planet. She placed the coffees carefully around the edge of the table.

'It all sounds so exotic,' she said, sitting down. 'I wish I could remember more of the country where I was born.'

'And where was that?' Rosemary asked.

'Palestine.'

'Really?' There was a hint of disbelief in Rosemary's voice. 'That's extraordinary! Weren't you sorry to come to live in our freezing winters?'

'I had no choice in the matter,' Julia smiled, 'but I remember shivering throughout all my childhood. Even on some days in the summer.'

'And I...' Nadia raised her voice theatrically, her pony tail dancing, 'I was once entertained by one of the wealthiest Maharajas of India! In his own palace!'

Both Roger and Rosemary laughed, then he added indulgently,

'Are we now in the realms of fantasy?'

Nadia shook her head, laughing too.

'No, this is absolutely true!'

Roger looked to Miro and Stefan for confirmation. 'Were your parents diplomats? Or something?'

Now they all laughed.

'No,' Nadia said, seriously, 'they were war refugees. For a while we lived in Valivade in India. I was only a baby then, so I can't honestly say I had any awareness of any of it. But I can have a little boast, can't I?' she giggled again.

'And what about you? Miro and Stefan?' Roger asked. 'Were you there too?'

'We were both born in Austria,' Stefan said.

'Beautiful country. What made your parents decide to leave?'

'I think,' Stefan paused, a wry smile hesitant on his lips, 'I think when you've been forced into slave labour for five years, the beauty of the place gets somewhat overlooked. They left as soon as they were set free. By the British army, as it happened, in their region.'

'Well, fancy that!' Roger's surprise was genuine. 'And we thought we had it bad here in England!'

'It was bad enough for those who lost their families and their homes,' Miro reminded, 'whether it's thousands or just one person lost, it's still one too many. But listen everyone! How about changing the subject! Everyone tell a joke! And no excuses!'

The mood lightened as they drank their coffee, then Rosemary checked the time.

'It's been great, Miro, but we've got to go,' she said. 'It looks like it's good-bye for now, but not for long. We'll get together at Christmas, won't we?'

They all got up, tidied up the table, and between them carried all the things into the kitchen. Rosemary and Roger went through into the dining area. Miro's parents stood up from their tasks.

'It's been lovely,' Rosemary said, shaking hands with them. 'Thank you for inviting us.'

Roger followed suit. 'Indeed, much appreciated. The food's been delicious!'

Mrs. Anna looked pleased, a touch self-conscious.

'You are good friend to Miro,' she said.

'All best! At university,' Mr. Michal said, his eyes smiling. 'This for you. For pens and pencils.' He handed Rosemary a slim oblong wooden box with a lid, that had a carved pattern around the edge. 'I make it,' he added.

For once, the eloquent, sophisticated Rosemary appeared lost for words. In her astonishment, her mouth moved silently as she ran her finger along the surface of the box. 'I don't know what to say...' she said at last. 'It's a complete surprise. Thank you, thank you very much!'

Julia watched with a lightness inside her. She had nothing more to fear. It was not difficult to like Rosemary.

Miro went outside to see off his friends. Julia and Nadia stayed in the kitchen, washed up and dried, while Stefan made himself useful putting things away and entertaining them with tales of doctors and nurses.

They finished, Miro came back and it was time for Julia and Nadia to go too. Julia wished she could have stretched the evening a little longer, but good manners demanded that they should not overstay their welcome, just as good manners demanded that the boys should escort them home safely. They left with profuse thanks to Miro's parents.

The night was fragrant and warm, the street lights casting a discreet intimate glow. Nadia and Stefan went ahead. Miro clasped Julia's hand, and swung it gently in step, as he had done hundreds of times before, only now she felt an unspoken yet very real closeness between them. She cast him sideways glances. His features were blurred by the shadows.

'Next year,' he said, 'do you think your parents would allow you to go to France with me?'

'Next year?' Her heart flipped. Was he really thinking that far ahead? 'Miro, I'd love that. But I daren't even imagine it. You know what my Mama and Tato are like. It would be a job persuading them.'

'There'd be nothing improper,' he assured her, with a hint of amusement. 'We'd be staying with my cousin, a very strict and married lady, with two children of her own!'

'Very strict? Sounds frightening!' she giggled.

'Not with me around!' Then he was serious. 'Will you miss me Julia?'

Did he need to ask? Couldn't he guess how she felt?

'No, I won't in the least,' she teased, 'Miro, what do you think?'

'Just tell me.'

'You tell me first!'

They walked in silence, slowing down their pace so as not to reach the gate too soon, where Stefan and Nadia stood lost in animated talk.

'All right,' he said, 'I'll tell you. Then you can laugh at me!'

'Why do you think I'd ever do that!' her indignation must have reassured him.

'The thing is...' he hesitated, 'it's as if I'm obsessed. I can't stop thinking about you, Julia. I wake up, and there you are already in my mind. I think about you on my way to work, hundreds of times in the day, when I come home, when I cycle, run, walk, whatever I do, wherever I am...'

His words made her feel giddy.

'Miro, you've just described exactly how I feel too, about you,' she said.

'Really?' He sounded genuinely surprised 'Really?' there was a joyous catch in his voice. His hand tightened around hers, then he released it, threw his arm around her shoulders, drew her close to him, kissed her on the cheek and continued to walk with her hugged to his side. Everything was happening so fast she allowed herself to be carried along with his burst of euphoria. Then, as Stefan turned his head in their direction, Miro released her, slowly, his hand lingering over hers.

'I'll write to you,' he said.

'I hope so. It's only three weeks Miro. It's when you come back, that's when you'll be away for a really long time!'

'But I'll only be in London. I can jump on the train any time and be home in two hours.'

'What, and spend a fortune on the tickets?'

'I'll be saving every week.'

She knew the reality would be different; neither of them had money to throw away, but his words of comfort were like a declaration of his fidelity. He was hers. Happiness bubbled inside her.

Nadia and Stefan were too immersed in their own chatter to be aware of what had just passed between Julia and Miro, when they joined them at the gate to Julia's house.

'All good things…' Stefan quoted, sighing, evidently reluctant to let the moment go.

'Come to an end…' Nadia finished for him, 'but so do all the bad things. Hey, listen everyone, let's do this again soon. Get together. At the club next time. I'll bring Leon along.'

'Sure, the more the merrier,' Miro agreed. Did Julia detect a smidgen of sarcasm in his tone?

They said their 'goodbyes' and 'safe journeys' and though there was no chance for Miro and Julia to be alone again, she felt no pangs of regret. She knew there would be other times. This was just the beginning.

Indoors, it was all quiet with just the night light left on in the hallway. Her parents had gone to bed. Julia and Nadia undressed in silence and only when they lay back on the downy pillows, with just the moonlight filtering through the branches of the beech outside the window and falling on their cover in fuzzy circles, they began to whisper.

'Stefan's nice,' Nadia said, 'hasn't he got anyone?'

'I don't know. I don't think so.' Julia whispered back. 'It's because of his long course. Six years before he qualifies to practise. Apparently, he doesn't think it's fair to keep anyone waiting so long. And he wouldn't be able to support a wife while he's studying.'

'Silly man! He's missing out on all the fun! And his girl should support herself! I certainly wouldn't ever expect a man to keep me!'

Julia giggled. 'Nadia, it wouldn't be just any man! It would be your husband. And what about when you have small children?'

'That wouldn't be a problem for me. I would arrange my hours around the needs of my family.'

'Would Leon agree? What would his mother say?'

Nadia thought for a moment. 'I don't suppose she'll like anything that I do. She doesn't like me. Full stop. But Leon loves me. And that's all that matters.'

Julia squirmed. Her guilt deepened, especially now in the face of her own happiness. Miro was so certain. Like a rock. Unlike Leon. But before she could think of something to say, Nadia continued,

'He'd better have a jolly good excuse when I see him after church tomorrow. But I'll make him suffer. I'll taunt him, I'll tell him how much I enjoyed tonight and what he's missed!'

'Perhaps,' Julia suggested, 'you should hear him out first.'

'Yeees…' Nadia strung out the word with a hint of menace, 'now what about you and Miro. It's so obvious he's only got eyes for you.'

Julia laughed softly.

'We're happy as things are. There's a lot of waiting ahead of us yet.'

Nadia was quiet for a while.

'You know,' she said, 'sometimes I think that the best part is waiting. Letting your mind imagine all kinds of exciting situations. But once things happen, that's it. They never fit your expectations.'

Julia raised herself on her elbow.

'Nadia, don't say that. It's as if you've already given up. Things happen all the time. Some good. Some bad. But there's always the next time. And even if things turn out differently to what you've been expecting, they may be better for you in the long run.' God, this was the most veiled message she had ever delivered. Nadia would never be able to decipher the code.

'All I wish for myself,' Nadia said, 'is to be loved by Leon. And to be accepted by his mother.' She pulled herself up and leaned against the headrest. 'Julia, tell me honestly, am I so different from everyone else? Just because my parents had a different coloured skin and came from a different continent?'

Julia stroked her friend's hand.

'You know the answer to that. Do you know how I see people? Like flowers. The majority are the daisies and the buttercups. Then there are the ones that stand out. Roses, irises, lilies...'

'And what am I?' Nadia asked.

'I'll bring you a book from the library,' Julia answered without hesitation, 'I saw it last time. All about the bright colours in nature in the tropics. You'll be astonished at the incredible beauty of the flowers there. The one that stood out for me was called the bird of paradise.'

'You're making this up. Trying to humour me...' Nadia's whisper contained rebuke.

'See for yourself. It's so tall and splendid, it's not even aware of the silly stinging nettles around its base...'

Nadia slid down the pillow and settled beside Julia.

'I like this comparison,' she said with a smile in her whisper, 'I like it very much. Now I can go to sleep and dream of what I'm going to say tomorrow.'

'Good night.' Julia closed her eyes and thought about Miro.

CHAPTER 64

'Are you Julia? Oh, right. I'm Susan Grainger-Jones. Pleased to meet you. We've been assigned, that's Yvonne and myself, to get you acquainted with the layout of the school, the timetable of the day, and naturally, with the sixth form.'

'Hi Julia. I'm Yvonne Smith. Plain Smith.' Yvonne's eyes sparkled. 'What Susan means is that we'll be looking after you today.'

The two sixth formers who met Julia in the school's reception area, were as different as a poplar and a copper beech. Susan, tall, thin, her hair cut in a boyish style, looked more like a teacher than a pupil behind her black-rimmed glasses. Yvonne was smaller, with red hair bouncing round her freckled face and a ready smile.

'I've left my bicycle just outside the main entrance,' Julia worried.

'Now, that's something you must never do!' Susan admonished, her expression ambiguously deadpan. 'Follow me and I'll show you where to leave your bike, if you want to avoid getting black marks!'

Julia and Yvonne followed her outside, Yvonne suppressing a mischievous grin.

Julia had slept badly, waking up several times in the night to check the clock. Heaven forbid that she should be late on her first day! She jumped out of bed just after her parents had left for work at seven. Hurriedly she washed, dressed and ate quickly her breakfast of toast and coffee. Muszka jumped on her lap demanding attention, pushing her head in repetitive motion against Julia's chest.

'Later,' Julia promised, carrying the cat outside to the cat flap in the shed. She returned for the bowls of food and water. It was a glorious September morning with remnants of mist curling above the ground and beams of sunshine streaming through the trees.

Before leaving, Julia checked her hair, her face, her brushed teeth in the hallway mirror. It felt strange to be a schoolgirl again, in her navy uniform and a brimmed felt hat.

Nervousness would not leave her despite her concentration as she cycled along with the morning traffic. The flutters in her stomach increased when she dismounted her bicycle at the school gates. Numbers of girls were arriving at the same time, some milling around in the school grounds, some going inside through doors in different buildings.

She had followed Miss Ogden's instructions, and here she was, being chaperoned by two friendly girls. She breathed with relief.

'This is it!' Susan pointed to the sheltered area where bicycles were parked in a neat row. Julia left hers at the end, taking her satchel off the handle bar.

'Rightee-o!' Susan gave an encouraging smile. 'Now let's survey the rest of the campus!'

She led the way and Yvonne made an attempt at small talk, while Julia wondered how she was going to remember everything that was said and shown to her, teachers' names, room numbers, corridors in the entire complex of buildings that were joined by glass-walled passages all looking very much the same. The vast assembly hall needed no explanation and Julia particularly liked the library, an open space mezzanine, accessed by a circular wooden staircase. She noted with pleasurable anticipation a substantial section of illustrated Art books.

'Time to retreat to our classroom for registration,' Susan announced, checking her watch.

Julia was not prepared for the size of the classroom, nor the number of girls, nor the noise of excited talk between friends who had not seen each other all summer. As she stopped in the doorway she had the impression of looking down on a sea of very animated faces. There had only been twelve girls in her previous class at the convent.

Susan led the way to three empty desks at the back of the classroom.

'I thought,' she said, 'you may feel more at home, Julia, sitting between us on your first day.'

'And other days, if I may,' Julia added quickly.

They sat down, Julia in the middle, Susan and Yvonne moving their chairs close to her.

'So tell me, where are you from?' Susan asked, her eyes wide open behind her glasses.

Julia explained briefly, competing with the din. She did not mention her parents' enforced odyssey across distant, foreign lands.

'So, will you be going back home, at some stage?' Susan asked.

'Home?' Julia smiled at the misunderstanding. 'We have no home in Poland. Our home is here, in Rugby.'

'Do you not feel homesick, though?' Susan persisted, well-meaning.

'My parents may be homesick. For their home before the war. But I'm happy right here.'

Yvonne gave a warm smile, her red hair flouncing around her neck.

'Good. I hope we can be friends after school. That is, if you can put up with the crowd in our house. I've got two brothers and two sisters all younger than me!'

'Really?' Julia warmed to Yvonne in an instant. 'I envy you.'

'You wouldn't,' Yvonne laughed, 'if you had nowhere to escape from them. They're there all the time. Their incessant chatter drives me up the wall.'

'I'll change places with you any time,' Julia made it sound like a joke. Inwardly she wished she had been blessed with just one sibling, just one.

'Well…' Susan paused dramatically, waiting for their full attention, 'I have no such worries any more. The house is all mine. And my parents' attention. I have two brothers Julia. James is at Caius in Cambridge, spelt C.a.i.u.s, but pronounced Keys. That's how you distinguish the initiated from the ignoramus, the way they pronounce the name of his college.'

Julia had no idea what Susan was talking about, but she put on a suitably knowing expression and nodded.

'And my older brother Bruce is in London. In the stock exchange. Works really long hours. To keep up with the States. They burn themselves out, you know, these young men, before they're thirty!'

It was like listening to a foreign language which Julia did not understand. She looked to Yvonne for clarification. Yvonne grinned.

"You must stop him, Susan. *Toute suite!* We need all the young men we can get, don't we Julia?'

Julia agreed readily, mesmerised by this mysterious talk of young men burning in the stocks, which she believed had been abandoned to history.

'Where does your father work, Julia?' Yvonne asked.

'BTH,' Julia replied simply. There was no way she could glamorise his job.

'So does mine!' Yvonne's exclamation sounded like Eureka! 'Tool making. Takes Mum out every Friday, and us to the sea every summer. Wouldn't be much good to us, burning himself out!'

'Ah!' Susan lifted a finger, like a preliminary to a long speech. 'Not everyone could do my brother's job. This conversation is getting boring. Tell me Julia, which subjects have you chosen for your A's?'

'English, History and Art.'

'Good choices, the first two. You'll be with us. Intellectuals.' Susan nodded thoughtfully to fit in with that image.

Yvonne giggled.

'Don't be put off, Julia. It'll be fun. And the Art crowd are a crazy lot too. You'll love them. That girl over there, Leatitia, she makes regular petitions for a male nude model!'

Julia laughed. For the first time that morning. She could not tell if Yvonne was serious but it did not matter.

A sudden hush fell on the class. This was followed by chairs scraping on the floor as all the girls got up. Another hush, then,

'You may sit down!' A commanding voice from the teacher's desk in front of a wall blackboard.

The girls sat down and Julia saw above their heads a middle-aged woman in a grey suit, surveying the class through her thick rimmed spectacles and waiting pointedly till the very last murmur died down.

'Most of you know me,' she spoke very precisely, 'but for those who don't, I'll introduce myself. I'm Miss Beecham, your teacher of French, as well as, in this academic year, your very own form mistress. After registration, please acquaint yourself with your timetable, to enable smooth changes of rooms throughout the day. Copies for everyone are here on my desk. As usual, the ten past nine bell will signal time for assembly.'

Miss Beecham opened the class register and began to read out the names alphabetically. Julia waited with abated breath for hers. It got to J.

'...Dorothy Jackson...Sylvia Jennings...Julia Ka...Ka?..' Miss Beecham looked up, her gaze roaming the class.

Julia raised her hand.

'That's me. Julia Kalinska'.

All heads turned round. Julia felt suddenly very hot.

'Say it again, Julia,' Miss Beecham's eyes were unblinking.

'It's Kalinska. Ka..lin..ska'.

'Thank you. Right. Shirley Lennox... Margaret Lock...'

Julia did not hear the rest, only her own voice still resounding in her head. She felt a movement and looked sideways. Yvonne was smiling, then she mouthed silently to her, 'It's OK. Don't worry!'

Somehow she had lived through the first day at her new school. She was exhausted, cycling home through the late afternoon traffic congesting around her the closer she got to the town centre. The bright, slanting sunlight was blinding as it bounced off the white pavements and the pale stone buildings. She should have remembered her sunglasses. If only she could empty her tired mind of all the images and niggling thoughts, all the detritus of the events of the day, but they, like re-runs of scenes from a film, kept crowding back with unstoppable compulsion: the assembly in the big hall, six hundred girls standing to attention in absolute silence, and only Miss Ogden's heels tapping the wooden floor as she made her way in measured steps, in regal manner, up to the stage where the teaching staff were already assembled. Then later the classes and her new teachers, so different from her old teachers at the convent school, the revered pre-war Polish professors.

Julia had a good feeling about her new teachers: the young Miss Simpson, in her light grey suit and high heels, who had introduced the class to Napoleon's family origins in her first lecture; Mr. McBride, fatherly with his gentle voice and white moustache, a touch absent-minded, yet so precisely eloquent on the subject of Victorian poets; Mr. Donley, bearded like Van Gogh, flamboyant in his electric blue shirt and a fiery yellow cravat, who had nagged and cheered on the class to produce fast five-minute sketches of the objects displayed in still life, rather than fret over laborious overworked drawings.

Julia had been glad of Susan and Yvonne's company. At the end of the day they seemed like old friends, survivors with her of a harrowing shared adventure. It had been a strain all day having to focus her mind on every word spoken in class, on the banter between her friends, on formulating her own responses, so as not to appear like an idiot. Was her English good enough? Had she made a good impression? Would they still want to be her friends?

The last hour was Dance. At long last there was something she could feel confident about. She was well adept in all the popular dances, not to mention the Polish traditional *krakoviak*, the mazurka and the polonnaise, that she and her peers had been taught from their earliest years and performed annually at all the commemorative concerts, so emotionally charged for her parents' generation. But Dance at her new school was something else: the Gay Gordons, the Lambeth Walk, the square dance, the valeta… Julia had never heard of them before. She had clung to Yvonne, frantically memorising the steps and the formations so as not to let down her friend.

Escaping the town centre traffic, Julia cycled faster down Railway Terrace, the wind cooling her face. Miro came into her thoughts, his soft gaze caressing, his smile lifting her spirits. He was never faraway, appearing in her mind in hundreds of brief pauses throughout the day. He'd be writing to her now. Her heart skipped with anticipation of his letter. She too had so much to tell him. And her old friends, Lidia and Yagoda. How had they managed on their first day in a strange school? She'd write to them first thing tonight.

At least she'd be seeing Nadia at the weekend. Poor Nadia! She had gone to church on Sunday ready to deliver her rehearsed rebuke at Leon. This had been meant to shame him into meek submission and eternal acceptance of Nadia's prominence in his life. But Leon had been absent. Only his parents were there. Nadia had acknowledged them with a charming smile and a polite 'dzień dobry', but had thought better of asking them about Leon's whereabouts.

Julia passed by Miro's house, where the front windows, like mirrors, reflected the sky, the hanging basket looked thirsty in the heat, the climbing rose shaded the locked door. Julia felt a pang of emptiness.

Her squat concrete bungalow had trapped the heat all day. Julia opened wide the doors and windows and stood for a moment in the welcome draught, cooling her face, her arms and legs. Muszka pushed at her calves demanding noisily fresh food and drink. Julia filled her bowls with tinned cat food and water and hurried to change out of her school uniform. Navy and dark blue. Still a little strange after her old uniform of a sky blue tunic and ivory blouse. Holy Mary's colours. A tug of nostalgia took her by surprise. She pulled on her casual navy slacks and a sleeveless white cotton blouse, combed through her hair and went back to the kitchen.

Now that she was home for good, she mused, her Mama would never have to rush home from work to prepare the evening meals. From now on, Julia would do it all. For tonight they had fancied *placki*. She peeled the potatoes and began the grating process, careful not to cut her fingers. She wished she could hurry time. She had so much to tell her Mama and Tato. She knew they'd be pleased with her report of excellent discipline and high expectations in her new school.

Yesterday, when they came home from work, she had surprised them with her purchases from the market. Theo's face lit up when he examined the new, dual-purpose torch. But then he put it back in the box.

'My old torch is still working perfectly all right,' he said. 'You shouldn't have squandered your money so lightly, Julia. You'll need it for your own books and Art materials.'

That had not been Julia's expected reaction from him. She had anticipated a show of great pride in her, words of praise for having been so thoughtful.

'I agree with your Tato,' Mama confirmed as she handled with care the delicate china cups and saucers, with the gold rims and dancing shepherds and their fairy-like partners. 'These are beautiful things, but do we really need them? When will we use them, Julia? Such fine posh things in this humble dwelling?'

'For Christmas and for Easter,' Julia had suggested eagerly. 'For Roman and for Eva.'

Mama had put them back in the brown paper wrapping.

'Roman and Eva know me well enough. I don't need to impress them.'

'Then for us!' Julia would not give up, her heart dropping a little.

The cups and saucers had been put away, but next time anyone came, Julia promised herself, she would take them out and serve coffee or tea the elegant way.

At the end of the week Julia received letters from Lidia and Yagoda.

'ESCAPE at long last!' Lidia wrote, 'from every housework chore and NURSING Vittorio! I never imagined I'd be so glad about going back to school. My new best friend (we do French together) is Sophia, half Polish, half Italian like me. Vittorio is still with us, hobbling around on crutches, with just Nonna for company all day. Alberto would rather stay at home with him, but Papa keeps an eagle eye on them both! I have NO complaints. MARCELLO meets me from school every day and we walk home together, so he can fulfil his Christian obligation of visiting the sick. Wink, wink!'

Julia giggled, intending to ask Lidia to describe EVERYTHING about Marcello in her next letter.

She opened Yagoda's letter.

'Dear Julia, I dreaded my first day at the English Martyrs. But I needn't have worried. It's all so open and unrestricted and very noisy and jolly. It's strange to have a boy sitting next to me in class. Robert does Latin with me.

544

I was very shy at first, but he's just like you or Lidia, can be serious, but also very funny.

My best friend is Danuta, another Polish girl. I've already been invited to her house and force-fed by her doting Mama with gigantic portions piled on my plate. In Russia, she says, this food would have been devoured in seconds by the starving children.

Danuta and I have joined the Polish Youth Club, and already on Saturday evenings we're practising the *krakoviak* and the *polonez* dances for the 11ᵗʰ of November concert.

I'm making good progress in the Dance and Drama classes too. We're doing *Sleeping Beauty* for the Christmas Panto, with additional fairies. I'm one of them!'

Strange, Julia mused, how their lives were changing. Only three months ago they were three young schoolgirls on the threshold of the yet unchartered adulthood, and now life was carrying them along with unstoppable force. And the strange thing was, it was never quite how she had imagined things to turn out. What next? she wondered.

Julia could sense something was wrong the moment her parents came through the kitchen door. She was poised over the cooker, ready to start frying the *placki*, but seeing their expressions, she turned off the gas. Tato was quiet, his brow furrowed, his mouth set. Mama said simply,

'I've had a headache all day. I'll go and lie down first. Don't wait for me with the supper.' She dropped her bag on the kitchen chair and left them. Julia looked to Tato for an explanation. He stood at the sink and scrubbed his hands under running water, his clothes reeking with the chemical factory smell.

'I don't know Julia. I hope it's not that illness again. She says it's like a feeling of being afraid all the time. Like something dreadful waiting to happen. She says people talk about her. Behind her back.'

That sinking feeling again. Poor Mama! Well, she'd talk her out of it. She would start with an aspirin, to get rid of the headache.

Her Mama was lying on the bed in semi-darkness, with the curtains drawn. She had curled herself into a tight ball, her arms hugging her knees, her eyes were closed with deep lines around them.

'Mama,' Julia touched her shoulder, 'take the aspirin, it'll help with the headache.'

She uncurled herself slowly and raised herself on her elbow. She drank the whole glass in one go.

'I feel so worn out,' she said, retracting to her previous position and shutting her eyes.

Julia lingered, not knowing what else to do. She stroked her mother's shoulder, then her face gently, pushing back her hair behind the ear.

'Go and make the supper, Julia,' Mama whispered, 'I'll be all right now.'

Hesitant, with her stomach churning, Julia went back to the kitchen and started frying the small potato pancakes.

They ate in silence, Julia and her Tato. It was oppressive, it was as if her Mama was still in hospital. Tato had changed and washed and smelled soapy and clean, and was seemingly unaware of Julia's presence or of the delicious taste of the *placki* that she had fried. She waited for him to ask about school. She wanted his praise.

'Are they as good as Mama's?'

He looked up, as if he'd just only woken up.

'The *placki*,' she prompted. She saw a change in his expression. His eyes focused on her, a softness relaxed his face.

'They were very good, Julia, thank you…'

'I've got lots to tell you,' she said, looking for interest in his expression. He sat back, took a packet of Woodbines from his breast pocket and lit one, shrouding his face in smoke.

'Shall I tell you, then?'

'What?'

She told him as she cleared the table, washed up and dried. There was no response from him.

'Well, what do you think, Tato?' she turned round. She knew that expression when he was upset; watery eyes, pursed lips, holding back, quashing feelings that must not be exposed.

She sat down beside him.

'Tato, it's only a headache. We all get headaches sometimes. Mama will be all right.' He was quiet a moment longer as he drew on his cigarette.

'You know…' he sighed, 'I've come to the conclusion, and not for the first time, that someone up there hates us, and hates us, and hates us. Our generation has been through such a lot. And every time we settle and begin to think that life at last is coming back to normality something else happens and spoils everything again.'

He carried on smoking, thoughtful, resigned.

'If you like Tato, if it'll make you stop worrying, I'll go to the surgery and explain to the doctor your concerns. What do you want me to tell him exactly?'

His eyes came suddenly to life.

'Would you do that, Julia? Would you? Just tell him your mother acts as if she's imagining things. And combined with the headache I'm just very uneasy. I want to stop that illness before it gets hold of her again.'

It had not been a part of Julia's plan to spend half the evening in the doctor's surgery, but if the doctor's advice were to appease her Tato's fears and if she could get some medication to relieve her Mama's symptoms, then that was what she had to do.

The surgery on Craven Road was a downstairs back room of his private house, painted brown and cream and furnished with a row of chairs against each of the four walls. The official time of the evening surgery was from six to eight, but if at closing time there were still twenty people waiting to consult Dr. Hemmings, he would carry on till all his patients had been seen and dealt with.

Julia was used to waiting. She brought with her *A Tale of Two Cities* to read. It was different from Dickens' other novels, his mission-driven depiction of the injustices in Victorian England. She knew the story, she had seen the film, but that did not spoil her renewed interest in losing herself in Sydney Carton's world, the noble hero who had made her cry as he stood innocent at the guillotine prepared to save someone else's life with his. '*It is a far, far better thing that I do, than I have ever done, It is a far, far better rest that I go to, than I have ever known'*. Heart wrenching stuff. The words had stuck in her mind, as memorable as the last moment of the film, when Carton's eyes look up to heaven above the menacing shape of the guillotine.

It was half past eight by the time her turn came. Dr. Hemmings, elderly, bespectacled, with a gentle thoughtful manner listened and nodded as Julia described her and Tato's fears.

'I can't treat your mother without a proper diagnosis,' he said, 'I would need to see her. Headaches can be a symptom of a variety of ailments. However, since I know her recent medical history, I can prescribe a mild sedative to help her sleep through the night. This usually makes the patient feel so much better in the daytime. See if there's an improvement in the next few days. But if you're still worried, come back with your mother next time.'

At home, Tato was sitting by the radio with the volume turned down. The screech of jamming, even with the reduced noise level, rendered the programme unintelligible. Why was he bothering at all? Julia would never be able to understand him.

'She's better,' he said with an inflection of hope in his voice, 'just having her supper. What did the doctor say?' Julia told him briefly before joining Mama at the kitchen table. She was just finishing the last *platzek* on her plate.

'Not as good as fresh fried,' Julia said. 'How are you now, Mama?'

'The headache's gone, thank goodness.' Mama dabbed her mouth with a handkerchief before taking a sip of the lemon tea. She had not changed and there was a whiff of the factory smell in her dress, yet Julia was more aware of the familiar scent of the smooth skin on her browned arms and a trace of perfume in her hair. She met her Mama's gaze and something contracted in her stomach. Her mother's brown irises had a strange haunted look about them.

'Everything will be fine, Mama,' she said with forced brightness, 'I've got a prescription for you. The tablets will make you sleep better, and if you get a good night's rest, the doctor said, you'll feel better in the day.'

Mama's gaze became distant, increasing Julia's unease, but then she said,

'I'm all right, Julia, only I don't know what to do, to stop the others talking about me. Behind my back.'

'Who?' Julia was taken aback. 'Who's talking about you?'

'The people at work. They stand in groups and say things about me. All lies.' Julia felt a shiver down her spine. Her Mama continued, 'they turn away and disperse the moment they see me coming.'

'Mama, perhaps they're just talking about their own things. Why would they say things against you?' Julia reasoned.

Her Mama's expression flared up. She stood up and took her plate to the sink and began to wash it over the soaking frying pan. She spoke over her shoulder,

'You don't know anything, Julia, but life will teach you a few bitter lessons yet.'

That night in bed, after she had written to Lidia and Yagoda and made a few preliminary notes from the library book on the essay on Napoleon, Julia attempted to read, but it was hard going. Her mind was crowded with the events of the day, her stomach churned with anxiety over her Mama's strange behaviour. She had left her sitting in the armchair after supper, staring into the empty fire grate, listening to Viennese music, which mercifully had been allowed to replace the usual unbearable shrillness blaring from Radio Free Europe. Julia had made a few attempts to start a conversation. Tato responded with a few 'Ahems...' while his eyes scanned The Polish Daily, but Mama said nothing.

'Julia,' he said in the end, 'go, do your homework. I'll stay here with Nastusha.'

'I'm not an invalid!' Mama snapped.

It was quiet now. It was the silence of emptiness, of a feeling of having been abandoned in a vast desert. Everyone was so faraway. Miro, Nadia, Lidia and Yagoda. Even Sister Alicya. She never imagined she'd miss her, this authoritative disciplinarian. Always reliable. Secure.

Julia closed the book, switched off the light and rested her head on the pillow. She could not stop them, the hot tears, gathering, spilling out of her eyes. She wiped them away and blew her nose.

'Tomorrow,' she told herself, she'd be as strong as Scarlett, 'tomorrow would be another day.' The pills would help her mother. Life would be normal again.

CHAPTER 65

Late Saturday afternoon, Julia cycled to Nadia's house. It was a windy day, with billowing clouds chasing across a grey expanse of sky, torn here and there with shards of blue. It was hard work cycling up the hill and part of the way Julia made on foot pushing her bicycle with the overnight bag tucked inside the basket attached on the handle bar. She felt like a scarecrow with her hair blown in all directions, but there was no point fretting, till she got indoors.

Nadia's parents were in the front garden weeding and tidying up the rubbish that had been blown inside their gate. Uncle Henryk's hat was pulled right down to his ears, but Aunt Eva's hair, loosened from the tie at the back, flew around her face like sinuous sea-weed. In response to Julia's greeting she stopped, and resting on the rake attempted to push the hair off her face.

'*Co nowego?* How are things?' she asked. 'How's Nastusha today? She had me worried all week,' her blue eyes expressed genuine concern. Mama and Aunt Eva worked together. Their factory produced food tins.

'She was singing today,' Julia replied cheerfully. 'That's always a good sign.'

'Good, good,' Aunt Eva nodded, her eyes still thoughtful. 'It's a relief.'

Uncle Henryk stopped raking and lit a cigarette, after a few attempts, shielding the lighter with his cupped hand. He was a thin, wiry man with hard arms that looked as if chiselled in wood.

'I don't know why you're fretting so much,' he said to his wife. 'Everyone's got their good and bad days.'

'I'm not fretting!' Aunt Eva replied, more sharply, Julia thought, than his remark merited. 'It's natural to worry about your family and friends!'

'Well, don't worry, auntie,' Julia assured her, 'Mama's really so much better today.'

She excused herself, left them to their tasks and went round the back to leave her bicycle inside their shed. Indoors Marek was sitting at the table with open books spread out before him and Zloty at his feet. The dog gave out a happy greeting sound.

'Hi Marek. Hi Zloty!'

'Hi Julia!'

'Homework?'

Marek made a face. 'Only for a few more minutes. Then I'm off round to Stewart's.'

Julia ran up the stairs to Nadia's room. It smelled like the perfumery counter at Boots. Nadia turned round from the mirror. 'I'm a silly goose!' she rolled her eyes at herself.

'Why are you a silly goose?' Julia laughed, dropping down her bag by the bed and sitting down on the edge. Walking and cycling against the wind had made her hot. She slipped off her coat and ran her fingers through her hair.

'I shouldn't have fretted so much last weekend. About Leon. You were right. He was helping his sister with the decorating. He's sent me a note. He's painting the last room today. But he'll see me after church tomorrow.'

Julia felt a prick of guilt. She was pleased to see Nadia happy again, but she still had her doubts about Leon. When was the right time to tell her? And how? But perhaps she wouldn't have to, not when everything was all right between them.

The time for summer dresses was over. They both wore slacks and jumpers, Julia her favourite red, and Nadia, a snowy white that made her dark looks appear even more oriental.

'Your hair's a mess,' Nadia scrutinised Julia severely, 'but I've got just the thing for you! Look!' From a drawer in her dressing table she took out a soft angora beret with a pom-pom. Red. 'Just your colour. It was Stella's.'

Julia did not argue. She pulled it on. It felt luxurious. Like Stella. Like London.

'Not like that!' Nadia laughed, and adjusted the beret above Julia's left eye.

'There! Now you look like a chic Parisian girl!' Julia quite liked her reflection in the mirror.

They slipped on their gabardine raincoats and ran downstairs.

'Won't you take your little brother with you?' Marek teased, a mischievous grin splitting his face.

'Sorry! Girls' night only,' Nadia answered with the haughtiness of an older sister.

'Yuk!' he made a face of utter disgust.

They went outside giggling. Aunt Eva was taking down the washing that almost blew out of her grasp. Uncle Henryk was attempting to sweep up the path against the dust and the leaves whirling around him.

'What time will you be back?' he stopped and drew on his cigarette. The smoke billowed up to his eyes.

'The film finishes about ten thirty. Then we've got the bus to catch. About eleven?'

'I'll wait up for you,' he said in a tone that meant *don't be late!*

In town, there was time to visit the café in North Street before the film. They sat by the window and watched the people go by, and as Julia sipped slowly her expensive coffee, she imagined, with a feeling of unease, what Mama would have said. *Julia! How could you! You could have bought a JAR of coffee for that!*

Nadia did not appear to have any such qualms. She drank her coffee with an air of being accustomed to such treats and talked about Leon.

'You know…' her eyes were dreamy, 'I've got a feeling he'll propose to me soon. The sooner the better, I think. I like to know where I'm going. I like my life planned. Once we get engaged, we can start saving for a deposit for a house. And once we've got a house, we can get married!'

Julia put down her cup and watched Nadia's expressions change from excited to serious, to ecstatic, to practical.

'But Nadia,' she said at last, 'what's the hurry? You're only seventeen, for goodness sake!'

'Seventeen and a half,' Nadia corrected her, 'I'll be eighteen soon. Besides, I rather fancy being a teenage bride. So romantic!' her smile became kittenish, self-pleased. 'What about you? Are you and Miro..?' Her question was rhetorical against her all-knowing look. It made Julia laugh.

'Nadia, we're simply very good friends. Besides, we know what's expected of us first. We've got to finish our studies. Find jobs.'

'But all that waiting!' Nadia was sceptical. 'What if Miro gets fed up? What if he finds somebody else?'

Julia shrugged.

'Then I can't stop him, can I? If he's interested in me enough, then he'll wait.'

'Silly pride will get you nowhere,' Nadia pronounced, her dark eyes flashing. 'You must get clever, Julia. A little cunning will take you a long way!'

Julia laughed again. She felt contented. She had received Miro's letter in the morning. He had described humorously his unexpected, discovered skills of having to pit his ingenuity against the far superior artfulness of the two-year-old Jean-Pierre in his charge, of having to twist his tongue around his school French when shopping for his cousin Celine at the food market, of having to really stretch his mind in keeping up with his male cousins' jokes when going out with them in the evenings. 'But nothing compares,' he had written, 'with my time spent with you. I miss you, dear Julia. Can't wait to see you again.' She felt a glow inside her, just remembering his words.

The cinema was packed with the Saturday crowd when they arrived. They found two seats lower down in the auditorium and settled down to watching the newsreel already in progress. There was more trouble in the Belgian Congo; there were scenes from the closing ceremony at the Rome Olympics; someone called Cassius Clay had won the gold medal for boxing; and a representative from Penguin Publishers confirmed that they were prepared to face trial rather than abandon their plan to publish *Lady Chatterley's Lover*.

The B movie that followed was a charming tale about a family of otters.

There was a break before the main feature film. The lights came on, the usherettes appeared at all the doors with their trays of refreshments, queues formed down the aisles, cigarette smoke rose in broken wisps, and curled like milky ribbons around the spotlight beams, sweets and crisps papers scrunched around them. Julia and Nadia shared the fruit jellies they had bought earlier.

'This book, they're talking about,' Nadia said, 'surely it can't be that bad if Penguin want to publish it.'

'I've no idea,' Julia replied, 'It's D.H.Lawrence. I must remember to get one of his other books next time I go to the library.'

'Funny, isn't it,' Nadia mused, 'it's always the boring stuff that they force you to read at school. George Elliot. Gawd! All that thick prose. Pages of it!' Nadia made a suffering face.

'Jane Austen was OK.' Julia reminded her, 'I was in love with Captain Wentworth all through *Persuasion*'.

'Not a patch on Rhett Butler though. Why couldn't we have had that for our 'O' levels?'

'Why?' Julia laughed, 'American? In an English Lit. exam?' It was at that moment that Julia saw him, as her gaze wandered above Nadia's head and absentmindedly scanned the auditorium. Leon. In the highest, furthest corner. He was with Alison. Slowly, she brought her gaze down to Nadia's face. Her friend was absorbed with her own questions. 'And another thing...' she was saying, 'why do some people think they are above censorship, and above everyone else and that they will decide what the rest of us are allowed to read or not?'

It was important to keep Nadia talking, to keep her looking just one way, at Julia, opposite to where Leon was sitting right at the top.

'Yes, I absolutely agree with you Nadia,' Julia felt a sudden dryness in her mouth. 'Any jellies left?' *Please guardian angel, please don't let her turn around.*

Nadia's natural chatter was a godsend for a change. She did not appear to notice Julia's monosyllabic replies. It was a relief when the lights dimmed and the film started. *Room at the Top.* With Laurence Harvey and Simone Signoret. Julia had not been prepared for such explicit openness in exposing adult matters and was a little shocked by the unfolding scenes before her, but she would never have confessed that to Nadia. As she watched with bated breath, Sister Alicya came to her mind. The nun would have been shocked too. Very shocked. That a pupil of hers was watching such stuff. Julia smiled to herself, with a touch of guilt. Minutest guilt. She was an adult now. She could make her own decisions. Besides, the viewing was compulsive.

She liked Lawrence Harvey and the young girl, Heather Sears together, but wished that someone prettier had been chosen for Simone's part. Then her sympathies shifted as the film progressed. Lawrence turned out to be a two-timing rat! Like Leon! Making Heather pregnant and Simone so unhappy! He married Heather in the end. But so what! Julia wouldn't have gone anywhere near him, after what he'd done. But poor Heather had no choice.

'Wow! What a story!' Nadia's tone said it all when the film finished. Did she get the message? Julia wondered, her eyes scanning furtively the space high above Nadia's head when the lights came on. She had sat through the film with an invisible rod prodding her back, but now felt immediate relief, seeing Leon's place empty.

They got up and joined the crowd slowly moving down the aisles towards the exit doors, onto the brightly lit staircase that mirrored the staircase on the opposite side.

'I've just seen Leon!' Nadia exclaimed suddenly. 'Look Julia, there! On the other side!' She craned her neck above the crowd, excitement beaming from every part of her face. Julia saw him too, and Alison beside him.

Pressed by the crowd from all sides, she descended the steps with a feeling of dread, of an impending catastrophe. Like Sydney Carton going to the guillotine. But Nadia was like a live wire beside her, waving frantically above the crowd to catch his attention. Julia watched his face with morbid fascination; first the recognition, then the shock, then a broad smile as if his little charade had already been resolved.

'Leon! What a surprise!' Nadia barely contained her squeal, unable to stop in the crowd which carried them along into the foyer. 'What happened? I thought you were helping your sister today.'

Julia watched Alison's bemused expression.

'I was,' Leon looked over his shoulder, 'but I finished earlier than I thought I would.'

'Then why didn't you come over? We could have gone together.'

By now they were being pushed through the open doors and down the steps. They stopped on the pavement. The crowds, at long last, loosened around them and began to disperse. Except Alison. She stood close to Leon and hooked her arm around his. Nadia's joy turned to puzzlement.

'Hallo?' She acknowledged Alison with a nod, looking to Leon for an explanation.

'This is Alison,' he said, 'a friend from work.' No hesitation. Not a trace of embarrassment.

'Just a friend?' Alison teased and clung closer.

Julia could not bear to watch. Nadia's excitement crumbled and a look of bewilderment crept into her eyes.

'Leon?' she asked.

'Nadia,' Leon was suddenly impatient, 'I've promised Alison's parents to get her home at a certain time. I've really got to go. But I'll see you after church tomorrow. OK?'

Nadia did not reply, just watched him and Alison walk away. She did not say a word on the way to the bus; she was still deep in thought when they found a seat and Julia peered into the night through the bright reflections of the bus interior, glad of the murmur of other passengers' voices. She felt like Judas, like Brutus, like the worst friend, who by definition was not a friend at all.

'Nadia…' she whispered at last, aware of other people around them, not knowing what to say, wishing she possessed some magic to take Nadia's pain away. But Nadia gave a determined nod.

'I'll give him one chance to explain himself,' she spoke softly. 'There must be an explanation. We were so close, Julia. We couldn't have been any closer. He's mine. And I'm his. This Alison must be just who he says she is. Just a friend from work. She's got it all wrong if she thinks she's someone special. It must be just a silly misunderstanding, don't you think, Julia?'

Her intense eyes bore deeply into Julia's. Julia felt sick. There would never be the right moment to reveal the unpleasant truth. She would have to do it now, even if it made her feel like an executioner delivering the final blow.

'Nadia… I've seen them together before…' She waited for Nadia's explosion, but Nadia just kept looking into her eyes as if trying to make sense of her words.

'You saw them? When?..'

Julia told her. Once at the cinema, when Nadia was in London, and another time at Woolworths. She omitted to recount the detail of Leon's payment for Alison's purchase.

'You knew? And you never told me?' Her subdued reproach was worse than the twist of a knife.

'Nadia, and what was I supposed to say? That I was suspicious? That Leon was not to be trusted? Would you have liked me for that? Would you have believed me?'

'So how long were you going to wait before telling me?' All Nadia's hurt was expressed in those words.

'I don't know… I was hoping all the time that everything would be all right in the end…' her genuine excuse sounded hollow suddenly.

'A fine friend you are!' Nadia's bitterness felt like a blow.

'See?'

'See what?'

'He's already pushed a wedge between us. And neither of us have done anything wrong.'

Nadia bit her lip and turned away. She would still not speak when they walked home from the bus. The wind had died down, the sky had cleared as a bright moon kept watch over the silver edged houses. Julia took off the beret with the pompom and shook her hair loose. She did not feel glamorous any longer, all the fun of the evening had gone. She wished she could get her bicycle out and go home, but such rashness would have made both sets of parents angry; too many questions would be asked. She was stuck with Nadia's mood till the next day.

They let themselves into the house and found Nadia's father asleep on the sofa, the television light flickering over his still form. Nadia touched his shoulder.

'We're back,' she whispered, 'you can go to bed now.'

'Good night,' Julia said and followed her friend upstairs with a heavy heart.

The silence between them was like a suffocating smoke. And to think she'd been looking forward to this evening all week. In the dark, in Nadia's double bed, Julia was aware of her friend's proximity, yet she dared not move for fear of their arms brushing against each other. She lay still, stiff as if frozen, though it was not cold. After a while she knew Nadia was crying, silently into the pillow.

'Nadia...' she whispered touching her shoulder, expecting to be pushed away.

She felt Nadia sit up and lean against the headboard and dab her eyes with a handkerchief.

'I feel such a fool, Julia, such a fool!' her lowered voice was bursting with anger. 'I trusted him! I believed him! How could I have been so stupid? He was only after one thing. And once he'd got it, he moved onto someone else. And me? I'm nothing now. Soiled goods. That's all I am! No one will ever want me!'

'Shshsh...' Julia hugged her, 'you're still the same Nadia. Beautiful and funny and clever and practical...need I go on?'

'I know what you're doing, Julia, but you can't change facts! I'm a ruined woman!'

Julia bit her lip.

'Nadia,' she applied a reasoning, calming tone, 'you're in shock. That's understandable. Give it a day or two, when you've had time to think. Then you can decide what to do.'

'Do you think it's his mother? Put him off seeing me?' Nadia hadn't listened. She was clutching at straws.

'Even if it were, in the end it's only between you and him.'

'Then I'll give him one more chance. I love him so much, Julia. I can't bear it. I can't believe he'd do anything like that to me.'

It was obvious that Nadia was too upset to be receptive of any suggestions.

'Tomorrow,' Julia said, 'in bright daylight everything will look so much better.' She wished she could believe her own words.

In the church, the next day, Nadia chose to sit at the back. 'Good vantage point,' she whispered, 'we can watch everyone coming in.' Julia knew that her friend had only one person in mind.

Julia had marvelled at Nadia's composure at breakfast time; no red eyes, no blotchy face. She had put on her Sunday best, white blouse and a navy suit to please her parents, who too were dressed up in their best clothes for church. They asked about the film and Nadia responded glibly. It was a tale about a man who was loved by two women.

'How did he do that?' Uncle Henryk asked. Julia was pleased to note a spark in his usually dull eyes.

'You've got nothing to complain about,' Aunt Eva pointed out. 'You've got three adoring women.'

'And a man,' Marek added licking jam off his fingers, 'and a faithful dog.'

'*Dobrze.* Good. I get the picture,' Uncle Henryk gave a soft chuckle. It must have been one of his good days.

'So what happened in the end?' Aunt Eva wanted to know.

'One of them died.'

'How convenient for him!' Uncle Henryk remarked.

Only it hadn't been quite as simple as that. The older woman, Simone, had drowned her rejection in drink, crashed her car and got killed. But Nadia, Julia told herself, was far too sensible to do anything stupid over her split up with Leon.

He came into the church following his parents, noticed Nadia and Julia and greeted them with his charming smile. There was no denying it; he was exceptionally good looking. Nadia acknowledged him with a nod.

Julia's parents were already there, two rows up from the back, in Mama's favourite place, partly hidden by a column.

'Less conspicuous,' she had explained, 'when I miss communion.' Julia had often been tempted to abstain herself in solidarity with her mother, but that, she knew, would have only upset her Mama. Today, however, she was going to stay at the back to keep Nadia company. Poor Nadia, how was she ever going to confess her sin? There were no diminutive terms for fornication.

Miro's parents were there with his two brothers, and Roman with Joyce and Andrew, and a host of people Julia had known since her childhood days spent in the refugee camp near Husbands Bosworth, where life was lived in a close-knit community, where confidentiality was too irksome to observe, where everyone held strong opinions about everyone else's problems and affairs, where solutions were at hand without having to resort to lawyers and experts. Julia smiled every time she remembered this haven for gossip mongers. Life was never dull.

Her mind was unsettled throughout the service. It was hard to concentrate on the dry rhetoric of the sermon. If she ever got the chance, which of course she never would, because a) she was not a man, and b) because she'd never choose to become a priest, but if ever she did, she'd tell the people a short story with a happy ending, that would send them home feeling good about themselves and ready to tackle the demands of the week ahead of them.

The service finished with the hymn sung unfailingly in all the Polish churches throughout the world: '*Lord, return to us our dear country, free.*'

Nadia moved quickly before the congregation began to crowd the central aisle. Julia followed her out of the church, to where their bicycles were parked and chained together in a recess at the back of the church.

'Aren't you going to wait for Leon?' Julia asked, keeping up with her.

'Let him look for me!' Nadia wore a look of defiance.

And indeed, he appeared just as they had unlocked the chains and were about to walk away.

'Nadia, wait! What's the hurry?' his slick smile embraced them both. 'Can I walk you home? I can explain everything.'

She straightened up and lifted her face, unsmiling.

'Leon,' she said, 'listen carefully. I've only got one question for you. And your answer has got to be a Yes or a No. Do you understand? Just one word. Nothing more. OK?'

He shrugged with a show of goodwill, then his glance skimmed Julia.

'Wouldn't you like to leave this till we're alone?'

'I'm just going,' Julia said hastily, but Nadia stopped her, with a firm grasp of Julia's arm.

'No,' she said, 'I want Julia to hear this. Are you ready Leon? The simple question is, do you love me or not?'

His face crinkled in a smile of indulgent tolerance of her misunderstanding.

'Nadia... how can you even ask?'

'Yes or No, Leon'.

He shook his head in a show of bewilderment, lifting his hand to touch her. But she brushed him off and stepped back.

'Thank you Leon. That's all I wanted to know. Goodbye! For good!' She turned her back on him, grasped the handlebar of her bicycle and began to walk away. He dashed in front of her.

'Nadia, stop! Let me explain!'

Julia squirmed. It was embarrassing to watch.

'There's nothing more to explain. I understand everything,' Nadia replied pressing onwards.

'Has Julia been telling you things?' Julia felt his gaze on her, angry, accusing.

'She didn't have to Leon. You've done it all yourself. Now let me pass!'

They left him and did not look back, taking the path behind the church to avoid the crowd and the necessary polite talk with the people they knew. Julia was overawed with Nadia's silence. In Oak Street they mounted their bicycles and Julia found herself pedalling hard to keep up with Nadia's speed. Her friend stopped at the T-junction by the Rugby School playing fields and tilting her bicycle rested on her foot.

'Don't feel sorry for me, Julia,' she said with a hardness that made Julia wince, 'I simply did what had to be done.'

'Nadia, of course I feel sorry,' Julia replied in all honesty. 'It just all feels so sad. But you're amazing, Nadia. How do you stay so calm? I'd be screaming, I'd be calling him all the worst names!'

Nadia's mouth curved wryly. Julia did not like that look.

'I do. Inside my head. I call him a bastard. A *skurvysyn*. But what's the point? It's not going to bring him back to me. What's done is done. I suppose I should feel lucky I've escaped in time. And not ended up like Heather Sears... in the film...' So, she had got the message.

'Nadia, if you want me to go back with you, then I will,' Julia offered. Nadia lifted her chin with a touch of defiance. Julia glimpsed germinating plans in that faraway look of hers.

'Thanks, but there's really no need. You've got your own things to sort out for tomorrow and I've got mine for my duty tonight.'

'But that's hours yet!'

'I'll find things to do. I'll certainly not sit around crying!'

Julia felt like crying. She wanted to put her arms around her friend. It felt like a bereavement. Like a loss of something that had all the promise of goodness and permanency about it. It was gone. Just like that. How would she be able to bear it if something like that happened to her and Miro? But he was different, wasn't he? They had been friends for so long.

'Nadia,' she spoke gently, 'you know you can cycle over any time...'

'Thanks Julia. I will,' Nadia's eyes were thoughtful, 'but next weekend I'll go to London. To Stella. I won't give him the satisfaction of thinking that I'm sitting at home moping after him. HIM!' she hissed with disdain.

'Good for you!' Julia exclaimed with a cheer she did not feel. She hugged her friend in farewell, racked with helpless sympathy, 'I'll see you soon.'

Julia waited for her parents by the clock tower in the town centre. They always walked the same route to the church and back, one and a half miles each way. It was a pleasure on sunny days, but there had been times when they returned home in drenched clothes and squelching shoes.

'This is nothing, Julia,' Mama would say shaking the rain off her coat and hanging it to dry. 'In Poland, where we lived before the war, the public transport was very sparse between the villages. We simply walked everywhere. Or, if you were lucky, you'd get a lift on a horse-cart.'

They came from around the corner, Mama in her grey autumn coat and a matching hat (a self respecting woman always wore a hat to church) and Tato, with a cigarette between his fingers and sporting his grey suit, a white shirt and a dark fedora hat with the brim pulled down to his eyes. Tato and his friends dressed like those heroes in the war-time films, Humphrey Bogart and Trevor Howard. The church on Sundays was packed with their doubles.

Julia watched Mama with anxious keenness as they approached, but all seemed to be well. Mama's animated voice preceded her as she explained some family connection between Mrs. Sroka they had just met at the church, and

558

someone her Mama had known in the past. In Siberia. Then in Persia. During the war.

'*Wszystko dobrze?*' Mama asked, 'Did you have a nice time?'

Julia fell in step with them, pushing the bicycle with her overnight bag inside the basket attached to the handlebar. 'It was very good,' she said, 'a really interesting film. A slice of real life.'

'Real life... I could tell you a thing or two...' her Tato remarked to no one in particular.

'I didn't see you in church,' a hint of reprimand from Mama.

'That's because we were in the back, Mama. But I saw you.'

'So why didn't you go to communion?'

This was a hard one to explain.

'I kept Nadia company. She was a little upset.'

Mama's dark amber eyes widened with a question.

'So what has she been up to?'

'Oh, nothing major. Just a misunderstanding with Leon.'

Mama thought for a moment.

'Don't treat religion lightly, Julia,' she said. 'When you've got nothing left, that's the one thing that gets you through the worst.'

'Mama, as if I would!'

Tato coughed through the smoke.

'Roman's coming round later,' he said. 'It's ages since we've had a good game of chess.'

'I'd rather go for a walk with Joyce,' Mama said. 'Make the most of this weather while it lasts.'

It was indeed a complete change from the previous grey and windy day; the clear sky was one unblemished backdrop to the glowing globe of the sun that gilded the crowns of the trees down Park Road, and intensified the reds and the oranges of the flowerbeds in the park.

'I've still got an unopened jigsaw from last Christmas,' Julia remembered, 'Andrew may like to have a go.'

After their Sunday dinner, in the late afternoon, when Tato went outside for a smoke and Julia helped Mama to prepare the table for their friends, Julia was surprised and thrilled that Mama had unwrapped the new china cups. There was also a new serving plate with a matching set of side plates, decorated with pink roses.

'These are lovely,' she said smiling, as she wiped them clean. 'When did you get them?'

'Yesterday. At the market. For your sake Julia,' Mama gave her a wry smile, looking up from slicing her home-baked honey and apple cakes, 'so you don't feel ashamed of me.'

'Mama! How could you say such a thing!' Didn't she know how hurtful her words were? Mama shrugged and continued to arrange slices of cake on the serving plate. After a while she said,

'Sometimes I don't know what to think any more. Sometimes I'm not sure who's right and who's wrong. All I ever wanted, Julia, was to have an ordinary life, doing ordinary things, being able to do the right thing and not having to battle with obstacles all the time.'

Julia knew that Mama was referring to the ban on her receiving communion. Did she really think Julia would ever be ashamed of her?

'Mama,' she spoke fervently, 'Mama, you must know how much Tato and I love you. We'll always love you. And what about Eva? What about Roman? You couldn't have wished for better friends. They're like gold. A hundred percent true!'

'Yes… they are…' Mama appeared distracted. 'It's hard to explain… I just get so bogged down with all those thoughts in my head… and I can't get rid of them. At times I feel so worn out I wish I could just go to sleep and not wake up ever… not for a long time,' she corrected herself. 'Not until my mind is totally clear and my heart as light as a feather…'

Her Mama's words startled her. She had thought she knew her so well, yet she had not realised the full extent nor the unyielding tenacity of her mother's anguish.

'Mama,' she spoke gently, going up to her to give her a hug, 'please try to be happy today. It's always nice when Roman and Joyce are around. We'll go for a walk later. The fresh air will do us all good. Blow away the cobwebs.' She was babbling. She felt so inadequate. But Mama returned the hug and appeared to perk up suddenly.

'You're right, Julia. I'll just go, put some fresh lipstick on.'

When Roman, Joyce and Andrew arrived in their grey and maroon Hillman, Mama was ready for them, standing on the doorstep, leaning her hand on Tato's shoulder, waving away his cigarette smoke, a welcome smile lifting her face.

Julia's mind could not stop going over the events of the day when she was in bed that night, ready for Monday, her files and books sorted in the satchel, her laundered and ironed uniform draped over the chair. She had another week to finish her essays in English and in History. She was looking forward to seeing Susan and Yvonne and the double period of hockey and netball at the end of the afternoon.

It had been quite a weekend with all the drama around Nadia and Leon. She could not stop thinking about her friend and she wished Miro was here. She had reread his letter so many times, and each time his words, 'I miss you, dear Julia. Can't wait to see you again,' stood out off the page and made her tingle inside. And Mama, she had been so like her old self all afternoon, serving cake, pouring tea, remembering the 'good times' with Roman, doing her best in her broken English to engage with Joyce, and later, when the table had been cleared and the chessboard and the jigsaw came out, she had leaned over Andrew's shoulder helping him to find the correct pieces, despite his good-natured protestations and the involuntary tilt of his head to dodge her hand that would surreptitiously brush over his hair.

'Mama,' Julia said at last, laughing, 'what about your walk? Aren't you going?'

'Yes, I suppose I ought to,' Mama had replied, reluctantly drawing herself from the table. 'Shall we? *Pójdziemy?*' she asked Joyce.

'*Pójdziemy!*' Joyce replied naturally in Polish, with a pleased smile.

Julia was shaken awake from her deep sleep. She lifted herself up with a start, her mind still lingering behind in a dream. Automatically she switched on the bedside light. Mama was sitting beside her. The unexpected sight made her flinch.

'Mama! What's happened? What time is it?' The alarm clock showed twelve minutes past two.

Her mother was in her nightdress, her hair was dishevelled and flattened on one side, she had a wild terrified look in her eyes and she was gripping to her chest a wad of newspapers with both her hands.

'They're writing about me, Julia. And it's all lies!'

A strange sensation ran down Julia's spine, like an army of ants.

'What are you saying Mama?' she felt a quickened beat of her own heart.

'They are, Julia, I'm telling you, they are!' Mama's voice grew agitated.

Julia had to appease her. She softened her voice.

'Show me, Mama, show me. Where?' This was bizarre.

Mama's fingers loosened round the wad of newspapers. Julia took the copy from the top. She scanned the page with her feverish eyes for her mother's sake. It was an old newspaper from the end of August.

'Mama, it's all political stuff, look! Troubles in South Africa, troubles in Jordan. There's a bit about East Berlin. The border being closed to the West. Typical! I can't see your name written anywhere!' God, was she really saying this?

Mama shook her head at her and there was that frightening look in her eyes, that accused Julia of being insane.

'But that's obvious! Can't you see that Julia? Can't you see that it's all written in code? Those who are responsible for spreading those lies, know exactly how to get at me!'

This was turning into a nightmare. Julia felt cornered. Her unease was fast growing into panic.

'Shall I wake up Tato?' she asked.

Mama's expression changed, softened, her eyes slowly losing that intense, frightening look.

'What for? He needs his sleep.'

'You need it too, Mama. And so do I.'

Julia held her breath when Mama stood up, placed the newspapers on the dressing table, walked round to the other side of Julia's bed and slipped underneath the covers. Their sides were touching. Julia's body stiffened, as if she were touching a stranger.

'Switch off the light, Julia,' Mama said, her eyes already closed, and when Julia did, she said, 'hold my hand, just for a moment.'

In the dark, on top of the covers Julia's hand sought her mother's. She clasped it firmly. Mama gave out a deep shuddering sigh. Her hand was work-worn and rough like sand paper.

As Julia stroked her hand, her Mama's breathing became slow and rhythmic after a while. Her own jangled nerves settled slowly with this soothing motion. Something broke inside her. She could not stop the tears. Tears of terrible grief, for there had been a moment when a sudden fear had dominated her love for her mother.

CHAPTER 66

Mama was gone in the morning when the alarm clock woke Julia up at seven. So, all was as it should be then, she hoped, her Mama was at work, safe with Tato. Yet Julia felt no relief. The house was hollow without them. Dead.

She sat up and there was Muszka, nuzzling against her arm, her contented purring like a declaration of love. A rush of tenderness swept over Julia. She hugged the cat to her chest. Muszka did not change. She brought normality into Julia's shaky world.

All through the day, fear like a prickly ball of thistle rolled up and down her spine. She did her best to concentrate on taking notes on Napoleon's military campaigns. Miss Simpson spoke with great enthusiasm, like someone who knew her subject well. On reflection, (and Julia deliberately whipped up her indignation to stifle her personal turmoil) this great Napoleon was nothing more than a ruthless, power obsessed tyrant. How many millions suffered misery and death in the wake of his wars? Was this how Hitler and Stalin would be viewed by future generations? Skilful military strategists rather than genocide perpetrators?

Her head was still filled with thoughts of such injustices when she settled down to Mr. McBride's lecture on Dickensian London. Such abject poverty among the lowest class, such thoughtless exploitation of young children's labour! Thank goodness for philanthropists like Dickens himself or the noble lady Burdett Coutts! Mr. McBride's fluent eloquence conjured up harrowing images, yet even these could not eliminate Julia's anxieties over her Mama.

She managed to lose herself for a blissful short while in her painting of still life, an exercise to be judged for the use of complementary colours. Later, she forced mirth into her remarks and a look of avid attention when she listened to her friends' accounts of their weekend activities; Susan's day in Oxford concluding with theatre in the evening; Yvonne's family picnic in the country. Such pleasant, such sane things! How she envied them! She did not tell them about her Mama. She knew what she had to do. But would Mama listen? Would she agree to see Dr. Hemmings?

As the afternoon wore on, as home time got closer, the burden of the inevitable duty pressed heavy on her shoulders.

At home, before she set about dusting and ensuring the front room looked tidy to perfection, (would Mama notice?), she fetched some root vegetables from the back garden, potatoes, onions, carrots and turnips, washed them, peeled them, diced them as she had watched Mama do, and left them to simmer with the thickening barley and lentils.

There was a letter in the post for her parents, addressed in Sister Alicya's writing. Julia was intrigued. She could not imagine why her former class mistress would write to them and not to her.

Her heart beat faster at the sounds of her parents' voices outside the kitchen door. How to act? As if nothing had happened in the middle of the night? They came in and she hugged them in turn, afraid to look directly into Mama's eyes. But Mama went straight to the cooker.

'*Mmmm, coś dobrego*! Something smells good,' she said, lifting the lid off the pot, 'and it looks ready!' There was a smile on her face when she turned round. Julia smiled back, for the first time that day feeling strangely light-headed.

'*Jest list do was.* There's a letter for you Mama, and Tato,' she said. 'It looks like Sister Alicya's writing.'

Mama tore open the envelope and Tato looked over her shoulder as they both read. Their serious expressions relaxed slowly, then Mama nodded, giving Julia the letter.

'*Naturalnie*! Of course we'll do it. Read it Julia and tell me what you think.'

Sister Alicya was appealing to their kindness to host a pupil from the convent school for the week of the half-term break. 'Klara,' she wrote, 'would benefit much from a family atmosphere. Her own parents live in Germany. The distance and the prohibitive cost of travel reduce her visits home to just twice a year.'

Julia knew Klara, the sullen looking girl from a lower form. If only it had been someone else, someone closer to her age.

'It'll be like babysitting her all week,' she said.

'*Nie*, it shouldn't be,' Tato reasoned kindly, 'I'm sure you'll have plenty of ideas on how to entertain you both.'

'But Tato, you don't know what she's like! I've never seen her smile or be nice to anyone!'

'Well, there's a task for you then!' Tato replied, going to get changed.

Julia looked at Mama. Her deep amber eyes appeared distant. A prickle of fear again.

'Mama,' she risked, 'are you feeling all right?'

She came out of her trance.

'I'm just thinking Julia. So long after the war, and there are still families forced to live apart. There must be a reason why your friend is here, being cared for by the nuns, and not at home with her parents.'

'She's not really my friend, just a girl I know. She's only fourteen.'

'All the more reason why we should be kind to her and make her welcome,' Mama said with unexpected firmness, but Julia's mind was preoccupied with her own niggling thought. What if Mama had another strange turn during Klara's stay? Then the nuns would find out. Everyone would know. A sick feeling coiled inside her stomach.

'Mama, it's not too late to write back if it's not convenient,' she said, her voice trailing off small.

Mama turned from the door and gave Julia a puzzled look.

'*Nie martw się.* Don't worry. Everything will be fine. In fact,' her face suddenly lit up, 'I'll get some wool from the market and start knitting her something nice. What colour do you think she'd like?'

Julia was astonished at the change in Mama's mood. Perhaps, after all, this unplanned event would benefit everyone in the end.

'I've no idea, Mama,' she said, 'but I think that any pastel colour will be a hundred times better than all those depressing blacks and greys, and the horrible brown stockings.'

'That's settled then,' Mama said. 'Write to Sister Alicya tonight. Tell her, we'll be delighted.'

Julia did. Her mind was flooded with thoughts of her old school. Her friends, the strict, ordered timetable of the weekdays, the relaxed atmosphere at the weekends, the reading in bed for pleasure, the walks, the Girl Guides' open bonfires, the jolly sing-songs.

As she finished the letter and sealed the envelope she pondered about girls like Klara. There had been quite a few at her old school, their lives still overshadowed by the fallout from the war. Orphaned girls, fostered girls, adopted girls, girls from broken families. She had been perceived as one, from an 'irregular' family. That was ridiculous. She had both her parents. And she loved her Tato.

In bed that night, Julia fantasised about visiting Poland one day, perhaps even finding her father. She was not aware of any feelings towards him other than curiosity. He'd be forty- nine now, three years older than Mama. Was he tall? Slim? Good looking? Or worn, like most of her friends' parents she knew. Did he ever think about her? About his wife? What had possessed him to behave the way he did? His actions all those years ago still had the power to affect her mother.

But tonight, Julia cheered herself, Mama appeared well, even hummed to herself as she pruned and watered the house plants and did a little hand washing of a few small things. Julia closed her eyes and, drifting into sleep, prayed there wouldn't be any more wake-up calls in the middle of the night.

Miro had written, 'I'll be on the 8.30pm. train from London. Will you be able to meet me?'

It had thrilled her to know that of all people he had wanted her to be there.

Julia stood on the platform and watched the hands of the station clock jerk rhythmically towards the time of his arrival. Any minute now. Her excitement was overshadowed however with niggling thoughts that this was just a flying visit home, his return from France. On Sunday he'd be leaving again to start his very first term at the London School of Law.

She shivered. It was chilly on the dimly lit platform. First of October tomorrow. The prospect of the winter months, of the black long evenings, without him, touched her with a strange melancholy.

She had missed him, and she would miss him again. There had been evenings when she longed to escape Mama's erratic moods, to run down the road, round the corner, into the lively and warm atmosphere of Miro's home. She was certain his parents would have made her welcome, but without him there, it would have been thoughtlessly self-indulging to take up their time.

She worried about Mama. Her moods had become inconsistent for no apparent reason. Some evenings after work, she was apathetic and distant; on other evenings, she appeared possessed with unsettling energy, rushing about the house, cleaning and dusting, as if her life depended on it. Her initial, puzzling euphoria at the prospect of Klara's visit at half term had been short-lived. Julia had had to coax her to go to the market to buy some knitting wool. Finally, to Julia's relief, she allowed herself to be persuaded, and with Julia's discreet suggestions, she chose a soft blue pastel shade. Klara should be pleased. Some evenings when Mama sat knitting, lost in her own thoughts, therapeutic Julia had hoped, it felt almost like old times. Julia would rest beside her in breaks from writing essays and tell her about school and her friends. She would be rewarded with an occasional nod, while Mama's eyes stayed fixed on her busy hands.

Julia had looked to Tato for support, for his lead in persuading Mama to see Dr. Hemmings.

'You worry too much, Julia,' he reassured her when Mama was out of earshot one evening, scrubbing and bleaching the bathroom till the house smelled like a hospital. 'We all have our good and our bad days.'

'But Tato...', Julia pointed at the blaring radio and covered up her ears. He did not turn the volume down but rose and went into the kitchen. She followed him in a haze of cigarette smoke. When he sat down at the kitchen table, the front of his jumper sprinkled with cigarette ash, she resumed her plea. 'But Tato, it's not normal the way Mama is these days. Those awful silences. And then the frantic cleaning marathons. And the strange look in her eyes. As if she was somewhere else. It's scary! What are we going to do?'

He drew on his cigarette and studied the patterns on the tablecloth.

'Julia, if she doesn't feel like talking, why make her? If she feels like being busy, why stop her? She doesn't need people dictating to her. She's had enough of that in her life.'

'I'm not talking about the past, Tato. I'm worried about her now. She wasn't like this before…' how could she explain, without sounding peevish, that she needed her Mama to be like a proper mother, interested in her, supportive, sympathetic, demonstrative of her love. 'Tato, are you really happy with things as they are?'

He raised his grey eyes to her, wise, resigned.

'*Moja kochana*. My dear Julia, there have been many things in my life that I didn't like. You can't have always everything that you want. Your Mama's not doing anybody any harm. Let her be. Anyway, she enjoys Saturday evenings with Roman, doesn't she? There's nothing wrong with her then, is there?'

That was true enough. Roman came round to play chess, Mama's mood would perk up and they would reminisce over tea and cakes for hours about people they had known in the past. Hundreds of them. Sometimes Mama would be persuaded to accompany Tato to Roman's house. Julia was glad then. She knew Joyce's gentle manner would draw Mama out of her silent world.

One Saturday evening, when Julia had stayed in alone, Nadia had cycled over to see her. The weekend in London with Stella had been good, she said, the usual sparkle dimmed in her dark eyes, but, she had said, she could not afford such excursions every weekend.

'Anyway,' she had assured Julia, 'I'm well and truly over Leon. I don't need escapes from my own home town. You've not seen him by any chance?'

Julia had not. Not by chance nor in church.

'I wonder what he's up to these days?' Nadia could not help herself, 'I bet he's too ashamed to show his face!'

Julia wished she could have produced some words of wisdom that would stop Nadia all that scab-picking.

'Nadia, You're too good for him! Don't waste your feelings and your time on someone who's not worth it!' She almost winced at her own cliches but then pressed on. She had to. For Nadia's sake. 'You know what? I can see you going right to the top. It'll be Matron Bzovska, before long!'

This made Nadia laugh, but Julia glimpsed that familiar fire in her friend's dusky eyes.

'Do you really think so?'

'Of course I do! What's there to stop you?'

Nadia's expression took on a speculative, dreamy look and her lips curled at some imaginary scene in her mind.

On another occasion when Nadia had been still fretting about Leon, she had simply repeated Miss Ogden's message from the school assembly.

'You know what, Nadia? Our headmistress has just reminded us about Mrs. Pankhurst's achievements for womankind. She's just died. Seventy-eight. An extraordinary woman!'

'Who?'

'Emmeline Pankhurst. The suffragette.' Julia enunciated each word slowly.

Nadia's glazed look flared up.

'What's that got to do with me?'

'Everything! She fought for our rights, Nadia. For ordinary girls like you and me. Miss Ogden said we must not waste such a precious legacy.'

Nadia shook her head, still puzzled.

'She said,' Julia pursued with expressed patience, 'this was not just about our rights to vote. This was about us, women, and about how others perceive us, and for others to value us, we must value highly ourselves and our worth.'

Nadia thought for a moment.

'That's all very well, but how does that help us to get a man?'

Julia had laughed then.

'Nadia, *moja kochana*, you don't have to GET a man. He'll come looking for YOU. Especially when he believes he's getting a treasure.'

'Your Miss Ogden said all that?' Nadia was incredulous.

'Yes. She did,' Julia chuckled, 'in respect of our chosen careers.'

'A...h!' Nadia exclaimed, 'I thought so!'

At the sound of the approaching train all thoughts dispersed from Julia's mind and a thrilling shot of excitement buoyed her up as if she were about to fly. The bright yellow windows whizzed by like a film roll, slowing down, then coming to a stop. Doors were pushed open, a crowd spilled out of the carriages and for a split second Julia feared that Miro hadn't arrived. Then, a few doors down, she caught sight of a suitcase being thrust forward, with Miro behind it, holding on, balancing it down the two steps onto the platform.

'Miro! I'm here!' she ran towards him.

He responded by turning round with undisguised joy in his face.

'So you've come!'

And then he did something he had never done before. He opened his arms wide, wrapped them around her and drew her close to him, tight against his chest. She could feel his heartbeat, his energy rippling through his body, she inhaled the scent of him, a mixture of cigarette and train smell in his clothes, a whiff of lavender on his face. He made her tremble. It was all so unexpected. It was such bliss! She felt his warm breath against her hair as he spoke,

'I've missed you so much! Did you miss me?' He released her to look into her eyes.

'Did I miss you?' Julia laughed, throwing her head back, 'Miro, I've been counting the days, all the time you were away. And since yesterday, hours and minutes!'

'Really?' he asked, but she knew from the exhilaration in his voice that he knew how she felt.

And then they both laughed and both talked at once, oblivious of the crowd rushing to the exit, oblivious of the station master's whistle and the train's departing sounds.

When they were the only ones left on the platform, Miro spoke with laughter lingering in his voice,

'I suppose we better go.'

'I've got my bicycle outside,' Julia said, 'for your suitcase.'

They walked the short distance home with the bicycle between them and Miro's suitcase balancing across the seat and the handle bar. Julia did not like this part of the road just outside the station, dark and deserted at night time, hemmed in on one side by the factory walls, and on the other side cast in deep shadows of the tall hedgerow. Yet strangely, with Miro at her side she could have walked to the edge of England.

He described his stay in France with his cousins. It had been good, but as they all worked he had to make himself useful and help out with any jobs being done around their houses. He had become very fond of little Jean-Pierre, and naturally, he hoped his French had improved, but he had missed home.

'They were all very good to me,' he said, 'but I wanted to be here with you.'

'I wouldn't have made a very good French teacher,' Julia replied grinning. 'Besides, I've been very busy too.' She told Miro about her school work, about her teachers, about her friends. 'In addition, I've been worrying about my Mama. She's not been too well.'

'Isn't she supposed to be taking some medication?' Miro was serious now.

'She should. But she's not very communicative. I simply don't know how to approach her without having my head snapped off. And when I try to discuss it with Dad, he says I worry too much. He's a bit of an ostrich, I think, much as it hurts me to say that.'

'I'll see them tomorrow,' Miro promised brightly. 'Have a chat with them. And I think you need cheering up. How about going to the cinema?'

'That would be just lovely!' Julia exhaled with happiness.

They walked past the wide open playing field, its far end dissolving in the darkness, over the river bridge, from which the brighter lights and the row of local shops could be seen. Outside Miro's front gate, Julia felt a surge of regret at their parting.

'What time tomorrow?' she asked.

'Three? Four? As soon as I get myself sorted for Sunday. We could go for a walk round the town first,' he suggested, 'then coffee, then the cinema.'

'Yes, let's do that!'

He pulled the suitcase off the bicycle and placed it on the ground. She waited for his embrace, her body tingling. He held her close for a moment, too short a moment.

'I've got a book for you,' he said, 'I'll bring it tomorrow.'

'A trick book?' she laughed, remembering their childhood ruse of using a book as an excuse to see each other after school hours.

'A real book,' he chuckled, then added seriously, 'I think you'll like it.

Bonjour Tristesse, by Francoise Sagan. She's only in her early twenties, but already a big name in France.'

'Will I do her justice with my school French?'

'I got you the English version. And...' he smiled happily, 'a surprise present too.'

'What is it?'

'It won't be a surprise if I tell you now, will it?'

She wanted to hug him. 'Go inside Miro,' she said, 'your Mum and Dad have been waiting for you all evening.'

At home, having left her bicycle in the shed, Julia entered the house through the back door to the sounds of '*The Red Poppies of Monte Cassino*'. Tato had a selection of records with army and patriotic songs and played them often as an alternative to the Radio Free Europe. He was sitting in his armchair reading the story of Voytek the bear, the Polish army mascot, who had been rescued as a cub and had travelled with the army through all the tribulations of the war years, to enjoy his retirement in a Scottish zoo. Mama was knitting in her armchair. She did not look up when Julia came in.

'*Wszystko dobrze*? Everything all right? So, how's Miro?' Tato asked peering over the rims of his spectacles.

'*Wszystko dobrze*. Everything's fine. But I think he's glad to be home,' Julia replied smiling, willing Mama to look up at her. 'Not for long though. He's off again on Sunday. To start his first term in London. We thought, tomorrow, we'd go to the cinema.'

Mama continued to knit without a pause, but Tato asked,

'Anything good on at the cinema?'

'I don't know. It'll be just nice to have a change from doing schoolwork. The newsreel is always informative,' she added for good measure. 'Shall I make tea?'

She busied herself in the kitchen and came back with three lemon teas served in proper glasses she had bought at Woolworths.

She sat down next to her Mama and repeated an edited version Miro's account of his stay in France.

'He's a good lad,' Tato remarked, 'mature for his age.'

'Yes,' Julia agreed readily and looked into Mama's face waiting for her response. But Mama remained silent, only her hands working fast.

Mama was still quiet and preoccupied with her own thoughts the next morning. Julia waited till her parents got ready and went out to do their weekly shopping, then she set about the housework. To surprise and please Mama. She went round the linoleum floors with a damp mop and round all the surfaces with a duster. She cleaned the bathroom and the kitchen tops.

Then she sat down at her desk to add a page or two to her essay in progress. The title they'd been given was Napoleon's quote: 'If the English had let me, I would have lived in peace.' Discuss.' It was a challenge. It was like detective work, pulling together all the relevant facts, events, places and dates, building a narrative from pages of notes scribbled in Miss Simpson's lectures, and notes that she had gleaned from her own research. There were so many books on Napoleon; impossible to read them all.

'When you have five minutes,' Miss Simpson had suggested with a mischievous smile, 'read Thackeray's *Vanity Fair*. He captures wonderfully the spirit of the times. Wellington's officers attending a ball the night before Waterloo. I recommend particularly that chapter.'

Julia read avidly in bed every night, and this was the *up* side, she had to admit, of not having the distraction of television, yet she longed to own a set one day, every time her tired brain felt dizzy and her vision became blurred from scanning miles of print.

This morning, thoughts of Miro kept interrupting her concentration. Outside her window the rowan berries hung in deep red shiny clusters, just like the beads of a coral necklace. Miro had promised to replace the other, broken one. Did he still remember? It did not really matter now. Her mind was already racing ahead to the afternoon, to the leisurely walk in town, his hand holding hers, coffee by the clock tower, then the cinema. She could hardly wait. It was a perfect October day, sunny, with the remnants of summer still in the air.

Miro came round in the late afternoon, long after her parents' return from the town, long after lunch which she had prepared, which Mama did not comment about, nor about the polished surfaces around the house.

'Sorry Julia,' he sounded out of breath as if he'd been running, 'I just couldn't get away. So much to do before tomorrow. These are for you.' He handed her some French magazines with a wrapped package on the top. She guessed it was the book. There was excitement in his face and his eyes appeared eager for her approval.

'Thank you. Thanks a lot!' she smiled, her heart quivering between anticipation of the evening ahead of them and the anxiety about Mama's unresponsive behaviour. If they hurried now, there would be less chance of things going wrong.

She led Miro into the front room, where her Tato had spread out old Polish papers on the table and was cutting out articles for his scrap book. Mama was in the kitchen.

'Mama, Miro's here!'

Mama came out wiping her hands on her apron, her eyes on Miro, her face softening with a pale smile, but remained standing at the kitchen door. Miro greeted her parents, shook hands with them and was invited to sit down for a while. Julia felt flutterings of nervousness in her stomach, but Miro took

571

his time to observe the protocol of good manners and make polite conversation. Only with Miro it was not stilted or forced; his words flowed easily, he asked about their work and about their latest news. Julia watched Mama's reactions, willing her hard to be responsive and welcoming. It was a relief to see her nod and even smile a little, but there was something edgy about her stance.

'Miro, would you like coffee or tea?' she asked in the end.

He gave her a charming smile as he stood up.

'That's very kind,' he said, 'but no, thank you. We're just about to go off to town.'

It happened then: Mama's hands began to shake and a look of fear came into her eyes.

'I don't want you to go. I forbid it!' Her voice was shaky, desperate.

Julia felt her stomach twist. Miro's smile stiffened for a moment. Then his face became concerned. Julia threw Tato a desperate glance. He appeared frozen stooping over his cuttings on the table.

'Mama, what are you saying?' she spoke in her most pacifying tone. 'It's just us. Just Miro and me. We're not going anywhere far. Just into town.' She attempted to place her hand on Mama's arm, but was shrugged off in an agitated manner.

'You don't understand!' Mama cried, 'Nobody understands! You're in danger, Julia! I don't want you to go anywhere. I forbid it!'

Julia looked helplessly at Miro. Her lips trembled. He stepped close to her mother, and in a gentle voice he said,

'Mrs. Anastazia, I promise you, Julia will be absolutely safe with me. Please don't worry about her.'

Mama's eyes looked huge with some hidden terror, then in an electrifying moment, a sudden change swept over her. Her expression crumbled, like a child's, and she began to cry, loud, racking sobs.

'Mama!' Julia stretched out comforting arms, and this time there was no rejection. Her Mama allowed herself to be led to her armchair. She sat down, covered her face with her hands and rocked, her cries calming down, her pleading becoming intense.

'Don't go Julia, please don't go!'

Julia sat down beside her, her arm around Mama's shoulders.

'I won't go anywhere, Mama, I'll stop here with you.' She looked up into Miro's and Tato's concerned faces, and to her annoyance, felt tears prickle her eyes. She watched Miro beckon to Tato to follow him into the kitchen, she heard them whisper behind the half-closed door, but Mama seemed unaware of her surroundings. She held onto Julia's hand and rocked.

They came back after a short while and Tato said,

'I'll cycle over to the surgery. Miro's coming with me.'

Left alone with her mother, Julia felt crushed. It was as if normality was being destroyed around her. Why was this happening to them? Why couldn't her mother remain the gentle, loving Mama of her childhood? Like Aunt Eva. Or Mrs. Joyce. It was all so unfair!

She stroked Mama's hand, thin and scrawny, yet with shapely rounded nails, and watched her body calming down and becoming still. Mama rested her head against the back of the armchair and closed her eyes. Even in repose her face looked troubled. There were lines between her eyebrows, and creases around her mouth. Her young self looked down from the sepia photograph on the wall with those beautiful dark eyes. It was hard to imagine she had been that young girl once, like herself, Julia. What had been her dreams then? What had happened in between to turn her into this bewildering stranger?

Julia made a resolution to ask Mama about the diaries; soon, at the first opportune moment, on one of the good days when Mama could be approached without the fear of a backlash.

She could not stop the bitterness within her, as she imagined what her day could have been like. Instead, she felt like a prisoner in her own house.

Muszka materialised suddenly and rubbed herself against the furniture before jumping onto Julia's lap, which she kneaded for a short while before settling herself against Julia's stomach with much contented purring. Mama appeared asleep and unaware of the cat. Normally, no matter what mood, she never refused Muszka the fuss and the petting that the cat demanded of her.

Tato and Miro returned within forty minutes.

'The surgery's officially closed now for the weekend,' Miro said, 'but your Doctor Hemmings is a really decent man. He opened the door for us and when we explained the problem, he wrote out a prescription for the time being and made an appointment to see your Mama on Monday.'

Relief swept over her. Though nothing much had happened, there was hope of a change, at least.

'Thanks, Miro.' She appreciated his assistance, as she was sure that her Tato must have too, never too confident with his imperfect English.

Mama opened her eyes. She looked disorientated.

'Has anything happened?' she asked.

'Nastusha, *moja kochana*,' Tato stooped over her, 'we got you some medication. Dr. Hemmings says you must take two tablets now. They will make you sleep and you'll feel so much better afterwards.'

Mama's expression was riddled with uncertainty, then suddenly alertness returned to her eyes. She looked at Julia.

'Julia, you mustn't go anywhere. You must stay here, at home. You must listen to me. You must!'

Julia had no intention to argue. She had already given up on her planned day.

'Don't worry Mama, I'll stay at home.'

She watched Tato lead Mama away to the bedroom, and when she was left alone with Miro, she wanted to cry. Soon he'd be going too.

'I'm so sorry Miro, that it's worked out like this. Thanks again for helping out Dad.'

'Don't mention it,' he said with warmth, 'I'll just nip back home and bring a few things to show you.'

His words astonished her. Something soared inside her.

'You mean?.. you're coming back?'

'Of course I'm coming back,' he smiled. 'Where else would I want to go?'

'But I thought… the town… the cinema…'

'Julia, all those things were sort of planned, because of you. But whether it's in town or right here, it makes no difference to me, as long as we're together.'

'Really?' She wanted to throw her arms around him, to hold him close. She was aware of a change taking place within her. All the resentment and frustration were fading away and something else was filling their place, inflating her heart with happiness. She knew it was love. She was unshakeably certain. *I love* you she wanted to say, she wanted to repeat it again and again. But she could not say these words out loud, not before he said them first.

While her Mama slept and Tato pottered around the house, she and Miro sat at the kitchen table, with books and magazines spread out before them. Julia made tea and cut slices of apple and plum cakes, which her Mama had made two nights before on one of her action packed evenings.

Miro took a sip of tea, then fumbled in his breast pocket, a pleased, mysterious look on his face.

He placed a small white flat box in front of her.

'The surprise present,' he said.

This was indeed a surprise. She had forgotten about it in all the commotion before. With barely controlled anticipation she removed the lid and lifted the tissue paper. Coiled inside the box was a coral necklace, rich red, the beads perfect shiny globes, all the same size. She was breathless.

'I don't know what to say!'

'But do you like it?' His eyes sparkled, his smile was broad.

'Do I? Miro! It's just… but… the cost!'

He chuckled.

'Don't worry about that! I had some savings. And my cousin in France has contacts. In the jewellery business. He sorted it all out for me!' Miro picked the necklace out of the box and fastened it round Julia's neck, against her white jumper. She fingered it delicately, feeling its smoothness, like that of glass marbles, yet warm on her skin.

'How can I ever thank you enough?'

'Just enjoy wearing it,' he said. He picked her hand and pressed it to his lips, palm up. This send a tingle up her arm. Gently, she withdrew it. In case her Tato walked in.

They flicked through the magazines and talked and exchanged all the latest news and she giggled a lot at his descriptions of his cousins' romantically motivated escapades that somehow never quite had worked out as planned. They played scrabble and vied with each other for supremacy in coining new words. When it got dark, Tato settled down to his reading by the radio in the front room.

'I'll have to think of something for supper,' Julia said. 'Will you stay?'

Miro looked at his watch.

'Will you mind a lot if I go?'

Her heart sagged, but she forced a smile.

'Of course I'll mind, Miro. I don't want you to go, but you must. Your Mum and Dad need to see you too. Have Lukasz and Piotr missed you? You've no idea how lucky you are to have brothers!'

He laughed at that, heartily, as if she had said something amusing.

'You're welcome to them, Julia. No, I don't think they missed me. They were too busy playing pranks on each other and then sorting things out in their version of boxing. I could happily bang their heads together at times. It's so quiet, so serene in your house. Would there be room for me?'

This amused her. She felt a lightness within herself, a smoothing out of her worries.

'Julia', he said, his eyes already bright with anticipation, 'I'll come for you tomorrow morning and we can walk to church together. OK?'

'Very much OK.' she laughed. The long walk to church and afterwards back again would give them the chance to enjoy some time together.

She missed Miro the moment he left, but she had already something to look forward to. She cleared the table, set out the plates and the cutlery, grated the cheese and sliced the tomatoes. She looked into the front room. Tato was sitting reading by the fire, lost in a haze of smoke.

'I'm ready to boil the spaghetti,' she said. 'Shall I wake up Mama?'

He looked at his watch.

'She's had a good sleep,' he said, 'I suppose we ought to wake her up or she won't sleep at night.'

It was cold and dark in her parents' bedroom. Julia let the hall light in and switched on the bedside lamp. Mama was asleep on her side, covered up with a blanket up to her chin. She was so still that for a split second, for a terrifying moment, Julia thought she was dead. She brushed her hand against her mother's cool cheek.

'Mama, *kolacja*. It's suppertime,' she said and continued to stroke her mother's face.

Mama's eyes were suddenly wide open. She sat up with such a brisk movement that it startled Julia.

'*Co się stało?* What's happening?' She was agitated, her features tightening with fear.

'Nothing's happening, Mama, nothing,' Julia soothed her. 'It's time for you to have something to eat.'

Mama calmed down, her darting eyes coming to a stop on Julia's face.

'Is it night time?' she asked. 'It's so dark everywhere.'

'It's only seven, Mama. Come and sit with us in the kitchen. It's warm there. I'll have the spaghetti boiled in a few minutes.'

Mama threw back the cover and slid her legs off the bed. She was shivering slightly. Julia pulled a cardigan off the pile of clothes on the chair, and draped it over her mother's shoulders.

'I'll be all right now,' Mama said. 'Give me five minutes. You can start boiling.'

A little later, at the table, though Mama said nothing at first, Julia was pleased to see her enjoy the food which she had prepared, the freshly cooked spaghetti mixed with sliced tomatoes and grated cheese.

Tato made small talk with exaggerated cheerfulness, wording his questions cleverly so as to entice Mama into the conversation. Her reaction was sparse and lethargic, the odd nod, the pale smile, while her eyes appeared to study her embroidered tablecloth with intense concentration.

If Julia could have been granted one wish that evening, she thought, it would have been to see her Mama laugh, with happiness and pride in her eyes, the way she used to, when Julia, at five, had sung nursery rhymes.

CHAPTER 67

The worst thing was the uncertainty. It was like an invisible presence pressing constantly against Julia's stomach. Cycling home from school every afternoon, she braced herself against what may be awaiting her.

She hung on for normality to the regular patterns in her life; the school hours, the twice weekly letters from Miro, the Saturday evenings with Roman, the times spent together with Nadia, when her friend was off duty. Aunt Eva cycled over less frequently these days, now that the weather had changed and the autumnal wind and rain made outdoor pursuits less pleasant.

Julia had managed to persuade Mama to keep the appointment with Dr. Hemmings. He had prescribed additional medication, and stressed the importance of the regular daily intake. Julia reminded Mama punctually, but was often rebuked for being a pest. On occasions Mama considered her medication not at all necessary. Julia felt choked with utter helplessness and would cycle to school with a heavy heart. Mama's moods were erratic, alternating between stubbornly uncommunicative and disturbingly agitated, when any attempt at sensible reasoning would be rebuffed with a flash of anger.

Julia's escape was her bedroom, but it was hard to concentrate on her homework when her throat hurt with an acute tightness and her eyes prickled. Tato said very little from behind the paper, screening himself off in his radio corner. Julia had tried to convey her concerns to him, but he did not have the solutions that she was desperate for.

'Let her be, Julia,' he would say. 'What's the point of upsetting her even more? She's got her own convictions. No matter what you tell her, in the end she still does what she wants.'

But that was not quite true, Julia felt, because even when her entreaties were dismissed outright one day, they would be followed discreetly the following day. She made another appointment to see Dr. Hemmings.

'It's not about me,' she explained, 'it's about my mother. But it does concern me, because the way she is at the moment affects me and my step-father. All I want to know is what can be done to make things better for her and for us.'

Dr. Hemmings sat behind his desk, in his tweed jacket with the leather patches on the elbows, his white hair combed neatly across his head, his grey eyes, crinkled round the edges, peering over his half-moon spectacles.

'As you know,' he said in his always pleasant level voice, 'your mother has depression. There are no overnight cures for mental disorders. What you need is time. And a lot of patience. It's a slow progress. The medication will help. Does she take it as prescribed?'

'I do my best,' Julia said, 'I remind her all the time.'

His face softened and he nodded saying,

'I'm sure you do your best.'

'But,' she insisted, 'I need to do something practical. It's so frustrating, not knowing what else to do.'

His gaze scrutinised her for a moment, not unkindly, before he replied,

'I know it's hard,' he said. 'For a while, it may be a long while, it will feel as if there's no change at all, then one day, you'll suddenly notice it.'

His words lightened the burden inside her.

'How long will it take?' she asked.

He was slow to reply.

'That's not something that can be predicted precisely,' he said. 'It depends largely on your mother's response to this particular drug.'

'But will it really work?' she needed his reassurance.

'It's the best there is. That's why I've prescribed it. Give it a little time ...'
He nodded and rose from his seat to indicate he had the next patient to see.

This afternoon, as she cycled home from school, she was beset with thoughts that were as dark as the heavy clouds hanging low over the town. It was only half past four but already the dusk was coming down fast, activating the street lights, bringing forward the lighting-up time in the moving traffic. Julia was ready for the half-term break next week, for the simple physical comforts of not having to get up early and rush; it would all be so much more desirable, if only she could get rid of her worries. Klara. What would she do with her all week? Her Mama. How would she be? How would she behave? What would Klara think? The Youth Dance. Julia had been looking forward to it with impatience and fear in equal measures. Miro was coming home. Stefan was to join him. She and Nadia had been planning their outfits for weeks. But what if her Mama had another of her panic attacks and stopped her from going? Julia could not bear such a thought.

The house was in darkness when she arrived. Her first job was to light the fire. She put away her bicycle in the shed and let herself in through the kitchen door. She hated to be the first to come home, into the darkness and the cold. So different from the buildings at the convent school, always warm and brightly lit. She switched on the kitchen light, moved swiftly towards the front room and pushed open the door. Her fingers automatically ran up the wall feeling for the switch. The light came on. She jumped and screamed with fright. It was the unexpected sight that gave her the shock.

Sitting in the armchair, fully dressed in her coat, scarf and gloves, was her Mama, staring into the open, burning fire.

'Mama! You scared me! What are you doing sitting in the dark? Why aren't you at work? Aren't you feeling well?'

She looked hard into her mother's face, her heart pounding, her mouth dry. Mama did not react. Her gaze was fixed on the fire.

'Mama, please say something.' She moved close and squatted beside her mother, her unease sending currents of panic.

After a while Mama detached her gaze from the fire and slowly brought it round onto Julia's eyes.

'I've had a headache all day,' she said in a lifeless monotone. 'In the end I just walked out. I couldn't stand it any longer.'

'Oh Mama, what will they say at work?' Visions of reprimands and dismissal crossed Julia's mind.

Mama shrugged. 'Eva said she'd explain.'

Julia stood up.

'Did you take the aspirins?'

'No.'

'You should. I'll make hot tea. It's good you've started the fire.'

Mama sat up, livening up.

'I've burnt some rubbish that I found under your bed, Julia.'

Julia froze, except for her mind, racing, praying that she'd misheard. Then a sick feeling rose to her throat.

'What rubbish, Mama? I've not got any rubbish under my bed. Only my school things.' She rushed out, almost running the few paces to her bedroom. She knelt down on the floor and threw back the bed cover. She pulled out the three flat card boxes. One contained all her English work, files with essays and notes. They all seemed intact. Inside the History box, though the contents had been rearranged, they all appeared to be there. The Art box held files with her written work and a large folder with her paintings and sketches. With shaking hands she opened it and looked through her work. The set of five-minute sketches in charcoal was missing, also the set of paintings done as an experiment in complementary colours.

Julia's heart lodged in her throat as she rushed back to her mother.

'Mama! What have you done with them? I had some paintings here! And sketches!'

Her mother's eyes had a blank look.

'I burned them. I thought they were rubbish,' she said.

'But Mama! How could you think that! They were inside this file. Everything inside this file is my work. I have to save it for assessment. How can I hope to get good marks if half of it is missing?' She was on the brink of letting out a roar of sheer exasperation, but her mother's tone surprised her with its calm.

'Julia, be reasonable... tell me, who has ever seen blue bananas and purple oranges? And those scribbly and smudged drawings... You can do so much better than that ! How could you think of submitting work which is so below your usual high standard?'

Julia's eyes filled up. She turned round and rushed back to her room, closing the door behind her, shutting her mother out. She was overcome by an overwhelming, unstoppable grief. She sat down on her bed and let the tears flow down her face in copious streams. Her Mama did not come after her, to throw her arms around her, to hold her close, to apologise for the terrible thing she had done.

After a while, when all the sorrow had flowed out of her and she was left feeling hollow, she became aware of the coldness in her room, though she was still wearing her coat. A hot drink was what she needed. She got up from the bed, switched on the two-bar electric fire and braced herself against facing Mama. She was sitting still where she had left her and did not look up when Julia went by. She remained quiet when Julia placed the tea and the aspirin tablets beside her. Julia did not say anything either, before returning to her room.

She sat at her desk with her hands around the hot glass and thought hard. Mama's deed was not such a big disaster as she had thought at first. She would have to replicate the lost work, of course, but she could do it in her free periods at school. The problem was the storage afterwards. If Miro was at home, she'd have an immediate solution, he'd be discreet, but it was unthinkable to involve his parents. Nadia lived too faraway. There was Roman. She made up her mind to see him later in the evening. For the time being she needed to empty her mind of harrowing thoughts, and her chest of a gnawing pain.

She had always found solace in reading. She picked up one of the library books by her bedside. It was Baroness Orczy's *The Scarlet Pimpernel*. She read the first three pages and knew she was going to enjoy the book, yet she was not able to give the narrative her full attention. Mama was sitting alone in the front room. Her conscience pricked her. She closed the book, replaced it by her bedside, and went back to her.

Mama was flushed, so close to the fire.

'Mama, shall I hang up your coat?'

Her mother did not reply, just wriggled herself out of the coat, stuffed the gloves inside the pockets and removed her scarf. She sat back and closed her eyes.

Julia put away all the things in the hallway, then coming back she asked,

'What are we having for supper?'

Without opening her eyes, Mama replied,

'Whatever you fancy. Make something for yourself and your Tato. I'm not hungry.'

Julia had started to fry the sliced potatoes when Tato came home at the usual time of six-thirty. He had his cap pulled down to his eyes, his coat flapping about him in the gust of wind let in through the kitchen door. He gave it a strong energetic tug, closing it securely before turning round, slipping off his cap, smoothing down his hair and approaching Julia by the cooker, in a slow, tiptoeing manner.

'Eva's told me everything,' he spoke quietly. 'She waited for me at the factory gate.'

Julia noticed the lines between his eyebrows, the grooves at the side of his mouth.

'Mama's resting,' she said. 'She said she wasn't hungry. But maybe the cooking smells will make her change her mind.'

He went into the front room and she heard him coax her mother to lie down on the sofa. 'You'll be more comfortable with your feet up and your head on the pillow.'

He rejoined Julia in the kitchen after washing and changing into a fresh shirt. There were still feint traces of cigarette smoke and chemical factory smells as he moved past her.

'Nastusha's asleep,' he said, 'let's not disturb her. She may have an appetite later, when she's had a rest.'

It was a simple meal, quick to make, exactly what Julia liked; thinly sliced potatoes fried with onions, a bacon omelette and a green salad dribbled in oil and vinegar.

Her Tato ate with relish and praised Julia's cooking in superlatives, making her smile, despite her previous mood.

'Come on Tato, it'll pass, but it's not that fantastic!'

'Simple and fresh. That's the best Julia. You know, anything like this reminds me of the first meal we tasted on our first day of freedom. There are some aromas and flavours that you never forget.'

His train of thought, she sensed in anticipation, was already beginning to steer towards his wartime stories. She'd heard them all before.

'Tato,' she said resolutely, 'what are we going to do about Mama?'

He put down his knife and fork and looked at her.

'What do you mean, Julia? She's on medication. Give it a chance. Some things can't be rushed.'

She told him of the earlier incident.

'It scared me, Tato. I feel as if nothing's safe anymore.'

'Hmm...' he was thoughtful, 'it's how it started last time.' He resumed eating, chewing slowly.

'I've been thinking Tato,' she said, 'I'll go to see Roman and Joyce after supper. I'll ask them if I can keep my schoolwork at their house.'

His expression remained worried.

'Isn't it a lot of fuss? I don't like bothering other people.'

'Roman's not other people,' Julia rebuked him. 'He's your best friend. Besides, I need to go out. Even if just to clear my head a little.'

'Does it have to be tonight? It's like a hurricane outside.'

'Please Tato. I won't be long.'

He did not say No, but neither did he show any enthusiasm and it worried Julia that she may have hurt his feelings, preferring his friend's company to his. But how could she explain, without hurting him further, how claustrophobic she felt in her own home at times, and how disturbing she found her Mama's erratic moods, and the aura around them stifling all joy inside her.

'Tato,' she said, her tone conciliatory, 'teach me how to stay calm.'

He finished eating, lit a cigarette and sat back inhaling hard and long.

'Calm..?' he shrugged, 'my dear child, calm is what I'd like to be too. No, I'm not calm. Simply burnt out.'

'Burnt out? It sounds so old! I don't understand you Tato.'

'No you don't. How could you? At sixteen? You'd have to have had my experiences. And I wouldn't wish them on anyone!'

It was a cue, but Julia did not ask. She felt a strong need, a desire to get away, to be somewhere else. Outside the blustery wind rattled loose gates and whistled through the trees, and suddenly she longed for its force to pull her away free, to lift her like a bird.

'Tato, I'll just tidy up and then I'll go,' she said.

Roman and Joyce made her so welcome when she knocked on their door, it almost seemed as if they had been expecting her. Roman picked up her bicycle from the pavement and brought it indoors, inside the hall. His wife led Julia down the corridor towards the kitchen.

'Mrs Joyce,' Julia felt a strong compulsion to excuse herself and to explain, 'I'm really sorry to barge in like this. I won't stay long. I've got a little problem. I need your advice.'

Joyce turned her head and smiled.

'Don't fret Julia, you know you're always welcome.'

In the kitchen, all in neat pale green cupboards and wall units, Andrew was sitting at the table, finishing his meal.

'Please join us Julia,' his mother said. 'We've just finished eating. I was about to make a pot of tea.'

Roman came up behind them.

'Let's all sit down,' he said. 'A hot drink is just what we all need on a wild night like this.'

It was so pleasant, so easy in their house; why couldn't her home be so inviting?

Julia sat down beside Andrew.

'This is my second helping of chips,' he informed her. 'My favourite food, fritters and chips'.

'It should have put some pounds on you straight away,' Julia assured him, smiling.

He stretched out his thin arms before him and examined them.

'They're supposed to grow strong when I'm asleep. But sleep is so boring. I'd much rather do other things.'

'Lots of sleep and lots of exercise, my dear,' his mother said, placing a pot of tea on the table and a plate with sliced sponge cake. As always, she was neat and perfectly groomed in her fawn twin set and pearls and a dark brown pencil skirt. She sat down beside her husband and poured tea into dainty china cups with the blue willow motif.

'So Julia, what's the news?' Roman asked after she had taken a sip of tea. Her sigh came spontaneously, before she could stop it.

'It's Mama. I'm worried about her.'

Andrew sat up and stopped eating. Joyce looked from him to her husband.

'Roman, let Julia enjoy her tea and cake. There's plenty of time to talk about serious matters later.' Julia sent her a grateful look and chatted to Andrew about his school and friends till he was ready to leave the table. He lingered at the door.

'Mum, can I watch 'What's my line?' before I go upstairs?'

Joyce made a patient face.

'Andrew, reading a book is far better for you...'

Her son turned his entreating gaze at his step-father.

'Dad please, it's really interesting, and I'm getting better at guessing all the time. I always get the right answer long before the people on the panel!'

Roman smiled and looking at Joyce said,

'It looks as if Andrew is an excellent advocate in presenting his case. How could her ladyship refuse him?'

Joyce spread her hands.

'You're a witness Julia,' she said wryly, 'how these two manipulate me. All right then, Andrew, half an hour, and then I'm coming to check.'

When Andrew was out of earshot, Julia related the earlier incident with her mother to them, feeling relieved and at the same time like a traitor.

'I wish I didn't have to tell you all this. I just... I feel so lost, so inadequate...'

Joyce placed her hand over Julia's on the table.

'You did the right thing. Don't reproach yourself.'

Roman's eyes reflected the rich blue of the tablecloth and shone with some inner thoughts.

'Julia, I'm glad you came to us,' he said. 'I know it's hard for you and Theo. And I can understand how impatient you must be for things to get back to normal. They will. You'll see. Can you promise me just one thing?'

'What's that?' she asked, intrigued.

'It's simple,' he said. 'Just take one day at a time. What's the point of worrying in advance about things that may not happen?'

His words made sense, but if only things could be as simple as he suggested.

'I can't help it,' she said. 'It's like an obsession. It's like an attack of thoughts that fill up my head and I can't get rid of them.'

He nodded.

'It's natural, but try to fight such thoughts with pleasant images of your Mama, of how she really is, when she's well. The way she is now is only a wink against the whole of her life. I've known her since long before you were born. We've been through some rough times together. She's sensitive, but she can be tough. She'll get through this. As she did before. Many times.'

His words were like balm to Julia's troubled mind.

'Really, uncle, really?' A flutter in her chest lightened the weight.

He smiled reassuringly.

'Don't worry on your own Julia, you and Theo. You've got us. Any time. But first things first. We've got to be practical. Your schoolwork will be safe with us, here. For as long as necessary.'

'I was hoping you'd say that,' she formed her lips into a smile, yet she felt little relief. 'When can I bring my things over?'

'I'll fetch them tomorrow, in my car,' he offered.

'But what about Mama..? How do I explain? It'll be awkward.'

'No need to worry. I've got a gap between lectures tomorrow afternoon. I'll come round with Andrew when I've fetched him from school. Will that be all right?'

'Yes, thank you,' she nodded, 'I'm really grateful, but I've got this awful feeling, doing things behind my Mama's back.'

'Julia,' Joyce's voice was warm as she gave Julia's hand a gentle pat. 'Don't reproach yourself. None of this would be necessary if your Mum was well. This is just a sensible precaution. That's all. Everything will go back to how it was before, as soon as your Mum's better.'

Roman and Joyce were the best friends her parents could have wished for, then why was Julia experiencing this odd feeling that their support for her was like an invisible rift between her and her Mama? She may just as well have stood on a river bank and pushed out a raft, with her Mama alone on it.

Roman was talking to her,

'Every day Julia, try to think of all the good things that have happened to you. Trust me, this list will be longer than the list of negative things.'

She gave a weary sigh.

'I feel so bogged down with everything. When will I have time to think about positive and negative things?'

He smiled.

'It'll come naturally if you practise often enough, Julia. Believe me, bad things pass…'

'And good things too?' she prompted, with bitterness.

'Yes, to return in another form,' he answered unruffled. 'That's life, Julia. Constant change. In circles. Enjoy the good things when they come, but don't despair when things go against you. No doubt you've been told enough times that adversities make you stronger.'

'I don't want to be Hercules,' Julia replied, 'I just want to be me. Minus all the irritations.'

It was time to go. She bade them goodnight with profuse thanks and enjoyed the comfort of Joyce's embrace, in an aura of lavender soap and powdery makeup fragrance.

In Murray Road she cycled downhill towards the station, gripping the handlebars, her fingers pressing down the steadying brakes. The whistling wind shook the branches of the linden trees and threw busy patterns on the pavement around the poles of the street lights. It was exhilarating, refreshing, mind emptying, the force pushing against her back, blowing against her face. The ink black sky had been cleared of clouds and the luminous white moon appeared to soar above the stars. It was a beautiful night, fit for romantic walks across the fields. Julia thought of Miro and wondered if he too was looking up at the starry night and thinking of her.

Roman's words came back to her. She caught herself following his advice without even trying. It was quite true, that she could find pleasure in little things; lifting her face to the wind, lifting her eyes to the beauty in the sky. And come to think of it, most of her day had not been that bad, not until she had got home from school. She hoped now that her Mama would still be sleeping and there would not be any questions asked.

Mama was up, sitting by the fire reading the newspaper. Tato was listening to the radio, a Polish transmission from Paris that was free of jamming noise. He gave Julia an encouraging nod. This did not dispel her nervousness. With forced cheerfulness she asked,

'*Czy już jadłaś*? Have you eaten Mama?'

Her mother put down the newspaper in her lap and looked up. Her face was tired but relaxed.

'*Tak*. Yes. I've had a toast. That's enough for me,' she replied. 'How are they, Roman and *Joy*?'

Julia felt a weight lift off her chest.

'They're fine. They send their regards.'

Mama's amber eyes rested on her for a long uncomfortable while, before she said,

'They're good people Julia, they'd never let you down, if ever anything happened to me or your Tato. I feel happier knowing that and it's right that you visit them. Young people are usually too busy with their own things to think about us oldies.'

Mama's words, though serious, made Julia smile.

'Mama,' she sat down beside her, 'I never think of any of you as *oldies*.' This was a white lie, but she excused herself in this situation. In fact, her parents' generation, most of them still in their late forties, had that permanently worn and lined appearance that had made them look old even when Julia was a child. 'Is there anything you'd like me to do,' she asked, 'before I get on with my homework?'

Her mother gave her another long look, as if thinking was an effort.
'*Nie*. No,' she said, 'just get your things ready for tomorrow.'

Every afternoon for the rest of that week Julia returned home from school bracing herself against surprises, but the week passed smoothly, her mother took the prescribed pills regularly and did not resist Tato's and Julia's reminders; and though subdued, she was not unresponsive in her thoughtful, lethargic manner. On Friday night she set about dusting and cleaning the house and changing the bed linen. Julia helped her willingly, praying in her mind that her mother's improved condition would last out for another week, that nothing would go wrong during Klara's stay.

On Saturday morning Julia woke up with a start, her heart still pounding from the desperate run in her dream. She lay back against the pillow and steadied her breathing with deep, slow intakes of air. The bright light radiating from around the curtains indicated a sunny morning outside. She became aware of a sound. She listened with bated breath at first, then as it became clearer it was like a signal of long awaited good news. Her Mama was singing in the kitchen. The words were muffled but Julia knew them well and mouthed them to Mama's tone-perfect melody.

> A maiden was walking in the green wood
> She met a huntsman gallant and good
> Where is her street, where is her home?
> Where is the maiden whom I love so?

The tune was waltzy and light-hearted.

CHAPTER 68

It was an effort to warm to Klara at first sight. Her cheerless expression dampened any attempt at a sincere welcome.

'Good journey?' Julia asked, bright and chirpy. The crowd that got off the train milled around them for a few intensive seconds, then headed towards the exit. Julia picked up her young friend's battered old suitcase. Klara made a nervous movement towards her as if to pick up the suitcase herself. This came naturally, Julia knew, after years of training by the nuns, that instinctive readiness to serve others.

'It's all right,' Julia assured her, 'I've got the bike outside. It'll take the weight off our hands.'

Klara walked beside her, her small frame swamped in the long winter coat. Her dark eyes sent guarded glances from underneath her thick fringe, and the wide brim of her school hat. A walking mushroom, Julia thought waspishly, and immediately berated herself for her mean thoughts and willed herself to be especially nice to the guest who had been dumped on her.

'It's not far,' she said, when they were outside the station, with the bicycle between them and the suitcase resting on top of it. The air was balmy for a late October day. The gales earlier in the week had blown down much of the foliage off the trees, but what had been left glowed orange and red in the sun. There was a hint of mist above the playing fields as they passed them.

'We could go for a walk over there later,' Julia suggested. 'It's lovely by the canal.'

Klara shrugged.

'Maybe a walk into town?' Julia asked.

Klara nodded.

'What about the cinema tonight? They're showing *Robin Hood* with Richard Todd. And in the other one I think, it's *Lassie come Home*. Family films this week as it's half term.'

Klara looked up, her eyes squinting against the brightness.

'I like going to the cinema,' she said in a flat tone.

'That's settled then!' Julia spoke with relief. God, this was going to be hard work. Why couldn't it have been somebody else? Yagoda or Lidia? If only!

'Has Sister Alicya said anything? Sent any message?'

Klara shook her head.

'Only to give best wishes to your parents. And I'm to behave and be helpful and not be a nuisance to anyone.'

Julia laughed. Klara looked puzzled.

'It's all right,' Julia said smiling, 'I couldn't imagine you being anything else. We'll make the most of the daytime hours. Stay in, in the evenings OK? Have you any homework?'

Klara did not actually smile but there was a moment's animation in her delayed reaction.

'Sister Vespera has given us a book to read. And write notes on every chapter. *Pride and Prejudice*.

'You'll love it!' Julia enthused. 'I've got other books, if you like to read. What else do you like to do?'

She caught Klara's furtive gaze.

'Drawing and painting.'

'Excellent! You can use my paints!' Klara's expression remained shut.

'I hope you've got a good appetite,' she said, changing the subject and retaining the friendly manner despite a touch of resentment. 'My Mama will have lunch ready for us when we get home.'

Mama had been like her old self all morning. Almost. There had been moments of hesitancy in her responses to Julia's deliberately light-hearted talk, as they prepared food for cooking together. But when she talked about the people she had known in the past, especially the children, the war orphans who had been sent to New Zealand and Mexico, she spoke with optimism, rather than her usual bitterness and imagined how they had all made a new and better life for themselves after their wartime traumas. 'We must make Klara feel at home,' her mother had said. 'I'm sure she'd rather be with her own parents than us.' Mama's improved state of mind was amazing. If only, please God, it would stay permanent.

Tato was sweeping the path around the house, his white hair glowing in the sun, a ribbon of smoke unravelling from the cigarette in his mouth. He stopped, removed the cigarette from his lips and gave them a *Witam*, welcome smile.

'*Cudowny dzień*! A wonderful day! Ordered especially for you, Klara!'

She nodded, then timidly looked away.

Indoors, pleasant smells of cooking pervaded the house. Mama came out of the kitchen, a white apron covering her navy dress, looking so lovely and clean, Julia thought with pride, and watched her greet Klara with outstretched arms and a hug. For a brief moment Klara's reserve melted in that embrace as she leaned limp against Mama's chest.

'Lunch is ready,' Mama said, 'but you don't have to rush Klara, if you want to change out of your uniform first.'

In Julia's room Klara stopped at the dressing table and studied her serious face in the mirror for a long moment before looking around and memorising, it seemed, all the objects around her.

'I have my own room at home,' she said, 'but I'm hardly ever there. I'd love a room like yours.'

Was she serious?

'It's all second-hand furniture,' Julia giggled self consciously, 'and we'll have to share the bed.'

'No problem,' Klara said with that deadpan manner of hers. 'It's big. And looks comfortable.'

She took off her school hat and her coat, to reveal the sky blue tunic and the ivory white blouse, worn with a beige cardigan, intended for cold weather.

'I've kept my school uniform for a souvenir,' Julia said to make conversation, 'I can't imagine ever wearing it again, but it's kind of hard getting rid of it. I've left you some space and some hangers in the wardrobe.'

Klara opened her suitcase on the bed.

'I've not got a lot to hang up,' she said, 'two skirts, two blouses, and a cardigan which I'll be wearing anyway.' She took out those items one by one as she spoke.

'They're nice,' Julia wanted to sound pleasant as she noted the boring grey and navy pleated skirts. 'I'll go now to see if my Mum needs me. Come when you're ready.'

In the kitchen, there was nothing left for her to do, Mama had seen to everything. She looked so well. There was a liveliness about her which Julia had not seen for a long time. Julia felt a bubble in her chest, rising, expanding. She was afraid to burst it. She was afraid to be happy too soon.

'Mama, this is all lovely,' she said giving her mother a heartfelt hug. The table was covered with one of Mama's embroidered tablecloths and set neatly for four.

'I thought,' Mama said, checking the pots on the cooker, 'that we'd start with the chicken soup. Wholesome and warming.'

'Perfect!' Julia agreed.

Tato came in, scrubbed his hands at the sink and sat at the table. His clothes had retained the freshness of the outdoors and his face, a sunny expression. Klara appeared at the half open door hesitant, her eyes worried.

'Am I late? Have I kept you waiting?'

'Not at all,' Tato said, '*Prosze*. Please, do sit down.'

Her light brown plaits hung down on her chest, against the loose blouse, bought a size larger, no doubt, for growth. Her navy skirt, like a pleated tube, almost touched her ankles. Julia had a flash of memory of her own oversize coat at one stage, then at another, of being caught between a constricting liberty bodice that she had grown out of and being pulled up by the thick brown stockings that no longer reached the tops of her thighs. It had felt like being trapped inside a press.

She patted the seat next to hers. 'Will you sit beside me?'

Mama's chicken soup with vermicelli was savoured in approving silence, its delicate taste just right, its warmth spreading comfort through the body, before Tato initiated a friendly dialogue. That had been his intention, but Klara's curt *Tak* and *Nie*, Yes and No, soon transformed his efforts into a monologue, which did not put him off at all. He started on his favourite subject of the wartime years.

'Theo, please!' Mama gave him a meaningful look. 'Let's talk about the coming week. I'm sure the girls want to make plans, especially if the weather stays as beautiful as today.'

Klara got up abruptly and collected the empty soup plates.

'I'll wash up,' she said rushing to the sink.

'No need!' Julia and her mother tried to stop her. 'We'll do that afterwards,' Julia said and Mama added, 'Please Klara, you're our guest! Just sit down and enjoy the meal.'

The second course was chicken with buttered potatoes and beetroot served hot and sweet.

'Is it tasty?' Julia asked her.

With her mouth full, Klara nodded and kept her gaze down on the plate. Julia turned to Mama.

'It's excellent,' she said and was rewarded with a normal smile. Please God, she thought, let her stay like this.

'So, Klara,' Tato said, 'where were your parents during the war?'

She swallowed her mouthful and raised her guarded eyes.

'They were in a labour camp, in Germany,' she replied. 'Their own children, a boy and a girl died of typhoid there. The conditions were very bad. When the war finished and they were liberated, they adopted me.'

They all stopped eating. Julia was shocked. So, Klara had been a war orphan. Julia was amazed that she was opening up to them on such a personal matter. As her amazement subsided she became aware of a growing feeling of sympathy towards this strange girl and of displeasure with herself for her initial unkind thoughts. Of course, she wouldn't have had them in the first place, she absolved herself, if only Klara had been an easier person to like.

Theo began to eat and regained his voice.

'They were terrible times. I don't think there's one person that I know who hasn't suffered the loss of someone close to them. Still,' he said more cheerfully, 'all that is behind us now. Where is your home now?'

'Hannover.'

'And how do you like it here in England? At the convent school?'

Klara thought for a moment.

'I wouldn't be here if my Mama was well. She's had TB. Her lungs are still weak. She's often away at some sanatorium, even when I come home for the summer. Sometimes I'm sent away to some other people. Once I was sent away to a farm in Sweden.'

'Really? Was it exciting going abroad?' Julia's questioning was deliberately enthusiastic.

Klara stared at her.

'No. I hated it. I just wanted to stay at home.'

Julia squirmed at her own insensitivity.

'Of course you did,' she agreed eagerly, 'but couldn't you simply have refused to go?'

Klara shook her head.

'My Dad said I should be grateful for having such opportunities. The money was offered from the Polish Orphans' Fund. I wasn't ungrateful. I just wished I didn't have to go.'

Julia knew the feeling. Despite her school environment having been so palatial compared to her home surroundings, first in a Nissen hut then in a prefabricated bungalow, she had always yearned to be with her parents.

'You poor child,' Mama said with her normal motherly softness. 'Believe me Klara, time goes faster than you realise and things change.'

That was exactly what Roman had said. Looking at Klara's small pinched face, Julia thought suddenly how charmed her own life was, especially now, when her Mama appeared to be recovering so well.

'Klara,' she said, her voice lively to forestall her friend clamming up again, 'shall we go into to town after lunch?'

Klara had just finished eating. Her plate had been scraped clean.

'Would you like more?' Mama offered.

'Thank you. No. That was plenty. And very good.' She turned her grave face to Julia. 'Are there lots of shops in town?'

'Lots!' Julia smiled. 'But not as many as in Hannover, I imagine. Rugby's only a small place.'

Klara nodded.

When they were having plum cake with lemon tea, Mama left the table and came back with a small package.

'This is for you, Klara,' she said, anticipation lifting her cheeks.

'Me?' Klara's surprise was genuine. She took the package and unwrapped it. Julia watched her face for signs of joy or just a little excitement. There was a flicker of interest in her solemn eyes, but her mouth remained set when she examined the knitted gloves, the scarf and the beret all in soft pastel blue.

'I thought you may like to put them on for your walk into town,' Mama suggested.

'No,' Klara shook her head, 'I'll keep them for best. For church tomorrow. Thank you Mrs. Anastazia. Now, please tell me what can I do for you?'

Mama laughed softly.

'*Moja kochana*! My dear! You don't have to do anything for me. Just wear these things and enjoy them!'

In Boots in town, Klara smelled all the soaps, all different fragrances and brands, each claiming to be the best. Her eyes remained thoughtful throughout.

'I've got a little pocket money,' she confided, 'but I won't spend it until I've seen everything first.'

In Woolworths she lingered at the cheap jewellery counter.

'That butterfly brooch,' she said, 'would sit nicely on a polo neck jumper. But I've not got one yet. Everything's so expensive!'

'Not at the market,' Julia said, 'I'll take you there on Monday.'

'*Dobrze*. All right,' was all she said.

In Overs, the stationers, Klara spent much time examining pens and pencils and crayons and paints. In the end she chose a small sketchbook.

'I've got pencils,' she said.

'And I've got the paints,' Julia reminded.

'*Dobrze*. All right,' she replied.

Outside dusk was falling from a cloudless icy blue sky with the remnants of pink light low behind the rooftops. By the clock tower Julia asked,

'Not tired of walking yet?'

Klara shook her head. Julia suggested,

'I'll take you through the park, then. A bit bare looking at this time of the year, but still pleasant and quiet away from the traffic.'

'All right, then' Klara replied. She was no chatter-box, but she was agreeable. Perhaps, by the end of the week Julia could hope for a breakthrough in Klara's reticence.

Julia's bed was comfortably wide enough for them both. That night after they'd read for a long while, Julia for pleasure an Agatha Christie, and Klara *Pride and Prejudice* because Sister Vespera had told her to, Klara closed her book, lay back and shut her eyes. Her hand carried on stroking Muszka automatically, who had settled between them with an owner's assured possessiveness.

'Ready for lights out?' Julia asked.

'If you wish.'

Julia switched off the bedside light, and when her eyes got accustomed to the dark, she could see the shadows of the copper beech and the rowan tree shivering on the curtain. There was a slight breeze rustling outside, and the fabric glowed orange from the street lights.

She was surprised when Klara spoke.

'I like it here. I like your room. I like the shadows on the curtain. Dark and cold outside. So cosy in bed!'

'Good,' Julia replied, 'I'm glad you like it. I emulsioned the walls myself last year. And Mama made the curtains. Nothing as grand as our dormitories at school!'

'I sleep in a small room, when the girls are away,' Klara said. 'It's like a nun's cell. Just a bed and a locker. It's more fun when sometimes other girls stay behind. Marta and Dana sometimes do. Their parents live in Pakistan.'

'So what do you do? When you're just on your own?'

Klara was quiet for a moment.

'Sister Honorata is good to me. I help her in the sacristy. Or we sort books in the library. Sometimes we sew together. I love to embroider things. But she often has to go to prayers. With the other nuns. Then I go for a walk round the grounds by myself.'

An image appeared in Julia's mind, that of a solitary figure wandering about on her own, like Bambi, or the baby monkey, Fiki-Miki, whose mum was eaten by a snake. Impulsively she said,

'We'll have a nice week together, won't we?' She sought Klara's hand on the cover and gave it a sisterly pat.

Time passed quickly. Julia's initial reservations and resentment faded in the busy timetable and the quickly established routines. The mornings were devoted to schoolwork, the afternoons to walks into town or the library. They had been to see *Robin Hood* and *Lassie come Home*. They had been to the market and had found a polo-neck jumper for Klara, at a price she could afford. It was in pale peacock blue and did some mysterious enhancement to her chestnut brown colouring. Klara could look really pretty at times.

Tato had given them some pocket money. Julia saved hers; Klara bought a piece of black fabric for a grown-up, straight skirt. Mama cut it out to size and Julia machine-sewed it all in one evening. Worn with the new jumper, it certainly transformed Klara's appearance, from a schoolgirl into a young woman. Julia expected a cry of excitement, a look of joy on Klara's face, as she studied herself in the mirror but her set expression was like a shutter, hiding all her inner thoughts. Yet, night after night, she would put on her new jumper, with the much coveted butterfly brooch from Woolworths glittering at the neck, and her new skirt, keep them on for a few minutes, then hang them back in the wardrobe, like some priceless treasure.

She liked books. Every afternoon in town she would browse through books in the library or inside any shop that had a section with books. At night time, bathed and fragrant with the strong scented soap from the market, they would both read in bed, Klara's sporadic exclamations betraying her well guarded enjoyment. And afterwards, when the light was switched off, Julia would sense her turning towards her, and sidle up a fraction, with the same request every night.

'Tell me a story, Julia. A grown up story. With a happy ending. It's got to have a happy ending. OK?'

Julia plodded through *Gigi* and *Sabrina* and *Notre Dame de Paris*, till her throat felt dry. One night she asked,

'Aren't you bored yet, Klara, listening to all this?'

'No.'

'Surely you mean Yes.'

'No. I love happy endings.'

'Don't we all!'

'See!' there was a note of triumph in Klara's voice.

Julia could not deny she had dreams too; she wanted Miro's love, she wanted her Mama to be well, she wanted a settled future, an exciting job, an elegant house, and later, when she and Miro had saved enough, to travel and see the world.

'What's your dream Klara?' she asked. 'What would be your happy ending?'

There was a long silence before Klara answered,

'I'd like someone to be all mine. Just mine!'

Another of Klara's seeming pleasures was doing housework. It was her ever present readiness to start and then her diligence in accomplishing her tasks to perfection that made one wonder at the strange attraction for her of cleaning and polishing. Every evening before Julia's parents came home from work, though she did not voice her eagerness to help prepare the evening meal, she'd be first in the kitchen, putting her apron on, getting out the pots and pans, sorting the vegetables to peel. And when the pots were simmering, she would check them with nervous regularity, while looking for spots in the kitchen that needed scrubbing and wiping dry.

One morning when she had been dusting around Julia's open books and files with the zeal of a ferocious tornado, and after Julia had attempted for the tenth time to start on the next part of her essay, Julia's patience snapped.

'Klara, stop! For goodness sake!' This came out too sharp. Julia saw the startled look in Klara's eyes. She moderated her voice. 'Klara, please!… you're making my head spin. You're not our slave. You're our guest. You don't have to do any of this.'

Klara gave her a long thoughtful look.

'I don't want to be your guest,' she said, 'I want to be like you.' She looked down as if already regretting her words.

Julia was astonished. Without thinking she got up and automatically placed her arm around her friend's thin shoulders.

'Klara, of course you're like one of us,' she said. 'You don't have to do chores to prove yourself'.

Klara's lips remained set, her silence prompting Julia to say more.

'You know how highly my Mama and Tato think of you.' In fact, Julia thought, they lavished more praise on her than on their own daughter. 'You don't have to do anything else to make them like you more.' That was another strange thing, whenever Julia commented quietly on Klara's cheerless nature, they chided her for her lack of understanding and patience.

'Did they say they like me?' Klara asked.

'It's obvious, isn't it?'

She shrugged, but was there a flicker of liveliness in those unreadable eyes?

'Then...,' she hesitated, 'would they agree to my coming here again?'

Julia's smile stiffened. This was unbelievable! Why would Klara want to come back at all? It wasn't as if she had ever expressed ecstatic happiness at her stay with Julia. And besides, the next break would be Christmas. What would Julia do with her all fortnight? Miro would be home, and she would rather spend more time with him.

'Won't you be going home for Christmas?' she asked.

'No. It's not nice travelling abroad in the winter months. My Mama and Tato don't want me to be stuck in the middle of nowhere if the weather turned suddenly nasty, and they stopped running trains. And the sea can be rough. No, I've got to wait till Easter.'

'And what about the convent? Don't they make it a special time at Christmas?'

A deep, expressive sigh.

'They do. But it gets very busy with visiting guests. Lots of other church people. I don't fit in with anyone there.'

She raised her grave eyes and Julia felt a niggle of discomfort. One last try.

'Aren't there girls in your own class that you'd rather be with?'

Klara shook her head.

'I was once sent to Monika's, but she had her own friends where she lived. I was made to feel I was not part of her gang.' What a surprise! Julia knew when she was beaten. She knew what her parents would say to Klara's request.

'Well,' she said with a cheer she did not feel, 'you don't need to worry any more, Klara. My Mama and Tato would never turn anyone away at Christmas. Especially you.'

She forced a wide encouraging smile, but Klara's face remained serious.

'*Dobrze.* All right,' she said, 'now what I'd really like to do is to make *pierogi* for your Mama and Tato.'

This was so unexpected it made Julia laugh.

'Do you realise it'll take us all day?'

'I've had good practice,' Klara assured her, 'I can make them by myself.'

'It's all right. We'll make them together.' This had not been her plan for the day, but the idea was not so unattractive. She had always enjoyed making *pierogi* with Mama. It was not just because of the tactile pleasure of kneading the dough and rolling it out and cutting out little circles and pressing their sides together to make miniature parcels with the savoury cheese filling inside, it was more than that. While indulging in this relaxing activity, with the numbers of *pierogi* growing in neat rows, it felt during those moments of intimate chatter as if nothing else existed, as if her Mama was exclusively her own.

'It's a brilliant idea, Klara,' she said. 'That will really surprise them!'

That evening praise flowed for Klara's enterprise. 'Excellent!' Tato pronounced. 'Brings back memories of *Shtuka* in Lvov. The best eating place in town!'

Mama had a smile in her eyes and a lift in her face. Just as Julia loved her to be.

'What made you want to spend all your day cooking?' she asked, her voice caressing with approval.

She had been like her old self since Klara's arrival. Every day just as Julia had looked out for a hint of joy in Klara's face, so she had observed her mother for signs of change in her behaviour. To her daily relief, Mama's recovery appeared to be making steady progress. Some evenings she was tired and sleepy and retired to bed earlier blaming the pills, which she took regularly, accepting with grace Julia's automatic reminders. But the evenings when she stayed up longer and sat with the girls by the fire embroidering or darning socks or mending Tato's pockets, she would entertain them with colourful accounts of her teen years in Poland, of her travels in the Middle East during the war, of the huge numbers of people she had got to know because of the extraordinary circumstances that had thrown them together. She did not mention Dorotka. But she spoke with great sentiment about Pavel and Agata, two motherless children that she had fostered for a while. They were grown up now, married to each other, and living in Toronto, where their fathers had emigrated after the war. Julia had heard many of these stories before, but watching Klara's rapt expression, she listened too, intent on remaining within the orb of her Mama's attention. What mattered the most, was that Mama was well.

While Klara kept herself busy with her own activities, Julia worked on her History essay. Miss Simpson had challenged the class to a subject entirely of their own choice, pertaining to modern history. Julia entitled her essay: *Poland in Present Times*. Fifteen years after the war, and still in the grip of the Soviet Communism. The repression, the censorship of the press, the armies of the secret police, the spying, the arrests, the countless files kept on the minutest, inoffensive actions of ordinary citizens. Would Poland ever be free? Julia's imagined trip to her parents' country seemed so remote, as to be unattainable. Yet she still dreamed.

The much awaited Friday arrived. Miro was coming home. For the Saturday Youth Dance. Stefan was coming too. And Nadia. Julia was counting the hours. There was just one niggle. Klara. When her young friend was in the bathroom, she raised this matter with her parents.

'Of course you must take her,' Tato said.

'Couldn't you and Mama take her to the cinema?' Julia suggested feebly. 'Klara's only fourteen. What will she do there all night?'

'She'll enjoy just watching,' Mama said, 'as you did. Remember? When you were little and I helped with the refreshments.'

That was true. Just being there was exciting enough. The music, the dancing couples, the beautiful dresses.

'Oh well…' Julia sighed, giving up.

'Let's ask her,' Tato suggested. 'That's fair, isn't it?'

Julia guessed in advance Klara's choice.

'I've never been to a dance yet,' Klara said, her eyes, for once, sparkling, her hair a little damp from the bathroom steam, a scent of soap around her. 'I'd love to go with you, Julia.'

That was last night. This evening, when it got to eight o'clock, Julia said to her parents,

'Miro must be home by now. I'd like to see him. Make arrangements for tomorrow.'

'Don't stay too long,' Mama admonished. 'They've all had a long week.'

'I'll be quick,' Julia promised, wishing to be somewhere else, away from everything and everyone, just Miro and herself together.

Klara came with her and as they stood at Miro's door, as always, there were the sounds of a scuffle on the other side. The door opened with a yank to reveal Miro's brothers standing to pretend attention and snorting with suppressed giggles. They stopped, seeing Klara. Julia was amused by their sudden awareness of a newcomer. A girl. Close to their age.

'Is Miro home yet?' she asked.

'Yes. And Hi! Come in,' Lukasz invited, his eyes stuck on Klara.

They went inside. Mr. Michal was sitting at the table in the dining part of the room, chiselling and smoothing a piece of wood. He gave them a welcome wave and Mrs. Anna called out from the kitchen. Miro was there too, apparently making coffee.

'Hi Julia!' he came towards her, his face beaming. 'You beat me to it! I was just about to go over to yours.'

'Then come back with us,' she said. 'This is Klara. My young friend from my old school.'

Klara smiled shyly and looked away, avoiding Lukasz's gaze. Miro said,

'Since you're here, sit down and I'll make coffee for everyone.'

Julia and Klara took off their coats and hung them over the backs of the chairs. Lukasz and Piotr hovered close by as if bracing themselves for a speech or a performance. Then Lukasz said,

'Klara, do you like television? *Lone Ranger* is on right now.'

Klara nodded, said 'Yes,' and looked at Julia.

'Go on,' Julia said, 'it's your chance.'

The boys led her to the lounge part of the room and sat down cross-legged on the rug and leaned against the settee. Klara did the same, on the edge.

Miro brought the coffee in mugs, and sat at the table opposite Julia. She felt a surge of happiness. Just to be near him. She knew from his regular letters that he had settled well. Nevertheless, she wanted to hear it all again.

'Was it a wrench to tear yourself away from the metropolis?' she teased.

He rewarded her with his ever ready smile.

'Oh, absolutely! The peak of the high life, where I live!'

She knew his accommodation was a shared room in the Civil Service Hostel. Because it was the cheapest he could get.

'And your room-mate? Won't he miss you this weekend?'

Miro's eyes crinkled with amusement.

'Sure! Like a boil on the bum!'

A theatrical gasp from Miro's mother, who came to join them at the table. 'Miro! Mind your language!'

Julia could not help a giggle. She knew from Miro's accounts that his room mate worked for the Transport, that he had an obsession with maps, which were strewn all over the place, which he then marked with red pens, to suggest new routes. The poor man suffered with frequent boils, which he had to have lanced at the nearby St. Mary's Hospital.

'Poor old devil!' Miro had written. 'Twice my age! I've got to look after him, haven't I?' He'd treat him to a pint, and in return would be treated to a hot chocolate when writing up notes late into the night. None of this was mentioned now, not in front of Miro's parents. The conversation was steered towards lectures and lecturers and Miro's companion, Ralph Montague.

'Dad,' Miro said, 'his father and his two brothers are lawyers. Family firm. And they've got a house somewhere in Surrey. Sometimes he invites me to his digs. It's like a hotel. Someone makes him sandwiches and brings them up to his room. Can you believe it?!'

Miro's father grinned. 'Perhaps you should invite him over here. Show him the real world!'

Miro did not add, that on Friday nights, Ralph would take him to the *Brush and Palette* meeting place, where a drink could be enjoyed in the company of artists sketching a live model. 'Usually fat, with sagging breasts,' Miro had written.

Mrs. Anna asked Julia about her school and her friends. The conversation flowed smoothly, and when Julia glanced at the clock, she saw with regret it was time for her to go. Miro seemed to have guessed her thoughts.

'Let them watch to the end,' he referred to his brothers and Klara, 'I'll walk you home. Would Klara like to come here tomorrow night? There's always a good film on a Saturday night.'

Julia's heart skipped. She looked at Miro's parents for their reaction.

'But of course!' Mrs. Anna nodded. 'If Klara still wants to come after tonight. Those two can be a bit silly at times.'

'They're very entertaining!' Julia jumped to their defence. 'I'm sure Klara will find them amusing. But, we'd never want to impose in any way!'

'Not at all! See what she says,' Mrs. Anna smiled in their direction.

The film had just come to an end, with the credits rolling, and Lukasz leaned in front of his brother towards Klara.

'Did you enjoy that? Would you like to come again? We can play chess if you like. Or some other game. Monopoly or Scrabble. Or just look at comics. I've got a stack of them!' He certainly did not waste time.

Klara leaned back as if attempting to disappear into the sofa.

'I'm going back on Sunday,' she said.

'There's still tomorrow. Won't you come in the evening?' Lukasz raised his eyebrows and made a funny pleading face which, to Julia's surprise, made Klara laugh.

'It's just that,' she hesitated, 'I'm supposed to be going to a dance with Julia.' Her glance begged Julia for rescue. Julia stood up and walked over to them.

'Lukasz, it's really good of you to ask. We'll let you know as soon as we decide arrangements for tomorrow. OK?'

They were all up now, and Lukasz shrugged his shoulders in resignation.

'OK.' he said, 'but if you go with the oldies Klara, you'll regret it! You'll be a gooseberry all night!'

Too right! Julia thought, but laughed with the others. Even Klara smiled.

'Thank you,' she said, 'it's been a good film.'

She linked her arm with Julia's as Miro walked them home. It was a still black night with the mist forming orange halos around the street lights and the dampness settling into the fabric of their coats. At the gate, Julia gave Klara the key and waited for her to let herself in. She turned to Miro and longed for his embrace.

'We're too exposed here,' he whispered, 'but tomorrow night we'll find time on our own.'

'I've missed you,' she said.

'I've missed you too,' he clasped her hand in both his.

'What shall we do about Klara?'

He brushed her face with his lips. 'There will be a crowd of us. She'll have enough chaperones. Till tomorrow!' he said. And those last two words held a promise of everything she had been waiting for.

Tato was still listening to the radio, the volume surprisingly low, Muszka asleep on his lap, and Mama was knitting by the fire.

'Everything all right?' she asked.

Yes, Julia thought, as long as Mama was well, and Klara did not get in the way, and nothing happened tomorrow that could spoil the planned evening for her. She gave Mama a brief account of the visit to Miro's house.

'Lukasz and Piotr made Klara really welcome,' she said, sitting down close beside her. 'They've invited her tomorrow night.'

Her Mama rested the knitting in her lap and gave her full attention. Julia loved that soothing, comforting feeling, when Mama's face was relaxed, when her brown amber eyes were soft, taking in everything that Julia was telling her.

'We'll ask her,' Mama said. 'Give her the choice. She may just want to stay at home after all. Whatever. I want her to feel wanted, and her wishes respected. She's only been with us a few days. Then after that, her only certainty is the school. Then another place, new people, new adjustments.' She raised her eyebrows, counting on Julia's understanding.

'All right,' Julia agreed, resigned, but not resentful. She kissed her Mama goodnight and gave Tato a hug, before retiring to her room.

Klara was already in bed reading. She put her book down, her face showing animation, very seldom displayed.

'It was nice in their house, wasn't it?' she said. There was still hope. Julia undressed and put on her dressing gown.

'They're nice people, Klara.' She went to the bathroom, washed and brushed her teeth and joined Klara in bed. They read for a good hour before Klara tired. She yawned, put the book aside and slid down under the covers.

'Ready?' Julia asked. She switched off the light and lay back against the pillow. The dark, misty night threw the room into pitch blackness. Julia closed her eyes and thought about Miro. His smiling, lively face was like a bright imprint on her mind.

'Julia,' Klara's clear whisper startled her, 'I wish I didn't have to go back on Sunday.' Julia was astonished. Klara wanting to stay with her!

'Klara, we all have to go back. To school. To work. Miro to London. What would you do here on your own?'

'It's not that,' Klara said, 'I know we all have to get on with our things. I just wish...'

'What?'

'That this was my home.'

Had it been someone else saying these things, Julia would have suspected cruel ridicule. After all there was nothing of any great value in their possessions to make their home enviable. But it was not in Klara's nature, she was certain of that, to poke fun at others. She was speaking now in all earnestness. Quite unexpectedly Julia was touched by her candour.

'Klara, you've got a home. And your Mum and Dad love you. Let's call this your second home, shall we? You'll soon be back here for Christmas.'

'It's still such a long way away!'

'It'll go like lightning! You'll be surprised!'

Klara was quiet for a long while. Julia assumed she was falling asleep. Then her whisper came sharp and clear.

'Can you keep a secret?'

'I can. But don't tell me anything you may regret later.' Probably some silly tittle-tattle. Schoolgirl secrets. Julia smiled now at the memory of her own.

'I trust you,' Klara pursued. 'I've not told this to anyone.' Strange, how Klara always opened up in the dark.

'All right then, but only if you really must.'

'Well…' Klara took a deep breath, 'one day, when I was at home on my own, I was looking through one of the drawers, it had lots of old photographs. And all sorts of old papers and documents. I never took any notice of them before. I picked up a brown envelope and a photo fell out. It was of me. When I was a baby…'

'And..?'

'I took out the other papers. From the envelope. They were some official documents from the Red Cross. All about me. Before I got adopted…'

Julia found herself listening with interest now. 'Go on…'

'They were about my mother. My real mother. She was a worker in a labour camp. In Germany. There was nothing there about my real father. Only about this Frenchman that she met after I was born. He wanted to go back home to France. He wanted her, but not me.'

This was like something out of a book or a film.

'Are you sure Klara? Him not wanting you? A little baby?'

'I'm only repeating what it said in the papers,' Klara was matter of fact, 'and do you know what my mother did? Not my good Mama, but my real mother. She took me to the town centre and abandoned me in the pram all by myself!'

'Oh Klara!' Julia was shocked.

'But that's not the end, Julia! Some people found me and took me to the Red Cross. Somehow, they found my mother too and I was back with her. So, the next time, she threw me in the river! Pram and all!'

Julia sat up and switched on the bedside light. This was a bombshell!

Exposed to the light, Klara looked withdrawn again, her mouth pinched, her eyes fearful.

'You won't tell anyone, will you?' she whispered. 'No one must ever know, that I know.'

Julia knew instinctively that Klara was telling her the truth. This awful, painful truth. With a spontaneous reaction, she embraced her young friend and held her close as her Mama always did when she was upset. She was surprised and gratified when Klara relaxed and returned her hug, the first one all week. She smelled of soap and lavender talcum powder and other scents she'd been trying out for the past seven days.

'I'm glad you know,' she said. 'If I had a sister, I'd want her to be like you. Then we wouldn't have to have secrets. Would we? I don't like secrets. They sort of burn a hole in you, don't they?'

Despite herself Julia smiled. She gave her another hug. An empathy, an understanding, as clear as a beam of light entered her heart. She knew only too well all about the loneliness of being an only child.

'My dear Klara, you mustn't worry any more. Your secret is absolutely safe with me. We shall write to each other, won't we? Every week. Now, shall we get some sleep?'

They slid back under the covers and Julia switched off the light.

'Just one more thing,' Klara whispered, 'would I really be a gooseberry if I go with you tomorrow night?'

After such a revelation! How could Julia refuse her anything!

'No Klara, you'd never be a gooseberry. It's your last day tomorrow. All I want is for you to be happy.'

'Then, if it's OK. with you, I'd rather go round to Lukasz and watch a film with him.'

It was like any other Youth Dance held at St. Mary's Community Hall twice a year: popular music of the moment blaring at full volume, acrobatic rock-n-roll, jiving and twisting, high spirits, the atmosphere all the more feverish in the constantly changing colours of the spotlights scanning the darkened hall.

Julia loved it all.

They left their coats in the cloak room, Julia, Nadia, Miro and Stefan, and stopped in the doorway to accustom their senses to all the activity and noise. On the side, the drinks and food counter were brightly lit. Three ladies were busying themselves in the kitchen beyond. One of them was Leon's mother.

Nadia grabbed Julia's hand and pulled her along.

'Good evening, Mrs. Tarnovska!' she called over the pounding beat of *Rock around the Clock*, her face beaming a brilliant white smile. She looked indeed stunning, Julia thought, her dark looks enhanced by the glow of her red dress. She asked,

'Is Leon coming tonight? I've not seen him for ages!'

Leon's mother turned round and appeared speechless for a moment. Julia was aware of Miro and Stefan standing right behind them. Mrs. Tarnovska's gaze wandered up to the boys and lingered speculatively. Stefan was not unlike Leon in looks; tall, slim and blond, and eye-catching in his smart dark jacket, white shirt and tie.

'Good evening,' Julia added, 'I've missed him too.' A little white lie would soothe Mrs. Tarnovska's discomfort. She returned Julia's smile a little stiffly.

'Good evening,' she replied. 'Well, yes, he's a little too busy at the moment...'

'Still helping his sister?' Nadia asked innocently. 'Pity he couldn't come. We'd have such fun!'

They turned to walk away and Nadia whispered to Stefan. 'Indulge me please. I'll explain later. Just put your arm around my shoulders.'

He gave her a puzzled smile and did better: he slipped his arm around her waist and pulled her close to him. Julia could not resist a backward glance. Mrs. Tarnovska's eyes were glued to Nadia's retreating back.

They found a table in a corner and straightaway Miro pulled Julia out onto the crowded dance floor. They jived, hearts racing, limbs flying, lights and other dancers whizzing round them in a blur. The sheer exuberance of those moments filled Julia's heart with bursting happiness. Oh to be like this with Miro, forever!

And so it went on till the break, popular dances, traditional waltzes, polkas and tangos, till Julia's whole being tingled with exhaustion. Leaning on Miro each time, feeling his liveliness, his energy, as he led her back to their table after each dance, his hot palm on her bare shoulder, were delicious sensations.

At break the lights were switched on and a queue formed at the drinks and food counter. Miro and Stefan joined the queue. Julia and Nadia rested at the table, fanning their faces with the cork mats.

'It's the best dance that I've ever been to!' Nadia laughed, her almond eyes dreamy, her smile flash-white between her red lips.

'It's great!' Julia agreed excitedly. She would have said more about Leon, about Stefan, about forgetting, about moving forward, but there was no need. Nadia had sorted it all out herself. Julia said,

'I think we caused Leon's mother something of a surprise!'

Nadia's expression became a little serious, but not too much.

'D'you know? I have no more feelings on that matter. Nothing that upsets me, any way. Stefan tells me that being different from everyone else, makes me stand out. Makes me special.' She smiled. 'He's been telling me about his background. He said we have a lot in common. He and I.' Another self-pleased smile.

Julia was pleased for her too, perhaps because she was so happy herself.

'I told you so! Birds of Paradise! Remember?'

'I really feel like one tonight,' Nadia laughed, and fluttered her eyes with pretend self-flattery.

They looked around the hall, now noisy with excited talk at the round tables that lined all four sides. Julia recognised familiar faces from her young school days, their families now settled in Leicester or Coventry. Pity Yagoda had a bad cold and was not able to come. And Lidia lived so faraway!

When the boys returned with a plate of sandwiches and soft drinks, their talk turned naturally to their everyday lives: Stefan's arranged visits to various hospital units for observation, Miro's tales of his colleagues' wicked pranks at the Law School, Nadia's experiences in the male ward, under the Matron's ever watchful razor sharp gaze.

'It's like working inside a tiger's cage,' Nadia said. 'You never know when she's going to pounce on you!'

'Tell me about it!' Stefan laughed. 'We students are rated like amoebas. On good days!'

'We've not got a matron,' Miro said, 'but we all agree that our Mr.Prescott must have been one in his previous life! He's known lovingly as the *Hatchet*. Barks orders like a demented judge. I pity the few girl students who have to listen to his rantings. One got so flustered with his long winded questioning, that her answer was something like this: when a man has an erection in the middle of the road he has to have it lit up at night.'

Stefan and Nadia burst out laughing. Julia felt embarrassed.

'Exactly!' Miro picked up the story. 'Everyone just roared. But perversely, the *Hatchet* said, well done!'

'Well,' Julia said, 'I can't match any of your stories with equal sophistication. With me it's just schoolwork and more schoolwork. But what about Elizabeth Taylor? A MILLION dollars! For doing *Cleopatra!*

'Hollywood! Here I come!' Nadia raised her Babycham glass. 'Your last opportunity!'

'What about us?' Stefan teased.

'*Frankenstein* and the *Mummy*?' Miro suggested.

The talked turned to general matters and all the latest current affairs. Before the lights went down and the colourful spotlights were reactivated, Julia and Nadia rushed to the ladies to repair their make-up.

'Every minute counts!' Nadia said breathlessly. 'I wish it didn't have to end at midnight!'

At five minutes to midnight, the last waltz was announced. Miro held Julia tight to him, and it felt as if she was aware of every muscle in his body, every breath, every movement, his silence heavy with unspoken words. The music finished, the lights went out. And in the short moment of darkness, his lips touched hers. An electric current coursed through her body. A fire ignited in the deepest centre of her being. An exquisite sensation. A longing, a strange eagerness within her. She held on to him and returned the kiss. The lights came on. His eyes were intense, looking straight into hers. His lips mouthed,

'I love you.' He said it at last. Words she had been waiting for.

'Me too,' she mouthed. 'Love you.'

Then they had to separate and stand straight, next to each other, as the first notes of *God save our Gracious Queen* were played, followed immediately by the Polish anthem, *Poland shall never be destroyed as long as we shall live!*' All through the sung anthems, Miro's fingers played gently with hers.

The walk home was magical. As if nature had conspired in their favour. It was one of those rare mild autumn nights, with a soft breeze blowing scattered little clouds across a starry sky, and a bright moon gilding the outlines of buildings and trees, and showing the way along whitened pavements.

They took a short cut through Oak Street, past the elegant red-brick Rugby School buildings, the shiny slate-tiled roofs, casting deep shadows down the walls. The wide-spread chestnuts on the green whispered with their bare branches.

Julia and Miro walked in unison, their arms entwined round each other's waists. Their sides touching. Perfection. She adjusted her scarf and looked up at him. He brought his face down to touch hers. Bliss.

'I don't want this night to end,' she said.

'There will be others,' a buoyancy of promise in his voice, 'lots! Hundreds! This is just the beginning.'

Nadia and Stefan walked a little ahead, entranced in an animated talk, their clasped hands swinging in step.

'They've hit it off, haven't they?' Julia remarked with feeling.

'Good luck to them!' Miro replied.

'When will you come home again?'

Miro gave a sigh.

'I wish it could be every weekend. Too expensive. And I've got lots to cram. Before the end of the term exams.'

'How will I bear it that long?'

He chuckled.

'Making fun of me?'

She shook her head.

'If only you knew Miro, how lonely it can get sometimes. Especially when Mama's not too well.'

He picked up her free hand and pressed it to his lips.

'At Christmas, I'll see you every day. And in the Spring, when the weather gets warm you'll have to come down to London.'

The very thought quickened her pulse.

'Miro! That's a fantasy! You know my parents will never allow it!'

'They will. Because I'll invite Stefan and Nadia at the same time. There are always free rooms at the weekends. Mrs. Goodenough, true to her name, bless her, is in charge, but very kindly disposed towards me.'

'Oh Miro!' she was breathless just imagining that.

They talked in this excited vein all the way down Moultrie Road with its mansion-sized residences and down Bath Street with neat terraced houses flanking both sides, and made plans for next Summer, the walks, the cycling, the train rides. They talked about their studies, their friends and a hundred small, insignificant things, even their preferred toppings on toast.

'Gosh! I've not told you half the things I wanted to say,' Miro laughed when they turned into Julia's road. Nadia and Stefan were already at the gate, deep in whispered conversation, their heads almost touching. There were no other lights apart from the street lighting; all houses were quiet and dark, plunged in the night slumber.

'And I've got lots more to tell you,' Julia said. 'I don't think we'll ever be bored.'

Miro hugged her to him.

'Write to me every day.'

'And you too.'

At the gate, the four of them chatted in whispers, prolonging the moment of parting.

'We'll fetch you tomorrow,' Miro said, 'on the way to church.'

'Till tomorrow, then.' The boys waited and watched them let themselves in.

Indoors everyone was asleep. Julia and Nadia undressed in the dark and slipped into the double bed on each side of Klara.

'I'm just so happy!' Nadia whispered.

'Me too!' Julia hugged herself to hold the tingly feeling inside her.

In church, the next day, they sat together, Stefan and Nadia, Miro and Julia, and Klara on her other side. Julia did not resent her presence, nor the attention that Miro had lavished on them both in equal measures on the way to the church, as he amused them with stories of the boys' pranks at his old school. She was touched to note less guardedness in Klara's manner and a readiness to laugh at Miro's humour.

The Mass came to an end, and before the last hymn was sung, the congregation sat down for the notices. Miro's hand touched Julia's in the tight space between them, and it felt good to have that secret contact with him. And then, her ears pricked up with sudden alertness.

The priest's voice spoke out a familiar name. Leon Tarnovski. Nadia leaned forward and exchanged glances with her. The priest was reading the wedding bans. Leon Tarnovski and Alison Sommers. Nadia leaned forward again to catch Julia's eyes. She was smiling. Then she looked up at Stefan. She did not mind. She really did not mind.

When the congregation stood up to sing the last hymn, Julia turned her head and looked behind. Right by the arched doorway, flattened against the confessional, Leon and Alison stood together. His eyes were cast down. Julia caught Alison's gaze, gave her a nod and smiled. Alison returned the smile and smoothed down the flap of the coat over her thickened waist.

CHAPTER 69

Disaster struck without any warning. Swift, uncompromising, with a fatal blow. Only hours before, life was lived to familiar patterns and agreed time-tables, unaware of the impending devastation that was to leave a trail of pain and numbing bewilderment.

When Julia let herself in that chilly afternoon, there was nothing to indicate that within hours her life would be marked with a dividing moment of *before* and *after*. She was in good spirits, despite the pinching cold and that November darkness in the house. It was Friday, the start of the weekend. And there was a letter from Miro.

She switched on the lights, but delayed the pleasure of tearing open the envelope till after she had lit the fire, the dry wood and the scrunched paper she had left ready in the morning, till after she had filled Muszka's bowl, till she had made herself tea, and with her coat still on, she sat close to the fire, warming her hands on the hot mug.

Before long, the face-nipping cold air was softened by the hot-red glow. She put down the empty mug beside her and opened Miro's letter.

He had kept his promise and had written every day. He made her feel involved with his life in London. He made her feel as if she knew his friends, his lecturers, the route to the Law School, his room and his room-mate. Pity he was so faraway and they had to wait till Christmas before his next home-coming.

By the time Mama and Tato came home from work, the house had a warm, aromatic atmosphere, with Julia's prepared supper ready to serve: a simple meal of mashed potatoes, a cream sauce thick with mushrooms, and a green salad, one of the meatless Friday meals.

Julia had changed, a red polo-neck and black slacks, and had run a duster over all the exposed surfaces. For Mama. She had sorted out her schoolwork into manageable sections over the next two days. Tonight, she planned to tackle her Art assignment, then afterwards, read simply for pleasure. *The Go-between*. L.P. Hartley. A riveting tale of a young boy's innocent input into the forbidden love between a farm hand and the young lady from the manor.

Pity Nadia lived on the other side of the town. Friday night was a good time to meet, but then, she may have been on duty.

As soon as they sat down to eat, Mama complained of a headache. She looked flushed and her eyes were crinkled, as if warding off pain. She picked at her food, but was unable to swallow.

'I'm sorry Julia. I've got no appetite. It started this afternoon.'

'Don't worry, Mama,' Julia said brightly, anxiety pinching her stomach. 'I can warm up this for you later. Take a tablet and lie down.'

She dispensed tablets and water, while Tato fetched a blanket and a pillow from their bedroom. They made Mama comfortable on the sofa by the fire. She closed her eyes with a sigh of comfort.

They finished their supper, Tato and Julia, making small talk, pretending neither was worried about Mama's indisposition.

Later, after Julia had tidied and washed up, she entered her cold bedroom only long enough to collect her Art things. She spread herself out on the larger table in the front room. Tato retired to his armchair by the radio, the volume mercifully turned down, and read his Polish Daily. Mama slept. And Muszka, stealthily wedged between the blanket and the armrest, slept at Mama's feet.

Julia's assignment in Art was to design a textile pattern. She had looked for ideas in the library and had come across an illustrated book of William Morris patterns. Magical! She began to create her own patterns with coloured pencils and cut-outs in complementary and toning colours. Engrossing work. She lost track of time, until the stiffness in her neck and shoulders made her look at the clock. Almost nine. Time for tea and a biscuit. Mama was still sleeping, her position hardly changed since she lay down. Tato was reading his book, one of many he had ordered from the Polish Daily, diaries and memoirs of soldiers from Anders' army.

Julia tidied up and made three mugs of tea, placing two on the table. She left her Mama's close beside her on the little stool. Muszka stirred, yawned and stretched a paw.

'Mama. I've made tea.' Julia stroked her shoulder.

Mama's eyes fluttered and closed again.

'Mama? Are you awake?'

No response. Her face was flushed. The heat from the fire.

'Mama…' Julia stroked her face with the back of her hand. Still nothing. Cold fingers of unease prodded Julia's stomach.

'Tato,' she turned to him, 'can you speak to her?'

He was already getting up, his gaze concerned, fixed on Mama. He picked up her hand and gave it a gentle tug.

'Nastusha, you'll be better off in bed.' Her hand fell out of his and hung loose down the side of the sofa. Muszka made a leap, then a run to hide in the kitchen.

'Tato,' a jolt of panic, 'what's wrong with Mama?'

He stooped down and attempted to lift Mama's shoulders against the pillow. Her head drooped forward.

'We need an ambulance,' he said. The look of fear in his eyes scared her.

From that moment on, it was like responding to pre-programmed instincts. Her mind was in turmoil, yet she threw on her coat, checked the change in her pocket, bolted out of the front door and ran down the road as if a hurricane chased her. It was a raw, black night, with the street lights barely visible through pale, misty halos.

There were two young boys loitering by the phone box, the third having a smoke inside. They made stupid remarks as she ran up to them, but her panic over-rode her usual reluctance of any confrontation. She rapped her knuckles on the glass door.

'Please!' she shouted. 'My mother's just collapsed. She needs an ambulance!'

The jollity stopped, as if cut off with a knife. One of them yanked the door open and shouted to his mate,

'Gary! Get out! It's an emergency!'

Things happened fast. Automatically. In the smoke-filled cubicle, Julia dialled 999. A female voice answered.

'Which service do you need?'

'What?' It was all too much. 'My mother's just collapsed. We need help. Please!'

The female voice was calm. She asked for Julia's address. Then through her jumbled thoughts Julia heard her say,

'Go back to your mother now. The ambulance will be over as soon as possible.'

It must have been the relief of hearing these words. Something snapped inside her. Tears rolled down her face, as she shot out of the phone box and ran back. She did not hear one of the boys remark,

'Hey, this sounds like a bit of fun. Shall we go to watch?' They sprinted after her and stopped on the corner of Julia's road.

At home, there was no change in Mama. The rise and fall of her chest was a comforting sign. She was alive. Tato had put on his coat in readiness.

'I'm coming too,' Julia said.

The next ten minutes seemed interminable. Julia crouched beside Mama and stroked her head, because that made her feel as if she was doing something useful. Tato stood over them and checked his watch every few seconds, sighing and rubbing his forehead and muttering unintelligible words.

When the ambulance arrived, its luminous yellowness and flashing lights cutting through the black night, Julia ran out of the front door to meet the ambulance men. Just the sight of them was like a steadying hand on her shoulders.

'It's my mother!' she cried. They came in, two big men in uniforms, carrying a stretcher, their manner calm, friendly. One of them checked Mama's pulse and lifted an eyelid.

'What bad with her?' Tato's voice was shaking.

The man nodded sympathetically. 'They'll tell you at the hospital. Once they've checked her over.'

'May we come with you?' Julia asked, fearing his refusal.

'But of course!' he said kindly.

They carried Mama out, covered with a blanket up to her chin. It was frightening to see her so still. Tato followed and Julia came out last, pulling the door shut after her.

A familiar voice called out to her. Was she hallucinating? 'Julia! What's happening?'

She looked up and saw him standing next to the open back door of the ambulance. Miro. He was watching Mama being lifted and Tato climbing up beside her. She ran up the path to him.

'It's Mama. I'll explain later. But when did you get back?'

'Just now.' She noticed his small travel bag. He said, 'I'll come after you!'

There was no time for anything else. She climbed up and joined Tato by Mama's side, as one of the men stayed with them and closed the door. She felt drained and hollow. Automatically she placed her hand on top of Tato's tightly clasped hands in his lap. His face looked small and crumpled.

'They'll do everything they can,' the ambulance man assured them.

At the hospital of St. Cross, they were shown into a small waiting room, whitewashed, with brown wooden chairs arranged in groups of four, while Mama was being examined somewhere else, behind wide, double, closed doors. The nurse, a young girl no older than Nadia, asked them if they'd like a cup of tea.

The question was so unexpected, they stared at her as if rendered mute.

'You could do with one,' she decided for them.

The tea was hot and sweet, comforting to Julia's parched mouth. Her Tato did not speak, just stared into his cup with an occasional glance at the clock on the wall. It was only just after ten. It felt as if the evening had started days ago.

There was a movement at the half-open door. Julia leaned forward eagerly anticipating the doctor with some good news. It was Miro, smoothing his wind-swept hair with one hand and loosening the coat buttons with the other.

'I came as quickly as I could.'

She sprang up from her chair towards him. 'Miro! How did you?..'

He was not beaming his usual open smile. He came towards her and gave her a hug. In front of her Tato! But then he shook hands with him too.

'You're a good lad,' Tato cleared his throat, 'come, sit down with us.'

It did him good, her Tato, to open up and recount the events of the evening to Miro.

'Just waiting for the doctor,' he concluded. 'If they keep her in, a short stay in hospital will do her good.'

Julia agreed. Her mind raced ahead. She'd look after Mama. Take time off school. Until things improved. To Miro she said,

'I never expected to see you before Christmas!' It was a relief to talk about normal things. His smile was restrained.

'I got very homesick.' He looked straight into her eyes. She understood. Dear Miro.

'Homesickness…' her Tato picked up the theme, 'it never goes away. No matter how old you are.' Miro asked him about his home in Poland before the war. Tato talked, yet again, about all the things closest to his heart.

About half past ten, the doctor came in, accompanied by a senior looking sister. His pristine white coat and her neat navy uniform made them look important and businesslike. He held some papers in his hand.

'Mr. Lutovski,' he levelled his gaze at Tato. Tato stood up, and so did Julia and Miro. 'We've examined your wife. Anastazia.' He glanced at the papers. 'She has suffered a stroke.'

'What's that?' Julia asked.

'You're her daughter, I guess?' He spoke unhurriedly, his words precise. Julia nodded. 'In your mother's case, it's a brain haemorrhage.'

What did it mean? 'Can the blood be drained? Will she be all right?' Julia asked.

The sister looked at the doctor. He cleared his throat.

'It's serious. She is on medication. We can't do much else at the moment.'

'But medication,' Tato asked, 'it help? Yes?'

The doctor nodded. 'It'll ease the pressure on her brain. She's resting. She'll be monitored regularly. You can go and sit with her now.'

'For how long?' Julia asked. The Sister's features softened.

'All night, if you wish,' she said.

There were just four women patients in the small ward, all with curtains drawn around them and someone sitting at their beds.

Tato, Miro and Julia picked up a chair each from the stack by the door, and entered Mama's curtained cubicle. She had been changed into a blue hospital gown, and was resting against the pillows, her arms outstretched at her sides.

'Mama, we're here with you,' Julia said, as they sat down around her. All that could be heard were whispers and stirrings from the other corners of the room. They sat in silence for a long time just watching Mama's chest move up and down.

'Miro,' Tato was first to speak, 'there's no need for you to lose sleep tonight. Go home and get some rest.'

'I want to stay,' Miro replied, 'in case I can be of any help.'

'Thank you,' Tato said. 'We may yet have to rely on you tomorrow. For that reason you must be well rested.'

'Why Tato? What's on your mind?' Julia asked, anxiety snaking its way round her insides.

'I don't know,' Tato sighed, 'it just makes sense for at least one of us to be bright and alert tomorrow. You could go too, Julia…' She stopped him short with a vehement *no!*

'All right, I'll go,' Miro agreed with some reluctance, 'but I'll be back at the crack of dawn tomorrow!'

611

Julia kept dozing on and off, her head resting on the side of Mama's bed. She was vaguely aware of the nurse coming in regularly to check Mama's pulse and temperature. At about two, when the nurse came in again, she noticed that Tato was gone.

'Has he gone home? My Dad?' anxiety squeezed her stomach.

'No,' the nurse whispered softly, 'he's in the little waiting room. There are reclining seats there. More comfortable than these. You should do the same.'

'But my Mum...' Julia was uncertain. Mama was still, just as before.

'We'll come and tell you, if there's any change,' the nurse assured her.

Julia found Tato asleep in the reclining armchair. He stirred and opened his eyes when she sat down beside him.

'Has anything happened?' he asked. He looked tired, his clothes crumpled.

'No, I've just come to join you. How about you going home?'

He rubbed his eyes wearily. 'Not until there's a change.'

When Julia was woken up again, it was with a pat on her shoulder. The clock on the wall showed ten minutes to five and the nurse was peering down at her.

'You may like to see your mother now,' the nurse said. Tato was already up eager to go.

They followed the nurse down the corridor, Julia's mind lively with images of Mama sitting up in bed and waiting for them. She was surprised to find the doctor and the senior sister by Mama's bedside. Mama lay still, as before, sleeping. Only, on second glance, there was a stiffness about her, like a still from a film. A life stopped.

'Mr. Lutovski, Julia,' the doctor said in a grave tone, 'Anastazia has stopped breathing, a few minutes ago.'

CHAPTER 70

It was like watching herself from above, it was as if she was someone else, going about all the normal things, fulfilling all the demands and necessities of life, that carried on regardless, while she, Julia, nursed a pain as huge as the universe.

She went to school that Monday morning, with a letter from her Tato, composed by herself, informing Miss Beecham, her form mistress, of the family bereavement and requesting a few days compassionate leave for Julia. Tato had gone to work too, until his sister's arrival on Thursday. 'I may just as well,' he'd said, his eyes pink and watery, 'or I'll go mad all alone in this place all day!'

On the school bus out of town, a myriad of thoughts crammed Julia's mind, threatening to burst her brain. Last Saturday's events, like a film reel, kept replaying themselves countless times. Miro and Roman had been their guardian angels, Tato's and hers. In her bewildered state, she had no idea where to turn, what to do, after such a catastrophic event. Her Tato seemed to have lost his voice, and all the way to Roman's house, as they walked from the hospital, his gaze was on the ground, his eyes staring from a stony face.

In the dawn light on Saturday morning, there was little traffic about, but what struck Julia, was that everything looked exactly the same, calm and safe as yesterday. There was no mark, no sign anywhere of the cataclysm that had devastated their lives.

Roman and Joyce, in their dressing-gowns, received them like family. Joyce made hot tea and toast with jam, and Roman found it hard to compose himself as he listened to Tato's account of the night's events.

'Anastazia, my dear Anastazia!' Roman did not hide his anguish, 'I loved her like my own sister!'

Afterwards, he drove them home for a wash and a change of clothes. Miro had joined them too, having cycled to the hospital first, and learnt the terrible news.

The Registry Office was first on the list of the places to visit, then the Funeral Directors. Once the date of the funeral was agreed, Miro offered to go to the Post Office and send telegrams to Mama's two sisters in Germany, Hanna and Magda, and to Tato's sister Maria in Sweden. So much to think about! So much to organise! Julia stood dazed beside Miro as he made all the arrangements. Already they'd had replies from all three women: they were all coming to Mama's funeral.

613

Miro had cycled with Julia to Aunt Eva's. She had opened the door and her spontaneous welcome turned to concern when she saw their faces. A flood welled up inside Julia and forced its way out of her eyes, streaming down her cheeks. She heard Miro explain,

'Something terrible has happened, Mrs. Eva. Julia's Mama died this morning.'

'My God! Oh my God! What are you saying! How? When? O God!'

She ushered them indoors. Uncle Henryk got up from the table, his face grave. Marek peered from behind him, his eyes huge with interest. There was the sound of feet running down the stairs and Nadia burst into the room. She stopped as her eyes took in the scene.

Aunt Eva regained composure briefly, and organised everyone to sit round the table, while she and Nadia made coffee.

Between the sips of coffee Julia described what had happened to her Mama, her eyes filling up constantly, her voice breaking. They wanted to know every detail, repeated several times, as if they could not absorb what she was telling them the first time. Aunt Eva's eyes were red from crying and Uncle Henryk's lines deepened on his drawn face. He just shook his head now and again in disbelief.

Nadia sipped her coffee in silence, her distracted gaze wandering from Julia to Miro, her usual sparkle gone. She said in the end, after Julia's final account,

'I can't believe it! What did they say? What has actually caused it?'

Julia explained. What she thought she understood. What she found hard to understand. Words on paper. Regarding her Mama. Only it wasn't the Mama she knew.

'The statement on the Death Certificate says that Mama died of a stroke. A massive brain haemorrhage. It was also discovered that she'd had high blood pressure. And diabetes. She was never treated for anything like that!'

On alighting from the school bus, she stood back a little on the pavement, composing herself, allowing other girls to go by. She must not cry. She must not make a spectacle of herself. She clenched her teeth, hung her satchel over her shoulder and fell in step with the others.

At the school gate she came across Yvonne.

'Hi Julia!' As always, Yvonne greeted her with a friendly smile, her freckled cheeks raised, her fiery curls bouncing underneath the brim of her hat. 'Good weekend?'

Julia's lip trembled. She steadied it, pressing her mouth together. Then she replied,

'Not so good Yvonne. I'll explain later. I've got to see Miss Beecham first.'

'I'll come with you,' Yvonne offered. Her kindness threatened to shake Julia's composure. She nodded, nevertheless, and was aware of Yvonne's puzzled look as they proceeded towards the staff room. Julia knocked on the door and waited, avoiding Yvonne's gaze.

The door was opened by the young gym teacher, Miss Lewis.

'Can I help you?'

'Yes please,' Julia said politely, 'I need to see Miss Beecham.'

'Rightee-o!'

When Miss Beecham came to the door in her perennial brown suit and her short cut straight hair caught with a slide at the side, Julia was overcome with awe for a moment. She cleared her throat hurriedly.

'Miss Beecham, I've got a letter for you. From my father.'

'Oh, yes?' Miss Beecham took the letter and opened the envelope. Her serious expression remained unchanged, as she read it through. She folded it thoughtfully, before looking at Julia.

'I'm terribly sorry, Julia. Of course you must have time off. Wouldn't you rather go home now?'

'Thank you, but no. I'll stay, since I'm here.'

Miss Beecham gave her an approving look. 'That's the spirit!' she said, before closing the door.

Now it was Yvonne's turn, her eyes were probing for an explanation. Julia sighed.

'Yvonne, it's sad news. My Mum died on Saturday morning.'

Hearing herself stating this fact, evoked an attack of crying. She choked it all back, wishing now, she could be anywhere else but here. Yvonne's arm comforted her across her back and led her to their classroom.

She managed not to cry most of the day. She was able to lose herself in Mr. McBride's lecture on Victorian poets, pulling back her straying mind to concentrate. She was aware of Yvonne's and Susan's protectiveness towards her, their loyal company throughout the lunch break, their light-hearted but not frivolous talk. She was grateful. When Susan asked her plainly in the end, what had actually happened to her mother, Julia was able to compose herself enough to tell her.

In the afternoon, in the History period, the class received back their recent essays, and Julia hers, her dissertation on the state of affairs in the present-day, Soviet-run Poland. She was pleased with the mark, but puzzled by Miss Simpson's comment. '*I suggest you read widely around your subject in order to avoid forming one-sided views*'.

Julia cried then, discreetly, into her handkerchief, at the back of the classroom.

CHAPTER 71

When Julia was five a letter came for her Mama from the Red Cross. She remembered that day vividly. Her Mama laughed and cried all day and hugged Tato and cuddled her and talked and talked.

'Julia! You have two aunties! They've been found! Alive! Your Aunt Hanna and your Aunt Magda!'

For nine years her Mama knew nothing of her family, separated from them in 1940. Like her, they were deported too, in the opposite direction, to the west. They spent the war years in a German labour camp, where their parents died of malnutrition and ill health. Hanna and Magda survived with their children, and after the war settled in a small town, Munnerstadt, near Frankfurt. Both their husbands and their older brother Voytek had been killed in the 1939 September Campaign, a valiant but disastrous attempt at fending off the German invasion.

When Julia was eight, her Mama took her on a two-day train journey, which seemed interminable as they sat for long hours and slept on the hard wooden benches in the Third Class.

The town of Munnerstadt appeared to Julia like a fairy-tale town, with its pretty houses, colourful gardens, green parks, ornate churches, their interiors filled with gilded angels and cherubs. They stayed with Aunt Magda, who lived in a top floor flat, with two rooms and a spacious attic, where Julia practised cartwheels and headstands. Aunt Magda's twins, Tomek and Melania, were grown up at seventeen, and already working in their apprenticeships, car mechanics and tailoring respectively. Her aunt's rented flat seemed palatial in comparison to Julia's Nissen hut, with its corrugated iron body.

Aunt Hanna's accommodation was at the American base nearby. The American soldiers were seen everywhere, and the droning of their lorries could be heard most days, as they went out to practise their military manoeuvres. Aunt Hanna was employed in their kitchen. Her children, Yacek and Anna, at twenty-one and nineteen, considered themselves old enough to work away from home and had found jobs in Frankfurt. They came back to visit, nevertheless, and to meet their aunt from England.

Julia had vivid memories of that hot, dry summer. Aunt Magda's image remained that of a good-natured, softly spoken aunty, always ready with a hug and a kiss. Aunt Hanna was different. She had made her Mama cry. Julia still remembered words, which at the time she did not understand. *Time to cut the umbilical cord! Time to stop snivelling!*

Even now, as she stood on the cold, draughty platform waiting for the train from London, that instinctive resentment that she had felt at the time, surfaced again. Any minute now, after all the years, she'd be seeing her aunts again. It was an unusually blue sky for this mid-November day, that would be greeting them.

Aunt Hanna was unmistakeable, when she alighted first, amongst the crowd waiting to get on. Her slim black coat elongated her shape, her chin was hidden in the fur collar, and the brim of her black felt hat, shaded her very blue eyes and her very red mouth.

Aunt Magda's black attire contrasted sharply with her anaemic complexion, her grey eyes, and her pale hair, escaping in crimped curls the black angora beret. Her face, nevertheless, broke into a most welcoming smile on seeing Julia.

They each, in turn, held Julia in a long, strong embrace. Words were not necessary. Julia picked up two of their bags and informed them,

'Our friend Roman is waiting outside the station. He'll take us home in his car.' It had been a lucky coincidence that their arrival was in his lunch hour.

Roman, as always, was charming, helpful, chatty, and Julia noticed Aunt Hanna's eyes darting to him with interest in the mirror, as he drove them home. Conversation was disjointed, with random questions, and Julia's attempted answers as more questions were thrown at her. Before dropping them off, Roman said,

'I'll be back for you tonight, ladies. My wife has prepared a room for you. It'll be comfortable, I promise. If you don't need anything out of your suitcases now, I'll take them with me.'

Julia's aunts kept their smaller bags with them and followed her indoors.

'We'd have been happy to stay here with you, Julia,' Aunt Magda said, taking off her coat and hat in the narrow hallway. Aunt Hanna shook her hair loose and checked herself in the mirror. Her hair had been obviously recently styled and rinsed dark blond, and fell in elegant waves around her face.

'I'd like that too,' Julia replied politely, 'but as you'll see, our house hasn't got a lot of space.' She opened the door to her room. Muszka was curled in a ball on her bed. 'We'd have to squash, all three of us. And Tato's sister is coming as well. She'll have my bed. And a resident cat, by the looks of it.'

'Rather her than me,' Aunt Hanna said. 'I hope she hasn't got fleas. The cat, I mean.'

'She's very clean!' Julia assured her, taking a mental note to keep Muszka away from her fastidious aunt.

She led them into the front room, where she'd covered the table with

Mama's embroidered tablecloth and set out the porcelain cups and saucers and plates. Aunt Magda sat down and looked around, her worn hands clasped tightly on the table. Aunt Hanna studied the photographs on the wall, pleased to see herself and all their family displayed. After a while she followed Julia into the kitchen and lifted the lid off the pot on the stove, as Julia was brewing tea.

'Smells good,' she said, 'did you cook it?' Her abrupt tone was a little grating.

Julia forced a smile. 'Like Mama's. Thick vegetable soup. We'll have chicken and a proper meal later.' She poured the soup into bowls and brought it over to the table together with thickly cut fresh bread and butter. It was a strange feeling, Mama's sisters sitting with her, and her Mama absent.

It pleased her that her aunts enjoyed her soup.

'You must have been very hungry,' she said.

'We took sandwiches and water with us, 'Aunt Magda said, in her soft, un-intrusive voice, 'but this is really good on a cold day. Tell us Julia, tell us everything from the beginning.'

Julia began with her Mama's stay in the hospital last summer, her puzzling, erratic behaviour, her promising recovery, and now, the unexpected blow.

'We were stunned when your telegram came,' Aunt Magda said. 'Nastusha was the youngest. And the first to go!' Her eyes looked watery.

'She was her own worst enemy!' Aunt Hanna stated.

'Too sensitive,' Julia remarked and could not help adding, 'for some people.'

They finished the soup and she collected the bowls. She came back with a pot of tea and an apple cake cut into squares. She poured the tea into her prized porcelain cups. Aunt Magda asked.

'And how's Theo taking it?'

Julia offered them cake, before replying, 'It's hard for my poor Tato.'

Aunt Hanna looked over the rim of her cup. Her gaze was meaningful.

'And what's going to happen now, Julia? You and Theo. Under the same roof. When he's not your true father.'

It was like a slap. Julia understood in a split second, how this woman's tongue had upset her Mama all those years ago. Her anger, for the moment, flared stronger than her grief. She cleared her throat.

'But he *is* my true father. My Tato. He's the one who brought me up.'

There was sympathy in Aunt Magda's expression, but Aunt Hanna had not finished yet.

'You're young, Julia. You know nothing about life!'

'I'm learning all the time.'

'It's better to be careful than sorry,' Aunt Hanna persisted.

'I'll bear that in mind.' God, she wasn't making it easy to like her.

Aunt Magda spoke softly across the table,

'Julia, my dear, we worry about you. You are our sister's child. Any time you need it, there will be a home waiting for you with us.' She meant well.

'Aunty,' Julia said with polite firmness, 'but there's really nothing for you to worry about. I couldn't wish for a kinder Tato. And I could never leave him now. Besides, my life is here. My school. My friends. Everything.' She did not tell them about Miro. She did not add that she could never contemplate moving to Germany. Of all places!

Over cake and tea, as Julia listened to their anecdotes of their young years at home, she relaxed and her annoyance subsided, but wariness of Aunt Hanna remained. Somehow through their constant mentioning of her Mama, it felt as if Mama was sitting there with them at the table. Perhaps she was. Julia's hand rested on the empty seat beside her.

Her aunts were not used to sitting around idle. After clearing up lunch things, they started looking round for jobs to do.

'No, please,' Julia pleaded, 'you are our guests. Let's go for a walk instead. While the sun shines. It'll get dark before long.' To her relief. Aunt Hanna agreed.

They dressed warmly, and muffled with scarves, walked down the country lane towards Old Brownsover, and on the bridge over the canal. Here in the open fields the air was bracing and the sun was low, making your eyes squint. Julia got secret little smiles from Aunt Magda, as Aunt Hanna's incessant chatter gave detailed accounts of all the different jobs she had been employed in over the years, and her opinions of the attitudes of her numerous employers: German, Russian, American, British. She was pleased with her present job.

'They care for their soldiers, the Americans do. It's really good stuff that we cook for them. No cutting corners. No rubbish there.'

She spoke of her children, Yacek and Anna, both married now, with two children each.

'Keeps me young,' she laughed, 'all this baby sitting!'

Aunt Magda's grandchildren were only babies still, Tomek had a daughter, and Melania a son. All Julia's cousins had German spouses. How strange were the whims of fate!

Back home, after a warming cup of tea, Aunt Hanna took over the kitchen.

'All I need are the basic ingredients, and I'll make you delicious cakes!' She brought out of her handbag little sachets of flavourings: vanilla, chocolate, lemon and orange. She held them up. 'Which do you fancy?'

'Hanna, you're always the best judge!' Aunt Magda stated, winking at Julia. She sat down beside her by the fire, leaving Aunt Hanna to take command of the kitchen. Aunt Magda took out her knitting from her bag, a lacy pattern in pink.

'For my little Dagmar,' she said, 'a most delightful little girl.' Julia did not doubt her, but the German name had a harsh sound for someone so small.

When her Tato came home from work at half past-six, the house was warm, smelling of baking, the supper cooked and ready to serve, the table set in the front room. Her aunts had known her Tato only from the photographs which her Mama sent regularly with the Christmas cards.

His face, pained and shrunken in the last few days, brightened and filled out at the sight of them, and a smile appeared as he hugged each of his wife's sisters in turn.

'It was so good of you to come,' he said. 'So much expense. And effort. But it helps here,' he beat his chest, 'to know that she was loved so much.'

He disappeared for a short while, to get washed and changed, as they sat waiting at the table.

'I like him already,' Aunt Magda said, her pallor tinged pink from the warmth in the room.

'Anastazia could have done much worse!' Aunt Hanna stated with the air of a sage, 'I could never understand what all the fuss was about!' It seemed Tato had won her approval too.

Later, Julia was pleasantly surprised, relieved, even comforted in her constant state of sadness. It cheered her to see the change in Tato. From the clammed up, shrinking, grieving man of the last few days, he emerged his nearly normal self, eager again to recall the war years, and amuse his wife's sisters with countless anecdotes of the numerous friendships forged in his wartime travels.

The conversation got livelier still, at the discovery of their common acquaintance with people and places back home in pre-war Poland.

Julia was content to sit back and listen, and in her mind talk to her Mama. If only she could be here. She would have enjoyed this. If only she could come back just for one moment to tell her, *I'm all right now.*

Muszka sneaked out from her imposed confinement in Julia's bedroom and quietly climbed onto her lap under the table. Julia stroked her warm softness and avoided Aunt Hanna's gaze.

On Thursday her Tato stayed at home. Together they went to the station to meet Aunt Maria off the London train. With a touch of nervous anticipation Julia wondered what Aunt Maria would be like. Aunt Hanna had already made herself the boss of their household. She and Aunt Magda had stayed at home, dusting and cleaning, despite Julia's polite protestations.

'We've got to do something!' Aunt Hanna insisted, a duster in her hand, her dark dress protected by Mama's floral apron. 'Roman's wife keeps their house so immaculate, there's nothing for us to do!'

They had stayed the nights with Roman and Joyce and had been impressed with Joyce's efforts to communicate with them in Polish.

'If only this was the summer, we'd do some gardening for them and for you!' Aunt Magda promised.

Today was a typical November day, dark and misty and oppressive. The cold on the platform penetrated the clothes and the flesh to the very bones. Julia couldn't control her shivering.

'Aunt Maria will get a shock,' she said for something to say, blowing warm breath into her gloved hands, 'I hope to God, the temperature will improve for tomorrow!'

'She's used to worse,' Tato said. 'It's much colder in Sweden.' He had his long, thick coat on, and a furry hat with ear flaps, from his Siberian times, he was proud to point out. It was useful today.

Tomorrow had been set for Mama's funeral. It felt unreal. It helped having her aunts around, but nothing could stop the sudden, overpowering waves of grief. There was a void in every part of the house, that confronted her wherever she went, a constant reminder that her Mama was gone. Sometimes, she had a feeling that if she looked up quickly from her writing desk, she'd see her Mama standing at the door. She tried that. Many times. Till her vision was blurred, till her throat ached.

She wished this was not real. But it was. The priest had announced it so. Last Sunday. The shock of the congregation was real. Aunt Eva's tears were real. Nadia was not her exuberant self as she patted and squeezed Julia's hand outside the church. They'll all be there tomorrow. All her Mama's fiends. And Miro. Dearest Miro. Her buffer. Her rock.

Tato and his sister fell into each other's arms and stood holding each other tight for a long time. Twenty years separated this moment from the last time they had been together.

'Good journey?' was all he said, standing back to have a better look at her.

'Yes. Considering the distance. All in one day. The flight and the train. And here I am!'

She turned her attention to Julia. She was like a character from a Tolstoy novel: a fur hat down to her eyes, fur collar and a long grey coat, almost touching the ground. Julia warmed to the expression in her light grey eyes, of interest and sympathy and understanding.

'Come here, my little offspring,' she said opening her arms wide. She pressed Julia to her chest, making her feel like a big cuckoo baby against her small frame. 'None of us in our family have been blessed with progeny. It gladdened my heart to know that my brother had found a blissful niche in his much fragmented life. And now yet again, fate is cruel to him.'

'I'm still here,' Julia said, returning the hug. Inexplicably she found Aunt Maria's slightly eccentric self-expression rather endearing. 'We'll continue looking after each other.'

She picked up the smaller bag, and her Tato the suitcase, which he secured on top of his bicycle outside the station. Julia found herself apologising for the dull and misty day, assuring Aunt Maria that November could surprise with a sudden burst of sunshine.

'Where I live, Julia,' Aunt Maria said, 'it's a continuous night from September till April. Big business in candles and table lamps. All through the winter months they are lit in the windows around the clock to create light inside and out.'

At home, Aunts Hanna and Magda were already waiting with a pot of tea and Hanna's cakes. After the usual welcome greetings and hugs, Julia showed Tato's sister into her room, which she had prepared, dusted and cleaned, and emptied of all her school things. She stacked them in grocery boxes in the corner under the window in the front room.

'It's so good of you, my sweet girl,' Aunt Maria said, 'but where will you sleep?'

'The sofa's quite comfortable,' Julia assured her, 'I'll manage quite well.'

At that moment Muszka made her appearance and rubbed herself against Aunt Maria's calf. Julia picked her up with apologies.

'She's supposed to stay in Tato's room.'

'She can stay here. I adore cats.' Aunt Maria stated with no fuss. Julia liked her.

They joined the others at the table, and again, Julia experienced a moment of contentment at the sight of the porcelain set. She was certain that despite her Mama's initial protestations, she would have been pleased now with Julia's efforts to entertain her family in style.

Aunt Maria was of a slight build. The woollen beige dress hung loose on her, but the fluffy cardigan in coffee brown added illusory bulk to her frame. Her hair, which may have been dark blond once, was predominantly grey, combed back off her face and twisted in a chignon on her nape. The string of pearls and the pearl earrings added grace to her understated elegance.

She sat down at the table, and immediately talk flowed, while Aunt Hanna poured tea and Aunt Magda cut the cake. Julia listened, glad to have a rest from the effort of having to make conversation. Their subjects were inexhaustible: Poland before the war, the war years, the people they knew, hundreds, the present situation in their country, the speculations for the future.

The room got very warm. Aunt Maria took off her cardigan and draped it over the back of the chair. And that was the moment when everyone saw it, when she rested her hands on the table: the black tattooed number above her wrist.

'Quite a memento they've left you, Maria,' Tato remarked drily. 'The bastards!' Tato did not swear often. She rubbed her wrist and turned it over so that the tattoo would not be visible.

'Yes... Ravensbruck. How could I ever forget?'

'We heard...' Aunt Magda said softly, 'but not until the end of the war. How did you survive such things?'

Aunt Maria shook her head and pulled the sleeve down over her hand. Her story was similar to thousands of other tales of survival, that gradually unravelled in shocking numbers and testified to the unimaginable cruelty that humans are capable of.

Her husband, a lawyer, and she a Classics teacher had been arrested by the Gestapo and sent to Auschwitz first. 'We were separated and I never saw my Zbyszko again. For two years I worked with other women digging ditches and building roads. In the most appalling conditions. Rain, mud, snow, frost, that threatened the loss of your fingers. Hundreds of women died. Then one day, out of the blue, a large group of us was packed on the train and sent to Ravensbruck.' She gave a shrug of disbelief. 'Why me? Why us? We weren't given any information. This camp was just for women. Ukrainian, Jewish, Romanian, Polish. Conditions here were just as bad as before. The barracks were dirty and infested with lice. We slept two, sometimes three to a bed.' Her gaze became distant. 'I once slept with a dead girl for three nights before they took her body away. It was terrifying. I couldn't sleep at all, fending off the rats that were after her…'

Julia shivered. It was unimaginable, looking at this neat woman.

'It was common knowledge,' Aunt Maria continued, 'that some women were beaten to death. Some sent to be gassed. No rhyme or reason to any of it. Except their own secret plan. Some women were used for medical experiments. Like rabbits. Most of those died. Those that survived were left damaged with missing body parts… an amputated arm or a leg.'

Aunt Magda gave a shuddering sigh. 'And you survived all that?'

'I almost didn't. I had frequent infections. And very little food. But they approved of my workmanship. I worked in a place where all the clothes taken off the dead people or stolen from ghettos had to be altered to strict specifications. A week before liberation, at the end of April in 1945, we didn't know, of course, how close we were to freedom, I caught pneumonia. In the brief, lucid moments, I really believed that it was the end for me. It was like a miracle when the Swedish white ambulances arrived and took us away from that hell on earth…'

The little group round the table fell quiet. Julia could only wonder at their own personal memories of their past.

'And how are things now?' she asked tentatively. 'Are you happy in Sweden?'

Aunt Maria's features softened as she turned her attention to her.

'My dear Julia, in life, as you'll learn, if you can't have what you love, then you love what you have. Sweden's been good to me. I shall forever be grateful. I have work. I can afford to rent a flat. I have friends. It would be a sin to complain now. After everything that's happened …'

'Do you miss teaching?' Julia asked. Maria smiled.

'Slavonic Studies don't feature high on the Swedish curriculum. In any event, I enjoy my work. In the summer months I work on a farm. Rearing chickens and geese. It's only for half a year. Then from September, through the dark winter months, I do sewing. I get more than enough orders. Women's clothes and soft furnishings.'

'Really?' Julia's interest perked up, 'I've always fancied being a fashion designer!'

Aunt Maria laughed. 'It's not quite like that. But I still get a lot of pleasure when my customers walk away happy.'

That night, after Roman's brief visit to collect Aunts Hanna and Magda, and after her Tato and Aunt Maria had retired to their rooms, Julia lay on the sofa, covered up to her chin, in the faint but still warm glow from the dying fire and Muszka curled against the crook of her bent legs. It felt good to have her close, yet nothing could bring her relief from the oppressing sadness. She would have given anything for a brief moment with Mama. Just one touch. One word.

Tomorrow was so close. So final. She could not imagine ever being cured of the pain buried deep inside her.

CHAPTER 72

The day of the funeral was a fragmented chain of impressions. The opening words of the funeral service distressed her. All about sins and sinners and praying for Anastazia's soul, so that she could be absolved of all her failings and led by Angels to heaven. A week too late. Where would her Mama have been all this time? Julia was certain she was already in heaven.

She cried when the coffin was carried out of the church. She choked back her reflex to howl when the coffin was lowered into the ground. Tato and her aunts looked down, ashen-faced, grief frozen in their faces. Against the grey sky, the tall cypresses stood still around them, not a breath of a breeze rustling their branches. People sprinkled handfuls of soil, that made thudding noises on the coffin. She and her aunts had prepared a basket of chrysanthemum heads, which shone like stars at the bottom of the pit. Gratitude to her aunts warmed her tired heart for this simple idea. Mama had loved flowers.

Afterwards, they walked the short distance from the cemetery along Clifton Road to Roman and Joyce's house. Their lounge accommodated adequately the gathering of the closest friends. Eva's face was blotchy with crying. Henryk spoke hardly at all. Stella had come up from London, doll-like in her short, black velvet coat, a soft velvet beret-style hat, and high boots. A stylish city girl with stunning looks. Julia's weary mind could not summon up the usual fanciful ideas that Stella's glamorous image usually evoked. She was vaguely aware of Stella and Nadia's subdued talk as she and Miro followed them. His warm hand holding on to hers was so comforting, she did not want their hands to part.

Indoors, inside Joyce's front room she looked around and wondered if her Tato was feeling as utterly miserable as she did. Did Mama's sisters? They all looked just the same as before, as they stood or sat in small groups; Tato deep in conversation with his sister Maria, Hanna and Magda with Henryk and Stella, Miro's parents Michal and Anna with Roman, while Eva and Nadia went round with platefuls of sandwiches and slices of cake brought along by everyone present. Her Mama's last party with her loved ones.

Julia and Miro helped Mrs. Joyce to make coffee and tea, and distribute the cups from the trays. It felt as if she was in a trance, as if separated from everyone by a pane of glass. Miro's face appeared close to hers regularly with whispered words of encouragement. She loved his face, she loved his eyes, shiny like chestnuts, full of concern. She wished everything would just fade away, and it was just him and her, and she could fall into his arms and cry and cry till all the pain poured out of her, and only peace was left.

'I wish I could have more time with you,' she said when they were alone in the passage between the kitchen and the front room. He brushed her cheek with his lips.

'We will make time. I promise. When this is over,' he said.

Julia dedicated Saturday to her aunts, Hanna and Magda. She showed them round the shops in town. They were delighted with the small gifts that they found for their grandchildren. Julia missed Miro and struggled with the urge to go to his house in the evening. But the evening, her last with her Mama's sisters, turned out better than her dreaded expectation of it. They sat round the table after the evening meal and reminisced and Julia listened, her heart lifting at each mention of her Mama's name. It was good for Tato. His drawn face relaxed occasionally and even managed a smile. And Aunt Hanna, for once, said nice things to everyone.

On Sunday morning, Roman brought back her Mama's sisters for the last time, and after their tearful goodbyes with Tato and Maria, Julia and Miro accompanied them on their first leg of the train journey to Victoria in London.

Aunt Hanna quizzed Miro incessantly; about his family, their past, his studies, his future plans. He answered all questions with good grace. In the end, she could not help herself. She asked,

'And what are your intentions towards Julia?' Her blue eyes challenged him from underneath the brim of her hat.

Julia's toes curled as she glanced sideways at Miro. But he smiled politely.

'My intentions are all good,' he said, 'and my plans are to complete my studies, to qualify, to find a job, and then,' he looked at Julia again, 'then we'll plan together.' She felt a pleasant flutter in her stomach. And pride, as she gave Aunt Hania a quick glance.

Aunt Hanna pursed her red lips and gave him a challenging stare. But Aunt Magda intervened.

'I'm pleased for you both. Please write to me often, and keep me informed.'

They said their final goodbyes at Victoria, and then Julia and Miro watched the Dover train move slowly out of the station. They waved till Hanna and Magda's window receded into the distance and became just a reflecting strip of glass.

'Alone at last!' Miro exhaled and laughed and held Julia close to him in his arms, with hundreds of travellers milling around them.

'You've handled her well,' Julia managed a small laugh in this rare moment of lightness. 'Did you mean all that?'

'Julia,' he was serious, 'you must know me by now. I don't trifle with serious matters.' But then a wide smile split his face. 'Hey, lets's go! Lets get some ham and cheese rolls and go to my place. I'll make coffee. We'll have a feast!' It was the way he said it. She felt a fizz of anticipation. Her spirit soared. It felt as if he was promising her the best restaurant in town.

'Dare I?' she asked. 'Alone? In a bachelor pad? What would people say?' She said it flippantly, but she needed reassuring.

Miro laughed. 'But you won't be on your own! You'll be with me!' Then seeing her expression he added, 'Julia, I'd never do anything to upset you or your family. Trust me.' He pulled her hand gently saying, 'Let's go! Let's enjoy the little time we've got.'

They took a tube to Lancaster Gate. The stately looking house, in the 19th century stuccoed terrace, stood three storeys high over the basement, which served as the kitchen and the canteen for its inhabitants.

'There won't be anyone about in the day,' Miro said, leading Julia inside the entrance hall. 'We only use the canteen at breakfast and in the evenings. But we all have a kettle in our rooms.'

Julia followed him up the sturdy, dark wood stairs, with a rectangle of hard-wearing linoleum on each tread. Excitement rose above her prevailing oppressive mood. She and Miro had never been like this, together, alone, in a strange house.

Miro unlocked his door and let her in. His room-mate was away for the weekend. The room looked symmetrical with each side copying the other: two beds against opposite walls, two wardrobes at the end, two desks with chairs close to the window. In the corner behind the door, there was a small sink with a mirror above it, a small worktop with a kettle and an electric ring, and a wooden box for storing the basics, such as coffee, tea, sugar and biscuits.

'Here we are!' Miro said smiling, taking off his coat and Julia's, to put them away in his wardrobe. Julia noticed that the base, apart from his spare shoes, was stacked with books and files.

'Heavy day tomorrow?' she asked.

'Thankfully, no. Just two hours in the afternoon. I'll have the morning to sort myself out. But first things first, Julia. I'll make coffee and you can sit down at the table. Be my guest!'

She managed a laugh.

'Any plates?' she asked.

'No such luxuries here, just two saucers,' he replied, filling the kettle with water. She placed the saucers on his desk and the filled bread rolls beside them. They chatted while he made coffee in two mugs. She looked out of the window at the long narrow strip of lawn below, surrounded by high walls. Drab and forlorn on this grey November day.

'It's certainly very private here,' Julia remarked.

'Claustrophobic,' Miro replied bringing the coffee to his desk. 'I often go to the park. Such wide open spaces there. You wouldn't believe this was London. Visit me in the summer Julia, there's so much to see!'

627

'Really?' she teased, wishing that could be as easy as his words.

They sat down opposite each other. The sip of coffee tasted good, sweet and not too strong. She took a bite of the bread-roll. She chewed, feeling no hunger.

'You'll have to help me with the second one,' she said. 'I'll never manage both.'

'With pleasure,' Miro replied, his eyes shining. He ate with the eagerness of a hungry man.

An amicable silence followed. Julia allowed him to enjoy his food. There was so much she had been wanting to tell him, and now, that they were alone, she did not know where to begin. The one prevalent sensation was that she was hurting, it seemed in every part of her. If only someone or something could relieve her of that ache. Her eyes prickled and blurred and before she could control yet another spasm of grief, tears trickled down her face. She wiped them away with her sleeve.

'Julia,' his voice was gentle and he placed his hand over hers, 'you've had a ghastly week!'

She gave a shuddering sigh.

'I just want my Mama back.'

She cried then, uncontrollably into her hands, cupped over her face. She was aware of Miro getting up, coming to her side, placing his arm around her shoulders and saying,

'Come, sit down with me, and cry as much as you need.'

He led her to his bed, and when they sat down on the edge, he held her close to his chest, like a child in need of comfort. The fit of grief subsided, she wiped her eyes and blew her nose and felt she could attempt a normal talk with him again.

'Now, I'm such a mess!' She looked up at him. He kissed her on both cheeks.

'Let's sit back comfortably,' he said, wriggling up to lean against the wall. Julia settled beside him and moulded herself into the arc of his arm. She loved the sensation, the feel of his closeness, the warmth, the comfort.

'I wish I didn't have to leave,' she said.

'Julia,' he hugged her, 'grief is like an illness. You've not had any time yet to start dealing with it.'

'What if it's incurable? '

He hugged her again.

'You've got to take your mind off it. Think of positive things. Give your Dad a thought. He is hurting too. You've got to be strong for him...'

'And who's going to be strong for me?' It was peevish, she knew, but she had to say it.

He removed his arm from her shoulders, cupped her face in his hands and kissed her on the lips. 'I'll be strong for you.' He kissed her again, his lips moving gently over hers, the sensation sending shivers up her spine, yet a warmth spreading out from the centre of her being, her mind floating effortlessly in space.

'Miro, oh Miro!' she whispered between their kisses.

'I love you,' he said simply, 'I'll never let you down.' He moved his face back to look at her. 'How about, if we have another coffee and afterwards walk across the park, before I take you to the station?'

'It sounds very sensible,' she said in mock seriousness, yet grateful and loving him all the more for not pushing her to do things she was not ready for.

CHAPTER 73

Julia walked briskly from the station along the deserted, dimly-lit route, eerie with its shadowy recesses, close to the factory walls. Further, when she reached the playing fields, the vast blackness hanging above them felt menacing. No one else in sight, only the occasional car on this bleak road, that would be transformed in the morning with thousands of BTH employees rushing to work.

It was a relief to reach her street and run up the short distance to her gate. Tato and Aunt Maria had finished their meal earlier. There was a lingering, pleasant aroma of frying and baking. Homely and comforting. As soon as Julia took off her coat, and went to warm her hands by the fire, she noticed changes in the front room. Mama's iron beadsted, freshly made up, stood against the wall next to the narrow dresser, with Muszka already in possession of her new sleeping place.

'What's been happening?' Julia asked.

'Just practicalities,' Aunt Maria called from the kitchen. There was the hissing sound from the frying pan. 'We'll tell you Julia, all about it in a minute. You've had a long day. You must eat first.'

'Tato?' Julia looked at him. He was sitting in his armchair by the radio, sorting out the week's editions of the Polish Daily. He took off his glasses. His grey eyes were tired and watery. There were deep lines around his mouth. He rubbed his forehead wearily.

'Maria wants you to have your own room back. That's all. You need to have your own space, Julia, to study.'

'You can't forever sleep on the sofa!' Aunt Maria called from the kitchen.

Julia had not minded, but in truth, she had missed the privacy of her own room. She was so thoughtful, Aunt Maria.

Her Tato asked about Hanna and Magda and she assured him they got off all right. Aunt Maria brought Julia's supper, ready on a plate, and placed it before her.

'I should be waiting on you, auntie,' Julia said self-consciously.

'And I don't want to be treated like a guest forever,' Maria said, sitting down opposite her. 'I want us to be like a family. Eat my dear. You've probably been hungry all day.'

The pork chop, fried potatoes and carrots looked appetizing. Julia cut the meat and tasted it.

'Thank you,' she said, 'this is very good.'

Aunt Maria nodded, looking gratified, and rested her palms on the table, one cupped inside the other. Her nails were oval-shaped, neatly manicured and varnished pale pink. Despite the prevailing smell of cooked food, there was a hint of perfume about her. She leaned forward as if taking Julia into her confidence.

'We had time for a long talk today, Theo and I,' she said, 'about the future. Our future, Julia. The three of us.' Julia raised her eyes with interest. There was an earnestness about Aunt Maria's manner, as if she was trying hard to convey that all her intentions were meant well. 'We know it's hard for you Julia,' she continued, 'and it won't be better straight away. But in time... believe me, it won't be as awful as it is now.'

Julia ate slowly, her throat feeling tight.

'We've all lost someone we loved,' Aunt Maria said. 'All three of us now are orphans.'

Julia had never thought of adults as being orphans. Did they feel pain as deep as hers? And if they did, how did they cope with it? Her gaze wandered towards her Tato, sitting in his corner with his pile of newspapers. There was something infinitely wistful about him, his white hair all fluffy without the flattening hair cream. Poor Tato. He'd lost his first wife and his little son. And now Mama. And Aunt Maria her husband.

'How do you get over it?' Julia asked.

'You never do, Julia,' Aunt Maria said. 'It always stays in your heart. But your Mama would not want you to spend your life grieving. She'd want you to do well at school. Do something worthwhile with your life. Otherwise, all her previous efforts of providing for you would have been for nothing.'

Yes, Julia thought, with a sudden lift in her thoughts, that's exactly what her Mama would have expected of her. Carrying on with her life, as normally as possible, would not have been a betrayal to her Mama's memory, but a tribute. Such a simple but such an uplifting thought!

'Julia,' Tato spoke from his corner, lighting a cigarette, 'always appreciate the good things in your life. No matter how small. Better to have had even a little than nothing at all.'

Twelve years with Mama, that's all Tato had. That would never be enough for her, but she kept her thoughts to herself.

'Julia,' Aunt Maria ran her hand over her smooth hair, 'we've been thinking, Theo and I. How would you feel about my staying with you for a little longer?'

How would she feel? Aunt Maria's company would be a blessing in the terrible void Julia felt around her.

'How long can you stay?' she asked.

'Till after Christmas.'

Julia's mind raced. All the things she had been dreading, the long dark evenings, the cold, empty house each afternoon, Tato's isolation and the screeching radio, her escape from her own loneliness into the emptiness of her room… all those things need not be as bad with Aunt Maria here. Relief lifted her spirit.

'That would be wonderful,' she said with all the sincerity she felt, 'but what about your work?'

Aunt Maria smiled.

'My dear child, I've not had a break for fifteen years. No one's waiting for me.'

'Then stay as long as you can,' Julia invited fervently, getting up to take the empty plate away.

When Aunt Maria brought tea and cake to the table, Tato joined them saying,

'We've discussed the possibility, Julia, of Maria's longer stay with us. But there are formalities to be overcome first. And the authorities are well known for their delaying tactics.'

Aunt Maria's eyes sparkled as she poured tea. 'I intend to lodge an application for a permanent residency in this country. How would you feel about that?'

'Great!' Julia's cry was spontaneous.

Aunt Maria took a hurried sip and her face was animated with anticipation.

'Julia, I think we have a good chance. On compassionate grounds. Remember, two, three years ago? Polish families were given permission to reunite. Those scattered all over Europe. A lot of people came over here from Poland.'

Yes, Julia remembered the new girls at her old school, appearing from out of nowhere in the middle of the term. She had viewed them at first through her Mama's rosy and romantic notions of her old country. She had perceived them as mysterious and exotic. The lively ones had been strictly monitored by Sister Alicya against possible communist influences.

They were different. They didn't fit in. Julia had felt sorry for them. It must have been really hard for them to leave their friends behind. To be taken away from everything familiar. And to have to call a stranger they had never met, their Dad.

She turned to Aunt Maria. 'How will you feel about leaving your home?'

'Home?' Aunt Maria shrugged with a wistful smile, 'I've lost that already. We all did. Our generation. I'm just a visiting guest now, wherever I go.'

'Do you feel like that here? With us?'

Maria's features softened.

'No, Julia, it's different here. It feels good. I've felt it even in this short space of time. You two are the only family I've got. I can't go back to my sisters in Poland. They depend on my help. On my staying in the West. God only knows when I'll be able to see them again.'

It was a revelation. Aunt Maria needed them.

'You really want to come and live with us? For good? In this tiny place?'

632

Aunt Maria sat up with a surge of energy.

'I've been thinking, Julia. I've got some savings too. And with both combined, Theo's and mine, we may just about have enough for a deposit for a house.'

This was fantasy! A house!

'Maria's getting ahead of herself,' Tato was down to earth.

'Don't mind him,' Aunt Maria spoke with good humour. 'We've got to start somewhere. We've got to draw up a plan, haven't we?'

Julia agreed. She remembered one of her Mama's sayings: *when one door closes another one opens.* Now, even in her sadness, she felt a sudden lift as she was drawn into Aunt Maria's vision.

'I'll do all the decorating,' she volunteered, 'I love to emulsion the walls!'

'We're not there yet,' Tato said, 'and in any event, it'll most likely be one of those titchy terraced houses in Wood Street. If that!'

'Oh Tato! So what?' Julia chided him. 'But we'll all have a room of our own. And a front room. And a dining room. And a kitchen. All separate. And all that space!'

'Julia,' Tato lit another cigarette after his cake and tea, 'it's all such a long way in the future. Just concentrate on your studies for now.'

'I will.'

Aunt Maria gave her an approving smile.

Julia looked at the clock.

'Time for me to get things ready for school tomorrow,' she said. 'God, how I dread going back!'

'You mustn't worry in advance. Waste of time,' Aunt Maria said. 'I'm sure everyone will be understanding.'

'I've got two very good friends.'

'Then you must invite them over.'

Julia cringed. 'Aunty, they both live in beautiful houses.'

Aunt Maria gave her a gently reprimanding look. 'Julia, true friends love you for yourself, not for your possessions.'

Julia did not argue. She knew too well the wide gap between theory and practice. She got up instead and insisted on tidying and washing up herself. When the jobs were done, she bid Tato and Aunt Maria good night, still in deep discussion at the table.

'Julia,' Tato turned to her, 'I've left some things for you on your bed. Your Mama's Post Office savings book…'

She interrupted him, 'But Tato, *you*'ll need that…'

'No.' His tone was adamant. 'This money is yours. You'll need it. Especially later, when you carry on studying. There's also a box. With Mama's diaries. She wanted you to have them.'

The diaries. Julia had been curious about them for a long time. And now she would have been prepared to wait another fifty years, if that would bring her Mama back.

In her room, Julia switched on the electric bar. It usually took about twenty minutes to warm up the air. In that time she would take a hot bath and then escape fast to her bed under the feather eiderdown. Tonight, the temptation to examine the things on her bed was stronger than her need to escape the cold. She had a quick peep at the savings book. Six hundred pounds! It was a lot of money! She would never squander it! Her Mama's savings. There was only one thing she'd like to buy herself. A small television set. Even a second-hand one would do. Already in her mind she saw Nadia staying overnight on Saturdays and the two of them watching romantic or thriller films into the small hours.

She then lifted the lid off the shoe box, which was large and square and must have contained a pair of boots originally. It was filled with an assortment of notebooks and exercise books, the buff covers yellowed, the corners dog-eared. They were marked with bold numerals in black ink, and her parents' names: Julian and Anastazia. She sorted them in consecutive order and replaced them in neat piles inside the box. She picked up the first one from the top. Julian No.1. She looked at the first page. It was covered in dense lines of slightly slanting writing. Her father's. It was a strange sensation holding in her hand something that had been handled by him. The only link between them. Old paper and invisible imprints of his fingers on it.

With a beating heart she read the first paragraph.

10th February 1940. I'm yanked out of sleep by a frightening din. Someone is yelling and hammering at the door, and Korek is barking like mad.

Her father wrote that. She'd have to read on. If only in part, to get to know the stranger who had denied her that natural right of a love between a father and daughter.

There was also a large brown envelope. Julia lifted the flap and shook out its contents on the bed. Old sepia photographs, with serrated edges and upturned corners. She recognised aunts Hanna and Magda. There were family groups. And an elderly couple, her Mama's parents. She must have missed them with the same ache that Julia was feeling now.

A small flat object, wrapped in tissue paper, was wedged at the bottom of the envelope. Julia took it out. It was a little white bonnet. Like a doll's. Dorotka's.

For a split second Julia had a feeling of being transfixed with her Mama's grief. Then slowly, she collected all photographs back into the envelope, pushed in gently the only memento she had of her sister, and placed the envelope on top of the diaries. So much sadness. So much heart-ache. Her Mama's life history contained in a shoe box.

CHAPTER 74

It was a revelation. And Julia had thought that she knew it all! She had heard these stories since her earliest childhood. Things that had happened long before she was born. History. Distant past. Nothing to do with her present life. She was now tormented with inconsolable remorse and regret. That she had not listened. Shown no understanding, no sympathy. There was no escape from that.

The compulsion to read, to find out more, was like a fever that took hold of her every night, when the house was quiet, when Tato and Aunt Maria had gone to bed, when she had finished her schoolwork and prepared things for the next day. How could she have been so stupid, so insensitive to her Mama's need of sharing her painful past with her? Now, too late, she knew what grief was.

She hid her distress from Tato and Aunt Maria with talk of school in the evenings; and at school with her friends, with amicable responses of a listener to their dialogues, for Susan and Yvonne were both eloquent speakers, happy to have an audience. She could not expect them or anyone to sustain their patience with a tedious cry-baby.

Every night, with Muszka settled beside her, she told herself she would read just one more section, then stop. Take a break for a few days, or this reading would drive her mad. And every night, when the time came to switch off the light, the temptation was so strong she could not resist it. It was like a drug, bringing temporary relief, then leaving her tormented.

She surprised herself with the change in her perception of her father. Julian. He was no longer that vague figure, a soldier in uniform she had only seen once in her early childhood. He was a real person. He had loved and cared for people. And then something awful happened. Through no fault of his own. He was unable to care for his own wife and child. She could not love him the way she loved her Tato, but that indifference born of a child's unarticulated sense of injustice was now dissolving in sympathy for him.

The germinating idea of visiting Poland as soon as she turned eighteen, grew in her mind to a determined plan. She fantasised about finding her father, but then what? Did satisfying her curiosity merit the heartache such a meeting could cause? She had no answers. But she had time, she did not have to make any decisions yet.

And then, there was the BIG SECRET. Aunt Eva's secret. Julia was terrified of dropping the tiniest hint that she knew. Yet every time she was in Nadia's house she could not think of anything else. Nadia should know the truth, she reasoned. That she was not a foundling, that Eva was her mother. But such a revelation could damage their family. Julia shivered with dread at the very thought. Perhaps one day, when she and Nadia were two old ladies she'd be able to tell her then. But that would be too late. Too late for her and Eva to form that special bond.

The only person she trusted to raise her dilemma with was Roman. Particularly now that she knew of his past. He was never ordained as a priest, but there was something about him, something she had sensed even as a child that inspired open discussion in the sure knowledge that he would honour one's trust. Like a confession.

She met him in town one Saturday at the beginning of December. The town looked festive with fairy lights festooned around display windows, and with garish Christmas-themed cut-outs, stuck to glass panes and doors, proclaiming best ideas for presents. At half past three it was already dark, but the town was a-buzz with hurrying crowds, their preoccupied faces reflecting the bright glow from the open stores.

'Julia!' he stopped her by the clock tower. His hands were weighed down with bulging bags, a roll of wrapping paper sticking out of one. As always, there was a note of warm affection in his manner, as if he were Julia's relative. 'Have you got much more to do?'

'No, I'm just window shopping. Just needed to clear my head and stretch my legs a bit. It's all that sitting over my school work.'

'Then come along with me,' he invited. 'I'm just on my way home. Joyce and Andrew will be pleased to see you.'

Their talk was disjointed as they dodged other people, until they got out of the crowds near the Lawrence Sherriff School. Here the pavement was wide and the pedestrians sparse. Now was her chance.

'Uncle Roman. There's something I've got to ask you. That no one else must know.' She slowed down and looked hard at him. He shortened his long strides, giving her full attention.

'What is it?'

'I've read Mama's diaries. And my father's.'

Roman's face lit up. 'I'm so glad to hear that, Julia. They've listened to me, after all! I've been keeping notes too. So important! They were unusual times!'

'But, Uncle Roman, I don't think that Mama had ever expected me to read them so soon…'

'When is soon, too soon or too late?' he asked. 'You're an adult Julia. You'll appreciate and cherish such an unusual legacy.'

'Oh but I do, I do! Every time I read one of the notebooks it's like having contact with Mama. And even with my father.'

Roman gave her a sympathetic look.

636

'Don't judge him too harshly,' he said. 'He was a good man. Things happened to him. Things he hadn't asked for. He was a changed man after the war. We all were.'

'I'm trying to understand that,' Julia said. 'But it's not even that, that is bothering me so much. I've discovered a secret,' she lowered her voice, fearing even now, in this quiet street, that she may say too much. 'It's one person's secret, but I feel very strongly that another person should know. What should I do?'

'Hmmm...' he thought for a moment, as they strode along together, the street lights throwing fuzzy circles of light on the pavement, between the shadows of the bare linden trees. Then he looked at her. 'Julia, you mustn't worry about it. Just think, if your Mama was still here, you wouldn't have access to her diaries for maybe a very long time yet. The secret you worry about would still be confined to her diaries. So what's the hurry now?'

'It's just that,' she said, 'every time I look at that person, I feel it's that person's right to know what I know.'

'Then you must act like a priest,' he chuckled, and she understood the reference. 'It's not your secret to tell. You're absolved from that responsibility. All right?'

'All right,' she agreed reluctantly, for this seemed the only resolution at the moment, but one day in the future, she would remind him of this conversation and press him for a more satisfactory answer.

They reached his front door.

'Come in for a hot drink. And leave all your woes outside!' he said.

Whenever she went round to Nadia's, she noticed Aunt Eva's manner had become softer and kinder of late, not just to herself, but also to her family. Not, that she had ever been unkind. She had been like a second mother to Julia all her childhood. Incredibly now, even Uncle Henryk would join them at the table and contribute to the conversation with his cryptic but amusing dry humour.

Nadia remained unchanged, except in Julia's mind. She was in love with Stefan. It was the real thing. Leon was history, she assured Julia. She and Stefan spent Saturdays together and, to please her parents, Stefan would always return her home at the agreed time in the evening. 'They like him,' she said confidently, 'they may even approve his overnight stay with us in the Christmas break,' she promised herself with much hope and anticipation.

Incredibly time moved on. Days passed, then weeks, with the winter running relentlessly its pre-ordained course of long frosty nights, short days, clear icy blue skies or choked with a solid grey mass, heralding imminent snow.

It helped, it helped enormously that Aunt Maria was living with them. She was the much needed companion for Tato in the evenings. The radio screeched less these days, as Tato sat at the table with his sister and they reminisced about their home and their childhood days in Poland. It helped on dark cold days, with her fingers and toes numbed to the bone, to arrive to a warm and lit up house, with Aunt Maria waiting to give her hot tea and sympathy and ask her about her school work.

The house was in ship-shape order now. In her quiet, pensive manner, Aunt Maria was continuously on the go. Even when resting, she would read or knit or repair holes in Tato's pockets or darn his socks. Every Monday she would come back from the market with a piece of cloth and make it up into a garment. Before long Julia became the happy recipient of her aunt's talents: new blouses and skirts, and for Christmas, a woollen dress in cherry red, with a white collar and cuffs.

Aunt Maria made it so easy to love her. Julia was often reminded of Sister Alicya's saying: 'God takes with one hand and gives with the other.' She just wished He had been that little bit more generous and had left her Mama alone. For no one in the world could replace her.

She visited her Mama's grave on Saturday mornings, a compulsive detour on the way to town. It brought a passing relief to the constant ache inside her, to leave a posy of chrysanthemums on top of the freshly dug soil, the only nicety left which she could still do for her Mama.

It helped to write to Miro every day. His daily letters brought sunshine to her troubled mind and filled it with thoughts of Christmas and then of plans for the summer, and all the things he promised they'd do together. His presence in her mind was like a solid signpost directing them on a long shared road into the future.

There had been letters from all her friends and from Sister Alicya, well meaning with comforting words, but nothing could soothe the rawness of her grief. She had written to Pavel and Agata, who had been strangers until she had read her Mama's diaries. They had kept in touch all those years, and now she understood why. They were both thirty now, married to each other, with two children of their own, little Daniel and Marysia, named after the siblings so cruelly lost in Siberia. 'It was because of your Mama that we survived. We owe her so much. And because of that Julia, our home will always be yours.' Julia vowed to herself, she'd never lose contact with them. In Mama's memory.

Close to the end of the term, Christmas cards started to arrive; from Aunts Hanna and Magda, from Mama's wartime friend Mr. Ostrovski in Warsaw, from Tato's sisters in Lodz, and from Yagoda and Lidia.

Yagoda's came first. 'Dearest Julia,' she wrote, 'you're in my thoughts every day. Your Mama is close to you too, even if you can't see her. She'd want you to be happy. So, the first weekend you're free, jump on the train and come to Leicester. We'll have great time together, I promise!' Dear Yagoda. Julia felt a strong yearning to see her old friend. She could not picture the new Yagoda without her plaits. She read on: 'The Panto was a success. I made a passable fairy. Everyone screamed with laughter at the kitchen hands throwing pies at each other. But my Mama cried, and could not stop talking afterwards about all that food wasted!'

Lidia's card and letter came a day later. 'Dearest Julia, it's been a tough time for you. Here's a thought: when it gets to Spring and the weather gets warmer, come down for a weekend here. We'll take a train to London (minutes from us) and meet up with Miro. Marcello will come too, but sadly you'll be deprived of Vittorio's company. He's gone home at last, all in one piece, much to Mama's great relief and with Papa's blessing.'

Both letters buoyed Julia's spirit with their promise of better times ahead.

On the last day of the term in Julia's school, the sixth formers, two parallel classes, were given permission to change out of their uniforms for the afternoon Christmas party. Julia was pleased with her appearance and felt quite presentable in her cherry red dress, until she saw other girls emerging from the cloakroom. Some she could hardly recognise with their faces caked in heavy make-up, and their hair back-combed and piled into gigantic beehives on top of their heads. She felt suddenly artless and insignificant, a veritable Cinderella. But then Yvonne came along, her ginger colouring enhanced by an emerald taffeta dress, her freckles left un-powdered and her curls dancing untamed around her face with her every step. Susan was not seduced by make-up either; her sleek hair was cut short like a choir boy's with a thick fringe sweeping across her forehead; she wore a crisp white blouse with a navy bow at the collar that matched her long velvet skirt. Julia was glad to be in their company.

However, she was still cringing at the memory of her faux pas; at her ignorance of a certain English custom. When she arrived in class in the morning, she had found thirty-five Christmas cards addressed to her on her desk, from every single girl in class. She had brought none. The Polish custom was to send cards only to those people you were unable to see personally throughout the year. She vowed, she'd never be caught out like that again!

The party tables, covered in white and decorated with red and gold crackers, were set out in long rows in the assembly hall. The food that was already laid out was colourful and appetising: small triangular sandwiches, miniature sausages, diced pork pies, individual jellies in paper cups, little fairy cakes dotted with glittery 'hundreds and thousands', and orange juice drinks.

The background music played traditional carols and Christmas songs made popular by performers like Bing Crosby and Harry Belafonte.

It was strange to have the Staff members mingle with the girls and sit with them at the tables; all except Miss Ogden. Julia's segment in the long row of tables had Miss Peterson allotted to them, a young teacher of English in the lower classes. She was very attractive with her thick blond hair tumbling around her shoulders and a bright red lipstick drawing the eye to her perfect teeth when she smiled. She chose a place between Yvonne and Julia, with Susan on Julia's other side.

The head-girl, an impossibly mature looking girl in her black evening dress and high heels, declared the official start of the party from the stage, after which the murmur rose to a lively crescendo of animated voices as the food was politely passed around.

'So, Julia...' Miss Peterson turned her inquisitive blue eyes at her, 'is this similar to how you party in your school at home?'

Julia felt her cheeks turning pink. She liked Miss Peterson, who had a friendly manner and was, no doubt, well intentioned to make the most of this rare casual encounter between the girls and the staff, but it was clear that she perceived Julia just as a passing visitor in this country.

'I honestly don't know,' Julia answered truthfully, 'I've never lived in Poland.'

'How so?' Miss Peterson's eyes widened. Julia sighed inwardly. Full explanation? That would take days.

'I live here permanently,' Julia explained. 'My parents were war refugees. They came and they stayed.'

'You must miss your country a lot, no doubt.'

Julia smiled, a shy, polite smile.

'This is my country, here. I don't know any other.'

'I see...'

They chewed daintily on their thin cucumber sandwiches, while Yvonne and Susan talked to the other girls across the table.

'So, will your Christmas be like ours?' Miss Peterson asked.

'Not quite...' Julia went on to explain about Vigilia and the Midnight Mass, and the first and the second days of Christmas, when not only the families but close friends got together too.

'It sounds like a lot of hard work,' Miss Peterson's tone was touched with sympathy, 'I'm going away for Christmas with friends. Skiing. In France!'

'Wow!' Julia exclaimed spontaneously and made Miss Peterson smile, 'I mean,' she corrected herself, 'it must be quite wonderful!'

'It is. This year there's been a lot of snow. So it bodes well.'

'That's something I've never done. Something I definitely must write on my list of *to do* things,' Julia said to be pleasant, thinking she would prefer warm sand and peaceful lapping water to shivering in the cold. From her earliest childhood, winters equated with the misery of frozen fingers and toes, icy winds penetrating her clothes to the bone, earaches and head colds. Even now, as she sat at the table chatting to Miss Peterson, she was aware of her itchy toes pushed tightly inside her shoes.

'Will you be going away anywhere after your Christmas festivities?' Miss Peterson asked.

'Maybe only to Leicester. To visit a friend. I'll be also having a friend from my previous school staying with us. It'll be quite busy.'

Miss Peterson gave her a thoughtful look. 'Your parents must be very kind,' she said.

'Yes, I suppose they are,' Julia was modest with her acknowledgement, omitting to explain the family situation. It was not just kindness, she reflected, that drove them to acts of generosity, it was a strong feeling of duty to support the less fortunate than themselves. *We are all orphans*, Aunt Maria had said, *if we don't stick together, our future is bleak.*

When Miss Peterson's attention was required by another girl, Julia's mind turned to the coming week. Soon Miro would be home. She was counting the days. It felt like waiting for medication that would alleviate her pain. And on Saturday Klara would be home. She had grown fond of her younger friend through their regular correspondence and could not imagine now Klara not being part of her life.

Vigilia. Their front room looked crammed with the table set for eight, and with the Christmas tree filling the corner above the chest of drawers, normally the spot occupied by Tato's radio. But the air was warm with the heat from the open fire and impregnated with scents of fresh fir and baking, and no one minded sitting squashed together around the table: Roman, Joyce and Andrew, Tato and Aunt Maria, and Klara and Julia. There was an eighth place setting, traditionally left empty for anyone arriving unexpectedly at the door. Room prepared at the inn on this magical night. It should have been Mama's place. The pang of grief was so strong, it had made Julia's eyes sting earlier. Tato and Aunt Maria had shed tears too, inevitably, when the wafer was broken and shared by everyone at the start of the feast.

But now, halfway through, the atmosphere was lively with much general talk, interspersed with praise from the adults for Klara's enthusiastic input in making *uszka* for the *barszcz, pierogi, gołąbki,* salads and fish, and helping out Aunt Maria to bake the cheese and the poppy seed cakes. Julia did not mind her being singled out, though she, herself had done just as much. She knew the adults' intention was to make Klara feel at home.

Klara sat with her eyes cast down, her dark blond hair caught in a high pony tail and tied with a white ribbon, which matched the crispness of the collar and cuffs of her new dress. Aunt Maria had made it for her, a soft blue colour, that Klara had chosen herself. She would only relax when the attention was turned away from her, and only then would she attempt a conversation with Andrew. Comparing schools was an easy topic.

Aunt Maria excelled herself with her coffee gateau, made with ground hazelnuts instead of flour, and decorated with coffee cream. Julia's absolute favourite. As she delighted in the taste of this delicacy, her eyes kept wandering to the empty seat. It was like a magnet. The emptiness holding its breath back, as if at any moment Mama would appear to take her rightful place.

Roman clapped his hands and made her jump. 'Right! How about a carol concert? Who's going to sing first?'

Klara withdrew within herself and bent her head. 'I couldn't possibly,' she said in advance.

'Of course you can sing!' Roman chivvied her, as he did Andrew, who shook his head with much giggling and hid behind Joyce's shoulder. Roman looked at Julia.

'You won't let me down will you? Your Mama was a good singer. She'd be singing all evening tonight.'

That was true. If only her Mama could be here. If only she could give her a sign. Just one.

'Yes, I'll sing,' she said.

They cleared the table first of all other dishes, leaving just the cakes and the pot of tea. Julia was pleased with the sight of the porcelain cups and saucers on the white cloth with small twigs from the fir tree scattered at random. It all looked so festive. Perhaps her Mama's spirit was here, after all. Perhaps she could see it all too.

When everyone was ready, Julia stood up in front of the Christmas tree, feeling presentable in her cherry red dress and her hair back-combed into a spherical bob. She intoned *Silent Night*, her Mama's favourite tune. Her voice was not as strong and mellow as her Mama's, but it was clear and she reached the high notes without any effort. She stopped before the second verse and invited Klara to join her. Surprisingly, Klara agreed. Together, they made a reasonable sound, she thought, Klara's voice a clear, melodious soprano. She saw Aunt Maria wipe away a tear and Joyce's mouth tremble. The adults' loud ovation broke through the emotionally charged tension, and after that they all sang a few carols together.

Later, when all the remnants of the feast were put away and everything was washed up and dried, Aunt Maria and Joyce sat by the fire with a glass of sherry each, Tato and Roman got out the chess, and on the other side of the table, Julia spread out the 500-piece jig-saw puzzle. It was a picture of a sea-side view, with the sand and sea, multicoloured boats drying out on the shingle, a lighthouse and people on the promenade, and a sky dotted with clouds and sea-gulls.

'Blimey!' Andrew exclaimed. 'All the pieces look the same!'

'Not quite,' Julia laughed, 'but that's the idea. Otherwise it wouldn't be a challenge.'

Klara, in her usual serious mood, set about her task with tight-lipped concentration, and within minutes produced a section of the drying boats. Not to be beaten, Andrew offered hurriedly,

'I'll start on the light-house bit, shall I?'

'Great!' Julia encouraged him. 'And I'll attempt the sea.'

There was something mesmeric and soothing in matching the pieces and fitting them together. Joyce and Aunt Maria chatted by the fire, in Joyce's best effort with the Polish words and Aunt Maria's limited English; Tato and Roman reminisced as always, between the moves of their Kings and Queens; and Klara and Andrew became mute with concentration. There was a calm to this evening which made it perfect, Julia thought, except for the absence of one person. Would the ache inside her ever go away?

At a quarter past eleven she heard the laughter outside their front door. Miro and Stefan, punctual, as arranged. With a spurt in her step she went to let them in, but they declined on account of their snow-caked boots. They called out their greetings from the threshold while Julia got herself dressed in her outdoor clothes. Tato and Roman went up to them to shake hands.

'We'll see you at the church, then.' Roman said. His car could not accommodate them all, so Julia, rather gladly, had volunteered to walk.

The night outside was icy, the sky inky black, the stars like shards of glass above the snow covered land.

'Brrr...' Julia shivered, feeling the cold penetrating her clothes. She had sacrificed her precisely styled hair in the name of common sense, by pulling on the woollen hat, scarf and mittens knitted by her Mama. The boys, dressed in their thick dark duffel coats and Sherlock Holmes hats with ear flaps, got hold of her hands, and together they ran the full length of the street. Her heart beat so fast she could hardly catch her breath.

'Enough! Enough!' she pleaded. 'Or I'll drop dead!'

They stopped, with much merriment, and after that walked briskly, three abreast, on the main road, which was totally free of traffic at this time of the night. Julia felt the warmth from her effort spread to her hands and feet.

'We should have gone in the van with your Dad,' she suggested. Stefan's family had come over for Christmas to Miro's parents.

'What, and miss all this fun?' Stefan picked up a handful of snow and aimed it at a bare tree trunk below the bridge. 'Fancy a fight?'

'Not tonight, thank you,' Julia laughed and dodged him.

'He wouldn't dare that with me!' Miro caught up with her. 'He knows who'd be the winner!'

'All right!' Stefan picked up a handful of snow, 'I challenge you then, Miroslavski! How about tomorrow? Duel at dawn? We'll soon separate the men from the boys!'

It was all such silly juvenile fun, but that was just the antidote Julia craved for the depressive mood of the last few weeks. Flanked by them, as they walked past the factory walls, she felt safe and secure and listened with amusement to their ridiculous word sparring.

The town centre was lit up but virtually deserted, bar the odd pedestrian here and there, as alone looking as they were.

'I love Christmas,' Julia said, 'but it's like living in perpetual darkness at this time of the year. The days are so short and dark.'

'We'll make the most of the next few days, I promise,' Stefan said. He was referring to Nadia's invitation for the Christmas evening at her house. Also, they had planned a long walk together on Boxing Day. To her surprise, Klara had happily declared that she would stay in with Aunt Maria and go with her and Tato round to Roman's. Julia rather guessed that Klara enjoyed her aunt's attention and cherished the moments of exclusive companionship.

Nadia was waiting for them inside the main entrance porch of the church, her family already inside, including Stella and Jack. On seeing Stefan, her face broke into a wide, ecstatic smile, which was rewarded with a hug from him. They found a space in one of the back pews, from which they could view the whole congregation: men's Crombie or long gabardine coats, women's woollens and furs, a variety of hats, scarves and wraps, and always, that hint of mothballs.

It was the traditional High Mass, sung throughout, with a rather too long homily, carols and prayers, and at the end, a Christmas hymn, *God is born, All force is struck down...*, replacing the usual, *God, who has guarded Poland for centuries...*

It was when everyone turned round to leave, that Julia saw Leon, tucked in the corner between the entrance portal and the confessional box. He was on his own. Spontaneously she waved to him. He smiled back and waited. She must congratulate him. His wedding was to take place on Boxing Day.

When she and Miro reached him, with Nadia and Stefan close behind, carried along by the crowd, he fell in step beside them, and slowly they made their way out of the church. The congregation was reluctant to disperse; groups stood around in the lit-up forecourt, wishing each other a merry Christmas with much hugging and shaking of hands.

'Leon,' Julia spoke first, when they stepped aside, 'I'm really happy for you. Congratulations!' She meant it. The memory of his kindness that day, when he drove her on his motorbike to visit her Mama in hospital, came back with a rush of emotion. She could have hugged him now. And with no sense of betrayal any more, as to her loyalty to Nadia. Nadia had found happiness with Stefan.

'Congratulations,' Miro repeated shaking Leon's hand.

'Is Alison all right?' she asked.

'Yes, thank you. She just needs more rest.' He then added quickly, 'before the big day.'

'Of course, she must look her best!'

There was an awkward pause, before he spoke again.

'I was so sorry to hear about your mother.'

'I know,' she said, 'everyone's been so kind. I'm lucky...' she looked at Miro.

'It is in times of crises,' Leon said, 'that you discover how much you need friends.' He looked beyond Julia's shoulder. 'I hate making enemies. It's not in my nature. Believe me.'

644

Julia turned her head towards where Nadia stood with Stefan, his arm hugging her to his side. 'Go and talk to her,' she said to Leon.

They walked over together, Leon squeezing his hat in his hands.

'Hi Nadia. Stefan. Will you permit me to wish you a happy Christmas?'

Her smile was genuine and her voice was warm when she spoke. 'Of course, Leon, and I wish you all the best too. Congratulations! There must be a state of high fever in your house at the moment. With all the preparations for the wedding!'

'Well, actually no,' Leon cleared his throat, 'it's going to be a modest wedding, with just the two families present.'

Nadia gave a nod and her tone was approving, 'I'm sure it'll be beautiful, Leon. I wish you and Alison all the best.'

'Thank you.' He said that with feeling, as if a problem was resolved. He walked away without a backward glance.

'That was kind, Nadia.' Julia praised her.

Nadia shrugged. 'It's all history now.' She pressed her face against Stefan's arm.

People were slowly dispersing. They were approached first by Roman then by Stefan's step-father, Mr. Franek with offers of lifts home. They declined with thanks, and Miro whispered with a mischievous grin.

'They're intent on sabotaging our walk home!'

Klara waved, walking arm in arm with Aunt Maria, accompanied by Joyce and Andrew, on their way to the car. Julia waved back. Miro turned to Stefan,

'Now it's my turn. Will you be all right walking home by yourself all the way from Nadia's house?'

'I'll decide when I get there,' Stefan grinned. 'If there's an inch of space on the sofa, then I'll crash out till it gets light.'

'Oh, yes, yes, do that Stefan!' Nadia skipped like a little girl, 'Mama won't mind at all. We are all very prim and proper in our house! Separate rooms for boys and girls! You'll just have Zloty for company downstairs. He'll lick you to sleep with joy!'

'Great! It'll save on having a wash in the morning,' Stefan laughed.

'Take my key then,' Miro offered, 'and no gong banging when you let yourself in!'

Nadia gave Julia a hug. Happiness shone in her smile, in her sparkling eyes.

'I'll see you tomorrow,' she said, 'five o'clock at my house.' She clutched Stefan's hand and they walked down the path towards the main road. The snow lay soft and untouched between the dark tombstones in the cemetery surrounding the church.

Julia and Miro walked in the opposite direction, taking a short cut up Oak Street, towards the section in this area, consisting exclusively of the Rugby School buildings. In the holidays only the housemasters and their families would remain in these elegant and imposing premises, but at this hour there was not one light to give any indication of a human presence there. The absolute quiet made Julia feel as if she and Miro were the only two people left in this town, yet, it was not a feeling of unease; it was a feeling of calm and intimacy. She wanted to walk with him in this peace all night, with the luminous snow lighting the way for them.

'You know,' she said, 'this is the first time since Mama died that I'm beginning to feel normal again. It's hard to explain. All the while, it's been like looking down at myself from above, or like sensing something about to happen, or like listening to a void, or like being pressed down by an invisible weight. All those feelings are gone for the moment. And it feels so good.'

Miro stopped, wrapped his arms round her and held her close to him. Then he kissed her gently on her lips before releasing her.

'I'm glad,' he said, 'it's been quite an ordeal. Ghastly! I thought about you every single day, Julia, and I felt so useless not being able to help you at this awful time.'

'But you did help me, Miro! You did! Your letters were like a daily fix for me!'

'Really?' he sounded surprised and pleased at the same time.

'I just wished,' she said, 'that London was not so far away. I'd give anything to see you every day.'

He hugged her again, as if he could not stop himself. They crossed Hillmorton Road and walked down the short Moultrie Road with the grand mansions, looking like fairy castles surrounded by the snow.

'I'm home till after the New Year,' he said. 'We'll do something nice together every day. OK?' Just hearing him say that filled her with hope, and anticipation of happier days.

They walked in silence for a while before Miro spoke again. The snow crunched under their boots.

'We'll make plans for the summer. It's good to have something to look forward to.'

'If only I could hurry time!' Julia wished.

'It'll come. You can't stop it,' he assured her. 'And do you know what else I've been thinking about? Next year this time you'll be thinking about your eighteenth birthday. We'll get your naturalisation forms at the beginning of January. So you can send them off as soon as possible. Then we'll apply for your British passport. It should all be sorted by the summer.'

Julia's mind spun with a myriad of thoughts. She hardly noticed her surroundings, as they walked down Bath Street, with the row of cars parked along the pavement, their tops hidden underneath deep caps of snow.

'Miro, this is a brilliant idea! Then we can start planning our trip to Poland! Our first ever!'

'Yes!' he sounded animated. 'I know Roman is planning to go too. With

Joyce and Andrew naturally. I've not asked him yet, but if he likes my idea, then he could take us along and we'd share the cost of the journey.'

'Oh Miro! You're a genius!' Spontaneously she hugged him to her, 'I like it! I like it very much. In fact, so much, I'm already worrying it might not happen, because I want it so much!'

He stifled his laughter in the absolute quiet of the street.

'Julia, you're such a funny girl! I love it! Of course it'll happen! It's just a matter of time!'

Excitedly they discussed all the places they were going to see. Warsaw and Krakow were a must. Then Czestochowa with the miraculous Black Madonna.

'I don't mind, in fact,' Julia said, 'where we go and what we see. It'll be wonderful to simply be there. All my childhood when Mama talked about her home in Poland, it seemed so impossible that I could ever be there. And now, I can hardly believe how close it is within my reach.'

'I shall have to visit my parents' friends from the war years,' Miro reflected, 'and no doubt take them sack-fulls of stuff. My mother often talks about her friend Maryla, who was like a second mother to me.'

'And I'll have to see my Tato's sisters in Lodz. Roman will need a trailer for all our stuff,' Julia joked. Then her thoughts became serious. She braced herself to speak them aloud. 'Miro, I've also wondered, many times, if there's any possibility of finding my father?'

He slowed down his step to look at her.

'You know my reservations, Julia, but only because I don't want you to get hurt. However, I can well imagine how curious I'd be in your place. So if you still want it that much, when the time comes, I'll help you with your search.' He squeezed her hand affectionately.

She was suddenly buoyed by a burst of exhilaration, like a kite on a gust of wind.

They had walked past the factory walls, past the open playing field, now like a white lake, and carried on at a brisk pace till they reached her street. At the gate, Miro hugged her long and hard and kissed her goodnight. The whole neighbourhood with its squat bungalows covered in snow was plunged in silence, and everything was still like a scene on a postcard.

'Miro,' Julia whispered, 'it's been so good to talk. I can't wait for tomorrow. I won't be able to sleep!'

'You will, Julia,' his mouth was warm against her cheek, 'and dream of our big adventure.' He waited at the door till she let herself in.

CHAPTER 75

POLAND – SUMMER 1962

Everything had gone according to Miro's meticulous plans. She was now in possession of the British passport which had made this longed-for trip possible. Nevertheless, even as British citizens, they had been treated with the same indifference and disregard as everyone else on the East German- Polish border. They waited all the morning for hours in a miles-long queue together with hundreds of cars and lorries to be passed through. The August sun bore down on them from the blinding-white sky. Julia longed for the cooling wind they had left behind on the English Channel, as she stood at the side of the open car, her blouse and her slacks stuck to her in clammy discomfort. Everyone, hundreds of travellers, had got out of their vehicles leaving the doors wide open to encourage even just a breath of fresh air in this searing heat.

Miro stood beside her, his red face streaked with sweat, his arms akimbo to dry off the wet patches down the sides of his shirt. They looked around, squinting their eyes and shading them with their palms. On the other side of the car, Joyce was sponging Andrew's face with bottled water, herself looking crumpled, not at all the usually immaculately-attired lady. Roman had left them for a moment in search of a private place on this busy, heavily used route with not a building in sight with fresh water or toilet facilities. Only vast fields of corn on both sides.

The trodden verges on both sides were littered with paper and remnants of rotting food, which attracted clouds of black, malevolent buzzing flies. Deeper into the field, behind the screen of tall leafy stalks, Julia discovered the ground covered with human dirt and stepped carefully over the mounds till she found an as yet unvisited spot for her own need. Descriptions of similar situations in her Mama's diary came back to her mind, except that this was not some forgotten place in the remotest corner of the Soviet continent twenty years ago; this was the present day Russian-controlled state.

Back at the car Joyce remarked,

'I hate looking so frightful,' as she smudged her meticulously applied make-up with the back of her hand.

'We're all looking the same.' Julia made light of it, feeling her scalp prickle.

Roman and Miro appeared stoical in accepting all the discomforts of the imposed wait, and having given up on preserving the appearance of their shirts, used their sleeves for continuous wiping of their foreheads and hair.

'This is the worst bit,' Roman did his best to remain positive, 'believe me, once we're through, it'll be like a joy ride all the way to Adam's house!' Adam was Roman's brother, whom he had not seen for twenty-two years.

'There's no excuse for any of this!' Joyce said tersely.

Foot by foot, the long convoy of cars moved up all morning to the checkpoint. Here, the land was flat and bleak, with just a couple of brick buildings on each side of the strong metal barrier, spanning the width of the road, barbed wire marking the border, and a watch tower dominating all. Two armed guards stood at the barrier.

Despite the heat, Julia shivered.

A number of guards loitered at the dark entrances of the buildings and among them Russian uniforms could be glimpsed with their round flat hats like pancakes.

'What now?' Julia whispered.

One of those men walked over and ordered them out of the car. As they stood in a silent group, he checked each of their passports and read each page meticulously, as if it were a book. He ordered them to open the boot and pointed at Julia's suitcase.

'Open!' His voice was gruff.

Julia was disgusted by the sight of his fingers rummaging through her neatly folded things. Then he ordered them back in the car, said a few words in German to Roman and walked away to disappear inside the shadowy entrance of the brick building.

'Can we go now?' Andrew asked, his damp hair plastered to his forehead.

'Not yet. He wants us to fill in some forms.'

'Why?'

'No idea.'

Julia marvelled at Roman's calm.

The heat was stifling, and the official's disappearance stretched into long minutes. When he reappeared, nonchalantly oblivious to the rising temperature of the mood of those waiting behind Roman's car, he spoke briefly to Roman, then walked away.

'I don't believe it!' Miro hissed in exasperation. 'What is it this time?'

Roman gave a short laugh.

'He says the forms haven't been printed yet.'

'This is preposterous!' Joyce cried in disbelief. 'What game is he playing?'

'Don't worry, he'll come back. I'll just do as Adam's instructed.'

Sure enough, after a patience-testing while, the official returned with a sheet of paper and passed it to Roman through the open window.

'You're very lucky!' he announced. 'This is the last printed form left. Fill it in and add your passengers' names and addresses at the bottom of the page.'

Roman did that, while the man kept guard at the open window. Roman folded the paper in half and placed a ten dollar note inside. The guard fingered it, nodded and waved them off.

'Pass!'

They all heaved a sigh of relief when the barrier lifted.

'This is daylight robbery!' Miro muttered.

'Of course it is! But who's going to stop them? They all take a cut. Right up to the top man!'

Roman accelerated across the fifty-metre strip of no-man's-land, only to be stopped at the barrier of the Polish border. The same scene again, armed guards, brick buildings, barbed wire, a watch tower, Polish armed guards and Russian uniforms amongst them.

'What, all that again?' Julia cried in dismay.

'I've got everything ready,' Roman assured her.

He handed over their passports on demand, with another ten dollar note inside his.

The young, pock-marked guard stretched out his authority for some very long tense minutes, as he studied their passports. Then suddenly he snapped them shut, returned them and ordered Roman to drive on. The first real Pole, on the first real spot of Polish soil.

After several hours drive from the border to Warsaw, they reached the suburbs in the evening. Here was one of the very few areas that had escaped total destruction by the German bombers. Fashionable before the war, with its elegant villas set back from the boulevard, and amidst lush greenery, municipal gardens and parks, it was now a mish-mash of crumbling old houses flanked by cheap-looking blocks of flats, angular, soul-less, with rusty window frames and cracked walls, erected in haste in the immediate post-war era, to house the thousands who had been left homeless. Groups of children could be seen playing ball games in the pebbly yards close to the buildings.

The warm evening air was hazy and throat-scratching, impregnated with fumes from the exhausts of the traffic, second- and third-rate cars and lorries and vans. Roman's commentary got ever more excited as he recognised his old childhood haunts.

'Here, in this park, I used to cycle with my friends, and on this pond, look just there, we used to skate in the winter, and there on those trees, we used to play Tarzan, and build dens and dangle from ropes!'

His excitement rubbed off on his passengers and suddenly the tiredness that had begun to drag Julia down lifted as she joined the others in spontaneous comments on the landmarks they passed. There was an abundance of half-built unfinished buildings on both sides of the wide boulevard.

'Lack of materials,' Roman explained. 'Everything is taken east. They have rebuilt the old city, but do you know at what cost? By demolishing old historical buildings in Wroclaw, Stetin and Poznan, and using their authentic Gothic bricks! Can you imagine such cannibalism?' he shrugged. 'They made an excellent job of it, though. Rebuilding Warsaw from scratch.'

Roman couldn't imagine, he said, strangers living now in their family home. So dire was the destruction that thousands were left living in ruins, shelters and shacks. All pre-war private properties were requisitioned by the state and the space in them divided to house homeless families.

Roman's family home, when they arrived, was a two-storey house with a third floor in the loft, judging by the row of sky lights in the roof. The stucco, clinging in crumbling patches to the brick walls must have been white a long time ago. The thick dark wood window-frames were held together with uneven layers of putty, and the massive front door, now left wide open, was rough and cracked, the once black glossy veneer, reduced to dull, peeling flakes.

The house resounded with a cacophony of noise and from its open windows there wafted a mixture of cooking smells. It had once stood in its own grounds. It was now surrounded by a wide dirt track, where groups of children were engaged in a variety of games, their excited voices echoing round the neighbourhood. A row of poplars nearby screened off a concrete block of flats.

The children stopped their games and gathered to watch Julia's party climb out of the car. A foreign car. It was bliss to stretch her legs and she longed to plunge herself in cold water. She smiled at Miro and Joyce, who like herself, looked creased and damp and in need of a good scrub.

A man in his middle forties ran out of the front door, his face transfixed with an ecstatic smile. Though there was no immediate resemblance between his blond looks, his sturdier build and Roman's finer features, Julia guessed this was his brother, Adam.

'Roman! Welcome man! It's been an age! A century!'

They fell into each other's arms and remained in a strong bear-hug for a long, mute moment, only their shoulders heaving.

The children in the yard moved closer, their curious eyes large in their dust-smudged faces. An attractive woman appeared in the doorway and ran lightly down the steps, her dark hair bouncing around her face, her cotton dress falling loosely around her feminine plumpness.

'Kasia!' Roman cried. 'My dearest Kasia! You were just a slip of a girl last time I saw you. And look at you now!' He stretched out his arm to his sister-in-law and the three of them clung together.

Then he stepped back and introduced his family. Adam and Kasia hugged them naturally, as if they had known Joyce and Andrew all their lives.

After that it became a melee of introductions, of disjointed talk, Adam helping Roman to empty the boot, his teenage son Bronek joining to help Miro and Julia with their luggage. Together, laden with suitcases and bags, they made their way indoors.

Inside the entrance hall, a dark, lofty space, lightened up with daylight from the open doors, Adam directed,

'Bronek, take Julia and Miro upstairs. Roman and Joyce, follow me this way.' He then led his group to the flat on the right.

The central staircase, a sturdy, mahogany structure, worn dusty grey with decades of use, led to the upper floor, then further up to the attic. As Julia and Miro climbed up behind their leader Bronek, Julia glimpsed scenes of life inside the rooms that they passed by. The house was full of people, crammed in their allotted spaces, stopping what they did to look at the procession heading upstairs. Cooking smells and music from radios, loud discussions and children's voices followed them up into the loft.

A young girl, of about fourteen, greeted them at the top of the stairs.

'My sister Beata,' said Bronek, lugging up Julia's suitcase. Beata had her mother's dark curly hair and her uncle Roman's violet eyes.

'I've prepared your beds for you,' she said pleasantly, after introductions, her eagerness to please evident in her expression. The beds were mattresses placed directly on the wooden floor, and made up invitingly with pristine white bedding. There were six of them. 'It's for us, younger people,' she explained. 'The rooms downstairs are not big enough'.

'It's lucky,' Bronek added wiping sweat off his forehead with the back of his hand, 'that we've been allowed to keep half the attic for our use. The other half is our neighbours.' It was curtained off with a hessian drape.

The sloping walls between the skylights were lined with stacked storage cartons and all kinds of objects stuffed on top of them. The wooden floor looked scrubbed clean, and there was adequate space between each mattress for access.

'May I sleep next to you?' Beata asked Julia. 'And Miro on your other side?'

'Of course!' Julia laughed, amused. Judging by the spark in Miro's eyes, he too saw the humour of their situation: with four gooseberries around them, their virtue and their good names were going to be preserved. Even when they slept side by side!

'And then Bronek, and Yarek and Andrew,' Beata pointed out the mattresses. It turned out that their younger brother was twelve, the same age as Andrew.

While Julia and Miro arranged their luggage on the side, Beata suggested, 'I expect you're dying for a wash?'

'I can't think of anything else!' Julia replied, taking out her toiletries bag.

'We've got our own bathroom in our flat downstairs,' Bronek said, 'but I expect it'll be in full use now. There's a communal bathroom on the first floor. It's quite awful, I must warn you, but it should be free before the late evening rush.'

'I'll go now,' Julia said. She could not wait another minute to get out of her sweat-saturated clothes and splash herself all over with cooling water.

The bathroom must have been a spacious room originally, but the toilet had been partitioned off later and had a separate door. The bath and the washbasin, both comfortably large objects must have been of the best quality in their hey-day, with sturdy chrome taps and sturdy chrome feet supporting the bath.

Now, the sight of them filled Julia with revulsion. The washbasin was discoloured with rusty streaks running down the curved sides, over the network of hair-line cracks. The bath was in an even worse state. The only enamel left clung to the surrounding ledge; the rest of the bath was sheer rusting metal.

For a moment Julia could not think how she was going to wash. The simplest solution was to tackle the problem head on, get in the bath, and crouching over its rough surface, splash herself all over with running water. And that was what she did.

Invigorated, fragrant, with her clean hair drying fast, she returned to the attic in a fresh change of underwear, a fresh white blouse and a pink gingham skirt. She was not unaware of Beata's admiring gaze.

'Brace yourself!' she warned Miro.

'I told you!' Bronek laughed.

As she chatted with him and Beata while waiting for Miro, she was touched by their natural friendliness; there were no awkward pauses, it was as if they had been friends for a very long time.

Miro too looked pleased when he returned refreshed.

'Sheer bliss!' he exhaled with feeling, before folding away his used things. He brought out his Brownie camera. Before going downstairs Julia extracted from her suitcase a prepared bag of small gifts, that she and Miro had bought jointly: tea and coffee, also a few little luxuries; good quality soaps, splash-on aftershave, fragrant moisturising cream, nylon stockings and men's socks, pens and biros, and for Yarek, a school writing set.

Downstairs, Adam's family occupied just a quarter of their original home. It had once been a substantially large room with high ceilings. Adam had divided it up with wooden partitions and created smaller areas for specific purposes: a living and kitchen space and two bedrooms. Beata, Julia discovered later, would normally sleep on the sofa-bed. Also, to avoid queuing up for the disgusting bathroom in the mornings, Adam had measured out a square metre of space in one corner and constructed a cubicle with a toilet and a shower.

Julia caught a glimpse of its incredibly compact size when she entered the room, just as Joyce was coming out transformed, back to her meticulously groomed self. She gave Julia a wide smile of satisfaction.

They all sat round the table, covered over with a white tablecloth and laden with a mouth-watering spread. The atmosphere was charged with uncontained happiness and the talk flowed unrestrained. Roman and Adam, their faces animated with permanent smiles, seemed to anticipate each other's thoughts, both talked at once and affectionately slapped each other on the shoulder. Joyce listened with a bright, well-meaning look in her eyes, her English politeness allowing Kasia to have her say at length, without interruptions. Yarek had Andrew already engaged in a book of mathematical puzzles. The language barrier appeared to be no deterrent to their growing friendship. Bronek and Beata flanked Julia and Miro in protective hospitality as if their sole purpose was to look after them.

'Please, tuck in everyone,' Kasia invited.

The spread was indeed sumptuous: sliced cold meats, pieces of roast chicken, boiled sausages, a variety of salads, the sour dough bread delicious on its own or with dripping. As they began to serve themselves, Adam filled the adults' liqueur glasses with a ruby coloured drink.

'Cheers! *Na zdrowie!*' He raised his glass. 'Down the hatch!'

The liquid ran like wild-fire down Julia's throat. Spirit and plum juice. She gasped and cooled it with soda water, much to Adam's amusement. When he refilled the glasses, she turned hers upside down.

'That's plenty for me, thank you,' she declined, her eyes still watering. 'Now I must give Mrs. Kasia's splendid feast all the attention it deserves.' She tasted the mixed vegetable salad. 'Perfect! How did you manage to get everything you needed?'

Her hostess looked pleased.

'We have our ways and means,' her cheeks dimpled in a smile.

Later Julia discovered that the chronic shortages in the shops had turned the housewives into formidable strategists: they bought whatever was available at any given time and then exchanged the goods among themselves. And when visitors from abroad were to be entertained, families and friends rallied round to ensure food on the table.

Yarek and Andrew finished first and begged to be excused in order to join in the football game that continued tirelessly outside. When they left, Kasia closed the door behind them and Adam got up to close the window.

'You never know who's listening,' he said. It was common knowledge that hundreds of secret agents were being employed by the SB, the Ministry of Public Security to snitch on their neighbours about the most trivial matters. He returned to the table and refilled the glasses.

'*Za Ruską flotę. Do dna!* The Russian fleet! To the bottom! Now we can talk!'

After that, conversation flowed freely, the men putting the world to rights, each with his own unbending ideas on politics and improving the economy, and Joyce and Kasia comparing the availability of various household items and the prices. Bronek and Beata asked Julia about school and holidays. They were surprised that Julia and Miro worked in their official breaks from studies. A serving girl in Woolworths? A law student labouring in a quarry? No, they had their holidays organised by the state: summer camps for their pupils. Thank goodness, Julia reflected, there was at least one good thing in this communist-run state.

At one point, when there happened to be a surprising gap in the men's prevailing, heated monologues, Julia addressed Adam.

'I'm so grateful to you for finding my father's address. I wouldn't know where to begin.'

He smiled mysteriously and touched his nose.

'It helps to have contacts.'

'There's a special station on the radio,' Kasia added, 'that is dedicated entirely to searching for lost people. All that time after the war and people are still looking for each other! There's also a page in the national newspaper that lists hundreds of names. But it takes months, sometimes years, before people find each other. '

'And isn't it fortunate,' Julia said, 'that it's so close to Warsaw! It could have been anywhere in the whole of the country!'

'It's fortunate,' Adam agreed, 'but not at all surprising. Warsaw was so badly destroyed that anyone coming from abroad was pressurised into helping rebuild the capital city first. Afterwards, some moved away and settled elsewhere, but many stayed. Hence the proliferation of the abominable concrete blocks!'

'Don't beat yourself up about it,' Kasia said firmly. Adam was an architect. She looked around the table. 'You can't make a purse out of a sow's ear. The materials they were allowed were the cheapest of the kind. I don't have to spell out who had the benefit of our best productions. And can I just remind you Adam, how happy people were to have a place of their own, no matter how minute or ugly it was!'

He gulped down another swig of the firewater.

'Concrete! Everywhere you go there's concrete!' He made a face. 'The old town's not bad, though. Even a sour malcontent such as I has to admit they did a good job of it. Surprising for the dim-wits who make decisions at the top. We'll go there tomorrow. You'll see for yourselves.'

'And Lazienki Palace,' Kasia smiled in anticipation. She looked at Julia. 'Your visit to your father's will have to wait till the evening. There may not be anyone there in the daytime.'

Later, when the younger contingent relocated themselves to the attic for the night, and Andrew and Yarek wore themselves out with giggling over misunderstandings of English and Polish words, and Bronek and Beata gave in finally to sleep, and the whole house, full of people, fell quiet in the dark, Julia felt Miro's hand over hers on the cover. He stroked it and whispered,

'It's been quite a day! Sleep well.'

'I'm so tired,' she whispered back, 'but how can I sleep, thinking about tomorrow?'

CHAPTER 76

This was the moment, the moment Julia had imagined hundreds of times. Now it was here, she still did not trust the reality of it. Perhaps, she thought with a quickened heartbeat, this was just the end part of a dream that would vanish with her waking up?

The door in front of her was a faded peaty brown, scratched and scuffed at the bottom, one of many such doors in a lobby on the sixth storey, with a concrete floor and peeling walls. The creaking lift, as it went up and down, swallowed and disgorged in turn worn and oppressed looking people.

Their wide-eyed curiosity was unabashed, as they stared at them in passing. Julia felt conspicuous in her smart navy dress with a white Peter Pan collar (material from the market and made up by kind Aunt Maria) and her shiny patent sandals. Miro and Roman were undeniably the visitors from the West in their crisp shirts and light-weight casual jackets. The strangers' prolonged gazes filled Julia with sympathy for them, and guilt at her own good fortune.

Roman gave her a reassuring smile.

'Don't worry, everything will be fine.' They had agreed Roman would speak first, her father's old friend.

And then what? Julia had fretted. Then, Roman had soothed her, they'd let things unfold naturally.

There was the sound of the key in the lock, then of the bolts being pulled back. She glanced at Miro. He touched her hand. Who would it be first? Her father? His wife? Their child?

Here she was now, on the brink of her discovery. The shabby brown door creaked noisily and an old lady appeared. Her grey hair was parted in the middle and pulled back into a bun at the back. She peered at them through her owl-eyes spectacles.

'I'm very sorry to disturb you,' Roman's voice was all charm, 'we've been given this address as my friend's. Julian Kalinski. Does he live here?'

She stared at him, weighing him up, then shook her head. Her features were wizened and when she spoke her teeth were exposed, uneven and yellowed.

'No, they moved out some time ago.'

Julia's heart dropped. *I knew it! It was all too easy to be true!*

'Do you know where to?' Roman asked.

'Yes!' The woman nodded, then pointed up. 'Two floors up. Number six. We needed a larger flat and they were relocated to a smaller one. After he died.'

Her words did not register at first. Nor, it seemed with Roman either.

'Died? Who? Julian Kalinski?'

'Yes,' the woman straightened up her small frame, suddenly the bearer of important news. 'But that's all I know. I only ever see them in passing.'

It was not a pang of grief that hit her, for how does one grieve for a stranger? But Julia was so overwhelmed with dismay, that it brought tears to her eyes. She felt Miro's arm around her, just as Roman was expressing his thanks and the old woman closed the door.

Roman looked crestfallen. 'Who would have thought it! Poor Julian! He'd only be just over fifty now...'

They stood in stunned silence for a moment, until a couple of noisy young boys ran past them to the lift.

'What now?' Julia asked 'Is that it?'

'We're going up!' Miro said decisively.

'To his family..?' Julia was suddenly anxious.

'I'll speak to them,' Roman said, 'I need to know more.'

They went up in the lift together, Julia with grave misgivings, and then she and Miro waited at the far end of the dim corridor, while Roman knocked on number six. He knocked a few times, but there was no response. He raised his shoulders with an expression of defeat. They came back to him.

'Let's ask the neighbours,' Miro suggested.

They knocked on the nearest door and it was opened by a middle-aged man in faded shirt and trousers. He pushed back his hair that kept falling in streaks over his forehead. Roman did his polite, charming explanation again, while the man's eyes travelled over each one of them in turn, slowly taking in their appearance.

'Yes, Mrs. Kalinska is our neighbour,' he said, 'but she's not here at the moment.'

'Do you know what time she'll be back?' Roman asked.

'What time? No, she won't be back tonight.' He turned his head and called out, 'Ada! Is it Friday that Irena's coming back?'

From the depths of their abode, redolent with cooked cabbage, a woman's voice replied, confirming this information.

'Thank you so much,' Roman said,' we've still got much travelling to do. But now that we know we don't have to waste time hanging around.'

As if encouraged by Roman's openness, the man added,

'She's visiting relatives in Bialystok. Most likely her cousin will be coming back with her. She often looks after the kids in the holidays. Who shall I say has been asking about her?'

Roman smiled.

'Her husband's friend. We were together in the army. All those years ago.'

The man's eyes widened with interest.

'Is that so? That'll certainly be a surprise for her!'

More like a shock, Julia thought.

On the first day of their visit, Adam and Kasia took time off work to guide them around Warsaw. Kasia was the manager of a small hotel. *Mainly party people and a few Russians. Who else could afford such a luxury?*

With Roman's Hillman safely locked away, (*too eye-catching*, Adam warned), they travelled to the centre of the city on the tram. All ten of them.

'Not quite like the underground,' Julia whispered to Miro, discreetly amused by the plump lady squashed against her, with a live goose poking out its head from the woman's shopping bag. Andrew was mesmerised by the playful poodle trying to escape his owner's tight embrace, and Joyce sat straight and prim in her white slacks, her feet hemmed in by a large open bag that breathed out all the smells of an allotment produce: onions, garlic, cabbage, swedes and pungent soil, stuck to the newly-dug potatoes.

The Palace of Culture in the centre of Warsaw was impossible to miss. The massive edifice styled on the New York sky-scrapers dominated the city and all the suburbs for miles around.

'But that's breath-taking!' Julia commented, looking up into the sky, where the central tower rose 187 metres high.

'Ugly monstrosity,' Kasia hissed. 'A gift from the Soviet people to the Poles. What insolence! Who wants their gifts when they're stealing everything else from us?'

She was in her element in the Royal Lazienki Park, competing with Adam to point out the architectural attributes of the Belvedere Palace, a regal white building with a grand colonnaded entrance.

'Once a residence of the Polish kings! And now, not at all scorned by the party leaders of this communist state!'

The Lazienki Park was truly spectacular with its acres of woodland and its central lake with an island on which stood the romantic Palace on the Water. Andrew and Yarek ran ahead, away from Adam's inevitable historical lecture, and Bronek and Beata fell back too, to talk with Julia and Miro as they strolled along the water's edge.

Further up the hill, they came across Chopin's monument, a dramatic sculpture of a wind-blown tree with Chopin in a pensive, perhaps creative mood, resting beneath it.

'I can't believe I'm here!' Julia said in awe. 'And to think, all those years, when I murdered his pieces on the piano... he was here, here all the time, and I never imagined it..!'

This feeling of wonder stayed with her all day.

In the late afternoon, with the slanting sun still hot in the cloudless sky, and long hours of sightseeing behind them, they sought respite in the shade of the Barbican wall. An ice-cream kiosk nearby provided much needed refreshment for their parched throats, and a low wall surrounding a patch of green with a tree in the middle proved to be a godsend for their weary limbs. They sat down with their walking partners, Roman with Adam, Joyce with Kasia, Andrew with Yarek, and Beata with Bronek flanked Julia and Miro.

For the first few moments they rested in a dreamy silence, licking ice-creams, taking sips of soda water, even Andrew and Yarek, so lively all day, were wilting now with fatigue.

Julia's tired feet tingled. Her mind turned like a kaleidoscope of images stored throughout the day: the Old Town with its market square, the facade of the tall, ornate buildings, so faithfully rebuilt to their original appearance, the flower stalls, their colours dazzling in the sun, the iconic Zygmunt's Column in the Palace Square, the Barbican medieval gateway into the city, its ancient stonework preserved at the base of the reconstructed walls, and *doroshki*, the horse-drawn carriages, romantic relics of a bygone age. Before today, all this had been just a dot on the map. Her Mama's native country. Her home.

'Are you tired?' Beata's voice cut into her thoughts. The others were slowly reviving, Adam lighting a cigarette and Bronek explaining to Miro some intricacies of his friend's motorbike engine.

'No,' Julia replied. 'I'm not tired. Just totally overwhelmed and charmed. I can't believe I'm really here!'

'I understand perfectly,' Beata assured her. 'My dream is to see London.'

CHAPTER 77

Julia and Miro had promised on Scout's honour to visit their parents' families and friends while holidaying in Poland. First, Mr. Ostrovski in Warsaw, her Mama's wartime friend, then Maryla and Bazylka, Mrs. Anna's companions throughout their slave labours in Nazi occupied Austria, then Tato's and Aunt Maria's sisters in Lodz, and at the end, Miro's parents' families near Krakow.

Visiting Mr. Ostrovski required just one evening out of their first week. Bronek was their guide and went with them on a tram to another suburb of Warsaw, tall concrete blocks, hundreds of them in rows, the ground lines softened somewhat by trees and shrubs.

Bronek helped them to find the block marked thirty-six, then once inside its dark lobby, to decipher the correct floor number, before they entered the metal lift.

'Claustrophobic,' Julia shuddered feeling her legs turn rubbery as the lift creaked upwards.

Bronek laughed. 'It's fun! I envied all my friends who lived in high-rise blocks. We'd play tig in the lifts. Up one and down the other.'

'How exciting!' Julia mocked.

'It was!' he assured her with a grin.

Julia's legs were shaky when they stepped out on the twelfth floor.

The knock on Mr. Ostrovski's door had a prompt effect. An elderly lady opened it a fraction and peered at them from inside the gap.

'Good evening,' Julia said, 'I'm looking for Mr. Ostrovski. He was my mother's friend during the war. I'm Julia Kalinska.'

There was a moment's hesitation in the lady's expression, then her face relaxed and she greeted them with a surprisingly youthful smile. A row of good teeth.

'Well I never!' she opened the door wide, 'Julia! Marcin never stops talking about your mother. Anastazia, right? Come in, please come in!'

She was in her early seventies, a plump maternal type, with short white hair and a dark navy dress, long sleeves, despite the hot weather. The three of them followed her inside. The kitchen, as they passed, was perhaps one metre by two with just enough space for one person to turn around in the middle.

A glass door opened into a living room that was no bigger than Nadia's boxroom at her house. All furniture looked downsized to fit in snugly and on the whole the impression was that of taste and care. Small original oils and watercolours adorned the walls and embroidered white linen headrests on the two miniature sofas gave the appearance of orderly comfort.

'Zygmuś! Marcin! We've got visitors!' their hostess called out, her voice vibrant with excitement. She led them towards a lace-curtained glass door that stood open, revealing a small balcony and two elderly gentlemen sipping tea over a miniature low table.

They placed their cups down, stood up and entered the room. They were evidently brothers, each with a shock of white hair and similarity in their features of high foreheads and Roman noses. One was smaller and stockier than his thin, tall brother. Julia guessed that this one had been her Mama's dear friend.

'Mr. Ostrovski,' she addressed him and surprised herself with a strong punch of emotion, 'I'm Julia, Anastazia's daughter. Mama's told me so much about you!'

She saw how his face dropped its guard, how his lip quivered, how his eyes glistened. He stretched out his arms and embraced her holding her close to his chest.

'My dear child! It's like having Anastazia back.'

After that all other introductions followed, and fresh tea on the table, and home-baked cake, and talk, everyone talking at once, which never failed to amuse Julia.

'You're getting quite good at that,' she often teased Miro.

'No match for you,though,' he would retort.

They all became pensive when Mr. Ostrovski began to recount his return to Poland from India after the war, with his two small, orphaned grandsons.

'Warsaw was in ruins, but my family was here. I had nowhere else to go. Besides,' he glanced at his brother and his sister-in-law, 'Zygmuś and Emilia helped me with my little boys, as their own grandchildren grew up. We all had to work very hard, to rebuild the city. It went on for years. But the important thing was, we were together.'

He spoke proudly of his grandsons Maks and Aleks, who were now twenty-six and twenty-four, both married with a child each. Maks was living in Bielsk Podlaski near the eastern border, working in furniture production. Aleks had just been employed in the delivery section of the first ever supermarket, newly opened in June.

'I can die happy now,' Mr. Ostrovski said smiling, 'knowing they've both found a place for themselves on this earth.'

'Who's talking of dying!' his brother intervened, his eyes creased with good humour. 'We're like youngsters again! Free to do as we please!'

Julia had kept contact with Mr. Ostrovski after her Mama's death, writing him Christmas and Easter cards. He asked her about Eva and Stella. She told him all the latest news.

'They were like coveted dolls in Uzbekistan,' he reminisced, 'with their white-blond-hair and those clear blue eyes. So noble of Eva to have adopted Nadia. A little Indian girl!'

'Yes, it was,' Julia agreed heartily, 'where else would I find such a good friend? My best!'

She was glad no one was able to read her thoughts and find, like a tiny grain hidden in her mind the secret she could not share with anyone. Only with Miro, one day, when she became officially his wife.

They parted with promises of keeping in touch and the Ostrovski trio were overwhelmed with Julia's standard gifts of coffee and tea and toiletries, stockings, socks and scarves, things she could afford to buy at the Rugby market, their quality far exceeding anything available here in the shops.

Miro's mother had written to her friends Maryla and Bazylka, informing them of Miro's imminent visit, but she was not able to specify the exact day or time.

'I'd like to telephone them,' Miro said at the breakfast table, 'Bazylka's husband Tomasz works in a surgery. I've got his number.'

'The nearest telephone booth is at our local post office,' Kasia said, stopping to pour tea, 'Bronek can take you there after breakfast. If you ask for *błyskawiczny*, the 'lightning service', they'll connect you as soon as a line is free.'

Julia accompanied the boys to the post office. It was a large, yellow stone building on the main street, stained in brown streaks with age. The interior was dark wood, giving it a sombre atmosphere, despite a rose-shaped skylight in the domed roof, and a patterned tiled floor, the surface of which had been worn down over decades of use.

The far end was one continuous counter with windows behind which sat the serving staff. The side walls were lined with telephone cubicles, five on each side, every single one occupied, and the waiting people forming a congesting crowd.

'You have to get your queue number first,' Bronek informed them and led them to the shortest line at the serving windows.

Their queue moved at a snail's pace together with parallel queues of dejected looking people, helplessly resigned to the 'lightning system'. Julia, Miro and Bronek entertained themselves with subdued chatter, mindful not to irritate the finely tuned sensibilities of those around them. After forty five minutes they reached the counter.

The strange thing about the serving windows was their position, set down at chest level, so that every single person speaking through the gap just above the desk was forced to bend down and speak up with their neck twisted at an unnatural angle. Not to mention, as Miro pointed out later with a large dose of amusement, having to inspect the contents of the nostrils of the serving person.

The big woman behind the glass wore the unsmiling mask of officialdom, making her painted arched eyebrows all the more startling.

'I'm listening,' she gave Miro a bored stare.

He explained his mission.

'That'll be ten *zlotys* for five minutes. Your conversation will be monitored and you'll be automatically cut off.'

Miro paid her. She gave him two printed numbers.

'The black numeral is your queue number. The red numeral is the number of your booth. Your numbers will be called out on the megaphone. You'll then proceed to booth number five.'

The 'lightning' service kept them waiting over two hours and each time a new announcement was made on the loudspeaker, they braced themselves for a lightning dash to booth number five. Finally, incredibly, it was Miro's turn.

Tomasz, Bazylka's husband answered his call. His presence there was no coincidence, for as the rural doctor's assistant, he had to be prepared to step inside any other role demanded of him; that of a receptionist, a nurse, a midwife, and often a vet.

Miro held the receiver to his ear, listened, answered, nodded, smiled, then a look of surprise stopped on his face.

'They cut me off! Just like that!' his lips parted in indignation.

'That's normal,' Bronek shrugged.

'Normal? Preposterous!' Miro's expression said it all.

'Hey you! Have you finished?' Someone was already pushing into the booth.

Outside, Julia fretted.

'But Miro, did you manage to say everything?'

'Yes. It's all arranged. They'll be waiting for us tomorrow afternoon.'

CHAPTER 78

Julia knew of Maryla and Bazylka's past from Mrs. Anna's frequent tales of their wartime years spent together in Nazi-enforced labour on an Austrian farm.

When they were liberated by the British in May 1945, they were dispatched with hundreds like them, displaced refugees, to the Polish Army centres set up along the Adriatic coast of Italy. The men joined Anders' army, and the women with their children were left in the camps to await decisions as to their future.

The Yalta agreement earlier that year in February, had pandered to Stalin's demands, and while Europe celebrated the end of the war, Poland was left in Russian control. The Poles were faced with a terrible dilemma: to return or to distance themselves from home? Despite the threat of persecution from the new communist government in Poland, some people decided to go back. Their longing to be reunited with their families proved stronger than their fear. Bazylka and Maryla, together with their fiancés, went back to look for their parents.

Now, Bazylka and Tomasz lived in a small village near Krasna, forty kilometres east of Warsaw. Maryla and Ludwik lived almost next door in the adjoining village.

This had not always been so. The first ten years after their return, they laboured long hours, both men and women alike, in rebuilding Warsaw as well as constructing high raised blocks for the thousands crammed in shared rooms, basements, shelters, lean-tos and garages. Then good fortune smiled on them, when their boss's greed turned in their favour. He coveted their flats for his own relatives. A party member with useful connections, he arranged for the four of them to be transferred to the country. Not everyone's dream, with the state-owned rural industries limping at best, and at worst grinding to a halt after three consecutive seasons of exceptionally bad weather.

But the two couples did as they were ordered while rejoicing secretly. After years of back-breaking work, the four frustrated scholars, whose studies had been severed by the outbreak of war, were at long last allowed to step into positions closer to their liking. The timing was fortunate. In order to support the ailing rural industry, funds were suddenly made available by the Party for the benefit of the proletariat. New village schools were built, surgeries set up, as well as state run village shops and services.

Maryla was appointed to assist the single teacher and head in running the small village school. Tomasz and Bazylka, with their medical training interrupted and never allowed to be completed, were found positions as assistants in the village surgery, that met the needs of several other villages and hamlets in the radius of some ten miles. And Ludwik, with his once youthful dreams of designing bridges, was given a post at a railway depot in Tluszcz, overseeing repair works of engines and carriages.

The village of Krasna was set in a landscape of woods and meadows, overhung with willow trees, and ripe cornfields, that undulated in the breeze like a honey-coloured sea. The country roads were dusty, beaten tracks, uneven with potholes, challenging Roman's driving skills.

They drove through villages, some with just a few houses like log cabins, some with thatched roofs shading the walls, all looking sleepy in the oppressive heat. Occasionally a family of ducks or geese would waddle noisily across the track, a goat or a cow tethered and grazing close to the house would look up, distracted by the car's sound. There was the odd pig in its pen, practically on the doorstep, its smell pervading the air, and hens roaming freely in and out of the open doors.

'Of course,' Roman explained, 'one's not allowed to compete with the state farms. Only enough livestock for one's own family. God forbid any excess for sale!'

'Incredible!' Joyce commented. 'Such a beautiful country. So much potential!' In her crisp white blouse, cream slacks and cream pumps she looked dressed up for lunch in a city hotel.

'I just want cold water, when we get there,' Andrew said, rubbing his sweaty forehead against his arm. 'Gallons and gallons!'

'Not much further now. But I think we'll have to drink vodka first,' Roman teased.

Julia licked her parched lips.

'How can they drink so much? And how can they afford it?'

'They make their own.' Roman said. 'Their own medicine. For the doldrums.'

Bazylka and Tomasz's house was charming in its simplicity: wooden walls, greyed with age were shadowed by a thick overhanging thatch that was held in place with wire netting. The door, the window-frames and the shutters, now pushed back flat against the walls, glossy and crisp blue, had the appearance of recent paintwork.

The cottage was set back from the dirt track by a wide stony drive. A low wooden fence on one side held in masses of tall hollyhocks, dark red and pink, and thickly growing lupins, their spiry stalks covered in blossom of vivid blues and purples. At the end of the fence, facing the road, was a little wooden shrine with a statuette of Our Lady, surrounded by freshly cut flowers in glass jars.

On the other side of the house stood a wooden shed with a deep, sloping roof. Outside its closed double door, an old Trabant was parked.

Roman's Hillman crunched to a halt in front of the house, the dust rising in a cloud from underneath the tyres. A man and a woman appeared in the open door of the house and came towards them, their smiles sincere and welcoming. Julia guessed they were Tomasz and Bazylka. She had heard so much about them. He was indeed handsome, in his early forties, tall and hard-muscled, his tawny hair thick and falling in a wave across his forehead. Bazylka was a strong looking woman, used to hard work. Her eyes were indeed the lightest brown with tints of green and her titian hair was un-fussily swept back, coiled and held in place with pins.

Miro jumped out of the car first and rushed towards them. He was heartily embraced, first by Tomasz and then by Bazylka, who appeared reluctant to let him go.

'Look at you, Miro!' she stood back and held him at arm's length, 'I remember vividly, as if it was only yesterday, when your Mama brought you home, a young girl, younger than you are now. A tiny little scrap. And look at you now! A handsome young man!' Her green eyes shone, her voice was filled with pride. She hugged him again and Miro laughed and returned her embrace with a kiss on her cheek to her delight.

All the usual introductions followed and handshakes and small talk, after which Tomasz and Bazylka invited them indoors. Their sons Karol and Krystian, fifteen and thirteen, hovered at the door, preparing themselves for their appointed task, Julia discovered later, of looking after Joyce ad Andrew with their smattering of English. Their relief and surprise were evident when Joyce greeted them in Polish.

Their front room was modestly furnished with just the basic, most needed furniture: thick-set wooden table and heavy wooden chairs to match, and a small low table close to the sofa and two arm chairs. Family portraits adorned the walls, a cross, a gilt-edged picture of the Black Madonna, and two original oils of the Polish landscape. The sombre impression of the room was lifted with white accents: white lace curtains, white lace head-rests on the sofas, and a white tablecloth underneath the already prepared food, making it look all the more appetising.

'Maryla and Ludwik should be here any minute now,' Bazylka said, filling the glasses on the table with fruit juice. 'Please, take one, you must be so thirsty!'

Andrew drank his in one go and his face lit up when his glass was promptly filled again.

'Thank you so much!' His prim politeness made Karol and Krystian smile.

They all picked up their drinks and were invited to follow through the kitchen into the garden at the back. The area close to the house was a carpet of pansies and nasturtiums.

'Beautiful!' Joyce said, her eyes reflecting the bright colours.

'All my artistic wife's work!' Tomasz said with a sparkle. 'I'm just the digger!'

He remained with Joyce and Roman close to the house, chatting, his gesticulating hands emphasising the points he made, while Bazylka linked her arms with Miro and Julia, naturally like their aunt, and led them deeper into their long garden.

'Tell your Mama,' she said to Miro, 'not to worry about us any more. We've had some hard times, but things are better now. We've been allotted reasonable accommodation and this piece of land for our use.'

They walked along the path close to mature fruit trees, apple, pear and plum, where four hens roamed about freely scratching and clucking importantly.

'I love hens,' Julia said with feeling. 'My Mum kept hens, just four like these, when I was a child.' And for a split second an image of her Mama passed through her mind, her Mama with a seed bowl in her hand, the chickens pushing at her feet and the joy on her Mama's face.

'And my Dad kept rabbits,' Miro added, 'to feed us three boys. Forever ravenous and forever like locusts hanging around my Mum's cooking pots!'

'We learned all the tricks on the Austrian farm,' Bazylka said, taking them through a well-maintained vegetable plot. 'We grow enough here to see us through the winter months. And besides, we are a small and close community here. We exchange things all the time.'

It was so peaceful, so beautiful here. A perfect place for her Mama, Julia thought. Would she have been happier returning to Poland? Julia could not imagine now her own home anywhere else but in England.

They all walked back to the front of the house when Maryla and Ludwik arrived with their daughters, Krysia and Vanda, fourteen and ten. Their Syrena's dull green body was dotted with patches of beige, to cover the eroding damage of rust.

There followed another round of introductions and handshakes, after which Maryla, just like Bazylka before, embraced Miro and would not let him go, much to his amusement.

'Where's that little baby of mine?' she looked up into his face, her head barely reaching his shoulder. 'I carried you in my basket everywhere I went to give your poor Mama a break. You slept like the little baby Moses beside us, while we worked and worked in the fields.' There was almost a touch of nostalgia in her words as she remembered the harshness of those times.

She was just as Julia had imagined her from Mrs. Anna's descriptions, a small, slight woman, light blonde hair, cut in a neat bob, and clear blue eyes, that had not gone unnoticed by their sleazy employer at that Austrian farm. Her husband Ludwik had retained his dark looks that had gained him the nickname of 'Gipsy' in his young days. His handsome symmetrical face showed worry lines between his eyebrows, etched by the hardship of the years of strife.

Their daughters did not look much like sisters. The older Krysia, had inherited her father's dark looks, the younger Vanda was as fair as her mother, but both were pretty. Their chirpiness embraced their cousins immediately and included Andrew in their eagerness to tell them their latest news.

'May we show Andrew around the village?' Krysia's face was alive with anticipation.

'But you've not eaten yet!' Bazylka fretted.

'We will! When we get back! We won't be long!'

Julia wondered at Andrew's reaction to being abducted in this unexpected way, but he looked bemused and sending his mother a quick smile, he went along with his new friends.

The adults were vigorously invited by Bazylka to go inside and take places at the table. Inevitably, the liqueur glasses were filled, clinked with *Na zdrowie*! And emptied in one gulp.

'No more!' Roman protested laughing. 'I've got to get my cargo safely back home tonight!'

'Plenty of room here, to sleep it off,' Tomasz said, matter- of- fact, and filled another round.

Julia grinned at Miro. They had worked out their own defence. A full glass untouched could not be refilled. Joyce followed suit with a conspiratorial glance at Julia, but then she charmed her hosts with her praise, spoken in Polish.

'This is very good. You are wonderful hosts. A lot of trouble for you, all this.' She waved her hand over the food so attractively prepared.

'Nothing is trouble,' Tomasz raised his glass, 'when you have good friends. One thing socialism teaches you is to value your friends.'

'And contacts and backhanders,' Ludwik added drily, his dark eyes smiling, nevertheless.

'We all know each other in this place,' Tomasz assured him.

'Just as well,' Ludwik exhaled an expressive sigh.

Miro, his parents' emissary, asked Bazylka and Maryla everything his mother wanted to know. 'Right to the very end,' he said, 'they thought you'd change your mind and come to England with them.'

'It was a hard decision,' Maryla said, cutting her buttered bread, 'but nothing mattered so much at the time as going back to find our parents.'

'We got a shock, as soon as we arrived in Warsaw,' Bazylka picked up the story. 'Militia men were already waiting on the platform, and every single person on that train was escorted to their headquarters to be questioned for hours on end. Were we Anders' spies? Who sent us? Who were our contacts? Why did we really come back? On and on and on. I must admit, I did think then, that we'd made our biggest mistake.'

'I told them again and again,' Maryla put her knife and fork down, ' that we missed our families, that we missed our home, that we came back to rebuild our city. Especially that we had already been pestered by their people in Italy to do exactly that!'

'The first night,' Tomasz gulped down another mouthful of the firewater, 'was one of the worst nights of my life. And I've lived through a few,' he smiled wickedly, and Julia remembered Mrs. Anna's account of how they, the three girls, had found him one day wounded and hiding in the nearby forest. 'We were released at long last from the militia headquarters into a totally black night. The war was over, but there were no street lights left. We held onto each other, the four of us, and foot by foot, we felt our way along the jagged edges of dilapidated buildings. We found a hole in the wall. We climbed in, only to discover the shelter was full of people. Somebody woke up and swore at us. I begged him to let us stay. Just till the morning.' Tomasz took another swig.

'How did you find your parents?' Miro asked.

'We found them, but not straight away,' Bazylka said. 'Dear God! Those first few weeks were a nightmare. You'd have to see it to believe how badly ruined the city was. People lived in any possible space, with just a board or a piece of metal sheet over their heads. Anything that could be salvaged was turned into a makeshift shelter. We went looking for work the very next day. Everyone was employed in building, men on the actual building sites and women in warehouses and in transporting the materials. We carried cement bags all day, Maryla and I, and loaded them onto lorries.'

'I still get back-ache just thinking about it,' Maryla said, and Julia could not imagine Maryla's small hands doing such heavy work. 'But the good thing was, that as soon as we got registered for work, they sent us to some army barracks that night, so we did not have to sleep under the stars.'

'Every night after work,' Ludwik said, passing her the salad, 'we were forced to report at the Militia Bureau. The questioning was the same, night after night, till you felt physically worn out, till your brain turned to mince. Then one night they asked me to be their informant. I thought I'd explode! But calmly, with the greatest effort, I told them they'd be wasting their time with me, since we were new and I didn't know anyone and there was no time left in the evenings to even get to know other people. Surprisingly, they left us alone.'

'They had new victims by then,' Tomasz said.

'To cut a long story short,' Maryla got back to Miro's question, 'we found our mothers, not all three at once, but when we were looking around for a basement flat. Basements withstood destruction and were in great demand, while people waited for new blocks to be finished. Unfortunately none of our fathers returned from the war.' There was a sad pause, which Joyce broke gently.

'They must be so happy visiting you here.'

'Yes, very much,' Bazylka smiled at her. 'They love the freedom and the fresh air of the country, but would you believe it, they miss their M One.'

'M One?' Joyce asked.

'One-room flats. The running water. The bathroom. The warm radiators in winter. There are some rewards in those giant hen coops.'

Ludwik lit a cigarette and exhaled expansively.

'We've got a lot to be thankful for,' his manner was deadpan. 'Tomasz examines sticky ears, Bazylka sows' bottoms, Maryla wipes snotty noses and I oil rusty engines! Exactly what we had all dreamed of!'

Maryla winced, her expression reprimanding, but Tomasz slapped Ludwik's shoulder playfully. 'Come now Ludwik, we've not done so badly, considering everything else! Considering *everyone* else!'

'Well, do you know what?' Ludwik sat up, his dark, alert eyes wandering round their faces, 'I sometimes get a little tired of having to feel grateful for things I've never asked for!'

'Ludwik,' Tomasz filled his glass, 'this is what you need, boy, to stop this maudlin nonsense! Drink up and be merry! There's a few more crates of the stuff! Who's going to help me, if you don't?'

Ludwik indulged his brother-in-law by allowing himself to be jollied, drank in one gulp, made a comically pained face, spread out his hands helplessly.

'*Vox populi*... who am I to argue!'

Talk continued about what was and what could have been. The children returned from their walk, the boys hot and red faced, the girls pretty and cool in their pastel cotton dresses. Bazylka sent them straight to the washroom to wash their hands. At the table, they all drank thirstily, before considering the food.

Andrew looked pleased. 'I saw a pig,' he told Joyce, pinching his nose. 'She had little piglets. They were so sweet, but the smell!' He laughed.

'My dear fellow,' Roman said, 'you've got to be tough to be a country squire!'

Andrew rolled his eyes.

'Dad, you know very well I want to be a cricketer!'

The evening passed pleasantly with not a moment's break in the talk that evolved into separate, concurrent strands. Julia studied her hosts, warm and hospitable people, who had been her and Miro's age when their lives had been fragmented like a jig-saw, and never rearranged in quite the same way. Miro and she had their own dreams now; she shuddered at the thought of some cataclysm turning their world upside down.

When the time came to say farewells, Miro presented Maryla and Bazylka with packages prepared by his parents.

'A few useful things,' he said with a smile.

'For the impoverished relatives,' Ludwik teased, but with no real malice.

'No, not at all!' Miro protested hotly. 'They care about you all, Mr. Ludwik, I know how much they feel for you and remember the old times. No, you're all like their family. And the invitation stands. Always and at any time!'

Ludwik threw his arm around Miro's shoulders and drew him close.

'I know, my dear lad, I know! This bloody system makes malcontents of all of us. Some hide it better than others!'

On Thursday that week Julia and Miro travelled to Lodz on the train. Roman offered to drive, but Julia insisted that he should spend some time with his brother without the perpetual company of others.

It was a welcome breathing space too, for herself and Miro. Since their arrival in Warsaw, they were never alone, not even when they slept. It did not matter; just sharing this amazing adventure together was happiness enough. At night time in the dark, when their hands met across the floor, and she sensed his energy transferring itself and tingling up her arm, her heartbeat quickened at this small act of intimacy, as she listened amused to the youngsters' chatter before they wore themselves out.

Tato's sisters, Veronika and Sabina, shared an apartment in one of the formidable pre-war buildings that formed an imposing, grand facade on both sides of one of the mid-city boulevards. On this hot day, the sun was distant and hazy amidst the fumes from the exhaust pipes of the slow-moving traffic, congesting all four lanes. All windows high up in the apartments were open, airing the rooms in stoical optimism.

Julia and Miro found the address; it was a tall, wide, double-fronted door, grey and peeling, left ajar, revealing a massive staircase underneath which, in the dark recess, some bicycles were chained to the wall.

The building was three storeys high, with an additional floor in the attic. The aunts' apartment was on the second floor, the name card close to the bell displaying their names. Julia had posted them a letter, immediately on arrival in Poland, and now kept her fingers crossed that they were at home.

Sounds of clicking footsteps preceded the opening of the door. Julia recognised Veronika, for her striking resemblance to Tato and Aunt Maria. Sabina hurried close behind her, smaller, plumper, on high heels. They both cried, 'Welcome! Welcome!' and threw themselves at Julia and Miro in an aura of soap and talcum powder scents, and embraced them in fervent hugs before leading them inside.

It was a spacious room with a high ceiling, furnished predominantly in brown, pre-war table, chairs and a dresser, brown sofa and matching armchairs, brown and cream patterned wall-paper and a yellowed lampshade, gathered like a skirt around the hanging bulb.

They led Julia and Miro straight to the table covered with a white cloth and set with porcelain plates and cups.

'Please, sit down my dear young people,' Veronika's hand moved languidly, her fingers stained with tobacco. 'Tea will be ready in a moment.' She went over to the kitchen corner and lit the gas burner underneath the kettle.

'And a home-made cake!' Sabina added, her eyes smiling as she turned to the sideboard.

Their sibling likeness was strongest in their blue-grey eyes, like Tato's, and the gentle arcs of their eyebrows. Veronika was taller, hints of dark blond mingling with grey in her hair, parted in the middle and twisted into a knot at the back. Her slow, lingering smile revealed stained teeth of a smoker.

Sabina's teeth were short, like a child's and she did not stop laughing and chirping all the while she busied herself with bringing out the cake and carrying it like treasure over to the table.

'Coffee and hazelnut,' she announced with pride.

'My favourite!' Julia exclaimed to please her. Sabina looked pleased, her short curls bouncing around her face.

'My mouth's already watering,' Miro gave her a wide smile, 'but for lunch, I'll be the cook! I insist! Only the best restaurant for Julia's aunties!'

This produced a burst of mirth from them both. Julia and Miro watched amused.

'A restaurant! My dear children, of course, how would you know?' Sabina recovered first. 'Best restaurants? Only in hotels. For the Party people. Only they can afford to go there. In any event, I wouldn't want to be seen with them. No, for us, it's the works' canteen! But there's no need, really. Believe me, Veronika and I are dab hands at improvising meals. Dear God!' she raised her eyes to heaven. 'All those hard times, and we managed. As long as you had an egg, you could make a meal of anything you found in the pantry.'

'That is why,' Miro gave her a persuasive smile, 'I insist all the more that we take you out for a meal! '

Sabina peered down at Miro with unabashed admiration.

'Is he always like this, Julia?'

Julia laughed, pleasantly touched by Sabina's approval of him.

'Miro? We get along fine!'

'I think, I will too.' Sabina winked at him.

Veronika came over with the pot of tea. As they enjoyed it at leisure with the deliciously creamy gateau, both aunts showered Julia with questions, wanting to know everything about Theo and Maria and her Mama.

'Who would have thought it!' Veronika mused, lighting a cigarette, 'all those fragmented lives! And all those new lives, formed and put together out of the remnants of our former lives! We were so happy for Theo,' her smile spread slowly across her face, 'so happy, that after all the wartime setbacks he had found peace at last with your Mama.'

Peace? Julia wondered, but there was no point raking up her Mama's demons. She reinforced Veronika's belief.

'Tato says he's had twelve good years with my Mama. He says he's grateful for that. That would never be enough for me! And he never complained!'

'A lot of people had less,' Veronika said quietly. Her husband and Sabina's

672

had been high ranking officers in the army, when Poland was attacked. After the tragic September Campaign, all contact with them was lost. Their bodies were discovered later in the mass grave in the Katyn forest. 'But let's not talk today about sad things.' Her hand waved away bad thoughts together with the cigarette smoke. 'Tell me, where have you been so far, what have you seen and what are your other plans?'

Julia gave them an account of their travels to date, leaving out any mention of her father. Miro added,

'Next Monday we're planning to go down to Krakow. My parents' families live in that area.'

'And on the way, we plan to stop at Czestochova,' Julia said, her voice reflecting her eagerness.

'Wonderful!' Sabina cried. 'Make sure to time it with the exposition of the holy icon. It's an experience you mustn't miss. You'll never forget it!'

Veronika watched them through a haze of smoke. In her unhurried manner she asked,

'Julia, tell me, but only if you want to, have you ever thought about looking for your own father?'

It was a surprise question. Julia was stumped for a moment, but there was no point avoiding the subject. She nodded.

'I've only ever met him once,' she said. 'I've never had any feelings about him, except curiosity. In fact, Roman's brother did some research before we arrived, and I've actually got his address. Legionovo, close to Warsaw. We went there last Monday, but they weren't there. His family, that is. We heard from the neighbour that my father died some time ago.'

'Oh, I'm sorry,' Veronika gave her a sympathetic glance, 'it is all so sad!'

Julia nodded.

'It's sad for his family. But for me..? I'm in two minds if I should go there at all.'

'But you must, Julia, you must!' Sabina's grey curls bounced vigorously round her face. 'Go to his grave, at least. Who knows? Perhaps he missed you all those years. And his family... they are yours too, your step-siblings. Don't write them off lightly!'

Julia's expression was polite.

'I've thought about everything, auntie, all aspects of this situation. All the pros and cons.'

'Then you must do it!' Sabina was adamant. 'And what did Theo say?'

'Tato? I think he may have worried a little. But deep down he knows there's only one Tato for me. And Aunt Maria was exactly of the same mind as you.'

The mention of their older siblings brought an avalanche of memories from their childhood days. When their morning stretched past their lunchtime hour, Miro looked pointedly at the old ticking clock on top of the bookcase.

'Shall we go?'

'Yes, two minutes,' Sabina twittered, 'you'll see where we work.' Veronika and Sabina worked in a hosiery factory. Their husbands, if they were alive, would have considered it an affront to their officers' honour. 'We love it there, don't we Veronika? Can't complain about perks. Reject yarns and fabrics for our own use, for just a few *groshe*, and the boss... a party man, but quite human.'

'And not averse to your gifts,' Veronika added drily. 'How many thousand bottles have you given him now?'

'Come now, Veronika,' Sabina would not be browbeaten, 'how else would we have swapped days and have today free?'

'My dear aunties,' Julia said contritely, 'I never imagined our visit would cause you bother.'

'No bother at all!' Sabina laughed. 'Nothing is a bother in our system if you have good contacts!'

Before they got themselves ready to go out, Julia emptied the carrier bag she had brought with her: the ever-in-demand coffee and tea, shawls, stockings and fragrant toiletries. Tato and Aunt Maria had also sent them angora cardigans; a silver grey for Veronika and a pale sage green for Sabina. Veronika held hers against herself and nodded with approval.

'Maria always had good taste.'

Sabina squealed with delight and rubbed the soft wool against her face.

'We've got something for you too.' She laughed like a young girl and clicked on her high heels to the adjoining room. She came back with a carton of miscellaneous objects: family photographs in silver frames, a white tablecloth embroidered with pale blue flowers, a crystal bowl, brooches and bracelets in a lidless wooden box, an unopened bottle of vodka, a porcelain milk jug, a pewter vase, and other treasures.

'It's all for you,' Sabina said,' but if you can't take it all at once, choose anything you fancy for now.'

'Auntie,' Julia smiled uncertainly, taken aback by such generosity, 'just one of the photographs, if I may, would be lovely!'

The photographs had a nostalgic, pre-war feel about them, all the four siblings together, on different occasions. Theo, the eldest, Maria, Veronika and Sabina.

'They are lovely! They are absolutely lovely!' Julia said with feeling. 'I'll take this one back for Tato and Aunt Maria. It'll go straight up on the wall in our front room!'

Sabina gurgled with delight. 'Then you must also take this bottle for Theo. And the tablecloth for Maria. And you, Julia, you must choose something from the jewellery. We insist, don't we, Veronika?'

Veronika stood a little aside, on account of her smoking, but she peered over Sabina's shoulder. 'Of course Julia, dear child, pick anything you like.'

Julia was drawn to a filigree silver bracelet with cornelian stones. She picked it out and held it delicately between her fingers.

'Exquisite!'

'Then you must put it on.' Sabina fastened it around Julia's wrist. 'Such a thin wrist! Just like mine when I was your age. It fits you perfectly. But there's one more thing I want you to have!' She trotted off to the adjoining room and came back with a bulging cotton sack, like a pillow-case. She pulled out of it something very shaggy.

'Look!' she cried with pride, draping the fox stole around Julia's shoulders. 'And for you Miro, a rug!' She spread out the rectangular shape made of rabbit's fur, at Miro's feet.

For a moment Julia was speechless, and could only stand still, paralysed with revulsion at the fox's head and feet dangling down her front.

'Dear aunty,' she managed after recovering somewhat, 'I'm overwhelmed, but I couldn't possibly accept such a generous gift.'

'But why not? But you must!' Sabina's eyes were round in earnestness. 'Who else have we got to leave this to?'

Miro cleared his throat.

'Julia is right. Your gifts are far too generous. Their bargaining power may yet prove very useful here. Who knows? And if not, they'll still be here when we come next time.'

Sabina was not convinced and looked crestfallen, but Veronika intervened.

'Sabina, let them be. They're young, fashions change all the time. Have you seen any youngsters in furs?'

'That's because they are expensive. And rare!' Sabina would not give up.

'And old-fashioned,' Veronika stated with another puff of smoke.

Sabina accepted defeat with a shrug of shoulders and Julia felt immediate regret.

'Aunty, we are enormously grateful. But truly, the furs have a much greater value here than they would have in England.' As she helped Sabina to fold the furs gently back into the cloth sack, she caught Veronika's amused grin.

'Shall we go?' Miro invited, and his smile promised them a delightful afternoon.

Later, in the evening, on the train back to Warsaw, Julia and Miro relived their day with the two sisters. *Priceless*, she thought of them affectionately. There was so much to tell Tato and Aunt Maria!

CHAPTER 79

Take two. The long concrete floor, peeling walls, two rows of shabby doors. The same scene as five days before.

Roman knocked, a purposeful strong rap, and stood back. Julia and Miro stood beside him. She was apprehensive. Who would it be? His wife? Or one of the children? There were two, the neighbour had said. Her half-siblings. Extraordinary!

As before she had put on her best dress and puffed out her freshly washed hair into a neat bob. And clipped the single pearls to her earlobes. She wanted to impress.

There was the sound of a key being turned in the lock and of a bolt being pushed back. The door was swung open and in its frame stood a young woman. Roman gasped and looked at Julia. She felt Miro's suppressed reaction.

It was like coming face-to-face with her twin. The same oval face, the same dark eyes, earnest underneath the straight line of eyebrows, a small mouth, pursed in expectation, even her hair was styled in the fashionable bob.

The girl's gaze swept over Roman and Miro, then stopped on Julia's face. She looked as startled as Julia was.

'Who are you?' she asked. Her consonants were soft, East European.

Roman regained his composure.

'I've been told Julian Kalinski's family live here. I'm an old friend. We were in the army together. And before that in Siberia. I'm Roman Zastavny.'

'In Siberia?' she latched on this word. 'Siberia?' Her deep breaths quickened, 'Then you may just be the person I'm looking for!' Her gaze remained intense on Julia's face. 'And who are you?' she asked again.

Julia stared. She was unable to speak.

'My friends from England.' Roman said.

'England?' She took a deep breath.

A boy of about fourteen and a girl of maybe ten came up behind her.

'Who is it?' the boy asked. He was tall with dark-blond hair and light-brown eyes. His sister, with two plaits, had similar colouring. His eyes widened with surprise when he looked at Julia.

'Who's this lady?' he asked.

Julia swallowed hard, cleared her throat, and at last managed to speak.

'My name's Julia. Can you tell me yours?'

'Julia? It's like my dad's. Julian. My name's Vladek.' He followed Julia's gaze. 'My sister Grazyna. And my big sister Dorota.'

There was a moment's pause in which Julia's heart dropped right down to her shaking legs. Through the whooshing in her ears she heard Roman stutter,

'Bbb...ut that's im...impossible! You were dead! I saved you from being thrown away with dead bodies!'

'Then it was you? You saved my life!' Another long, electrifying pause. Then slowly she smiled. It was Mama's smile. It was like a pang of pain and immense joy at the same time. Tears sprang to Julia's eyes.

'Our likeness is so extraordinary,' Dorota said, 'we must be sisters!'

Julia nodded, shedding tears down her face. Wordlessly, Dorota stretched out her arms. Julia embraced her. There was a choked silence as they hugged. Dorota recovered first.

'Please, come in,' she said, looking at Miro and Roman, 'I think we've got lots to tell each other.'

They followed, Roman looking dumbstruck.

It was a tiny flat, like Ostrovski's, with colourful throws and rugs to cover the cheapness of the furniture.

'Please, sit down,' Dorota invited, 'I'll make tea. Irena won't be back till later. She's a nurse...' her voice trailed off as her eyes followed Julia. She looked distracted. 'Vladek... please look after the guests. And Grazyna, will you help me make tea?'

Julia's gaze was fixed on her, till she disappeared in the kitchen. This was her Mama's little Dorotka, the baby she had lost in Siberia.

They sat down at the table, with Vladek hovering round them, doing his best as the stand-in host.

'I don't understand, I can't believe it!' Roman regained his composure, his eyes in a daze.

Julia felt Miro's hand on hers. His face expressed tenderness and his support. A silence overcame them. Gallantly, young Vladek attempted small talk, and his eyes lit up when Miro asked him about school and his friends.

Dorota came in with a tray of tea and sliced fruitcake, Grazyna close behind her. She responded to Dorota's instructions, and proudly set out the cups and saucers and the small plates. The closeness between all three siblings was evident, and Julia felt a twinge of envy.

As if by a signal, they all said things at the same time which became a jumble of random remarks.

'I think,' Roman took control and gave Dorota his charming smile, 'I think, what we want to know, is how you survived.'

She finished pouring tea for everyone and placed the pot down before looking at him.

'I'll tell you everything,' her voice was like a sigh, 'but I need to know about my Mama first.' She turned her eyes to Julia.

'It's a long story,' Julia said.

'Please…' She leaned intensely across the table, clasping her hands together.

Roman and Miro remained quiet throughout Julia's abbreviated account of her mother's travels and her recent years. Dorota stopped her now and again, asked questions, fell into thoughtful silences, dabbing her nose and her eyes with a handkerchief.

All the while that Julia spoke, Vladek and Grazyna ate their cake and sipped their tea unobtrusively, their attention totally fixed on Julia's tale. There was a long silent pause when Julia finished. Miro placed a slice of sponge cake on her plate.

'Thanks,' she said, taking a sip of tea.

Roman looked at Dorota.

'And your story?..' he pleaded, 'for me, it's like a miracle. Seeing you today.'

Her sad features softened, and when she raised her eyes to his, there was the unmistakeable expression of wonder and gratitude in them.

'I too, never imagined that one day I'd find my saviour.'

Roman shook his head, 'I just want to know how you survived.'

'Because of you.' Dorota began her story with a nod in his direction. The Russian couple to whom Roman had entrusted her body, believing her to be dead, took her home, with the intention of giving her a decent burial, a promise made to Roman, who had entreated them with the gift of a silver chain and cross. But as soon as they placed her on a seat in the warm room, she began to stir and whimper.

'But how's that possible?' Julia cried, her throat recovering after a few sips of tea.

'Apparently,' Dorota said, 'these things happen in Siberia, where temperatures fall so low that the human body, when threatened with freezing to death, sometimes goes into a state of hibernation. *Letarg*, they call it. They believed that this was what happened to me. '

'Incredible! A miracle!' Roman kept repeating.

'They were good people, I'm sure,' Dorota continued. 'They had promised to bury a dead child. But raising me as their own, on top of their own five, in those awful conditions… that was simply beyond their means. They guessed I was a Polish child. The note that they found inside my wrap stated my name, my date of birth and my parents' names.'

'I did that,' Roman said. 'In my wildest hope, I imagined a cross on your grave with your name on it.'

'I owe you so much,' Dorota said, her voice unsteady. 'Because of that, they travelled to the nearest labour camp, hoping there'd be some Polish families there. My adopted parents, Zbyszek and Zofia accepted me gladly, despite the harsh conditions and their own sacrifices to provide for me. Their own two little boys had died of scarlatina, and lack of medication more likely,

678

and they looked on this chance as a sign from heaven. But they never hid from me who my real parents were.' She paused and her smile was sad. 'We missed the news of the amnesty. No one bothered to inform us. We stayed in Siberia till 1957. It was something to do with reuniting the families after the war. The war!' she said wryly. 'The war that had been over for years!'

Roman shook his head. 'How did you manage to survive that long?'

She sighed.

'It wasn't all bad, not for us, children, who did not understand our parents' problems. As time went on, the Poles were allowed to create their own, self-contained community. We had our own school, our own surgery, even a shop, but most people grew their own things and exchanged goods and services among themselves. Life went on. My parents had two more boys after adopting me. We returned to Lukov, to their family. That's where we live now.'

Vladek and Grazyna sat still all the while, listening to Dorota's narrative with rapt attention, nibbling the cake, sipping the tea, Vladek sometimes reminding Dorota of details she'd missed out. Julia liked him. She liked the little girl too, with her shy manner, reminding her of herself in her infant years.

'It wasn't any easier here, when we returned,' Dorota continued, 'my parents had to find work, my younger brothers a school, and I was eighteen, I wanted to go on to further education. We were called the *Ruskis*... That was especially hard for my younger brothers. You know how cruel kids can be at school.' She took a sip of tea. 'It's all behind us now. We're all well settled in. I've finished the Academy of Physical Training...'

'Really..?' Julia's mood lifted with interest. 'What was your favourite discipline?'

Dorota gave a low, self-deprecating laugh.

'Gymnastics and dance. But don't get excited! I teach Russian now, that's what I was ordered to do. Because of my background and my good knowledge of the language. But who wants to learn Russian in Poland today? Can you imagine the challenge? Every day it's like pushing a river up a mountain!'

'Is there room for me in your class?' Miro asked softly, with an impish smile. Then his tone was serious. 'Surely, learning any language can only be an asset.'

'Try telling that to the people,' Roman said, 'the people who are tired, frustrated, fed up to the core with anything Russian.'

Julia felt a sudden rush of sympathy for Dorota.

'So what do you do?'

'I bribe them!' Dorota gave her an intimate smile. 'No. Czes helps me. He's my fiancé.' She twiddled the ring on her engagement finger. 'He's the sports teacher at our school. He organises additional activities on Saturdays for kids who do well in my subject. And can you believe it? His class is usually full. And my reputation saved!'

They enjoyed the cake and tea for a while, before Julia asked her burning question,

'How did you find your father, in the end? Our father,' she corrected herself.

Dorota lifted her eyes, so like her own, dark and direct.

'I've always thought about it,'she cleared her voice. 'Even when we still lived in Russia. As soon as we settled here I started writing to various places. The Red Cross. The radio. The national newspaper. Thousands of people are still doing it. Looking for their lost relatives. It took over two years before there was a breakthrough. Someone in this block heard his name on the radio.' Dorota took a deep breath and her eyes softened. 'I shall never forget that day. His condition when I found him. And the fact that my own mother was dead!'

'Dead? Is that what he told you?'

Dorota shook her head.

'No. It was what he didn't say. He was very ill by that time. Ravaged by cancer. He couldn't bear to talk about the past. I did not have the heart to press him. And Irena would not say anything either at the time. I assumed... Siberia and all that. Thousands had died...'

Why had Irena been so cruel? Keeping the truth back from Dorota, Julia wanted to ask. But she was aware of two pairs of innocent eyes looking at her.

'So how did you find out?' she asked Dorota, instead.

'Irena told me everything. After father died. I started my second search straight away. I wrote to the Red Cross in England. To Radio Free Europe. To the Polish Daily. All the information I have got so far, is that there was an Anastazia Kalinska in Hertford Bridge in 1948.'

'Her name changed when she married Theo,' Julia said, and Roman added,

'A lot of people emigrated to the States and Canada, at that time.'

'But tell me, Dorota, tell me, what was he like? Our father. Was there a time when he was happy?'

'Yes!' Vladek spoke, suddenly enlivened. 'My Dad wasn't sad all the time. He took us sledging in the winter. And camping in in the summer. At the Kampinovski Park, not far from here, where he worked as a forester.'

'He got his old job back?' For some strange reason this information pleased Julia.

'Yes,' Dorota confirmed, 'after slaving for years on building sites, he got his old job back.'

Vladek and Grazyna slid off their chairs and fetched two photograph albums from a drawer in the dresser.

'This blue one is all about me,' Vladek explained, but there are lots of photos of my Dad.' He placed his album in front of Julia, and Miro relieved Grazyna of hers, giving her a friendly smile.

Vladek could hardly contain his eager, running commentary, as Julia turned the pages of the album. So many unknown people, strange faces, but for her, only one person stood out, his familiarity strengthening with every turned page. Her heart quickened at every new image of him, in photographs that chronicled family events, yet she could not contain the creeping bitterness, that she and her Mama were missing from all those special, recorded moments of his life.

They went for a walk in a nearby park, an expanse of green edged with trees and shrubs, an oasis of freshness amongst the forest of concrete blocks. It was early evening, warm, still and balmy. Old people sat on benches, mothers pushed prams, dog lovers exercised their pets, children played games.

Roman and Miro engaged in a ball game with Vladek, much to his boyish, exuberant delight. Grazyna stayed with her big sister, holding onto her hand, listening quietly to Dorota and Julia's talk, as they strolled around the park.

The first shock of their mutual discovery had passed. They described their separate lives, again and again, asking new questions, discovering new things about each other. It was extraordinary, how in such a short space of time, Julia already felt a strong affinity growing between them. Dorota asked her about Miro.

'I love him. He's the one.' Julia answered simply and saw affection in Dorota's eyes.

'And I like him too,' she said. 'You must meet my Czes. And my family, my parents and brothers. Will you have time to go with me to Lukov? Before you go home?'

'We'll make time,' Julia assured her, 'after our trip to Krakow. And next summer Dorota, you and Czes must do everything to visit us in England.'

Spontaneously Dorota hugged her. It felt for a brief moment like having her Mama back.

Then she stooped down to a pair of mesmerised eyes looking up at her.

'And you too, Grazynka, and Vladek, you'll come one day to visit me. Would you like that?'

Grazyna smiled shyly and nodded. Julia stroked her head. A feeling of tenderness swept over her.

Dorota checked her watch.

'I'll go ahead now,' she said. 'Irena will be home soon. I'll warn her. Plus, she will be wondering where all that food came from.'

Prior to their walk, Roman and Miro had bought fresh ham, cheese, tomatoes and bread for the evening snack.

Julia watched little Grazyna skip away holding onto Dorota's hand. Her sisters! She then strolled over to the boys, where they were still chasing after the ball, seemingly tireless.

Irena was as Mama had described her in her notes, dark-blonde hair, swept up at the sides and pinned, regular, attractive features, yet now the skin grooved and hardened by years of strife. Early forties, Julia thought.

They shook hands, Irena's a firm, nurse's grip. Strange, shaking hands with Mama's rival. Was it a betrayal? *Should she hate her? For all Mama's suffering?* Irena's manner was tense when she asked them to sit at the table. Her hand trembled when she accepted the cigarette offered by Roman. He lit hers and his. She inhaled hard, her eyes half shut. She breathed out slowly.

'Pity, he didn't live to see this day,' she said. 'I had a feeling, always, that one day you'd come looking for him, Julia.' Her direct gaze conveyed regret and sympathy.

'Why didn't *he* try to find me?' *His child*, Julia wanted to add. *Had he no feelings?*

Irena's shoulders sagged.

'I asked him that. Many times. After our life became a little more normal. After all the horrors at the beginning. He clammed up each time and would not be drawn even into the slightest discussion. It was as if he wanted to erase his past. Completely.'

'But why?' It was like a denial of her own existence.

'Sometimes,' Roman said, 'remembering is so painful, that blanking out things from your mind is the only antidote left to put a stop to the relentless torture.'

'Me? A torture to him?' Julia was dismayed.

'No, not you, Julia,' Irena said quietly. 'It was everything. The upheaval. The war. The head wound. What followed afterwards. With us... He blamed himself for everything...' she drew on her cigarette and kept her eyes down. 'He needed to forget.'

'And you, Mrs. Irena?' Julia meant, *did you not blame yourself for any of it?*

Irena's brow was crinkled, as if staving off a headache,

'I did not ask for any of that. I was just his nurse. He needed me. I grew to love him.'

There it was, so simply stated. As if nothing else mattered. All her Mama's suffering dismissed in a few words. She should hate this woman.

Julia looked around, all eyes on her, even Vladek's and his little sister's, trying to make sense of this extraordinary meeting. Her wish had been to find her father. Too late for him, but she found the truth. And so much more besides. Her two young half-siblings and Dorota. A tangible link with her Mama. A never dreamed of, astonishing gift! Someone up there cared for her. She had so much to be thankful for. Miro, and Theo and kind Aunt Maria and now this! Dearest Mama, she thought, forgive me for being civil to *her*.

'But, Mrs. Irena...' she said, 'did you not sometimes, just sometimes, think about my Mama?'

Irena's cigarette was shaky between her fingers, sending the smoke up like a wavy streamer and shedding the ash on the white surface. Her face contorted with her thoughts and emotions and there was a pause before she controlled herself. Her voice was husky, when she spoke.

'What can I say? That I have regrets?' A pause. A nod. 'Yes, I have regrets. Many! About the terrible circumstances that threw your father and me together.' A shrug of shoulders, a pained expression. 'I never set out with plans to steal someone else's husband or a child's father.' She shook her head nervously. 'I never stopped regretting that. But caring for him, and afterwards... our children... how could I ever regret that?'

Little Grazyna linked her arm with her mother's and rested her head on her mother's shoulder with a gesture of belonging.

Was this Irena's apology? Trite words, they seemed, for all the years of Mama's suffering. But in truth, there was nothing Irena could have said or done now, to repair the damage caused in the past. Julia's heart ached for her Mama and she felt that out of loyalty she should treat Irena with utter disdain. But seeing her now in this stark reality, a widow struggling to bring up her children, her father's children, on reduced means, Julia simply could not whip up feelings of hatred against her. *I'm sorry, Mama, I'm so sorry!*

She cleared her throat.

'Mrs. Irena,' she said, 'we can't change the past. But the present and the future... it's up to us now... We are bound together, whether we like it or not.' She looked at her half-siblings.

Irena's shoulders dropped. She gave a nod, then drew hard on her cigarette. Julia caught approval in Roman's gaze, just as Miro's hand covered hers, resting in her lap.

They went to the cemetery the next day. Joyce and Andrew came along too. Joyce had been so moved by Julia's discovery, she wanted to meet Dorota and her step-family. She walked with Irena and the children ahead, Julia and Dorota in the middle, and Miro with Roman behind.

It all seemed so unreal, walking like this with her father's family. Perhaps, because she was still under the influence of shock, she felt no strong feelings of resentment towards Irena, only the overwhelming feeling of wonder, at being reunited so miraculously with Dorota.

The cemetery was like a flower garden, the colours brilliant in the sun, the graves covered in bouquets or surrounded with potted roses, dahlias and asters.

'How can people afford all this?' Julia asked, enchanted by the view around her.

Dorota tightened her linking arm around Julia's. 'You know, there are many things people can't afford. But flowers for the grave are a matter of honour. Everyone does their best. You should see the cemetery on All Saints Day. It's an ocean of colour and candlelight. Not at all spooky or sad. Families come together and visit their loved ones. Those who have already gone.'

Their father's grave was like hundreds of others, a layer of white pebbles held in by a rectangular stone edge, and a stone cross with a photograph of him set behind a small pane of glass.

They laid down their flowers and Irena arranged them between the pots of bright red geraniums. Roman stooped down to look at the photograph.

'It was taken,' Irena said, 'just after he'd started his job at the Kampinoski Park. He was very happy then.'

Julia looked closer. Her father was about forty-four at the time, and though not smiling directly, looked relaxed, his eyes creased with some held back amusement, his hair curling round his temples.

'That's how I like to think of him,' Dorota said, 'before the illness took away his good looks.'

Julia read the inscription. A life enclosed in a few words. The date of his death took on a sudden meaning. 10.10.1960.

'That's just a month before Mama died!' she cried. She stood at the grave and said quiet prayers for the peaceful repose of his soul. A thought came into her mind. It was a pleasant thought and she felt her spirit lifting. She recalled her Mama's face, as she remembered her from her childhood, radiant with contentment, and she had a strong feeling of belief that her Mama was happy now. Reunited with her true husband. For all eternity.

CHAPTER 80

A week later, with her mind reeling with all the impressions of her travels in the past two weeks, Julia was deposited at her front door.

The house, in which she now lived with her Tato and Aunt Maria, was a small terraced house on Wood Street facing the junction with Park Road. Things had gone well for them in the past two years; Aunt Maria had obtained permanent residency in England and, together, they had enough saved for a deposit for their own property.

The front wall was pebble-dash painted in white. Indoors, the passage led to the front room, the dining room and the kitchen at the back. Upstairs, they each had their own bedroom and the use of a tiny bathroom off the landing. It had been Aunt Maria's Swedish influence to go against the trend of patterened wallpapers and to paint all the rooms in the palest pastel primrose, thus giving their small house a feeling of space.

Her Tato and Aunt Maria must have heard them arrive, for they came out with open arms and greeting smiles. Muszka had been sitting on the doorstep, but with a sudden recognition, jumped up, ran up to Julia and started pushing herself against Julia's ankle.

Tato and Aunt Maria stopped by the car and Tato spoke to Roman through the wound-down window.

'Welcome back, intrepid travellers! I want to hear all about it! Lunch here tomorrow, after church, all right? Is that a yes? Good! It's a yes!'

Miro helped Julia with her suitcase inside the hall. He pulled her to him and held her close.

'I'll see you tomorrow.'

'It'll seem strange now after two weeks together,' she said.

'It's just a short parting. I love you, Julia. I couldn't imagine my life without you.' He kissed her on the lips. It was a seal. Of their mutual love. For ever.

Aunt Maria busied herself in the kitchen straight away, declining Julia's help and inviting her to sit at the table with Theo. Julia gave her Tato a long, heartfelt hug, comfortable, as always, in the familiar scents of soap and hair cream and tobacco.

'I've missed you, so much!' she said.

He returned her embrace, pleased and self-conscious at the same time.

'Well, I'm glad you're back. All in one piece!'

Their talk was incessant over the meal, Dorota's story causing much astonishment. But what evidently gave them the most joy, was Julia's report of her visit to their sisters in Lodz.

'As soon as it's made possible,' Theo said, his eyes dreamy with anticipation, 'they'll have to come for a visit.' He then got up and handed Julia her post that had arrived in her absence. 'The two letters on the top,' he said, 'I think are important.' They were. Two brown envelopes. The first she opened had her A-level exam results. They all held their breath.

Julia's eyes scanned the page, impatient for only one thing: the pass percentages. They were good results; English and History 80% and Art 85%. Julia smiled and their faces lit up with relief. A big boulder fell off her chest.

'It's all good. I've passed well,' she confirmed. She held out the sheet of paper for them to see. The second letter informed her of the starting date at the Leicester College of Art.

'I've been accepted! I start the last week of September!' Glowing inside with contentment, she asked, 'And what's been happening here, while I've been away?'

Aunt Maria cleared her throat and raised her eyebrows in preparation for an announcement.

'Well, actually, something has happened. Could have been far worse! But thank God, it's not tragic!'

'What?' The old anxiety was back in a flash.

'It's Eva,' Tato said, 'she had an accident.'

'Bad?' Julia swallowed hard.

'Knocked down by a car. When she was cycling,' Aunt Maria said. 'A cracked pelvis. And of course, cuts and bruises. Has to be kept still.'

'Poor Aunt Eva!' Julia cried, 'I must go to see her. How's everyone else? It must be awful for them!'

'Yes,' Aunt Maria said, 'It must be. Stella's down from London and Nadia came here last night. She wanted to know when you were coming back. She'll be here later.'

'Nadia? Tonight?'

'Yes, and she's staying over.'

This was good news. Julia had so much to tell her.

Nadia gave her a long hug, as if she could not let her go.

'I've missed you,' she said, her voice shaky, unlike hers.

'I've missed you too,' Julia assured her, 'Tell me, how's your Mama?'

She led her to the front room, where Tato and Aunt Maria looked up from their reading and wanted to know the latest news.

'She's improving, but it'll take a while before she's allowed home.'

'And how are you all coping?' Aunt Maria asked with concern.

Nadia gave a wan smile.

'We're managing, thank you. Even my Dad has surprised us. He can actually make toast and fry an egg. Marek is very helpful. And now we've got Stella too.'

'Won't she mind you leaving her?' Julia asked.

'She's got Jack with her. And I needed to get out. To clear my head!'

Upstairs, in Julia's bedroom, Muszka had already made herself comfortable on the edge of the bed and did not stir from her slumber. Nadia sat down beside her and stroked her in an absent manner. Julia sat down at her desk.

'You'll never guess! Not in a million years!' Nadia began, but there was something tense in her familiar preamble.

'The suspense is killing me!' Julia egged her on as always, but Nadia did not smile. Her dark, almond-shaped eyes suddenly filled with tears.

'Nadia! What is it? Is it Stefan?'

Nadia shook her head, spilling her tears down her cheeks.

'No. It's much worse than that!'

'What?!'

'It's awful! I'm not who *you* thought I was! Everything's changed. I don't know any more who anyone really is!'

'What are you talking about? Nadia!' It was all so muddled.

Nadia wiped her eyes and blew her nose.

'It's all come out because of the accident!'

'What?' Julia was beginning to guess and felt unease creeping up her tightening stomach.

'Julia, you'd never guess,' Nadia paused dramatically, 'but my Mama, Eva, is actually my real, my natural, my birth mother! Only she's kept it a secret all this time and invented this whole adoption story because of my Dad. And now, when she thought she might die, she told him the whole truth!'

Julia's gasp was genuine, part shock, part relief that the secret was no longer hers to keep.

'Oh Nadia! How did he take it?'

'You'll never believe it! He says he knew it all the time!'

Incredible! 'And he never said anything?!'

Her face looked tired and distracted.

'He says that bloody war ruined so many lives. He says, there was no point in raking up the past and tormenting yourself with what could have been and was not. He says, he's had enough torment in his life. All he wants now is peace and just getting on with what he's got.'

It sounded very much like her own father; with the past so painful, it was better to forget. She moved over to Nadia, and gave her a heart-felt sisterly embrace.

'So what now?'

Nadia's sigh was weary.

'I should be happy, shouldn't I? But I can't get used to the new me. Everything was so straightforward before. I was their adopted child. I loved them both the same. Now, I feel as if it's only my Dad who is real. And my Mama is a stranger. And when I think of her... and that other man... I shudder, to think they made me!' She rubbed her temples . 'I wish I could erase him from my mind. Every time I look at her, I think of it. And every time she looks at me, she must hate me!'

'Oh Nadia, Nadia, hush...' Julia rocked her in her arms, 'you know that's not true. Your Mama loves you. Why else would she have gone through this charade for so many years? We all love you. You're exactly the same person as you were yesterday and ten years ago and when we were kids in the Infants. What does Stefan say?'

Nadia looked up and there was a softening in her expression.

'He still loves me.'

'Still?'

'Always, he says.' A nod and the beginning of a smile.

'There you are! And what about Stella? And Marek?'

Nadia looked bemused.

'It's strange, you know. I could swear they are trying hard to be nice to me, like I'm some sort of a lost relative that they have found. But it's *him!* *Him* that bothers me. My natural father. I feel nothing but hatred for him. And that's so horrible!'

Julia had no wise words of advice. One thing she knew from her Mama's notes was that Selim had been smitten with Eva. What a pity that his final act was so despicable it ruled out any belief in his nobler feelings. And like any other person, he must have had some good sides to his nature. But he'd be remembered just for this one evil deed.

'Nadia, if only I could wave a magic wand...' Julia sighed, 'but hey, listen! It's a waste of time tormenting yourself like this. And for what? For driving yourself batty? Your Dad is right. Listen to him! And think how lucky you are to have your very own Mum. I'd do anything to have mine back!'

Nadia looked at her and her gaze remained thoughtful for a long while.

'I know. I know all this. I just wish life wasn't such a pain!'

'You're made of strong stuff!' Julia told her sternly.

'What do you mean?' Nadia flashed her a suspicious glance.

'Your Mum, Nadia, your Mum! She has always been a brave woman. Now it's your turn to be tough. And not even in the middle of a desert without food and water!' Julia fixed Nadia with a compelling stare till her friend relented and granted her a nod. Julia reciprocated with a satisfied smile. 'Nadia you'll never guess! Not in a million years! The story I've got to tell you!'

That night in bed, after they had watched an old film with Rock Hudson and Jayne Wyman, a weepie called *The Magnificent Obsession*, (which did Nadia a lot of good), and she was finally asleep beside her, and Muszka was purring contentedly at the foot of the bed, Julia was still awake, though this must have been her longest day that summer.

There was a bright moon shining against the floral pattern of the curtain, which filtered and diffused the light over the objects in the room. There was soothing quiet around her, like an extension of the peace and happiness she felt within. So much had happened in the last two weeks, all of it good. Tato and Aunt Maria were pleased with her success. Tomorrow she would write to Dorota. Tomorrow she would visit Aunt Eva. Cheer her up with her own incredible story. Tomorrow she would spend the evening with Miro. And after that… thoughts of the future crowded Julia's mind. A new phase in her life was about to begin, yet she felt no fear of the unknown. Not the slightest touch of anxiety. Bubbling inside her was a feeling of anticipation, as if she were about to embark on a new and adventurous journey. Rather than looking back, she had so much to look forward to. She was ready.

EPILOGUE

There is a corner at a cemetery in Rugby shaded by solemn cypress trees. The inscriptions on tomb stones and crosses bear Polish names.

The gold lettering on a black marble cross reads thus:

IN LOVING MEMORY
OF
ANASTAZIA LUTOVSKA
BORN 10.4.1913 IN POLAND
DIED 5.11.1960 IN RUGBY
THOUGH MY FEET HAVE WALKED THOUSANDS OF MILES
MY HEART REMAINS CLOSE TO MY HOME
R.I.P.

Two young women place flowers on the grave and stand silent for a long while. When they lift their eyes and face each other, there is peace and contentment in their appearance, a wordless understanding that their quest is fulfilled.

AUTHOR'S NOTE

In 1940, on Stalin's orders, mass deportations of civilians took place along the belt of East European countries bordering with Russia.

In Poland alone there were several such deportations:

Feb. 1940 – 140,000 people
April 1940 – 61,000 people
June 1940 – 85,000 people

In 1941 another massive deportation of 85,000 people took place, plus a number of smaller groups, bringing the total to almost 400,000.

In the first wave of deportations 11,000 people died en route or on arrival at the labour camps.

When 'amnesty' was declared, a cynical misnomer since none of these people were criminals, it was estimated that there were 292,000 civilian Poles in labour camps and 97,000 Polish POWs in gulags.

In August 1942 only 100,000 civilians were evacuated and led to freedom by the forming Polish army under the command of General Anders.

* *Information sourced from Wikipedia.*

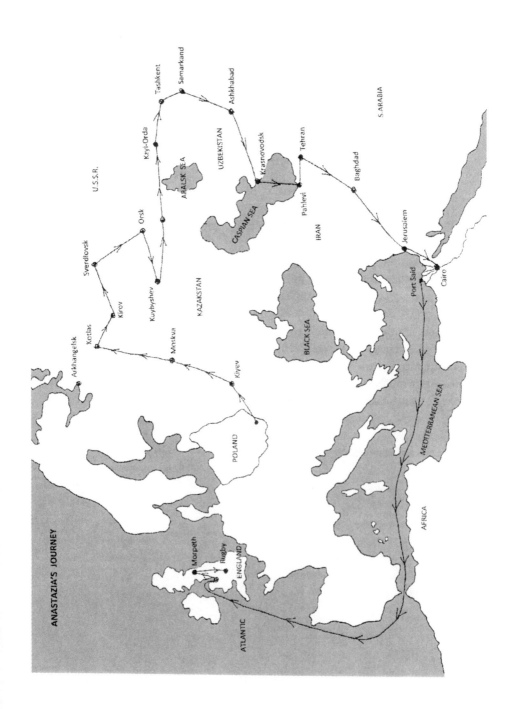

ANASTAZIA'S JOURNEY

Morpeth
Rugby
ENGLAND
ATLANTIC

Arkhangelsk
Kotlas
Kirov
Sverdlovsk
Orsk
Kuybyshev
Moskva
Kiyev
POLAND
U.S.S.R.
KAZAKSTAN
Kzyl-Orda
Tashkent
Samarkand
Ashkhabad
UZBEKISTAN
ARALSK SEA
CASPIAN SEA
Krasnovodsk
Pahlevi
Tehran
Baghdad
IRAN
S.ARABIA
BLACK SEA
Jerusalem
Port Said
Cairo
MEDITERRANEAN SEA
AFRICA

Acknowledgements

With my thanks and gratitude to:
  My husband Michael for his tireless research,
  My children Liz, Andrew and Jonathan, and my friends Krystyna Kogut and Agata Szostek for their support and practical help,
  My colleagues at the Peatling Magna Writers and at the Leicester Writers' Club for their patient listening and constructive remarks.

I am especially grateful to the people listed below who, like my parents and their friends, had survived the Siberian odyssey, and were willing to share their experiences with me:

Marta Brzezinska, Halina Chruscik, Lucyna and Gienek Cieplowski, Ala Dzik-Jurasz, Stefan Goryn, Ryszard Grzybowski, Sister Jadwiga, Maria Kalus, Lucyna Kaminska, the Kmiec Family – Janina, Staszek and Mila, Krystyna and Czeslaw Kogut, Janina Kulbicka, Genowefa Kumigiel, Barbara Wieclawska, Danuta Wojciechowicz.

My grateful thanks to the poet Martin Stepek and Fleming Publications for their kind permission to include his poem 'I lay down on the shores of Pahlevi – Soliloquy' in my novel. The poem appears in a volume of his poems *For there is Hope* published by Fleming Publications, ISBN number 978-0-9556507-3-4